CHRISTOPHE
MERRY C
JAN, PAUL
COURTENAY, ASHLEIGH & TYLER

THE
BOLITHO OMNIBUS

THE
BOLITHO OMNIBUS

Stand into Danger
In Gallant Company
Sloop of War

Alexander Kent

HUTCHINSON

London Sydney Auckland Johannesburg

The right of Alexander Kent to be
identified as Author of this work has been asserted
by Alexander Kent in accordance with the
Copyright, Designs and Patents Act, 1988

This edition first published in 1991 by
Hutchinson

Random Century Group Ltd
20 Vauxhall Bridge Road, London SW1V 2SA

Random Century Australia (Pty) Ltd
20 Alfred Street, Milsons Point, Sydney, NSW 2061, Australia

Random Century New Zealand Ltd
PO Box 40–086, Glenfield, Auckland 10, New Zealand

Random Century South Africa (Pty) Ltd
PO Box 337, Bergvlei, 2012, South Africa

Incorporating

STAND INTO DANGER
First published by Hutchinson and Co (Publishers) 1980
© Highseas Authors Ltd 1980

IN GALLANT COMPANY
First published by Hutchinson and Co (Publishers) 1977
© Bolitho Maritime Productions Ltd 1977

SLOOP OF WAR
First published by Hutchinson and Co (Publishers) 1972
© Alexander Kent 1972

BRITISH LIBRARY CATALOGUING-IN-PUBLICATION DATA
Kent, Alexander
   The Bolitho omnibus: Stand into Danger/In Gallant
   Company/Sloop of War.
   I. Title
   823[F]

ISBN 0–09–175118–7

Photoset in Sabon by Speedset Ltd, Ellesmere Port
Printed and bound in Great Britain by
Clays Ltd, St Ives PLC

STAND INTO DANGER

I

Welcome Aboard

Richard Bolitho thrust some coins into the hand of the man who had carried his sea-chest to the jetty and shivered in the damp air. It was halfway through the forenoon, and yet much of the land and the sprawling houses of Plymouth were hidden in drifting mist. No wind at all to speak of, so that the mist made everything look eerie and dismal.

Bolitho squared his shoulders and stared across the swirling water of the Hamoaze. As he did so he felt the unfamiliar touch of his lieutenant's uniform which, like everything in his sea-chest, was new: the white lapels of his coat, the cocked hat set squarely across his black hair. Even his breeches and shoes had come from the same shop in Falmouth, in his own county just across the river, from the tailor whose family had been making clothing for sea officers since anyone could remember.

It should be his proudest moment. All he had worked and hoped for. That first, seemingly impossible step from midshipman's berth to wardroom, to become a King's officer.

He tugged his hat more firmly across his forehead as if to make himself believe it. It *was* his proudest moment.

'Be you joinin' th' *Destiny*, zur?'

Bolitho saw that the man who had carried the chest was still beside him. In the dull light he looked poor and ragged, but there was no mistaking what he had once been: a seaman.

Bolitho said, 'Yes, she's lying out there somewhere.'

The man followed his glance across the water, his eyes faraway.

'Fine frigate, zur. Only three years old, she be.' He nodded sadly. 'She's bin fittin' out for months. Some say for a long voyage.'

Bolitho thought of this man and all the hundreds like him who roamed the shorelines and harbours looking for work, yearning for the sea which they had once cursed and damned with the best of them.

But this was February 1774, and to all accounts England had been at peace for years. Wars still erupted around the world, of course, but always in the name of trade or self-preservation. Only the old enemies remained the same, content to bide their time, to seek out the weakness which might one day be exploited.

Ships and men, once worth their weight in gold, were cast aside. The vessels to rot, the seamen, like this ragged figure with all the fingers missing from one hand and a scar on his cheek as deep as a knife, left without the means to live.

Bolitho asked, 'What were you in?'

Astonishingly, the man seemed to expand and straighten his back as he answered, 'Th' *Torbay*, zur. Cap'n Keppel.' Just as quickly he slumped down again. 'Any chance of a berth in your ship, zur?'

Bolitho shook his head. 'I'm new. I don't know the state aboard *Destiny* as yet.'

The man sighed. 'I'll call 'e a boat then, zur.'

He put his good hand in his mouth and gave a piercing whistle. There was an answering clatter of oars in the mist, and very slowly a waterman's boat nudged towards the jetty.

Bolitho called, '*Destiny*, if you please!'

Then he turned to give some more coins to his ragged companion, but he had vanished into the mist. Like a ghost. Gone perhaps to join all the others.

Bolitho clambered into the boat and drew his new cloak around him, his sword gripped between his legs. The waiting was done. It was no longer the day after tomorrow and then tomorrow. It was now.

The boat dipped and gurgled in a cross-current, the oarsman watching Bolitho with little enthusiasm. Another young luff going to make some poor jack's life hell, he thought. He wondered if the young officer with the grave features and black hair tied to the nape of his neck was so new he would not know the proper waterman's fare. But then again, this one had a West Country touch in his voice, and even if he was a 'foreigner' from across the border in Cornwall, he would not be fooled.

Bolitho went over all that he had discovered about his new ship. Three years old, the ragged man had said. He would know. All Plymouth probably pondered over the care which was being taken to equip and man a frigate in these hard times.

Twenty-eight guns, fast and agile, *Destiny* was what most young officers dreamed of. In time of war, free of the fleet's apron strings, swifter than any larger vessel, and more heavily armed than anything smaller, a frigate was a force to be reckoned with. Better hopes of promotion, too, and if you were lucky enough ever to reach the lofty peak of command, so too would a frigate offer the chance of action and prize-money.

Bolitho thought of his last ship, the seventy-four-gun *Gorgon*. Huge, slow-moving, a teeming world of people, miles of rigging, vast spans of canvas, and the spars to carry it. It was also a schoolroom, where the young midshipmen learned how to control and sustain their unwieldy charge, and they learned the hard way.

Bolitho looked up as the waterman said, 'Should be seeing her about now, sir.'

Bolitho peered ahead, glad of the interruption to his thoughts. As his mother had said when he had left her in the big grey house at Falmouth, '*Put it behind you. Dick. You cannot bring him back. So take care of yourself now. The sea is no place for the unwary.*'

The mist darkened and edged aside as the anchored ship loomed into view. The boat was approaching her starboard bow and past the long tapering jib-boom. Like Bolitho's new uniform on the wet jetty, the *Destiny* seemed to shine through the drifting murk.

From her lithe black and buff hull to her three mastheads she was a thoroughbred. All her shrouds and standing rigging were freshly blacked down, her yards crossed, and each sail neatly furled to match its neighbour.

Bolitho raised his eyes to the figurehead as it reached out as if to greet him. It was the most beautiful one he had ever seen. A bare-breasted girl with her out-thrust arm pointing to the next horizon. In her hand she held the victor's crown of laurels. Only the laurels and her unwavering blue stare had been inserted to break her white purity.

The waterman said between pulls, 'They *say* that the woodcarver used his young bride to copy for that, sir.' He showed his teeth in what might have been a grin. 'I reckon he had to fight a few away from *her*!'

Bolitho watched the frigate slipping past the boat, the occasional activity on her nearest gangway and high above the deck.

She was a beautiful ship. *He was lucky.*

'Boat ahoy!'

The waterman bawled in reply, 'Aye, aye!'

Bolitho saw some movement at the entry port, but not enough to excite much attention. The waterman's answer to the challenge had said it all. An officer was joining the ship, but nobody senior enough to bother about, let alone her captain.

Bolitho stood up as two seamen leapt into the boat to help make fast and to collect his chest. Bolitho glanced at them quickly. He was not fully eighteen years old, but he had been at sea since he was twelve and had learned to assess and measure the skills of sailormen.

They looked tough and hardy, but the hull of a ship could hide a lot. The sweeping of jails and assize courts, being sent to sea to serve the King rather than face deportation or a hangman's halter.

The seamen stood aside in the pitching boat as Bolitho handed the oarsman some money.

The man pushed it into his jerkin and grinned. '*Thankee*, sir. Good luck!'

Bolitho climbed up the frigate's tumblehome and stepped through the entry port. He was astonished at the difference even though he had been expecting it. After a ship of the line, the *Destiny* seemed crowded to a point of confusion. From the twenty twelve-pounders on her gun deck to the smaller weapons further aft every inch of space seemed to have a purpose and to be in use. Neatly flaked lines, halliards and braces, tiered boats and racks of pikes at the foot of each mast, while in and around every item were men he must soon know by name.

A lieutenant stepped through the side party and asked, 'Mr Bolitho?'

Bolitho replaced his hat. 'Aye, sir. Come aboard to join.'

The lieutenant nodded curtly. 'Follow me. I'll have your gear taken aft.' He said something to a seaman and then shouted, 'Mr Timbrell! Put some more hands in the foretop. It was like bedlam up there when I last inspected it!'

Bolitho just remembered in time to duck his head as they walked aft beneath the quarterdeck. Again the ship appeared to be crowding in on him. More guns, firmly tethered behind each sealed port, the aromas of tar and cordage, fresh paint and crowded humanity, the smells of a living vessel.

He tried to assess the lieutenant who was leading him aft to the wardroom. Slim and round-faced, with that harassed look of a man left in charge.

'Here we are.'

The lieutenant opened a screen door and Bolitho stepped into his new home. Even with the black muzzled twelve-pounders along one side, a reminder, if one was needed, that there was no place in a ship-of-war which was safe when the iron began to fly, it looked surprisingly comfortable. A long table, with high-backed chairs instead of benches like those endured by lowly midshipmen. There were racks for drinking glasses, others for swords and pistols, and on the deck there was a covering of painted canvas.

The lieutenant turned and studied Bolitho thoughtfully. 'I'm Stephen Rhodes, second lieutenant.' He smiled, the change making him more youthful than Bolitho had realized. 'As this is your first ship as lieutenant, I'll try to make the way as easy as I can. Call me Stephen, if you wish, but sir in front of the hands.' Rhodes threw back his head and yelled, 'Poad!'

A scrawny little man in a blue jacket bustled through a screen door.

'Some wine, Poad. This is the new third lieutenant.'

Poad bobbed. 'Pleasure, sir, I'm sure.'

As he hurried away Rhodes remarked, 'Good servant, but light-fingered, so don't leave anything too valuable lying about.' He became serious again. 'The first lieutenant is in Plymouth, doing something or other. His name is Charles Palliser, and might seem a bit stiff at first meeting. He's been in *Destiny* with the captain from her first commissioning.' He changed tack suddenly. 'You were lucky to get this appointment.' It sounded like an accusation. 'You're so young. I'm twenty-three, and was only promoted to second lieutenant when my predecessor was killed.'

'*Killed?*'

Rhodes grimaced. 'Hell, it was nothing heroic. He was thrown off a horse and broke his neck. Good fellow in many ways, but there it is.'

Bolitho watched the wardroom servant putting goblets and a bottle within Rhodes' reach.

He said, 'I *was* surprised to get this appointment myself.'

Rhodes eyed him searchingly. 'You don't sound too sure? Don't you *want* to join us? God, man, there are a hundred who would jump at the chance!'

Bolitho looked away. A bad beginning.

'It's not that. My best friend was killed a month back.' It was out in the open. 'I just can't believe it.'

Rhodes' eyes softened and he pushed a glass towards him.

'Drink this, Richard. I didn't understand. Sometimes I wonder why we do this work when others live easily ashore.'

Bolitho smiled at him. Except for his mother's benefit he had not smiled much lately.

'What are our orders, er, Stephen?'

Rhodes relaxed. 'Nobody really knows except the lord and master. A long haul to the south'rd is all I *do* know. The Caribbean, maybe further still.' He shivered and glared at the nearest gunport. 'God I'll be glad to see the back of this wet misery here!' He took a quick swallow. 'We've a good company for the most part, but with the usual seasoning of gallows-birds. The sailing master, Mr Gulliver, is newly promoted from master's mate, but he's a fine navigator, even if he is a bit awkward amongst his betters. By tonight we shall have a full complement of midshipmen, two of whom are twelve and thirteen respectively.' He grinned. 'But don't be slack with 'em, Richard, just because you were one yourself a dog-watch ago. Your head will be on the block, not theirs!'

Rhodes tugged a watch from his breeches. 'First lieutenant will be coming off shortly. I had better chase up the hands. He likes a smart display when he steps aboard.'

He pointed to a small screened cabin. 'That one is yours, Richard. Tell Poad what you need and he will get the other servants to deal with it.' Impulsively he thrust out his hand. 'Good to have you with us. Welcome aboard.'

Bolitho sat in the empty wardroom listening to the clatter of blocks and rigging, the unending slap of feet above his head. Hoarse voices, the occasional trill of a boatswain's call as a piece of gear was piped up from a boat alongside, to be stored and checked into its own special place in the hull.

Soon Bolitho would know their faces, their strengths and weaknesses. And in this low-beamed wardroom he would share his hopes and daily life with his fellows. The two other lieutenants, the marine officer, the newly appointed sailing master, the surgeon and the purser. The select few in a company which was listed as being 200 souls.

He had wanted to ask the second lieutenant about *the lord and master*, as he had described him. Bolitho was very young for his rank, but not so much that he did not know it would have been wrong. To share a confidence and to give a personal opinion of *Destiny*'s captain would be little short of madness from Rhodes' point of view when he had only just met the new arrival.

Bolitho opened the door of his tiny cabin. About the length of the swinging cot and enough room to sit down. A place for privacy, or as near to it as one could get in a small, bustling man-of-war. After the midshipman's berth on the orlop deck it was a palace.

His advancement had been very swift, as Rhodes had remarked. But for all that, if the unknown lieutenant had not been killed by a fall from his horse the vacancy for third lieutenant would not have been posted.

Bolitho unlocked the top half of his sea-chest and then hung a mirror on one of the massive timbers beside his cot. He looked at himself, seeing the small lines of strain around his mouth and grey eyes. He was leaner, too, honed down to a youthful toughness which only shipboard food and hard work could produce.

Poad peered at him. 'I could pay a waterman to go into town and purchase some extra victuals for you, sir.'

Bolitho smiled. Poad was like a stall-holder at a Cornish fair.

'I have some coming aboard directly, thank you.' He saw the disappointment and added, 'But if you see that it's stowed properly I'll be *obliged*.'

Poad nodded quickly and scuttled away. He had made his play. Bolitho's reaction had been the right one. There would be payment somewhere along the way if Poad looked after the new lieutenant's personal stores.

A door crashed open and a tall lieutenant strode into the wardroom, hurling his hat on one of the guns and yelling for Poad in one breath.

He examined Bolitho very slowly, his eyes taking in everything from his hair to his new buckled shoes.

He said, 'I'm Palliser, the senior.'

He had a crisp way of speaking. He glanced away as Poad ran through the door with a jug of wine.

Bolitho watched the first lieutenant curiously. He was very tall, so that he had to stoop between the deckhead beams. In his late twenties, but with the experience of a man far older. He and Bolitho wore the same uniform, but they were so far apart they could have been standing on either side of an abyss.

'So *you're* Bolitho.' The eyes swivelled back towards him above the rim of the goblet. 'You have a fair report, in *words*, that is. Well, this is a frigate, Mr Bolitho, not some overmanned third-rate. I need every officer and man working until this ship, *my* ship, is ready to weigh.' Another fierce swallow. 'So report on deck, if you please. Take the launch and get yourself ashore. You must know the lie of the land around here, eh?' He gave a fleeting smile. 'Lead a recruiting party to the west bank and examine those villages. Little, gunner's mate, will assist. He understands the game. There are some posters you can put up at the inns as you go. We need about twenty sound hands, no rubbish. We are up to full complement, but at the end of a long passage that's another matter. We shall lose a few, have no doubt of it. Anyway, the captain wants it done.'

Bolitho had been thinking of unpacking, of meeting his companions, of having a meal after the long coach journey from Falmouth.

To settle things quite firmly, Palliser said offhandedly, 'This is Tuesday, be back aboard noon on Friday. Don't lose any of your party, and *don't* let them pull the wool over your eyes!'

He banged out of the wardroom, calling for somebody else.

Rhodes appeared in the open door and smiled sympathetically. 'Hard luck, Richard. But his manner is rougher than his thoughts. He has picked a good shore-party for you. I've known some first lieutenants who would give a new junior a collection of moonstruck felons for company, just to give him hell when he returned.' He winked. 'Mr Palliser intends to have a command of his own soon. Bear that in mind at all times as I do, it helps considerably!'

Bolitho smiled. 'I'd better go at once, in that case.' He hesitated. 'And thank you for making me welcome.'

Rhodes sank down in a chair and thought about the noon meal. He heard the clatter of oars alongside and the shout of the launch's coxswain. What he had seen of Bolitho he liked. Young certainly, but with the restless quality of one who would do well in a tight corner or in a screaming hurricane.

It was strange how you never considered the worries and problems of your betters when you were a midshipman. A lieutenant, junior or not, was a kind of superior being. One who berated and was quick to find fault with the youthful beginners. Now he knew better. Even Palliser was frightened of the captain. Probably the lord and master was terrified of upsetting his admiral, or someone higher still?

Rhodes smiled. But for a few more precious moments there was peace.

*

Little, the gunner's mate, stood back, his broad hands on where his hips should have been, and watched as one of his men tacked up another recruiting poster.

Bolitho pulled out his watch and looked across the village green as a church clock chimed midday.

Little said gruffly, 'Mebbee time for a wet, sir?'

Bolitho sighed. Another day, after a sleepless night in a tiny, none too clean inn where he worried that his small recruiting party might desert, in spite of what Rhodes had said about their selection. But Little had made sure that part had gone well. He was totally at odds with his name; squat, overweight, even gross, so that his belly sagged heavily over his cutlass belt like a sack. How he managed it on purser's rations was a marvel. But he was a good hand, seasoned and experienced, and would stand no nonsense.

Bolitho said, 'One more stop, Little. Then. . . ,' he gave a rueful smile, 'I'll buy you all a drink.'

They brightened up immediately. Six seamen, a marine corporal and two drummer boys who looked like toy soldiers freshly out of a box. They did not care about the miserable results of their trek from one village to the next. Usually the sight of Bolitho's party aroused little interest, except amongst the children and a few snapping dogs. Old habits died hard so near to the sea. Many still recalled the dreaded press-gangs when men could be torn from their families and put in a King's ship to suffer the harsh conditions of a war which few understood even now. And a goodly number had never come back at all.

Bolitho had managed to obtain four volunteers so far. Four, and Palliser was expecting twenty. He had sent them back with an escort to the boat in case they should have a change of heart. Two of them were seamen, but the others were labourers from a farm who had lost their jobs, 'unfairly', they both said. Bolitho suspected they were willing to volunteer for a more pressing reason, but it was no time to ask questions.

They tramped across the deserted green, the muddy grass splashing up from Bolitho's shoes and on to his new stockings.

Little had already quickened his pace, and Bolitho wondered if he had done the right thing to offer them all a drink.

He shrugged inwardly. So far nothing had gone right. Matters could hardly get much worse.

Little hissed, 'There be some men, sir!' He rubbed his big hands together and said to the corporal, 'Now, Dipper, get your little lads to strike up a tune, eh?'

The two minute marines waited for their corporal to relay the order, then while one beat a lively tap on his drum the other drew a fife from his cross-belt and broke into what sounded like a jig.

The corporal's name was Dyer. Bolitho asked, 'Why do you call him Dipper?'

Little grinned, baring several broken teeth, the true mark of a fighter.

'Bless you, sir, 'cause he were a pickpocket afore he saw the light and joined the bullocks!'

The little group of men by the inn seemed to melt away as the seamen and marines drew near.

Two figures remained, and a more incongruous pair it was hard to imagine.

One was small and darting, with a sharp voice which carried easily above the fife and drum. The other was big and powerful, stripped to the waist, his arms and fists hanging at his sides like weapons waiting to be used.

The small man, a barker, enraged earlier by the sudden departure of his audience, saw the sailors and beckoned excitedly.

'Well, well, well, wot 'ave we 'ere then? Sons of the sea, the British Jack Tar!' He doffed his hat to Bolitho. 'An' a real gentleman in command, no doubt of that!'

Bolitho said wearily, 'Fall the men out, Little. I'll have the landlord send some ale and cheese.'

The barker was shouting, 'Which one of you brave lads will stand up to this fighter of mine?' His eyes darted amongst them. 'A *guinea* for the man who can stand two minutes against 'im!' The coin flashed between his fingers. 'You don't 'ave to win, my brave boys, just stand and fight for *two minutes*!'

He had their full attention now, and Bolitho heard the corporal murmur to Little, 'Wot about it, Josh? A 'ole bleedin' guinea!'

Bolitho paused by the inn door and glanced at the prize-fighter for the first time. He looked as strong as ten, and yet there was something despairing and pathetic about him. He was not looking at any of the seamen but apparently staring into space. His nose had been broken, and his face showed the punishment of many fights. Country fairs, for the farming gentry, for anyone who would wager on seeing men fight for a bloody victory. Bolitho was not certain which one he despised more, the man who lived off the fighter or the one who laid bets on his pain.

He said shortly, 'I shall be inside, Little.' All at once the thought of a glass of ale or cider beckoned him like a wilful spirit.

Little was already thinking of other things. 'Aye, sir.'

It was a friendly little inn, and the landlord hurried to greet Bolitho, his head almost brushing the ceiling. A fire burned brightly in its box, and there was a smell of freshly baked bread and smoked hams.

'You sit down there, Lieutenant. I'll see to your men presently.' He saw Bolitho's expression. 'Begging your pardon sir, but you're wasting your time hereabouts. The war took too many away to follow the drum, an' those what came back went elsewhere to the big towns like Truro an' Exeter to get work.' He shook his head. 'Me now, if I was twenty years younger I might have signed on.' He grinned. 'Then again . . .'

Some while later, Richard Bolitho sat in a high-backed chair beside the fire, the mud drying on his stockings, his coat unbuttoned to allow for the excellent pie the landlord's wife had brought for him. A big, elderly dog lay by his feet, pulsating gently as it enjoyed the heat and dreamed of some past exploit.

The landlord whispered to his wife, 'Did you *see* him? A King's officer, no less. Lord, he looks more like a boy!'

Bolitho stirred from his drowsiness and yawned. Then his arms froze in mid air as he heard loud shouts of anger interposed with laughter. He jumped to his feet, groping for his sword and hat and trying to button his coat at the same time.

He almost ran to the door, and when he stumbled into the keen air he saw the seamen and marines falling against each other, convulsed with laughter, while the little barker screamed, 'You *cheated*! You *must* 'ave cheated!'

Little spun the gold guinea and caught it deftly in his palm. 'Not me, matey. Fair an' square, that's Josh Little!'

Bolitho snapped, 'What's going on?'

Corporal Dyer said between gasps of laughter, ' 'E put the big prize-fighter on 'is back, sir! Never seen the like!'

Bolitho glared at Little. 'I'll speak to you later! Now fall the men in, we've miles to go to the next village!'

He swung round and stared with astonishment as the barker turned on the fighter. The latter was standing as before, as if he had never moved, let alone been knocked down.

The barker picked up a length of chain and screamed, '*This* is for yer bloody stupidity!' The chain slashed across the man's naked back. '*This* is for losin' my money!' *Crack.*

Little glanced at Bolitho uneasily. ''Ere, sir, I'll give the bugger 'is money, I'll not see that poor devil beaten like a cur!'

Bolitho swallowed hard. The big fighter could have killed his tormentor with one blow. Perhaps he had been on the way down for so long he no longer felt pain or anything else.

But it was more than enough for Bolitho. His bad beginning aboard *Destiny*, his failure to find the required volunteers were all he could take. This degrading sight tipped the balance completely.

'You there! Belay that!' Bolitho strode forward, watched with both awe and amusement by his men. 'Put down that chain at once!'

The barker quailed and then quickly regained his earlier confidence.

He had nothing to fear from a young lieutenant. Especially in a district where he was often paid for his services.

'I've me rights!'

Little snarled, 'Let me 'andle the bugger, sir! I'll give 'im bloody rights!'

It was all getting out of hand. Some villagers had appeared, too, and Bolitho had a mental picture of his men having a pitched battle with half the countryside before they could get to the launch.

He turned his back on the defiant barker and faced up to the fighter. Near to he was even bigger, but in spite of his size and strength Bolitho saw only his eyes, each of which was partly hidden by lids battered shapeless over the years.

'You know who I am?'

The man nodded slowly, his gaze fixed on Bolitho's mouth as if he was reading every word.

Gently Bolitho asked, 'Will you volunteer for the King's service? Join the frigate *Destiny* at Plymouth,' he hesitated, seeing the painful understanding in the man's eyes, 'with me?'

Then just as slowly as before he nodded, and without a glance at the gaping barker he picked up his shirt and a small bag.

Bolitho turned to the barker, his anger matched only by his feeling of petty triumph. Once clear of the village he would release the fighter anyway.

The barker yelled, 'You can't do that!'

Little stepped forward threateningly. 'Stow the noise, matey, an' show respect for a King's officer, or . . .' He left the rest in little doubt.

Bolitho licked his lips. 'Fall in, men. Corporal, take charge there!'

He saw the big fighter watching the seamen and called, 'Your name, what is it?'

'Stockdale, sir.' Even the name was dragged out. His chords must have been mangled in so many fights that even his voice was broken.

Bolitho smiled at him. 'Stockdale. I shall not forget you. You will be free to leave us whenever you wish.' He glanced meaningly at Little. 'Before we reach the boat.'

Stockdale looked calmly at the little barker who was sitting on a bench, the chain still dangling from his hand.

Then he wheezed very carefully, 'No, sir, I'll not leave you. Not now. Not never.'

Bolitho watched him join up with the others. The man's obvious sincerity was strangely moving.

Little said quietly, 'You've no need to worry. This'll be all round the ship in no time.' He leaned forward so that Bolitho could smell the ale and cheese. 'I'm in your division, sir, an' I'll beat the block off any bugger who tries to make trouble!'

A shaft of watery sunlight played across the church clock, and as the recruiting party marched stoically towards the next village Bolitho was glad of what he had just done.

Then it began to rain, and he heard Little say, 'Not much further, Dipper, then back to the ship for a wet!'

Bolitho looked at Stockdale's broad shoulders. Another volunteer. That made five in all. He lowered his head against the rain. Fifteen to go.

The next village was even worse, especially as there was no inn, and the local farmer only allowed them to sleep for the night in an unused barn, and that was with obvious reluctance. He claimed his house was full of visitors, and anyway. . . . That word 'anyway' spoke volumes.

The barn leaked in a dozen places and stank like a sewer, and the sailors, like most of their kind, used to the enforced cleanliness of living in close quarters, were loud voiced in their discontent.

Bolitho could not blame them, and when Corporal Dyer came to tell him that the volunteer Stockdale had vanished, he replied, 'I'm not surprised, Corporal, but keep an eye on the rest of the party.'

He thought about the missing Stockdale for a long time, and wondered at his own sense of loss. Perhaps Stockdale's simple words had touched him more deeply than he had realized, that he had represented a change of luck, like a talisman.

Little exclaimed, 'God Almighty! *Look at this!*'

Stockdale, dripping with rain, stepped into the lantern light and placed a sack at Bolitho's feet. The men crowded round as the treasures were revealed in the yellow glow. Some chickens, fresh bread and crocks of butter, half a meat pie and, more to the point, two big jars of cider.

Little gasped, 'You two men, start plucking the chickens, you, Thomas, watch out for unwanted visitors.' He faced Stockdale and thrust out the guinea. ''Ere, matey, you take it. You bloody earned it!'

Stockdale barely heard. As he bent over his sack he wheezed, 'No. 'T'were '*is* money. You keep it.'

To Bolitho he said, 'This is for you, sir.'

He held out a bottle which looked like brandy. It made sense. The farmer was probably mixed up with the smuggling 'trade' hereabouts.

Stockdale watched Bolitho's face searchingly, then he added, 'I'll make you comfortable, you see.'

Bolitho saw him moving about amongst the busy seamen as if he had been doing it all his life.

Little said quietly, 'Reckon you can stop frettin' now, sir. Old Stockdale will be worth fifteen men all on his bloody own, by my reckonin'!'

Bolitho drank some of the brandy, the grease from a chicken leg running unheeded across the cuff of his new shirt.

He had learned a lot today, not least about himself.

His head lolled, and he did not feel Stockdale remove the cup from his fingers.

And there was always tomorrow.

Leave the Past Behind

Bolitho pulled himself up the *Destiny*'s side and raised his hat to the quarterdeck. Gone was the mist and dull cloud, and the houses of Plymouth beyond the Hamoaze seemed to be preening themselves in hard sunshine.

He felt stiff and tired from tramping from village to village, dirty from sleeping in barn and inn alike, and the sight of his six recruits being mustered and then led forward by the master-at-arms did little to raise his spirits. The sixth volunteer had come up to the recruiting party less than an hour before they had reached the long-boat. A neat, unseamanlike figure aged about thirty, who said he was an apothecary's assistant but needed to gain experience on a long voyage so that he might better himself.

It was as unlikely a story as that of the two farm labourers, but Bolitho was too weary to care.

'Ah, I see you are back, Mr Bolitho!'

The first lieutenant was standing at the quarterdeck rail, his tall figure framed against the washed-out sky. His arms were folded and he had obviously been watching the new arrivals from the moment the returning launch had been challenged.

In his crisp voice he added, 'Lay aft, if you please.'

Bolitho climbed to the larboard gangway and made his way to the quarterdeck. His companion of three days, the gunner's mate Little, was already bustling down a ladder, going to take a 'wet' with his mates, no doubt. He was lost amongst his own world below decks, leaving Bolitho once more a stranger, little different from the moment he had first stepped aboard.

He confronted the first lieutenant and touched his hat. Palliser looked composed and extremely neat, which made Bolitho feel even more like a vagrant.

Bolitho said, 'Six hands, sir. The big man was a fighter, and should be a welcome addition. The last one worked for an apothecary in Plymouth.'

His words seemed to be falling like stones. Palliser had not moved and the quarterdeck was unnaturally quiet.

Bolitho ended, 'It was the best I could do, sir.'

Palliser pulled out his watch. 'Good. Well, the captain has come aboard in your absence. He asked to see you the moment you returned.'

Bolitho stared at him. He had been expecting the heavens to fall. Six men instead of twenty, and one of those would never make a sailor.

Palliser snapped down the guard of his watch and regarded Bolitho coolly. 'Has the long sojourn ashore rendered you hard of hearing? The captain wishes to see you. That does not mean now; aboard this ship it means the moment that the captain *thought* of it!'

Bolitho looked ruefully at his muddy shoes and stockings. 'I'm – I'm sorry, sir, I thought you said . . .'

Palliser was already looking elsewhere, his eyes busy on some men working on the forecastle.

'I told you to obtain twenty men. Had I ordered you to bring six, how many would you have found? Two? None at all?' Surprisingly he smiled. 'Six will do very well. Now be off to the captain. Pork pie today, so be sharp about your business or there'll be none left.' He turned on his heel, yelling, 'Mr Slade, what *are* those idlers doing, damn your eyes!'

Bolitho ran dazedly down the companion ladder and made his way aft. Faces loomed past him in the shadows between the decks, voices fell silent as they watched him pass. *The new lieutenant. Going to see the captain. What is he like? Too easy or too hard?*

A marine stood with his musket by his side, swaying slightly as the ship tugged at her anchor. His eyes glittered in the lantern which spiralled from the deckhead, as it did night and day when the captain was in his quarters.

Bolitho made an effort to straighten his neckcloth and push the rebellious hair from his forehead.

The marine gave him exactly five seconds and then rapped smartly on the deck with his musket.

'Third lieutenant, *sir*!'

The screen door opened and a wispy-haired man in a black coat, probably the captain's clerk, gave Bolitho an impatient, beckoning gesture. Rather like a schoolmaster with a wayward pupil.

Bolitho tucked his hat more firmly beneath his arm and entered the cabin. After the rest of the ship it was spacious, with a second screen separating the stern cabin from the dining space, and what Bolitho took to be the sleeping quarters.

The slanting stern windows which crossed the complete rear of the cabin shone in the sunlight, giving an impression of warmth, while the overhead beams and the various pieces of furniture rippled cheerfully in the sea's reflections.

Captain Henry Vere Dumaresq had been leaning against the sill,

apparently peering down at the water, but he turned with unusual
lightness as Bolitho entered through the dining space.

Bolitho tried to appear calm and at ease, but it was impossible. The
captain was like nobody he had ever seen. His body was broad and
thickset, and his head stood straight on his shoulders as if he had no
neck at all. It was like the rest of the man, powerful and giving an
impression of immense strength. Little had said that Dumaresq was
only twenty-eight years old, but he looked ageless, as if he had never
changed and never would.

He walked to meet Bolitho, putting each foot down with forceful
precision. Bolitho saw his legs, made more prominent by his expensive
white stockings. The calves looked as thick as a man's thigh.

'You appear somewhat knocked about, Mr Bolitho.'

Dumaresq had a throaty, resonant voice, one which would carry
easily in a full gale, yet Bolitho suspected it might also convey quiet
sympathy.

He said awkwardly, 'Aye, sir, I – I mean, I was ashore with the
recruiting party.'

Dumaresq pointed to a chair. 'Sit.' He raised his voice very slightly.
'Some claret!'

It had the desired effect, and almost immediately his servant was
busily pouring wine into two beautifully cut glasses. Then just as
discreetly he withdrew.

Dumaresq sat down opposite Bolitho, barely a yard away. His power
and presence were unnerving. Bolitho recalled his last captain. In the big
seventy-four he had always been remote, aloof from the happenings of
wardroom and gunroom alike. Only at moments of crisis or ceremony
had he made his presence felt, and then, as before, always at a distance.

Dumaresq said, 'My father had the honour of serving with yours
some years back. How is he?'

Bolitho thought of his mother and sister in the house at Falmouth.
Waiting for Captain James Bolitho to return home. His mother would
be counting the days, perhaps dreading how he might have changed.

He had lost an arm in India, and when his ship had been paid off he
had been told he was to be placed on the retired list indefinitely.

Bolitho said, 'He is due home, sir. But with an arm gone and no
chance to remain in the King's service, I'm not certain what will become
of him.' He broke off, startled that he had spoken his thoughts aloud.

But Dumaresq gestured to the glass. 'Drink, Mr Bolitho, and speak as
you will. It is more important that I should know you than you should
care for my views.' It seemed to amuse him. 'It comes to all of us. We
must consider ourselves fortunate indeed to have *her*!' His big head
swivelled round as he looked at the cabin. He was speaking of the ship,
his ship, as if he loved her more than anything.

Bolitho said, 'She is a fine vessel, sir. I am honoured to join her.'
'Yes.'

Dumaresq leaned over to refill the glasses. Again he moved with catlike ease, but used his strength, like his voice, sparingly.

He said, 'I learned of your recent grief.' He raised one hand. 'No, not from anyone in this ship. I have my own means, and I like to know my officers just as I know my command. We shall be sailing shortly on what may prove a rewarding voyage, then again it may be fruitless. Either way it will not be easy. We must put old memories behind us, reserve not forget them. This is a small ship and each man in her has a part to play.

'You have served under some distinguished captains and you obviously learned well from your service. But in a frigate there are few passengers, and a lieutenant is not one of them. You will make mistakes, and I will allow for that, but misuse your authority and I will fall upon you like a wall of rock. You must avoid making favourites, for they will end up using you if you are not careful.'

He chuckled as he studied Bolitho's grave features.

'There is more to being a lieutenant than growing up. The people will look to you when they are in trouble, and you will have to act as you think best. Those other days ended when you quit the midshipman's berth. In a small ship there is no room for friction. You have to become a *part* of her, d'you see?'

Bolitho found himself sitting on the end of his chair. This strange man gripped his attention like a vice. His eyes, set wide apart, equally compelling, insistent.

Bolitho nodded. 'Yes, sir. I do.'

Dumaresq looked up as two bells chimed out from forward.

'Go and have your meal. I've no doubt you're hungry. Mr Palliser's crafty schemes for recruiting new hands usually bring an appetite if nothing more.'

As Bolitho rose to his feet Dumaresq added quietly, 'This voyage will be important to a lot of people. Our midshipmen are mostly from influential parents who are eager to see they get a chance to distinguish themselves when most of the fleet is rotting or laid up in-ordinary. Our professional warrant officers are excellent, and there is a strong backbone of prime seamen. The rest will learn. One last thing, Mr Bolitho, and I trust I will not have to repeat it. In *Destiny*, loyalty is paramount. To me, to this ship, and to His Britannic Majesty, *in that order*!'

Bolitho found himself outside the screen door, his senses still reeling from the brief interview.

Poad was hovering nearby, bobbing excitedly. 'All done, sir? I've 'ad yer gear stowed where it'll be safe, just like you ordered.' He led the way to the wardroom. 'I managed to 'old up the meal 'til you was ready, sir.'

Bolitho stepped into the wardroom and, unlike the last time, the place was noisy with chatter and seemingly full of people.

Palliser stood up and said abruptly, 'Our new member, gentlemen!'

Bolitho saw Rhodes grinning at him and was glad of his friendly face.

He shook hands and murmured what he hoped was the right thing. The sailing master, Julius Gulliver, was exactly as Rhodes had described him, ill at ease, almost furtive. John Colpoys, the lieutenant who commanded the ship's marine contingent, made a splash of scarlet as he shook Bolitho's hand and drawled, 'Charmed, m'dear fellah.'

The surgeon was round and jolly-looking, like an untidy owl, with a rich aroma of brandy and tobacco. There was Samuel Codd, the purser, unusually cheerful for one of his trade, Bolitho thought, and certainly no subject for a portrait. He had very large upper teeth and a tiny receding chin, so that it looked as if half of his face was successfully devouring the other.

Colpoys said, 'I hope you can play cards.'

Rhodes smiled. 'Give him a chance.' To Bolitho he said, 'He'll have the shirt off your back if you let him.'

Bolitho sat down at the table next to the surgeon. The latter placed some gold-rimmed glasses on his nose. They looked completely lost above his red cheeks.

He said, 'Pork pie. A sure sign we are soon to leave here. After that' — he glanced at the purser — 'we will be back to meat from Samuel's stores, most of it condemned some twenty years ago, I daresay.'

Glasses clinked, and the air became heady with steam and the smell of food.

Bolitho looked along the table. So this was what wardroom officers were like when out of sight of their subordinates.

Rhodes whispered, 'What did you make of him?'

'The captain?' Bolitho thought about it, trying to keep his memories in their proper order. 'I was impressed. He is so, so . . .'

Rhodes beckoned Poad to bring the wine jug. 'Ugly?'

Bolitho smiled. 'Different. A bit frightening.'

Palliser's voice cut through the conversation. 'You will inspect the ship when you have eaten, Richard. Truck to keel, fo'c'sle to taffrail. What you cannot understand, ask me. Meet as many of the junior warrant officers as you can, and memorize your own divisional list.' He dropped one eyelid to the marine but not quickly enough for Bolitho to miss it. 'I am certain he will wish to see that his men measure up to those he so skilfully brought us today.'

Bolitho looked down as a plate was thrust before him. There was little of the actual plate left visible around the pile of food.

Palliser had called him by his first name, had even made a casual joke about the volunteers. So these were the real men behind the stiff attitudes and the chain of command on the upper deck.

He raised his eyes and glanced along the table. Given a chance he would be happy amongst them, he thought.

Rhodes said between mouthfuls, 'I've heard we're sailing on Monday's tide. A fellow from the port admiral's office was aboard yesterday. He is usually right.'

Bolitho tried to remember what the captain had said. *Loyalty*. Shelve all else until there was time for it, when it could do no damage. Dumaresq had almost echoed his mother's last words to him. The sea is no place for the unwary.

Feet clattered overhead, and Bolitho heard more heavy nets of stores being swayed inboard to the twitter of a call.

Away from the land again, from the hurt, the sense of loss. Yes, it would be good to go.

True to Lieutenant Rhodes's information, His Britannic Majesty's Ship *Destiny* of twenty-eight guns made ready to weigh anchor on the following Monday morning. The past few days had gone so swiftly for Bolitho he thought life might be quieter at sea than it had been in harbour. Palliser had kept him working watch-on, watch-off with hardly a break. The first lieutenant took nothing at face value and made a point of questioning Bolitho on his daily work, his opinions and suggestions for changing some of the men around on the watch and quarter bills. If he was swift with his sarcasm, Palliser was equally quick to put his subordinate's ideas to good use.

Bolitho often thought of Rhodes's words about the first lieutenant. *After a command of his own.* He would certainly do his best for the ship and her captain, and be doubly quick to stamp on any incompetence which might eventually be laid at his door.

And Bolitho had worked hard to know the men he would deal with directly. Unlike the great ships of the line, a frigate's survival depended on her agility and not the thickness of her timbers. Likewise, her company was divided into divisions where they could work with the best results for the ship's benefit.

The foremast, with all its spread of canvas, course and topsail, topgallants and royals, with the additional foresails, jib and flying jib provided the means to turn with haste, through the wind's eye if need be, or to luff and cut across an enemy's vulnerable stern. At the opposite end of the ship the helmsmen and sailing master would use each mast, each scrap of canvas to lay the vessel on the course required with the least need for manoeuvre.

Bolitho was in charge of the mainmast. The tallest in the ship, it too was graded like the men who would soon be swarming aloft when ordered, no matter how they felt or what the weather threw against them.

The nimble topmen were the cream of the company, while on the deck itself, working at braces and halliards and manning the capstan bars, were the landmen, the newly recruited, or old sailors who could no longer be expected to fight salt-hardened canvas a hundred feet and more above the hull.

Rhodes had the fore, while a master's mate took charge of the mizzen-mast, supposedly the easiest one in any ship with its limited sail plan and where bodily strength was the first requirement. The afterguard, marines and a handful of seamen were sufficient to attend the mizzen.

Bolitho made a point of meeting the boatswain, a formidable-looking man named Timbrell. Tall, weather-beaten and scarred like an ancient warrior, he was the king of the vessel's seamen. Once clear of the land, Timbrell would work under the first lieutenant to rectify storm damage, repair spars and rigging, maintain the paintwork, ensure all seams were free of leaks, and generally keep an eye on the professionals who would carry out those needs. The carpenter and his crew, the cooper and the sailmaker, the ropemaker and all the rest.

A seaman to his fingertips, he was a good friend to a new officer, but could be a bad enemy if provoked.

This particular Monday morning had begun early, before daybreak. With the cook providing a hasty meal, as if he too was conscious of the need to get under way.

Lists were checked yet again, names to match voices, faces to put into jobs where they belonged. To a landsman it would have looked like chaos, with lines snaking across the decks, men working aloft astride the great yards as they loosened the sails, hardened overnight by an unexpected frost.

Bolitho had seen the captain come on deck several times. Speaking with Palliser or discussing something with Gulliver, the master. If he was anxious he did not show it, but strode around the quarterdeck with his sure-footed tread like a man thinking of something else beyond the ship.

The officers and warrant officers had changed into their faded sea-going uniforms, so that only Bolitho and most of the young midshipmen looked alien in their new coats and shining buttons.

Bolitho had received two letters from his mother, both together from the Falmouth Mail. He could picture her as he had last seen her. So frail, and so lovely. The lady who had never grown up, some local people said. The Scottish girl who had captivated Captain James Bolitho from their first meeting. She was really too frail to carry the weight of the house and the estate. With his elder brother Hugh at sea somewhere, back aboard his frigate after a short period in command of the revenue cutter *Avenger* at Falmouth, and their father not yet home, the burden would seem doubly hard. His grown-up sister Felicity had already left home to marry an army officer, while the youngest in the family, Nancy, should have been thinking of a coming marriage of her own.

Bolitho crossed to the gangway where the hands were stowing the hammocks brought up from below. Poor Nancy, she would be missing Bolitho's dead friend more than anyone, and with nothing to keep her mind free of her loss.

Someone stood beside him and he turned to see the surgeon peering at the shore. The time he had found to speak with the rotund surgeon had been well spent. Another strange member in their company. Ship's surgeons, in Bolitho's experience, had been of the poorest quality, butchers for the most part, and their bloody work with knife and saw was as feared by sailors as any enemy broadside.

But Henry Bulkley was a world apart. He had been in a comfortable living in London, at a prestigious address where his clients had been wealthy but demanding.

Bulkley had explained to Bolitho during the quiet of a dog-watch, 'I got to hate the tyranny of the sick, the selfishness of people who are only content if they are ill. I came to sea to escape. Now I *repair* and do not have to waste my time on those too rich to know their own bodies. I am as much a specialist as Mr Vallance, our gunner, or the carpenter, and I share their work in my own way. Or poor Codd, the purser, who frets over each mile logged and sets it against his stores of cheese and salt beef, candles and slop clothing.'

He had smiled contentedly. 'And I enjoy the pleasure of seeing other lands. I have sailed with Captain Dumaresq for three years. He, of course, is never sick. He would not *permit* it to happen!'

Bolitho said, 'It is a strange feeling to leave like this. To an unknown destination, a landfall which only the captain and two or three others may know. No war, yet we sail ready to fight.'

He saw the big man called Stockdale mustering in line with the other seamen around the trunk of the mainmast.

The surgeon followed his glance and observed, 'I heard something of what happened ashore. You have made a firm convert in that one. My God, he looks like an oak. I say that Little must have tripped him to win his money.' He shot a glance at Bolitho's profile. 'Unless he wanted to come with you? To escape from something, like most of us, eh?'

Bolitho smiled. Bulkley did not know the half of it. Stockdale had been allotted to the mizzen-mast for sail drill, and the quarterdeck six-pounders when the ship cleared for action. It was all in writing and signed with Palliser's slashing signature.

But somehow Stockdale had managed to alter things. Here he was in Bolitho's division, and would be stationed on the starboard battery of twelve-pounders which were in Bolitho's charge.

A quarter-boat pulled strongly from the shoreline, all the others having been hoisted inboard on their tier before the first cock had even considered crowing.

The last link with the land. Dumaresq's final letters and despatches for the courier. Eventually they would end up on somebody's desk at the Admiralty. A note would be passed to the First Sea Lord, a mark might be made on one of the great charts there. A small ship leaving under sealed orders. It was nothing new, only the times had changed.

Palliser stroke to the quarterdeck rail, his speaking trumpet beneath his arm, his head darting around like a bird of prey seeking the next victim.

Bolitho looked up at the mainmast truck and was just able to discern the long red masthead pendant as it snapped out towards the quarter. A north-westerly wind. Dumaresq would need at least that to work clear of the anchorage. Never easy at the best of times, and after three months without sea-going activity, it would only require some forgetful seaman or petty officer to relay the wrong order and a proud exit might become a shambles in minutes.

Palliser called, 'All officers lay aft, if you please.' He sounded irritable, and was obviously conscious of the importance of the moment.

Bolitho joined Rhodes and Colpoys on the quarterdeck, while the master and the surgeon hovered slightly in the background like intruders.

Palliser said, 'We shall weigh in half an hour. Take up your stations, and watch every man. Tell the boatswain's mates to start anyone shirking his work, and take the name of each malingerer for punishment.' He glanced at Bolitho curiously. 'I have put that Stockdale man with you. I am uncertain as to why, but he seemed to feel it was his place. You must have some special gift, Mr Bolitho, though for the life of me I cannot see it!'

They touched their hats and walked away to their various stations.

Palliser's voice followed them, hollow and insistent through the speaking trumpet.

'Mr Timbrell! Ten more hands on the capstan! Where is that damn shantyman?'

The trumpet swivelled round like a coachman's blunderbuss. 'Hell's teeth, Mr Rhodes, I want the anchor hove short this morning, *not next week*!'

Clink, clink, clink, the pawls on the capstan moved reluctantly as the men threw themselves on the bars. Whippings and lashings had been cast off from the various coils of halliards and other running rigging, and while the officers and midshipmen were placed at intervals along the decks, like blue and white islets amongst a moving tide of seamen, the ship seemed to come alive, as if she too was aware of the time.

Bolitho darted a glance at the land. No more sun, and a light drizzle had begun to patter across the water, touching the ship and making the waiting men shiver and stamp their bare feet.

Little was whispering fiercely to two of the new seamen, his big hands stabbing out like spades as he made some point or other. He saw Bolitho and sighed.

'Gawd, sir, they're like blocks o' wood!'

Bolitho watched his two midshipmen and wondered how he should break the barrier which had sprung up as he had appeared on deck. He had spoken only briefly to them the previous day. *Destiny* was the first ship to both of them, as she was to all but two of the 'young gentlemen'. Peter Merrett was so small he seemed unable to find a place amid the straining ropes and panting, thrusting seamen. He was twelve years old, the son of a prominent Exeter lawyer, who in turn was the brother of an admiral. A formidable combination. Much later on, if he lived, little Merrett might use such influence to his own advantage, and at the cost of others. But now, shivering and not a little frightened, he looked the picture of misery. The other one was Ian Jury, a fourteen-year-old youth from Weymouth. Jury's father had been a distinguished sea officer but had died in a shipwreck when Ian had still been a child. To the dead captain's relatives the Navy must have seemed the obvious place for Jury. It would also save them a great deal of trouble.

Bolitho nodded to them.

Jury was tall for his age, a pleasant-faced youth with fair hair and a barely controlled excitement.

Jury was the first to speak. 'Do we know where we are bound, sir?'

Bolitho studied him gravely. Under four years between them. Jury was not really like his dead friend, but the hair was similar.

He cursed himself for his brooding and replied, 'We shall know soon enough.' His voice came out more sharply than he had intended and he said, 'It is a well-kept secret as far as I am concerned.'

Jury watched him, his eyes curious. Bolitho knew what he was thinking, all the things he wanted to ask, to know, to discover in his new, demanding world. As he had once been himself.

Bolitho said, 'I shall want you to go aloft to the maintop, Mr Jury, and watch over the hands as they work. You, Mr Merrett, will remain with me to pass messages forrard or aft as need be.'

He smiled as their eyes explored the towering criss-cross of shrouds and rigging, the great main-yard and those above it reaching out on either beam like huge long-bows.

The two senior midshipmen, Henderson and Cowdroy, were aft by the mizzen, while the remaining pair were assisting Rhodes by the foremast.

Stockdale happened to be nearby and wheezed, 'Good mornin' for it, sir.'

Bolitho smiled at his battered features. 'No regrets, Stockdale?'

The big man shook his head. 'Nah. I needs a change. This will do me.'

Little grinned from across a long twelve-pounder. 'Reckon you could take the main-brace all on yer own!'

Some of the seamen were chattering or pointing out landmarks on the shore as the light began to strengthen.

From the quarterdeck came the instant reprimand. 'Mr Bolitho, sir, keep those hands in order! It is more like a cattle-fair than a man-o'-war!'

Bolitho grimaced. 'Aye, aye, sir!'

He added for Little's benefit, 'Take the name of anyone who . . .'

He got no chance to finish as Captain Dumaresq's cocked hat appeared through the after companion and then with apparent indifference his bulky figure moved to one side of the quarterdeck.

Bolitho whispered fiercely to the midshipmen, 'Now listen, you two. Speed is important, but not more so than getting things done correctly. Don't badger the men unnecessarily, most of them have been at sea for years anyway. Watch and learn, be ready to assist if one of the new hands gets in a tangle.'

They both nodded grimly as if they had just heard words of great wisdom.

'Standing by forrard, sir!'

That was Timbrell, the boatswain. He seemed to be everywhere. Pausing to put a new man's fingers properly around a brace or away from a block so that when his companions threw their weight on it he would not lose half of his hand. He was equally ready to bring his rattan cane down with a crack on somebody's shoulders if he thought he was acting stupidly. It brought a yelp of pain, and unsympathetic grins from the others.

Bolitho heard the captain say something, and seconds later the red ensign ran smartly up to the peak and blew out in the wind like painted metal.

Timbrell again. 'Anchor's hove short, sir!' He was leaning over the beak-head, peering intently at the current as it swirled beneath the bowsprit.

'Stand by on the capstan!'

Bolitho darted another glance aft. The place of command. Gulliver with his helmsmen, three today at the big double wheel. Taking no chances. Colpoys with his marines at the mizzen braces, the midshipman of the watch, and the signals midshipman, Henderson, still staring up at the wildly flapping ensign to make sure the halliards had not fouled. With the ship about to leave port, it would be more than his life was worth.

At the quarterdeck rail, Palliser with a master's mate, and slightly apart from them all, the captain, stout legs well braced, hands beneath his coat-tails, as he stared the full length of his command. To his astonishment, Bolitho saw that Dumaresq was wearing a scarlet waistcoat beneath his coat.

'*Loose heads'ls!*'

The men up forward stirred into life, an unwary landman almost getting trampled underfoot as the great areas of canvas flapped and writhed in their sudden freedom.

Palliser glanced at the captain. There was the merest nod. Then the first lieutenant lifted his speaking trumpet and yelled, 'Hands aloft there! *Loose tops'ls!*'

The ratlines above either gangway were filled with seamen as they rushed up like monkeys towards the yards, while other fleet-footed topmen dashed on higher still, ready to play their part when the ship was under way.

Bolitho smiled to hide his anxiety as Jury sped after the clawing, hurrying seamen.

By his side Merrett said horsely, 'I feel sick, sir.'

Slade, the senior master's mate, paused and snarled, 'Then contain it! Spew up 'ere, my lad, an' I'll stretch you across a gun an' give you six strokes to sharpen your wits!' He hurried on, snapping orders, pushing men to their proper stations, the small midshipman already forgotten.

Merrett sniffed. 'Well, I *do* feel sick!'

Bolitho said, 'Stand over there.'

He peered towards the speaking trumpet and then aloft at his men strung out along the yards, the great billowing mass of the main-topsail already catching pockets of wind and trying to wrench itself free.

'Man the braces! Stand by . . .'

'*Anchor's aweigh, sir!*'

Like a released animal the *Destiny* paid off into the wind, her sails thundering out from her yards, banging and puffing in a frenzy until with the men straining at the braces to haul the yards round and the helm hard over she came under command.

Bolitho swallowed bile as a man slipped on the mainyard but was hauled to safety by one of his mates.

Round and further still, so that the land seemed to be whirling past the bows and the graceful figurehead in a wild dance.

'More hands to the weather forebrace! Take that man's name! Mr Slade! See to the anchor and lively now!'

Palliser's voice was never still. As the anchor rose dripping to the cathead and was swiftly made fast to prevent it battering at the ship's hull, more men were rushed elsewhere by his demanding trumpet.

'Get the fore and main-courses set!'

The biggest sails boomed out from their yards and hardened like iron in the driving wind. Bolitho paused to straighten his hat and draw breath. The land where he had searched for volunteers was safely on the opposite beam now, and with her masts lining up to the wind and rudder *Destiny* was already pointing towards the narrows, beyond which the open sea waited like a field of grey.

Men fought with snaking lines while overhead blocks screamed as braces and halliards took on the strain of muscle against the wind and a growing pyramid of canvas.

Dumaresq had not apparently moved. He was watching the land sliding abeam, his chin tightly jammed into his neckcloth.

Bolitho dashed some rain or spray from his eyes, feeling his own excitement, suddenly grateful he had not lost it. Through the narrows and into the Sound, where Drake had waited to match the Armada, where a hundred admirals had pondered and considered their immediate futures. And where after that?

'Leadsman in the chains, Mr Slade!'

Bolitho knew he was in a frigate now. No careful, portly manoeuvre here. Dumaresq knew there would be many eyes watching from the land even at this early hour. He would cut past the headland as close as he dared, with just a fathom between the keel and disaster. He had the wind, he had the ship to do it.

Behind him he heard Merrett retching helplessly and hoped Palliser would not see him.

Stockdale was bending a line round his palm and elbow in a manner born. On his thick arm it looked like a thread. He and the captain made a good pair.

Stockdale said huskily, 'Free, that's what I am.'

Bolitho made to reply but realized the battered fighter was speaking for his own benefit.

Palliser's tone stung like a lash. 'Mr Bolitho! I shall tell you *first*, as I need the t'gan'sls set as soon as we are through the narrows! It may give you time to complete your dream and attend to your duties, sir!'

Bolitho touched his hat and beckoned to his petty officers. Palliser was all right in the wardroom. On deck he was a tyrant.

He saw Merrett bending over a gun and vomiting into the scuppers.

'Damn your eyes, Mr Merrett! Clean up that mess before you dismiss! And control yourself!'

He turned away, confused and embarrassed. Palliser was not the only one, it seemed.

3

Sudden Death

The week which followed *Destiny*'s departure from Plymouth was the busiest and the most demanding in Richard Bolitho's young life.

Once free of the land's protection, Dumaresq endeavoured to set as much canvas as his ship could safely carry in a rising wind. The world was confined to a nightmare of stinging, ice-cold spray, violent swooping thrusts as the frigate smashed her way through troughs and rearing crests alike. It seemed as if it would never end, with no time to find dry clothing, and what food the cook had been able to prepare and have carried through the pitching hull had to be gulped down in minutes.

Once as Rhodes relieved Bolitho on watch he shouted above the din of cracking canvas and the sea surging inboard along the lee side, 'It's the lord and master's way, Dick! Push the ship to the limit, find the strength of every man aboard!' He ducked as a phantom of freezing spray doused them both. 'Officers, too, for that matter!'

Tempers became frayed, and once or twice small incidents of insubordination flared openly, only to be quenched by some heavy-fisted petty officer or the threat of formal punishment at the gratings.

The captain was often on deck, moving without effort between compass and chartroom, discussing progress with Gulliver, the master, or the first lieutenant.

And at night it was always worse. Bolitho never seemed to get his head buried in a musty pillow for his watch below before the hoarse cry was carried between deck like a call to arms.

'All hands! All hands aloft an' reef tops'ls!'

And it was then that Bolitho really noticed the difference. In a ship of the line he had been forced to claw his way aloft with the rest of them, fighting his loathing of heights and conscious only of the need not to show that fear to others. But when it was done, it was done. Now, as a lieutenant, it was all happening just as Dumaresq had prophesied.

In the middle of one fierce gale, as *Destiny* had tacked and battered her way through the Bay of Biscay, the call had come to take in yet another reef. There had been no moon or stars, just a rearing wall of broken water, white against the outer darkness, to show just how small their ship really was.

Men, dazed by constant work and half blinded by salt spray, had staggered to their stations, and then reluctantly had begun to drag themselves up the vibrating ratlines, then out along the topsail yards. The *Destiny* had been leaning so steeply to leeward that her main-yard had seemed to be brushing the broken crests alongside.

Forster, the captain of the maintop, and Bolitho's key petty officer, had yelled, 'This man says 'e won't go aloft, sir! No matter what!'

Bolitho had seized a stay to prevent himself from being flung on his face. 'Go yourself, Forster! Without you up there God knows what might happen!' He had peered up at the remainder of his men while all the time the wind had moaned and shrieked, like a demented being enjoying their torment.

Jury had been up there, his body pressed against the shrouds by the force of the wind. On the foremast they had been having the same trouble, with men and cordage, sails and spars all pounded together while the ship had done her best to hurl them into the sea below.

Bolitho had then remembered what Forster had told him. The man in question had been staring at him, a thin, defiant figure in a torn checkered shirt and seaman's trousers.

'What's the matter with you?' Bolitho had had to yell above the din.

'I can't go, sir.' The man had shaken his head violently. '*Can't!*'

Little had come lurching past, cursing and blaspheming as he helped to haul some new cordage to the mainmast in readiness for use.

He had bellowed, 'I'll drag 'im aloft, sir!'

Bolitho had shouted to the seaman, 'Go below and help relieve the pumps!'

Two days later the same man had been reported missing. A search of the ship by Poynter, the master-at-arms, and the ship's corporal, had revealed nothing.

Little had tried to explain as best as he knew how. 'It were like this, sir. You should 'ave *made* 'im go aloft, even if 'e fell and broke 'is back. Or you could 'ave taken 'im aft for punishment. 'E'd 'ave got three dozen lashes, but 'e'd 'ave been a *man*!'

Bolitho had reluctantly understood. He had taken away the seaman's pride. His messmates would have sympathized with a man seized up at the gratings and flogged. Their contempt had been more than that lonely, defiant seaman had been able to stand.

On the sixth day the storm passed on and left them breathless and dazed by its intensity. Sails were reset, and the business of clearing up and repairing put aside any thought of rest.

Now, everyone aboard knew where the ship was first headed. To the Portuguese island of Madeira, although what for was a mystery still.

Except to Rhodes, who had confided that it was merely to lay in a great store of wine for the surgeon's personal use.

Dumaresq had obviously read the report of the seaman's death in the log, but had said nothing of it to Bolitho. At sea, more men died by accident than ever from ball or cutlass.

But Bolitho blamed himself. The others, Little and Forster, years ahead of him in age and experience, had turned to him because he was their lieutenant.

Forster had remarked indifferently, 'Well, 'e weren't much bloody good anyway, sir.'

All Little had offered had been, 'Could 'ave been worse, sir.'

It was amazing to see the difference the weather made. The ship came alive again, and men moved about their work without glancing fearfully across their shoulders or clinging to the shrouds with both arms whenever they went aloft to splice or reeve new blocks.

On the morning of the seventh day, while the smell of cooking started the wagers going as to what the dish would eventually be, the masthead lookout yelled, 'Deck there! Land on the lee bow!'

Bolitho had the watch, and beckoned Merrett to bring him a telescope. The midshipman looked like a little old man after the storm and a week of back-breaking work. But he was still alive, and was never late on watch.

'Let me see.' Bolitho levelled the glass through the black shrouds and past the figurehead's curved shoulder.

Dumaresq's voice made him start. 'Maderia, Mr Bolitho. An attractive island.'

Bolitho touched his hat. For so heavy a man the captain could move without making a sound.

'I – I'm sorry, sir.'

Dumaresq smiled and took the telescope from Bolitho's hands. As he trained it on the distant island he added, 'When I was a lieutenant I always made sure that somebody in my watch was ready to warn me of my captain's approach.'

He glanced at Bolitho, the wide, compelling eyes seeking something. 'But not you, I suspect. Not yet anyway.'

He tossed the glass to Merrett and added, 'Walk with me. Exercise is good for the soul.'

So up and down along the weather side of the quarterdeck the *Destiny*'s captain and her most junior lieutenant took their stroll, their feet by-passing ring-bolts and gun-tackles without conscious effort.

Dumaresq spoke briefly of his home in Norfolk, but only as a place. He did not sketch in the people there, his friends, or whether he was married or not.

Bolitho tried to put himself in Dumaresq's place. Able to walk and speak of other, unimportant things while his ship leaned to a steady wind, her sails set one above the other in ordered array. Her officers, her seamen and marines, the means to sail and fight under any given condition, were all his concern. At this moment they were heading for an island, and afterwards they would sail much further. The responsibility seemed endless. As Bolitho's father had once wryly remarked, 'Only one law remains unchanged for any captain. If he is successful others will reap the credit. If he fails he will take the blame.'

Dumaresq asked suddenly, 'Are you settled in now?'

'I think so, sir.'

'Good. If you are still mulling over that seaman's death, I must ask you to desist. Life is God's greatest gift. To risk it is one thing, to throw it away is to cheat. He had no *right*. Best forgotten.'

He turned away as Palliser appeared on deck, the master-at-arms bringing up the rear.

Palliser touched his hat to the captain, but his eyes were on Bolitho.

'Two hands for punishment, sir.' He held out his book. 'You know them both.'

Dumaresq tilted forward on his toes, so that it appeared as if his heavy body would lose its balance.

'See to it at two bells, Mr Palliser. Get it over and done with. No sense in putting the people off their food.' He strode away, nodding to the master's mate of the watch like a squire to his gamekeeper.

Palliser closed his book with a snap. 'My compliments to Mr Timbrell, and ask him to have a grating rigged.' He crossed to Bolitho's side. 'Well, now?'

Bolitho said, 'The captain told me of his home in Norfolk, sir.'

Palliser seemed vaguely disappointed. 'I see.'

'Why does the captain wear a red waistcoat, sir?'

Palliser watched the master-at-arms returning with the boatswain. 'Really, I am surprised your confidences did not extend that far.'

Bolitho hid a smile as Palliser strode away. He did not know either. After three years together that was something.

Bolitho stood beside Rhodes at the taffrail and watched the colourful activity of Funchal Harbour and its busy waterfront. *Destiny* lay at her anchor, with only the quarter-boat and the captain's gig in the water alongside. It did not look as if anyone would be allowed ashore, Bolitho thought.

Local boats with quaint curling stems and stern-posts milled around the frigate, their occupants holding up fruit and bright shawls, big jars of wine and many other items to tempt the sailors who thronged the gangways or waved from the shrouds and tops.

Destiny had anchored in mid-afternoon, and all hands had stayed on deck to watch the final approach, drinking in the beauty of what Dumaresq had rightly described as an attractive island. The hills beyond the white buildings were filled with beautiful flowers and shrubs, a sight indeed after the wild passage through the Bay. That, and the two floggings which had been carried out even as the ship had changed tack for their final approach, were forgotten.

Rhodes smiled and pointed at one boat. It contained three dark-haired girls who lay back on their cushions and stared boldly up at the young officers. It was obvious what they hoped to sell.

Captain Dumaresq had gone ashore almost as soon as the smoke of the gun salute to the Portuguese governor had dispersed. He had told Palliser he was going to meet the governor and pay his respects, but Rhodes said later, 'He's too excited for a mere social visit, Dick. I smell intrigue in the air.'

The gig had returned with instructions that Lockyer, the captain's clerk, was to go ashore with some papers from the cabin strong-box. He was down there now fussing about with his bag of documents while the side-party arranged for a boatswain's chair to sway him out and down into the gig.

Palliser joined them and said disdainfully, 'Look at the old fool. Never goes ashore, but when he does they have to rig a chair in case he falls and drowns!'

Rhodes grinned as the clerk was finally lowered into the boat. 'Must be the oldest man aboard.'

Bolitho thought about it. That was something else he had discovered. It was a young company, with very few senior hands like those he had known in the big seventy-four. The sailing master of a man-of-war was usually getting on in years by the time he was appointed, but Gulliver was under thirty.

Most of the hands lounging at the nettings or employed about the decks looked in good health. It was mostly due to the surgeon, Rhodes had said. That was the value of a medical man who cared, and who had the knowledge to fight the dreaded scurvy and other diseases which could cripple a whole ship.

Bulkley was one of the few privileged ones. He had gone ashore with orders from the captain to purchase all the fresh fruit and juices he thought necessary, while Codd, the purser, had similar instructions on the matter of vegetables.

Bolitho removed his hat and let the sun warm his face. It would be good to explore that town. Sit in a shady tavern like those Bulkley and some of the others had described.

The gig had reached the jetty now and some of *Destiny*'s marines were making a passage through a watching crowd for old Lockyer to get through.

Palliser said, 'I see that your shadow is nearby.'

Bolitho turned his head and saw Stockdale kneeling beside a twelve-pounder on the gun-deck. He was listening to Vallance, the ship's gunner, and then making gestures with his hand beneath the carriage. Bolitho saw Valance nod and then clap Stockdale on the shoulder.

That was unusual. He already knew that Vallance was not the easiest warrant officer to get along with. He was jealous about everything in his domain, from magazine to gun crews, from maintenance to the wear and tear of tackle.

He came aft and touched his hat to Palliser.

'That new man Stockdale, sir. He's solved a problem with a gun I've been bothered with for months. It was a replacement, y'see. I've not been happy about it.' He gave a rare smile. 'Stockdale thinks we could get the carriage reset by . . .'

Palliser spread his hands. 'You amaze me, Mr Vallance. But do what you must.' He glanced at Bolitho. 'Your man may not say much, but he is certainly finding his place.'

Bolitho saw Stockdale looking up at him from the gun-deck. He nodded and saw the man smile, his battered face screwed up in the sunlight.

Jury, who was the midshipman of the watch, called, 'Gig's shoved off, sir!'

'That was quick!' Rhodes snatched a telescope. 'If it's the captain coming back already, I'd better . . .' He gasped and added quickly, 'Sir, they're bringing Lockyer with them!'

Palliser took a second glass and levelled it on the green-painted gig. Then he said quietly, 'The clerk's dead. Sergeant Barmouth is holding him.'

Bolitho took the telescope from Rhodes. For the moment he could see nothing unusual. The smart gig was pulling strongly towards the ship, the white oars rising and falling in perfect unison, the crew in their red checkered shirts and tarred hats a credit to their coxswain.

Then as the gig swung silently to avoid a drifting log, Bolitho saw the marine sergeant, Barmouth, holding the wispy-haired clerk so that he would not fall into the sternsheets.

There was a terrible wound across his throat, which in the sunlight was the same colour as the marine's tunic. Rhodes murmured, 'And the surgeon's ashore with most of his assistants. God, there'll be hell to pay for this!'

Palliser snapped his fingers. 'That man you brought aboard with the other new hands, the apothecary's assistant? Where is he, Mr Bolitho?'

Rhodes said quickly, 'I'll fetch him, sir. He was doing some jobs in the sick-bay, just to test him out, the surgeon said.'

Palliser looked at Jury. 'Tell the boatswain's mate to rig another tackle.' He rubbed his chin. 'This was no accident.'

The local boats parted to allow the gig to glide to the main chains.

There was something like a great sigh as the small, untidy boat was hauled up the side and swung carefully above the gangway. Some blood ran down on to the deck, and Bolitho saw the man who had joined his recruiting party hurrying with Rhodes to take charge of the corpse.

The apothecary's assistant's name was Spillane. A neat, self-contained man, not the sort who would leave security to seek adventure or even experience, Bolitho would have thought. But he seemed competent, and as he watched him telling the seamen what to do, Bolitho was glad he was aboard.

Sergeant Barmouth was saying, 'Yessir, I'd just made sure that the clerk was safely through the crowd, an' was about to take my stand on the jetty again, when I 'eard a cry, then everyone started yellin' an' carryin' on, you know, sir, like they does in these parts.'

Palliser nodded abruptly. 'Quite so, Sergeant. What then?'

'I found 'im in an alley, sir. 'Is throat was slit.'

He paled as he saw his own officer striding angrily across the quarterdeck. He would have to repeat everything for Colpoys's sake. The marine lieutenant, like most of his corps, disliked interference by the sea officers, no matter how pressing the reason.

Palliser said distantly, 'And his bag was missing.'

'Yessir.'

Palliser made up his mind. 'Mr Bolitho, take the quarter-boat, a midshipman and six extra hands. I'll give you an address where you will find the captain. Tell him what has happened. No dramatics, just the facts as you know them.'

Bolitho touched his hat, excited, even though he was still shocked by the suddenness of Lockyer's brutal death. So Palliser did know more of what the captain was doing than he proclaimed. When he looked at the scrap of paper which Palliser thrust into his hand he knew it was not the governor's residence, or any other official place for that matter.

'Take Mr Jury, and select six men yourself. I want them smartly turned out.'

Bolitho beckoned to Jury and heard Palliser say to Rhodes, 'I might have sent you, but Mr Bolitho and Jury have newer uniforms and may bring less diccredit on my ship!'

In next to no time they were being pulled across the water towards the shore. Bolitho had been at sea for a week, but it seemed longer, so great was the change in his surroundings.

Jury said, 'Thank you for taking me, sir.'

Bolitho thought of Palliser's parting shot. He could not resist a sarcastic jibe. And yet he had been the one to think of Spillane, the one to see what Stockdale was doing with the gun. A man of many faces, Bolitho thought.

He replied, 'Don't let the men wander about.'

He broke off as he saw Stockdale, half hidden by the boat's oarsmen. Somehow he had found time to change into his checked shirt and white trousers and equip himself with a cutlass.

Stockdale pretended not to see his surprise.

Bolitho shook his head. 'Forget what I said. I do not think you will have any trouble after all.'

What had the big man said? *I'll not leave you. Not now. Not never.*

The boat's coxswain watched narrowly and then thrust the tiller bar hard over.

'Toss yer oars!'

The boat came to a halt by some stone stairs and the bowman hooked on to a rusty chain.

Bolitho adjusted his sword-belt and looked up at the watching townspeople. They appeared very friendly. Yet a man had just been murdered a few yards away.

He said, 'Fall in on the jetty.'

He climbed up the stairs and touched his hat to Colpoys's pickets. The marines looked extremely cheerful, and despite their rigid attitudes in front of a ship's officer, they smelled strongly of drink, and one of them had a flower protruding from his collar.

Bolitho took his bearings and strode towards the nearest street with as much confidence as he could muster. The sailors tramped behind him, exchanging winks and grins with women on balconies and in windows above the street.

Jury asked, 'Who would want to kill poor Lockyer, sir?'

'Who indeed?'

Bolitho hesitated and then turned down a narrow alley where the roofs nodded towards each other as if to blot out the sky. There was a heady scent of flowers, and he heard someone playing a stringed instrument in one of the houses.

Bolitho checked his piece of paper and looked at an iron gate which opened on to a courtyard with a fountain in its centre. They had arrived.

He saw Jury staring round at the strangeness of everything, and remembered himself in similar circumstances.

He said quietly, 'You come with me.' He raised his voice. 'Stockdale, take charge out here. Nobody is to leave until I give the word, understood?'

Stockdale nodded grimly. He would probably batter any would-be troublemaker senseless.

A servant led them to a cool room above the courtyard where

Dumaresq was drinking wine with an elderly man who had a pointed white beard and skin like finely tooled leather.

Dumaresq did not stand. 'Yes, Mr Bolitho?' If he was startled by their unheralded arrival he hid it very well. 'Trouble?'

Bolitho glanced at the old man but Dumaresq said curtly, 'You are with friends here.'

Bolitho explained what had happened from the moment the clerk had left the ship with his bag.

Dumaresq said, 'Sergeant Barmouth is nobody's fool. If the bag had been there he would have found it.'

He turned and said something to the courtly gentleman with the beard, and the latter showed a brief flash of alarm before regaining his original composure.

Bolitho pricked up his ears. Dumaresq's host might live in Madeira, but the captain was speaking in Spanish, unless he was much mistaken.

Dumaresq said, 'Return to the ship, Mr Bolitho. My compliments to the first lieutenant and ask him to recall the surgeon and any other shore party immediately. I intend to weigh before nightfall.'

Bolitho closed his mind to the obvious difficulties, to say nothing of the risk of leaving harbour in the dark. He sensed the sudden urgency, the apprehension which Lockyer's murder had brought amongst them.

He nodded to the elderly man and then said to Dumaresq, 'A lovely house, sir.'

The old man smiled and bowed his head.

Bolitho strode down the stairs with Jury in his shadow, sharing every moment without knowing what was happening.

Bolitho wondered if the captain had noticed. That his host had understood exactly what he had said about his fine house. So if Dumaresq had spoken to him in Spanish it was so that neither he nor Jury should understand.

He decided it was one part of the mystery he would hold to himself.

That night, as promised, Dumaresq took his ship to sea. In light airs, and with all but her topsails and jib brailed up, *Destiny* steered slowly between other anchored vessels, guided by the ship's cutter with a lantern close to the water like a firefly to show her the way.

By dawn, Madeira was just a purple hump on the horizon far astern, and Bolitho was not certain if the mystery still remained there in the alley where Lockyer had drawn his last breath.

4

Spanish Gold

Lieutenant Charles Palliser closed the two outer screen doors of Dumaresq's cabin and said, 'All present, sir.'

In their various attitudes the *Destiny*'s lieutenants and senior warrant officers sat and watched Dumaresq expectantly. It was late afternoon, two days out of Madeira. The ship had a feeling of leisurely routine about her, as with a light north-easterly wind laying her on a starboard tack she cruised steadily into the Atlantic.

Dumaresq glanced up at the skylight as a shadow moved past it. Most likely the master's mate of the watch.

'Shut that, too.'

Bolitho glanced at his companions, wondering if they were sharing his growing sense of curiosity.

This meeting had been inevitable, but Dumaresq had taken great pains to ensure it would come well after his ship had cleared the land.

Dumaresq waited for Palliser to sit down. Then he looked at each man in turn. From the marine officer, past the surgeon, the master and the purser, finally to his three lieutenants.

He said, 'You all know about the death of my clerk. A reliable man, even if given to certain eccentricities. He will be hard to replace. However, his murder by some persons unknown means more than the loss of a companion. I have been under sealed orders, but the time is come to reveal some of the task we shall soon be facing. When two people know something it is no longer a secret. An even greater enemy in a small ship is rumour, and what it can do to idle minds.'

Bolitho flinched as the wide, compelling eyes paused on him momentarily before passing to some other part of the cabin.

Dumaresq said, 'Thirty years ago, before most of this ship's company had drawn breath, one Commodore Anson took an expedition south around Cape Horn and into the Great South Sea. His purpose was to harry Spanish settlements for, as you should know, we were then at war with the Dons.' He nodded grimly. 'Again.'

Bolitho thought of the courtly Spaniard in the house behind the harbour at Funchal, the secrecy, the missing bag for which a man had died.

Dumaresq continued, 'One thing is certain. Commodore Anson may have been courageous, but his ideas of health and caring for his people were limited.' He looked at the rotund surgeon and allowed his features to soften. 'Unlike us, maybe he had no proper doctors to advise him.'

There were several chuckles, and Bolitho guessed the remark had been made to put them more at their ease.

Dumaresq said, 'Be that as it may, within three years Anson had lost all of his squadron but his own *Centurion*, and had left thirteen hundred of his people buried at sea with his various escapades. Most of them died from disease, scurvy and bad food. It is likely that if Anson had returned home without further incident he would have faced a court martial and worse.'

Rhodes shifted in his chair, his eyes shining as he whispered, 'I *thought* as much, Dick.'

Dumaresq's glance silenced whatever it was Rhodes had been about to impart.

The captain brushed some invisible dust from his red waistcoat and said, 'Anson fell in with a Spanish treasure ship homeward bound with bullion in her holds valued at more than a million guineas.'

Bolitho vaguely remembered reading of the incident. Anson had seized the ship after a swift fight, had even broken off the action in order that the Spaniards could douse a fire which had broken out in their rigging. He had been that eager and desperate to take the treasure ship, *Nuestra Señora de Covadonga*, intact. Prize courts and the powers of Admiralty had long looked on such captures as of greater value than the lives lost to obtain them.

Dumaresq cocked his head, his calm attitude momentarily lost. Bolitho heard the hail from the masthead to report a sail far off to the north. They had already sighted it twice during the day, for it seemed unlikely there would be more than one vessel using this same lonely route.

The captain shrugged. 'We shall see.' He did not elaborate but continued, 'It was not known until recently that there was another treasure ship on passage to Spain. She was the *Asturias*, a larger vessel than Anson's prize, and therefore more heavily laden.' He darted a glance at the surgeon. 'I can see *you* have heard of her?'

Bulkley sat back and interlaced his fingers across his ample stomach. 'Indeed I have, sir. She was attacked by an English privateer under the command of a young Dorset man, Captain Piers Garrick. His letter of marque saved him many times from the gallows as a common pirate, but today he is Sir Piers Garrick, well respected, and the past holder of several government posts in the Caribbean.'

Dumaresq smiled grimly. 'True, but I suggest you confine your other suspicions to the limits of the wardroom! The *Asturias* was never found, and the privateer was so damaged by the engagement that she too had to be abandoned.'

He looked round, irritated as the sentry called through the door, 'Midshipman of the watch, *sir!*'

Bolitho could picture the anxiety on the quarterdeck. Should they disturb the meeting below their feet and risk Dumaresq's displeasure? Or should they just note the strange sail in the log and hope for the best?

Dumaresq said, 'Enter.' He did not seem to raise his voice and yet it carried to the outer cabin without effort.

It was Midshipman Cowdroy, a sixteen-year-old youth who Dumaresq had already punished for using unnecessary severity on members of his watch.

He said, 'Mr Slade's respects, sir, and that sail has been reported to the north'rd again.' He swallowed hard and seemed to shrink under the captain's stare.

Dumaresq said eventually, 'I see. We shall take no action.' As the door closed he added, 'Although I fear that stranger is not astern of us by coincidence.'

A bell chimed from the forecastle and Dumaresq said, 'Recent information has been found and sworn to that most of the treasure is intact. A million and a half in bullion.'

They stared at him as if he had uttered some terrible obscenity.

Then Rhodes exclaimed, 'And we are to discover it, sir?'

Dumaresq smiled at him. 'You make it sound very simple, Mr Rhodes, perhaps we shall find it so. But such a vast amount of treasure will, and has already, aroused interest. The Dons will want it back as their rightful property. A prize court will argue that as the ship had already been seized by Garrick's privateer before she managed to escape and hide, the bullion is the property of His Britannic Majesty.' He lowered his voice. 'And there are some who would seize it to further a cause which would do us nothing but harm. So, gentlemen, now you know. Our outward purpose is to complete the King's business. But if the news of this treasure is allowed to run riot elsewhere, I will want to know who is responsible.'

Palliser rose to his feet, his head bowed uncomfortably between the deckhead beams. The rest followed suit.

Dumaresq turned his back and stared at the glittering water which stretched to the horizon astern.

'First we go to Rio de Janeiro. Then I shall know more.'

Bolitho caught his breath. The South Americas, and Rio was all of 5000 miles from his home at Falmouth. It would be the furthest he had yet sailed.

As they made to leave Dumaresq said, 'Mr Palliser and Mr Gulliver, remain, if you please.'

Palliser called, 'Mr Bolitho, take over my watch until I relieve you.'

They left the cabin, each immersed in his own thoughts. The far-off destination would mean little to the ordinary sailor. The sea was always there, wherever he was, and the ship went with him. Sails had to be trimmed and reset at all hours, no matter what, and a seaman's life was hard whether the final landfall was in England or the Arctic. But let the rumour of treasure run through the ship and things might be very different.

As he climbed to the quarterdeck Bolitho saw the men assembling for the first-watch looking at him curiously, then turning away as he met their eyes, as if they already knew.

Mr Slade touched his hat. 'The watch is aft, sir.'

He was a hard master's mate and unpopular with many of the people, especially those who did not rise to his impressive standards of seamanship.

Bolitho waited for the helmsmen to be relieved, the usual handing over from one watch to the next. A glance aloft at the set of the yards and sails, examine the compass and the chalked notes on the slate made by the midshipman on duty.

Gulliver came on deck, banging his palms together as he did when he was worried.

Slade asked, 'Trouble, sir?'

Gulliver eyed him warily. He had been in Slade's position too recently to take any comment as casual. Seeking favours perhaps? Or a way of suggesting that he was out of his depth with the wardroom officers aft?

He snapped, 'At the next turn of the glass we will alter course.' He peered at the tilting compass, 'Sou'-west by west. The captain intends to see the t'gan'sls, though with these light winds under our coat-tails I doubt if we can coax another knot out of her.

Slade squinted up at the masthead lookout. 'So the strange sail means something.'

Palliser's voice preceded him up the companion ladder. 'It *means*, Mr Slade, that if that sail is still there tomorrow morning she is indeed following us.'

Bolitho saw the worry in Gulliver's eyes and guessed what Dumaresq must have said to him and Palliser.

'Surely there is nothing we can do about that, sir? We are not at war.'

Palliser regarded him calmly. 'There is quite a lot we can do about it.' He nodded to emphasize the point. 'So be ready.'

As Bolitho made to leave the quarterdeck in his care Palliser called after him, 'And I shall be timing those laggards of yours when all hands are piped to make more sail.'

Bolitho touched his hat. 'I am honoured, sir.'

Rhodes was waiting for him on the gun-deck. 'Well done, Dick. He'll
respect you if you stand up to him.'

They walked aft to the wardroom and Rhodes said, 'The lord and
master is going to take that other vessel, you know that, don't you,
Dick?'

Bolitho threw his hat on to one of the guns and sat down at the
wardroom table.

'I suppose so.' His mind drifted back again, to the coves and cliffs of
Cornwall. 'Last year, Stephen, I was doing temporary duty aboard a
revenue cutter.'

Rhodes was about to make a joke of it but saw the sudden pain in
Bolitho's eyes.

Bolitho said, 'There was a man then, a big and respected landowner.
He died trying to flee the country. It was proved he had been smuggling
arms for an uprising in America. Maybe the captain thinks this is
similar, and all this time that gold has been waiting for the right use.' He
grimaced, surprised at his own gravity. 'But let's talk about Rio. I am
looking forward to that.'

Colpoys strolled into the wardroom and arranged himself carefully in
a chair.

To Rhodes he said, 'The first lieutenant says you are to select a
midshipman to assist with the clerical duties in the cabin.' He crossed
his legs and remarked, 'Didn't know the young fellas could write!'

Their laughter died as the surgeon, unusually grim-faced, entered,
and after a quick glance around to make certain they were undisturbed,
said, 'The gunner's just told me something interesting. He was asked by
one of his mates if they would need to move some of the twelve-pounder
shot forward to make room for the bullion.' He let his words sink in.
'How long has it been? Fifteen minutes? Ten? It must be the shortest
secret of any day!'

Bolitho listened to the regular creak and clatter of rigging and spars,
the movement of the watch on deck overhead.

So be ready, Palliser had said. It had suddenly adopted another
meaning altogether.

The morning after Dumaresq's disclosures about the treasure ship
found the strange sail still lying far astern.

Bolitho had the morning-watch, and had sensed the growing tension
as the light hardened across the horizon and faces around him took on
shape and personality.

Then came the cry, 'Deck there! Sail to th' nor'-east!'

Dumaresq must have been ready for it, expecting it. He came on deck
within minutes, and after a cursory glance at the compass and the
flapping sails, observed, 'Wind's dropping off.' He looked at Bolitho.

'This is a damnable business.' He recovered himself instantly. 'I shall have breakfast now. Send Mr Slade aloft when he comes on watch. He has an eye for most craft. Tell him to study that stranger, though God knows she is cunning enough to keep her distance and still not lose us.'

Bolitho watched him until he had disappeared below and then looked along *Destiny*'s full length. It was the ship's busiest time, with seamen at work with holy-stones on the deck planking, others cleaning guns and checking running and standing rigging under Mr Timbrell's critical eye. The marines were going through one of their many, seemingly complicated drills with muskets and fixed bayonets, while Colpoys kept at a distance, leaving the work to his sergeant.

Beckett, the carpenter, was already directing some of his crew to begin repairs on the larboard gangway which had been damaged when a purchase had collapsed under the weight of some incoming stores. The upper deck with its double line of twelve-pounders was like a busy street and a market-place all in one. A place for hard work and gossip, for avoiding authority or seeking favour.

Later, with the decks cleaned up, the hands were piped to sail drill with Palliser at his place on the quarterdeck to watch their frantic efforts to knock seconds off the time it took to reef or make more sail.

And all the while as they lived through the daily routine of a man-of-war, that other sail never left them. Like a tiny moth on the horizon it was always there. When *Destiny* shortened sail and the way fell from beneath her beakhead, the stranger too would follow suit. Spread more canvas and the lookout would immediately report a responding action by the stranger.

Dumaresq came on deck as Gulliver was just completing his supervision of the midshipman's efforts as they took the noon sights to fix the ship's position.

Bolitho was close enough to hear him ask, 'Well, Mr Gulliver, how will the weather favour us tonight?' He sounded impatient, even angry that Gulliver should be doing his normal duties.

The sailing master glanced at the sky and the red masthead pendant. 'Wind's backed a piece, sir. But the strength is the same. Be no stars tonight, too much cloud in the offing.'

Dumaresq bit his lip. 'Good. So be it.' He swung round and called, 'Pass the word for Mr Palliser.' He saw Bolitho and said, 'You have the dog-watches today. Make certain you gather plenty of lanterns near the mizzen. I want our "friend" to see our lights later on. They will give him confidence.'

Bolitho watched the change in the man, the power running through him like a rising wave, a need to crush this impudent follower.

Palliser came striding aft, his eyes questioning again as he saw Dumaresq speaking with his junior lieutenant.

'Ah, Mr Palliser, I have work for you.'

Dumaresq smiled, but Bolitho could see from the way a nerve was
jumping at the corner of his jaw, the stiffness in his back and broad
shoulders, that his mind was less relaxed.

Dumaresq made a sweeping gesture. 'I shall require the launch ready
for lowering at dusk, earlier if the light is poor. A good man in charge, if
you please, and extra hands to get her mast stepped and sails set as soon
as they are cast off.' He watched Palliser's inscrutable face and added
lightly, 'I want them to carry several of the large lanterns, too. We shall
douse ours and darken ship completely as soon as the launch is clear.
Then I intend to beat hard to wind'rd, come about and *wait*.'

Bolitho turned to look at Palliser. To tackle another vessel in the dark
was not to be taken flippantly.

Dumaresq added, 'I shall flog any man aboard who shows so much as
a glow-worm.'

Palliser touched his hat. 'I'll attend to it, sir. Mr Slade can take charge
of the boat. He's so keen on promotion it'll do him good.'

Bolitho was astounded to see Dumaresq and the first lieutenant
laughing together like a pair of schoolboys, as if this was an everyday
occurrence.

Dumaresq looked at the sky and then turned to stare astern. Only
from the masthead could you see the other vessel, but it was as if he was
able to reach beyond the horizon itself. He was calm again, in control of
his feelings.

He said, 'Something to tell your father about, Mr Bolitho. It would
appeal to him.'

A seaman tramped past carrying a great coil of rope across his
shoulder like a bundle of dead snakes. It was Stockdale. As the captain
vanished below he wheezed, 'We goin' to fight that one, sir?'

Bolitho shrugged. 'I – I think so.'

Stockdale nodded heavily. 'I'll grind an edge on my blade, then.' That
was all it apparently meant to him.

Left alone to his thoughts, Bolitho crossed to the rail and looked
down at the men already working to free the launch from the other
boats on the tier. Did Slade, he wondered, yet realize what might
become of him? If the wind rose after they had dropped the launch,
Slade could be driven miles off course. It would be harder than finding a
pin in a hayrtack.

Jury came on deck, and after some hesitation joined him by the rail.

Bolitho stared at him. 'I thought you were sent aft to do poor
Lockyer's work?'

Jury met his gaze. 'I asked the first lieutenant if he would send Mr
Midshipman Ingrave instead.' Some of his composure collapsed under
Bolitho's gaze. 'I'd prefer to stay in your watch, sir.'

Bolitho clapped him on the shoulder. 'On your head be it.' But he felt pleased all the same.

The boatswain's mates hurried from hatchway to hatchway, their silver calls trilling in between their hoarse cries for the watch below to assist in swaying out the launch.

Jury listened to the shrill whistles and said, 'The Spithead nightingales are in full cry this evening, sir.'

Bolitho hid a smile. Jury spoke like an old sailor, a real sea-dog.

He faced him gravely. 'You'd better go and see what is being done about the lanterns. Otherwise Mr Palliser will have the both of us in full cry, I'm thinking.'

As dusk came down to conceal their preparations the masthead lookout reported that the other sail was still in sight.

Palliser touched his hat as the captain came on deck. 'All ready, sir.'

'Very well.' Dumaresq's eyes shone in the reflected glare from the array of lanterns. 'Shorten sail and stand by to lower the boat.' He looked up as the main-topsail filled and boomed sullenly from its yard. 'After that, every stitch she can carry. If that ferret back there is a friend, and merely seeking our protection on the high seas, we shall know it. If not, Mr Palliser, he shall know *that*, I promise you!'

An anonymous voice whispered, 'Cap'n's comin' up, sir!'

Palliser turned and waited for Dumaresq to join him by the quarterdeck rail.

Gulliver's shadow moved through the gloom. 'South by east, sir. Full and bye.'

Dumaresq gave a grunt. 'You were right about the clouds, Mr Gulliver, though the wind's fresher than I expected.'

Bolitho stood with Rhodes and three midshipmen at the lee side of the quarterdeck ready to execute any sudden order. More to the point, they were able to share the drama and the tension. Dumaresq's comment had sounded as if he blamed the master for the wind.

He looked up and shivered. *Destiny*, after thrashing and beating her way to windward for what had seemed like an eternity, had come about as Dumaresq had planned. With a stiff wind sweeping over the larboard quarter she was plunging across a procession of breaking white-horses, the spray rising above the weather rigging and sweeping on to the crouching seamen like tropical rain.

Destiny had been stripped down to her topsails and jib with her big forecourse holding two reefs in readiness for a swift change of tack.

Rhodes murmured, 'That other vessel is out there somewhere, Dick.'

Bolitho nodded and tried not to think of the launch as it had vanished into a deepening darkness, the lanterns making a lively show on the water.

It was an eerie feeling, with the ship so quiet around him. Nobody spoke, and the heavily greased gear was without its usual din and clatter. Just the sweeping sea alongside, the occasional rush of water through the lee scuppers as *Destiny* dropped her bows into a deep trough.

Bolitho wanted to forget what was happening around him and to concentrate on what he had to do. Palliser had selected the best seamen in the ship for a boarding party if it came to that. But the sudden upsurge of wind might have changed Dumaresq's ideas, he thought.

He heard Jury moving restlessly by the nettings, and Rhodes' midshipman, Mr Cowdroy, who had been in the ship for two years. He was a haughty, bad-tempered youth of sixteen who would be impossible as a lieutenant. Rhodes had had cause to report him to the captain more than once, and the last time he had been ignominiously caned across a six-pounder by the boatswain. It did not seem to have changed him. Little Merrett made up the trio, trying to keep out of sight, as usual.

Rhodes said softly, 'Soon now, Dick.' He loosened the hanger in his belt. 'Might be a slaver, who knows?'

Yeames, master's mate of the watch, said cheerfully, 'Not likely, sir. You'd *smell* a blackbirder by now!'

Palliser snapped, 'Be silent there!'

Bolitho watched the sea curling above the dipping side in a frothing white bank. Beyond it there was nothing but an occasional jagged crest. As black as a boot, as Colpoys had remarked. His marksmen were already aloft in the tops, trying to keep their muskets dry and watching for the first sight of the stranger.

If the captain and Gulliver had timed it correctly, the stranger should appear on *Destiny*'s starboard bow. The frigate would hold the wind-gage and the other vessel would have no chance of slipping away. The men at the starboard battery were ready, the gun captains on their knees as they prepared to run out as soon as the word came from aft.

To a civilian sitting by his hearth in England it might all seem like a kind of madness. But to Captain Dumaresq it was something else entirely, and it mattered. The other vessel, whatever she was, was interfering with the King's affairs. That made it personal, not to be taken lightly.

Bolitho gave another shiver as he recalled his first meeting with the captain. *To me, to this ship, and to His Britannic Majesty, in that order*!

Destiny raised her quivering jib-boom like a lance and seemed to hang motionless on the edge of another trough before she plunged forward and down, her bows smashing through solid water and flinging spray high above the forecastle.

From one corner of his eye Bolitho saw something fall from overhead. It hit the deck and exploded with a loud bang.

Rhodes ducked as a ball whined dangerously past his face and gasped, 'A damned bullock has dropped his musket!'

Startled voices and harsh accusations erupted from the gundeck, and Lieutenant Colpoys ran to the quarterdeck ladder in his haste to deal with the culprit.

It all happened in a swift sequence of events. The sudden explosion as *Destiny* ploughed her way towards the next array of crests, the attention of officers and seamen distracted for just a few moments.

Palliser said angrily, 'Stop that noise, damn your eyes!'

Bolitho turned and then froze as out of the darkness, running with the wind, came the other vessel. Not safely downwind to starboard, but right here, rising above the larboard side like a phantom.

'*Put up your helm!*' Dumaresq's powerful voice stopped some of the startled men in their tracks. 'Man the braces there, stand by on the quarterdeck!'

Rearing and plunging, her sails booming and thundering in wild confusion, *Destiny* began to swing away from the oncoming vessel. Gun crews who minutes earlier had been nursing their weapons in readiness for a fight were caught totally unawares, and even now were tumbling across to help the men on the opposite side where the twelve-pounders still pointed at their sealed ports.

More spray burst over the quarterdeck as another sea surged jubilantly across the nettings and drenched the men nearby. Order was being restored, and Bolitho saw seamen straining back on the braces until they seemed to be touching the deck itself.

He shouted, 'Stand to, men!' He was groping for his hanger even as he realized that Rhodes and his midshipman had already gone running to the bows. 'She'll be into us directly!'

A shot echoed above the din of sea and wind, but whether fired by accident or by whom, Bolitho did not know or care.

He felt Jury by his side.

'What'll we do, sir?'

He sounded frightened. As well he might, Bolitho thought. Merrett was clinging to the nettings as if nothing would ever shift him.

Bolitho used something like physical strength to control his stampeding thoughts. He was in charge. Nobody else was here to lead, to advise. Everyone on the upper deck was too occupied with his own role.

He managed to shout, 'Stay with me.' He pointed at a running figure. 'You, clear the starboard battery and prepare to repel boarders!'

As men floundered cursing and shouting in all directions, Bolitho heard Dumaresq's voice. He was on the opposite side of the deck, yet seemed to be speaking into Bolitho's ear.

'*Board*, Mr Bolitho!' He swung round as Palliser sent more men to shorten sail in a last attempt to delay the impact of collision. 'She must not escape!'

Bolitho stared at him, his eyes wild. 'Aye, sir!'

He was about to draw his hanger when with a thundering crash the other vessel drove hard alongside. But for Dumaresq's quick action she would have rammed into the *Destiny*'s broadside like a giant axe.

Yells changed to screams as a tumbling mass of cordage and broken spars crashed on and between the two hulls. Men were knocked from their feet as the sea lifted the vessels together yet again, bringing down another tangle of rigging and blocks. Some men had fallen, too, and Bolitho had to drag Jury by the arm as he shouted, 'Follow me!' He waved his hanger, keeping his eyes away from the sea which appeared to be boiling between the two snared hulls. One slip and it would be all over.

He saw Little brandishing a boarding axe, and of course Stockdale holding his cutlass like a dirk against his massive frame.

Bolitho gritted his teeth and leapt for the other vessel's shrouds, his legs kicking in space as he struck out seeking a foothold. His hanger had gone from his hand and swung dangerously from his wrist as he gasped and struggled to hold on. More men were on either side of him, and he retched as someone fell between the two vessels, the man's scream cut off abruptly like a great door being slammed shut.

As he dropped to the unfamiliar deck he heard other voices and saw vague shapes rushing across the fallen wreckage, some with blades in their fists, while from aft came the sharp crack of a pistol.

He groped for his hanger and shouted, 'Drop your weapons in the King's name!'

The roar of voices which greeted his puny demand was almost worse than the danger. Perhaps he had been expecting Frenchmen or Spaniards, but the voices which yelled derision at his upraised hanger were as English as his own.

A spar plunged straight down into the dark, momentarily separating the two opposing groups and smashing one of the figures to pulp. With a final quiver the two vessels wrenched themselves apart, and even as a sword-blade darted from the shadows towards him, Bolitho realized that *Destiny* had left him to fend for himself.

5

Blade to Blade

Calling to each other by name, and matching curses with their unknown adversaries, the *Destiny*'s small boarding party struggled to hold together. All the while the deck was flung about by the sea, the motion made worse by fallen spars and great creepers of rigging which trailed over the bulwarks and pulled the hull into each trough like a sea-anchor.

Bolitho slashed out at someone opposite him, his blade jarring against steel as he parried away another thrust. Bolitho was a good swordsman, but a hanger was a poor match for a straight blade. Around him men were yelling and gasping, bodies interlocked while they fought with cutlass and dirk, boarding axe and anything which they could lay hands on.

Little bellowed, 'Aft, lads! Come on!' He charged along the littered deck, hacking down a crouching shadow with his axe as he ran, and followed by half of the party.

Near Bolitho a man slipped and fell, and then rolled over, protecting his face from the one who stood astride him with a raised cutlass. Bolitho heard the swish of steel, the sickening thud of the blade driving into bone. But when he turned he saw Stockdale wrenching his own blade free before tossing the dead man unceremoniously over the side.

It was a wild, jumbled nightmare. Nothing seemed real, and Bolitho could feel the numbness thrusting through his limbs as he fought off another attacker who had slithered down the shrouds like an agile ape.

He ducked, and felt the man slice above his head, the breath rasping out of him from the force of his swing. Bolitho punched him in the stomach with the knuckle-bow of his hanger, and as he reeled away hacked him hard across the neck, the pain lancing up his arm as if he had been the one to be cut down.

Despite the horror and the danger, Bolitho's mind continued to respond, but like that of an onlooker, somebody uninvolved with the bloody hand-to-hand fighting around him. The vessel was a brigantine, her yards in disarray as she continued to fall downwind. There was a smell of newness about her, a freshly built craft. Her crew must have been dumbfounded when *Destiny*'s canvas had loomed across their bows, and that shock was the only thing which had so far saved the depleted boarding party.

A man bounded forward, regardless of the slashing figures and sobbing wounded who were being trampled underfoot.

Through his reeling mind one more thought came to Bolitho. This gaunt figure in a blue coat and brass buttons must be the vessel's master.

The brigantine was temporarily out of control, but within hours that could be put right. And *Destiny* was nowhere to be seen. Perhaps her damage was much worse than they had thought. You never really considered it might happen to your own ship. Always to another.

Bolitho saw the dull glint of steel and guessed dawn was not far away. Surprisingly, he thought of his mother, glad that she would not see his body when he fell.

The gaunt man yelled, 'Drop your sword, rot you!'

Bolitho tried to shout back at him, to rally his men, to give himself a last spur of defiance.

Then the blades crossed, and Bolitho felt the strength of the man through the steel as if it was an extension of his own arm.

Clash, clash, clash. Bolitho parried and cut at the other man, who took every advantage to press and follow each attack.

There was a clang, and Bolitho felt the hanger torn from his fingers, the lanyard around his wrist severed by the force of the blow.

He heard a frantic voice yell, 'Here, sir!' It was Jury, as he hurled a sword across the writhing bodies hilt-fist.

Bolitho's desperation came to his aid. Somehow he caught it, twisting it in his grip as he felt its balance and length. Tiny pictures flashed through his mind. His father teaching him and his brother Hugh in the walled kitchen-garden at Falmouth. Then later, matching careful movements against each other.

He sobbed as the other man's sword cut through his sleeve just below his armpit. Another inch and. . . . He felt the fury sweeping everything else aside, an insanity which seemed to give him back his strength, even his hope.

Bolitho locked blades again, feeling his opponent's hatred, smelling his strength and his sweat.

He heard Stockdale calling in his strange, husky voice and knew he was being pressed too hard to reach his side. Others had stopped fighting, their wind broken as they stared with glazed eyes at the two swordsmen in their midst.

From another world, or so it seemed, came the crash of a single cannon. A ball hissed over the deck and slammed through a flapping sail like an iron fist. *Destiny* was nearby, and her captain had taken the risk of killing some of his own men to make his presence felt and understood.

Some of the brigantine's men threw down their weapons instantly. Others were less fortunate and were felled by the inflamed boarders even as they tried to grasp what was happening.

Bolitho's adversary shouted wildly, 'Too late for you, *sir*!'

He thrust Bolitho back with his fist, measured the distance and lunged.

Bolitho heard Jury cry out, saw Little running towards him, his teeth bared like a wild animal.

After all the agony and the hate, it was too easy and without any sort of dignity. He held his balance and did not even have to guide his feet and arms as he stepped aside, using the other man's charge to flick his blade in one ringing encounter and then drive his own beneath the lost guard and into his chest.

Little dragged the man away and raised his bloodied axe as he tried to struggle free.

Bolitho shouted, 'Belay that! Let him be!'

He looked round, feeling dazed and sick, as some of his men gave a wild cheer.

Little let the man fall to the deck and wiped his face with the back of his wrist, as if he too was slowly but reluctantly letting go of the madness. Until the next time.

Bolitho saw Jury sitting with his back against a broken spar, his hands clasped across his stomach. He knelt down and tried to drag Jury's fingers away. Not him, he thought. Not so soon.

A seaman Bolitho recongnized as one of his best maintopmen bent down and jerked the midshipman's hands apart.

Bolitho swallowed hard and tore the shirt open, remembering Jury's fear and his trust at the moment of boarding. Bolitho was young, but he had done this sort of thing before.

He peered at the wound and felt like praying. A blade must have been stopped by the large gilt plate on Jury's cross-belt, he could see the scored metal even in the poor light. It had taken the real force, and the attacker had only managed to scar the youth's stomach.

The seaman grinned and fashioned a wad from Jury's torn shirt. 'He'll be all right, sir. Just a nick.'

Bolitho got shakily to his feet, one hand resting on the man's shoulders for support.

'Thank you, Murray. That was well said.'

The man looked up at him as if trying to understand something.

'I saw him throw that sword to you, sir. It was then that some other bugger made his play.' He wiped his cutlass absently on a piece of sailcloth. 'It was the last bloody thing he *did* do on this earth!'

Bolitho walked aft towards the abandoned wheel. Voices from the past seemed to be following him, reminding him of this particular moment.

They will be looking to you now. The fight and fury has gone out of them.

He turned and shouted, 'Take the prisoners below and put them under guard.'

He sought out a familiar face from others who had followed him blindly without really knowing what they were doing.

'You, Southmead, man the wheel. The rest go with Little and cut free the wreckage alongside.'

He glanced quickly at Jury. His eyes were open and he was trying not to cry out from the pain.

Bolitho forced a smile, his lips frozen and unreal. 'We have a prize. Thank you for what you did. It took real courage.'

Jury tried to reply but fainted away again.

Through the wind and spray Bolitho heard the booming challenge of Captain Dumaresq's voice through a speaking trumpet.

Bolitho called to Stockdale, 'Answer for me. I am spent!'

As the two vessels drew closer, their fine lines marred by broken spars and dangling rigging, Stockdale cupped his big hands and yelled, 'The ship is ours, sir!'

There was a ragged cheer from the frigate. It seemed obvious to Bolitho that Dumaresq had not expected to find a single one of them left alive.

Palliser's crisp tones replaced the captain's resonant voice. 'Lay to if you are able! We must recover Mr Slade and his boat!'

Bolitho imagined he could hear someone laughing.

He raised his hand as the frigate tacked slowly and awkwardly away, men already working on her yards to haul up fresh canvas and reeve new blocks.

Then he looked at the brigantine's deck, at the wounded men who were moaning quietly or trying to drag themselves away like sick animals will do.

There were some who would never move.

As the light continued to strengthen, Bolitho examined the sword which Jury had flung to save him. In the dull light the blood was like black paint, on the hilt and up to his own wrist.

Little came aft again. The new third lieutenant was young. In a moment he would fling the sword over the side, his guts soured by what they had done together. That would be a pity. Later he would want it to give his father or his sweetheart.

Little said, ''Ere, sir, I'll take that an' give it a shamper for you.' He saw Bolitho's hesitation and added affably, 'It's bin a real mate to you. Always look after yer mates, that's what Josh Little says, sir.'

Bolitho handed it to him. 'I expect you're right.'

He straightened his back, even though every muscle and fibre seemed to be cutting him like hot bands.

'Lively, men! There's much to do.' He recalled the captain's words. 'It won't do it by itself!'

From beneath the foremast and its attendant pile of fallen debris Stockdale watched him and then gave a satisfied nod. One more fight had ended.

Bolitho waited wearily by Dumaresq's table in *Destiny*'s cabin, his aching limbs at odds with the frigate's motion Dull daylight had revealed the brigantine's name to be *Heloise*, outward bound from Bridport in Dorset to the Caribbean, by way of Madeira to take on a cargo of wine.

Dumaresq finished leafing through the brigantine's log-book and then glanced at Bolitho.

'Do sit, Mr Bolitho. Before you fall down.'

He rose and walked to the quarter windows, pressing his face against the thick glass to seek out the brigantine which was lying in *Destiny*'s lee. Palliser and a fresh boarding party had gone across earlier, the first lieutenant's experience in much demand as they sought to repair the damage and get the vessel under way again.

Dumaresq said, 'You performed well. Extremely so. For one so young and as yet inexperienced in leading men, you achieved more than I'd dared to hope.' He clasped his powerful hands behind his coat-tails as if to contain his anger. 'But seven of our people are dead, others badly injured.' He reached up and banged the skylight with his knuckles. '*Mr Rhodes!* Be so good as to find out what the damned surgeon is about!'

Bolitho forgot his tiredness, his previous resentment at being ordered from his prize to make way for the first lieutenant. It was fascinating to watch the slow rise of Dumaresq's anger. Like a smouldering fuse as it edges towards the first cask of powder. It must have made poor Rhodes jump to hear his captain's voice rising from the deck at his feet.

Dumaresq turned to Bolitho. 'Good men killed. Piracy and murder, no less!'

He had made no mention of the miscalculation which all but wrecked or dismasted both ships.

He was saying, 'I knew they were up to something. It was evident at Funchal that too many ears and eyes were abroad.' He ticked off the points on his strong fingers. 'My clerk, just to get the contents of his satchel. Then the brigantine, which must have quit England about the same time as we left Plymouth, *happens* to be in harbour. Her master must have known I could not beat to wind'rd and make a chase of it. So long as he kept his distance he was safe.'

Bolitho understood. If *Destiny* had clawed round to approach the other vessel in daylight, the *Heloise* would have had the advantage of the wind and the distance. The frigate could outpace her in any fair chase, but under cover of darkness the brigantine would easily slip away if expertly handled. Bolitho thought of the gaunt man he had cut down in the fight to hold the deck. He could almost pity him. Almost. Dumaresq had ordered him to be brought across so that Bulkley, the surgeon, could save his life, if that were possible.

Dumaresq added, 'By God, it proves something, if more proof were needed. We are on the right scent.'

The marine sentry called, 'Surgeon, sir!'

Dumaresq glanced at the perspiring surgeon. 'And about bloody time, man!'

Bulkley shrugged, either indifferent to Dumaresq's explosive temper or so used to it that it meant nothing to him.

'The man is alive, sir. A bad wound but a clean one.' He glanced curiously at Bolitho. 'He's a strong fellow, too. I'm surprised and gratified to see you in one portion!'

Dumaresq snapped, 'Never mind all that. How dare that ruffian interfere with a King's ship. He'll get no mercy from me, be certain of it!'

He calmed slowly. It was like watching the sea receding, Bolitho thought.

'I must find out what I can from him. Mr Palliser is searching the *Heloise*'s hull, but in view of what Mr Bolitho took pains to discover, I think it unlikely we will gain much. According to the log she was launched last year and completed just a month back. Though she's hardly big enough for useful commerce, I'd have thought.'

Bolitho wanted to leave, to try and wash the strain of combat from his hands and mind.

The surgeon remarked, 'Mr Jury is well enough. A nasty cut, but he is a healthy boy. There'll be no after effects.'

Dumaresq gave a smile. 'I spoke with him when he was brought up from the cutter. A touch of hero-worship there, I think, Mr Bolitho?'

'He saved my life, sir. He's no cause to praise me for that.'

Dumaresq nodded. 'Hmmm. We shall see.'

He changed tack. 'We shall be sailing in company before nightfall. Keep all hands busy, that's the thing. Mr Palliser will need to rig a jury topgallant mast on that damned pirate, but it must be done.' He glanced at Bolitho. 'Pass the word to the quarterdeck. Change masthead lookouts every hour. We'll use this enforced respite to keep our eyes open for other would-be followers. As it stands, we have a fine little prize, and nobody yet knows anything about it. It might assist in some way.'

Bolitho stood up, his legs heavy again. So there was to be no rest.

Dumaresq said, 'Turn up the hands at noon to witness burial, Mr

Bolitho. We'll send the poor fellows on their last journey while we lie to.' He scattered the sentiment by adding, 'No sense in wasting time once we are under way.'

Bulkley followed Bolitho past the sentry and towards the ladder which led below to the main-deck.

The surgeon gave a sigh. 'He has the bit between his teeth now.'

Bolitho looked at him to try and understand his feelings. But it was too dark between decks, with only the ship's sounds and smells rising around them for company.

'Is it the bullion?'

Bulkley lifted his head to listen to the muffled shouts from a boat coming alongside, booming against the hull in the deep swell.

'You are still too young to understand, Richard.' He laid a plump hand on Bolitho's sleeve. 'And that was no sort of criticism, believe me. But I have met men such as our captain, and I know him better than many. He is a fine officer in most respects, if a trifle headstrong. But he *yearns* for action like a drunkard craves the bottle. He commands this fine frigate, but he feels deep down that it is too late or too early for him. With England at peace, the chances of distinction and advancement are few. It suits me very well, but. . . ,' he shook his head. 'I have said enough, but I know you will respect my confidence.'

He ambled to the ladder, leaving an aroma of brandy and tobacco to join the other smells already present.

Bolitho walked forward into the daylight and then ran quickly up a ladder to the quarterdeck. He knew that if he did not keep moving he would fall asleep on his feet.

Destiny's gundeck was littered with broken rigging, amidst which the boatswain and the ropemaker stood and discussed what might still be saved. Above the decks the seamen were busy splicing and hammering, and the torn sails were already brought down to be patched and stowed away for emergencies. A ship-of-war was self-sufficient. Nothing could be wasted. Some of that canvas would soon be gliding into the sea-bed, weighted down with round shot to carry the dead to the place where there was only darkness and peace.

Rhodes crossed to his side. 'Good to have you back, Dick.' He dropped his voice as they both turned to look across at the drifting brigantine. 'The lord and master was like an enraged lion after you'd broken free from the side. I shall tread very warily for the next week.'

Bolitho studied the other vessel. It was more like a dream than ever now. It was hard to believe he had managed to rally his men and take the *Heloise* after all which had happened. Men had died. He had probably killed at least one of them himself. But it had no meaning. No substance.

He walked to the rail and saw several of the faces on the deck below turn up towards him. What did they think, he wondered? Rhodes seemed genuinely pleased for him, but there would be envy, others might feel he had been too lucky, too successful for one so junior.

Spillane, the surgeon's new helper, appeared on the lee gangway and threw a parcel over the side.

Bolitho felt sick. What was it? An arm or a leg? It could have been his.

He heard Slade, the master's mate, yelling abuse at some unfortunate seaman. The *Destiny*'s recovery of the launch and the thankful shouts of the exhausted crew when she had eventually discovered them had apparently done nothing to make Slade any gentler.

In due course the dead men were buried, while the living stood with bared heads as the captain read a few words from his prayer book.

Then, after a hasty meal and a welcome tot of brandy, the hands turned to again, and the air was filled with the noise of saws and hammers, with strong smells of paint, and tar for the seams, to mark their progress.

Dumaresq came on deck at the end of the afternoon-watch and for several minutes looked at his ship and then at the clearing sky which told him more than any instrument.

He said to Bolitho, who was once more officer of the watch, 'Look at our people working. Ashore they are branded as hawbucks and no-good drunkards. But give 'em a piece of rope or a span of timber an' you'll see what they can do.'

He spoke with such feeling that Bolitho ventured to ask, 'Do you think another war is coming, sir?'

For an instant he thought he had gone too far. Dumaresq turned quickly on his thick legs, his eyes hard as he said, 'You have been speaking with that damned sawbones, eh?'

Then he gave a deep chuckle. 'There is no need to answer. You have not yet learned deceit.' He moved to the opposite side for his usual stroll, then added, 'War? I am depending on it!'

Before darkness closed in to hide one ship from another, Palliser sent word to say he was ready to proceed and would repair the less important damage in the days on passage for Rio.

Slade had gone across to the *Heloise* to take charge of the prize crew, and Palliser returned in the quarter-boat even as nightfall joined the sky to the horizon like a curtain.

Bolitho marvelled at the way Palliser kept going. He showed no sign of tiredness, and did not spare himself as he bustled about the ship using a lantern to examine every repair and shouting for the culprit if he discovered something which he considered to be shoddy workmanship.

Thankfully Bolitho climbed into his cot, his coat on the deck where it had fallen. Around him *Destiny* shivered and groaned as she rode a quarter sea without effort, as if she too was grateful for a rest.

It was the same throughout the hull. Bulkley sat in his sick-bay drawing on a long clay pipe and sharing some of his brandy with Codd, the purser.

Outside, barely visible on the orlop deck, the remaining sick and wounded slept or whimpered quietly in the darkness.

In the cabin Dumaresq was at his table writing busily in his personal diary, without a coat, and with his shirt open to the waist. Occasionally he glanced at the screen door as if to pierce it and see the length of his command, his world. And sometimes he looked up at the deckhead as Gulliver's footsteps told him that the master was still brooding over the collision, fearful the blame might be laid at his door.

Throughout the main-deck, where there was barely room to stand upright, the bulk of the ship's company swung in their hammocks to *Destiny*'s regular plunging motion. Like lines of neat pods, waiting to give birth in an instant if the wind so ordered or the drums beat to quarters.

Some men, unable to sleep or working their watch on deck, still thought of the short, bitter fight, of moments when they had known fear. Of familiar faces which had been wiped away, or of the prize money the handsome brigantine might bring them.

Tossing in his cot in the sick-bay, Midshipman Jury went over the attack yet again. Of his desperate need to help Bolitho as the lieutenant's hanger had been hurled away, of the sudden agony across his stomach like a hot iron. He thought of his dead father whom he could scarcely remember and hoped he would have been proud of what he had done.

And *Destiny* carried them all. From the grim-faced Palliser who sat opposite Colpoys in the deserted wardroom, the cards mocking him from the table, to the servant, Poad, snoring in his hammock, they were all at her mercy as her figurehead reached out for the horizon which never drew any nearer.

Two weeks after seizing the brigantine, *Destiny* crossed the Equator on her way south. Even the master seemed pleased with their progress and the distance covered. A convenient wind and milder, warmer air did much to raise the men's spirits and keep them free of illness.

Crossing the line was a new experience for over a third of the ship's company. Boisterous horse-play and skylarking which accompanied the ceremony were encouraged by a four days' allowance of wine and spirits for everybody.

With Little, the gunner's mate, making a formidable Neptune in a painted crown and a beard of spun-yarn, accompanied by his bashful queen in the shape of one of the ship's boys, all the newcomers to his kingdom were soundly ducked and abused.

Afterwards, Dumaresq joined his officers in the wardroom and stated his satisfaction with the ship's performance and swift passage. They had left the *Heloise* far astern, with some of her damage still being repaired. Dumaresq was obviously in no mood to delay his own landfall, and had ordered Slade to meet him off Rio with all the haste he could manage.

On most days *Destiny* pushed her way along under all plain sail, and would have made a fine sight had there been any other vessel to share their ocean. Working high above the decks, or employed in regular sail and gun drill, the new hands began to fit into the routine, and Bolitho saw the pallid shins of those who had come from the debtors' jails or worse taking on a deeper hue as the sun grew stronger with each passing day.

Another of the men who had been wounded in the fight had died, bringing the total to eight. Watched night and day by one of Colpoy's marines, the *Heloise*'s master continued to regain his strength, and Bolitho imagined Dumaresq was set on keeping him alive if only to see him hang for piracy.

Midshipman Jury had been allowed to return to duty, but was confined to working on deck or standing his watch aft. Strangely enough, their brief moment of shared danger and courage seemed to hold him and Bolitho apart, and although they met several times every day, Bolitho could sense a certain discomfort between them.

Maybe the captain had been right. Perhaps Jury's hero-worship, as he had termed it, had created an embarrassment rather than a bond.

Little Merrett, on the other hand, seemed to have gained more confidence than anyone would have thought possible. It was as if he had expected to be killed, and that now he was convinced nothing worse could ever happen to him. He ran up the shrouds with the other midshipmen, and during the dog-watches his shrill voice was often heard in some contest or argument with his companions.

One evening, as the ship ghosted along under her courses and topsails and Bolitho took over the first watch for Lieutenant Rhodes, he saw Jury watching the other midshipmen skylarking in the fighting tops, probably wishing he was up there with them.

Bolitho waited for the helmsman to call, 'Steady as she goes, sir! Sou'-sou'-west!' Then he crossed to the midshipman's side and asked, 'How is the wound?'

Jury looked at him and smiled. 'It no longer hurts, sir. I am lucky.' His fingers strayed to his leather cross-belt and touched the scar on the gilt plate. 'Were they really pirates?'

Bolitho shrugged. 'I believe they were intent on following us, spies perhaps, but in the eyes of the law they will be seen as pirates.'

He had thought a great deal about it since that terrible night. He suspected Dumaresq and Palliser knew a lot more than they were telling, that the captured brigantine was deeply involved with *Destiny*'s secret mission and her brief stay at Funchal.

He said, 'But if we maintain this pace we shall be in Rio in a week's time. Then I daresay we shall learn the truth.'

Gulliver appeared on the quarterdeck and peered up at the hardening canvas for a long minute without speaking. Then he said, 'Wind's getting up. I think we should shorten sail.' He hesitated, watching Bolitho's face. 'Will you tell the captain, or shall I?'

Bolitho looked at the topsails as they filled and tightened to the wind. In the dying sunlight they looked like great pink shells. But Gulliver was right, and he should have seen it for himself.

'I'll tell him.'

Gulliver strode to the compass, as if unable to contain his restlessness. 'Too good to last. I knew it.'

Bolitho beckoned to Midshipman Cowdroy who was temporarily sharing his watches until Jury was fully recovered.

'My respects to the captain. Tell him the wind is freshening from the nor'-east.'

Cowdroy touched his hat and hurried to the companion. Bolitho bit back his dislike. An arrogant, intolerant bully. He wondered how Rhodes put up with him.

Jury asked quietly, 'Are we in for a storm, sir?'

'Unlikely, I think, but it's best to be prepared.' He saw something glitter in Jury's hand and said, 'That is a fine looking watch.'

Jury held it out to him, his face filled with pleasure. 'It belonged to my father.'

Bolitho opened the guard carefully and saw inside a tiny but perfect portrait of a sea officer. Jury was already very like him.

It was a beautiful watch, made by one of the finest craftsmen in London.

He handed it back and said, 'Take good care of it. It must be very valuable.'

Jury slipped it into his breeches pocket. 'It is worth a great deal to me. It is all I own of my father.'

Something in his tone affected Bolitho deeply. It made him feel clumsy, angry with himself for not seeing beyond Jury's eagerness to please him. He had no one else in the world who cared.

He said, 'Well, my lad, if you keep your wits about you on this voyage it will stand you in good stead later on.' He smiled. 'A few years ago who had even heard of James Cook, I wonder? Now he is the country's hero, and when he returns from his latest voyage, I've no doubt he'll be promoted yet again.'

Dumaresq's voice made him spin round. 'Do not excite the boy, Mr Bolitho. He will want my command in no time!'

Bolitho waited for Dumaresq's decision. You never knew where you were with him.

'We shall shorten sail presently, Mr Bolitho.' He rocked back on his heels and examined each sail in turn. 'We'll run while we can.'

As he disappeared through the companion, the master's mate of the watch called, 'The cutter is workin' free on the boat tier, sir.'

'Very well.' Bolitho sought out Midshipman Cowdroy again. 'Take some hands and secure the cutter, if you please.' He sensed the midshipman's resentment and knew the reason for it. He would be glad to be rid of him from his watch.

Jury had guessed what was happening. 'I'll go, sir. It's what I should be doing.'

Cowdroy turned on him and snapped, 'You are unwell, *Mr* Jury. Do not strain yourself on our behalf!' He swung away, shouting for a boatswain's mate.

Later, as true to Gulliver's prediction the wind continued to rise and the sea's face changed to an angry array of white crests, Bolitho forgot about the rift he had created between the two midshipmen.

First one reef was taken in, then another, but as the ship staggered and dipped into a worsening sea, Dumaresq ordered all hands aloft to take in all but the main-topsail, so that *Destiny* could lie to and ride out the gale.

Then, to prove it could be gentle as well as perverse, the wind fell away, and when daylight returned the ship was soon drying and steaming in the warm sunshine.

Bolitho was exercising the starboard battery of twelve-pounders when Jury reported that he had been allowed to return to full duty and was no longer to bunk in the sick-bay.

Bolitho had a feeling that something was wrong, but was determined not to become involved.

He said, 'The captain intends that ours will be the smartest gun salute they have ever seen or heard in Rio.' He saw several of the bare-backed seamen grinning and rubbing their palms together. 'So we'll have a race. The first division against the second, with some wine for the winners.' He had already asked the purser's permission to grant an extra issue of wine.

Codd had thrust out his great upper teeth like the prow of a galley and had cheerfully agreed. 'If you pay, Mr Bolitho, *if you pay!*'

Little called, 'All ready, sir.'

Bolitho turned to Jury. 'You can time them. The division to run out first, twice out of three tries, will take the prize.'

He knew the men were getting impatient, fingering the tackles and handspikes with as much zeal as if they were preparing to fight.

Jury tried to meet Bolitho's eyes. 'I have no watch, sir.'

Bolitho stared at him, aware that the captain and Palliser were at the quarterdeck rail to see his men competing with each other.

'You've lost it? Your father's watch?' He could recall Jury's pride and his sadness as he had shown it to him the previous evening. 'Tell me.'

Jury shook his head, his face wretched. 'It's gone, sir. That's all I know.'

Bolitho rested his hand on Jury's shoulder. 'Easy now. I'll try to think of something.' Impetuously he tugged out his own watch, which had been given to him by his mother. 'Use mine.'

Stockdale, who was crouching at one of the guns, had heard all of it, and had been watching the faces of the other men nearby. He had never owned a watch in his life, nor was he likely to, but somehow he knew this one was important. In a crowded world like a ship a thief was dangerous. Sailors were too poor to let such a crime go unpunished. It would be best if he was caught before something worse happened. For his own sake as much as anybody's.

Bolitho waved his arm. '*Run out!*'

The second division of guns won easily. It was only to be expected, the losers said, as it contained both Little and Stockdale, the two strongest men in the ship.

But as they shared out their mugs of wine and relaxed beneath the shade of the main-course, Bolitho knew that for Jury at least the moment was spoiled.

He said to Little, 'Secure the guns.' He walked aft, some of his men nodding at him as he passed.

Dumaresq waited for him to reach the quarterdeck. 'That was smartly done!'

Palliser smiled bleakly. 'If we must bribe our people with wine before they can handle the great guns, we shall soon be a dry ship!'

Bolitho blurted out, 'Mr Midshipman Jury's watch has been stolen.'

Dumaresq eyed him calmly. 'And so? What must I do, Mr Bolitho?'

Bolitho flushed. I'm sorry, sir. I – I thought . . .'

Dumaresq shaded his eyes to watch a trio of small birds as they dashed abeam, seemingly inches above the water. 'I can almost smell the land.' He turned abruptly to Bolitho again. 'It was reported to you. Deal with it.'

Bolitho touched his hat as the captain and first lieutenant began to pace up and down the weather side of the deck.

He still had a lot to learn.

6

A Matter of Discipline

With all her canvas, except topsails and jib, clewed up, *Destiny* glided slowly across the blue water of Rio's outer roadstead. It was oppressively hot with barely enough breeze to raise much more than a ripple beneath her beakhead, but Bolitho could sense the expectancy and excitement around him as they made their way towards the protected anchorage.

Even the most experienced seaman aboard did not deny the impressive majesty of the landfall. They had watched it grow out of the morning mist, and it was now spread out on either beam as if to enfold them. Rio's great mountain was like nothing Bolitho had seen, dwarfing all else like a giant boulder. And beyond, interspersed with patches of lush green forest, were other ridges, steep and pointed like waves which had been turned to stone. Pale beaches, necklaces of surf, and nestling between hills and ocean the city itself. White houses, squat towers and nodding palms, it was a far cry from the English Channel.

To larboard Bolitho saw the first walled battery, the Portuguese flag flapping only occasionally above it in the hard sunlight. Rio was well defended, with enough batteries to dampen the keenest of attackers.

Dumaresq was studying the town and the anchored vessels through his glass.

He said, 'Let her fall off a point.'

'West-nor'-west, sir!'

Palliser looked at his captain. 'Guard-boat approaching.'

Dumaresq smiled briefly. 'Wonders what the hell we are doing here, no doubt.'

Bolitho plucked his shirt away from his skin and envied the half-naked seamen while the officers were made to swelter in their heavy dress-coats.

Mr Vallance, the gunner, was already checking his chosen crews to make sure nothing went wrong with his salute to the flag.

Bolitho wondered how many unseen eyes were watching the slow approach of the English frigate. A man-of-war, what did she want? Was she here for peaceful purposes, or with news of another broken treaty in Europe?

'Begin the salute!'

Gun by gun the salute crashed out, the heavy air pressing the thick smoke on the water and blotting out the land.

The Portuguese guard-boat had turned in her own length, propelled by great sweeps, so that she looked like a giant water-beetle.

Somebody commented, 'The Bugger's leadin' us in.'

The last gun recoiled and the crews threw themselves on the tackles to sponge the smoking muzzles and secure each weapon as a final gesture of peaceful intentions.

A figure waved a flag from the guard-boat, and as the long sweeps rose dripping and still on either beam, Dumaresq remarked dryly, 'Not too close in, Mr Palliser. They're taking no chances with us!'

Palliser raised his trumpet to his mouth. 'Lee braces there! Hands wear ship!'

Like parts of an intricate pattern the seamen and their petty officers ran to their stations.

'Tops'l sheets!' Palliser's voice roused the sea-birds from the water upon which they had only just alighted after the din of the salute. 'Tops'l clew-lines!'

Dumaresq said, 'So be it, Mr Palliser. Anchor.'

'Helm a'lee!'

Destiny turned slowly into the wind, the way going off her as she responded to the helm.

'*Let go!*'

There was a splash from forward as the big anchor plummeted down, while strung out on the topsail yards the seamen deftly furled the sails as if each mast was controlled by one invisible hand.

'Away gig's crew! Away quarter-boat!'

Bare feet stampeded across the hot decks while *Destiny* took the strain of her cable and then swung to the pull of the ocean.

Dumaresq thrust his hands behind his back. 'Signal the guard-boat alongside, if you please. I shall have to go ashore and pay my respects to the Viceroy. It is best to get such ponderous matters over and done with.'

He nodded to Gulliver and his mates by the wheel. 'Well done.'

Gulliver searched the captain's face as if expecting a trap. Finding none, he replied thankfully, 'My first visit here as master, sir.'

Their eyes met. Had the collision been any worse it would have been the last time for both of them.

Bolitho was kept busy with his own men and had little time to watch the Portuguese officers come aboard. They looked resplendent in their proud uniforms and showed no discomfort in the blistering heat. The town was almost hidden in mist and haze, which gave it an added air of enchantment. Pale buildings, and craft with colourful sails and a rig not unlike Arab traders which Bolitho had seen off the coast of Africa.

'Dismiss the watch below, Mr Bolitho.' Palliser's brisk voice caught him off guard. 'Then stand by with the marine escort to accompany the captain ashore.'

Bolitho ducked thankfully beneath the quarterdeck and made his way aft. In contrast with the upper deck it seemed almost cool.

In the gloom he all but collided with the surgeon as he clambered up from the main-deck. He seemed unusually agitated and said, 'I must see the captain. I fear the brigantine's master is dying.'

Bolitho went through the wardroom to his tiny cabin to collect his sword and his best hat for the journey ashore.

They had discovered little about the *Heloise*'s master, other than he was a Dorset man named Jacob Triscott. As Bulkley had remarked previously, it was not much incentive to stay alive when only the hangman's rope awaited him. Bolitho found that the news troubled him deeply. To kill a man in self-defence, and in the line of duty, was to be expected. But now the man who had tried to cut him down was dying, and the delay seemed unfair and without dignity.

Rhodes stamped into the wardroom behind him. 'I'm parched. With all these visitors aboard, I'll be worn out in no time.'

As Bolitho came out of his cabin Rhodes exclaimed, 'What is it?'

'The brigantine's master is dying.'

'I know.' He shrugged. 'Him or you. It's the only way to see it.' He added, 'Forget about it. The lord and master will be the one to get annoyed. He was banking on getting information from the wretch before he expired. One way or another.

He followed Bolitho through the screen door and together they looked forward, to the waiting glare of the upper deck.

Rhodes asked, 'Any luck with young Jury's watch?'

Bolitho smiled grimly. 'The captain told me to deal with it.'

'He would.'

'I expect he's forgotten about it by now, but I must do something. Jury has had enough trouble already.'

Johns, the captain's personal coxswain, dressed in his best blue jacket with gilt buttons, strode past. He saw Bolitho and said, 'Gig's in the water, sir. You'd best be there, too.'

Rhodes clapped Bolitho on the shoulder. 'The lord and master would not take kindly to being kept waiting!'

As Bolitho was about to follow the coxswain, Rhodes said quietly, 'Look, Dick, if you'd like me to do something about that damned watch while you're ashore . . .'

Bolitho shook his head. 'No, but thank you. The thief is most likely from my division. To search every man and turn his possessions out on the deck would destroy whatever trust and loyalty I've managed to build up so far. I'll think of something.'

Rhodes said, 'I just hope young Jury has not merely mislaid the timepiece; a loss is one thing, a theft another.'

They fell silent as they approached the starboard gangway where the side-party had fallen in to pay its respects to the captain.

But Dumaresq was standing with his thick legs apart, his head jutting forward as he shouted to the surgeon, 'No, sir, *he shall not die!*' Not until I have the information!'

Bulkley spread his hands helplessly. 'But the man is *going*, sir. There is nothing more I can do.'

Dumaresq looked at the waiting gig and at the quarter-boat nearby with Colpoys's marine escort already crammed aboard. He was expected at the Viceroy's residence, and to delay might provoke bad feelings which he would certainly wish to avoid if he needed Portuguese co-operation.

He swung on Palliser. 'Dammit, *you* deal with it. Tell that rogue Triscott that if he will reveal the details of his mission and his original destination I shall send a letter to his parish in Dorset. It will ensure that he is remembered as an honest man. Impress upon him what that will mean to his family and his friends.' He glared at Palliser's doubtful features. 'God damn it, Mr Palliser, think of something, will you?'

Palliser asked mildly, 'And if he spits in my face?'

'I'll hang him here and now, and see how his family like *that*!'

Bulkley stepped forward. 'Be easy, sir, the man is dying, he cannot hurt anyone.'

'Go back to him and do as I say. That is an order.' He turned to Palliser. 'Tell Mr Timbrell to rig a halter to the main-yard. I'll run that bugger up to it, dying or not, if he refuses to help!'

Palliser followed him to the entry port. 'It will be a signed declaration, sir.' He nodded slowly. 'I'll get a witness and have his words written down for you.'

Dumaresq smiled tightly. 'Good man. See to it.' He saw Bolitho and snapped, 'Into the gig with you. Now let us see this Viceroy, eh?'

Once clear of the side Dumaresq turned to study his ship, his eyes almost closed against the reflected glare.

'A fine surgeon is Bulkley, but a bit of an old woman at times. Anyone would think we are here for our health, instead of seeking a hidden fortune.'

Bolitho tried to relax, his buttocks burning on the sun-heated thwart as he attempted to sit as squarely as his captain.

The brief confidence led him to ask, 'Will there really be any treasure, sir?' He was careful to keep his voice low so that the stroke oarsman should not hear him.

Dumaresq tightened his fingers around his sword hilt and stared at the land.

'It is somewhere, that I do know. In what form it now is remains to be seen, but that is why we are here. Why we were in Madeira when I went to the house of a very old friend. But something immense is happening. Because of it my clerk was killed. Because of it the *Heloise* played the dangerous game of trying to follow us. And now poor Bulkley wants me to read a prayer for a rogue who may hold a vital clue. A man who nearly killed my young and *sentimental* third lieutenant.' He turned and regarded Bolitho curiously. 'Are you still in irons over Jury's watch?'

Bolitho swallowed. The captain had not forgotten after all.

'I am going to deal with the matter, sir. Just as soon as I can.'

'Hmmm. Don't make a drudgery of it. You are one of my officers. If a crime is committed the culprit must be punished. Severely. These poor fellows have barely a coin between them. I'll not see them abused by some common thief, though God knows many of them began life like that!'

Dumaresq did not raise his voice nor look at his coxswain, but said, 'See what you can do, Johns.'

It was all he said, but Bolitho sensed a powerful bond between the captain and his coxswain.

Dumaresq stared towards the landing-stairs. There were more uniforms and some horses. A carriage, too, probably to carry the visitors to the residency.

Dumaresq pouted and said, 'You can accompany me. Good experience for you.' He chuckled. 'When the treasure ship *Asturias* broke off the engagement all those thirty years ago, it was later rumoured she entered Rio. It was also suggested that the Portuguese authorities had a hand in what happened to the bullion.' He smiled broadly. 'So some of the people on that jetty are probably more worried than I at this moment.'

The bowman raised his boat-hook as with oars tossed the gig moved against the landing-stairs with barely a quiver.

Dumaresq's smile had gone. 'Now let us get on with it. I want to get back as soon as possible and see how Mr Palliser's persuasion is progressing.'

At the top of the stairs a file of Colpoys's marines, their faces the colour of their coats in the blazing sunshine, snapped to attention. Opposite them, in white tunics with brilliant yellow trappings, was a guard of Portuguese soldiers.

Dumaresq shook hands and bowed to several of the waiting dignitaries as greetings were formally exchanged and translated. A crowd of onlookers stood watching nearby, and Bolitho was struck by the number of black faces amongst them. Slaves or servants from the big estates and plantations. Brought thousands of miles to this place where, with luck, they might be bought by a kind master. If unlucky, they would not last very long.

Then Dumaresq climbed into the carriage with three of the Portuguese while others mounted their horses.

Colpoys sheathed his sword and glared up at the Viceroy's residence
on a lush hillside and complained, 'We shall have to march, dammit! I
am a marine, not a bloody foot-soldier!'

By the time they reached the fine-looking building Bolitho was
soaking with sweat. While the marines were led to the rear of the house
by a servant, Bolitho and Colpoys were ushered into a high-ceilinged
room with one side open to the sea and a garden of vivid blossoms and
shady palms.

More servants, soft-footed and careful to keep their eyes averted
from the two officers, brought chairs and wine, and above their heads a
great fan began to sway back and forth.

Colpoys stretched out his legs and swallowed the wine with relish.
'Sweet as a hymn in chapel!'

Bolitho smiled. The Portuguese officials, the military and traders
lived well here. They would need something to sustain them against the
heat and the risk of fever and death in a dozen forms. But the wealth of
the growing empire was said to be too vast to be assessed. Silver,
precious stones, strange metals and miles of prospering sugar plantations, no wonder they needed an army of slaves to satisfy the demands
from far-off Lisbon.

Colpoys put down his glass and got to his feet. In the time it had taken
them to march up from the jetty to the residence, Dumaresq had
apparently completed his business.

From his expression as he appeared through an arched doorway,
Bolitho guessed he was far from satisfied.

Dumaresq said, 'We shall return to the ship.'

The farewells were completed at the residence this time, and Bolitho
began to realize that the Viceroy was not in Rio, but would return as
soon as he was told of *Destiny*'s visit.

Dumaresq explained as much as he strode into the sunlight, touching
his hat to the saluting guards as he went.

He growled in his resonant voice, 'That means he *insists* I wait for his
return. I was not born yesterday, Bolitho. These people are our oldest
allies, but some of them are not above a little piracy. Well, Viceroy or
not, when *Heloise* catches up with us I shall weigh when I'm good and
ready!'

To Colpoys he said, 'March your men back.' As the scarlet coats
moved away in a cloud of dust, Dumaresq climbed into the carriage.
'You come with me. When we reach the jetty I want you to take a
message for me.' He pulled a small envelope from his coat. 'I had it
ready. I always expect the worst. The coachman will carry you there,
and I have no doubt the news of your visit will be all over the town

within an hour.' He smiled grimly. 'But the Viceroy is not the only man with cunning.'

As they clattered past Colpoys and his sweating marines, Dumaresq said, 'Take a man with you.' He glanced at Bolitho's expectant face. 'A body-guard, if you like. I saw that prize-fighting fellow in the quarter-boat. Stockdale, that's his name? Take him.'

Bolitho marvelled. How *could* Dumaresq contain so many things at once? Out there a man was dying, and Palliser's own life would not be worth much if he failed to obtain some information. There was someone in Rio who must be connected with the missing bullion, but not the one for whom he was carrying Dumaresq's letter. There was a ship, her people and the captured *Heloise*, and thousands of miles still lay ahead before they knew success or failure. For a post-captain of twenty-eight, Dumaresq certainly carried a great burden on his shoulders. It made Jury's missing watch seem almost trivial.

A tall, black-haired half-caste with a basket of fruit on her head paused to watch the carriage as it rolled past. Her bare shoulders were the colour of honey, and she gave a bold smile as she saw them watching her.

Dumaresq said, 'A fine-looking girl. And a prouder pair of catheads I never did see. It would be worth the risk of a painful payment later on just to relish her!'

Bolitho did not know what to say. He was used to the coarse comments of sailors, but from Dumaresq it seemed vulgar and demeaning.

Dumaresq waited for the carriage to stop. 'Be as fast as you can. I intend to take on fresh water tomorrow and there's a lot to be done before that.' He strode to the stairs and vanished into his gig.

Later, with Stockdale sitting opposite him and filling half the carriage, Bolitho directed his coachman to the address on the envelope.

Dumaresq had thought of everything. Bolitho or any other stranger might have been stopped and questioned here. But the sight of the carriage with the Viceroy's insignia on either door was enough to gain access anywhere.

The house where the carriage eventually pulled to a halt was a low building surrounded by a thick wall. Bolitho imagined it was one of Rio's oldest houses, with the additional luxury of a large garden and a well-tended driveway to the entrance.

A Negro servant greeted Bolitho without a flicker of surprise and led them into a great circular entrance hall with some marble vases which contained flowers like those he had seen in the garden and several statues which stood in separate alcoves like amorous sentries.

Bolitho hesitated in the centre of the hall, uncertain of what to do next. Another servant passed, eyes fixed on some distant object as he ignored the letter in Bolitho's hand.

Stockdale rumbled, 'I'll go an' stir their stumps for 'em, sir!'

A door opened noiselessly, and Bolitho saw a slightly built man in white breeches and a deeply frilled shirt watching him.

He asked, 'Are you from the ship?'

Bolitho stared. He was English, 'Er, yes, sir. I am Lieutenant Richard Bolitho of His Britannic . . .'

The man came to meet him, his hand outstretched. 'I *know* the name of the ship, Lieutenant. All Rio knows it by now.'

He led the way to a book-lined room and offered him a chair. As the door was closed by an unseen servant, Bolitho saw Stockdale standing massively where he had left him. Ready to protect him, to tear the house down brick by brick, he suspected.

'My name is Jonathan Egmont.' He smiled gently. 'That will mean nothing to you. You must be very young for your rank.'

Bolitho rested his hands on the arms of the chair. Heavy, well carved. Like the house, it had been here for a long time.

Another door opened and a servant waited for the man named Egmont to notice him.

'Some wine, Lieutenant?'

Bolitho's mouth was like a kiln. He said, 'I would welcome a glass, sir.'

'Rest easy then, while I read what your captain has to tell me.'

Bolitho glanced around the room as Egmont walked to a desk and slit open Dumaresq's letter with a gold stiletto. Shelf upon shelf of books, while on the floor were several rich-looking carpets. It was difficult to see very much because his eyes were still half blinded by the sun's glare, and anyway the windows were so heavily shaded that it was almost too dark to study his host. An intelligent face, he thought. A man about sixty, although he had heard that in such a climate men could age rapidly. It was hard to guess what he was doing here, or how Dumaresq had discovered him.

Egmont laid the letter carefully on the desk and looked across at Bolitho.

'Your captain has said nothing of this to you?' He saw Bolitho's expression and shook his head. 'No, of course he would not, and it was wrong of me to ask.'

Bolitho said, 'He wished me to bring the letter without delay. That is all I know.'

'I see.' For a few moments he looked unsure, even apprehensive. Then he said, 'I shall do what I can. It will take time, of course, but with the Viceroy away from his residence I have no doubt your captain will wish to remain for a while.'

Bolitho opened his mouth and then shut it as the door swung inwards and a woman entered the room carrying a tray.

He got to his feet, very conscious of his crumpled shirt, of his hair plastered to his forehead by the sweat of the journey. Set against what he was certain was the most beautiful creature he had ever seen, he felt like a vagrant.

She was dressed all in whi!e, the waist of her gown nipped in with a thin golden belt. Her hair was jet black like his own, and although held in check by a ribbon at the nape of her neck, was arranged to fall on her shoulders, the skin of which looked like silk.

She glanced at him and then studied him from top to toe, her head slightly on one side.

Egmont was also on his feet and said stiffly, 'This is my wife, Lieutenant.'

Bolitho bowed. 'I am honoured, ma'am.' He did not know what to say. She made him feel clumsy and unable to form his words, and all without saying anything to him.

She placed the tray on a table and raised her hand towards him.

'You are welcome here, Lieutenant. You may kiss my hand.'

Bolitho took it, feeling her softness, her perfume which made his head spin.

Her shoulders were bare, and despite the darkened room he saw that she had violet-coloured eyes. She was beautiful and more. Even her voice as she had offered her hand to him was exciting. How could she be his wife? She must be many years younger. Spanish or Portuguese, certainly not English. Bolitho would not have cared if she had just stepped from the moon.

He stammered, 'Richard Bolitho, ma'am.'

She stood back and put her fingers to her mouth. Then she laughed. 'Bo-li-tho! I think it will be easier for me to call you Lieutenant.' She swung her gown across the floor, her eyes moving to her husband. 'Later, I think I may call you Richard.'

Egmont said, 'I will write a letter for you to take with you, Lieutenant.' He seemed to be looking past, even through her. As if she was not there. 'I will do what I can.'

She turned to Bolitho again. 'Please call on us while you are in Rio. Our house is yours.' She gave a slow curtsy, her eyes on his face, until she said softly, 'I have *enjoyed* our meeting.'

Then she was gone, and Bolitho sat down in the chair as if his legs had broken under him.

Egmont said, 'I shall be a few moments. Enjoy the wine while I put pen to paper!'

Eventually it was done, and as he sealed the envelope with scarlet wax Egmont remarked distantly, 'Memory has a long reach. I have been here for many years and have rarely strayed but for the needs of my business. Then one day there comes a King's ship, commanded by the son of a man once dear to me, and now everything is changed.' He stopped abruptly and then said, 'But you will be in a hurry to return to your duties.' He held out the letter. 'I bid you good day.'

Stockdale eyed him curiously as he left the book-lined room. 'All done, sir?'

Bolitho paused as another door opened and he saw her standing there, her gown making her look like another perfect statue against the dark room beyond. She did not speak, or even smile, but just looked at him, directly, as if, Bolitho thought, she was already committing herself to something. Then her hand moved and stayed momentarily at her breast, and Bolitho felt his heart pounding as if trying to join hers in her hand.

The door closed, and he could almost believe he had imagined it or that the wine had been too strong.

He glanced at Stockdale and saw the look on his battered face and knew it was no lie.

'We had better get back to the ship, Stockdale.'

Stockdale followed him towards the sunlight. Not a bit too soon, he thought.

It was dusk by the time the boat from the landing-stairs made fast to the main chains. Bolitho climbed up to and through the entry port thinking of the beautiful woman in the white gown.

Rhodes was waiting with the side-party and whispered quickly, 'The first lieutenant is looking for you, Dick.'

'Lay aft, Mr Bolitho!' Palliser's brusque tones silenced Rhodes before he could say more.

Bolitho climbed to the quarterdeck and touched his hat. 'Sir?'

Palliser snapped, 'I have been *waiting* for you!'

'Yes, sir. But the captain ordered me on an errand.'

'And a fine time it has taken you!'

Bolitho controlled his sudden anger with an effort. Whatever he did or tried to do, Palliser was never satisfied.

He said quietly, 'Well, sir, I am here now.'

Palliser peered at him as if to seek out some kind of insolence.

Then he said, 'During your absence ashore, the master-at-arms, who was acting upon my orders, searched some of the people's messes.' He waited for Bolitho to react. 'I do not know what kind of discipline you are trying to instil into your division, but let me assure you it will take a lot more than a bribe of spirits and wine to achieve it! Mr Jury's watch was found in the possession of one of your maintopmen, Murray, so what say you?'

Bolitho stared at him incredulously. Murray had saved Jury's life. But for his swift action on the *Heloise*'s deck that night, the midshipman would be dead. And if Jury had not thrown the sword to replace Bolitho's lost hanger, he too would be a corpse. It had been their bond, of which none of them had spoken.

He protested, 'Murray is a good hand, sir. I cannot see him as a thief.'

'I'm certain of *that*. But you have a lot to learn, Mr Bolitho. Men like Murray would not dream of thieving from a messmate, but an officer, even a lowly midshipman, is fair game.' He controlled his voice with an obvious effort. 'But that is not the worst part. Mr Jury had the impertinence, the monstrous audacity, to tell me he had given the watch to Murray as a gift! Can you, *even you*, Mr Bolitho, believe it?'

'I can believe he said it to save Murray, sir. He was wrong, but I can well understand.'

'Just as I thought.' He leaned forward. 'I will see that Mr Jury is put ashore for passage to England the moment we are in company with some higher authority, and what do you think of that?'

Bolitho said hotly, 'I think you are acting unfairly!'

He could feel his anger giving way to despair. Palliser had tried to provoke him, but this time it had got suddenly out of hand.

He said, 'If you are trying to discredit me through Mr Jury, then you are succeeding. But even to contemplate it, knowing he has no family, and that he will give his very soul to the Navy, is damnable! And if I were you, *sir*, I'd be sick with shame.'

Palliser stared at him as if he had been struck. '*You what!*'

A small figure bobbed from the shadows. It was Macmillan, the captain's servant.

He said, 'Beg pardon, gentlemen, but the cap'n would like you in 'is cabin at once.'

He shrank back as if expecting to be knocked senseless.

Dumaresq was standing in the centre of the day-cabin, legs apart, hands on hips, as he glared at his two lieutenants.

'I'll not have you brawling on my quarterdeck like a pair of louts! What in hell's name has got into you?'

Palliser looked shocked, even pale, as he said, 'If you had heard what Mr Bolitho said, sir . . .'

'Heard? *Heard?*' Dumaresq jabbed one fist towards the skylight. 'I'd have thought the whole ship *heard* well enough!'

He looked at Bolitho. 'How dare you show insubordination to the first lieutenant. You will obey him without question. Discipline is paramount if we are not to become a shambles. I expect, no, I *demand* that the ship is at all times ready to act as I dictate. To bicker over some petty matter within earshot of anyone present is a madness, and I'll not tolerate it!' He examined Bolitho's face and added in a calmer tone, 'It must not happen again.'

Palliser tried again. 'I was telling him, sir . . .' He fell silent as the compelling eyes turned on him like lamps.

'You are my first lieutenant, and I shall uphold what you do under my command. But I will not have you using your temper on those too junior to hit back. You are an experienced and skilled officer, whereas Mr Bolitho is new to the wardroom. As for Mr Jury, he knows nothing of the sea but that which he has learned since we left Plymouth; would you say that is a fair assessment?'

Palliser swallowed hard, his head bowed beneath the beams as if he was in prayer.

'Yes, sir.'

'Good. That is something we agree upon.'

Dumaresq walked to the stern windows and stared at the reflected lights on the water.

'Mr Palliser, you will pursue the matter of the theft. I do not wish a useful hand like Murray punished if he is innocent. On the other side of the coin, I'll not see him evade it if he is guilty. The whole ship knows what has happened. If he walks free from this because of our inability to discover the truth, there will be no controlling the real trouble-makers and sea-lawyers amongst us.' He held out his hand to Bolitho. 'You have a letter for me, I expect.' As he took it he added slowly, 'Deal with Mr Jury. It is up to you to treat him fairly but severely. It will be as much a test for you as it is for him.' He nodded. 'Dismiss.'

As Bolitho closed the door behind him he heard Dumaresq say, 'That was a fine statement you took from Triscott. It makes up for the earlier set-back.'

Palliser mumbled something and Dumaresq replied, 'One more piece and the puzzle may be solved more quickly than I thought.'

Bolitho moved away, conscious of the sentry's eyes as they followed him into the shadows. He entered the wardroom and sat down carefully, like a man who has just fallen from a horse.

Poad said, 'Somethin' to drink, sir?'

Bolitho nodded, although he had barely heard. He saw Bulkley seated against one of the ship's great timbers and asked, 'Is the *Heloise*'s master dead?'

Bulkley looked up wearily and waited for his eyes to focus.

'Aye. He passed away within minutes of putting his name to the statement.' The surgeon's voice was very slurred. 'I hope it was worth it.'

Colpoys came from his cabin and threw one elegant, white-clad leg over a stool.

'I am growing sick of this place. anchored right out here. Nothing to do . . .' He looked from Bolitho to Bulkley and said wryly, 'I was wrong it seems. Here we have gaiety a-plenty!'

Bulkley sighed. 'I heard most of it. Triscott was making the one voyage as master. It seems he was ordered to join us at Funchal and determine what we were about.' He accidentally knocked over a goblet of brandy but did not appear to notice as the spirit ran over his legs. 'Having seen us on our way, he was supposed to head for the Caribbean and hand over the vessel to her new owner, the one who had paid for her to be built.' He coughed and dabbed his chin with a red handkerchief. ''Stead o' that, he got too nosey and tried to follow us.' He peered vaguely aft as if to seek Dumaresq through the bulkhead. 'Imagine that? The mouse hunting the tiger! Well, now he's paid for it in full.'

Colpoys asked impatiently, 'Well then, who is this mysterious buyer of brigantines?'

Bulkley turned towards the marine, as if it hurt him to move. 'I thought you were cleverer than that. Sir Piers Garrick, o' course! One-time privateer in the King's name and a damned pirate in his own!'

Rhodes entered the wardroom and said, 'I heard that. I suppose we should have known, as the lord and master was so careful to mention him. All those years ago. He must be over sixty now. And d'you really believe he still knows what happened to the *Asturias*'s bullion?'

Colpoys said wearily, 'The sawbones has dozed off, Stephen.'

Poad, who had been hovering close by, said, 'Fresh pork tonight, gentlemen. Sent off shore with the compliments of a Mr Egmont.' He waited for just the right moment. 'The boatman said it was to mark Mr Bolitho's visit to 'is 'ouse.'

Bolitho flushed as they all stared at him.

Colpoys shook his head sadly. 'My God, we've only just arrived here and I see a woman's hand in all this.'

Rhodes took him aside as Gulliver joined Colpoys and the purser at the table.

'Was he hard on you, Dick?'

'I lost my temper.' Bolitho smiled ruefully. 'I think we all did.'

'Good. Stand up to him. Don't forget what I said.' He made sure nobody else was listening. 'I've told Jury to wait for you in the chartroom. You'll be uninterrupted there for a while. Get it over with. I've been through all this myself.' He sniffed and exclaimed, 'I can smell that pork, Dick. You *must* have influence.'

Bolitho made his way forward to the small chartroom which was just beside the main companion. He saw Jury standing by the empty table, probably seeing his career wiped away like Gulliver's calculations.

Bolitho said, 'I was told what you did. Murray's case will be investigated, the captain has given his word. You will not be put ashore when we join the nearest squadron. You are staying in *Destiny*.' He heard Jury's quick intake of breath and said, 'So it's up to you now.'

'I – I don't know what to say, sir.'

Bolitho could feel his determination crumbling. He had once been like Jury, and knew what it was like to face apparent disaster.

He made himself say, 'You did wrong. You told a lie to protect a man who may well be guilty.' He silenced Jury's attempted protest. 'It was not your place to act for one in a way you might not have acted for another. I was equally at fault. If I was to be asked if I would have cared as much if Murray had been one of the bad apples in the barrel, or had you been like one of the other midshipmen, I should have had to admit to being biased.'

Jury said tightly, 'I am sorry for the trouble I have caused. Especially to you.'

Bolitho faced him for the first time, seeing the pain in his eyes.

'I know. We have both learned something from all this.' He hardened his tone. 'If not, we are neither of us fit to wear the King's coat. Carry on to your berth, if you please.'

He heard Jury leave the chartroom and waited for several minutes to recover his composure.

He had acted correctly, even if he had been late. In future Jury would be on his guard and less willing to depend on others. Hero-worship, the captain had termed it.

Bolitho sighed and walked to the wardroom. Rhodes looked up at him as he opened the door, his eyes questioning.

Bolitho shrugged. 'It was not easy.'

'It never is.' Rhodes grinned and twitched his nose again. 'It will be a delayed dinner because of the pork's late arrival in our midst, but I feel the waiting will put a worthwhile edge to the appetite!'

Bolitho took a goblet of wine from Poad and sat in a chair. It was better to be like Rhodes, he thought. Live for today, with no care for the next horizon and what it might bring. That way, you never got hurt. He thought of Jury's dismayed features and knew otherwise.

7

Divided Loyalties

Two more days passed with no sign that the Portuguese Viceroy had returned, or, if he had, that he intended to receive Dumaresq.

Sweltering under a blazing sun, the seamen went about their work with little enthuasiam. Tempers flared, and on several occasions men were taken aft to be awarded punishment.

And as the bell chimed each passing watch, Dumaresq, whenever he appeared on the quarterdeck, seemed to be growing more intolerant and angry. A seaman was given extra work merely for staring at him, and Midshipman Ingrave, who had been acting as his clerk, was sent back to his normal shipboard duties with 'Too stupid to hold a pen!' still ringing in his unhappy ears.

Even Bolitho, who had little experience of the politics used in foreign ports, was aware of *Destiny*'s enforced isolation. A few hopeful craft hovered near the ship with local wares for barter, but were openly discouraged by the vigilant guard-boat. And there had certainly been no message sent by the man called Egmont.

Samuel Codd, the purser, had gone aft to complain about his inability to preserve his supply of fresh fruit, and half of the ship must have heard Dumaresq's fury break over him like a tidal wave.

'What do you take me for, you miser? D'you think I have nothing to do but buy and sell like a common tinker? Take a boat and get ashore yourself, and *this* time tell the merchant the stores are for *me*!' His powerful voice had pursued Codd from the cabin. 'And don't return empty-handed!'

In the wardroom the atmosphere was little changed. The usual grumbles and exaggerated yarns about what had happened during the daily routine. Only when Palliser appeared did the climate become formal, even strained.

Bolitho had seen Murray and had confronted him with the accusation of theft. Murray had firmly denied any part of it, and had pleaded with Bolitho to speak on his behalf. Bolitho was deeply impressed by the man's sincerity. Murray was more resentful at the prospect of an unjust flogging than fearful. But that would come unless something could be proved.

Poynter, the master-at-arms, was adamant. He had discovered the watch in Murray's ditty-box during a quick search of several messes. Anybody could have put it there, but what was the point? It was obvious that something would be done to discover the missing watch. A careful thief would have hidden it in one of a hundred secret places. It did not make any sense.

On the evening of the second day the brigantine *Heloise* was sighted heading for the land, her sails shining in the dying sunlight as she completed a leisurely tack for the final approach.

Dumaresq watched her with his telescope and was heard to mutter, 'Taking his damn time. He'll have to do better if he wants promotion!'

Rhodes said, 'Have you noticed, Dick? The freshwater lighters have not been sent out to us as promised? Our stocks must be running low. No wonder the lord and master grows pink with anger.'

Bolitho recalled what Dumaresq had told him. That *Destiny* was to take on water the day after anchoring. He had forgotten, with so much else to occupy his thoughts.

'Mr Rhodes!' Dumaresq strode to the quarterdeck rail. 'Signal *Heloise* to anchor in the outer roadstead. Mr Slade'll not likely attempt an entrance in the dark, but just to be sure, send a boat with my instructions to moor clear of the headland.'

The trill of calls brought the boat's crew running aft. There were several groans when they saw how far the brigantine was standing from the land. A long, hard pull in two directions.

Rhodes sought out the midshipman of the watch. 'Mr Lovelace, go with the boat.' He kept his face straight as he looked at Bolitho. 'Damned midshipmen, eh, Dick? Must keep 'em busy!'

'Mr Bolitho!' Dumaresq was watching him. 'Come here, if you please.'

Bolitho turned aft until they were both at the taffrail, well out of earshot of everyone.

'I have to tell you that Mr Palliser is unable to discover any other culprit.' He watched Bolitho closely. 'That troubles you, I see.'

'Yes, sir. I have no proof either, but I am convinced Murray is innocent.'

'I'll wait until we are at sea. Then punishment will be carried out. It does no good to flog men before the eyes of foreigners.'

Bolitho waited, knowing there was more to come.

Dumaresq shaded his eyes to stare up at the masthead pendant. 'A fair breeze.' Then he said, 'I shall need another clerk. There is more writing and copying in a man-of-war than powder and shot.' His tone hardened. 'Or fresh water, for that matter!'

Bolitho stiffened as Palliser came aft and then paused as if at an invisible line.

Dumaresq said, 'We are done. What is it, Mr Palliser?'

'Boat approaching, sir.' He did not look at Bolitho. 'It is the same one which brought the pork for cabin and wardroom.'

Dumaresq's brows lifted. 'Really? That interests me.' He turned on his heel, then said, 'I shall be in my quarters. And on the matter of my clerk, I have decided to put the surgeon's new helper, Spillane, to the task. He seems educated and well-disposed to his betters, and I'll not *spoil* the good surgeon by overloading him with aid. He has enough loblolly boys to run his sick-bay.'

Palliser touched his hat. 'So be it, sir.'

Bolitho walked to the larboard gangway to watch the approaching boat. Without a glass he could see no one aboard he recognized. He felt like mocking himself for his stupidity. What had he expected? That the man, Jonathan Egmont, would be coming out to see the captain? Or that his lovely wife would take the fatiguing and uncomfortable journey just to wave to him? He was being ridiculous, childish. Perhaps he had been at sea too long, or his last visit to Falmouth which had brought so much unhappiness had left him open to fantasy and impossible dreams?

The boat came to the main chains, and after a great deal of sign language between the oarsmen and a boatswain's mate an envelope was passed up to Rhodes and then carried aft to the cabin.

The boat waited, idling a few yards from the frigate's hull, the olive-skinned oarsmen watching the busy sailors and marines and probably assessing the strength of *Destiny*'s broadside.

Eventually Rhodes returned to the entry port and handed another envelope down to the boat's coxswain. He saw Bolitho watching and crossed to join him by the hammock nettings.

'I know you will be sorry to hear this, Dick.' He could not prevent his mouth from quivering. 'But we are invited ashore to dine tonight. I believe you know the house already?'

'Who will be going?' Bolitho tried to control his sudden anxiety.

Rhodes grinned. 'The lord and master, *all* of his lieutenants, and, out of courtesy, the surgeon.'

Bolitho exclaimed. 'I cannot believe it! Surely the captain would never leave his ship without at least one lieutenant aboard?' He looked round as Dumaresq appeared on deck. 'Would he?'

Dumaresq shouted, 'Fetch Macmillan and my new clerk, Spillane!' He sounded different, almost jubilant. 'I shall require my gig in half an hour!'

Rhodes hurried away as Dumaresq added loudly, 'I want you and Mr Bolitho and our gallant redcoat ready and presentable at that time!' He smiled. 'The surgeon, too.' He strode away as his servant scurried in his wake like a terrier.

Bolitho looked at his hands. They appeared steady enough, and yet, like his heart, they seemed to be out of control.

In the wardroom there was complete confusion as Poad and his assistants tried to produce clean shirts, pressed uniform coats and generally attempted to transform their charges from sea officers into gentlemen.

Colpoys had his own orderly and was cursing like a trooper as the man struggled with his gleaming boots while he examined himself in a hand-mirror.

Bulkley, as owl-like and crumpled as ever, muttered, 'He's only taking me because of the wrong he did in my sick-bay!'

Palliser snapped, 'For God's sake! He probably doesn't trust you alone in the ship!'

Gulliver was obviously delighted to be left aboard in temporary command. After the long passage from Funchal he had seemingly gathered more confidence, and anyway he hated 'the ways of the quality', as he had once confided to Codd.

Bolitho was the first at the entry port. He saw Jury taking over the watch on the quarterdeck, their eyes met and then moved on. It would all be different once the ship was at sea again. Working together would drive away the differences, except that there was still Murray's fate to be considered.

Dumaresq came on deck and inspected his officers. 'Good. Quite good.'

He looked down at his gig alongside, at the oarsmen in their best checked shirts and tarred hats, with his coxswain ready and waiting.

'Well done, Johns.'

Bolitho thought of the other time he had gone ashore here with Dumaresq. How he had casually asked Johns to look into the matter of Jury's missing watch. Johns, as captain's coxswain, was held in great respect by the petty officers and senior hands. A word in the right place, and a hint to the master-at-arms, who never needed much encouragement when it came to harrying the people, and a swift search had done the rest.

'Into the boat.'

In strict order of seniority, and watched from the gangway by several of the off-duty seamen, *Destiny*'s officers descended into the gig.

Last of all, resplendent in his gold-laced coat with the white lapels, Dumaresq took his place in the stern-sheets.

As the boat moved carefully away from the frigate's hull, Rhodes said, 'May I say, sir, how grateful we are to be invited?'

Dumarasq's teeth showed very white in the gloom. 'I asked all my officers to join me, Mr Rhodes, because we are of one company.' His grin broadened. 'Also, it suits my purpose for the folk ashore to know we are *all* present.'

Rhodes answered lamely, 'I see, sir.' Clearly he did not.

In spite of his earlier misgivings and worries, Bolitho settled down
and watched the lights on the land. He was going to enjoy himself. In a
foreign, exotic country which he would remember and describe in detail
when he returned to Falmouth.

No other thought would interfere with this evening.

Then he recalled the way she had looked at him when he had left the
house, and felt his resolve giving way. It was absurd, he told himself, but
with that glance she had made him feel like a man.

Bolitho stared along the loaded table and wondered how he would
manage to do justice to so many glistening dishes. He was already
wishing he had heeded Palliser's curt advice as they had climbed ashore
from the gig. 'They'll try to make you drunk, so take care!' And that had
been nearly two hours ago. It did not seem possible.

The room was large with a curved ceiling and hung around with
colourful tapestries, the whole made even more impressive by hundreds
of candles, glittering chandeliers at regular intervals overhead, while
along the table's length were some candelabra which must be solid gold,
Bolitho thought.

The *Destiny*'s officers had been carefully seated, and made patches of
blue and white, separated by the richer clothing of the other guests. They
were all Portuguese, most of whom spoke little English and shouted at one
another to demand an instant translation or a means of making a point
clear to the visitors. The commandant of the shore batteries, a great
hogshead of a man, was matched only by Dumaresq in voice and appetite.
Occasionally he would lean towards one of the ladies and bellow with
laughter, or thump the table with his fist to emphasize his remarks.

A parade of servants came and went, ushering an endless procession
of dishes, which ranged from succulent fish to steaming platters of beef.
And all the time the wine continued to flow. Wine from their homeland
or from Spain, sharp-tasting German hocks and mellow bottles from
France. Egmont was certainly generous, and Bolitho had the impression
that he was drinking little as he watched over his guests with an
attentive smile on his lips.

It was almost too painful to look at Egmont's wife at the opposite end
of the table. She had nodded to Bolitho when he had arrived, but little
else. And now, squashed between a Portuguese ship-chandler and a
wrinkled lady who never seemed to stop eating, even to draw breath,
Bolitho felt ignored and lost.

But just to look at her was breathtaking. Again she was dressed in
white, against which her skin seemed golden by contrast. The gown was
cut very low across her breasts, and around her neck she wore a
double-headed Aztec bird with trailing tail feathers, which Rhodes had
knowledgeably identified as rubies.

As she turned her head to speak with her guests the ruby tails danced between her breasts, and Bolitho swallowed another glass of claret without realizing what he had done.

Colpoys was already half drunk and was describing at some length to his lady companion how he had once been caught in a woman's chamber by her husband.

Palliser on the other hand seemed unchanged, eating steadily but sparingly, and careful to keep his glass always half filled. Rhodes was less sure of himself now, his voice thicker, his gestures more vague than when the meal had begun. The surgeon held his food and drink very well, but was sweating badly as he tried to listen to the halting English of a Portuguese official and answer a question from the man's wife at the same time.

Dumaresq was incredible. He turned nothing away and yet seemed completely at ease, his resonant voice reaching along the table to keep a lagging conversation alive or to arouse one of his worse for wear officers.

Bolitho's elbow slipped from the table and he almost fell forward amongst the decimated dishes. The shock helped to steady him, to realize just how badly the drink had taken effect. Never again. Never, *never* again.

He heard Egmont announce, 'I think, gentlemen, if the ladies are about to withdraw, we should transfer to a cooler room.'

Somehow Bolitho managed to get to his feet in time to assist the wrinkled lady from her chair. She was still chewing as she followed the others through a door to leave the men at their ease.

A servant opened another door and waited for Egmont to lead his guests into a room which looked out over the sea. Thankfully, Bolitho walked on to the terrace and leaned on a stone balustrade. After the heat of the candles and the power of the wine the air was like water from a mountain stream.

He looked at the moon and then across the anchorage where the lights from *Destiny*'s open gun-ports glittered on the water as if the ship was burning.

The surgeon joined him by the balustrade and said heavily, '*That* was a meal of substance, my boy!' He belched. 'Enough to feed a village for a month. Just imagine it. All that way from France or Spain, no expense spared. When you consider some people are lucky to get a loaf of bread, it makes you wonder.'

Bolitho looked at him. He had thought about it, although not from the point of injustice. How could a man like Egmont, a stranger in this foreign land, make so much wealth? Enough to obtain anything he wanted, even a beautiful wife who must be half his age. The double-headed bird about her throat was gold, a fortune in its own right. Was that part of the *Asturias*'s treasure? Egmont had known Dumaresq's father, but had obviously never met his son before. They had barely spoken, when you thought about it, and when they had it seemed to be through one of the others, light and trivial.

Bulkley leaned forward and adjusted his spectacles. 'There's a work-hungry master, eh? Can't wait for the morning tide.'

Bolitho turned and looked at the anchorage. His practised eye soon discovered the moving vessel, in spite of the queasiness in his stomach.

A vessel under way, her sails making a flitting shadow against the riding lights of other anchored craft as she headed out into the roadstead.

Bulkley said vaguely, 'Local man, must be. Any stranger'd go aground here.'

Palliser called from the open doorway. 'Come in and join us.'

Bulkley chuckled. 'Always a generous fellow when it's someone else's cellar!'

But Bolitho remained where he was. There was enough noise coming from the room anyway, laughter and the clink of glasses, and Colpoys's voice rising higher and higher above the rest. Bolitho knew his absence would not be noticed.

He walked along the moonlit terrace, letting the sea air cool his face.

As he passed another room he heard Dumaresq's voice, very close and very insistent.

'I did not come all this way to be fobbed off with excuses, Egmont. You were in it up to the neck right from the beginning. My father said as much before he died.' The contempt in his voice was like a whip. 'My father's "gallant" first lieutenant who held off when he was sorely needed!'

Bolitho knew he should draw back, but he could not move. The tone of Dumaresq's voice seemed to chill his spine. It was something which had been pent-up for years and now could not be restrained.

Egmont protested lightly, 'I did *not* know. You must believe me. I was fond of your father. I served him well, and always admired him.'

Dumaresq's voice was muffled. He must have turned away with impatience, as Bolitho had seen him do often enough aboard ship.

'Well, my father, whom you so much *admired*, died a pauper. But then, what could you expect for a discarded sea-captain with one arm and one leg, eh? But he kept your secret, Egmont, he at least understood the meaning of loyalty! This could be the end of everything for you.'

'Are you threatening me, sir? In my own home? The Viceroy respects me, and will soon have something to say if I choose to complain!'

'Really?' Dumaresq sounded dangerously calm. 'Piers Garrick was a pirate, of gentle birth maybe, but a bloody pirate for all his manners. If the truth had leaked out about the *Asturias*, even his *letter of marque* would not have saved his neck. The treasure ship put up a good fight, and Garrick's privateer was severely damaged. Then the Don struck his colours, probably did not realize that Garrick's hull was so badly shot through. That was the worst thing he ever did in his life.'

Bolitho waited, holding his breath, fearful that the sudden silence meant they had somehow discovered his presence.

Then Dumaresq added quietly, 'Garrick scuttled his own command and took control of the *Asturias*. He probably butchered most of the Spaniards, or left them to rot somewhere where they could not be found. It was all made so simple for him. He sailed the treasure ship into this port on some excuse or other. England and Spain were at war, *Asturias* would be allowed to remain here for a short while, outwardly to effect repairs, but really to prove she was afloat after Garrick's alleged encounter with her.'

Egmont said shakily, 'That is surmise.'

'Is it? Let me continue, and then you shall decide if you intend to call for the Viceroy's aid.'

His voice was so scathing that Bolitho could almost feel pity for Egmont.

Dumaresq continued, 'A certain English ship was sent to investigate the loss of Garrick's vessel and the escape of the treasure which should rightfully have been a King's prize. That ship was commanded by my father. You, as his senior, were sent to take a statement from Garrick, who must have realized that without your connivance he was for the gallows. But his name was cleared, and while he gathered up his gold from where he had hidden it after destroying the *Asturias*, you resigned from the Navy, and quite mysteriously rose to the surface right here in Rio where it all began. But this time you were a rich man, a *very* rich man. My father, on the other hand, continued to serve. Then in '62, when he was with Rear-Admiral Rodney at Martinique, driving the French from their Caribbean islands, he was cruelly wounded, broken for life. There is a moral in that, surely?'

'What do you want me to do?'

He sounded dazed, stunned by the completeness of Dumaresq's victory.

'I shall require a sworn testimony to confirm what I have just said. I intend to enlist the Viceroy's aid if need be, and a warrant will then be sent from England. The rest you can well imagine for yourself. With your statement and the power invested in me by His Majesty and their lordships, I intend to arrest *Sir* Piers Garrick and take him to England for trial. I want that bullion, or what is left of it, but most of all I want *him*!'

'But why do you treat me like this? I had no part in what happened to your father at Martinique. I was not then in the Navy, you know that yourself!'

'Piers Garrick was supplying weapons and military stores to the French garrisons at Martinique and Guadeloupe. But for him my father might have been spared, and but for *you*, Garrick would not have had the chance to betray his country a second time!'

'I – I must have time to think, to . . .'

'It has all run out, Egmont. All thirty years of it. I require to know Garrick's whereabouts and what he is doing. Anything you can tell me about the bullion, *anything*. If I am satisfied, I will sail from here and you shall not see me again. If not . . .' He left the rest unsaid.

Egmont said, 'Can I trust you?'

'My father trusted *you*.' Dumaresq gave a short laugh. 'Choose.'

Bolitho pressed his shoulder against the wall and stared up at the stars. Dumaresq's energy was not merely inspired by duty and an eagerness for action. Hate had kept him sifting vague information, hate had made him hunt down the key which would unlock the mystery surrounding Garrick's rise to power. No wonder the Admiralty had selected Dumaresq for the task. The added spur of revenge would put him leagues ahead of any other captain.

A door banged open and Bolitho heard Rhodes singing and then protesting as he was dragged bodily back into the room.

He walked slowly along the terrace, his mind reeling from what he had heard. The enormity of the secret was unsettling. How could he go about his duties without giving away what he had discovered? Dumaresq would see through him in seconds.

He was suddenly completely sober, the dullness gone from his mind like a sea mist.

What would become of her if Dumaresq carried out his threat?

He swung angrily on his heel and made his way towards the open doors. When he entered he realized that some of the guests had already gone, and the commandant of the batteries was bowing almost to the floor as he swept his hat across his corpulent belly.

Egmont was there with his wife, his face pale but otherwise impassive.

Dumaresq too seemed as before, nodding to the departing Portuguese, kissing the gloved hand of the chandler's lady. It was like seeing two different people from the ones he had overheard just a few rooms away.

Dumaresq said, 'I think my officers are unanimous in their delight at your table, Mr Egmont.'

His glance settled on Bolitho for a second. No more, but Bolitho sensed the question as if it had been shouted aloud.

'I hope we can repay your kindness. But duty is duty, as you will know from experience.'

Bolitho glanced round, but nobody had noticed the sudden tension between Egmont and the captain.

Egmont turned away and said, 'We will say good-night, gentlemen.'

His wife came forward, her eyes in shadow as she held out her hand to Dumaresq.

'It is good-morning now, no?'

He smiled and kissed her hand. 'You are a delight to see at any hour, ma'am.'

His gaze lingered on her bared bosom, and Bolitho flushed as he recalled what Dumaresq had said about the girl who had watched their carriage.

She smiled at the captain, her eyes clear now in the candlelight. 'Then I think you have seen enough for one day, sir!'

Dumaresq laughed and took his hat from a servant while the others made their farewells.

Rhodes was carried bodily from the house and laid in a waiting carriage, a blissful smile on his face.

Palliser muttered, 'Damned disgrace!'

Colpoys, whose pride was the only thing which prevented his collapsing like Rhodes, exclaimed thickly, 'A fine night, ma'am.' He bowed and almost fell over.

Egmont said tersely, 'I think you had better go inside, Aurora, it grows damp and chill.'

Bolitho stared at her. *Aurora.* What an exquisite name. He retrieved his hat and made to follow the others.

'Well now, Lieutenant, have you nothing to say to me?'

She looked at him as she had the first time, her head slightly on one side. He saw it in her eyes, the dare, the challenge.

'I am sorry, ma'am.'

She held out her hand. 'You must not apologize so often. I wish we had had more time to speak. But there were so many.' She tossed her head and the ruby tails flashed on her bosom. 'I hope you were not too bored?'

Bolitho realized that she had removed her long white glove before she offered her hand.

He held her fingers and said, 'I was not bored. I was in despair. There is a difference.'

She withdrew her hand, and Bolitho thought he had ruined everything by his clumsiness.

But she was looking at her husband who was listening to Bulkley's parting words. Then she said softly, 'We cannot have you in despair, Lieutenant, now can we?' She looked at him steadily, her eyes very bright. 'It would never do.'

Bolitho bowed and murmured, 'May I see you?'

Egmont called, 'Come along, the others are leaving.' He shook Bolitho's hand. 'Do not delay your captain. It does not pay.'

Bolitho walked out to one of the waiting carriages and climbed inside. She knew and understood. And now, after what he had overheard, she would need a friend. He stared blindly into the darkness, remembering her voice, the warm touch of her fingers.

'Aurora.' He started, realizing he had spoken her name aloud.

But he need not have bothered, his companions were already fast asleep.

She was twisting in his arms, laughing and provoking him as he tried to hold her, to feel the touch of her bare shoulder against his lips.

Bolitho awoke gasping in his cot, his head throbbing wildly as he blinked at the lantern above his face.

It was Yeames, master's mate, his eyes curious as he watched the lieutenant's confusion, his reluctance to let go of a dream.

Bolitho asked, 'What time is it?'

Yeames grinned unsympathetically. 'Dawn, sir. The 'ands is just turnin' to to 'olystone and scrub down.' He added as an afterthought, 'The cap'n wants you.'

Bolitho rolled out of his cot and kept his feet well apart on the deck for fear of falling. The brief respite on Egmont's cool terrace had gone, and his head felt as if it contained a busy anvil, while his throat tasted vile.

Dawn, Yeames had said. He had not been in his cot for more than two hours.

In the next cabin he heard Rhodes groaning as if in agony, and then yelping in protest as an unknown seaman dropped something heavy on the quarterdeck overhead.

Yeames prompted, 'Better 'urry, sir.'

Bolitho tugged on his breeches and groped for his shirt which had been tossed in one corner of the tiny space. 'Trouble?'

Yeames shrugged. 'Depends wot you mean by trouble, sir.'

To him Bolitho was still a stranger and an unknown quantity. To share what he knew, merely because Bolitho was worried, would be stupid.

Bolitho found his hat, and tugging on his coat he hurried through the wardroom and blundered aft towards the cabin.

The sentry called, 'Third lieutenant, *sir*!' and Macmillan, the captain's servant, opened the screen door as if he had been waiting behind it.

Bolitho stepped through into the after cabin and saw Dumaresq by the stern windows. His hair was awry, and he looked as if he had not found time to undress after his return from Egmont's house. In a corner by the quarter windows, Spillane, the newly appointed clerk, was scratching away with his pen, trying to show no concern at being called at such an early hour. The other two present were Gulliver, the master, and Midshipman Jury.

Dumaresq glared at Bolitho. 'You should have come immediately! I do not expect my officers to dress as if they are going to a ball when I need them!'

Bolitho glanced down at his crumpled shirt and twisted stockings. Also, with his hat clamped beneath one arm, his hair was falling over his face, just as it had been on the pillow. Hardly suitable for a ball.

Dumaresq said, 'During my absence ashore, your seaman Murray escaped. He was not in his cell, but being taken to the sick-bay because he had complained about a severe pain in his stomach.' He turned his wrath on the master. 'God damn it, Mr Gulliver, it was obvious what he was doing!'

Gulliver licked his lips. 'I was in charge of the ship, sir. It was my responsibility. I saw no cause for Murray to suffer, an' the man not yet found guilty as charged.'

Midshipman Jury said, 'The message was brought aft to me, sir. It was my fault.'

Dumaresq replied tersely, 'Speak when you are addressed. It was not your fault, because midshipmen do not *have* responsibility. Neither do they possess the wit or the brains to be in a position to say what this or that man shall do!' His eyes trained round on Gulliver again. 'Tell Mr Bolitho the rest.'

Gulliver said harshly, 'The ship's corporal was escorting him when Murray pushed him down. He was outboard and swimming for the shore before the alarm was raised.' He looked downcast and humiliated at having to repeat his explanation for a junior lieutenant's benefit.

Dumaresq said, 'So there it is. Your trust in that man was wasted. He escaped a flogging, but when he is taken he will hang.' He glanced at Spillane. 'Note it in the log. Run.'

Bolitho looked at Jury's dismay. There were only three ways for a man to quit the Navy, and they were noted as R, D, or DD. *Run* implied desertion, D stood for discharged. Murray's next entry would be the last. *Discharged – Dead.*

And all because of a watch. And yet, in spite of the disappointment over his trust in Murray, Bolitho was strangely relieved at what had happened. The punishment for a man he had known and liked, who had saved Jury's life, was no longer a threat. And its aftermath of suspicion and bitterness had been averted.

Dumaresq said slowly, 'So be it. Mr Bolitho, you will remain. The others may carry on.'

Macmillan closed the door behind Jury and Gulliver. The master's shoulders were stiff with resentment.

Dumaresq asked, 'Hard, you are thinking? But it may prevent weakness later on.'

He calmed as only he could, the rage falling away without apparent effort.

'I am glad you carried yourself well last night, Mr Bolitho. I hope you kept your eyes and ears open?'

The sentry's musket thumped on the deck again. 'First lieutenant, *sir*!'

Bolitho watched as Palliser entered the cabin, his routine list of work for the day beneath his arm. He looked gaunter than usual as he said, 'The water lighters may come out to us today, sir, so I shall tell Mr Timbrell to be prepared. Two men are to see you for promotion, and there is the question of punishment for the ship's corporal for negligence and allowing Murray to desert.'

His eyes moved to Bolitho and he gave a curt nod.

Bolitho wondered if it was mere chance that Palliser always seemed to be nearby whenever he was with the captain.

'Very well, Mr Palliser, though I'll believe those water lighters when I see them.' He looked at Bolitho. 'Go and put your appearance to rights and take yourself ashore. Mr Egmont has a letter for me, I believe.' He gave a wry smile. 'Do not dally too long, although I know there are many distractions in Rio.'

Bolitho felt his face going hot. 'Aye, sir. I'll leave directly.'

He hurried from the cabin and heard Dumaresq say, 'Young devil!' But there was no malice in his voice.

Twenty minutes later Bolitho was sitting in the jolly-boat being pulled ashore. He saw that Stockdale was acting as boat's coxswain, but did not question him on this. Stockdale seemed to make friends easily, although his fearsome appearance might also have something to do with his apparent freedom of movement.

Stockdale called hoarsely, 'Easy all!'

The oars rose dripping in the rowlocks, and Bolitho realized that the jolly-boat was losing way in order not to be run down by another vessel. She was a brig, a sturdy, well-used vessel with patched canvas and many a scrape on her hull to mark encounters with sea and weather.

She had already spread her topsails, and there were men sliding down backstays to the deck to set the forecourse before she cleared the rest of the anchored vessels nearby.

She moved slowly between *Destiny*'s jolly-boat and some incoming fishermen, her shadow falling across the watching oarsmen as they rested on their looms and waited to proceed.

Bolitho read her name across the counter, *Rosario*. One of hundreds of such craft which daily risked storm and other dangers to trade and to extend the outposts of a growing empire.

Stockdale growled, 'Give way all!'

Bolitho was about to turn his attention to the shore when he saw a movement at the stern windows above the name *Rosario*. For an instant he imagined he was mistaken. But he was not. The same black hair and oval face. She was too far off for him to see the violet of her eyes, but he saw her looking towards him before the brig changed tack and the sunlight made the windows into a fiery mirror.

He was heavy-hearted when he reached the house with the age-old wall around it. Egmont's steward told him coolly that his master had departed, his wife, too. He did not know their destination.

Bolitho returned to the ship and reported to Dumaresq, expecting a further eruption of fury at this latest set-back.

Palliser was with him as Bolitho blurted out what he had discovered, although he did not mention he had seen Egmont's wife in the *Rosario*.

He did not need to. Dumaresq said, 'The only vessel to leave here was the brig. He must be aboard. Once a damned traitor always a traitor. Well, he'll not escape this time, by God no!'

Palliser said gravely, 'So this was the reason for the delay, sir. No fresh water, no audience with the Viceroy. They had us over a gate.' He sounded suddenly bitter. 'We can't move, and they know it!'

Surprisingly, Dumaresq gave a great grin. Then he shouted, 'Macmillan, I want a shave and a bath! Spillane, prepare to write some orders for Mr Palliser.' He walked to the stern windows and leaned on the sill, his massive head lowered towards the rudder. 'Select some prime seamen, Mr Palliser, and transfer to the *Heloise*. Do not rouse the guard-boat's attention with too much fuss, so take no marines. Weigh and chase that damned brig, and don't lose her.'

Bolitho watched the change in the man. It explained why Dumaresq had stopped Slade from entering the protected anchorage. He had anticipated something like this and had a trick to play, as always.

Palliser's mind was already busy. 'And you, sir?'

Dumaresq watched his servant as he prepared a bowl and razor by his favourite chair.

'Water or no water, Mr Palliser, I shall weigh tonight and come after you.'

Palliser eyed him doubtfully. 'The battery might open fire, sir.'

'In daylight maybe. But there is a lot of so-called honour at stake here. I intend to test it.' He turned away, dismissing them, but added, 'Take the third lieutenant. I shall require Rhodes, even if his head is still falling apart from his drinking, to assume your duties here.'

At any other time Bolitho would have welcomed the offer gladly. But he had seen the look in Palliser's eyes, and remembered the face at the brig's cabin windows. She would despise him after this. Like the dream, it was over.

8

The Chase

Lieutenant Charles Palliser strode to the *Heloise*'s compass box and then consulted the masthead pendant.

To confirm his fears, Slade, the acting-master, said dourly, 'The wind's backed a piece, but it's also falling away.'

Bolitho watched Palliser's reactions and compared him with Dumaresq. The captain was in Rio aboard *Destiny*, outwardly dealing with the ship's affairs, even to the extent of seeing two seamen who had been put up for promotion. Fresh water, the prospect of a summons from the Portuguese Viceroy, it would mean nothing to most of the frigate's company. But Bolitho knew what was really uppermost in Dumaresq's thoughts: Egmont's refusal to yield and his sudden departure in the brig *Rosario*. Without Egmont, Dumaresq would have little choice but to seek higher naval authority for instructions, and in that time the scent would go cold.

Slade had said that the brig had been steering north-north-east as she had cleared the roadstead. Egmont was heading along the coast, probably all the way to the Caribbean. In a small trading vessel like that it would be extremely uncomfortable for his lovely wife.

Palliser crossed to his side. On the brigantine's confined deck he looked like a giant, but unusually content, Bolitho thought. Palliser was free of his captain's word, could act as he pleased. Always provided he did not lose the *Rosario*. And with the wind dropping fast, that was a possibility.

He said, 'They'll not be expecting a chase. That is all we have on our side.'

He glanced up, irritated, as the forecourse boomed and flapped, empty of wind and allowing the heat to seek out the men on deck.

'*Damn!*' Then he said, 'Mr Slade says the brig will stay inshore. Unless the wind shifts, I accept that. We shall continue as we are. Change the lookouts as you think fit, and have the weapons which are still aboard this vessel inspected.' He clasped his hands behind him. 'Don't work the people too hard.' He saw the surprise on Bolitho's face and gave a thin smile. 'They will have to take to the oars shortly. I intend to warp *Heloise* with the boats. They'll need all their muscle for that!'

Bolitho touched his hat and walked forward. He should have guessed. But he had to confess admiration for Palliser's preparations. He thought of everything.

He saw Jury and Midshipman Ingrave waiting for him by the foremast. Jury looked tense but Ingrave, who was a year older, could barely conceal his delight at being freed from his task of acting-clerk for the captain.

Beyond them were other familiar faces amongst the hastily selected hands. Josh Little, gunner's mate, his stomach hanging over his cutlass-belt. Ellis Pearse, boatswain's mate, a bushy-browed man who had shown the same satisfaction as Bolitho that Murray had deserted. Pearse would have been the man to flog him, and he had always liked Murray. And of course, there was Stockdale, his thick arms folded over his chest as he surveyed the brigantine's deck, remembering perhaps that fierce, desperate struggle when Bolitho had fought hand to hand with the vessel's master.

Dutchy Vorbink, foretopman, who had left the East India Company and exchanged their ordered and well-paid life for that of a man-of-war. He spoke little English, unless he wanted to, so nobody had discovered his true reason for volunteering.

There were faces which had now become people to Bolitho. Some coarse and brutalized, others who would brawl with the best of them but were equally quick to put right a wrong for a less outspoken messmate.

Bolitho said, 'Mr Spillane, examine the arms chest and make a list of weapons. Little, you had better go through the magazine.' He looked around at the few swivel guns, two of which had been sent across from *Destiny*. 'Hardly enough to start a war.'

It brought a few grins and chuckles, and Stockdale muttered, 'There's still some prisoners battened below, sir.'

Bolitho looked at Little. He had forgotten about the *Heloise*'s original company. Those not killed or wounded had been detained here. Safe enough, but in the event of trouble they would have to be watched.

Little showed his uneven teeth. 'All taken care of, sir. I got Olsson on guard. They'd be too scared to challenge 'im!'

Bolitho agreed. Olsson was a Swede and was said to be half mad. It shone from his eyes which were like washed-out blue glass. A good seaman who could reef and steer and turn his hand to anything, but when they had boarded this same brigantine Bolitho had chilled to Olsson's crazy screams as he had cleaved his way through his opponents.

He forced a grin. 'I'd think twice myself.'

Pearse groaned as the sails shivered and then flapped dully against rigging and spars.

'There goes the bloody wind.'

Bolitho crossed to the bulwark and leaned out over the blue water. He saw the wind's ripple on the surface moving away far ahead of the bows like a great shoal of fish. The brigantine lifted and sighed in the swell, blocks and sails clattered in protest as the power went with the wind.

'Man your boats!' Palliser was watching from beside the helmsmen.

Bare feet padded over the hot deck seams as the first crews went away in the quarter-boat, as well as *Destiny*'s cutter which they had kept in tow beneath the counter.

It took far too long to lay out the towing warps and pass them to the boats. Then with each boat angled away on either bow the painful, dreary business began.

They could not hope to make any speed, but it would prevent the vessel from drifting completely out of command, and when the wind came they would be ready.

Bolitho stood above the larboard anchor and watched the towlines tautening and then sagging beneath the glittering water as the oarsmen threw their weight into play.

Little shook his head. 'Mr Jury's no 'and for this, sir. 'E'll need to use 'is starter on that lot.'

Bolitho could see the difference between the two towing boats. Jury's was yawing badly, and a couple of the oars were barely cutting beneath the surface. The other boat, with Midshipman Ingrave in charge, was making better progress, and Bolitho knew why. Ingrave was not a bully, but he was well aware of his superiors watching from the brigantine, and was using a rope's end on some of his men to make them work harder at the oars.

Bolitho walked aft and said to Palliser, 'I'll change the crews in an hour, sir.'

'Good.' Palliser was watching the sails and then the compass. 'She's got steerage-way at least. Few thanks to the larboard boat.'

Bolitho said nothing. He knew only too well what it was like as a midshipman to be suddenly thrown into an unpopular job. But Palliser did not press the point, which was something. Bolitho thought of his own sudden acceptance of his new role. He had not asked Palliser about changing the boats' crews, he had told him, and the first lieutenant had accepted without question. Palliser was as wily as Dumaresq. In their very different ways they were able to draw out exactly what they required from their subordinates.

He glanced at Slade, who was shading his eyes to peer at the sky. A man who wanted promotion above all else. Dumaresq used that too, to extract the best from the intolerant master's mate, which in turn would aid him when his chance of advancement finally came. Even Palliser had his mind set on his own command, and this temporary duty in charge of *Heloise* would stand very well on his record.

All through the day the relentless boat-pulling went on, while not even a faint breeze came to revive the sails. They hung from the yards, limp and useless, like the men who tumbled aboard from the boats as soon as they were relieved. Too exhausted to do much more than gulp down a double ration of wine which Slade had broached from the hold, they fell about like dead men.

In the cabin aft, tiny as it was, but adequate when compared with the rest of the space between decks, the relieved midshipmen and their lieutenants tried to find escape from the heat and the dangerous need to drink and keep on drinking.

With Palliser asleep and Slade on watch, Bolitho sat at the small table, his head lolling as he tried to keep his mind awake. Opposite him, his lips cracked from the sun's glare, Jury rested his head on his hands and looked into space.

Ingrave was away with the boats again, but even his keenness was flagging badly.

Bolitho asked, 'How do you feel?'

Jury smiled painfully. 'Dreadful, sir.' He tried to straighten his back and plucked his sodden shirt away from his skin.

Bolitho pushed a bottle towards him. 'Drink this.' He saw the youth hesitate and insisted, 'I'll stand your trick in the boats if you like. It's better than sitting here and waiting.'

Jury poured a cup of wine and said, 'No, sir, but thank you. I'll go when I'm called.'

Bolitho smiled. He had toyed with the idea of telling Stockdale to go with the midshipman. One sight of him would put a stopper on any slackness or insubordination. But Jury was right. To make it easy for him when he most needed confidence and experience would only lay a snare for later on.

'I – I was thinking, sir.' He looked across guardedly. 'About Murray. D'you think he'll be all right?'

Bolitho thought about it. Even that was an effort. 'Maybe. Provided he stays away from the sea. I've known men who have quit the Navy to return and find security under a different name in the service they had originally reviled. But that can be dangerous. The Navy is a family. There is always a familiar face and a memory to match it.'

He thought of Dumaresq and Egmont. Each linked by Dumaresq's dead father, just as he was now involved with whatever they might attempt.

Jury said, 'I often think about him. Of what happened on deck.' He glanced up at the low beams as if expecting to hear the ring of steel, the desperate shuffle of men circling each other for a kill. Then he looked at Bolitho and added, 'I'm sorry. I was told to put it from my mind.'

A call shrilled and a voice yelled, 'Away boats' crews! Lively there!'

Jury stood up, his fair hair brushing the deckhead.

Bolitho said quietly, 'I was told much the same when I joined the *Destiny*. Like you, I still have the same difficulty.'

He remained at the table, listening to the thump of boats alongside, the clatter of oars as the crews changed around yet again.

The door opened, and bent double like a crippled sailor, Palliser groped his way to a chair and thankfully sat down. He too listened to the boats thrashing away from the hull, the sluggish response from the tiller-head as the brigantine submitted to the tow.

Then he said flatly, 'I'm going to lose that devil. After getting this far, it's all been cut from under me.'

Bolitho could feel the disappointment like a physical thing, and the fact Palliser had made no effort to hide his despair was strangely sad.

He pushed the bottle and cup across the table. 'Why not take a glass, sir.'

Palliser looked up from his thoughts, his eyes flashing. Then he smiled wearily and took the cup.

'Why not, Richard?' He slopped the wine carelessly over the rim. 'Why not indeed?'

While the sun moved towards the opposite horizon, the two lieutenants sat in silence, occasionally taking a sip of the wine which by now was as warm as milk.

Then Bolitho dragged out his watch and said, 'One more hour with the boats and then we shall secure for the night, sir?'

Palliser had been in deep thought and took several seconds to reply.

He said, 'Yes. There's nothing else we *can* do.'

Bolitho was stunned by the change in him, but knew if he tried to cheer him up the truce would be shattered.

Feet shuffled through the main-deck and Little's great face squinted in at them.

'Beg pardon, sir, but Mr Slade sends 'is respects and says 'e can 'ear gunfire to the north'rd!'

An empty bottle rolled across the deck at the lieutenants' feet and clinked against the side as the cabin suddenly tilted.

Palliser stared at the bottle. He was still seated, but his head was touching a beam without difficulty.

He exclaimed, '*The wind!*' The damned, wonderful wind!' He clawed his way to the door. 'Not a moment too soon!'

Bolitho felt the hull give a shiver, as if it was awakening from a deep sleep. Then with a bound he hurried after the lanky Palliser, sobbing with pain as his skull came in contact with a ring-bolt.

On deck the men were staring around with disbelief as the big forecourse filled and boomed noisily from its yard.

Palliser yelled, 'Recall the boats! Stand by to come about!' He was peering at the compass and then up at the masthead pendant, just visible against the early stars.

Slade said, 'Wind's shifted, sir, veered a little, sou'-west.'

Palliser rubbed his chin. 'Gunfire, you say?'

Slade nodded. 'No doubt. Small pieces is my guess.'

'Good. As soon as the boats are secured, get under way again and lay her on the larboard tack. Steer nor'-west by north.'

He stood aside as the men ran through the deepening shadows to their stations.

Bolitho tested their new relationship. 'Will you not wait for *Destiny*, sir?'

Palliser held up his hand and they both heard the muted sounds of gunfire.

Then he said tersely, 'No, Mr Bolitho, I will not. Even if my captain succeeds in leaving harbour, and is able to discover more favourable winds than ourselves, he'll not thank me for allowing the evidence he so sorely needs to be destroyed.'

Pearse yelled, 'Boats secured aft, sir!'

'Man the braces! Stand by to come about!'

The wind hissed over the water and thrust against the canvas with new strength, pushing the brigantine over as a white froth gathered around her stem.

Palliser said sharply, 'Darken ship, Pearse! I want nothing to betray our presence!'

Slade said, 'It might be over an' done with before dawn, sir.'

But the new Palliser snapped, 'Nonsense! That vessel is being attacked, probably by pirates. They'll not risk a collision in darkness.' He turned to seek out Bolitho and added, 'Not like us, eh?'

Little shook his head and breathed out noisily. Bolitho could smell the drink on his breath, as strong as an open cellar door.

'Gawd, Mr Bolitho, 'e's really 'appy at last.'

Bolitho thought suddenly of the face he had seen aboard the ship now under attack.

'Please God we shall be in time.'

Little, not understanding, walked away to join his friend Pearse for another 'wet'.

So the new third lieutenant was as eager as the captain for prize money, he thought, and that could not be such a bad thing for the rest of them.

Palliser prowled across the poop like a restless animal.

'Shorten sail, Mr Bolitho. Take in the t'gan'sls and stays'l. Roundly now!'

Men groped their way to halliards and belaying-pins while others ran swiftly up the ratlines and out along the topgallant yard.

Bolitho always marvelled at the little time it took trained seamen to get used to a strange vessel, even in the dark.

It would soon be dawn, and he could feel the previous day's weariness and hours without sleep clawing at his resistance. Palliser had kept his small company on the move throughout the night. Changing tack, altering course, retrimming sails, as he plotted and estimated the whereabouts of the other vessels. Several times there had been short exchanges of gunfire, but Palliser had said it was more to deter a possible chase than with any hope of close action. One thing had been proved by the occasional cannon fire. There were at least three vessels out there beyond the *Heloise*'s taut jib. Like wolves around a wounded beast, waiting for it to falter or make one fatal mistake.

Little called hoarsely, 'All guns loaded, sir!'

Palliser replied, 'Very well.' In a lower tone to Bolitho he added, '*All* guns. A few swivels and about enough canister to disturb a field of crows!'

Midshipman Ingrave said, 'Permission to run up the colours, sir?'

Palliser nodded. 'Yes. This is a King's ship for the present, and we're not likely to meet another.'

Bolitho recalled some of the muttering he had heard during the night. A few of the hands were troubled at the prospect of engaging pirates or anyone else with so puny an armament.

Bolitho darted a quick glance to starboard. Was there a faint lightening on the horizon? There was a good lookout aloft, and he was their best hope of taking the other vessel by surprise. It was unlikely that pirates intent on capturing and plundering a trader would be bothered about keeping a watch elsewhere.

He heard Slade whispering with Palliser. He was another one who was unhappy about the coming confrontation.

Palliser said fiercely, 'Keep an eye on your course and be ready to change tack if we outrun the enemy. Leave the rest to me, see?'

Bolitho felt his limbs shiver. *The enemy*. Palliser had no doubts anyway.

Stockdale came from the shadows, his great frame angled against the deck as the wind held them over.

'Them buggers are usin' chain-shot, sir. Once or twice I 'eard it when I was aloft.'

Bolitho bit his lip. So they intended to cripple the *Rosario*'s rigging and then pound her into submission with less risk to themselves. They would get a shock when they saw *Heloise* bearing down on them. For a short while anyway.

He said, 'Maybe *Destiny*'s already chasing after us.'

'Mebbee.'

Bolitho turned away as Jury came to join him. Stockdale did not believe that, any more than he did.

Jury asked, 'Will it take much longer, sir?'

'Dawn comes up swiftly. You'll see their topsails or upper yards at any minute now. If one of them fires again, we should be able to plot his bearing.'

Jury watched him in the gloom. 'It does not trouble you, sir?'

Bolitho shrugged. 'Not now. Later perhaps. We are committed, or soon will be.' He turned and put his hand on the midshipman's shoulder. 'Just remember something. Mr Palliser has picked some very experienced hands for this work. But his officers are somewhat youthful.' He saw Jury nod. 'So keep your head and be where you can be seen. Leave the miracles to Mr Palliser.'

Jury smiled and then winced as his cracked lips reminded him of the previous day's boatwork.

He said, 'I'll stay with you.'

Stockdale chuckled. 'Beggin' yer pardon, young gentleman, but don't you be gettin' in my way.' He swung a cutlass across the bulwark like a scythe. 'Wouldn't want you to lose yer 'ead, so to speak!'

Palliser called, 'Stand by to take in the forecourse! Keep it quiet!'

The boatswain's mate pointed abeam. 'Dawn, sir!'

Palliser rasped, 'God dammit, Pearse, we're neither blind nor bloody deaf!'

Pearse grinned at Palliser's back. 'Palliser, you're a real pig!' But he was careful that nobody should hear him.

'Deck there! Sail on the starboard bow! And 'nother to larboard!'

Palliser clapped his hands together. 'We did it! Damn their eyes, we're into them!'

At that moment a gun fired, making an orange flash on the dark water.

Slade said anxiously, 'There's a third to wind'rd!'

Bolitho gripped his hanger and pressed its scabbard against his thigh to calm himself.

Three vessels, the centre one was doubtless the *Rosario*, with her two attackers standing off to form one great triangle. He heard a slithering sound and then a splintering crash, and vaguely through the darkness ahead he saw a jagged patch of spray as some spars and rigging hit the water.

Stockdale nodded. 'Chain-shot right enough, th' buggers.'

'Stand by on deck! Watch your slow-matches!'

There was no need for stealth now. Bolitho heard a shrill whistle from the nearest vessel and the crack of a pistol. It had either exploded in error or had been used as a signal to warn their consort.

With their muskets and powder-horns ready to use, cutlasses and boarding pikes within easy reach, the *Destiny*'s seamen peered into the darkness.

'Take in the forecourse!'

Men ran to obey, and as the great sail was brailed up to its yard the growing light revealed the crouching figures and trained swivels like the rising of a curtain.

There was a series of bangs, and Bolitho heard the chain-shot screeching overhead like tormented spirits in hell.

Little said between his teeth, 'Too 'igh, thank the livin' Jesus!'

The deadly chain-shot threw up broken spray far to starboard, but in direct line with the brigantine's two masts.

'Lee helm!' Palliser was gripping a backstay as he studied the enemy's blurred outline. 'As close to the wind as you can!'

'*Man the braces!*'

The brigantine crept round, until her remaining sails were rippling in protest.

'Nor'-west by west, sir! Full an' bye!'

The other vessel fired and a ball slammed down within twenty feet of the *Heloise*'s bow and hurled spray high over the beak-head.

Then firing began in earnest, the balls wide and haphazard as the gun crews tried to guess what the newcomer was trying to do.

Another ball ripped through the driver and left a jagged hole in the canvas large enough for a man's head.

Palliser exploded, 'That bloody fool brig fired at *us*.'

Little grinned. 'Thinks we're pirates, too!'

'I'll give him pirates!'

Palliser pointed at the vessel which was rising out of the darkness to larboard and shortening as she changed tack to run down on the brigantine's impudent approach.

'Schooner! Take her first!'

Little cupped his hands. 'On the uproll, lads!'

Men were still dragging one of the swivels across to mount it on the opposite side and yelled at Little to give them more time.

But Little knew his trade well.

'Easy, lads!' It was like hearing a man quietening a beast. '*Fire!*'

Like glow-worms the matches plunged down and the swivels barked viciously at the oncoming vessel. A murderous hail of closely packed canister swept across her forecastle, and Bolitho thought he heard screams as it found a target.

'Stand by to come about!' Palliser's voice carried easily even without his speaking trumpet. 'Lee braces!'

Palliser walked jerkily down the sloping deck to join Slade by the helm. 'We'll go for another one. Put up your helm.'

Heeling hard over, the brigantine ran to leeward, her canvas banging lustily until the seamen had hauled the yards round again. The second vessel seemed to pivot across the jib-boom until she lay to larboard, her stern end on to the charging *Heloise*.

Palliser yelled, 'Rake her poop, Little!' He swung on Slade and his gasping helmsmen. 'Steady as she goes, you fool!'

Bolitho found time to pity Slade's concern. The *Heloise* was rushing down on the other vessel's stern as if she was about to smash bodily through her quarter like an axe.

'*Fire!*'

Flashes lit up the decks of both vessels as their guns spat out darting orange tongues, accompanied by the crash of iron hitting home. *Heloise*'s canister must have wiped the other vessel's poop clean. Helmsmen, gun crews, there was not enough room to escape as the 'daisy cutters' jagged charges swept amongst them. She began to fall downwind, to be raked yet again by Little's other swivels.

'Set the forecourse!' Palliser's voice was everywhere.

Bolitho could see him clearly now, his lean body moving about the poop and framed against the brightening sea like an avenger.

'*Fire!*'

More balls shrieked overhead, and Bolitho guessed that their first target had regained his courage and was closing to the aid of his companions.

He saw the *Rosario* for the first time, and his heart sank at the spectacle. Her foremast had gone completely, and only half of her main appeared to be standing. Wreckage and severed rigging trailed everywhere, and as the sun lifted above the horizon Bolitho saw the thin scarlet threads which ran down from each scupper. It was as if the ship herself and not her defenders was bleeding to death.

'*Hands wear ship!*'

Bolitho jabbed a seaman's shoulder and yelled, 'Join the others!' He felt the man jump before he ran to throw his weight on the braces. He had imagined it to be hot iron and not his hand.

There was a tremendous crash, and Bolitho almost fell to his knees as two hits were scored on the *Heloise*'s hull.

Bolitho saw Ingrave staring at the nearest vessel, wide-eyed and unable to move.

He shouted, 'Get below and attend to the damage!' He strode to the midshipman and gripped his sleeve and shook him like a doll. '*At once, Mr Ingrave! Sound the well!*'

Ingrave stared at him vacantly, and then with unexpected determination ran to the companion.

Stockdale unceremoniously dragged Bolitho's arm and held him aside as a massive block fell from aloft, broken cordage whipping behind it. It struck the bulwark and bounced over the side.

Palliser shouted, '*Stand to!*' He had drawn his sword. 'Ready to larboard!'

Against the schooner's cannon, small though they were, the swivels sounded insignificant. Bolitho saw the canister blast through the schooner's fore-sail and hurl two men into bloody bundles before more balls smashed through *Heloise*'s lower hull. He heard the havoc tearing between decks, the crack of splinters and collapsing timbers, and knew they had been badly hit.

Someone had managed to get the pumps going, but he saw two men fall bleeding badly, and another who had been working on the topsail yard trying to lower himself to safety with one leg hanging to his body by a muscle.

Palliser shouted, 'Come aft!'

As Bolitho hurried to join him he said, 'We're doing no good. Get below yourself and report the damage.' He blinked as more shots thudded into the reeling hull, and somewhere a man shrieked in agony. 'Feel her? She's going!'

Bolitho stared at him. It was true. The *Heloise*'s agility had given way to an ungainly response to both helm and wind. It did not seem possible. So quickly, and their roles had changed. There was no aid at hand, and their enemies would not let them die easily.

Palliser snapped, 'I'm going to steer for the brig. With our men and her guns there's still a chance.' He looked steadily at Bolitho. 'Now be a good fellow and get below.'

Bolitho hurried to the companion, his quick glance taking in the splintered deck planking and stark bloodstains. They had fought here before. Surely that was enough? Perhaps fate had always intended they should end thus?

He called to Jury, 'Come with me.' He peered down into the darkness, dreading the thought of being trapped below if the ship went down. He spoke carefully to hide his anxiety. 'We will examine the damage together. Then if I fall . . .' He saw Jury gasp. So he had not yet accepted the idea of death. '. . . you will relay the details to Mr Palliser.'

Once down the companion ladder he lit a lantern and led the way forward, careful to avoid some of the jagged splinters which had been smashed through from the deck above. The sounds were muffled but filled with menace as the ship shook and buckled to the bombardment.

The two attacking vessels were working round on either beam, heedless of the danger of hitting each other in their eagerness to destroy the little ship with the scarlet ensign at her peak.

Bolitho dragged open a lower hatch and said, 'I can hear water.'

Jury whispered, 'Oh, dear God, we're foundering!'

Bolitho lay down and dipped his lantern through the hatch. It was a scene of complete chaos. Shattered casks and remnants of canvas floated amongst splintered wood, and as he watched he imagined he saw the water rising still further.

He said, 'Go to the first lieutenant and tell him there's no hope.' He restrained Jury, feeling his sudden surge of fear as more balls cracked into the hull. '*Walk*. Remember what I said. They'll be looking to you.' He tried to smile, to show that nothing mattered. 'All right?'

Jury backed away, his eyes moving from the open hatch to Bolitho. 'What will *you* do?'

Bolitho turned his head sharply as a new sound echoed through the listing hull like a giant's hammer. One of the anchors had broken free and was smashing into the bows with every roll. It could only speed their end.

'I'll go to Olsson. We must release the prisoners.'

And then Bolitho was alone. He swallowed deeply and tried to keep his limbs from shaking. Then very slowly he groped his way aft again, the regular boom of the anchor against the hull following him like an execution drum.

There was another thud against the hull, but it was followed instantly by a loud crack. One of the masts, or part of it, was coming down. He tensed, waiting for the final crash as it hit the deck or plunged over the side.

The next instant he was spread-eagled in the darkness, the lantern gone from his hand, although he did not feel anything, nor did he recall the moment of impact.

All he knew was that he was pinned beneath a mass of wreckage and unable to move.

He pressed his ear to a ventilation grating and heard the surge of water as it battered through the bilges and lower hold, He was on the edge of terror, and knew that in seconds he could be screaming and kicking in a hopeless attempt to free himself.

Thoughts crowded through his mind. His mother as she had watched him leave. The sea below the headland at Falmouth where he and his brother had first ventured out in a fisherman's boat, and his father's wrath when he had discovered what they had done.

His eyes smarted, but when he tried to move his fingers to his face the fallen debris held him as cruelly as any trap.

The anchor had stopped its incessant boom against the hull, which meant it was probably under water with the forepart of the vessel.

Bolitho closed his eyes and waited, praying that his nerve would not break before the end.

9

Palliser's Ruse

Bolitho felt a growing pressure against his spine as some of the fallen timber shifted to the brigantine's motion. He heard a scraping sound somewhere overhead, the clang of metal as one of the guns broke free and tumbled across the deck. The angle was more acute, and he could hear the sea piling against the hull, but much higher than before as the vessel continued to settle deeper and deeper.

There was still some shooting, but it seemed as if the victors were standing off to wait for the sea to complete their work for them.

Slowly, but with mounting desperation, Bolitho tried to wriggle free from the debris across his body. He could hear himself groaning and pleading, gasping meaningless words as he struggled to rid himself of the trap.

It was useless. He only succeeded in dislodging some more broken woodwork, a piece of which ploughed past his head like a spear.

With something like panic he heard sounds of a boat being manned, some hoarse cries and more musket shots.

He clenched his fists and pressed his face against the deck planking to prevent himself from screaming. The vessel was going fast and Palliser had ordered her to be abandoned.

Bolitho tried to think clearly, to accept that his companions were doing what they must. It was no time for sentiment or some useless gesture. He was already as dead as the others who had been shot down in the heat of the fighting.

He heard voices and someone calling his name. Needles of light probed through the tangled wreckage, and as the deck gave another lurch Bolitho shouted, '*Go back! Save yourselves!*'

He was shocked and stunned by his words and the strength of his voice. More than anything he had wanted to live until he had realized someone had cared enough to risk death for his sake.

Stockdale's throaty voice said, ''Ere, work that spar clear!'

Somebody else said doubtfully, 'Too late, by the looks of it, mate. We'd best get aft.'

Stockdale rasped, 'Take 'old like I told you! Now, together, lads! *'Eave!'*

Bolitho cried out as the pain pushed harder into his spine. Feet moved down from the other side of the pile and he saw Jury on his knees peering through a gap to look for him.

'Not long, sir.' He was shaking with fear but trying to smile at the same time. 'Hold on!'

As suddenly as it had smashed him down the weight of broken planking and one complete spar were levered and hoisted clear.

A man seized Bolitho's ankles and dragged him roughly up the sloping deck, while Stockdale appeared to be holding back a wall of wreckage all on his own.

Jury gasped, 'Quickly!' He would have fallen but for a seaman's ready grip, and then they were all staggering and lurching like drunks running from a press-gang.

On deck at last, Bolitho forgot the pain and the lurking moments of bare terror.

In the strengthening light he saw that the *Heloise* was already a total wreck, her fore-topmast gone completely and her main nothing more than a jagged stump. Her canvas, broken spars and an entangled mesh of fallen rigging completed the scene of devastation.

To drive it home, Bolitho saw that both boats were manned and standing clear, and the nearer of the two was already higher than the *Heloise*'s lee side.

Palliser stood in the cutter directing some of his men to use their muskets on one of the schooners. The dying brigantine acted as a barrier, the only thing which still stood between the enemy and their chance to run down on the boats and finish the one-sided fight.

Stockdale grunted, 'Over th' side, lads!'

His mind reeling, Bolitho saw that two of the men who had come back for him were Olsson, the mad Swede, and one of the farm-workers who had volunteered to his Plymouth recruiting party.

Jury kicked off his shoes and secured them inside his shirt. He looked at the water as it came swirling over the bulwark and exclaimed huskily, 'It's a long swim!'

Bolitho flinched as a musket ball smacked into the deck and raised a splinter as high as a goose quill within feet of where they were standing.

'Now or never!' He saw the sea thundering through the companion and turning one of the corpses in a wild dance as it forced the bows deeper and deeper below the surface.

With Stockdale panting and floundering between them, Bolitho and Jury sprang into the water. It seemed to take an age to reach the nearest boat, and even then they had to join the others who were hanging to the gunwales and trying not to hamper the oarsmen as they headed for the dismasted *Rosario*.

Most of the men around Bolitho were strangers, and he realized they must be the released prisoners. Olsson had looked so wild it was a wonder he had not left them to drown with their ship.

Then all at once the brig's side towered above them. She was a small vessel, but viewed from the water as he fought for breath and clung to a thrown line, Bolitho thought she looked as big as a frigate.

Eventually they were pushed, dragged and man-handled up and over the side where they were confronted by the brig's own company, who stared at them as if they had come from the sea itself.

Palliser left nobody in doubt as to who was in command.

'Little, take the prisoners below and put them in irons. Pearse, discover the chance of a jury-rig, anything to give us steerage-way!' He strode past some dazed and bleeding men and snapped, 'Have these guns loaded, d'you hear? God dammit, you're like a pack of old women!'

A man of some authority pushed through his sailors and said, 'I am the master, John Mason. I know why you're here, but I give thanks to God for it, sir, though I fear we are no match for them pirates.'

Palliser eyed him coldly. 'We shall see about that. But for now, do as I direct. How you and your people behave today may decide what happens to you.'

The man gaped at him. 'I don't understand, sir?'

'Do you have a passenger, one Jonathan Egmont?'

Bolitho leaned on the bulwark sucking in great gulps of air, the sea-water streaming from his limbs to mingle with the blood around the nearest gun.

'Aye, sir, but . . .'

'*Alive?*'

'Was when I last saw him. I put my passengers below when the attack began.'

Palliser gave a grim smile. 'That is fortunate. For both of us, I think.' He saw Bolitho and added sharply, 'Make sure Egmont is secure. Tell him nothing.' He was about to turn his attention to one of the schooners but instead watched the *Heloise*'s final moment, as with a last burst of spray from her hatches she plunged to the bottom. He said, 'I am glad you were able to stay with us. I ordered the vessel to be abandoned.' His eyes rested momentarily on Jury and Stockdale. 'However . . .'

Bolitho staggered to an open hatch, his bruised mind still grappling with the *Rosario*'s lay-out as she pitched about in the swell.

The brig had taken a terrible beating. Upended guns, corpses and pieces of men lay strewn with the other debris, ignored in the frantic efforts to keep their attackers from boarding.

A seaman with one hand wrapped in a crude bandage, the other gripping a pistol, called, 'Down 'ere, sir!'

Bolitho clambered down a ladder, his stomach rebelling against the stench of pain and suffering. Three men lay unconscious or dying, another was crawling back to his station as best he could in makeshift dressings and a sling.

Egmont stood at a table, wiping his hands on a rag, while a seaman trimmed a lantern for him.

He saw Bolitho and gave a tired shrug. 'An unexpected meeting, Lieutenant.'

Bolitho asked, 'Have you been attending the wounded?'

'You know the Navy, Lieutenant. For me it is a long, long time ago since I served your captain's father, but it is something you never lose.'

Bolitho heard the urgent clank of pumps, the sounds of blocks and tackles being hauled noisily across the upper deck. The *Destiny*'s seamen were working again, and he was needed up there to help Palliser, to keep them at it, driving them by force if necessary.

They had been in a savage fight and some had died, as he had nearly done. Now they were needed again. Let them falter and they would drop. Allow them time to mourn the loss of a friend and they would lose the stuff of fighting.

But he asked, 'Your wife, is she safe?'

Egmont gestured towards a bulkhead door. 'In there.'

Bolitho thrust his shoulder against it, the fear of being trapped below decks still scraping at his mind.

By lantern-light in a sealed, airless cabin he saw three women. Aurora Egmont, her maid and a buxom woman he guessed to be the master's wife.

He said, 'Thank God you're safe.'

She moved towards him, her feet invisible in the cabin's gloom so that she appeared to be floating.

She reached up and felt his wet hair and his face, her eyes large as she said quietly, 'I thought you were still in Rio.' Her hands touched his chest and his arms as they hung at his sides. 'My poor lieutenant, what have they done to you?'

Bolitho could feel his head swimming. Even here, amidst the stench of bilge and death, he was conscious of her perfume, the cool touch of her fingers on his face. He wanted to hold her, to press her against his body like the dream. To share his anxiety for her, to reveal his longing.

'*Please!*' He tried to step away. 'I am filthy. I just wanted to be sure you were safe. Unhurt.'

She pushed his protest aside and put her hands on his shoulders. 'My brave lieutenant!' She turned her head and called sharply to her maid, 'Stop weeping, you silly girl! Where is your pride?'

In those few seconds Bolitho felt her breast press against his wet shirt, as if there was nothing between their bodies.

He murmured, '*I must go.*'

She was staring at him as if to memorize everything about him. 'Will you fight again? Do you have to?'

Bolitho felt the strength returning to his body. He could even smile as he said, 'I have someone to fight *for*, Aurora.'

She exclaimed, 'You remembered!'

Then she pulled his head down and kissed him firmly on the mouth. Like him, she was shaking, her earlier anger with her maid a pretence like his own.

She whispered, 'Be careful, Richard. My young, *so*-young lieutenant.'

With Palliser's voice ringing in the distance, Bolitho walked back to the ladder and ran to the upper deck.

Palliser was examining the two big schooners with a telescope, and without lowering it he asked dryly, 'May I assume that all is well below?'

Bolitho made to touch his hat, but remembered it had gone a long time ago.

'Aye, sir. Egmont is helping the wounded.'

'Is he indeed?' Palliser closed his glass with a snap. 'Now listen. Those devils will try to divide our defences. One will stand off while the other attempts to board.' He was thinking aloud. 'We may have survived one fight, but they will see *Heloise*'s loss as their victory. They'll give no quarter now.'

Bolitho nodded. 'We might hope to hold them off if we had every gun fully manned, sir.'

Palliser shook his head. 'No. We are adrift and cannot prevent one or both of them from raking our stern.' He glanced at some of the brig's seamen as they staggered past with a trailing serpent of rigging. 'These people are done for, no stomach left. It's up to us.' He nodded firmly, his mind made up. 'We shall allow one of the buggers to grapple. Divide them and see how they like *that*.'

Bolitho looked at the fallen masts and sprawled bodies, among which *Destiny*'s seamen moved like scavengers on a battle-field. Then he touched his mouth with his fingers, as if he expected to feel a difference there where she had kissed him with such fervent passion.

He said, 'I'll tell the others, sir.'

Palliser eyed him bleakly. 'Yes. Just *tell* them. Explanations may come later. If they do, we shall know we have won. If not, they won't matter.'

Palliser lowered his telescope and said bitterly, 'They are better manned than I thought.'

Bolitho shaded his eyes to watch the two schooners, their big fore and aft sails like wings against the bright sky as they tacked slowly to windward of the helpless brig.

The larger of the two vessels, her canvas pock-marked by their canister-shot during the dawn engagement, was a topsail schooner. She touched off a memory and Bolitho said, 'I think she was the one I saw leaving harbour when we were at Egmont's house. I recognize her rig.'

'Most probably. Not many of them in these waters.'

Palliser was studying the schooners' methodical approach. One standing well up to windward, the other manoeuvring towards the *Rosario*'s larboard bow where she would be best shielded from her remaining guns. They were sturdy six-pounders, and under Little's skilled supervision could still make a mark on anything which ventured too close.

Palliser handed Bolitho the glass. 'See for yourself.' He walked over to speak with the brig's master and Slade by the compass box.

Bolitho held his breath and steadied the glass on the nearest schooner. She was weather-worn and ill-used, and he could see the many men who were staring across at the defiant, mastless brig. Some were waving their weapons, their jeers and threats lost only in distance.

He thought of the girl in the cabin, what they would do to her, and gripped his hanger so tightly that it hurt his palm.

He heard the brig's master say, 'I can't argue with a King's officer to be sure, but I'll not answer for what may happen!'

And Slade said urgently, 'We'll never hold 'em, sir, and it's not right to put it to the test!'

Palliser's voice was flat and uncompromising. 'What do you suggest? Wait for a miracle perhaps? Pray that *Destiny* will rise from the deep and save all our wretched souls?' He did not conceal his sarcasm or his contempt. 'God damn your eyes, Slade, I'd have expected better from you!'

He turned and saw Bolitho watching the tense little group. 'In about fifteen minutes that cut-throat will try to grapple us. If we drive him off he will stand clear and the both of them will rake us for a while. Then they will try again. And again.' He waved his arm slowly towards the torn decks and weary, red-eyed seamen. 'Do you see these people holding out?'

Bolitho shook his head. 'No, sir.'

Palliser turned away. 'Good.'

But Bolitho had seen the expression on his face. Relief perhaps, or surprise that someone was agreeing with him in spite of the terrible odds.

Then Palliser said, 'I am going below. I must speak with the prisoners we took from *Heloise*.'

Little said quietly to his friend the boatswain's mate, 'Them stupid clods won't know wot side they be on, eh, Ellis?' They both guffawed as if it was some huge joke.

Jury asked, 'What will we do next?'

Ingrave suggested shakily, 'Parley, sir?'

Bolitho watched the approaching schooner, the expert way her mainsail was being reset to give her a perfect heading for the last half cable.

'We shall meet them as they attempt to board.'

He saw his words moving along the littered deck, the way the seamen gripped their cutlasses and axes and flexed their muscles as if they were already in combat. The brig's men were only hired hands, not professional and disciplined like *Destiny*'s people. But the latter were tired, and there were too few of them when set against the threatening mob aboard the schooner. He could hear them now, yelling and jeering, their combined shouts like an animal roar.

If there had been only one vessel they might have managed. Perhaps it would have been better to die with the *Heloïse* rather than prolong the agony.

Palliser returned and said, 'Little, stand by the forrard guns. When I so order, fire at will, but make quite certain the shots do no real damage.' He ignored Little's disbelief. 'Next, load the remainder with a double charge of grape and canister. At the moment of coming alongside I want those bastards raked.' He let his words drive home. 'If you lose every man in doing it, I need those guns to fire!'

Little knuckled his forehead, his heavy features grim with understanding at last. The brig's bulwark offered little protection, and with the other vessel grinding alongside to grapple them together, the gun crews could be cut down like reeds.

Palliser unclipped his scabbard and tossed it aside. He sliced his sword through the air and watched the bright sunlight run along the blade like gold.

'It will be warm work today.'

Bolitho swallowed, his mouth horribly dry. He too drew his hanger and removed the leather scabbard as he had seen Palliser do. To lose a fight was bad enough, to die because you had tripped over your scabbard was unthinkable.

Muskets banged across the narrowing strip of water between the two hulls, and several men ducked as the balls struck the timbers or whined menacingly overhead.

Palliser sliced down an imaginary foe with his sword and then said sharply, '*Fire!*'

The leading guns hurled themselves inboard on their tackles, the smoke billowing back through the ports as their crews did their best to follow Little's orders.

A hole appeared in the schooner's big fore-sail, but the other shots went wide, throwing up spindly waterspouts nearer to the other vessel than the one which was bearing down on them.

There were wild cheers and more shots, and Bolitho bit his lip as a seaman was hurled back from the bulwark, his jaw smashed away by a musket ball.

Palliser called, 'Stand by to repel boarders!'

All at once the long schooner was right there opposite them, and Bolitho could even see his own shadow on her side with those of his companions.

Musket shots whipped past him and he heard another man cry out, the sound of the ball smashing into his flesh making Ingrave cover his face as if to save himself from a similar fate.

The sails were falling away, and as the tide of men surged across the schooner's deck grapnels soared above them to clatter and then grip the *Rosario*'s hull like iron teeth.

But someone aboard the schooner must have anticipated a last trick from men who could fight like this. Several shots swept through the crouching gun crews and two men fell kicking and screaming, their blood marking their agony until they lay still.

Bolitho glanced quickly at Jury. He was holding his dirk in one hand, a pistol in the other.

Between his teeth Bolitho said, 'Keep with me. Don't lose your footing. Do what you told me to do.' He saw the wildness in Jury's eyes and added, '*Hold on!*'

There was a great lurch as with a shuddering crash the schooner came hard downwind and continued to drive alongside until the grapnel lines took the strain and held her fast.

'*Now!*' Palliser pointed with his sword. '*Fire!*'

A gun belched flame and smoke and the full charge exploded in the exact centre of the massed boarders. Blood and limbs flew about in grisly array, and the momentary terror changed to a wild roar of fury as the attackers formed up again and hurled themselves over the side and on to the brig's hull.

Steel scraped on steel, and while a few men tried to fire and reload their muskets, others thrust wildly with pikes, flinging shrieking boarders between the two hulls to be ground there like bloody fenders.

Palliser yelled, '*Another!*'

But Little and his men were cut off on the forecastle, a wedge of slashing, yelling figures already on the deck between them and the remaining unfired cannon. Its crew lay sprawled nearby, either dead or dying Bolitho did not know. But without that final burst of grape and canister they were already beaten.

A seaman crawled towards the gun, a slow-match gripped in one fist, but he fell face down as an attacker vaulted over the bulwark and hacked him across the neck with a boarding axe. But the force of the blow threw him off balance and he slipped helplessly in his victim's blood. Dutchy Vorbink shouldered Jury aside and charged forward, his jaws wide in a soundless oath as he struck the scrambling figure on the head with his cutlass. The blade glanced from his skull, and Bolitho saw an ear lying on the deck even as Vorbink finished the job with a carefully measured thrust.

When he looked again, Bolitho saw Stockdale by the abandoned gun, his shoulder bleeding from a deep cut, but apparently oblivious to it as he swept up the slow-match and jabbed it to the gun.

The explosion was so violent that Bolitho imagined it must have split the barrel. A whole section of the schooner's bulwark had vanished, and amidst the charred woodwork and cut rigging the men who had been waiting their chance to leap across were entwined in a writhing heap.

Palliser yelled, '*At 'em, lads!*' He cut down a running figure and fired his pistol into the press of boarders as the thin line of defenders surged to meet it.

Bolitho was carried forward with the rest, his hanger rasping against a cutlass, the breath burning in his lungs as he parried the blade clear and slashed a wild-eyed man across his chest. A pistol exploded almost in his ear, and he heard Jury cry out to someone to watch his back as two kicking, yelling boarders cut their way through the exhausted seamen.

A pike slid past Bolitho's hip and pinioned a man who had been trying to follow his comrades through the breach. He was still screaming and dragging at the pike with his bloodied fingers as Stockdale loomed out of the throng and killed him with his cutlass.

Midshipman Ingrave was down, holding his head with both hands as the fight-maddened figures lurched over him in a tide of hatred.

Above it all Bolitho heard Palliser's voice. 'To me, my lads!' It was followed by a burst of cheering and wild cries, and with amazement he saw a tightly packed crowd of men surge through the companionway and forward hatch to join Palliser amidships, their bared blades already clashing with the surprised boarders.

'Drive 'em back!' Palliser pushed through his men, and this seemed to inflame them to greater efforts.

Bolitho saw a shadow waver towards him and struck out with all his strength. The man coughed as the hanger's blade took him right across the stomach and fell to his knees, his fingers knitted across the terrible wound as the cheering sailors blundered over him.

It could not be happening, but it was. Certain defeat had changed to a renewed attack, and the enemy were already falling back in a broken rout as the wave of men charged into them.

Bolitho understood that they must be the prisoners, the *Heloise*'s original crew, which Palliser had released and had put to his own use. But it was all confused in his mind as he cut and thrust with the rest, his shoulder knotted in pain, his sword-arm like solid lead. Palliser must have offered them something, as Dumaresq had done for their master, in exchange for their aid. Several had already fallen, but their sudden arrival had put back the heart into the *Destiny*'s men.

He realized too that some of the pirates had gone over the side, and when he lowered his guard for the first time he saw that the lines had been severed and the schooner was already drifting clear.

Bolitho let his arm fall to his side and stared at the other vessel spreading her sails and using the wind to stand away from the mastless blood-stained but victorious brig.

Men were cheering and slapping each other on the back. Others ran to help their wounded companions, or called the names of friends who would never be able to answer.

One of the pirates who had been feigning death ran for the bulwark when he finally realized his own vessel was breaking off the battle. It was Olsson's moment. With great care he drew a knife from his belt and threw it. It was like a streak of light, and Bolitho saw the running man spin round, his eyes wide with astonishment as the haft quivered between his shoulders.

Little jerked out the knife and tossed it to the pale-eyed Swede. 'Catch!' Then he picked up the corpse and pitched it over the bulwark.

Palliser walked the length of the deck, his sword over his shoulder where it made a red stain on his coat.

Bolitho met his gaze and said huskily, 'We did it, sir. I never thought it would work.'

Palliser watched the released prisoners handing back their weapons and staring at each other as if stunned by what they had done.

'Nor I, as a matter of fact.'

Bolitho turned and saw Jury tying a bandage round Ingrave's head. They had survived.

He asked, 'D'you think they'll attack again?'

Palliser smiled. 'We have no masts. But they have, with the masthead lookouts who can see far further than we. I have no doubt we owe our victory to more than a momentary and unorthodox ruse.'

Palliser, as always, was right. Within the hour *Destiny*'s familiar pyramid of sails was etched against the horizon in bright sunshine. They were no longer alone.

No Childish Desire

The *Destiny*'s stern cabin seemed unnaturally large and remote after the embattled brig.

In spite of what he had endured, Bolitho felt wide awake, and wondered what had given him this renewal of energy.

All day the frigate had been hove to with the mastless *Rosario* wallowing in her lee. While the rest of Palliser's party and the wounded had been ferried across to *Destiny*, other boats had been busy carrying men and material to help the brig's company set up a jury-rig and complete minimum repairs to take them into port.

Dumaresq sat at his table, a litter of papers and charts scattered before him, all of which Palliser had brought from the *Rosario*. He was without his coat, and sitting in his shirt, his neckcloth loosely tied, he looked anything but a frigate captain.

He said, 'You did well, Mr Palliser.' He looked up, his widely spaced eyes turning on Bolitho. 'You also.'

Bolitho thought of that other time when he and Palliser had been demolished by Dumaresq's scathing attack.

Dumaresq pushed the papers aside and leaned back in the chair. 'Too many dead men. *Heloise* gone, too.' He brushed the thought aside. 'But you did the *right* thing, Mr Palliser, and it was bravely done.' He gave a grin. 'I will send *Heloise*'s people with the *Rosario*. From what we have discovered, it would seem that their part in all this was of no importance. They were hired or bribed aboard the brigantine, and by the time they realized they were not going on some short coastal passage they were well out to sea. Their master, Triscott, and his mates, took care to ensure they remained in ignorance. So we'll release them into *Rosario*'s care.' He wagged a finger at his first lieutenant. '*After* you have selected and sworn in any good hands you can use to replace those lost. A spell in the King's service will make a lively change for them.'

Palliser reached out and took a glass of wine as Dumaresq's servant hovered discreetly beside his chair.

'What of Egmont, sir?'

Dumaresq sighed. 'I have ordered that he and his wife be brought across before nightfall. Lieutenant Colpoys has them in his charge. But I wanted Egmont to remain to the last moment so that he could see what his greed and treachery has cost the brig's company as well as my own.' He looked at Bolitho. 'Our plump surgeon has already told me about the vessel you both saw leaving Rio with such stealth. Egmont was safe while he lay hidden, but whoever gave the order for the *Rosario* to be waylaid and seized *wanted him dead*. According to the brig's charts, her final destination was St Christopher's. Egmont was prepared to pay the master anything to take him there, even to avoid his other ports of call in order that he should reach St Christopher's without delay.' He gave a slow smile. 'So that is where Sir Piers Garrick will be.' He nodded as if to emphasize his confidence. 'The hunt is almost over. With Egmont's sworn evidence, and he has no choice left now, we shall run that damn pirate to earth once and for all.' He saw Bolitho's open curiosity and added, 'The Caribbean has seen the making of much wealth. Pirates, honest traders, slavers and soldiers of fortune, they are all there. And where better for *old enemies* to simmer undisturbed?'

He became business-like again. 'Complete this coming and going without too much delay, Mr Palliser. I have advised *Rosario* to return to Rio. Her master will be able to relate his tale to the Viceroy, whereas I was unable to tell mine. He will know that a guise of neutrality must not be so one-sided in future.' As Palliser and Bolitho stood up he said, 'I am afraid we are short of fresh water because of my hasty departure. Mr Codd was able to get all the yams, greens and meat he could desire, but water will have to found elsewhere.'

Outside the cabin Palliser said, 'You are temporarily relieved of your duties. Even extreme youth has a limit. Go to your quarters and rest while you can.' He saw Bolitho's uncertainty. 'Well?'

'I – I was wondering. What will become of Egmont?' He tried to keep his voice unconcerned. 'And his wife?'

'Egmont was a fool. By remaining quiet he aided Garrick. Garrick was trying to help the French at Martinique against us, and that makes Egmont's silence all the more serious. However, if he has any sense he will tell the captain all he knows. But for us he'd be dead. He'll be thinking of that just now.'

He turned to leave, his movements showing little of the strain he had been under. He was still wearing his old sea-going coat which now had the additional distinction of a blood-stain on one shoulder where he had rested his sword.

Bolitho said, 'I should like to put Stockdale's name forward for advancement, sir.'

Palliser came back and lowered his head to peer at Bolitho beneath a deck-beam.

'Would you indeed?'

Bolitho sighed. It sounded rather like the old Palliser again.

But Palliser said, 'I've already done that. Really, Mr Bolitho, you'll have to think more quickly than that.'

Bolitho smiled, despite the ache in his limbs and the confusion in his thoughts which the girl named Aurora had roused with a kiss.

He entered the wardroom, his body swaying to the frigate's heavier motion.

Poad greeted him like a warrior.

'Sit you down, sir! I'll fetch something to eat and drink.' He stood back and beamed at him. 'Right glad we are to see you again, sir, an' that's the truth!'

Bolitho lay back in a chair and allowed the drowsiness to flow over him. Above and around him the ship was alive with bustling feet and the clatter of tackle.

A job had to be done, and the seamen and marines were used to obeying orders and holding their private thoughts to themselves. Across the darkening water the brig was also busy with working sailors. Tomorrow the *Rosario* would make her way towards safety, where her story would be retold a thousand times. And they would speak of the quiet Englishman with the beautiful young wife who had lived amongst them for years, keeping to themselves and outwardly content with their self-imposed exile. And of the frigate with her grotesque captain which had come to Rio and had slunk away in the night like an assassin.

Bolitho stared up at the deckhead, listening to the ship's noises and the sound of the ocean against her hull. He was privileged. He was right in the midst of it, of the conspiracy and the treachery, and very soon now *she* would be here, too.

When Poad returned with a plate of fresh meat and a jug of madeira he found the lieutenant fast asleep. His legs were out-thrust, the breeches and stockings torn and stained with what appeared to be blood. His hair was plastered across his forehead and there was a bruise on his hand, the one which had been gripping his hanger at the start of the day.

Asleep, the third lieutenant looked even younger, Poad thought. Young, and for these rare moments of peace, defenceless.

Bolitho walked slowly up and down the quarterdeck, avoiding flaked lines and the mizzen bitts without conscious effort. It was sunset and a full day since they had parted company with the battered *Rosario* to leave her far astern. She had looked forlorn and as mis-shapen as any cripple with her crude jury-rig and such a sparse display of sails it would take her several days to reach port.

Bolitho glanced aft at the poop skylight and saw the glow of lanterns reflecting on the driver-boom above it. He tried to picture the dining cabin with her there and the captain sharing his table with his two guests. How would she feel now? How much had she known from the beginning, he wondered?

Bolitho had seen her only briefly when she had been brought across from the brig with her husband and a small mountain of luggage. She had seen him watching from the gangway and had made to raise one gloved hand, but the gesture had changed to less than a shrug. A mark of submission, even despair.

He looked up at the braced yards, the topsails growing darker against the pale fleecy clouds which had been with them for most of the day. They were steering north-north-east and standing well out from the land to avoid prying eyes or another would-be follower.

The watch on deck were doing their usual rounds to inspect the trim of the yards and the tautness of running and standing rigging alike. From below he heard the plaintive scrape of the shantyman's fiddle, the occasional murmur of voices as the hands waited for their evening meal.

Bolitho paused in his restless pacing and grasped the nettings to steady himself against the ship's measured roll and plunge. The sea was already much darker to larboard, the swell in half shadow as it cruised slowly towards their quarter to lift *Destiny*'s stern and then roll beneath her keel in endless procession.

He looked along the upper deck at the regularly spaced guns lashed firmly behind the sealed ports, through the black shrouds and other rigging to the figurehead's pale shoulder. He shivered, imagining it to be Aurora reaching out like that, but for him and not the horizon.

Somewhere a man laughed, and he heard Midshipman Lovelace reprimanding one of the watch who was probably old enough to be his father. It sounded even funnier in his high-pitched voice, Bolitho thought. Lovelace had been awarded extra duties by Palliser for skylarking during the dog-watches when he should have been pondering on his navigational problems.

Bolitho recalled his own early efforts to study, to keep awake and learn the hard-won lessons laid down by his sailing master. It all seemed so long ago. The darkness of the smelly orlop and the midshipman's berth, trying to read the figures and calculations by the flickering light of a glim set in an old oyster shell.

And yet it was no time at all. He studied the vibrating canvas and marvelled at the short period it had taken to make so great a step. Once he had stood almost frozen with fear at the prospect of being left alone in charge of a watch. Now he felt confident enough, but knew if the time came he would and must call the captain. But no one else. He could not turn any more to seek out his lieutenant or some stalwart master's mate for aid or advice. Those days were gone, unless or until he committed some terrible error which would strip him of all he had gained.

Bolitho found himself examining his feelings more closely. He had been afraid when he had believed he was going to go down, trapped below decks in the *Heloise*. Perhaps the closest to terror he had ever been. And yet he had seen action before, plenty of times, even as a twelve-year-old midshipman in his first ship he had gritted his teeth against the thunder of the old *Manxman*'s massive broadside.

In his cot, with the flimsy screen door of his cabin shut to the rest of the world, he had thought about it, wondered how his companions saw and judged him.

They never seemed to worry beyond the moment. Colpoys, bored and disdainful, Palliser, unbreakable and ever-watchful over the ship's affairs. Rhodes appeared carefree enough, so perhaps his own ordeal in the *Heloise* and then aboard the brig had made a deeper impression than he had thought.

He had killed or wounded several men, and had watched others hack down their enemies with apparent relish. But surely you could never get used to it? The smell of a man's breath against your own, the feel of his body heat as he tried to break your guard. His triumph when he thought you were falling, his horror as you drove your blade into muscle and bone.

One of the two helmsmen said, 'Steady as she goes, sir. Nor'-nor'-east.'

He turned in time to see the captain's thickset shadow emerging from the companionway.

Dumaresq was a heavy man but had the stealth of a cat.

'All quiet, Mr Bolitho?'

'Aye, sir.' He could smell the brandy and guessed the captain had just finished his dinner.

'A long haul yet.' Dumaresq tilted on his heels to study the sails and the first faint stars. He changed the subject and asked, 'Are you recovered from your little battle?'

Bolitho felt stripped naked. It was as if Dumaresq had been reading into his very thoughts.

'I think so, sir.'

Dumaresq persisted. 'Frightened, were you?'

'Part of the time.' He nodded, remembering the weight across his back, the roar of water through the deck below where he had been trapped.

'A good sign.' Dumaresq nodded. 'Never become too hard. Like cheap steel, you'll snap if you do.'

Bolitho asked carefully, 'Will we be carrying the passengers all the way, sir?'

'To St Christopher's at least. There I intend to enlist the governor's aid and have word sent to our senior officer there or at Antigua.'

'The treasure, sir. Is there still a chance of recovering it?'

'Some of it. But I suspect we may recognize it in a very different form from that originally intended. There is a smell of rebellion in the air. It has been growing and smouldering since the end of the war. Sooner or later our old enemies will strike at us again.' He turned and stared at Bolitho as if trying to make up his mind. 'I read something of your brother's recent success when I was at Plymouth. Against another of Garrick's breed, I believe? He caught and destroyed a man who was fleeing to America, a man once respected but who proved to be as rotten as any common felon.'

Bolitho replied quietly, 'Aye, sir. I was there with him.'

'Indeed?' Dumaresq chuckled. 'There was no mention of *that* in the Gazette. Your brother wanted all the glory for himself perhaps?'

He turned away before Bolitho could ask of the connection, if there was one, between the dash down the Channel just a few months back and the mysterious Sir Piers Garrick.

But Dumaresq said, 'I am going to play cards with Mr Egmont. The surgeon has agreed to partner him, whereas I shall have our gallant marine for mine.' He gave a rich chuckle. 'We might empty one of Egmont's money-boxes before we drop anchor off Basseterre!'

Bolitho sighed and walked slowly to the quarterdeck rail. Half an hour and the watch would change. A few words with Rhodes, then down to the wardroom.

He heard Yeames, master's mate of the watch, murmur with unusual politeness, 'Why, good *evenin'*, ladies.'

Bolitho swung round, his heart pounding in immediate response as he saw her moving carefully along the side of the quarterdeck, her arm entwined with that of her maid.

He saw her hesitate and was of two minds what to do next.

'Let me assist you.'

Bolitho crossed the deck and took her proffered hand. Through the glove he felt the warmth of her fingers, the smallness of her wrist.

'Come to the weather side, ma'am. There is less spray and a far better view.'

She did not resist as he led her up the sloping deck to the opposite side. Then he pulled out his handkerchief and bound it quickly round the hammock nettings.

He explained as calmly as he could that it was to protect her glove from tar or any other shipboard substance.

She held herself close to the nettings and stared abeam across the dark water. Bolitho could smell her fragrant perfume, just as he was very aware of her nearness.

Then she said, 'A long way to St Christopher's Island, is it not?' She had turned to look at him but her eyes were in shadow.

'It will take us over two weeks, according to Mr Gulliver, ma'am. It is a good three thousand miles.'

He saw her teeth white in the gloom, but did not know if she was showing dismay or impatience.

'A *good* three thousand miles, Lieutenant?' Then she nodded. 'I understand.'

Through the open skylight Bolitho heard Dumaresq's deep laugh and Colpoys saying something in reply. Dealing his cards, no doubt.

She had heard too and said quickly to her maid, 'You may leave us. You have worked hard today.'

She watched the girl reaching for the companionway and added, 'She has lived all her life on hard dry land. This ship must be strange to her.'

Bolitho asked, 'What will you do? Will you be safe after all that has happened?'

She tilted her head as Dumaresq laughed again. 'That will depend on *him*.' She looked past Bolitho, her eyes shining like the spray alongside as she asked, 'Does it matter so much to you?'

Bolitho said, 'You know it does. I care terribly.'

'You do?' She reached out and gripped his arm with her free hand. 'You are a kind boy.' She felt him stiffen and added gently, 'I apologize. You are a man to have done what you did back there when I thought I was going to be killed.'

Bolitho smiled. 'I am the one to apologize. I want you to like me so much that I act like a fool.'

She twisted round and moved closer to look at him. 'You mean it. I can tell that, if nothing else.'

'If only you could have remained in Rio.' Bolitho was searching his mind for some solution which might help. 'Your husband should not have risked your life.'

She shook her head, the movement of her hair striking at Bolitho's heart like a dagger.

'He has been good to me. Without him I would have been lost long ago. I was a stranger in Rio. I am of Spanish blood. When my parents died I was to have been bought as a wife by a Portuguese trader.'

She gave a shudder. 'I was only thirteen. He was like a greasy pig!'

Bolitho felt betrayed. 'Was it not love which made you marry your husband?'

'Love?' She tossed her head. 'I do not find men very attractive, you know. So I was content with his arrangements for me. Like his many fine possessions, I think he sees me as a decoration.' She opened the shawl which she had carried on deck. 'Like this bird, yes?'

Bolitho saw the same two-headed bird with the ruby tail feathers she had worn at her house in Rio.

He said fervently, 'I love you!'

She tried to laugh but nothing came. She said, 'I suspect you know even less about loving than I do.' She reached up and touched his face. 'But you meant what you said. I am sorry if I hurt you.'

Bolitho grasped her hand and pressed it firmly against his cheek. She had not laughed or piled scorn on him for his clumsy advances.

He said, 'You will be left in peace soon.'

She sighed. 'And then you will come like a knight on your charger to save me, yes? I used to dream of such things when I was a child. Now I think as a woman.'

She pulled his hand down and pressed it against her skin, so that the warmth of the jewelled bird on his fingers was like a part of her.

'Do you feel that?' She was watching him intently.

He could feel the urgent beat of her heart rising to match his own as he touched the smooth skin and the firm curve of her breast.

'That is no childish desire.' She made to move away but when he held her she said, 'What is the use? We are not alone to act as we please. If my husband thinks I am betraying him, he will refuse to help your captain.' She put her hand on his lips. 'Hear me! Dear Richard, do you not see what that would mean? My husband thrown into some English prison to await trial and death. I, as his wife, might be taken also, or left destitute to await another Portuguese trader, or worse.' She waited for him to release her and then murmured, 'But do not think I would not or could not love you.'

Voices echoed along the deck and Bolitho heard a boatswain's mate calling out names as the watch trooped aft to relieve his own men.

In those few seconds Bolitho found himself hating the boatswain's mate with all his soul.

He exclaimed, 'I must see you again.'

She was already making her way to the opposite side, her slim outline like a ghost against the dark water beyond.

'Three thousand miles you said, Lieutenant? It is such a long way. Each day will be torture.' She hesitated and glanced back at him. 'For both of us.'

Rhodes clattered up through the companionway and stood aside to let her pass. He nodded to Bolitho and remarked, 'A beauty indeed.' He seemed to sense Bolitho's mood, that he was prepared to be hostile if he mentioned her again.

He added, 'That was clumsy of me. Stupid, too.'

Bolitho pulled him to one side, oblivious of the watch mustering beyond the quarterdeck rail.

'I am in hell, Stephen! I can tell no one else. It is driving me mad.'

Rhodes was deeply moved by Bolitho's sincerity and by the fact he was sharing his secret with him.

He said, 'We shall think of something.' It sounded so unconvincing in the face of his friend's despair that he said, 'A lot can happen before we sight St Christopher's.'

The master's mate touched his hat. 'The watch is aft, sir.'

Bolitho walked to the companionway and paused with one foot on the ladder. Her perfume was still hanging there, or if not it must be clinging to his coat.

Aloud he exclaimed, 'What can I do?'

But the only answer came from the sea and the rumble of the rudder beneath Dumaresq's cabin.

The first week of the *Destiny*'s passage passed swiftly enough, with several blustery squalls to keep the hands busy and to hold back the scorching heat.

Up and around Cabo Branco then north-west for the Spanish Main and the Indies. There were longer periods of low breezes, and some of no wind at all when the boats were put down and the gruelling work of warping the ship by muscle and sweat was enforced.

Fresh water ran lower as a direct consequence, and with neither rain nor the prospect of an early landfall it was rationed. After a week it was cut further still to a pint a day per man.

During his daily watches under the blazing sun, Bolitho saw very little of Egmont's wife. He told himself it was for her good as well as his own. There were troubles enough to contend with. Outbreaks of insubordination which ended in fists and kicks or the use of a petty officer's starter. But Dumaresq refrained from having any of his men flogged, and Bolitho wondered if it was because he was eager to keep the peace or holding his hand for his passengers' benefit.

Bulkley was showing signs of anxiety, too. Three men had gone down with scurvy. In spite of his care and the regular issue of fruit juice, the surgeon was unable to prevent it.

Once, while he had been lingering in the shadow of the big driver, Bolitho had heard Dumaresq's voice through the cabin skylight, dismissing Bulkley's pleas, even blaming him for not taking better precautions for his sick seamen.

Bulkley must have been examining the chart, because he had protested, 'Why not Barbados, Captain? We could anchor off Bridge-town and arrange for fresh water to be brought out to us. What we have left is crawling with vermin, and I'll not answer for the people's health if you insist on driving them like this!'

'God damn your eyes, sir! I'll tell you who you shall answer to, believe me! I'll not go to Barbados and shout to the whole world what we are doing. You attend to your duties and I shall do the same!'

And there it had ended.

Seventeen days after parting from the *Rosario* the wind found them

again, and with even her studding-sails set *Destiny* gathered way like
the thoroughbred she was.

But perhaps it was already too late to prevent some kind of explosion.
It was like a chain reaction. Slade, the master's mate, still brooding over
Palliser's contempt, and knowing it would likely hinder, even prevent
any chance of promotion, poured abuse on Midshipman Merrett for
failing to calculate the ship's noon position correctly. Merrett had
overcome his early timidity, but he was only twelve years old. To be
berated so harshly in front of several hands and the two helmsmen was
more than enough for him. He burst into tears.

Rhodes was officer of the watch and could have intervened. Instead
he remained by the weather side, his hat tilted against the sun, his ears
deaf to Merrett's outburst.

Bolitho was below the mainmast watching some of his topmen
reeving a new block at the topgallant yard and heard most of it.

Stockdale was with him, and muttered, 'It's like an overloaded
waggon, sir. Somethin's got to give.'

Merrett dropped his hat and was rubbing his eyes with his knuckles
when a seaman picked up the hat and handed it to him, his eyes angry as
he glanced at the master's mate.

Slade yelled, 'How dare you interfere between your betters?'

The seaman, one of the after-guard, retorted hotly, 'Dammit, Mr
Slade, 'e's doin' 'is best! It's bad enough for the bloody rest of us, let
alone fer 'im!'

Slade seemed to go purple.

He screamed, 'Master-at-arms! Secure that man!' He turned on the
quarterdeck at large. 'I'll see his backbone at the gratings!'

Poynter and the ship's corporal arrived and seized the defiant
seaman.

The latter showed no sign of relenting. 'Like Murray, eh? A good 'and
an' a loyal shipmate, and they were goin' to flog 'im, too!'

Bolitho heard a growl of agreement from the men around him.

Rhodes came out of his torpor and called, 'Pipe down there! What's
going on?'

Slade said, 'This man defied me, and swore at me, so he did!' He was
becoming dangerously calm and glaring at the seaman as if he would
strike him dead.

Rhodes said uncertainly, 'In that case . . .'

'In *that* case, Mr Rhodes, have the man put in irons. I'll have no
defiance in my ship.'

Dumaresq had appeared as if by magic.

Slade swallowed and said, 'This man was interfering, sir.'

'I heard you.' Dumaresq thrust his hands behind his back. 'As did the whole ship, I would imagine.' He glanced at Merrett and snapped, 'Stop snivelling, boy!'

The midshipman stopped, like a clock, and looked about him with embarrassment.

Dumaresq eyed the seaman and added, 'That was a costly gesture, Adams. A dozen lashes.'

Bolitho knew that Dumaresq could do nothing but uphold his subordinates, right or wrong, and a dozen lashes was minimal, just a headache, the old hands would term it.

But an hour later, as the lash rose and then cracked with terrible force across the man's naked back, Bolitho realised just how frail was their hold over the ship's company with land so far away.

The gratings were unrigged, the man named Adams was carried below grunting with pain to be revived with a wash-down of salt water and a liberal dose of rum. The spots of blood were swabbed away, and to all intents everything was as before.

Bolitho had relieved Rhodes in charge of the watch, and heard Dumaresq say to the master's mate, 'Discipline is upheld. For all our sakes.' He fixed Slade with his compelling stare. 'For your own safety, I would suggest you stay out of my way!'

Bolitho turned aside so that Slade should not see him watching. But he had seen Slade's face. Like that of a man who had been expecting a reprieve only to feel his arms being pinioned by the hangman.

All that night Bolitho thought about the girl named Aurora. It was impossible to get near her. She had been given half of the stern cabin, while Egmont made the best of a cot in the dining space. Dumaresq slept in the chartroom nearby, and there was always the servant and the marine sentry to prevent any casual caller from entering.

As he lay in his cot, his naked body sweating in the unmoving air, Bolitho pictured himself entering her cabin and holding her in his arms. He groaned at the torment, and tried to ignore the thirst which had left his mouth like a kiln. The water was foul and in short supply, and to keep drinking wine as a substitute was inviting disaster.

He heard uncertain footsteps in the wardroom and then a gentle tap on his screen door.

Bolitho rolled out of the cot, groping for his shirt as he asked, 'Who is it?'

It was Spillane, the captain's new clerk. Despite the hour he was neat and tidy, and his shirt looked as if it had just been washed, although how he had managed it was a mystery.

Spillane said politely, 'I have a message for you, sir.' He was looking at Bolitho's tousled hair and casual nakedness as he continued, 'From the lady.'

Bolitho darted a quick glance around the wardroom. Only the

regular creaks and groans of the ship's timbers and the occasional murmur of canvas from above broke the silence.

He found he was whispering. 'Where is it, then?'

Spillane replied, 'By word of mouth, sir. She'd not put pen to paper.'

Bolitho stared. Now Spillane was a conspirator whether he wanted to be or not.

'Go on.'

Spillane lowered his voice further still. 'You take over the morning-watch at four o'clock, sir.' His precise, landsman's expression made him seem even more out of place here.

'Aye.'

'The lady will endeavour to come on deck. For a breath of air, if someone is bold enough to question her.'

'Is that all?'

'It is, sir.' Spillane was watching him closely in the faint light from a shuttered lantern. 'Did you expect more?'

Bolitho glanced at him guardedly. Was that last remark a show of familiarity, a testing insolence because of their shared conspiracy? Maybe Spillane was nervous, eager to get it over with.

He said, 'No. Thank you for telling me.'

Bolitho stood for a long moment, his body swaying to the motion, as he went over everything Spillane had said.

Later, he was still in the wardroom, sitting in a chair, the same shirt dangling from his fingers as he stared into the shadows.

A boatswain's mate found him and whispered, 'I see you don't need a call, sir. The watch is musterin' now. Fair breeze up top, but another blazin' day is my guess.'

He stood back as Bolitho pulled on his breeches and fumbled around for a clean shirt. The lieutenant was obviously half asleep still, he decided. It was a cruel waste to don any clean garment for the morning-watch. It would be a wet rag by six bells.

Bolitho followed the man on deck and relieved Midshipman Henderson with the briefest possible delay. Henderson was next in line for lieutenant's examination and Palliser had allowed him to stand the middle-watch on his own.

The midshipman almost fled from the deck, and Bolitho could well imagine his thoughts as he tumbled into his hammock on the orlop. His first watch alone. Reliving it. What had nearly gone wrong, when he had nearly decided to rouse Palliser or the master. The feeling of triumph as Bolitho had appeared, knowing the watch was ended without mishap.

Bolitho's men settled down in the shadows, and after checking the compass and the set of the topsails he walked towards the companion-way.

Midshipman Jury crossed to the weather side and wondered when he would get his chance to stand a watch unaided. He turned and saw Bolitho moving aft by the mizzen-mast, and then blinked as another pale figure glided to meet him.

He heard the helmsmen whispering together and noticed that the boatswain's mate of the watch had moved discreetly to the weather gangway.

'Watch our helm there!' Jury saw the seamen stiffen at the great double-wheel. Beyond them the two pale figures seemed to have merged into one.

Jury walked to the quarterdeck rail and gripped it with both hands.

To all intents he *was* standing his first watch unaided, he thought happily.

11

A Close Thing

Under topsails, forecourse and jib only, the *Destiny* headed slowly towards the green humpbacked island. So gentle was the breeze that her progress was a snail's pace, an impression which grew as she approached the small ridge of land.

The masthead had sighted it the previous day, just before dusk, and throughout the night-watches until the break of dawn there had been a buzz of speculation from wardroom to messdeck.

Now, in the harsh forenoon sunlight it lay across their bows and shimmered in a low haze, as if it might vanish at any second like a mirage.

It was higher towards its centre, where thick clusters of palms and other foliage were bunched together, to leave the slopes and the tiny, crescent-shaped beaches totally devoid of cover.

'*Deep six!*'

The hollow chant from a leadsman in the chains reminded Bolitho of the shallows nearby, the hint of a reef lying to starboard. A few sea-birds dotted the water, and others cruised watchfully around the topgallant mastheads.

Bolitho heard Dumaresq conferring with Palliser and the master. The island was marked on the chart but apparently unclaimed. The known survey was poor, and Dumaresq was probably regretting his impulse to touch land in search for water.

But the ship was down to her last barricoes of water, and the contents were so vile that Bulkley and the purser had joined forces in another plea to the captain for him to seek a new supply. Enough at least to take them to their destination.

'By th' mark seven!'

Gulliver tried to relax his stance as the keel glided into deeper water. The ship was still standing two cables clear of the nearest beach. If the wind rose or changed direction, *Destiny* might be in trouble with no depth at all to beat free of the land and out-thrust reef.

Every man but the cook and the sick ones in Bulkley's care was on deck or clinging to the shrouds and ratlines, strangely silent as they peered towards the little island. It was one of hundreds in the Caribbean, but the hint of fresh, drinkable water made it appear special and priceless.

'By th' mark five!'

Dumaresq grimaced at Palliser. 'Hands wear ship. Stand by to anchor, if you please.'

With her sails barely flapping in the intense heat, the frigate turned wearily on the blue water until the order to let go was yelled along the deck. The anchor splashed down, pushing great circles away from the bows and churning up pale sand from the bottom.

Once anchored the heat seemed to force into the ship still more, and as Bolitho made his way to the quarterdeck he saw Egmont and his wife standing right aft by the taffrail, sheltering beneath a canvas awning which George Durham, the sailmaker, had rigged for them.

Dumaresq was studying the island slowly and methodically with the signal midshipman's big telescope.

He remarked, 'No smoke, or signs of life. Can't see any marks on the beach either, so there aren't any boats on this side.' He handed the glass to Palliser. 'That ridge looks promising, eh?'

Gulliver said cautiously, 'Could be water there, right enough, sir.'

Dumaresq ignored him and turned instead to his two passengers. 'Might be able to stretch your legs ashore before we weigh.' He chuckled.

He had addressed both of them, but Bolitho somehow knew that his words had been aimed at the woman.

He thought of that one moment when she had come on deck to see him. It had been unreal but precious. Dangerous, and all the more exciting because of it.

They had spoken very little. All through the following day Bolitho had thought about it, relived it, hung on to each moment for fear of losing something.

He had held her close to his body while the ship had ploughed into the first misty light of dawn, feeling her heart beat against his, wanting to touch her and afraid he would spoil it with his boldness. She had freed herself from his arms and had kissed him lightly on the mouth before merging with the remaining shadows to leave him alone.

And now, just to hear Dumaresq's casual familiarity towards her, his mention of stretching her legs, was like a barb, a spur of jealousy which he had never known before.

Dumaresq broke his thoughts. 'You will take a landing-party, Mr Bolitho. Determine if there is a stream or any useful rock pools. I will await your signal.'

He walked aft, and Bolitho heard him speaking again with Egmont and Aurora.

Bolitho flinched. He saw Jury watching him and imagined for an instant he had again spoken her name aloud.

Palliser snapped, 'Get a move on. If there is no water, we'd best know about it quickly.'

Colpoys was standing languidly by the mizzen. 'I will send some of my fellows as pickets, if you wish.'

Palliser exclaimed, 'Hell's teeth, we're not expecting a pitched battle!'

The cutter was hoisted outboard and lowered alongside. Stockdale, now promoted to gun-captain, was already detailing some hands for the shore-party, while the boat's coxswain supervised the loading of extra tackle for the water-barricoes should they require them.

Bolitho waited until the boat was manned and then reported to Palliser. He saw the girl watching him, the way one hand was resting on her necklace, remembering perhaps, or reminding him that his had once lain there.

Palliser said, 'Take a pistol. Fire it if you find anything.' His eyes narrowed against the fierce glare. 'Once the casks are filled they'll discover something else to grumble about!'

The cutter pulled away from the side, and Bolitho felt the sun burn across his neck as they left the *Destiny*'s protective shadow.

'Give way all!'

Bolitho trailed his arm over the side, feeling the sensual touch of cool water, and imagined her with him, swimming and then running hand in hand up the pale beach to discover each other for the first time.

When he looked over the gunwale he saw the bottom quite clearly, dotted with white stones or shells, and isolated humps of coral, deceptively harmless in the shimmering reflections.

Stockdale said to the coxswain, 'Looks like nobody's ever been 'ere, Jim.'

The man eased the tiller-bar and nodded, the movement bringing a trickle of sweat from under his tarred hat.

'Easy all! Bowman, boat yer oar!'

Bolitho watched the cutter's shadow rising to meet them as the bowman vaulted over the side to guide the stem into the sand while the others hauled their blades inboard and hung panting over the looms like old men.

And then there was total stillness. Just a far-off murmur of surf on a reef, the occasional gurgle of water around the grounded cutter. No bird lifted from the crowded hump of palms, not even an insect.

Bolitho climbed over the gunwale and waded to the beach. He was wearing an open shirt and breeches, but his body felt as if he was dressed in thick furs. The thought of tearing off his crumpled clothing and running naked into the sea mingled with his earlier fantasy, and he wondered if she was watching from the ship, using a telescope to see him.

Bolitho realized with a start that the others were waiting.

He said to the coxswain, 'Remain with the boat. The crew, too. They may have to do several journeys yet.' To Stockdale he said, 'We'll take the others up the slope. It's the shortest way and probably the coolest.'

He ran his eye over the small landing-party. Two of them were from the *Heloise*'s original company, now sworn-in members of His Majesty's Navy. They still appeared dazed at their swift change of circumstances, but they were good enough seamen to avoid the harsher side of the boatswain's tongue.

Apart from Stockdale, there was none of his own division in the group, and he guessed there had been little enthusiasm for volunteering to tramp round an uninhabited island. Later, if they discovered water, it would be very different.

Stockdale said, 'Follow me!'

Bolitho walked up the slope, his feet sinking in the loose sand, the pistol in his belt burning his skin like a piece of hot iron. It felt strange to walk here, he thought. A tiny, unknown place. There might be human bones nearby. Shipwrecked mariners, or men cast adrift and marooned by pirates to die horribly without hope of rescue.

How inviting the palms looked. They were moving gently, and he could hear them rustling as he drew nearer. Once he stopped to look back at the ship. She seemed far away, balanced perfectly on her own reflection. But in distance she had lost her rakish lines, and her mast and loosely furled sails seemed to be swaying and bending in the haze, as if the whole ship was melting.

The small party of seamen tramped gratefully into a patch of shade, their ragged trousers catching in some large fronds which displayed teethlike barbs around the edges. There were different smells here, too, of rotting undergrowth, and from vividly coloured blossoms.

Bolitho looked up at the sky and saw a frigate-bird circling high overhead, its scimitar-shaped wings motionless as it ghosted on the hot current. So they were not completely alone.

A man called excitedly, 'Look yonder, sir! *Water!*'

They pressed forward, all tiredness momentarily forgotten.

Bolitho looked at the pool with disbelief. It was shivering slightly, so he guessed there was some sort of underground source close by. He could see the surrounding palms reflected on its surface and the images of his men as they peered down at the water.

Bolitho said, 'I'll have a taste.'

He clambered along the sandy bank and dipped his hand into the water. It was a false impression, but it felt as cold as a mountain stream. Hardly daring to hope, he raised his cupped hand to his lips and after a slight hesitation swallowed deeply.

He said quietly, 'It's pure.'

Bolitho watched the seamen throwing themselves down on their chests and scooping the water over their faces and shoulders, swallowing great gulps of it in their eager excitement.

Stockdale wiped his mouth with satisfaction. 'Good stuff.'

Bolitho smiled. Josh Little would have called it a 'wet'.

'We'll stand easy a while, then signal the ship.'

The seamen drew their cutlasses and drove them into the sand before squatting down against the palms or leaning over the shimmering water as if to make sure it was still there.

Bolitho walked away from them, and as he examined his pistol to ensure that it was free of sand and damp he thought of that moment when she had joined him on *Destiny*'s quarterdeck.

It must not end, it could not be allowed to die.

'Something wrong, sir?' Stockdale lumbered up the slope.

Bolitho realized he must have been frowning in concentration. 'Not wrong.'

It was uncanny how Stockdale always seemed to know, to be ready in case he was needed. Yet it was something very real between them. Bolitho found it easy to talk to the big, hoarse prize-fighter, and the reverse was true also, without any hint of subservience or as a means to gain favour.

Bolitho said, 'You go and make the signal.' He watched the pistol half disappear in Stockdale's great fist. 'I need to think about something.'

Stockdale watched him impassively. 'You're young, an' beggin' yer pardon, sir, I think you should *stay* young for as long as you can.'

Bolitho faced him. You never really knew what Stockdale meant with his brief, halting sentences. Had he implied that he should keep away from a woman who was ten years older than he was? Bolitho refused to think about it. Their life was now, when they could find it. They could worry about differences later.

He said, 'Be off with you. I wish it was that simple.'

Stockdale shrugged and strode down the slope towards the beach, his broad shoulders set in such a way that Bolitho knew he was not going to let it rest there.

With a great sigh Bolitho walked back towards the pool to warn his men that Stockdale was about to fire the pistol. Sailors cooped up in a ship-of-war often became nervous of such things when they were put ashore.

One of the seamen had been lying with his face half under the water, and as Bolitho approached he stood up dripping and grinning with pleasure.

Bolitho said, 'Be ready, men . . .' He broke off as someone gave a piercing scream and the seaman who had been grinning at him pitched forward into the water.

All at once there was frantic pandemonium amounting to panic as the sailors scrabbled in the sand for their weapons and others stared with horror at the drifting corpse, the water reddening around it from a spear thrust between the shoulders.

Bolitho swung round, seeing the sunlight partially broken by running, leaping figures, the glitter of weapons and a terrifying scream of combined voices which made the hair rise on his neck.

'*Stand to!*'

He groped for his hanger and gasped with shock as another seaman rolled down the slope, kicking and spitting blood as he tried to tug a crude shaft from his belly.

'*Oh, God!*' Bolitho shaded his eyes against the bars of sunlight. Their attackers had it behind them and were closing in on the stampeding seamen, that terrible din of screaming voices making it impossible to think or act.

Bolitho realized they were black men, their eyes and mouths wide with triumph as they hacked down another sailor and pounded his face to a bloody pulp with a piece of coral.

Bolitho ran to meet the attack, dimly aware that more figures were rushing past him as if to separate him from his remaining seamen. He heard someone shrieking and pleading, the sickening sound of a skull splintered open like a coconut.

He found he had his back to a tree and was striking out wildly, wasting his strength, leaving himself open for one of those fire-hardened spears.

Bolitho saw three of his men, one of whom had been wounded in the leg, standing together, hemmed in by screaming, slashing figures.

He pushed himself away from the tree, hacked open a black shoulder with his hanger and bounced across the trampled sand to join the embattled seamen.

One cried, "S'no use! Can't 'old th' buggers!'

Bolitho felt the hanger knocked from his hand and realized he had not fastened the lanyard around his wrist.

He searched desperately for another weapon, seeing that his men were breaking and running towards the beach, the injured one hopping only a few paces before he too was cut down.

Bolitho got a terrifying impression of two staring eyes and bared white teeth, and saw the savage charging towards him, scooping up a discarded cutlass as he came.

Bolitho ducked and tried to leap to one side. Then came the impact, too great for pain, too powerful to measure.

He knew he was falling, his forehead on fire, while in another world he could hear his own voice calling out, brittle with agony.

And then, mercifully, there was nothing.

When consciousness finally returned, the agony which accompanied it was almost unendurable.

Bolitho tried to force open his eyes, as if by doing so he could drive away the torment, but it was so great he could feel his whole body contracting to withstand it.

Voices murmured above his head, but through his partially closed eyes he could see very little. A few hazy shapes, the darker shadows of beams directly overhead.

It was as if his head was being crushed slowly and deliberately between two heated irons, torturing his cringing mind with probing pains and brilliant flashes like lighting.

Cool cloths were being dabbed over his face and neck and then across his body. He was naked, not pinioned by force but with hands touching his wrists and ankles in case he struggled.

Another thought made him cry out with terror. He was badly injured elsewhere than in his head and they were getting ready for him. He had seen it done. The knife glittering in the feeble lanterns, the quick cut and turn of the blade, and then the saw.

'*Easy*, son.'

That was Bulkley, and the fact he was here helped to steady him in some way. Bolitho imagined he could smell the surgeon, brandy and tobacco.

He tried to speak but his voice was a hoarse whisper. 'What happened?'

Bulkley peered over his shoulder, his owl-like face with the little spectacles poised in the air like a comic bladder.

'Save your breath. Breathe slowly.' Bulkley nodded. 'That's it.'

Bolitho gritted his teeth as the pain tightened its hold. It was worse above his right eye where there was a bandage. His hair felt tight, matted with blood. Vaguely the picture re-formed, the bulging eyes, the cutlass swinging towards him. Oblivion.

He asked, 'My men, are they safe?'

Bolitho felt a coat sleeve brush against his bare arm and saw Dumaresq looking down at him, his shape made more grotesque by the angle. The eyes were no longer compelling, but grave.

'The boat's crew are safe. Two of your original party reached it in time.'

Bolitho tried to move his head, but someone held it firmly.

'Stockdale? Is he. . . ?'

Dumaresq smiled. 'He carried you to the beach. But for him all of the people would have been lost. I shall tell you later. Now you must endeavour to rest. You have lost a lot of blood.'

Bolitho could feel the darkness closing over him again. He had seen the quick exchange of glances between Dumaresq and the surgeon. It was not over. He might die. The realization was almost too much and he felt the tears smarting in his eyes as he gasped, 'Don't . . . want . . . to . . . leave . . . *Destiny*. Mustn't . . . go . . . like . . . this.'

Dumaresq said, 'You will recover.'

He rested his hand on Bolitho's shoulder so that he could feel the strength of the man, as if he were transferring some of his power into him.

Then he moved away, and Bolitho realized for the first time that he was in the stern cabin and that beyond the tall windows it was pitch-dark.

Bulkley watched him and said, 'You have been unconscious all day, Richard.' He wagged his finger at him. 'You had me somewhat troubled, I can tell you.'

'Then you are not worried for me now?' Again he tried to move, but the hands gripped him firmly like watchful animals.

Bulkley made a few adjustments to the bandages. 'A severe blow to the head with a heavy blade is never a thing to be scoffed at. I have done some work on you, the rest will depend on time and care. It was a close-run fight. But for Stockdale's courage and his determination to rescue you, you would be dead.' He glanced round as if to ensure that the captain had gone. 'He rallied the remaining seamen when they were about to flee from the beach. He was like a wild bull, yet when he carried you aboard he did it with the gentleness of a woman.' He sighed. 'It must be the costliest cargo of fresh water in naval history!'

Bolitho could feel a new drowsiness closing in to withstand the pounding anguish in his skull. Bulkley had given him something.

He whispered, 'You would tell me if . . .'

Bulkley was wiping his fingers. 'Probably.' He looked up and added, 'You are being well cared for. We are about to weigh anchor, so endeavour to rest yourself.'

Bolitho tried to keep a grip on his senses. About to weigh anchor. Here all day. So the water must have been obtained. Men had died. Many more afterwards, he thought, when Colpoys's marines took their revenge.

He spoke very slowly, knowing his words were getting slurred, but knowing too that he must make himself understood.

'Tell Aur . . . tell Mrs Egmont that . . .'

Bulkley leaned over him and pulled at his eyelids. 'Tell her yourself. She has been with you since you were brought aboard. I told you. You are well cared for.'

Then Bolitho saw her standing beside him, her black hair hanging down over either shoulder, glossy in the lantern light.

She touched his face, her fingers brushing his lips as she said softly, 'You can sleep now, my lieutenant. I am here.'

Bolitho felt the hands relax their hold from his wrists and ankles, and sensed the surgeon's assistants withdrawing into the shadows.

He murmured faintly, 'I – I did not want you to see me like this, Aurora.'

She smiled, but it made her look incredibly sad.

'You are beautiful,' she said.

Bolitho closed his eyes, the strength gone from him at last.

By the screen door Bulkley turned to look at them. He should be used to pain and the gratitude of recovery, but he was not, and he was moved by what he saw. It was more like a painting from mythology, he thought. The lovely woman weeping by the fallen body of her hero.

He had not lied to Bolitho. It had been very close, and the cutlass had not only made a deep scar above the eye and into the hairline but had scored the bone beneath. Had Bolitho been an older man, or the cutlass expertly used, it would have ended there.

She said, 'He is asleep.' But she was not speaking to Bulkley. She removed her white shawl and very gently spread it across Bolitho's body, as if his nakedness, like her words, was something private.

In *Destiny*'s other, ordered world a voice bellowed, '*Anchor's aweigh*, sir!'

Bulkley put out a hand to steady himself as the deck tilted to the sudden pressure of wind and rudder. He would go to his sick-bay and have several long drinks. He had no wish to see the island as it fell astern in the dusk. It had given them fresh water, but had taken lives in exchange. Bolitho's party at the pool had been massacred but for Stockdale and two others. Colpoys had reported that the savages who had attacked them were once slaves who had possibly escaped when on passage to an island plantation.

Seeing Bolitho and his men approaching, they had doubtless imagined they were there to hunt them down and award some brutal reprisal. When *Destiny*'s boats, roused by the pistol-shot from the beach and the sudden panic amongst the cutter's crew, had reached the shore, those same slaves had run towards them. Nobody knew if they had realized *Destiny* was not a 'blackbirder' after all and were trying to make recompense. Colpoys had directed the swivel guns and musketoons which were mounted in each boat to rake the beach. When the smoke had drifted away there had been nobody alive to explain.

Bulkley paused at the top of the ladder and heard the clatter of blocks, the pad of bare feet as the seamen hauled at halliards and braces to set their ship on her true course.

To a man-of-war it was only an interlude. Something to be written up in her log. Until the next challenge, the next fight. He glanced aft at the swaying deckhead lantern and the red-coated sentry beneath it.

And yet, he decided, there had been a lot of worthwhile things, too.

12

Secrets

The days which immediately followed Bolitho's return to the living were like parts of a dream. From the age of twelve, since he had first gone to sea as a midshipman, he had been used to the constant demands of a ship. Night or day, at any hour and under all conditions he had been ready to run with the others to whatever duty was ordered, and had been under no illusions as to the consequences if he failed to obey.

But as *Destiny* sailed slowly northwards through the Caribbean he was forced to accept his inactivity, to remain still and listen to the familiar sounds beyond the cabin or above his head.

The dream was made more than bearable by the presence of Aurora. Even the terrible pain which struck suddenly and without mercy she somehow held at bay, just as she saw through his pitiful attempts to hide it from her.

She would hold his hand or wipe his brow with a damp cloth. Sometimes when the agony probed his skull like a branding iron she put her arm beneath his shoulders and pressed her face to his chest, murmuring secret words into his body as if to still the torment.

He watched her whenever she was in a position where he could see her. While his strength held he described the shipboard sounds, the names of the sailors he knew, and how they worked together to make the ship a living thing.

He told her of his home in Falmouth, of his brother and sisters and the long Bolitho ancestry which was part of the sea itself.

She was always careful not to excite him with questions, and allowed him to talk as long as he felt like it. She fed him, but in such a fashion that he did not feel humiliated or like a helpless child.

Only when the matter of shaving arose was she unable to keep a straight face.

'But, dear Richard, you do not seem to *need* a shave!'

Bolitho flushed, knowing it was true, as he usually shaved but once a week.

She said, 'I will do it for you.'

She used the razor with great care, watching each stroke, and occasionally glancing through the stern windows to see if the ship was on even keel.

Bolitho tried to relax, glad that she imagined his tenseness was out of fear of the razor. In fact, he was more than aware of her nearness, the pressure of her breast as she leaned over him, the exciting touch on his face and throat.

'There.' She stood back and studied him approvingly. 'You look very . . .' she hunted through her vocabulary '. . . distinguished.'

Bolitho asked, 'Could I see, please?' He saw the uncertainty. '*Please.*'

She took a mirror from the cabin chest and said, 'You are strong. You will get over it.'

Bolitho stared at the face in the mirror. It was that of a stranger. The surgeon had sheared away his hair from the right temple, and the whole of his forehead from eyebrow to where the hair remained was black and purple with savage bruising. Bulkley had appeared content when he had removed the dressing and bandages, but to Bolitho's eyes the length and depth of the scar, made more horrific by the black criss-cross of the surgeon's stitches, was repellent.

He said quietly, 'It must sicken you.'

She removed the mirror and said, 'I am proud of you. Nothing could spoil you in my heart. I have stayed with you from that first moment when you were carried here. Have watched over you, so that I know your body like my own.' She met his gaze proudly. 'That scar will remain, but it is one of honour, not of shame!'

Later she left his side in answer to a summons from Dumaresq.

The cabin servant, Macmillan, told Bolitho that *Destiny* was due to sight St Christopher's on the following day, so it seemed likely that the captain was about to clarify Egmont's statement and make certain he would stand by it.

The hunt for the missing bullion, or whatever form it had taken since Garrick's seizure of it, seemed of no importance to Bolitho. He had had plenty of time to think about his future as he sweated in pain or had found recovery in her arms. Perhaps too much time.

The idea of her stepping ashore, to rejoin her husband in whatever new enterprise he dictated, and not to see her ever again, was unbearable.

To mark the progress of his recovery he had several visitors. Rhodes, beaming with pleasure to see him again, unabashed as ever as he said, 'Makes you look like a real terror, Richard. That'll get the doxies jumping when we reach port!' He was careful not to mention Aurora.

Palliser came too and made as close as he knew how to an apology.

'If I had sent a marine picket as Colpoy suggested, none of it would have happened.' He shrugged and glanced round the cabin, at the female attire draped near the windows after being washed by the maid. 'But it apparently has its brighter aspects.'

Bulkley and Dumaresq's clerk supervised the first walk away from the cabin. Bolitho felt the ship responding beneath his bare feet, but knew his weakness, the dizziness which never seemed far away, no matter how hard he tried to conceal it.

He cursed Spillane and his medical knowledge when he said, 'Might be a severe fracture there, sir?'

Bulkley replied gruffly, 'Nonsense. But still, it's early days.'

Bolitho had expected to die, but with recovery apparently within his grasp it seemed unthinkable there was yet another course he might have to take. To be sent home in the next available ship, to be removed from the Navy List and not even retained on half-pay to give some hope of re-employment.

He wished he could have thanked Stockdale, but even his influence had so far failed to get him past the sentry at the door.

All the midshipmen, with the noticeable exception of Cowdroy, had been to visit him, and had stared at his terrible scar with a mixture of awe and commiseration. Jury had been quite unable to hide his admiration and had exclaimed, 'To think that I cried like a baby over my pin-prick!'

It was late evening before she returned to the cabin, and he sensed the change in her, the listless way she arranged his pillow and made certain his water-jug was filled.

She said quietly, 'I shall leave tomorrow, Richard. My husband has signed his name to the documents. It is done. Your captain has sworn that he will leave us to go as we please once he has seen the governor of St Christopher's. After that, I do not know.'

Bolitho gripped her hand and tried not to think of Dumaresq's other promise to the *Heloise*'s master before he had died. Had died from Bolitho's own blade.

He said, 'I may have to leave the ship, too.'

She seemed to forget her own troubles and leaned over him anxiously.

'What is this? Who said you must go?'

He reached up carefully and touched her hair. Like silk. Warm, beautiful silk.

'It doesn't matter now, Aurora.'

She traced a pattern on his shoulder with her finger.

'How can you say that? Of course it *matters*. The sea is your world. You have seen and done much, but all your life still lies before you.'

Bolitho felt her hair touch his skin and shivered.

He said firmly, 'I shall quit the Navy. I have made up my mind.'

'After all you have told me of your family tradition, you would throw it all away?'

'For you, yes, I will.'

She shook her head, the long black hair clinging to him as she protested, 'You must not speak like this!'

'My brother is my father's favourite, and always has been.' It was strange that in moment of crisis he could say it without bitterness or remorse, even knowing it was the truth. 'He can uphold the tradition. It is you I want, you I love.'

He said it so fiercely that she was obviously moved.

Bolitho saw her hand rest on her breast, a pulse beating in her throat which made her outward composure a lie.

'It is madness! I know all about you, but of me you know nothing. What sort of life would you have, watching me grow older while you yearn for the ships, for the chances you threw away?' She placed her hand on his forehead. 'It is like a fever, Richard. Fight it, or it will destroy both of us!'

Bolitho turned his face away, his eyes pricking as he said, 'I could make you happy, Aurora!'

She stroked his arm, soothing his despair. 'I never doubted it. But there is more to life than that, believe me.' She backed away, her body moving in time with the ship's gentle roll. 'I told you earlier. I could love you. For the past days and nights I have watched you, touched you. My thoughts were wicked, my longing greater than I would dare admit.' She shook her head. 'Please, do not look at me like that. Perhaps, after all, the voyage took too long, and tomorrow comes too late. I no longer know anything.'

She turned, her face in shadow as she was framed against the salt-stained windows.

'I shall never forget you, Richard, and I will probably damn myself for turning your offer aside. But I am asking for your help. I cannot do it alone.'

Macmillan brought the evening meal and said, 'Beg pardon, ma'am, but the cap'n an' 'is officers send their respects, an' will you dine with them tonight? It bein' the last time, so to speak.'

Macmillan was really too old for his work, and served his captain in the same fashion as a respected family retainer. He was totally unaware of the tension, the huskiness in her voice as she replied, 'I will be honoured.'

Nor did he see the despair on the lieutenant's face as he watched her walk into the screened-off part of the cabin where her maid spent most of the day.

She paused. 'The lieutenant is stronger now. He will manage.' She turned away, her words muffled. 'On his own.'

*

With Bulkley's supporting hand at his elbow, Bolitho ventured on to the quarterdeck and looked along the ship's length towards the land.

It was very hot, and the scorching noon sun made him realize just how weak he still was. Seeing the bare-backed seamen bustling about the upper deck, others straddled along the yards as they shortened sail for the final approach, he felt lost, out of things in a way he had not known before.

Bulkley said, 'I have been to St Christopher's previously.' He pointed towards the nearest headland with its writhing line of white surf. 'Bluff Point. Beyond it lies Basseterre and the main anchorage. There will be King's ships a'plenty, I've no doubt. Some forgotten flag-officer who'll be anxious to tell our captain what to do.'

Some marines marched past, panting loudly in the red coats and heavy equipment.

Bolitho gripped the nettings and watched the land. A small island, but an important link in Britain's chain of command. At another time he would have been excited at a first visit. But now as he stared at the nodding palms, the occasional glimpse of native boats, he could only see what it represented. Here they would part. Whatever his own fate might be, here it was ended between them. He knew from the way Rhodes and the others avoided the subject that they were probably thinking he should be thankful. To have lived through that murderous attack and then be nursed by so beautiful a woman should be enough for any man. But it was not.

Dumaresq came on deck and glanced briefly at the compass and at the set of the sails.

Gulliver touched his hat. 'Nor'-nor'-east, sir. Steady as she goes.'

'Good. Prepare a salute, Mr Palliser. We shall be up to Fort Londonderry within the hour.'

He saw Bolitho and held up his hand. 'Stay if you wish.' He crossed the deck to join him, his glance taking in Bolitho's eyes, dulled by pain, the horrible scar laid bare for all to see. He said, 'You will live. Be thankful.'

He beckoned the midshipman of the watch. 'Get aloft with you, Mr Lovelace, and spy out Fleet Anchorage. Count the ships, and report to me as soon as you are satisfied.' He watched the youth swarm up the ratlines and said, 'Like the rest of our young gentlemen, he has grown up on this voyage.' He glanced at Bolitho. 'That applies more to you than anyone.'

Bolitho said, 'I *feel* a hundred, sir.'

'I expect so.' Dumaresq grinned. 'When you get your own command you will remember the pitfalls, I *hope*, but I doubt if you will pity your young lieutenants any more than I do.'

The captain turned aft, and Bolitho saw his eyes light up with interest.

Without looking he knew she had come on deck to see the island. How would she see it? As a temporary refuge or a prison?

Egmont seemed unchanged by his ordeal. He walked to the side and remarked, 'This place has altered little.'

Dumaresq kept his voice matter of fact. 'Garrick will be here, you are certain.'

'As sure as anyone can be.' He saw Bolitho and nodded curtly. 'I see you are recovered, Lieutenant.'

Bolitho forced a smile. 'Thank you, sir, yes. I ache, but I am in one piece.'

She joined her husband and said steadily, 'We both thank you, Lieutenant. You saved our lives. We cannot repay that.'

Dumaresq watched each in turn, like a hunter. 'It is our purpose. But some duties are more rewarding than others.' He turned away. 'To see Garrick taken is all I ask, damn him. Too many have died because of his greed, too many widows are left by his ambitions.'

Palliser cupped his hands. 'Take in the forecourse.'

Dumaresq's calm was slipping as he snapped, 'God damn his eyes, Mr Palliser, what *is* Lovelace doing up there?'

Palliser peered up at the mainmast cross-trees where Midshipman Lovelace sat precariously balanced like a monkey on a stick.

Egmont forgot Bolitho and his wife as he picked upon the captain's changed mood.

'What is worrying you?'

Dumaresq clasped and unclasped his strong fingers across the tails of his coat.

'I am not worried, sir. Merely *interested*.'

Midshipman Lovelace came sliding down a backstay and landed on the deck with a thud. He swallowed hard, visibly shrinking under their combined stares.

Dumaresq asked mildly, 'Must we wait, Mr Lovelace? Or is it something so stupendous you cannot bear to call it from the masthead?'

Lovelace stammered, 'B-but, sir, you told me to c-count the vessels yonder?' He tried again. 'There is only one man-o'-war, sir, a large frigate.'

Dumaresq took a few paces back and forth to clear his thoughts. 'One, y'say?' He looked at Palliser. 'The squadron must have been called elsewhere. East to Antigua to reinforce the admiral perhaps.'

Palliser said, 'There may be a senior officer here, sir. In the frigate maybe.' He kept his face immobile. Dumaresq would not take kindly to being outranked by another captain.

Bolitho did not care. He moved closer to the quarterdeck rail and saw her put her hand on it.

Dumaresq shouted, 'Where is that damned quill-pusher? Send for Spillane at once!'

To Egmont he said, 'I must discuss a few trivial matters before we anchor. Please come with me.'

Bolitho stood beside her and briefly touched her hand with his. He felt her tense, as if she shared his pain, and said quietly, 'My love, I am in hell.'

She did not turn to look at him but said, 'You promised to help me. *Please*, I will shame us both if you continue.' Then she did look at him, her eyes steady but just too bright as she said, 'It is all wasted if you are to be unhappy and your life spoiled because of something we both value.'

Palliser yelled, 'Mr Vallance! Stand by to fire the salute!'

Men ran to their stations while the ship, indifferent to all of them, continued into the bay.

Bolitho took her arm and guided her to the companionway. 'There will be a lot of smoke and dust directly. You had best go below until we are closer inshore.' How was it possible to speak so calmly on unimportant matters? He added, 'I must talk with you again.'

But she had already gone down into the shadows.

Bolitho walked forward again and saw Stockdale watching from the starboard gangway. His gun was not required for the salute, but he was showing his usual interest.

Bolitho said, 'It seems I am at a loss when it comes to finding the right words, Stockdale. How can I thank you for what you did? If I offered you reward, I suspect you would be insulted. But words are nothing for what I feel.'

Stockdale smiled. 'You bein' 'ere for us all to see is enough. One day you'll be captain, sir, an' grateful I'll be. You'll be needin' a good cox'n then.' He nodded towards Johns, the captain's own coxswain, smart and aloof in his gilt-buttoned jacked and striped trousers. 'Like old Dick yonder. A man o' leisure!' It seemed to amuse him greatly, but the rest of his words were lost in the controlled crash of gun-fire.

Palliser waited for the fort by the anchorage to reply and then said, 'Mr Lovelace was right about the frigate.' He lowered the telescope and glanced grimly at Bolitho. 'But he failed to note that she is wearing Spanish colours. I doubt that the captain will be greatly amused!'

Bulkley said anxiously, 'I think you should rest. You have been on deck for hours. What are you trying to do, kill yourself?'

Bolitho watched the clustered buildings around the anchorage, the two forts, each well placed at either side like squat sentinels.

'I'm sorry. I was thinking only of myself.' He reached up and gingerly touched the scar. Perhaps it would be completely healed, or partially covered by his hair before he saw his mother again. What with her husband returning home with one arm, and now a disfigured son, she would have more than enough to face up to.

He said, 'You did so much for me, too.'

'*Too?*' The surgeon's eyes twinkled behind his glasses. 'I think I understand.'

'Mr Bolitho!' Palliser appeared through the companionway. 'Are you fit enough to go ashore?'

'I must protest!' Bulkley pushed forward. 'He is barely able to stand up!'

Palliser stood facing them, his hands on his hips. Ever since the anchor had been dropped and the boats put down alongside, he had been called from one crisis to another, but mostly down to the great cabin. Dumaresq was extremely angry, if the loudness of his voice was anything to go by, and Palliser was in no mood for argument.

'Let *him* decide, dammit!' He looked at Bolitho. 'I am short-handed, but for some reason the captain requires you to go ashore with him. Remember our first meeting? I need every officer and man *working* in my ship. No matter how you feel, you keep going. Until you drop, or are incapable of movement, you are still one of my lieutenants, is that plain?'

Bolitho nodded, somehow glad of Palliser's temper. 'I'm ready.'

'Good. Then get changed.' As an afterthought he said, 'You may *carry* your hat.'

Bulkley watched him stride away and exploded angrily, 'He is beyond understanding! By God, Richard, if you feel unsteady I will demand that you stay aboard! Young Stephen can take your place.'

Bolitho made to shake his head but winced as the pain stabbed back at him.

'I shall be all right. But thank you.' He walked to the companionway adding, 'I suspect there is some special reason for taking me with him.'

Bulkley nodded. 'You are getting to know our captain very well, Richard. He never acts without a purpose, never offers a guinea which will not profit him two!'

He sighed. 'But the thought of leaving his service is worse than tolerating his insults. Life would seem very dull after Dumaresq's command!'

It was almost evening by the time Dumaresq decided to go ashore. He had sent Colpoys with a letter of introduction to the governor's house, but when the marine returned he had told him that there was only the acting-governor in residence.

Dumaresq had commented sharply, 'Not another Rio, I trust?'

Now, in the captain's gig, with a hint of cooler air to make the journey bearable, Dumaresq sat as before, with both hands gripped around his sword, his eyes fixed on the land.

Bolitho sat beside him, his determination to withstand the pain and the recurring dizziness making him break out in a sweat. He concentrated on the anchored vessels, and the comings and goings of *Destiny*'s boats as they ferried the sick and wounded ashore and returned already loaded with stores for the purser.

Dumaresq said suddenly, 'A mite to starboard, Johns.'

The coxswain did not even blink but moved the tiller accordingly. From one corner of his mouth he muttered, 'You'll get a good look at 'er presently, sir.'

Dumaresq nudged Bolitho sharply with an elbow. 'He's a rascal, eh? Knows my mind better than I!'

Bolitho watched the anchored Spaniard as she towered above them. She was more like a cut-down fourth-rate than a frigate, he thought. Old, with elaborately carved and gilded gingerbread around her stern and cabin windows, but well-maintained, with an appearance of efficiency which was rare in a Spanish ship.

Dumaresq was thinking the same and murmured, 'The *San Augustin*. She's no local relic from La Guaira or Porto Bello. Cadiz or Algeciras is my guess.'

'Will that make a difference, sir?'

Dumaresq turned on him angrily, and just as swiftly let his temper subside.

'I am bad company. After what you have suffered under my command, I can spare you civility at least.' He watched the other vessel with professional interest, as Stockdale had studied the other gun crews. 'Forty-four guns at least.' He seemed to recall Bolitho's question. 'It might. Weeks and months ago there was a secret. The Dons suspected there was evidence available as to the *Asturias*'s lost treasure. Now it seems they have more than mere suspicions. *San Augustin* is here to mime *Destiny*'s role and to prevent His Most Catholic Majesty's displeasure if we do not share our confidences.' He gave a grim smile. 'We shall see about that. I have no doubt that a dozen telescopes are watching us, so look no more. Let them worry about us.'

Dumaresq noticed that the landing-place was only fifty yards away and said, 'I brought you with me so that the governor would see your scar. It is better proof than anything else that we are working for our masters in Admiralty. Nobody here need know you gained so distinguished a wound whilst seeking water for our thirsty people!'

A small group was waiting for the boat to manoeuvre to the landing-place, some red uniforms amongst them. It was always the same. News from England. Word from the country which had sent them this far, anything which might maintain their precious contact.

Bolitho asked, 'Will the Egmonts be allowed to go, sir?' He lifted his chin, surprised at his own impudence as Dumaresq's gaze fastened on him. 'I should like to know, sir.'

Dumaresq studied him gravely for several seconds. 'It is important to you, I can see that.' He untangled the sword from between his legs in readiness for climbing ashore. Then he said bluntly, 'She is a very desirable woman, I'll not argue.' He stood up and straightened his hat with elaborate care. 'You need not gape like that. I'm neither completely blind nor insensitive, you know. If I'm anything, it's most likely envious.' He clapped him on the shoulder. 'Now, let's deal with the acting-governor of this seat of empire, Sir Jason Fitzpatrick, and afterwards I may consider *your* problem!'

Grasping his hat in one hand, and supporting his sword in the other, Bolitho followed the captain out of the boat. Dumaresq's casual acceptance of his feelings for another man's wife had completely taken the wind from his sails. No wonder the surgeon could not face the prospect of a quieter and more predictable master.

A youthful captain from the garrison touched his hat and then exclaimed, 'My God, gentlemen, that is a bad wound!'

Dumaresq glanced at Bolitho's discomfort and might even have winked.

'The price of duty.' He gave a solemn sigh. 'It makes itself felt in many ways.'

13

Place of Safety

Sir Jason Fitzpatrick, the acting-governor of St Christopher's, looked like a man who lived life to excess. Aged about forty, he was extremely fat, and his face, which had seemingly defied the sun over the years, was brick-red.

As Bolitho followed Dumaresq across a beautifully tiled entrance hall and into a low-ceilinged room, he saw plenty of evidence of Fitzpatrick's occupation. There were trays of bottles set around, with neat ranks of finely cut glasses close to hand, presumably ready for the acting-governor to slake his thirst with the shortest possible delay.

Fitzpatrick said, 'Be seated, gentlemen. We will taste some of my claret. It should be suitable, although in this damnable climate, who can say?'

He had a throaty voice, and incredibly small eyes which were almost hidden in the folds of his face.

Bolitho noticed the tiny eyes more than anything. They moved all the time, as if quite independent of the heavy frame which supported them. Dumaresq had told him on the way from the water-front that Fitzpatrick was a rich plantation owner, with other properties on the neighbouring island of Nevis.

'Here, master.'

Bolitho turned and felt his stomach contract. A big Negro in red jacket and loose white trousers was holding a tray towards him. Bolitho did not see the tray or the glasses upon it. In his mind's eye he could picture that other black face, hear the terrible scream of triumph as he had hacked him down with a seaman's cutlass.

He took a glass and nodded his thanks while his breathing returned to normal.

Dumaresq was saying, 'By the authority entrusted in me, I am ordered to complete this investigation without further delay, Sir Jason. I have the written statements required, and would like you to furnish me with Garrick's whereabouts.'

Fitzpatrick played with the stem of his glass, his eyes flitting rapidly round the room.

'Ah, Captain, you are in a great hurry. You see, the governor is absent. He was stricken with fever some months back and returned to England aboard an Indiaman. He may be on his way back by now. Communications are very poor, we are hard put to get our mail on time with all these wretched pirates on the rampage. Honest craft sail in fear of their lives. It is a pity their lordships of Admiralty do not put their minds to *that*.'

Dumaresq was unmoved. 'I had hoped that a flag-officer would be here.'

'As I explained, Captain, the governor is away, otherwise . . .'

'Otherwise there'd be no damned Spaniard anchored here, I'm certain of that!'

Fitzpatrick forced a smile. 'We are not at war with Spain. The *San Augustin* comes in peace. She is commanded by *Capitán de Navio* Don Carlos Quintana. A most senior and personable captain, who is also entrusted with his country's authority.' He leaned back, obviously pleased with his advantage. 'After all, what evidence do you really have? The statement of a man who died before he could be brought to justice, the sworn testimony of a renegade who is so eager to save his own skin he will say anything.'

Dumaresq tried to hide the bitterness as he answered, 'My clerk was carrying further documents of proof when he was murdered in Madeira.'

'Indeed I am genuinely sorry about that, Captain. But to cast a slur against the name of so influential a gentleman as Sir Piers Garrick without evidence would be a criminal act in itself.' He smiled complacently. 'May I suggest we await instructions from London? You may send your despatches on the next home-bound vessel, which will probably be from Barbados. You could anchor there and be ready to act when so instructed. By then, the governor may have returned, and the squadron too, so that you will have senior naval authority to uphold your actions.'

Dumaresq snapped angrily, 'That could take months. By then, the bird will have flown.'

'Forgive my lack of enthusiasm. As I told Don Carlos, it all happened thirty years ago, so why this sudden interest?'

'Garrick was a felon first, a traitor second. You complain about the flocks of pirates who roam the Main and the Caribbean, who sack towns and plunder the ships of rich traders, but do you ever wonder where they find their own vessels? Like the *Heloise*, which was new from a British yard, sent out here with a passage crew, and for what?'

Bolitho listened entranced. He had expected Fitzpatrick to leap to his feet and summon the garrison commander. To plan with Dumaresq how they would seek and detain the elusive Garrick, and *then* wait for further orders.

Fitzpatrick spread his red hands apologetically. 'It is not within my province to take such action, Captain. I am in a temporary capacity, and would receive no thanks for putting a match to the powder-keg. You must of course do as you think fit. You say you had hoped for a flag-officer to be here? No doubt to take the responsibility and decision from *your* shoulders?' When Dumaresq remained silent he continued calmly, 'So do not pour scorn on me for not wishing to act unsupported.'

Bolitho was astounded. The Admiralty in London, some senior officers of the fleet, even the government of King George had been involved in getting the *Destiny* here. Dumaresq had worked without respite from the moment he had been told of his assignment, and must have spent many long hours in the privacy of his cabin pondering on his own interpretation of his scanty collection of clues.

And now, because there was no naval authority to back his most important decision, he would either have to kick his heels and wait for orders to arrive from elsewhere, or take it upon himself. At the age of twenty-eight, Dumaresq *was* the senior naval officer in St Christopher's, and Bolitho found it impossible to see how he could proceed with a course of action which might easily destroy him.

Dumaresq said wearily, 'Tell me what you know of Garrick.'

'Virtually nothing. It is true he has shipping interests, and has taken delivery of several small vessels over the months. He is a very rich man, and I understand he intends to continue trading with the French in Martinique, with a view to extending commerce elsewhere.'

Dumaresq stood up. 'I must return to my ship.' He did not look at Bolitho. 'I would take it kindly if you would accommodate my third lieutenant who has been wounded, and all to no good purpose, it now appears.'

Fitzpatrick lifted his bulk unsteadily. 'I'd be happy to do that.' He tried to hide his relief. Dumaresq was obviously going to take the easier course.

Dumaresq silenced Bolitho's unspoken protest. 'I'll send some *servants* to care for your wants.' He nodded to the acting-governor. 'I shall return when I have spoken with the *San Augustin*'s captain.'

Outside the building, his features hidden in the gloom, Dumaresq gave vent to his true feelings. 'That bloody hound! He's in it up to his neck! Thinks I'll stay anchored and be a good little boy, does he? God damn his poxy face, I'll see him in hell first!'

'*Must* I stay here, sir?'

'For the present. I'll detail some stout hands to join you. I don't trust that Fitzpatrick. He's a local landowner, and probably as thick as thieves with every smuggler and slaver in the Caribbean. Play the innocent with me, would he? By God, I'll wager he knows how many new vessels have fetched up here to await Garrick's orders.'

Bolitho asked, 'Is he still a pirate, sir?'

Dumaresq grinned in the darkness. 'Worse. I believe he is directly involved with supplying arms and well-found vessels for use against us in the north.'

'America, sir?'

'Eventually, and further still if those damned renegades have their way. Do you think the French will rest until they have rekindled the fires? We kicked them out of Canada and their Caribbean possessions. Did you imagine they'd put forgiveness at the top of their list?'

Bolitho had often heard talk of the unrest in the American colony which had followed the Seven Years War. There had been several serious incidents, but the prospect of open rebellion had been regarded by even the most influential newspaper as bluster.

'All these years Garrick has been working and scheming, using his stolen booty to best advantage. He sees himself as a leader if a rebellion comes, and those in power who believe otherwise are deluding themselves. I have had plenty of time to mull over Garrick's affairs, and the cruel unfairness which made him rich and powerful and left my father an impoverished cripple.'

Bolitho watched the gig approaching through the darkness, the oars very white against the water. So Dumaresq had already decided. He should have guessed, after what he had seen and learned of the man.

Dumaresq said suddenly, 'Egmont and his wife will also be landing shortly. They are outwardly under Fitzpatrick's care, but post a guard for your own satisfaction. I want Fitzpatrick to know he is directly implicated should there be any attempt at treachery.'

'You think Egmont is still in danger, sir?'

Dumaresq waved his hand towards the small residency. 'Here is a place of safety. I'll not have Egmont on the run again with some mad scheme of his own. There are too many who might want him dead. After I have dealt with Garrick, he can do as he damn well pleases. The quicker the better.'

'I see, sir.'

Dumaresq signalled to his coxswain and then chuckled. 'I doubt that. But keep your ears open, as I believe things will begin to move very shortly.'

Bolitho watched him climb into the gig and then retraced his steps to the residency.

Did Dumaresq care what happened to Egmont and his wife? Or, like the hunter he was, did he merely see them as bait for his trap?

There were two or three small dwellings set well apart from the residency, and which were normally used for visiting officials or militia officers and their families.

Bolitho assumed that these visitors were rare, and when they came were prepared to supply their own comforts. The building allotted to him was little more than the size of a room. The frames around the shutters were pitted with holes, made by a tireless army of insects, he thought. Palms tapped against the roof and walls, and he guessed that in any heavy rainstorm the whole place would leak like a sieve.

He sat gingerly on a large, hand-carved bed and trimmed a lantern. More insects buzzed and threw themselves at the hot glass, and he pitied the less fortunate people on the island if the governor himself could be struck down by fever.

Planks creaked outside the loosely fitting door and Stockdale peered in at him. With six other men, he had come ashore, to keep a weather-eye on things, as he put it.

He wheezed, 'All posted, sir. We'll work watch an' watch. Josh Little will take the first one.' He leaned against the door and Bolitho heard it groan in protest. 'I've put two 'ands near the other place. It's quiet enough.'

Bolitho thought of the way she had looked at him as she and her husband had been hurried into the next dwelling by some of the governor's servants. She had appeared worried, distressed by the sudden change of events. Egmont was said to have friends in Basseterre, but instead of being released to go to them, he was still a guest. A prisoner, more likely.

Bolitho said, 'Get some sleep.' He touched the scar and grimaced. 'I feel as if it happened today.'

Stockdale grinned. 'Neat bit o' work, sir. Lucky we've a good sawbones!'

He strolled out of the door, and Bolitho heard him whistling softly as he found his own place to stretch out. Sailors could sleep anywhere.

Bolitho lay back, his hands behind his head, as he stared up at the shadows above the lantern's small glow.

It was all a waste. Garrick had gone from the island, or that was what he had heard. He must be better informed than Dumaresq had believed. He would be laughing now, thinking of the frigate and her unwanted Spanish consort lying baffled at anchor while he . . .

Bolitho sat up with a jerk, reaching out for his pistol, as the planks outside the door squeaked again.

He watched the handle drop, and could feel his heart pounding against his ribs as he measured the distance across the room and wondered if he could get to his feet in time to defend himself.

The door opened a few inches and he saw her small hand around its edge.

He was off the bed in seconds, and as he opened the door he heard her gasp, 'Please! Watch the light!'

For a long, confused moment they clung together, the door tightly shut behind them. There was no sound but their breathing and Bolitho was almost afraid to speak for fear of smashing this unbelievable dream.

She said quietly, 'I had to come. It was bad enough on the ship. But to know you were in here, while . . .' She looked up at him, her eyes shining. 'Do not despise me for my weakness.'

Bolitho held her tightly, feeling her soft body through the long pale gown, knowing they were already lost. If the world fell apart around them, nothing could spoil this moment.

How she had got past his sentries he could not understand, nor did he care. Then he thought of Stockdale. He should have guessed.

His hands were shaking badly as he held her shoulders and kissed her hair, her face and her throat.

She whispered, 'I will help you.' She stood back from him and allowed the gown to fall to the floor. 'Now hold me again.'

In the darkness, somewhere between the two small buildings, Stockdale propped his cutlass against a tree and sat down on the ground. He watched the moonlight as it touched the door he had seen open and close just an hour ago and thought about the two of them together. It was probably the lieutenant's first time, he thought comfortably. He could have no better teacher, that was certain.

Long before dawn the girl named Aurora slipped quietly from the bed and pulled on her gown. For a while more she looked at the pale figure, now sleeping deeply, while she touched her breast as he had done. Then she stooped and kissed him lightly on the mouth. His lips tasted of salt, perhaps from her own tears. Without another glance she left the room and ran past Stockdale, seeing nothing.

Bolitho walked slowly from the doorway and stepped down on to the sun-hardened ground as if he was walking on thin glass. Although he had donned his uniform he still felt naked, could imagine their embrace, the breathtaking demands of their passion which had left him spent.

He stared at the early sunlight, at one of his guards who was watching him curiously as he leaned on a musket.

If only he had been awake when she had left him. Then they would never have parted.

Stockdale strolled to meet him. 'Nothin' to report, sir.'

He eyed Bolitho's uncertainty with quiet satisfaction. The lieutenant was different. Lost, but alive. Confused too, but in time he would feel the strength she had given him.

Bolitho nodded. 'Muster the hands.'

He went to raise his hat to his head and remembered the scar which throbbed and burned at the slightest touch. She had even made him forget about that.

Stockdale stooped down and picked up a small piece of paper which had dropped from inside the hat. He handed it over, his face expressionless.

'Can't read meself, sir.'

Bolitho opened the paper, his eyes misty as he read her few brief words.

Dearest, I could not wait. Think of me sometimes and how it was.

Beneath it she had written, *The place your captain wants is Fougeaux Island.*

She had not signed her name, but he could almost hear her speaking aloud.

'You feelin' weak, sir?'

'No.'

He re-read the small message once again. She must have carried it with her, knowing she was going to give herself to him. Knowing too that it was ending there.

Feet grated on sand and he saw Palliser striding along the path, Midshipman Merrett trotting in his wake and hard put to keep up with the lanky lieutenant.

He saw Bolitho and snapped, 'All done.' He waited, his eyes wary.

Bolitho asked, 'Egmont and his wife, sir. What's happened?'

'Oh, didn't you know? They've just boarded a vessel in the bay. We sent their luggage across during the night. I'd have thought you would be better informed.'

Bolitho hesitated. Then very carefully he folded the paper and removed the lower half, with the island's name written on it.

Palliser examined it and said, 'It'll be the one.'

He refolded the paper and handed it to Merrett. 'Back to the ship, my lad, and present this with my respects to the captain. Lose it, and I promise you a hideous death!' The youth fled down the path and Palliser said, 'The captain was right after all.' He smiled at Bolitho's grave features. 'Come, I'll walk back with you.'

'You say they've already boarded a vessel, sir?' He could not accept it. 'Where bound?'

'I forget. Is it important?'

Bolitho fell in step beside him. She had provided the information as repayment, perhaps for saving her life, or for sharing his love with her. Dumaresq had used both of them. He felt his face sting with anger. A place of safety, he had called it. More likely one of deceit.

When he reached the ship he found the hands turned-to, the sails loosely brailed and ready to set at short notice.

As instructed, Bolitho presented himself in the cabin where Dumaresq and Gulliver were studying some charts with elaborate care.

Dumaresq told the master to wait outside and then said bluntly, 'In order to avoid my having to punish you for insubordination, let me speak first. Our mission in these waters is an important one for so small a vessel. I have always believed it, and now with that final piece of intelligence I know where Garrick has made his headquarters, his storehouse for arms, unlawful supplies and vessels to disperse them. It *is* important.'

Bolitho met his gaze. 'I *should* have been told, sir.'

'You enjoyed it, did you not?' His voice softened. 'I know what it's like to be in love with a dream, and that is all it could have been. You are a King's officer, and may amount to being a fair one, given time and a bit of common sense.'

Bolitho looked past him towards the windows, at the moored vessels there, and wondered which, if any of them, was Aurora's

He asked, 'Is that all, sir?'

'Yes. Take charge of your division. I intend to weigh as soon as my quill-pusher has made copies of my despatches for the authorities and for London.' He was lost in his thoughts, the hundred and one things he must do.

Bolitho blundered from the cabin and into the wardroom. It was impossible to picture the cabin as it had been. Her clothes hung neatly to dry, the young maidservant always near in case she was needed. Perhaps Dumaresq's way was the best, but need it be so brutal and without feeling?

Rhodes and Colpoys rose to greet him, and they solemnly shook hands.

Bolitho touched the piece of paper in his pocket and felt stronger. Whatever Dumaresq and the others thought, they could never be certain, or really know how it was.

Bulkley entered the wardroom, saw Bolitho and was about to ask him how his wound was progressing, but Rhodes gave a slight shake of his head and the surgeon called Poad for some coffee instead.

Bolitho would get over it. But it would take time.

'Anchor's aweigh, sir!'

Dumaresq walked to the rail and stared across at the Spaniard, as with her sails booming in a lively breeze *Destiny* tacked round towards the open sea.

He said, 'That will rile the Don. He's half of his people ashore gathering supplies and will not be able to follow us for hours!' He threw back his head and laughed. 'Damn you, Garrick! Make the most of your freedom!'

Bolitho watched his men setting the main-topgallant sail, calling to each other as if they were infected by Dumaresq's excitement. Death, prize-money, a different landfall, it was all meat to them.

Palliser shouted from the quarterdeck, 'Chase up those hands, Mr Bolitho, they have lead in their limbs today!'

Bolitho turned aft, his mouth framing an angry retort. Then he shrugged. Palliser was trying to help him in the only way he knew.

Skirting the treacherous shallows off Bluff Point, *Destiny* spread more sails and headed away towards the west. Later, when Bolitho took over the afternoon-watch, he examined the chart and Gulliver's carefully written calculations.

Fougeaux Island was very small, one of a scattered group some 150 miles west-north-west of St Christopher's. It had been claimed by France, Spain and England in turn, even the Dutch had been interested for a time.

Now it owed allegiance to no country, for to all intents it had no real use. It lacked timber for firewood or repairs, and according to the navigational notes it had less than its share of water. A bare, hostile place with a lagoon shaped like a reaping-hook as its one asset. It could provide shelter from storms, if little else. But as Dumaresq had observed, what else did Garrick require?

Bolitho watched the captain as he prowled restlessly about the deck, as if he could not bear the restraint of his quarters now that his goal was so close. Adverse winds were making progress hard and frustrating, with the ship tacking back and forth for several miles to gain a few cables advance.

But the mention of lost bullion, and the prospect of some share in it, seemed to make up for the back-breaking work of trimming the yards and resetting the sails again and again.

Suppose the island proved to be empty or the wrong one? Bolitho guessed it to be unlikely. Aurora must have known that Garrick's capture was the only way of preventing him from taking his revenge on her husband and herself. Also that Dumaresq had no intention of freeing them without solid information.

The next day found *Destiny* drifting becalmed, her sails hanging flat and devoid of movement.

Far away to starboard was the vague shape of another islet, but otherwise they had the sea to themselves. It was so hot that feet stuck to the deck seams, and the gun barrels felt as if they had been firing in battle.

Gulliver said, 'If we had taken a more northerly passage we'd have been in better luck for a wind, sir.'

'I know that, damn you.' Dumaresq turned on him hotly. 'And risk losing my keel as well, is that what you want? This is a frigate, not some damned fishing boat!'

All that day, and for half of the next, the ship rolled uneasily in the swell. A shark moved cautiously beneath her counter, and several of the hands tried their luck with hooks and lines.

Dumaresq never seemed to leave the deck, and as he passed Bolitho during his watch he saw that his shirt was black with sweat, and there was a livid blister on his forehead which he did not seem to notice.

Halfway through the afternoon-watch the wind felt its way slowly across the glittering water, but with it came a surprise.

'Ship, sir! Fine on the larboard quarter!'

Dumaresq and Palliser watched the tan-coloured pyramid grow above the horizon, the great scarlet cross clearly etched on her forecourse to dispel any doubt.

Palliser exclaimed bitterly, 'The Don, blast his soul!'

Dumaresq lowered the glass, his eyes like stones. 'Fitzpatrick. He must have told them. Now they're hot for blood.' He looked past his officer. 'If Don Carlos Quintana interferes now, it will be his own blood!'

'Man the braces there!'

Destiny shivered and tilted steadily to a freshening breeze, her renewed strength tossing spray up and around her white figurehead.

Dumaresq said, 'Put the people to gun-drill, Mr Palliser.' He stared astern at the other vessel. She already seemed to be drawing much closer.

'And run up the colours, if you please. I'll have no damned Spaniard crossing my bows!'

Rhodes dropped his voice. 'He means it too, Richard. This is his moment. He'd die rather than share it!'

Some of the men near the quarterdeck glanced at each other and murmured apprehensively. Their natural contempt for any navy but their own had been somewhat blunted by the brief stay at Basseterre. The *San Augustin* carried at least forty-four guns against their own twenty-eight.

Dumaresq shouted, 'And get those dolts to work, Mr Palliser! This ship is getting like a sty!'

One of Bolitho's gun-captains muttered, 'I thought we was only after a pirate.'

Stockdale showed his teeth. 'An enemy's an enemy, Tom. When did a flag make any difference?'

Bolitho bit his lip. This was the true responsibility of command at close quarters. If Dumaresq did nothing he could be court-martialled for incompetence or cowardice. If he crossed swords with a Spanish ship he might be blamed for provoking a war.

He said, 'Stand to, lads. Cast off the breechings!'

Maybe Stockdale was right. All you had to worry about was winning.

*

The following day the hands were sent to breakfast and then the decks swabbed down before the sun had crept fully over the horizon.

The breeze, though light, was steady enough, and had shifted during the night watches to south-westerly.

Dumaresq was on deck as early as anyone, and Bolitho saw the impatience in his thick-set figure as he strode about the deck glancing at the compass or consulting the master's slate by the wheel. He probably saw none of these things, and Bolitho could tell from the way that Palliser and Gulliver gave him a wide berth that they knew the measure of his moods of old.

With Rhodes, Bolitho watched the boatswain detailing his working parties as usual. The fact that a larger man-of-war than their own was trailing astern, and that the little known Fougeaux Island lay somewhere beyond the lee bow made no difference to Mr Timbrell's routine.

Palliser's brusque tones made Bolitho start. 'Rig top-chains before all else, Mr Timbrell.'

Some of the seamen looked up at the yards. Palliser did not explain further, nor did he need to for the older hands. The chains would be rigged to sling each yard, as the cordage which normally held them might be shot away in any sort of battle. Then the nets would be spread across the upper deck. The slings and the nets were the only protection to the men below from falling spars and riggings.

Perhaps it was the same aboard the Spaniard, Bolitho thought. Although he had seen little evidence so far. In fact, now that she had caught up, the *San Augustin* seemed content to follow and watch events.

Rhodes turned abruptly and headed for his own part of the ship, hissing quickly, 'Lord and master!'

Bolitho swung round and came face to face with the captain. It was unusual to see him away from the quarterdeck or poop, and the seamen working around him seemed to press back as if they too were awed by his presence.

Bolitho touched his hat and waited.

Dumaresq's eyes examined his face slowly, without expression.

Then he said, 'Come with me. Bring a glass.' Tossing his hat to his coxswain, he added. 'A climb will clear the head.'

Bolitho stared as Dumaresq began to haul himself out and on to the shrouds, his broad figure hanging awkwardly as he peered up at the spiralling masthead.

Bolitho hated heights. Of all the things which had encouraged him to work for advancement to lieutenant, he thought it was probably that. No longer needed to swarm aloft with the hands, no ice-cold terror as the wind tried to cut away your grip on frozen ratlines, or throw you out and into the sea far below.

Perhaps Dumaresq was goading him, provoking him, if only to relieve his own tension.

'Come along, Mr Bolitho! You are in stays today!'

Bolitho followed him up the vibrating shrouds, foot by foot, hand over hand. He told himself not to look down even though he could picture *Destiny*'s pale deck tilting away beneath him as the ship drove her shoulder into a steep roller.

Disdaining the lubber's hole, Dumaresq clawed his way out on the futtock shrouds so that his mis-shapen body was hanging almost parallel to the sea below. Then up past the main-top, ignoring some startled marines who were exercising with a swivel gun, and towards the topgallant yard.

Dumaresq's confidence gave Bolitho the will to climb faster than he could recall. What did Dumaresq know about love, or whether he and Aurora could have overcome all the obstacles together?

He barely noticed the height and was already peering up towards the main-royal yard when Dumaresq paused, one foot dangling in space as he observed, 'You can get the *feel* of her from here.'

Bolitho clung on with both hands and stared up at him, his eyes watering in the fierce sunlight. Dumaresq spoke with such conviction, and yet with a warmth which was almost akin to love itself.

'Feel her?' Dumaresq seized a stay and tugged it with his fist. 'Taut and firm, equal strain on all parts. As she should be. As any good vessel ought to be, properly cared for!' He looked at Bolitho's upturned face. 'Head all right?'

Bolitho nodded. In his mixture of resentment and anger he had forgotten about his wound.

'Good. Come on then.'

They reached the cross-trees where a lookout slithered down to make room for his betters.

'Ah.' Dumaresq unslung a telescope, and after wiping the lens with his neckcloth trained it across the starboard bow.

Bolitho followed his example, and then felt a touch of ice at his spine, despite the sun and the wind which hissed through the rigging like sand.

It was like nothing he had ever seen. The island seemed to be made entirely of coral or rock, obscenely stripped bare like something which was no longer alive. In the centre was a ridge, rather like a hill with the top sliced off. But misty in distance, it could have been a giant fortress, and the low island there merely to support it.

He tried to compare it with the sparse details on the chart, and guessed from the bearing that the sheltered lagoon was directly beneath the hill.

Dumaresq said hoarsely, 'They're there right enough!'

Bolitho tried again. The place appeared deserted, stamped in time by some terrible natural disaster.

Then he saw something darker than the rest before it was lost in the heat-haze. A mast, or several masts, while the vessels lay hidden by the protective wall of coral.

He looked quickly at Dumaresq and wondered how differently he saw it.

'Little pieces of a puzzle.' Dumaresq did not raise his voice above the murmur of rigging and canvas. 'There are Garrick's ships, his little armada. No line of battle, Mr Bolitho, no flagship with the admiral's proud flag to inspire you, but just as deadly.'

Bolitho took another look through his glass. No wonder Garrick had felt so safe. He had known of their arrival at Rio, and even before that at Madeira. And now Garrick had the upper hand. He could either send his vessels out at night or he could stay put like a hermit-crab in a shell.

Again Dumaresq seemed to be speaking to himself. 'All the Don cares about is the lost bullion. Garrick can go free as far as he is concerned. Quintana believes that he will excise those carefully selected vessels and what booty remains without firing a shot.'

Bolitho asked, 'Perhaps Garrick knows less than we think, sir, and may try to bluff it out?'

Dumaresq looked at him strangely. 'I am afraid not. No more bluff now. I tried to explain Garrick's mind to the Spaniard at Basseterre. But he would not listen. Garrick helped the French and in any future war Spain will need an ally like France. Be certain that Don Carlos Quintana is mindful of that, too.'

'Cap'n, sir!' The lookout beneath sounded anxious. 'The Don's makin' more sail!'

Dumaresq said, 'Time to go.' He looked at each mast in turn and then at the deck below.

Bolitho found he could do the same without flinching. The fore-shortened blue and white figures of the officers and midshipmen on the quarterdeck, the changing patterns of men as they moved around the double line of black cannon.

For those few moments Bolitho shared an understanding with this devious, determined man. She was his ship, every moving part of her, every timber and inch of cordage.

Then Dumaresq said, 'The Spaniard may attempt to enter the lagoon before me. It is dangerous folly because the entrance is narrow, the channel unknown. Without hope of surprise he will be depending on his peaceful intentions, with a show of force if that fails.'

He climbed with surprising swiftness down to the deck, and when Bolitho reached the quarterdeck Dumaresq was already speaking with Palliser and the master.

Bolitho heard Palliser say, 'The Don is standing inshore, sir.'

Dumaresq was busy with his telescope again. 'Then he stands into danger. Signal him to sheer off.'

Bolitho saw the other faces nearby, ones he had come to know so well. In a few moments it might all be decided, and it was Dumaresq's choice.

Palliser shouted, 'He ignores us, sir!'

'Very well. Beat to quarters and clear for action.' Dumaresq clasped his hands behind him. 'We'll see how he likes *that*.'

Rhodes gripped Bolitho's arm. 'He must be mad. He can't fight Garrick and the Dons.'

The marine drummer boys began their staccato beat, and the moment of doubt was past.

14

Last Chance

'The Don is shortening sail, sir.'

'We shall do likewise.' Dumaresq stood in the centre of the quarterdeck just forward of the mizzen, like a rock. 'Take in the t'gan'sls.'

Bolitho shielded his eyes as he peered up through the tracery of rigging and nets as his own men began to fist and fight the rebellious canvas. In less than an hour the tension had risen like the sun, and now, with *San Augustin* firmly placed on the starboard bow, he could feel it affecting every man who was near him. *Destiny* had the wind-gage, but by overhauling the Spanish captain had placed himself between her and the approaches to the lagoon.

Rhodes strolled aft and joined him between two of the twelve-pounders.

'He's letting the Don get away with it.' He grimaced. 'I must say I approve. I don't fancy a one-sided fight unless the odds are in *my* favour.' He glanced quickly at the quarterdeck and then lowered his voice. 'What do you make of the lord and master *now*?'

Bolitho shrugged. 'I am bounced between contempt and admiration. I despise the way he used me. He must have known Egmont would not betray Garrick's island on his own.'

Rhodes pursed his lips. 'So it *was* his wife.' He hesitated. 'Are you over it, Dick?'

Bolitho looked across at the *San Augustin*, her streaming pennants and the white ensign of Spain.

Rhodes persisted. 'In all this, with the prospect of being blown to gruel because of some stupid event of long ago, you can still fret for the love of a woman?'

Bolitho faced him. 'I'll not get over it. If only you could have seen her . . .'

Rhodes smiled sadly. 'My God, Dick, I'm wasting my time. When we return to England I'll have to see what I can do to roust you out of it.'

They both turned as a shot reverberated across the water. Then there was a splash as the ball threw up a spindly waterspout in direct line with the Spaniard's bowsprit.

Dumaresq snapped, 'God in heaven, the buggers have fired first!'

Several telescopes were trained on the island, but nobody was able to sight the hidden cannon.

Palliser said dourly, 'That was a warning. I hope the Don has the sense to heed it. This calls for stealth and agility, not a head-on charge!'

Dumaresq smiled. 'Does it indeed? You begin to sound like an admiral, Mr Palliser. I shall have to watch myself!'

Bolitho studied the Spanish ship closely. It was as if nothing had happened. She was still steering for the nearest finger of land where the lagoon began.

A few cormorants arose from the sea when the two ships sailed past, like heraldic birds as they circled watchfully overhead, Bolitho thought.

'Deck there! Smoke above th' hill, sir!'

The telescopes trained round like small artillery.

Bolitho heard Clow, one of the gunner's mates, remark, 'That be from a bloody furnace. Them devils is heatin' shot to feed the Dons.'

Bolitho licked his lips. His father had told him often enough about the folly of setting a ship against a sited shore battery. If they used heated shot it would turn any vessel into a pyre unless it was dealt with immediately. Sun-dried timbers, tar, paint and canvas would burn fiercely, while the wind would do the rest.

Something like a sigh transmitted itself along the deck as the *San Augustin*'s ports lifted in unison, and then at the blast of a trumpet she ran out her guns. In the far distance they looked like black teeth along her tumblehome. Black and deadly.

The surgeon joined Bolitho by the twelve-pounders, his spectacles glinting in the sun. Out of deference for the men who might soon need his services he had refrained from wearing his apron.

'I am as nervous as a cat when this is dragging on.'

Bolitho understood. Down on the orlop deck below the waterline, in a place of spiralling lanterns and entrapped smells, all the sounds were distorted.

He said, 'I think the Spaniard intends to force the entrance.'

As he spoke the other ship reset her topgallants and tacked very slightly to take advantage of the south-westerly wind. How fine her gingerbread looked in the sun's glare, how majestic were the proud pennants and the scarlet crosses on her courses. She was like something from an old engraving, Bolitho thought.

She made the lean and graceful *Destiny* appear spartan by comparison.

Bolitho walked aft until he stood directly below the quarterdeck rail. He heard Dumaresq say, 'Another half-cable, and then we'll see.'

Then Palliser's voice, less certain. 'He might just force the entrance, sir. Once inside he could wear ship and rake the anchored vessels, even use them to protect himself from the shore. Without craft, Garrick is a prisoner.'

Dumaresq considered it. 'That part is true. I have only heard of one man who successfully walked on water, but we need another sort of miracle today.'

Some of the nine-pounder crews nearby rocked back on their knees, grinning and prodding each other over the captain's humour.

Bolitho marvelled that it could be so easy for Dumaresq. He knew exactly what his men needed to keep them alert and keen. And that was what he gave them, neither more nor a fraction less.

Gulliver said to nobody in particular, 'If the Don succeeds, that's a farewell to our prize-money.'

Dumaresq looked at him, his teeth bared in a fierce grin. 'God, you are a miserable fellow, Mr Gulliver. How you can find your way about the ocean under such a weight of despair I cannot fathom!'

Midshipman Henderson called, 'The Spaniard has passed the point, sir!'

Dumaresq grunted, 'You have good eyes.' To Palliser he added, 'He is on a lee shore. It will be now or not at all.'

Bolitho found that he was gripping his hands together so tightly that the pain helped to calm him. He saw the reflected flashes from the *San Augustin*'s hidden gunpoints, the great gouts of smoke, and then seconds later came the rumbling crash of her broadside.

Puffs of smoke and dust rose like plumes along the hill-side, and several impressive avalanches of rocks tumbled down towards the water.

Palliser said savagely, 'We shall have to come about shortly, sir.'

Bolitho looked up at him. After *Destiny*, Palliser had been hoping for a command. He had made little secret of the fact. But with hundreds of sea officers on the beach and on half-pay, he needed more than an empty commission to carry him through. The *Heloise* could have been a stepping-stone for him. But promotion boards had short memories. *Heloise* lay on the bottom and not in the hands of a prize court.

If Don Carlos Quintana succeeded in vanquishing Garrick's defences, all the glory would go to him. The Admiralty would see too many red faces for Palliser to be remembered as anything but an embarrassment.

There was a solitary bang, and another waterspout shot skywards, well clear of the Spaniard's hull.

Palliser said, 'Garrick's strength was a bluff after all. Damn him, the Dons must be laughing their heads off at us. We found their treasure for them and now we're made to watch them take it!'

Bolitho saw the Spaniard's yards swinging slowly and ponderously, her main-course being brailed up as she edged past another spine of coral. To the anchored vessels in the lagoon she would make a fiercesome spectacle when she presented herself.

He heard someone murmur, 'They'm puttin' down boats.'

Bolitho saw two boats being swayed out from the *San Augustin*'s upper deck and then lowered alongside. It was not smartly done, and as the men tumbled into them and cast off, Bolitho guessed that their captain had no intention of heaving to on a lee shore, with the added threat of a heavy cannon nearby.

Instead of making for the spur of coral or for the island's main foreshore, the boats forged ahead of their massive consort and were soon lost from view.

But not from the masthead lookout, who soon reported that the boats were sounding the channel with lead and line to protect their ship from running aground.

Bolitho found he could ignore Palliser's bitter outbursts, just as he could admire the Spaniard's skill and impudence. Don Carlos had likely fought the British in the past, and this chance of humiliating them was not to be missed.

But when he glanced aft he saw that Dumaresq appeared unworried, and was watching the other vessel more as a disinterested spectator.

He was waiting. The thought struck Bolitho like a fist. Dumaresq had been pretending all along. Goading the Spaniard rather than the other way round.

Bulkley saw his expression and said thickly, 'Now I think I understand.'

The Spaniard fired again to starboard, the smoke gushing downwind in an unbroken bank. More fragments and dust spewed away from the fall of shot, but no terrified figures broke from cover, nor did any gun fire back at the brightly flagged vessel.

Dumaresq snapped, 'Let her fall off two points to starboard.'

'*Man the lee braces!*'

The yards squeaked to the weight of men at the braces, and leaning very slightly *Destiny* pointed her jib-boom towards the flat-topped hill.

Bolitho waited for his own men to return to their stations. He must be mistaken after all. Dumaresq was probably changing tack in readiness to come about and make a circular turn until they were back on their original approach.

At that moment he heard a double explosion, like a rock smashing through the side of a building. As he ran to the side and peered across the water he saw something leap in the air ahead of the Spanish ship and then drop from view just as quickly.

The masthead yelled, 'One o' th' boats, sir! Shot clean in 'alf!'

Before the men on deck could recover from their surprise the whole
hill-top erupted with a line of bright flashes. There must have been seven
or eight of them.

Bolitho saw the water leap and boil around the Spaniard's counter
and a jagged hole appear in a braced topsail.

Without a telescope it looked dangerous enough, but he heard
Palliser shout, 'That sail's smouldering! Heated shot!'

The other balls had fallen on the ship's hidden side, and Bolitho saw
the flash of sunlight on a glass as one of her officers ran to peer at the
hill-top battery.

Then, as the *San Augustin* fired again, the carefully sited battery
replied. Against the Spaniard's heavy broadside, the returned fire was
made at will, each shot individually laid and aimed.

Smoke spurted from the ship's upper deck, and Bolitho saw objects
being flung outboard and more smoke from her poop as flames took
hold.

Dumaresq was saying, 'Waited until she had passed the point of
reason, Mr Palliser. Garrick is not such a fool that he wants his channel
blocked by a sunken ship!' He thrust out his arm, pointing at the smoke
as the vessel's foretopgallant mast and yard plunged down into the
water. 'Look well. That is where *Destiny* would have been if I had
yielded to temptation!'

The Spaniard's firing was becoming haphazard and wild, and the
shots were smashing harmlessly into solid rock or ricocheting across the
water like flying fish.

From *Destiny*'s decks it appeared as if the *San Augustin* was
embedded in coral as she drove slowly into the lagoon, the hull trailing
smoke, her canvas already pitted with holes.

Palliser said, 'Why doesn't he come about?'

All his anger for the Spaniards had gone. Instead he was barely able to
hide his anxiety for the stricken ship. She had looked so proud and
majestic. Now, marked down by the relentless bombardment, she was
heading into helpless submission.

Bolitho turned as he heard the surgeon murmur, 'A sight I'll not
forget. Ever.' He removed his glasses and polished them fiercely. 'Like
something I was once made to learn.

> Far away where sky met sea
> A majestic figure grew
> Pushed along by royal decree
> Her aggressive pennants flew.'

He smiled sadly. 'Now it sounds like an epitaph.'

A rumbling explosion echoed against *Destiny*'s hull, and they saw black smoke drifting above the lagoon and blotting out the anchored vessels completely.

Dumaresq said calmly, 'She'll strike.' He ignored Palliser's protest. 'Her captain has no choice, don't you see that?' He looked along his own ship and saw Bolitho watching him. 'What would you do? Strike your colours or have your people burn?'

Bolitho heard more explosions, either from the battery or from within the Spaniard's hull. Like Bulkley, he found it hard to believe. A great ship, beautiful in her arrogance, and now this. He thought of it happening here, to his own ship and companions. Danger they could face, it was part of their calling. But to be changed in the twinkling of an eye from a disciplined company to a rabble, hemmed in by renegades and pirates who would kill a man for the price of a drink, was a nightmare.

'Stand by to come about, Mr Palliser. We will steer east.'

Palliser said nothing. In his mind's eye he was probably seeing the utter despair aboard the Spanish ship, although with a more experienced understanding than Bolitho's They would see *Destiny*'s masts turning as she stood away from the shore, and in that they would recognize their own defeat.

Dumaresq added, 'Then I shall explain what I intend.'

Bolitho and Rhodes looked at one another. So it was not over. It had not even begun.

Palliser closed the screen door quickly, as if he expected an enemy to be listening.

'Rounds completed, sir. The ship is completely darkened as ordered.'

Bolitho waited with the other officers and warrant officers in Dumaresq's cabin, feeling their doubts and anxieties, but sharing the chilling excitement nonetheless.

All day, *Destiny* had tacked slowly back and forth in the blazing sunshine, Fougeaux Island always close abeam, although not near enough to be hit by any battery. For hours they had waited, and some had hoped until the last that the *San Augustin* would emerge again, somehow freeing herself from the lagoon to join them. There had been nothing. More to the point, there had been no terrible explosion and the aftermath of flying wreckage which would have proclaimed the Spaniard's final destruction. Had she blown up, most of the anchored vessels in the lagoon would have perished, too. In some ways the silence had been worse.

Dumaresq looked around their intent faces. It was very hot in the sealed and shuttered cabin, and they were all stripped to their shirts and breeches. They looked more like conspirators than King's officers, Bolitho thought.

Dumaresq said, 'We have waited a whole day, gentlemen. It is what Garrick would have expected. He will have anticipated each move, believe me.'

Midshipman Merrett sniffed and rubbed his nose with his sleeve, but Dumaresq's eyes froze him into stillness.

'Garrick will have made his plans with care. He will know I have sent to Antigua for aid. Whatever chance we had of bottling him in his lair until that support arrived vanished when *San Augustin* made her play.' He leaned on his table, his hands encircling the chart he had laid there. 'Nothing stands between Garrick and his ambitions elsewhere but *this ship*.' He let his words sink in. 'I had few fears on that score, gentlemen. We can tackle Garrick's flotilla when it breaks out, fight them together, or run them down piecemeal. But things have changed. Today's silence has proved that.'

Palliser asked, 'D'you mean he'll use the *San Augustin* against us, sir?'

Dumaresq's eyes flashed with sudden anger at the interruption. Then he said almost mildly, 'Eventually, yes.'

Feet shuffled, and Bolitho heard several voices murmuring with sudden alarm.

Dumaresq said, 'Don Carlos Quintana will have surrendered, although he may have fallen in the first engagement. For his sake, I hope that was so. He will receive little mercy at the hands of those murdering scum. Which is something *you* will bear in mind, do I make myself clear?'

Bolitho found he was clenching and unclenching his hands. His palms felt clammy, and he knew it was the same sickness of fear which had followed the attack on the island. His wound started to throb as if to remind him, and he had to stare at the deck until his mind cleared again.

Dumaresq said, 'You will recall the first shots at the Spaniards? From a single cannon to the west'rd of the hill. They were deliberately fired badly to encourage the intruder into their trap. Once past the point they used the battery and some heated shot to create panic and final submission. It gives an ides of Garrick's cunning. He was prepared to risk setting her afire rather than allow her amongst his carefully collected flotilla. And Don Carlos might well have persevered against an ordinary bombardment, although I doubt if he would have succeeded.'

Feet moved overhead, and Bolitho imagined the men up there on watch, without their officers, wondering what schemes were being hatched, and who would pay for them with his life.

He could also picture the ship, without lights and carrying little canvas as she ghosted through the darkness.

'Tomorrow Garrick will still be watching us, to see what we intend. We shall continue throughout the day, patrolling, nothing more. It will do two things. Show Garrick that we expect assistance, also that we have no intention of leaving. Garrick will know time is running out and will endeavour to hasten things along.'

Gulliver asked uneasily, 'Won't that be the wrong thing to do, sir? Why not leave him be and wait for the squadron?'

'Because I do not believe the squadron *will* come.' Dumaresq eyed the master's astonishment blandly. 'Fitzpatrick, the acting-governor, may well delay my despatches until he is relieved of his own responsibility. By then it will be too late anyway.' He gave a slow smile. 'It is no use, Mr Gulliver, you must accept your fate, as I do.'

Palliser said, 'Us against a forty-four, sir? I've no doubt Garrick's other craft will be fairly well armed, and may be experienced in this sort of game.'

Dumaresq appeared to grow tired of the discussion. 'Tomorrow night, I intend to close the shore and drop four boats. I cannot hope to force the entrance myself, and Garrick will know this. He'll have guns laid on the channel anyway, so I'd still be at a grave disadvantage.'

Bolitho felt his stomach muscles tighten. A boat action. Always chancy, always difficult, even with the most experienced of hands.

Dumaresq continued, 'I will discuss the plans further when we see how the wind supports us. In the meantime, I can tell you this. Mr Palliser will take the cutter and the jolly-boat and land at the sou'-west point of the island. It is the best sheltered part and the least likeliest for an assault. He will be supported by Mr Rhodes, Mr Midshipman Henderson and . . .' his eyes moved deliberately to Slade, '. . . our senior master's mate.'

Bolitho glanced quickly at Rhodes and saw how pale his face seemed. There were tiny beads of sweat on his forehead, too.

The senior midshipman, Henderson, by comparison looked calm and eager. It was his first chance, and like Palliser he would soon be trying his luck for promotion. It would be uppermost on his mind until the actual moment came.

'There will be no moon, and as far as I can discover, the sea will be kind to us.' Dumaresq's stature seemed to grow and expand with his ideas. 'The pinnace will be lowered next, and will make for the reefs to the north-eastern end of the island.'

Bolitho waited, trying not to hold his breath. Knowing what was coming.

It was almost a relief when Dumaresq said, 'Mr Bolitho, you will take charge of the pinnace. You will be supported by Midshipmen Cowdroy and Jury, and an experienced gunner's mate with a complete gun's crew. You will find and seize that solitary cannon below the hill-side, and use it as I direct.' He smiled, but there was no warmth in his eyes. 'Lieutenant Colpoys can select a squad of picked marksmen and take them to cover Mr Bolitho's actions. You will please ensure that your marines discard their uniforms and make do with slop clothing like the seamen.'

Colpoys looked visibly shocked. Not by the prospect of being killed, but at the idea of seeing his marines clad in anything but their red coats.

Dumaresq examined their faces again. Perhaps to see the relief of the ones who would be staying, the concern of those detailed for his reckless plan of attack.

He said slowly, 'In the meantime, I shall prepare the ship to give battle. For Garrick will come out, gentlemen. He has too much to lose by staying, and as *Destiny* will be his last witness he will be eager to destroy us.'

He had their full attention.

'And that is what he will have to do, before I let him pass!'

Palliser stood up. 'Dismiss.'

They moved to the door, mulling over Dumaresq's words, trying perhaps to see a last glimmer of hope that an open battle might be avoided.

Rhodes said quietly, 'Well, Dick, I think I shall take a large drink before I stand my watch tonight. I do not feel like brooding.'

Bolitho glanced at the midshipmen as they filed past. It must be far worse for them.

He said, 'I have done a cutting-out expedition myself. I expect that you and the first lieutenant will be told to excise one of the anchored vessels.' He shivered in spite of his guard. 'I don't fancy the prospect of taking that cannon from under their noses!'

They looked at each other, and then Rhodes said, 'The first one of us to return buys wine for the wardroom.'

Bolitho did not trust himself to answer but groped his way to the companion-ladder and up to the quarterdeck to resume his watch.

A large shadow sidled from the trunk of the mizzen-mast and Stockdale said in a hoarse whisper, 'Tomorrow night then, sir?' He did not wait for a reply. 'Felt it in me bones.' His palms scraped together in the darkness. 'You'd not be thinkin' of takin' anyone else as a gun-captain?'

His simple confidence helped to disperse Bolitho's anxiety more than he would have thought possible.

'We'll stay together.' He touched his arm impulsively. 'After this, you'll lament the day you ever quit the land!'

Stockdale rumbled a chuckle. 'Never. 'Ere, a man's got room to breathe!'

Yeames, master's mate of the watch, grinned. 'I don't reckon that bloody pirate knows what 'e's in for, sir. Old Stockdale'll trim 'is beard for 'im!'

Bolitho walked to the weather side and began to pace slowly up and down. Where was she now, he wondered? In some ship heading for another land, a life he would never share.

If only she would come to him now, as she had on that other incredible night. She would understand. Would hold him tenderly and drive back the fear which was ripping him apart. And there was another long day to endure before they would begin the next act. He could not possibly survive this time, and he guessed that fate had never intended it otherwise.

Midshipman Jury shaded the compass-light with his hands to examine the swinging card and then looked across at the slowly pacing figure. Just to be like him would be the only reward he could ever want. So steady and confident, and never too impatient or hasty with a quick rebuke like Palliser, or scathing like Slade. Perhaps his father had been a bit like Richard Bolitho at that age, he thought. He hoped so.

Yeames cleared his throat and said, 'Best get ready to pipe the mornin'-watch, sir, though I fear it'll be a long day today.'

Jury hurried away, thinking of what lay ahead, and wondering why he was not apprehensive any more. He was going with the third lieutenant, and to Ian Jury, aged fourteen years, that was reward enough.

Bolitho had known the waiting would be bad, but throughout the day, as *Destiny*'s company laid out the equipment and weapons which would be required for the landing-parties, he felt his nerves stretching to breaking-point. Whenever he looked up from his work or came on deck from the cool darkness of one of the holds, the bare, hostile island was always there. Although his knowledge and training told him that *Destiny* covered and re-covered her track again and again during the day, it seemed as if they had never moved, that the island, with its fortress-like hill, was waiting, just for him.

Towards dusk, Gulliver laid the ship on a new tack to take her well clear of the island. The masthead lookouts had been unable to sight any sort of activity, so well sheltered was the lagoon, but Dumaresq had no doubts. Garrick would have watched their every move, and the fact *Destiny* had never tacked closer inshore might have helped to shake his confidence, to make him believe that help was already on the way for that solitary frigate.

Eventually, Dumaresq called his officers aft to the cabin. It was much as before, hot and clammy, the air penned in by the shutters so that they were all soon sweating freely.

They had gone over it again and again. Surely nothing on their part could go wrong? Even the wind favoured them. It remained from the south-west, and although slightly fresher than before, gave no hint that it might turn against them.

Dumaresq leaned on his table and said gravely, 'It is time, gentlemen. You will leave here to prepare your boats. All I can do is wish you well. To ask for luck would be an insult to each of you.'

Bolitho tried to relax his body, limb by limb. He could not begin the action like this. Any one fault would break him in pieces, and he knew it.

He plucked the shirt away from his stomach and thought of the time he had purposefully donned a clean one, just to meet her on deck. Perhaps this was the same hopeless gesture. Unlike changing into clean clothing before a battle at sea to avoid infecting a wound, this was something personal. There would be no Bulkleys on that evil island, no one to see the purpose of his reasoning, or to care.

Dumaresq said, 'I intend to lower the cutter and jolly-boat in an hour. We should be in position to drop the launch and pinnace by midnight.' His gaze moved to Bolitho. 'Although it will be a harder pull for your people, your cover will be better.' He checked off the points on his strong fingers. 'Make certain your muskets and pistols remain unloaded until you are sure there will be no accidents. Examine all the gear and tackle you need before you enter the boats. Talk to your people.' He spoke gently, almost caressingly. '*Talk* to them. They are your strength, and will be watching you to see how you measure up.'

Feet padded across the deck above and tackle scraped noisily along the planking. *Destiny* was heaving to.

Dumaresq added, 'Tomorrow is your worst day. You will lie in hiding and do nothing. If an alarm is raised, I cannot save you.'

Midshipman Merrett tapped at the door and then called, 'Mr Yeames's respects, sir, and we are hove to.'

With the cabin pitching unsteadily from side to side, it was rather unnecessary, and Bolitho was amazed to see several of those present grinning and nudging each other.

Even Rhodes, whom he knew to be worried sick about the coming action, was smiling broadly. It was that same madness returning. Perhaps it was better this way.

They moved out of the cabin and were soon swallowed up by their own groups of men.

Mr Timbrell's hoisting-party had already swayed out the jolly-boat, and the cutter followed shortly over the nettings and then into the slapping water alongside. There was suddenly no time for anything. In the enclosing darkness a few hands darted out for brief clasps, voices murmured to friends and companions, a 'good luck', or 'we'll show 'em'. And then it was done, the boats wallowing round in the swell before heading away towards the island.

'Get the ship under way, Mr Gulliver.' Dumaresq turned his back on the sea, as if he had already dismissed Palliser and the two boats.

Bolitho saw Jury talking with young Merrett, and wondered if the latter was glad he was staying aboard. It was incredible to consider how much had happened in so few months since they had all come together as one company.

Dumaresq moved silently to his side. 'More waiting, Mr Bolitho. I wish I could make her fly for you.' He gave a deep chuckle. 'But there never was an easy way.'

Bolitho touched his scar with one finger. Bulkley had removed the stitches, and yet he always expected to feel the same agony, the same sense of despair as when he had been cut down.

Dumaresq said suddenly, 'Mr Palliser and his brave fellows will be well under way by now. But I must not think of them any more. Not as people or friends, until it is over.' He turned away, adding briefly, 'One day you will understand.'

A Moment's Courage

Bolitho attempted to rise to his feet, gripping Stockdale's shoulder for support as the *Destiny*'s pinnace lifted and plunged across a succession of violent breakers. In spite of the night air and the spray which continually dashed over the gunwale, Bolitho felt feverishly hot. The closer the boat drew to the hidden island the more dangerous it became. And most of his men had thought the first part had been the worst. Being cast adrift by their parent ship and left to pull with all their might for the shore. Now they knew differently, not least their third lieutenant.

Occasionally, and now more frequently, jagged fangs of rock and coral surged past, the white water foaming amongst them to give the impression they and not the boat were moving.

Gasping and cursing, the oarsmen tried to maintain the stroke, but even that was broken every now and then as one of them had to lever his loom from its rowlock to save the blade from being splintered on a tooth of rock.

The yawing motion made thinking difficult, and Bolitho had to strain his mind to recall Dumaresq's instructions and Gulliver's gloomy predictions about their final approach. No wonder Garrick felt secure. No vessel of any size could work inshore amongst this strewn carpet of broken coral. It was bad enough for the pinnace. Bolitho tried not to think about *Destiny*'s thirty-four-foot launch which was following them somewhere astern. Or he hoped it was. The extra boat was carrying Colpoys and his marksmen, as well as additional charges of gunpowder. What with Palliser's large party which had already been put ashore on the south-west of the island, and Bolitho's own men, Dumaresq was short-handed indeed. If he had to fight, he would also need to run. The idea of Dumaresq fleeing in retreat was so absurd that it helped to sustain Bolitho in some way.

'Watch out, forrard!' That was the boatswain's mate Ellis Pearse up in the bows. A very experienced seamen, he had been sounding with a boat's lead-and-line for part of the way, but was now acting as a lookout as one more rock loomed out of the darkness.

The noise seemed so great that somebody on the shore must hear them. But Bolitho knew enough to understand that the din of the sea and surf would more than drown the clatter of oars, the desperate thrusts with boat-hooks and fists to fight their way past the treacherous rocks. Had there been even a glimmer of moon it might have been different. Strangely enough, a small boat stood out more clearly to a vigilant lookout than a full-rigged ship standing just offshore. As many a Cornish smuggler had found out to his cost.

Pearse called hoarsely, 'Land ahead!'

Bolitho raised one hand to show he had heard and almost tumbled headlong.

It had seemed as if the broken rocks and the mill-race of water amongst them would never end. Then he saw it, a pale suggestion of land rising above the drifting spray. Much larger close to.

He dug his fingers into Stockdale's shoulder. It felt like solid oak beneath his sodden shirt.

'Easy now, Stockdale! A little to starboard, I think!'

Josh Little, gunner's mate, growled, 'Two 'ands! Ready to go!'

Bolitho saw two seamen crouching over the creaming water and hoped he had not misjudged the depth.

Somewhere astern he heard a grating thud, and then some splashing commotion of oars as the launch regained her balance. It had probably grazed the last big rock, Bolitho thought.

Little chuckled. 'I'll bet that rattled the bullocks!' Then he touched the man nearest him. '*Go!*'

The seaman, as naked as the day he was born, dropped over the side, hung for a few moments kicking and spitting out water, and then gasped, 'Sandy bottom!'

'Easy all!' Stockdale swung the tiller-bar. 'Ready about!'

Eventually, stern on to the beach, the pinnace backed-water, and aided by two men gripping the gunwales surged the last few yards on to firm sand.

With the ease of a man lifting a stick from a pathway, Stockdale unshipped the rudder and hauled it inboard as the pinnace rose once again before riding noisily on to a small beach.

'Clear the boat!'

Bolitho staggered up the beach, feeling the receding surf dragging at his feet and legs. Men stumbled past him, snatching their weapons, while others waded into deeper water to guide the launch on to a safe stretch of sand.

The first seaman who had been detailed to go outboard from the pinnace was struggling to pull on his trousers and shirt, but Little said, 'Later, matey! Just shift yerself up to the top!'

Somebody laughed as the dripping seaman hopped past, and again

Bolitho marvelled that they could still find room for humour.

''Ere comes the launch!'

Little groaned. 'Hell's teeth! Like a pack o' bloody clergymen!' Hoisting his great belly over his belt, he strode down to the surf again, his voice lashing at the confusion of men and oars like a whip.

Midshipman Cowdroy was already clambering up a steep slope to the left of the beach, some men close at his heels. Jury remained by the boat, watching as the last of the weapons, powder and shot and their meagre rations were passed hand to hand to the shelter of the ridge.

Lieutenant Colpoys sloshed through the sand and exclaimed sharply, 'In God's name, Richard, surely there must be a better way of fighting a battle?' He paused to watch his marines as they loped past, their long muskets held high to escape the spray and sand. 'Ten good marksmen,' he remarked absently. 'Damn well wasted, if you ask me.'

Bolitho peered up at the ridge. It was just possible to see where it made an edge with the sky. They had to get over it and into their hiding-place without delay. And they had about four hours to do it.

'Come on.' He turned and waved to the two boats. 'Shove off. Good luck.'

He deliberately kept his voice low, but nevertheless the men nearest him stopped to watch the boats. Now it would be really clear to all of them. In an hour or two those same boats would be hoisted to the safety of their tier aboard *Destiny* and their crews would be free to rest, to put the tension and danger behind them.

How quickly they seemed to move, Bolitho thought. Without their extra passengers and weapons they were already fading into the shadows, outlined only occasionally by the spray as it broke over their oars.

Colpoys said quietly, 'Gone.' He looked down at his mixed garb of sea officer's shirt and pair of moleskin breeches. 'I'll never live this down.' Then, surprisingly, he grinned. 'But still, it will make the colonel sit up and take notice when I next see him, what?'

Midshipman Cowdroy came slithering back down the slope. 'Shall I send scouts on ahead, sir?'

Colpoys regarded him coldly. 'I shall send two of *my* men.'

He snapped out a curt order and two marines melted into the gloom like ghosts.

Bolitho said, 'This is your kind of work, John.' He wiped his forehead with his shirt-sleeve. 'Tell me if I do anything wrong.'

Colpoys shrugged. 'I'd rather have my job than yours.' He clapped him on the arm. 'But we stand or fall together.' He glared round for his orderly. 'Load my pistols and keep by me, Thomas.'

Bolitho looked for Jury but he was already there.

'Ready?'

Jury nodded firmly. 'Aye, ready, sir.'

Bolitho hesitated and peered down at the small sliver of sand where they had come ashore. The surf was still boiling amongst the reefs, but even the marks of the boats' keels had been washed away. They were quite alone.

It was hard to accept that this was the same small island. Four miles long and less than two miles from north to south. It felt like another country, somewhere which when daylight came would be seen stretching away to the horizon.

Colpoys knew his trade well. Bulkley had mentioned that the debonair marine had once been attached to a line regiment, and it seemed very likely. He threw out his pickets, sent his best scouts well ahead of the rest and retained the heavier-footed seamen for carrying the food, powder and shot. Thirty men in all, and Palliser had about the same number. Dumaresq would be thankful to get his boat crews back aboard, Bolitho thought.

And yet in spite of all the preparations, the confident manner in which Colpoys arranged the men into manageable files, Bolitho had to face the fact that he was in charge. The men were fanning out on either side of him, stumbling along on the loose stones and sand and content to leave their safety to Colpoys's keen-eyed scouts.

Bolitho controlled the sudden alarm as it coursed through him. It was like being on watch that first time. The ship running through the night with only you who could change things with a word, or a cry for help.

He heard a heavy tread beside him and saw Stockdale striding along, his cutlass across one shoulder.

Without effort Bolitho could picture him carrying his body down to the boat, to rally the remaining seamen and to call for assistance. But for this strange, hoarse-voiced man he would be dead. It was a comfort to have him at his side again.

Colpoys said, 'Not far now.' He spat grit from his teeth. 'If that fool Gulliver is mistaken, I'll split him like a pig!' He laughed lightly. 'But then, if he *is* wrong, I shall be denied that privilege, eh?'

In the darkness a man slipped and fell, dropping his cutlass and a grapnel with a clatter.

For an instant everyone froze, and then a marine called, 'All quiet, sir.'

Bolitho heard a sharp blow and knew that Midshipman Cowdroy had struck the awkward seaman with the flat of his hanger. If Cowdroy turned his back during any fighting, it was unlikely he would ever live to be a lieutenant.

Bolitho sent Jury on ahead, and when he returned breathless and gasping he said, 'We're there, sir.' He waved vaguely towards the ridge. 'I could hear the sea.'

Colpoys sent his orderly to halt the pickets. 'So far so good. We must be in the centre of the island. When it's light enough I'll fix our position.'

The seamen and marines, unused to the uneven ground and the hard march from the beach, crowded together beneath an overhanging spur of rock. It was cool and smelled damp, as if there were caves nearby.

In a matter of hours it would be a furnace.

'Post your lookouts. Then we'll issue food and water. It may be a long while before we get another chance.'

Bolitho unclipped his hanger and sat down with his back against the bare rock. He thought of his climb to the main cross-trees with the captain, his first sight of this bleak, menacing island. Now he was here.

Jury stooped over him. 'I'm not sure where to post the lookouts on the lower slope, sir.'

Bolitho pushed the weariness aside and somehow lurched to his feet.

'Come with me, I'll show you. Next time, you'll know.'

Colpoys was holding a flask of warm wine to his lips and paused to watch them vanish into the darkness.

The third lieutenant had come a long, long way since Plymouth, he thought. He might be young, but he acted with the authority of a veteran.

Bolitho wiped the dust from his telescope and tried to wriggle his prone body into a comfortable position. It was early morning, and yet the rock and sand were already hot, and his skin prickled so that he wanted to tear off his shirt and scratch himself all over.

Colpoys slid across the ground and joined him. He held out a fistful of dried grass, almost the only thing which survived here in little rock crannies where the rare rainfalls sustained it.

He said, 'Cover the glass with it. Any reflected light on the lens and the alarm will be raised.'

Bolitho nodded, sparing his voice and breath. Very carefully he levelled the glass and began to move it slowly from side to side. There were several small ridges, like the one which they were using to conceal themselves from enemy and sun alike, but all were dwarfed by the flat-topped hill. It shut off the sea directly ahead of his telescope, but to his right he could see the end of the lagoon and some six anchored vessels there. Schooners, as far as he could tell, pinned down by the glare, and with only one small boat cutting a pattern on the glittering water. Beyond and around them the curved arm of rock and coral ran to the left, but the opening and the channel to the sea were hidden by the hill.

Bolitho moved the glass again and concentrated on the land at the far end of the lagoon. Nothing moved, and yet somewhere there Palliser and his men were lying in hiding, marooned, with the sea at their backs. He guessed that the *San Augustin*, if she was still afloat, was on the opposite side of the hill, beneath the hill-top battery which had beaten her into submission.

Colpoys had his own telescope trained towards the western end of the island. 'There, Richard. Huts. A whole line of them.'

Bolitho moved his glass, pausing only to rub the sweat from his eyes. The huts were small and crude and without any sort of window. Probably for storing weapons and other booty, he thought. The glass misted over and then sharpened again as he saw a tiny figure appear on the top of a low ridge. A man in a white shirt, spreading his arms wide and probably yawning. He walked unhurriedly towards the side of the ridge, and what Bolitho had taken to be a slung musket proved to be a long telescope. This he opened in the same unhurried fashion and began to examine the sea, from side to side and from the shore to the hard blue line of the horizon. Several times he returned his scrutiny to a point concealed by the hill, and Bolitho guessed he had sighted *Destiny*, outwardly cruising on her station as before. The thought brought a pang to his heart, a mixture of loss and longing.

Colpoys said softly, 'That is where the gun is. *Our* gun,' he added meaningly.

Bolitho tried again, the ridges merging and separating in a growing heat-haze. But the marine was right. Just beyond the solitary lookout was a canvas hump. It was almost certainly the solitary gun which had made such a pretence at bad marksmanship to lure the Spaniard past the point.

Colpoys was murmuring, 'Put there to offer covering fire for any anchored prizes, I shouldn't wonder.'

They looked at each other, seeing the sudden importance of their part in the attack. The gun had to be taken if Palliser was to be allowed to move from his hiding-place. Once discovered, he would be pinned down by the carefully sited cannon and then slaughtered at leisure. As if to add weight to the idea, a column of men moved from the hill-side and made for the line of huts.

Colpoys said, 'God, look at 'em. Must be a couple of hundred at least!'

And they were certainly not prisoners. They strolled along in twos and threes, the dust rising from their feet like an army on the march. Some boats appeared in the lagoon and more men could be seen at the water's edge with long spars and coils of rope. It seemed likely they were about to rig sheer-legs in readiness for hauling cargo down to the boats.

Dumaresq had been right. Again. Garrick's men were preparing to leave.

Bolitho looked at Colpoys. 'Suppose we're wrong about the *San Augustin*? Just because we cannot see her doesn't mean she's disabled.'

Colpoys was still looking at the men by the huts. 'I agree. Only one way to find out.' He twisted his head as Jury came breathlessly up the slope. 'Keep down!'

Jury flushed and threw himself beside Bolitho. 'Mr Cowdroy wants to know if he can issue some more water, sir.' His eyes moved past Bolitho to the activity on the beach.

'Not yet. Tell him to keep his people hidden. One sight or sound and we'll be done for.' He nodded towards the lagoon. 'Then come back. Do you feel like a stroll?' He saw the youth's eyes widen and then calm again.

'Yes, sir.'

As Jury dropped out of sight, Colpoys asked, 'Why him? He's just a boy.'

Bolitho levelled his glass once again. 'At first light tomorrow *Destiny* will make a feint attack on the entrance. It will be hazardous enough, but if the *San Augustin*'s artillery is ranged on her as well as the hill-top battery, she could be crippled, even wrecked. So we have to know what we are up against.' He nodded towards the opposite end of the lagoon. 'The first lieutenant has his orders. He will attack the moment the island's defences are distracted by *Destiny*.' He met the marine's troubled gaze, hoping he looked more confident than he felt. 'And we must be ready to support him. But if I had to choose, I would say that yours is the greater value to this escapade. So I shall go myself and take Mr Jury as messenger.' He looked away. 'If I fall today . . .'

Colpoys punched his arm. 'Fall? Then we shall follow so swiftly, Saint Peter will need to muster all hands!'

Together they measured the distance to the other low ridge. Someone had rolled up part of the canvas and one wheel of a military cannon was clearly visible.

Colpoys said bitterly, 'French, I'll lay any odds on it!'

Jury returned and waited for Bolitho to speak. Bolitho unbuckled his belt and handed it to the marine.

To Jury he said, 'Leave everything but your dirk.' He tried to smile. 'We're travelling like gentlemen of the road today!'

Colpoys shook his head. 'You'll stand out like milestones!' He removed his flask and held it out to them. 'Douse yourselves and then roll in the dust. It will help, but not much.'

Eventually, dirty and crumpled, they were ready to go.

Colpoys said, 'Don't forget. No quarter. It's better to die than to be taken by those savages.'

Down a steep slope and then into a narrow gully. Bolitho imagined that every fall of loose stones sounded like a landslide. And yet, out of sight from the lagoon and the ridge where he had left Colpoys with his misgivings, it seemed strangely peaceful. As Colpoys had remarked earlier, there were no bird droppings, which implied that few birds came to this desolate place. There was nothing more likely to reveal their stealthy approach than some squawking alarm from a dozen different nests.

The sun rose higher, and the rocks glowed with heat which enfolded their bodies like a kiln. They stripped off their shirts and tied them around their heads like turbans, and each gripping his bared blade, ready for instant use, they looked as much like pirates as the men they were hunting.

Jury's hand gripped his arm. 'There! Up there! A sentry!'

Bolitho pulled Jury down beside him, feeling the midshipman's tension giving way to sick horror. The 'sentry' had been one of Don Carlos's officers. His body was nailed to a post facing the sun, and his once-proud uniform was covered in dried blood.

Jury said in a husky whisper, 'His eyes! They put out his eyes!'

Bolitho swallowed hard. 'Come on. We've a way to go yet.'

They finally reached a pile of fallen boulders, some of which were scarred and blackened, and Bolitho guessed they had been hurled down by *San Augustin*'s opening broadside.

He eased his body between two of the boulders, feeling their heat on his skin, the painful throbbing of the scar above his eye as he pushed and dragged himself into a cleft where he would not be seen. He felt Jury pressing behind him, his sweat mingling with his own as he slowly lifted his head and stared at the lagoon.

He had been expecting to see the captured Spaniard aground, or being sacked and looted by the victorious pirates. But there was discipline here, a purpose of movement which made him realize what he was watching. The *San Augustin* was at anchor, and her upper deck and rigging were alive with men. Splicing, hammering, sawing and hoisting fresh cordage up to the yards. She could have been any man-of-war anywhere.

Her fore-topgallant mast, which had been shot away in the short battle, was already being replaced by a professional-looking jury-rig, and from the way the men were working, Bolitho knew they must be some of her original company. Here and there about the ship's deck stood figures who did not take part in the frantic activity. They stood by swivel-guns or with muskets at the ready. Bolitho thought of the tortured, eyeless thing on the hill-side and tasted the bile in his throat. No wonder the Spaniards worked for their captors. They had been given an horrific lesson, and doubtless others besides, to break any resistance before it began.

Boats glided alongside the anchored ship, and tackles were lowered immediately, with big nets to hoist cases and great chests over her bulwarks.

One boat, separate from all the rest, was being pulled slowly around the *San Augustin*'s stern. A small, stiff-backed man with a neatly clipped beard was standing in the stern-sheets, pointing with a black stick, jabbing at the air to emphasize a point for the benefit of his companions.

Even in distance there was something autocratic and arrogant about the man. Someone who had gained power and respect from treachery and murder. It had to be Sir Piers Garrick.

Now he was leaning on the boat's gunwale, pointing with his stick again, and Bolitho saw that the *San Augustin*'s bilge was showing slightly, and Garrick was probably ordering a change of trim, some cargo or shot to be shifted to give his new prize the best sailing quality he could manage.

Jury whispered, 'What are they doing, sir?'

'The *San Augustin* is preparing to leave.' He rolled on his back, oblivious to the jagged stones as he tried to think clearly. '*Destiny* cannot fight them all. We must act now.'

He saw the frown on Jury's face. He had never thought otherwise. *Was I like him once? So trusting that I believed we can never be beaten?*'

He said, 'See? More boats are coming down to her. Garrick's treasure. It has all been for this. His own flotilla, and now a forty-four-gun ship to do with as he will. Captain Dumaresq was right. There is nothing to stop him.' He smiled gravely. 'But *Destiny*.'

Bolitho could see it as if it had already happened. *Destiny* standing close inshore to provide a diversion for Palliser, while all the time the captured *San Augustin* lay here, like a tiger ready to pounce. In confined waters, *Destiny* would stand no chance at all.

'We must get back.'

Bolitho lowered himself through the boulders, his mind still refusing to accept what had to be done.

Colpoys could barely hide his relief as they scrambled up to join him on the ridge.

He said, 'They've been working all the time. Clearing those huts. They've slaves with them too, poor devils. I saw more than one laid flat by a piece of chain.'

Colpoys fell silent until Bolitho had finished describing what he had seen.

Then he said, 'Look here. I know what you're thinking. Because this is a damnable, rotten useless island which nobody cares about and precious few have even heard of, you feel cheated. Unwilling to risk lives, your own included. But it's like that. Big battles and waving flags are rare. This will be described as a skirmish, an "incident", if you must know. But it *matters* if we think it does.' He lay back and studied Bolitho calmly. 'I say to hell with caution. We'll go for that cannon without waiting for the dawn tomorrow. They've nothing else which will bear on the lagoon. All the other guns are dug-in on the hill-top. It will take hours to shift 'em.' He grinned. 'A whole battle can be won or lost in that time.'

Bolitho took the telescope again, his hands shaking as he trained it on the ridge and the partly covered cannon. It was even the same lookout as before.

Jury said huskily, 'They've stopped work.'

'No wonder.' Colpoys shaded his eyes. 'See yonder, young fellow. Isn't that a cause enough for dying?'

Destiny moved slowly into view, her topsail and topgallants very pale against the hard blue sky.

Bolitho stared at her, imagining her sounds now lost in distance, her smells, her familiarity.

He felt like a man dying of thirst as he sees a wine jar in a desert's image. Or someone on his way to the gallows who pauses to listen to an early sparrow. Each knows that tomorrow there will be no wine, and no birds will sing.

He said flatly, 'Let's be about it then. I'll tell the others. If only there was some way of informing Mr Palliser.'

Colpoys backed down the slope. Then he looked at Bolitho, his eyes yellow in the sunlight.

'He'll know, Richard. The whole damned island will!'

Colpoys wiped his face and neck with his handkerchief. It was afternoon, and the blazing heat thrown back at them from the rocks was sheer torment.

But waiting had paid off. Most of the activity around the huts had ceased, and smoke from several fires drifted towards the hidden seamen and marines, bringing smells of roasting meat as an additional torture.

Colpoys said, 'They'll rest after they've eaten.' He glanced at his corporal. 'Issue the rations and water, Dyer.' To Bolitho he added quietly, 'I estimate that gun to be a cable's distance from us.' He squinted his eyes as he examined the slope and the steep climb to the other ridge. 'If we start, there'll be no stopping. I think there are several men with the cannon. Probably in some sort of magazine underground.' He took a cup of water from his orderly and sipped it slowly. 'Well?'

Bolitho lowered the telescope and rested his forehead on his arm. 'We'll risk it.'

He tried not to measure it in his mind. Two hundred yards across open ground, and then what?

He said tightly, 'Little and his crew can take care of the gun. We'll attack the ridge from both sides at once. Mr Cowdroy can take charge of the second party.' He saw Colpoys grimace and added. 'He's the senior one of the pair, and he's experienced.'

Colpoys nodded. 'I'll place my marksmen where they'll do the most good. Once you've taken the ridge, I'll support you.' He held out his hand. 'If you fail, I'll lead the shortest bayonet-charge in the Corps' history!'

And then, all of a sudden they were ready. The earlier uncertainty and tension was gone, wiped away, and the men gathered in their tight little groups with grim but determined faces. Josh Little with his gun-crew, festooned with the tools of their trade, and extra charges of powder and some shot.

Midshipman Cowdroy, his petulant face set in a scowl, had already drawn his hanger and was checking his pistol. Ellis Pearse, boatswain's mate, carried his own weapon, a fearsome, double-edged boarding-cutlass which had been made specially for him by a blacksmith. The marines had dispersed amongst the rocks, their long muskets probing the open ground and further towards the flat-topped hill-side.

Bolitho stood up and looked at his own men. Dutchy Vorbin, Olsson, the mad Swede, Bill Bunce, an ex-poacher, Kennedy, a man who had escaped jail by volunteering for the Navy, and many others he had come to know so well.

Stockdale wheezed, 'I'll be with you, sir.'

Their eyes met.

'Not this time. You stay with Little. That gun has got to be taken, Stockdale. Without it we might as well die here and now.' He touched his thick arm. 'Believe me. We are all depending on you today.'

He turned away, unable to watch the big man's pain.

To Jury he said, 'You can keep with Lieutenant Colpoys.'

'Is that an order, sir?'

Bolitho saw the boy's chin lift stubbornly. What were they trying to do to him?

He replied, 'No.'

A man whispered, 'The sentry's climbed down out of sight!'

Little chuckled. 'Gone for a wet.'

Bolitho found that his feet were already over the edge and his hanger glinting in the sunlight as he pointed towards the opposite ridge.

'Come on then! *At 'em, lads!*'

Heedless now of noise and deception, they charged down the slope, their feet kicking up dust and stones, their breath rasping fiercely, as they kept their eyes fixed on the ridge. They reached the bottom of the slope and pounded across open ground, oblivious to everything but the hidden gun.

Somewhere, a million miles away, someone yelled, and a shot whined across the hill-side. More voices swelled and faded as the men by the lagoon stampeded for their weapons, probably imagining that they were under attack from the sea.

Three heads suddenly appeared on the top of the ridge even as the first of Bolitho's men reached the foot. Colpoys's muskets banged seemingly ineffectually and from far away, but two of the heads vanished, and the third man bounded in the air before rolling down the slope amongst the British sailors.

'Come on!' Bolitho waved his hanger. '*Faster!*'

From one side a musket fired past him, and a seaman fell clutching his thigh, and then sprawled sobbing as his companions charged on towards the top.

Bolitho's breath felt like hot sand in his lungs as he leapt over a crude parapet of stone. More shots hammered past him, and he knew some of his men had fallen.

He saw the glint of metal, a wheel of the cannon beneath its canvas cover, and yelled, 'Watch out!'

But from beneath the canvas one of the hidden men fired a fully charged musketoon into the advancing seamen. One was hurled on his back, his face and most of his skull blasted away, and three others fell kicking in their own blood.

With a roar like an enraged beast, Pearse threw himself from the opposite side of the gun-pit and slashed the canvas apart with his double-edged blade.

A figure ran from the pit, covering his head with his hands and screaming, '*Quarter! Quarter!*'

Pearse threw back his arm and yelled, 'Quarter, you bugger! Take that!' The great blade hit the man across the nape of the neck, so that his head dropped forward on to his chest.

Midshipman Cowdroy's party swarmed over the other side of the ridge, and as Pearse led his men into the pit to complete his gory victory, Little and Stockdale were already down with the cannon, while their crew ran to discover if there was any life in the nearby furnace.

The seamen were like mad things. Yelling and cheering, pausing only to haul their wounded companions to safety, they roared all the louder as Pearse emerged from the pit with a great jar of wine.

Bolitho shouted, 'Take up your muskets! Here come the marines!'

Once again the seamen threw themselves down and aimed their weapons towards the lagoon. Colpoys and his ten marksmen, trotting smartly in spite of their borrowed and ill-matched clothing, hurried up to the ridge, but it seemed as if the attack had been so swift and savage that the whole island was held in a kind of daze.

Colpoys arrived at the top and waited for his men to take cover. Then he said, 'We seem to have lost five men. Very satisfactory.' He frowned disdainfully as some bloodied corpses were passed up from the gun-pit and pitched down the slope. 'Animals.'

Little climbed from the pit, wiping his hands on his belly. 'Plenty o' shot, sir. Not much powder though. Lucky we brought our own.'

Bolitho shared their madness but knew he must keep his grip. At any moment a real attack might come at them. But they had done well. Better than they should have been asked to do.

He said, 'Issue some wine, Little.'

Colpoys added sharply, 'But keep a clear eye and a good head. Your gun will be in action soon.' He glanced at Bolitho. 'Am I right?'

Bolitho twitched his nostrils and knew his men had the furnace primed-up again.

It was a moment's courage, a few minutes of reckless wildness. He took a mug of red wine from Jury and held it to his lips. It was also a moment he would remember until he died.

Even the wine, dusty and warm though it was, tasted like claret.

''Ere they come, sir! 'Ere come th' buggers!'

Bolitho tossed the mug aside and picked up his hanger from the ground.

'Stand to!'

He turned briefly to see how Little and his crew were managing. The cannon had not moved, and to create panic it had to be firing very soon.

He heard a chorus of yells, and when he walked to the crude parapet he saw a mass of running figures converging on the ridge, the sun playing on swords and cutlasses, the air broken by the stabbing crack of muskets and pistols.

Bolitho looked at Colpoys. 'Ready, marines?'

'*Fire!*'

16

Only a Dream

'*Cease firing!*'

Bolitho handed his pistol to a wounded seaman to reload. He felt as if every fibre in his body was shaking uncontrollably, and he could scarcely believe that the first attack had been repelled. Some of those who had nearly reached the top of the ridge were lying sprawled where they had dropped, others were still dragging themselves painfully towards safety below.

Colpoys joined him, his shirt clinging to his body like a wet skin. 'God!' He blinked the sweat from his eyes. 'Too close for comfort.'

Three more seamen had fallen, but were still alive. Pearse was already supplying each of them with spare muskets and powder-horns so that they could keep up a rapid fire for another attack. After that. . . ? Bolitho glanced at his gasping, cowering sailors. The air was acrid with powder-smoke and the sweet smell of blood.

Little bawled, ' 'Nother few minutes, sir!'

So fierce had been the attack that Bolitho had been forced to take men from the gun-crew to help repel the charging, yelling figures. Now, Little and Stockdale, with a few more picked hands, were throwing their weight on wooden staves and handspikes to work the cannon round towards the head of the anchorage.

Bolitho picked up the telescope and levelled it on the six motionless vessels. One, a topsail schooner, looked very like the craft which had put paid to the *Heloise*. None showed any sign of weighing, and he guessed that their masters were expecting the hill-top guns to smash this impudent invasion before more harm could be done.

He took a mug of wine from Pearse without seeing what he was doing. Where the hell was Palliser? Surely he must have realized what they were attempting? Bolitho felt a stab of despair. Suppose the first lieutenant believed the gunfire and pandemonium implied that Bolitho's party had been discovered and was being systematically wiped out. He recalled Dumaresq's own words before they had left the ship. *I cannot save you.* It was likely Palliser would take the same view.

Bolitho swung round, trying to hide his sudden desperation as he

called, 'How much *longer*, Little?' He realized that the gunner's mate
had only just told him, just as he knew that Colpoys and Cowdroy were
watching him worriedly.

Little straightened his back and nodded. 'Ready.' He stooped down
again, his eye squinting along the gun's black barrel. 'Load with powder,
lads! Ram the charge 'ome.' He was moving round the breech like a great
spider, all arms and legs. 'This 'as got to be done nice an' tidy like.'

Bolitho licked his lips. He saw two seamen taking a shot-carrier
towards the small furnace, where another man waited with a ladle in his
fists, ready to spoon the heated ball into the carrier. Then it was always
a matter of luck and timing. The ball had to be tipped into the muzzle
and tamped down on to a double-thick wad. If the gun exploded before
the rammer could leap clear he would be blown apart by the ball.
Equally, it might split the barrel wide open. No wonder captains were
terrified by using heated shot aboard ship.

Little said, 'I'll lay for the middle vessel, sir. A mite either way an' we
might 'it one or t'other.'

Stockdale nodded in agreement.

Colpoys said abruptly, 'I can see some men on the hill-top. My guess
is they'll be raking *us* presently.'

A man shouted, 'They're musterin' for another attack!'

Bolitho ran to the parapet and dropped on one knee. He could see the
small figures darting amongst the rocks and others taking up positions
on the hill-side. This was no rabble. Garrick had his people trained like
a private army.

'*Stand to!*'

The muskets rose and wavered in the glare, each man seeking out a
target amongst the fallen rocks.

A fusilade of shots ripped over the parapet, and Bolitho knew that
more attackers were taking advantage of covering fire to work around
the other end of the ridge.

He darted a quick glance at Little. He was holding out his hands like a
man at prayer.

'Now! *Load!*'

Bolitho tore his eyes away and fired his pistol into a group of three
men who were almost at the top of the ridge. Others were fanning out
and making difficult targets, and the air was filled with the unnerving
din of yells and curses, many in their own language.

Two figures bounded over the rocks and threw themselves on a
seaman who was frantically trying to reload a musket. Bolitho saw his
mouth open in a silent scream as one attacker pinioned him with his
cutlass and his companion silenced him forever with a terrible slash.

Bolitho lunged forward, striking a blade aside and hacking down the
man's sword-arm before he could recover. He felt the shock jar up his

wrist as the hanger cut through bone and muscle, but forgot the screaming man as he went for his companion with a ferocity he had never known before.

Their blades clashed together, but Bolitho was standing amongst loose stones and could barely keep his balance.

The deafening roar of Little's cannon made the other man falter, his eyes suddenly terrified as he realized what he had done.

Bolitho lunged and jumped back behind the parapet even before his adversary's corpse hit the ground.

Little was yelling, 'Look at that 'un!'

Bolitho saw a falling column of water mingled with steam where the ball had slammed down between two of the vessels. A miss maybe, but the effect would rouse panic quickly enough.

'Sponge out, lads!' Little capered on the edge of his pit while the men with the cradle dashed back towards the furnace for another ball. 'More powder!'

Colpoys crossed the blood-spattered rock and said, 'We've lost three more. One of my fellows is down, too.' He wiped his forehead with his arm, his gold-hilted sabre hanging from his wrist.

Bolitho saw that the curved blade was almost black with dried blood. They could not withstand another attack like the last. Although corpses dotted the slopes and along the broken rim of the parapet, Bolitho knew there were many more men already grouping below. They would be far more fearful of Garrick than a ragged handful of seamen.

'*Now!*' Little plunged his slow-match down and the gun recoiled again with a savage explosion.

Bolitho caught a brief blur of the ball as it lifted and then curved down towards the unmoving vessels. He saw a puff of smoke, and something solid detach itself from the nearest schooner and fly into the air before splashing in the water alongside.

'*A hit! A hit!*' The gun-crew, black-faced and running with sweat, capered around the gun like madmen.

Stockdale was already using his strength on a handspike to edge the muzzle round just that small piece more.

'She's afire!' Pearse had his hands above his eyes. 'God damn 'em, they're tryin' to douse it!'

But Bolitho was watching the schooner at the far end of the lagoon. She of all the vessels was in the safest anchorage, and yet even as he watched he saw her jib flapping free and men running forward to sever the cable.

He reached out, not daring to take his eyes from the schooner. '*Glass! Quickly!*'

Jury hurried to him and put the telescope in his fingers. Then he stood back, his eyes on Bolitho's face as if to discover what was about to happen.

Bolitho felt a musket-ball fan past his head but did not flinch. He must not lose that small, precious picture, even though he was in danger of being shot down while he watched.

Almost lost in distance, and yet so clear because he knew them. Palliser's tall frame, sword in hand. Slade and some seamen by the tiller, and Rhodes urging others to the halliards and braces as the schooner broke free and fell awkwardly downwind. There were splashes alongside, and for a moment Bolitho thought she was under fire. Then he realized that Palliser's boarders were flinging the vessel's crew overboard, rather than lose vital time putting them under guard.

Colpoys shouted excitedly, 'They must have swum out to the vessel! He's a cunning one is Palliser! Used our attack as the perfect decoy!'

Bolitho nodded, his ears ringing with the crack of musket-fire, the occasional bang of a swivel. Instead of steering for the centre of the lagoon, Palliser was heading directly for the schooner which had been hit by Little's heated shot.

As they tore down on her, Bolitho saw a ripple of flashes and knew that Palliser was raking the men on her deck, smashing any hope they might have had of controlling the flames. Smoke was rising rapidly from her hatch and drifting down towards the beach and its deserted huts.

Bolitho called, 'Little! Shift the target to the next one!'

Minutes later the heated ball smashed through a schooner's frail hull and caused several internal explosions which brought down a mast and set most of the standing rigging ablaze.

With two vessels burning fiercely in their midst, the remainder needed no urging to cut their cables and try to escape the drifting fireships. The last schooner, the one seized by Palliser's boarding party, was now under command, her big sails filling and rising above the smoke like avenging wings.

Bolitho said suddenly, 'Time to go.' He did not know why he knew. He just did.

Colpoys waved his sabre. 'Take up the wounded! Corporal, put a fuse to the magazine!'

Little's slow-match plunged down again, and another heated ball ripped across the water and hit the vessel already ablaze. Men were leaping overboard, floundering like dying fish as the great pall of smoke crept out to hide them from view.

Pearse lifted a wounded marine across his shoulder, but held his boarding-cutlass in his other hand.

He said, 'Wind's steady, sir. That smoke will blind the bloody battery!'

Panting like wild animals, the seamen and marines scrambled down the slope, keeping the ridge between them and the hill-top battery.

Colpoys pointed to the water. 'That'll be the closest point!' He fell on his knees, his hands to his chest. 'Oh God, they've done for me!'

Bolitho called two marines to carry him between them, his mind cringing to the din of musket-fire, the sound of flames devouring a vessel beyond the dense smoke.

There was shouting, too, and he knew that many of the schooner's people had been ashore when the attack had begun and were now running towards the hill-side in the hope of reaching the protection of the battery.

Bolitho came to a halt, his feet almost in the water. He could barely suck breath and his eyes streamed so badly he could see little beyond the beach.

They had done the impossible, and while Palliser and his men took advantage of their work, they were now able to go no further.

He knelt down to reload his pistol, his fingers shaking as he cocked it for one last shot.

Jury was with him, and Stockdale, too. But there seemed less than half of the party which had so courageously stormed the ridge and taken the cannon.

Bolitho saw Stockdale's eyes light up as the magazine exploded and hurled the gun bodily down the slope amidst a landslide of corpses and broken rocks.

Midshipman Cowdroy stabbed at the smoke with his hanger. '*Boat!* Look, there!'

Pearse lowered the marine to the ground and waded into the water, his terrible cutlass held above his head.

'We'll take it off 'em, lads!'

Bolitho could feel their desperation like a living force. Sailors were all the same in one thing. Get them a boat, no matter how small, and they felt they could manage.

Little dragged out his cutlass and bared his teeth. 'Cut 'em down afore they slips us!'

Jury fell against Bolitho, and for an instant he thought he had been taken by a musket-ball. But he was pointing incredulously at the smoke and the shadowy boat which was poking through it.

Bolitho nodded, his heart too full to understand.

It was Rhodes standing in the bows of the long-boat, and he saw the checkered shirts of *Destiny*'s seamen at the oars behind him.

'*Lively there!*' Rhodes reached down and seized Bolitho's wrist. 'All in one piece?' He saw Colpoys and shouted, 'Lend a hand there !'

The boat was so full of men, some of them wounded, that there was barely five inches of freeboard, as like a drunken sea-creature it backed-water and headed once more into the smoke.

Between coughs and curses Rhodes explained, 'Knew you'd try to reach us. Only chance. My God, you raised a riot back there, you rascal!'

A burning schooner drifted abeam, and Bolitho could feel the heat on his face like an inferno. Explosions rolled through the smoke, and he guessed it was either another magazine or the hill-top battery shooting blindly across the lagoon.

'What now?'

Rhodes stood up and gestured wildly to the coxswain. 'Hard a-starboard!'

Bolitho saw the twin masts of the schooner right above him, and with his men reached out to catch the heaving-lines which came through the smoke like serpents.

Groaning and crying out in pain, the wounded were pushed and hauled up the vessel's side, and even as the long-boat was cast adrift with a man who had died in sight of safety as her only passenger, Bolitho heard Palliser shouting orders.

Bolitho felt his way through the smoke and met Palliser and Slade by the tiller.

Palliser exclaimed, 'You look like an escaped convict, man!' He gave a brief smile, but Bolitho saw only the strain and the relief.

Rhodes was kneeling beside the marine lieutenant. 'He'll live if we can get him to old Bulkley.'

Palliser raised one hand and the helm went over very slightly. Another schooner was just abeam, her sails drawing well as she stood away from the blazing hulks and headed for the entrance.

Then he said, 'By the time they've discovered we've taken one of their own, we'll be clear.'

He turned sharply as the *San Augustin*'s towing masts broke above the smoke. She was still at anchor, and probably had every able man from the island on board waiting to fend off the drifting fire-ships and douse the results of any contact with them.

Palliser added, 'After that, it will be someone else's problem, thank God!'

A ball splashed down near the larboard bow, and Bolitho guessed that Garrick's gunners had at last realized what was happening.

As the smoke thinned, and parts of the island emerged, clean and pale in the sunlight, Bolitho saw they were already past the point.

He heard Pearse whisper, 'Look, Bob, there she be!' He lifted the head of a wounded seaman so that he could see *Destiny*'s braced topsails as Dumaresq drove her as close as he dared to the reefs.

Pearse, a boatswain's mate who had fought like a devil, who by command of his captain had laid raw the back of many a defaulter with his cat-o'-nine-tails, said very quietly, 'Poor Bob's dead, sir.' He closed the young seaman's eyes with his tarry fingers, adding, ''Nother minute and 'e'd 'ave bin fine.'

Bolitho watched the frigate shortening sail, the rush of men along her gangway as the two vessels tacked closer together. *Destiny*'s figurehead was as before, pure and pale, her victor's laurels held up as if in defiance to the smoke-shrouded island.

And all Bolitho could think of was the dead seaman named Bob, of a solitary corpse left drifting in the long-boat, of Stockdale's anxiety at being ordered away from his side when he was needed. Of Colpoys, and the corporal nicknamed Dipper, Jury and Cowdroy, and others who had been left behind.

'Take in the fores'l!' Palliser watched the *Destiny*'s wary approach with grim satisfaction. 'There were times when I never thought to see *that* lady again.'

Josh Little crossed to Pearse's side and said roughly, 'We'll 'ave a wet when we gets aboard, eh?'

Pearse was still looking at the dead seaman, 'Aye, Josh. An' one for 'im, too.'

Rhodes said, 'The lord and master will have his way now. A fight to the finish.' He ducked as a heaving-line soared aboard. 'But for myself, I wish the odds were fairer.' He looked across at the great pall of smoke which surrounded the flat-topped hill as if to carry it away. 'You're a marvel, Dick. You really are.'

They examined each other like strangers. Then Bolitho said, 'I was afraid you'd hold back. That you'd think we were all taken.'

Rhodes waved his arm to some of the seamen along *Destiny*'s gangway. 'Oh, didn't I tell you? We knew what you were doing, where you were, everything.'

Bolitho stared at him in disbelief. 'How?'

'Remember that main-topman of yours, Murray? He was their sentry. Saw you and young Jury as you left cover.' He gripped his friend's arm. 'It's true! He's below now with a splinter in his leg. Had quite a story to tell. Lucky for you and young Jury, eh!'

Bolitho shook his head and leaned against the schooner's bulwark to watch the two hulls come together in the swell.

Death had been that close, and he had known nothing about it. Murray must have taken the first available vessel out of Rio and had ended up with Garrick's pirates. He could have raised the alarm, or could have shot them both down and become a hero. Instead, something which they had once shared, another precious moment, had held them together.

Dumaresq's voice boomed through a speaking-trumpet. 'Roundly there! I shall be aground if you cannot shift yourselves!'

Rhodes grinned. '*Home*.'

Captain Dumaresq stood by the stern windows of his cabin, his hands behind him, as he listened to Palliser's account of the pitched-battle and their escape from the lagoon.

As he signalled for Macmillan to pass round more wine to his stained and weary officers, he said gravely, 'I put a landing-party ashore to prick Garrick's balloon. I did not expect you to make an invasion all on your own!' Then he smiled broadly, and it made him look sad and suddenly tired. 'I shall think of you and your lads at dawn tomorrow. But for you *Destiny* would have been met with such a resistance that I doubt I could have worked her clear. Things are still bad, gentlemen, but at least we *know*.'

Palliser asked, 'Do you still intend to despatch the schooner to Antigua, sir?'

Dumaresq regarded him thoughtfully. '*Your* schooner, you mean?' He moved to the windows and stared at the dying sun reflected from the water. Like red gold. 'Yes, I am afraid it is another prize I must take from you.'

Bolitho watched, his mind strangely alert in spite of the strain, the bitter memories of the day. He recognized the bond between captain and first lieutenant as if it were something solid and visible.

Dumaresq added, 'If *San Augustin* is little damaged we must fight her as soon as we can. When Garrick's lookouts see the schooner standing away he will know that time is running out, that I have sent for aid.' He nodded grimly. 'He will come out tomorrow. That is my belief.'

Palliser persisted, 'He will be supported by the other schooners, maybe two survived the fires.'

'I know. Better that than wait for Garrick to sail against us with a completely overhauled ship. I'd ask for better terms, but few captains get the chance to choose.'

Bolitho thought of the men who had been sent over to the schooner. All but a few were wounded, and yet there had been something defiant about them, something which had raised a cheer from *Destiny*'s gangways and rigging.

For reasons of his own, Dumaresq had sent Yeames, master's mate, in command of the prize. It must have been a hard blow for Slade.

Bolitho had been moved when Yeames had approached him before the last boatload had been ferried across. He had always liked the master's mate, but had thought little beyond that.

Yeames had held out his hand. 'You'll win tomorrow, sir, I've no doubt o' that. But mebbee we'll not meet again. In case we do, I'll want you to remember me, as I'd be proud to serve you when you gets your command.'

He had gone away, leaving Bolitho confused and proud.

Dumaresq's resonant voice broke through his thoughts. 'We shall clear for action at dawn tomorrow. I shall speak with the people before we close the enemy, but to you especially I give my thanks.'

Macmillan hovered by the screen door until he caught the captain's eye.

'Mr Timbrell's respects, sir, an' will you want to darken ship?'

Dumaresq shook his big head slowly. 'Not this time. I want Garrick to see us. To *know* we are here. His one weakness, apart from greed, is anger. I intend that he shall grow angrier before morning!'

Macmillan opened the door, and gratefully the lieutenants and midshipmen made to withdraw.

Only Palliser remained, and Bolitho guessed he would share the more technical details with the captain without their interruption.

With the door shut once more, Dumaresq turned to his first lieutenant and gestured to a chair.

'There's something else, isn't there?'

Palliser sat and thrust out his long legs. For a moment more he kneaded his eyes with his knuckles and then said, 'You were right about Egmont, sir. Even after you put him aboard a vessel outward-bound from Basseterre he tried to warn Garrick, or to reason with him. We'll probably never know. He obviously transferred to a smaller, faster vessel and took the northerly route through the island to reach here before us. Whatever happened, his words were lost on Garrick.'

He delved into his pocket and withdrew the gold necklace with its double-headed bird and gleaming ruby tails.

'Garrick had them butchered. I took this from one of our prisoners. The seaman I told you about explained the rest to me.'

Dumaresq picked up the heavy necklace and examined it sadly.

'Murray, he saw it?'

Palliser nodded. 'He was wounded. I sent him in the schooner before he could speak with Mr Bolitho.'

Dumaresq walked to the windows again and watched the little schooner turning stern on, her sails as gold as the necklace in his hand.

'That was thoughtful. For what he has said and done, Murray will be discharged when he reaches England. I doubt if his path will ever cross with Mr Bolitho's again.' He shrugged. 'If it does, the pain will be easier to bear by then.'

'You'll not tell him, sir? Not let him know that she is dead?'

Dumaresq watched the shadows reaching across the heaving water to cover the schooner's hull.

'He'll not hear it from me. Tomorrow we must fight, and I need every officer and man to give all he has. Richard Bolitho has proved himself to be a good lieutenant. If he survives tomorrow, he'll be an even better one.' Dumaresq raised one of the windows and without further hesitation tossed the necklace into *Destiny*'s wake. 'I'll leave him with his dream. It's the very least I can do for him.'

In the wardroom Bolitho sat in a chair, his arms hanging at his sides as the resistance ran out of him like fine sand from a glass. Rhodes sat opposite him, staring at an empty goblet without recognition.

There was still tomorrow. Like the horizon, they never reached it.

Bulkley entered and sat down heavily between them. 'I have just been dealing with our stubborn marine.'

Bolitho nodded dully. Colpoys had insisted on staying aboard with his men. Bandaged and strapped up so that he could use only one arm, he had barely the strength to stay on his feet.

Palliser came through the door and tossed his hat on to a gun. For a moment he looked at it, probably seeing it tomorrow with this place stripped bare, the screens gone, the little personal touches shut away from the smoke and fire of battle.

Then he said crisply, 'Your watch, I believe, Mr Rhodes? The master cannot be expected to do everything, you know!'

Rhodes lurched to his feet and grinned. 'Aye, aye, sir.' Like a man walking in his sleep he left the wardroom.

Bolitho barely heard them. He was thinking of her, using her memory to shield his mind from the sights and deeds of that day.

Then he stood up abruptly and excused himself from the others as he went to the privacy of his cabin. He did not want them to see his dismay. When he had tried to see her face there had been only a blurred image, nothing more.

Bulkley pushed a bottle across the table. 'Was it bad?'

Palliser considered it. 'It'll be worse yet.' But he was thinking of the jewelled necklace. On the sea-bed astern now. A private burial.

The surgeon added, 'I'm glad about Murray. It's a small thing in all this misery, but it's good to know he's clear of blame.'

Palliser looked away. 'I'm going to do my rounds and turn in for a few hours.'

Bulkley sighed. 'Likewise. I'd better request to borrow Spillane from clerk's duties. I shall be short-handed, too.'

Palliser paused in the doorway and regarded him emptily. 'You'd better hurry then. He'll maybe hang tomorrow. Just to stoke Garrick's anger further. He was his spy. Murray saw him searching old Lockyer's body at Funchal when it was brought aboard.' Weariness was slurring Palliser's words. 'Spillane guessed, and tried to incriminate him over Jury's watch. To drive a wedge between fo'c'sle and quarterdeck. It's been done before.' With sudden bitterness he added, 'He's as much a murderer as Garrick.'

He strode from the wardroom without another word, and when Bulkley turned his head he saw the first lieutenant's hat was still lying on the gun.

Whatever happened tomorrow, nothing would ever be the same again, he thought, and the realization saddened him greatly.

When darkness finally shut out the horizon and the flattened hill above Fougeaux Island had disappeared, *Destiny*'s lights still shone on the water like watchful eyes.

17

Into Battle

Overnight Fougeaux Island seemed to have shrunk in size, so that when the first faint light filtered down from the horizon it looked little more than a sand-bar across *Destiny*'s starboard bow.

Bolitho lowered his telescope and allowed the island to fall back into the shadows. Within an hour it would be bright sunlight. He turned his back and paced slowly up and down the quarterdeck. The business of preparing the ship for battle had been unreal, an almost leisurely affair carried out watch by watch during the night.

The seamen knew their way around the masts and hull so well that they had little left to do which required daylight. Dumaresq had thought that out with the same meticulous care he planned everything he did. He wanted his men to accept the inevitability of a fight, the fact that some if not all of them would never make another voyage in *Destiny*. There was only one alternative passage, and it was marked on the master's chart. Two thousand fathoms, straight down.

Also, Dumaresq intended his people to be as rested as possible, without the usual nerve-wrenching stampede of clearing for action when an enemy showed himself.

Palliser appeared on the quarterdeck, and after a cursory glance at the compass and each sail in turn he said, 'I trust the watch below is completing breakfast?'

Bolitho replied, 'Aye, sir. I have ordered the cooks to douse the galley fires as soon as they are done.'

Palliser took a glass from Midshipman Henderson, who had been assisting with the morning-watch.

Midshipman Cowdroy had been similarly employed during the night. As next in line for promotion, they might find themselves as acting-lieutenants before *Destiny*'s cooks relit their fires.

Palliser scrutinized the island carefully. 'Terrible place.' He returned the glass to Henderson and said, 'Aloft with you. I want to be told the moment Garrick tries to leave the lagoon.'

Bolitho watched the midshipman swarming up the ratlines. It was getting lighter rapidly. He could even see the boatswain's top-chains which he had slung on each yard, the additional tackles and lines hauled up to the fighting-tops for urgent repairs when needed.

He asked, 'You believe it is today, sir?'

Palliser smiled grimly. 'The captain is certain. That's enough for me. And Garrick will know it is his only chance. To fight and win, to get away before the squadron sends support.'

Vague figures moved about the upper deck and between the guns. Those black muzzles, now damp with spray and a night mist, would soon be too hot to touch.

Petty officers were already discussing last-moment changes to crews, to replace those who had died or were on their way to safety aboard the captured schooner.

Lieutenant Colpoys was right aft by the taffrail with his sergeant as seamen trooped along the gangways to pack the hammocks tightly in the nettings as protection for those who shared the quarterdeck in times like these. An exposed, dangerous place, vital to any ship, an aiming-point for marksmen and the deadly swivel-guns.

Midshipman Jury took a message at the quarterdeck ladder and reported, 'Galley fires doused, sir.'

He looked very young and clean, Bolitho thought, as if he had taken great care over his dress and bearing.

He smiled. 'A fine day for it.'

Jury looked up at the masthead, searching for Henderson. 'We have the agility if nothing else, sir.'

Bolitho glanced at him, but saw himself just a year or so back. 'That's very true.' It was pointless to add that the wind was only a breeze. To tack and wear with speed you required the sails drawing well. Wind and canvas were the stuff of a frigate.

Rhodes climbed up to the quarterdeck and glanced curiously at the smudge of land beyond the bowsprit. He was wearing his best sword, one which had belonged to his father. Bolitho thought of the old sword which his father wore. It appeared in most of the portraits of the Bolitho family at Falmouth. It was destined to be Hugh's one day, very soon now if his father was coming home for good. He turned away from Jury and Rhodes. Somehow, he did not have the feeling he would live to see it again. He was alarmed to discover he could accept it.

Palliser came back and said sharply, 'Tell Mr Timbrell to rig a halter from the main-yard, Mr Bolitho.' He met their combined stares. 'Well?'

Rhodes shrugged awkwardly. 'Sorry, sir. I just thought that at a time like this. . . .'

Palliser snapped, 'At a time like this, as you put it, one more corpse will hardly make much difference!'

Bolitho sent Jury for the boatswain and thought about Spillane and what he had done. He had had plenty of opportunity to steal information and pass it ashore in Rio or Basseterre. Like the captain's coxswain, the clerk was more free than most to move as he pleased.

Garrick must have had agents and spies everywhere, maybe even at the Admiralty where one of them had followed every move towards putting *Destiny* to sea. When the ship had made ready to sail from Plymouth, Spillane had been there. It would have been easy for him to discover the whereabouts of Dumaresq's recruiting parties. He had only to read the posters.

Now, like lines on a chart, they had all been drawn here to this place. A cross on Gulliver's calculations and bearings. Something destined rather than planned.

Most of the men on deck looked up as the boatswain's party lowered a hangman's noose from the main-yard to the gangway. Like Rhodes, they would have little stomach for a summary execution. It was outside their code of battle, their understanding of justice.

Bolitho heard one of the helmsmen mutter, 'Cap'n's comin' up, sir.'

Bolitho turned to face the companionway as Dumaresq, wearing a freshly laundered shirt, with his gold-laced hat set firmly on his head, strode on to the quarterdeck.

He nodded to each of his officers and the men on watch, while to Colpoys, who was attempting to draw himself to attention, he said curtly, 'Save your strength, you obstinate redcoat!'

Gulliver touched his hat. 'Nor' by east, sir. Wind's still light though.'

Dumaresq eyed him impassively. 'I can see that.'

He turned to Bolitho. 'Have the hands lay aft at six bells to witness punishment. Inform the master-at-arms and the surgeon, if you please.' He waited, watching Bolitho's emotions and his efforts to conceal them. 'You've still not learned deceit, it seems?' One of his feet tapped on the deck. 'What is it, the execution?'

'Yes, sir. It's like an omen. A superstition. I – I'm not sure what I mean.'

'Evidently.' Dumaresq walked to the rail and looked along the upper deck. 'That man tried to betray us, just as he attempted to destroy Murray and all he believed in. Murray was a good man, whereas —' He broke off to watch some marines beginning a slow climb to the fore and main-tops.

'I'd like to have seen Murray before he left, sir.'

Dumaresq asked sharply, 'Why?'

Bolitho was surprised at Dumaresq's reaction. 'I wanted to thank him.'

'Oh. That.'

Midshipman Henderson made all of them look up. 'Deck there! Ship standing out from the island, sir!'

Dumaresq dug his chin into his neckcloth. 'A last.'

He saw Midshipman Merrett by the mizzen. 'Go and fetch the Articles of War from my servant. We'll get this matter over with and then clear for action.'

He patted his scarlet waistcoat and gave a soft belch. 'That was a nice piece of pork. And the wine will help to start the day.' He saw Bolitho's uncertainty. 'Bring up the prisoner. I'd like him to see his master's ship before he swings, God rot him.'

Sergeant Barmouth placed a line of marines across the poop, and as the pipe for all hands to lay aft and witness punishment echoed between decks, Spillane, escorted by the master-at-arms and Corporal Dyer, appeared from the forecastle.

The seamen, already stripped to their trousers and ready for the drums to beat to quarters, parted to allow the little group through.

Beneath the quarterdeck rail they halted, and Poynter reported harshly, 'The prisoner, sir!'

Bolitho made himself look at Spillane's upturned face. If anything, it was completely empty, as if the neat and usually composed man was unable to accept what had happened.

Bolitho recalled how Spillane had come to his cabin with the message from *Aurora*, and wondered how much he had passed on to Garrick.

Dumaresq waited for his officers to remove their hats and then said in his resonant voice, 'You know why you are here, Spillane. Had you been a pressed man, or one forced into the King's service against your will it might have been different. You, however, volunteered, knowing you were intending to betray your oath and where possible bring disaster to your ship and your companions. Yours was a conspiracy to commit murder on a grand scale. Look yonder, man.'

When Spillane remained stricken and staring at him, Dumaresq snapped, 'Master-at-arms!' Poynter gripped the prisoner's chin and swung him round towards the bows.

'That ship is commanded by your master, Piers Garrick. Take a long look, and ask yourself now if the price of treachery was worthwhile!'

But Spillane's eyes were fixed on the swaying halter. It was doubtful if he saw anything else.

'Deck there!' Henderson's normally powerful voice sounded unsteady, as if he was afraid of breaking into the drama below him.

Dumaresq glared up at him. 'Speak, man!'

'The *San Augustin* has corpses hanging from her yards, sir!'

Dumaresq swarmed into the shrouds, snatching a telescope from Jury as he passed.

Then he climbed down to the deck very slowly and said, 'They are the ship's Spanish officers.' He darted a quick glance at Bolitho. 'Hung there as a warning, no doubt.'

But Bolitho had seen something else in Dumaresq's eyes. Just briefly, it had been relief, but why? What had he expected to see?

Dumaresq returned to the quarterdeck rail and replaced his hat. Then he said, 'Remove that halter from the main-yard, Mr Timbrell. Master-at-arms, put the prisoner down. He will await judgment with the others.'

Spillane's legs seemed to collapse under him. He clasped his hands together and said brokenly, 'Thank you, sir! The Lord bless you for your kindness!'

'Stand up, you bloody hound!' Dumaresq looked at him with disgust. 'To think that men like Garrick can corrupt others so easily. By hanging you, I would have been no better than he. But hear me. You will be able to listen to our progress today, and I suspect that will be an even greater punishment!'

As Spillane was hustled away, Palliser said bitterly, 'If we sink, that bugger will reach the bottom first!'

Dumaresq clapped him on the shoulder. 'Very true! Now, beat to quarters, if you will, and try to knock two minutes off your time!'

'Ship cleared for action, sir!' Palliser touched his hat, his eyes gleaming. 'Eight minutes exactly.'

Dumaresq lowered his telescope and glanced at him. 'Short-handed we may be, but each man-jack is working the harder for it.'

Bolitho stood below the quarterdeck watching his gun-crews by their tackles, seemingly relaxed, although the waiting was far from over.

The distant ship had spread more sail to stand well clear of the island, but as *Destiny* lifted and fell gently in the swell, the *San Augustin* appeared to be motionless. Would she turn and run for it? There was always a chance her stern-chasers might cripple the pursuing frigate with a lucky shot.

Midshipman Henderson, isolated from the preparations far below his perch, had reported that two other sail had cleared the lagoon. One was the topsail schooner, and Bolitho wondered how Dumaresq could be so sure Garrick was in the big man-of-war and not in the schooner. Perhaps he and Dumaresq were too much alike after all. Neither wishing to be a spectator, each eager to inflict a quick and undeniable victory.

Little walked slowly behind the starboard battery of twelve-pounders, stooping occasionally to check a tackle or to ensure that the ship's boys had sanded the decks sufficiently to prevent the crews from slipping when the pace grew warm.

Stockdale was at his own gun, his men dwarfed by his great bulk as he cradled a twelve-pound ball in his hands before replacing it in the shot-garland and selecting another. In a manner born, Bolitho thought. He had often seen old gun-captains do it. To make certain the first shots would be perfect. After the opening broadsides it was usually each crew to itself and devil take the hindmost.

He heard Gulliver say, 'We have the wind-gage, sir. We can always shorten sail if the enemy comes about.'

He was probably speaking merely to release his own anxieties or to await a suggestion from the captain. But Dumaresq remained silent, watching his adversary, glancing occasionally at the masthead pendant or the sluggish wave curling back from *Destiny*'s bows.

Bolitho looked forward and saw Rhodes speaking with Cowdroy and some of his gun-captains. The waiting was endless. It was what he expected, but he never grew used to it.

'The schooners have luffed, sir!'

Dumaresq grunted. 'Hanging back like jackals.'

Bolitho climbed to peer over the gangway which ran above the starboard battery to link quarterdeck to forecastle. Even with the packed hammock nettings and the nets spread above the deck there was little enough protection for the seamen, he thought.

Almost the worst part was the empty boat-tier. Apart from the gig and the quarter-boat towing astern, the rest had been left drifting in an untidy line. In action, flying splinters were one of the greatest hazards, and the boats made a tempting target. But to see them cast adrift put the seal on what they had to face.

Henderson called, 'The corpses have been cut down, sir!' He sounded hoarse from strain.

Dumaresq said to Palliser, 'Like so much meat. God damn his eyes!'

Palliser answered evenly, 'Maybe he wishes to see *you* angry, sir?'

'Provoke me?' Dumaresq's anger faded before it could spread. 'You could be right. Hell's teeth, Mr Palliser, it should be Parliament for you, not the Navy!'

Midshipman Jury stood with his hands behind his back watching the far-off ship, his hat tilted over his eyes as he had seen Bolitho do.

He said suddenly, 'Will they try to close with us, sir?'

'Probably. They have the numbers. From what we saw on the island, I would guess they outmatch us by ten to one.' He saw the dismay on Jury's face and added lightly, 'The captain will hole them off. Hit and run. Wear them down.'

He glanced up at Dumaresq by the rail and wondered. No emotion, and yet he must be scheming and planning for every possible set-back. Even his voice was as usual.

Jury said, 'The other two craft could be dangerous.'

'The topsail schooner maybe. The other one is too light to risk a close encounter.'

He thought of what would have happened but for their desperate action on the island. Was it only yesterday? There would have been six schooners instead of two, and the forty-four-gun *San Augustin* might have had time to mount more guns, maybe those from the hill-top battery. Now, whatever the outcome, their captured schooner would carry Dumaresq's despatches to the admiral at Antigua. Too late for them perhaps, but they would ensure that Garrick remained a hunted man for the rest of his life.

How clear the sky looked. Not yet too hot to be oppressive. The sea too was creamy and inviting. He tried not to think of that other time, when he had pictured himself running and swimming with her, finding happiness together, making it last.

Dumaresq said loudly. 'They will attempt to dismast us and lay us open to boarding. It is likely that the larger of the schooners has been armed with some heavier pieces. So make each shot tell. Remember that many of their gun-crews and seamen are Spaniards. Terrified of Garrick they may be, but they'll not wish to be pounded to gruel by you!'

His words brought a murmur of approval from the bare-backed gun-crews.

There was a ragged crash of cannon-fire, and Bolitho turned to see the *San Augustin*'s starboard guns shoot out long orange tongues, while the smoke rolled over the ship and partially hid the island beyond.

The sea foamed and shot skywards, as if the power was coming from beneath the surface instead of from the proud ship with the scarlet crosses on her courses.

Stockdale said, 'Rough.'

Several of the seamen around him shook their fists towards the enemy, although at three miles range it was unlikely anyone would see them.

Rhodes strolled aft, his beautiful sword at odds with his faded sea-going coat.

He said, 'Just to keep them busy, eh, Dick?'

Bolitho nodded. Rhodes was probably right, but there was something very menacing about the Spanish vessel for all that. Perhaps because of her extravagant beauty, the richness of her gilded carvings which even distance could not conceal.

He said, 'If only the wind would come.'

Rhodes shrugged. 'If only we were in Plymouth.'

Another broadside spouted from the Spaniard's hull, and some balls ricocheted across the sea's face and seemed to go on forever.

There was an even louder shout of derision, but Bolitho saw some of the senior gun-captains looking worried. The enemy's iron was dropping short and was not that well directed, but as both vessels were moving so slowly on what would likely remain a converging tack, it made each barrage more dangerous.

He pictured Bulkley and his loblolly boys on the shadowy orlop deck, the glittering instruments, the brandy to take away the agony, the leather strap to prevent a man biting through his tongue as the surgeon's saw did its work.

And Spillane, in irons below the waterline, what was he thinking as the thunder rolled against the timbers around him?

'Stand by on deck!' Palliser was staring down at the double line of guns. 'Run in and load!'

This was the moment. With fixed concentration each gun-captain watched as his men put their weight on the tackles and hauled them away from the sides.

Bulky cartridges were passed rapidly to each muzzle and rammed home by the loader.

Bolitho watched the one nearest to him as he gave the cartridge in his gun two extra sharp taps to bed it in. His face was so set, so absorbed, that it was as if he was about to take on an enemy single-handed. Then the wad, followed by a gleaming black ball for each gun. One more wad rammed down, just in case the ship should give an unexpected roll and tip the ball harmlessly into the sea, and they were done.

When Bolitho looked up again, the other ship seemed to have drawn much closer.

'Ready on deck!'

Each gun-captain held up his hand.

Palliser shouted, 'Open the ports!' He waited, counting seconds, as the port-lids rose along either side like re-awakened eyes. '*Run out!*'

The *San Augustin* fired again, but her master had let her fall off to the wind and the whole broadside fell a good half mile from *Destiny*'s larboard bow.

Rhodes was striding behind his guns, giving instructions or merely joking with his men, Bolitho could not tell.

With *San Augustin* now lying off their larboard bow on an invisible arrowhead, it was hard to keep his crews busy and prevent them from standing to look to the opposite side to see what was happening.

Palliser called, 'Mr Bolitho! Be ready to send some of your hands across to assist. Two broadsides and we will alter course to larboard and allow your guns a similar chance.'

Bolitho waved his hands. 'Aye, sir!'

Dumaresq said, 'Alter course three points to starboard.'

'Man the braces there! Helm a-weather!'

With her canvas flapping and cracking, *Destiny* responded, the *San Augustin* seeming to go astern as she showed herself to the crouching gun-captains.

'Full elevation! *Fire!*'

The twelve-pounders hurled themselves inboard on their tackles, the smoke rolling downwind towards the enemy in a frothing screen.

'Stop your vents!' Rhodes was striding more quickly now. 'Sponge out and load!'

The gun-captains had to work doubly hard, using a fist or two if necessary to contain their men's excitement. To put a charge into an unsponged barrel where some smouldering remains from the first shot were still inside was inviting sudden and horrible death.

Stockdale pounded the breeching-ring of his gun. 'Come on, boys! *Come on!*'

'Run out!' Palliser was resting his telescope on the hammock nettings to study the other ship. 'As you bear! *Fire!*'

This time the broadside was uneven, with each captain taking his time, choosing his own moment. But before they could watch the fall of shot men were already dashing to braces and halliards, while aft Gulliver urged his helmsmen to greater efforts as *Destiny* changed tack, standing as close to the wind as possible without losing her manoeuvrability.

Bolitho's mouth had gone dry. Without noticing he had drawn his hanger and was holding it to his hip as the deck tilted, and then slowly but steadily his gun-captains saw *San Augustin*'s gilded beak-head edge across their open ports.

'On the uproll!'

San Augustin's side erupted in darting tongues, and Bolitho heard the wild shriek of langridge or chain-shot passing high overhead. He found time to pity Midshipman Henderson clinging to the cross-trees with his telescope trained on the enemy while the murderous tangle of chain and iron bars swept past him.

'*Fire!*'

Bolitho saw the sea bursting with spray around the other ship, and thought he saw her main-course quiver as at least one ball ploughed through it.

As his men threw themselves on handspikes and rammers, yelling for powder and shot, oblivious to everything but the hungry muzzles and Palliser's voice from the quarterdeck, Bolitho glanced at the captain.

He was with Gulliver and Slade beside the compass, pointing at the enemy, the sails, at the drifting smoke, as if he held every act and each consequence in his palm.

'*Fire!*'

Down *Destiny*'s starboard side, gun by gun, the twelve-pounders crashed inboard, their trucks squealing like enraged hogs.

'Stand by to alter course! Be ready, Mr Rhodes! Larboard battery load with double-shot!'

Bolitho ducked away from running seamen and bellowing petty

officers. Their constant, aching drills on the long passage from Plymouth had taught them well. No matter what the guns were doing, the ship had to be worked and kept afloat.

Once again the guns roared out their challenge, a different sound this time, jarring and painful, as the double-shotted barrels responded to their charges.

Bolitho wiped his face with his wrist. He felt as if he had been in the sun for hours. In fact, it was barely eight bells. One hour since Spillane had been sent below.

Dumaresq was taking a risk to double-shot his guns. But Bolitho had seen the two schooners working their way to windward, as if to close with *Destiny* from astern. They had to hit *San Augustin*, and hit her hard, if only to slow her down.

Dumaresq shouted, 'Fetch the gunner! Lively there!'

Bolitho winced as water cascaded over the opposite gangway, and he felt the hull jump to a massive pounding. Two hits at least, perhaps on the waterline.

But the boatswain was already yelling orders, and his men were running past the marine sentries who guarded each hatchway, to examine the hull and to shore up any damage.

He saw the gunner, blinking like an owl in the sunlight, his face creased with anger at being called from his magazine and powder rooms even by the captain.

'Mr Vallance!' Dumaresq's face was split in a fierce grin. 'You were once the best gun-captain in the Channel Fleet, is that not so?'

Vallance shuffled his felt slippers, very necessary footware to avoid kicking up sparks in so lethal a place as the magazine.

'That be true, sir. No doubt on it.' Despite the noise, he was obviously pleased to be so remembered.

'Well, I want you to personally take charge of the bow-chasers and put paid to that topsail schooner. I'll bring the ship about.' He kept his voice level. 'You'll have to look alive.'

Vallance shuffled away, jerking his thumb to beckon two of the gun-captains from Bolitho's battery without even asking permission. Vallance was the best of his kind, even if he was usually a taciturn man. He did not need Dumaresq to elaborate. For when *Destiny* tacked round to engage the schooners she would present her full length to the enemy's broadside.

Destiny's bow-chasers were nine-pounders. Although not as powerful as several other naval guns, the nine-pounder was always considered to be the most accurate.

'*Fire!*'

Rhodes's crews were sponging out again, and the seamen shone with sweat which cut runnels through the powder-dirt on their bodies like marks of a lash.

The range was less than two miles, and when Bolitho looked up he saw several holes in the main-topsail and a few seamen working to replace some broken rigging while the battle raged across the narrowing strip of water.

Vallance was up in the bows now, and Bolitho could picture his grizzled head bobbing over the larboard nine-pounder, remembering perhaps when he had been a gun-captain himself.

Dumaresq's voice cut through a brief lull in the firing. 'When you are ready, Mr Palliser. It will mean five points to larboard.' He pounded his fists together. 'If only the wind would come!' He thrust his hands behind him again as if to control their agitation. 'Loose the t'gan'sls!'

Moments later, answering as best she could to the flapping canvas, *Destiny* tacked round to larboard, and in seconds, or so it seemed, the schooners lay across her bows.

Bolitho heard the crash of a nine-pounder, and then the other on the opposite bow as Vallance fired.

The topsail schooner seemed to stagger, as if she had run headlong on to a reef. Foremast, sails and yard all crumpled together to swamp her forecastle and slew her round out of command.

Dumaresq yelled, 'Break off the action! Bring her about, Mr Palliser!'

Bolitho knew that the second schooner was hardly likely to risk sharing her consort's fate. It was a masterful piece of gunlaying. He saw his men sliding down the stays to the deck after setting the extra sails, and wondered how *Destiny* would appear to the enemy's gun-crews as they peered through the smoke and saw one of their number crippled so easily.

It would hardly affect the difference of armament between the two ships, but it would put heart into the British seamen when they most needed it.

'Steady as she goes! Nor' by east, sir!'

Bolitho shouted, 'It'll be our turn next!' He saw several of the seamen turn to grin at him, their faces like masks, their eyes glazed by the constant crash of gunfire.

The deck seemed to leap beneath Bolitho's feet, and with astonishment he saw a twelve-pounder from the opposite battery toppled on to its side, two men crushed and screaming under it, while others ducked or fell sprawling to flying splinters.

He heard Rhodes yelling to restore order and the responding bang of several guns, but the damage had been bad, and as Timbrell's men ran to haul away the broken timber and upended gun, the enemy fired again.

Bolitho had no way of knowing how many of *San Augustin*'s shots found their mark, but the deck shook so violently he knew it was a massive weight of iron. Woodwork and pieces of broken metal clattered around him, and he covered his face with his arms as a great shadow swooped over the deck.

Stockdale pulled him down and croaked, 'Mizzen! They've shot it away!'

Then came the thundering crash as the complete mizzenmast and spars scythed across the quarterdeck and down over the starboard gangway, snapping rigging and entangling men as it went.

Bolitho staggered to his feet and looked for the enemy. But she seemed to have changed position, her upper yards misting over as she continued to shoot. *Destiny* was listing, the mizzen dragging her round as men ran and stumbled amongst the tangled rigging, their ears too defeaned by the noise to react to their orders.

Dumaresq came to the quarterdeck rail and retrieved his hat from his coxswain. He glanced quickly around the upper deck and then said, 'More hands aft! Cut that wreckage clear!'

Palliser seemed to rise out of the chaos like a spectre. He was gripping his arm which appeared to be broken, and he looked as if he might collapse.

Dumaresq roared, '*Move yourselves!* And another ensign to the mainmast, Mr Lovelace!'

But it was a boatswain's mate who swarmed up the shrouds through the smoke to replace the ensign which had been shot down with the mizzen. Midshipman Lovelace, who would have been fourteen years old in two weeks' time, lay by the nettings, torn almost in half by a trailing backstay.

Bolitho realized that he had been standing quite motionless while the ship swayed and shuddered about him to the jar of gun-fire.

He grasped Jury's shoulder and said. 'Take ten men and assist the boatswain!' He shook him gently. 'All right?'

Jury smiled. 'Yes, sir.' He ran off into the smoke, calling names as he went.

Stockdale muttered. 'We've less than six guns which'll bear on this side!'

Bolitho knew that *Destiny* would be out of control until the mizzen was hacked free. Over the side he could see a marine still clinging to the mizzen-top, another drowning as he watched, dragged under by the great web of rigging. He turned and looked at Dumaresq as he stood like a rock, directing the helmsmen, watching his enemy and making sure his own company could see him there.

Bolitho tore his eyes away. He felt shocked and guilty, as if he had accidentally stolen Dumaresq's secret.

So that was why he wore a scarlet waistcoat. So that none of his men should see.

But Bolitho had seen the fresh, wet stains on it which had run down on to his strong hands as his coxswain, Johns, supported him by the rail.

Midshipman Cowdroy clambered over the debris and yelled, 'I need more help forrard, sir!' He looked near to panic.

Bolitho said, 'Deal with it!' What Dumaresq had said to him about the stolen watch. *Deal with it.*

Axes rang through the smoke, and he felt the deck lurch upright as the broken mast and attendant rigging drifted clear of the side.

How bare it seemed without it and its spread of canvas.

With a start he realized that *San Augustin* lay directly across the bows. She was still firing, but *Destiny*'s change of direction which had been caused by the mizzen dragging her round, made her a difficult target. Balls slammed down close to the side or splashed in the sea on either beam. *Destiny*'s guns were also blind, except for the bow-chasers, and Bolitho heard their sharper explosions as they reopened fire in deadly earnest.

But another heavy ball smashed under the larboard gangway, toppling two guns and painting the decks red as it cut down a group of men already wounded.

Bolitho saw Rhodes fall, try to recover his stand by the guns and then drop to his side.

He ran to help him, shielding him from the billowing gun-smoke as the world went mad around them.

Rhodes looked directly at him, his eyes free of pain, as he whispered, 'The lord and master had his way, you see, Dick?' He looked up at the sky behind the rigging. 'The wind. Here at last but too late.' He reached up to touch Bolitho's shoulder. 'Take care. I always knew. . . .' His eyes became fixed and without understanding.

Blindly Bolitho stood up and stared around at the destruction and the pain. Stephen Rhodes was dead. The one who had first made him feel welcome, who had taken life at face value, day at a time.

Then, beyond the broken nettings and punctured hammocks he saw the sea. The sluggish swell was gone. He peered up at the sails. Holed they might by, but they were thrusting out like breast-plates as they pushed the frigate forward into the fight. They had not been beaten. Rhodes had seen it, *the wind*, he had said. The last thing he had understood on this earth.

He ran to the side and saw *San Augustin* startlingly close, right there on the starboard bow. Men were shooting at him, there was smoke and noise all around, but he felt nothing. Close to, the enemy ship was no longer so proud and invulnerable, and he could see where *Destiny*'s claws had left their mark.

He heard Dumaresq's voice following him along the deck, commanding, all powerful even in its pain. '*Ready to starboard, Mr Bolitho!*'

Bolitho snatched up Rhodes's beautiful sword and waved it wildly. '*Stand to! Double-shotted, lads!*'

Musket-balls hammered across the decks like pebbles, and here and there a man fell. But the rest, dragging themselves from the wreckage and leaving Rhodes's guns on the larboard side, shambled to obey. To load the remaining twelve-pounders, to crouch like dazed animals as foot by foot the *San Augustin*'s towering stern loomed over them like a gilded cliff.

'*As you bear!*'

Who was shouting the orders? Dumaresq, Palliser, or was he himself so stunned by the ferocity of the battle that he had called them himself?

'*Fire!*'

He saw the guns sliding inboard, the way their crews just stood and watched the destruction as every murderous ball ploughed through the Spanish man-of-war from stern to bow.

None of the gun-captains, not even Stockdale, made any attempt to reload. It was as if each man knew.

The *San Augustin* was drifting downwind, perhaps her steering shot away, or her officers killed by the last deadly embrace.

Bolitho walked slowly aft and on to the quarterdeck. Wood splinters were everywhere, and there were few men left at the six-pounders to cheer as some of the enemy's rigging collapsed in a welter of sparks and smoke.

Dumaresq turned stiffly and looked at him. 'I think she's afire.'

Bolitho saw Gulliver, dead by his helmsmen, and Slade in his place, as if he had been meant for master from the beginning. Colpoys, his red coat over his bandaged wounds like a cape, watching his men standing back from their weapons. Palliser, sitting on a cask, while one of Bulkley's men examined his arm.

He heard himself say, 'We'll lose the treasure, sir.'

An explosion shook the stricken *San Augustin*, and figures could be seen jumping over the side and trampling down anyone who tried to stop them.

Dumaresq looked down at his red waistcoat. 'So will they.'

Bolitho watched the other ship and saw the smoke thickening, the first glint of fire beneath her mainmast. If Garrick was still alive, he would not get far now.

Bulkley arrived on the quarterdeck and said, 'You must come below, Captain. I have to examine you.'

'*Must!*' Dumaresq gave his fierce grin. 'It is not a word I choose —' Then he fainted in his coxswain's arms.

After all that had happened it seemed unbearable. Bolitho watched as Dumaresq's body was picked up and carried carefully to the companionway.

Palliser joined him by the quarterdeck rail. He looked ashen but said, 'We'll stand off until that ship either sinks or blows up.'

'What shall I do, sir?' It was Midshipman Henderson, who had somehow survived the whole battle at the masthead.

Palliser looked at him. 'You will assume Mr Bolitho's duties.' He hesitated, his eyes on Rhodes's body by the foremast. 'Mr Bolitho will be second lieutenant.'

A greater explosion than all the previous ones shook *San Augustin* so violently that her fore and main-topmasts toppled into the smoke and the hull itself began to turn turtle.

Jury climbed up and joined Bolitho to watch the last moments of the ornate ship.

'Was it worth it, sir?'

Bolitho looked at him and at the ship around them. Already there were men working to put the damage to rights, to make the ship live again. There were a thousand things to do, wounded to care for, the remaining schooner chased and caught, prisoners to be rescued and separated from the Spanish sailors. A great deal of work for one small ship and her company, he thought.

He considered Jury's question, what it had all cost, and what they had discovered in each other. He thought too of what Dumaresq would have to say when he returned to duty. That was a strange thing about Dumaresq. Dying was like defeat, you could never associate it with him.

Bolitho said quietly, 'You must never ask that. I've learned, and I'm still learning. The ship comes first. Now let's be about it, otherwise the lord and master will have harsh words for all of us.'

Startled, he looked at the sword he still grasped in his hand.

Perhaps Rhodes had answered Jury's question for him?

Epilogue

Bolitho tugged his hat down over his eyes and looked up at the great grey house. There was a squall blowing up the Channel, and the rain which stung his cheeks felt like ice. All the months, all the waiting, and now he was home again. It had been a long, hard journey from Plymouth after *Destiny* had dropped her anchor. The roads were deeply rutted, and there had been so much mud thrown up on the coach windows Bolitho had found it difficult to recognize places which he had known since boyhood.

And now that he was back again he felt a sense of unreality, and, for some reason he could not determine, one of loss.

The house was unchanged, just as it had looked when he had last seen it, almost a year ago.

Stockdale, who had driven with him from Plymouth, shifted his feet uncertainly.

'Are you sure it's all right fer me to be 'ere, sir?'

Bolitho looked at him. It had been Dumaresq's last gesture before he had left the ship, before *Destiny* had been put into the hands of the dockyard for repair and a well-deserved overhaul.

'Take Stockdale. You'll be getting another ship soon. Keep him with you. A useful fellow.'

Bolitho said quietly, 'You're welcome here. You'll see.'

He climbed up the worn stone steps and saw the double-doors swing inward to greet him. Bolitho was not surprised, he had felt in the last few moments that the whole house had been silently watching him.

But it was not old Mrs Tremayne the housekeeper but a young maidservant he did not recognize.

She curtsied and blushed. 'Welcome, zur.' Almost in the same breath she added, 'Cap'n James is waitin' for you, zur.'

Bolitho stamped the mud from his shoes and gave the girl his hat and boat-cloak.

He strode through the panelled hall and stepped into the big room he knew so well. There was the fire, blazing brightly as if to hold the winter at bay, gleaming pewter, the filtered smells from the kitchen, security.

Captain James Bolitho moved from the fire and put his hand on his son's shoulder.

'My God, Richard, I saw you last as a scrawny midshipman. You've come home a man!'

Bolitho was shocked by his father's appearance. He had steeled himself against the loss of an arm, but his father had changed beyond belief. His hair was grey and his eyes were sunken. Because of his sewn-up sleeve he was holding himself awkwardly, something Bolitho had seen other crippled sailors do, fearful of having someone brush against the place where a limb had been.

'Sit down, my boy.' He watched Bolitho fixedly, as if afraid of missing something. 'That's a terrible scar you have there. I must hear all about it.' But there was no enthusiasm in his voice. 'Who was that giant I saw you arrive with?'

Bolitho gripped the arms of his chair. 'A man called Stockdale.'

He was suddenly aware of the quiet, the deadly, clinging silence.

He asked, 'Tell me, Father. Is something wrong?'

His father walked to a window and stared unseeingly through the sleet-washed glass.

'There have been letters, of course. They'll catch up with you one day.' He turned heavily. 'Your mother died a month ago, Richard.'

Bolitho stared at him, unable to move, unwilling to accept it.

'Died?'

'She had a short illness. A fever of sorts. We did all we could.'

Bolitho said quietly, 'I think I knew. Just now. Outside the house. She always gave the place light.'

Dead. He had been planning what he was going to tell her, how he would have quietened her concern over his scar.

His father said distantly, 'Your ship was reported some days back.'

'Yes. Then fog came down. We had to anchor.'

He thought suddenly of the faces he had left, how much he needed them at this moment. Dumaresq, who had gone to the Admiralty to explain the loss of the treasure, or to be congratulated for depriving a potential enemy of it. Palliser, who had got his command of a brig at Spithead. Young Jury, with a break in his voice when they had shaken hands for the last time.

'I heard of some of your exploits. It sounds as if Dumaresq made quite a name for himself. I hope the Admiralty see it that way. Your brother is away with the fleet.'

Bolitho tried to contain his emotion. Words, just words. He had known his father would be like this. Pride. It was always a question of pride with him, first and foremost.

'Is Nancy at home?'

His father looked at him distantly. 'You won't know that either. Your sister married the squire's son, young Lewis Roxby. Your mother said it was on the rebound after that other wretched business.' He sighed. 'So there it is.'

Bolitho leaned back against the chair, pressing his shoulders against the carved oak to control his sorrow.

His father had lost the sea. Now he was alone, too. This great house which looked across the slopes of Pendennis Castle or out across the busy comings and goings of Carrick Roads. Each a constant reminder of what he had lost, of what had been taken from him.

He said gently, '*Destiny* has paid off, Father. I can stay.'

It was as if he had shouted some terrible oath. Captain James strode from the window and stood looking down at him.

'I never want to hear that! You are *my* son and a King's officer. For generations we've left this house, and some have never come back. There's war in the air, and we'll need all our sons.' He paused and added softly, 'A messenger came here just two days back. An appointment already.'

Bolitho stood up and moved about the room, touching familiar things without feeling them.

His father added, 'She's the *Trojan*, eighty guns. There's going to be a war right enough if they're recommissioning *her*.'

'I see.'

Not a lithe frigate, but another great ship of the line. A new world to explore and master. Perhaps it was just as well. Something to fill his mind, to keep him busy until he could accept all which had happened.

'Now I think we should take a glass together, Richard. Ring for the girl. You must tell me all about it. The ship, her people, everything. Leave nothing out. It's all I have now. Memories.'

Bolitho said, 'Well, Father, it was a year ago when I joined *Destiny* at Plymouth under Captain Dumaresq. . . .'

When the young maidservant entered with the glasses and wine from the cellar, she saw the grey-headed Captain James sitting opposite his youngest son. They were talking about ships and foreign parts. There was no sign of grief or despair in their reunion.

But she did not understand. It was all a question of pride.

IN
GALLANT
COMPANY

I

Show of Strength

The stiff offshore wind, which had backed slightly to the north-west during the day, swept across New York's naval anchorage, bringing no release from the chilling cold and the threat of more snow.

Tugging heavily at her anchor cables, His Britannic Majesty's Ship *Trojan* of eighty guns might appear to a landsman's unpractised eye as indifferent to both wind and water. But to the men who continued with their work about her decks, or high above them on the slippery yards and rigging, her swaying motion made her anything but that.

It was March 1777, but to Lieutenant Richard Bolitho, officer of the afternoon watch, it felt like midwinter. It will be dark early, he thought, and the ship's boats would have to be checked, their moorings doubly secured before night closed in completely.

He shivered, not so much because of the cold, but because he knew there would be little relief from it once he was allowed to go below. For despite her massive size and armament, the *Trojan*, a two-decked ship of the line, whose complement of six hundred and fifty officers, seamen and marines lived out their lives within her fat hull, had no more than the galley fires and body-warmth to sustain them, no matter what the elements might do.

Bolitho raised his telescope and trained it towards the fading waterfront. As the lens passed over other anchored ships of the line, frigates and the general clutter of small supporting craft he found time to wonder at the change. It had been just last summer when *Trojan*, in company with a great fleet of one hundred and thirty ships, had anchored here, off Staten Island. After the shock of the actual revolution within the American colonies, the occupation of New York and Philadelphia with such a show of force had seemed to those involved as a start on the way back, a compromise.

It had been such a simple and leisurely affair at the time. After placing his troops under canvas along the green shoreline of Staten Island,

General Howe, with a token force of infantry, had gone ashore to take possession. All the preparations by the Continentals and local militia had come to nothing, and even the Staten Island force of four hundred men, who had been commanded by General Washington to defend the redoubts at all costs, had grounded their muskets and obligingly sworn allegiance to the Crown.

Bolitho lowered the glass as it blurred in drifting snow. It was hard to recall the green island and crowds of onlookers, the Loyalists cheering, the rest watching in grim silence. Now all the colours were in shades of grey. The land, the tossing water, even the ships seemed to have lost their brightness in the persistent and lingering winter.

He took a few paces this way and that across *Trojan*'s spacious quarterdeck, his shoes slipping on the planking, his damp clothing tugging at him in the wind. He had been in the ship for two years. It was beginning to feel a lifetime. Like many others throughout the fleet, he had felt mixed feelings at the news of the revolution. Surprise and shock. Sympathy and then anger. And above all the sense of helplessness.

The revolution, which had begun as a mixture of individual ideals, had soon developed into something real and challenging. The war was like nothing they had known before. Big ships of the line like *Trojan* moved ponderously from one inflamed incident to another, and were well able to cope with anything which was careless enough to stray under their massive broadsides. But the real war was one of communications and supply, of small, fast vessels, sloops, brigs and schooners. And throughout the long winter months, while the overworked ships of the inshore squadrons had patrolled and probed some fifteen hundred miles of coastline, the growing strength of the Continentals had been further aided by Britain's old enemy, France. Not openly as yet, but it would not be long before the many French privateers which hunted from the Canadian border to the Caribbean showed their true colours. After that, Spain too would be a quick if unwilling ally. Her trade routes from the Spanish Main were perhaps the longest of all, and with little love for England anyway, she would likely take the easiest course.

All this and more Bolitho had heard and discussed over and over again until he was sick of it. Whatever the news, good or bad, the *Trojan*'s role seemed to be getting smaller. Like a rock she remained here in harbour for weeks on end, her company resentful, the officers hoping for a chance to leave her and find their fortunes in swifter, more independent ships.

Bolitho thought of his last ship, the twenty-eight-gun frigate *Destiny*. Even as her junior lieutenant, and barely used to the sea-change from midshipman's berth to wardroom, he had found excitement and satisfaction beyond belief.

He stamped his feet on the wet planks, seeing the watchkeepers at the opposite side jerk round with alarm. Now he was fourth lieutenant of this great, anchored mammoth, and looked like remaining so.

Trojan would be better off in the Channel Fleet, he thought. Manoeuvres and showing the flag to the watchful French, and whenever possible slipping ashore to Plymouth or Portsmouth to meet old friends.

Bolitho turned as familiar footsteps crossed the deck from the poop. It was Cairns, the first lieutenant, who like most of the others had been aboard since the ship had recommissioned in 1775 after being laid up in Bristol where she had originally been built.

Cairns was tall, lean and very self-contained. If he too was pining over the next step in his career, a command of his own perhaps, he never showed it. He rarely smiled, but nevertheless was a man of great charm. Bolitho both liked and respected him, and often wondered what he thought of the captain.

Cairns paused, biting his lower lip, as he peered up at the towering criss-cross of shrouds and running rigging. Thinly coated with clinging snow, the yards looked like the branches of gaunt pines.

He said, 'The captain will be coming off soon. I'll be on call, so keep a weather-eye open.'

Bolitho nodded, gauging the moment. Cairns was twenty-eight, while he was not yet twenty-one. But the span between first and fourth lieutenant was still the greater.

He asked casually, 'Any news of our captain's mission ashore, sir?'

Cairns seemed absorbed. 'Get those topmen down, Dick. They'll be too frozen to turn-to if the weather breaks. Pass the word for the cook to break out some hot soup.' He grimaced. 'That should please the miserly bugger.' He looked at Bolitho. 'Mission?'

'Well, I thought we might be getting orders.' He shrugged. 'Or something.'

'He has been with the commander-in-chief certainly. But I doubt we'll hear anything stronger than the need for vigilance and an eye to duty!'

'I see.' Bolitho looked away. He was never sure when Cairns was being completely serious.

Cairns tugged his coat around his throat. 'Carry on, Mr Bolitho.'

They touched their hats to each other, the informality laid aside for the moment.

Bolitho called, 'Midshipman of the watch!' He saw one of the drooping figures break away from the shelter of the hammock nettings and bound towards him.

'Sir!'

It was Couzens, thirteen years old, and one of the new members of the

ship's company, having been sent out from England aboard a transport.
He was round-faced, constantly shivering, but made up for his
ignorance with a willingness which neither his superiors nor the ship
could break.

Bolitho told him about the cook, and the captain's expected return,
then instructed him to arrange for piping the relief for the first dog-
watch. He passed his instructions without conscious thought, but
watched Couzens instead, seeing not him but himself at that tender age.
He had been in a ship of the line, too. Chased, harried, bullied by
everyone, or so it had seemed. But he had had one hero, a lieutenant
who had probably never even noticed him as a human being. And
Bolitho had always remembered him. He had never lost his temper
without cause. Never found escape in humiliating others when he had
received a telling-off from his captain. Bolitho had hoped he would be
like that lieutenant one day. He still hoped.

Couzens nodded firmly. 'Aye, aye, sir.'

Trojan carried nine midshipmen, and Bolitho sometimes wondered
how their lives would take shape. Some would rise to flag rank, others
drop by the wayside. There would be the usual sprinkling of tyrants and
of leaders, of heroes and cowards.

Later, as the new watch was being mustered below the quarterdeck,
one of the lookouts called, 'Boat approaching, sir!' The merest pause.
''Tis the captain!'

Bolitho darted a quick glance at the milling confusion below the
quarterdeck. The captain could not have chosen a better time to catch
them all out.

He yelled, 'Pass the word for the first lieutenant! Man the side, and
call the boatswain directly!'

Men dashed hither and thither through the gloom, and while the
marines tramped stolidly to the entry port, their cross-belts very white
in the poor light, the petty officers tried to muster the relieving
watchkeepers into some sembance of order.

A boat appeared, pulling strongly towards the main chains, the
bowman already standing erect with his hook at the ready.

'Boat ahoy?'

The coxswain's cry came back instantly. *'Trojan!'*

Their lord and master was back. The man who, next to God,
controlled each hour of their lives, who could reward, flog, promote or
hang as the situation dictated, was amongst their crowded world once
more.

When Bolitho glanced round again he saw that where there had been
chaos there was order, with the marines lined up, muskets to their
shoulders, their commanding officer, the debonair Captain D'Esterre,
standing with his lieutenant, apparently oblivious to wind and cold.

The boatswain's mates were here, moistening their silver calls on their lips, and Cairns, his eyes everywhere, waited to receive his captain.

The boat hooked on to the chains, the muskets slapped and cracked to the present while the calls shrilled in piercing salute. The captain's head and shoulders rose over the side, and while he doffed his cocked hat to the quarterdeck he too examined the ship, his command, with one sweeping scrutiny.

He said curtly, 'Come aft, Mr Cairns.' He nodded to the marine officers. 'Smart turn-out, D'Esterre.' He turned abruptly and snapped, 'Why are *you* here, Mr Bolitho?' As he spoke, eight bells chimed out from the forecastle. 'You should have been relieved, surely?'

Bolitho looked at him. 'I think Mr Probyn is detained, sir.'

'Do you indeed.' The captain had a harsh voice which cut above the din of wind and creaking spars like a cutlass. 'The responsibility of watchkeeping is as much that of the relief as the one awaiting it.' He glanced at Cairns' impassive face. ''Pon my soul, Mr Cairns, not a difficult thing to learn, I'd have thought?'

They walked aft, and Bolitho breathed out very slowly.

Lieutenant George Probyn, his immediate superior, was often late taking over his watch, and other duties too for that matter. He was the odd man in the wardroom, morose, argumentative, bitter, although for what reason Bolitho had not yet discovered. He saw him coming up the starboard ladder, broad, untidy, peering around suspiciously.

Bolitho faced him. 'The watch is aft, Mr Probyn.'

Probyn wiped his face and then blew his nose in a red handkerchief. 'I suppose the captain was asking about me?'

Even his question sounded hostile.

'He noted you were absent.' Bolitho could smell brandy, and added, 'But he seemed satisfied enough.'

Probyn beckoned to a master's mate and scanned quickly through the deck log which the man held below a lantern.

Bolitho said wearily, 'Nothing unusual to report. One seaman injured and taken to the sick-bay. He fell from the boat tier.'

Probyn sniffed. 'Shame.' He closed his book. 'You are relieved.' He watched him broodingly. 'If I thought anyone was making *trouble* for me behind my back . . .'

Bolitho turned away, hiding his anger. Do not fret, my drunken friend. You are doing that for yourself.

Probyn's rumbling voice followed him to the companion as he put his men to their stations and allotted their tasks.

As he ran lightly down the companion ladder and made his way aft towards the wardroom, Bolitho wondered what the captain was discussing with Cairns.

Once below, the ship seemed to enfold him, contain him with her familiarity. The combined smells of tar and hemp, of bilge and packed humanity, they were as much a part of Bolitho as his own skin.

Mackenzie, the senior wardroom servant, who had ended his service as a topman when a fall from aloft had broken his leg in three places and made him a permanent cripple, met him with a cheery smile. If everyone else was sorry for him, Mackenzie at least was well satisfied. His injuries had given him as much comfort and security as any man could hope to find in a King's ship.

'I've some coffee, sir. Piping hot, too.' He had a soft Scottish accent which was very like Cairns'.

Bolitho peeled off his coat and handed it with his hat to Logan, a ship's boy who helped in the wardroom.

'I'd relish that, thank you.'

The wardroom, which ran the whole breadth of the ship's stern, was wreathed in tobacco smoke and touched with its own familiar aromas of wine and cheese. Right aft the great stern windows were already in darkness, and as the counter swung slightly to the pull of the massive anchor it was possible to see an occasional light glittering from the shore like a lost star.

Hutchlike cabins, little more than screens which would be torn down when the ship cleared for action, lined either side. Tiny havens which contained the owner's cot, chest and a small hanging space. But each was at least private. Apart from the cells, about the only place in the ship a man could be alone.

Directly above, and in a cabin which matched in size and space that which contained most of his officers, was the captain's domain. Also on that deck was the master and the first lieutenant, to be in easy reach of the quarterdeck and the helm.

But here, in the wardroom, was where they all shared their moments off-duty. Where they discussed their hopes and fears, ate their meals and took their wine. The six lieutenants, two marine officers, the sailing master, the purser and the surgeon. It was crowded certainly, but when compared with the below-the-waterline quarters of the midshipmen and other warrant officers and specialists, let alone the great majority of seamen and marines, it was luxury indeed.

Dalyell, the fifth lieutenant, sat beneath the stern windows, his legs crossed and resting on a small keg, a long clay pipe balanced in one hand.

'George Probyn adrift again, eh, Dick?'

Bolitho grinned. 'It is becoming a habit.'

Sparke, the second lieutenant, a severe-faced man with a coin-shaped scar on one cheek, said, 'I'd drag him to the captain if *I* were the senior here.' He returned to a tattered news-sheet and added vehemently, 'These damned rebels seem to do what they like! Two more transports seized from under our frigates' noses, and a brig cut out of harbour by one of their bloody privateers! We're too soft on 'em!'

Bolitho sat down and stretched, grateful to be out of the wind, even though he knew the illusion of warmth would soon pass.

His head lolled, and when Mackenzie brought the mug of coffee he had to shake his shoulder to awaken him.

In companionable silence the *Trojan*'s officers drew comfort from their own resources. Some read, others wrote home, letters which might never reach those for whom they were intended.

Bolitho drank his coffee and tried to ignore the pain in his forehead. Without thinking, his hand moved up and touched the rebellious lock of black hair above his right eye. Beneath it was a livid scar, the source of the pain. He had received it when he had been in *Destiny*. It often came back to him at moments like this. The illusion of safety, the sudden rush of feet and slashing, hacking weapons. The agony and the blood. Oblivion.

There was a tap at the outer screen door, and then Mackenzie said to Sparke, who was the senior officer present, 'Your pardon, sir, but the midshipman of the watch is here.'

The boy stepped carefully into the wardroom, as if he was walking on precious silk.

Sparke snapped curtly, 'What is it, Mr Forbes?'

'The first lieutenant's compliments, sir, and will all officers muster in the cabin at two bells.'

'Very well.' Sparke waited for the door to close. 'Now we will see, gentlemen. Maybe we have something of importance to do.'

Unlike Cairns, the second lieutenant could not conceal the sudden gleam in his eyes. Promotion. Prize money. Or just a chance for action instead of hearing about it.

He looked at Bolitho. 'I suggest *you* change into a clean shirt. The captain seems to have his eye on you.'

Bolitho stood up, his head brushing the deckhead beams. Two years in this ship, and apart from a dinner in the cabin when they had recommissioned the ship at Bristol, he had barely crossed one social barrier to meet the captain. He was a stern, remote man, and yet always seemed to possess uncanny knowledge of what was happening on every deck in his command.

Dalyell carefully tapped out his pipe and remarked, 'Maybe he really likes you, Dick.'

Rayne, the lieutenant of marines, yawned. 'I don't think he's human.'

Sparke hurried to his cabin, shying away from involvement with any criticism of authority. 'He is the captain. He does not require to be human.'

*

Captain Gilbert Brice Pears finished reading the daily log of events aboard his ship and then scrawled his signature, which was hastily dried by Teakle, his clerk.

Outside the stern windows the harbour and the distant town seemed far-away and unconnected with this spacious, well-lit cabin. There was some good furniture here, and in the neighbouring dining cabin the table was already laid for supper, with Foley, the captain's servant, neat as a pin in his blue coat and white trousers, hovering to tend his master's needs.

Captain Pears leaned back in his chair and glanced round the cabin without seeing it. In two years he had got to know it well.

He was forty-two years old, but looked older. Thickset, even square, he was as powerful and impressive as the *Trojan* herself.

He had heard gossip amongst his officers which amounted almost to discontent. The war, for it must now be accepted as such, seemed to be passing them by. But Pears was a realistic man, and knew that the time would eventually come when he and his command would be able to act as intended when *Trojan*'s great keel had first tasted salt water just nine years ago. Privateers and raiding parties were one thing, but when the French joined the fray in open strength, and their ships of the line appeared in these waters, *Trojan* and her heavy consorts would display their true worth.

He looked up as the marine sentry stamped his boots together outside the screen door, and moments later the first lieutenant rejoined him.

'I have passed the word to the wardroom, sir. All officers to be here at two bells.'

'Good.'

Pears merely had to look at his servant and Foley was beside him, pouring two tall glasses of claret.

'The fact is, Mr Cairns' – Pears examined the wine against the nearest lantern – 'you cannot go on forever fighting a defensive war. Here we are in New York, a claw-hold on a land which is daily becoming more rebellious. In Philadelphia things are little better. Raids and skirmishes, we burn a fort or an outpost, and they catch one of our transports, or ambush a patrol. What is New York? A besieged city. A town under reprieve, but for how long?'

Cairns said nothing, but sipped the claret, half his mind attending to the noises beyond the cabin, the sigh of wind, the groan of timbers.

Pears saw his expression and smiled to himself. Cairns was a good first lieutenant, probably the best he had ever had. He should have a command of his own. A chance, one which only came in war.

But Pears loved his ship more than hopes or dreams. The thought of Sparke taking over as senior lieutenant was like a threat. He was an efficient officer and attended to his guns and his duties perfectly. But imagination he had not. He thought of Probyn, and dismissed him just as quickly. Then there was Bolitho, the fourth. Much like his father, although he sometimes seemed to take his duties too lightly. But his men appeared to like him. That meant a lot in these hard times.

Pears sighed. Bolitho was still a few months short of twenty-one. You needed experienced officers to work a ship of the line. He rubbed his chin to hide his expression. Maybe it was Bolitho's youth and his own mounting years which made him reason in this fashion.

He asked abruptly, 'Are we in all respects ready for sea?'

Cairns nodded. 'Aye, sir. I could well use another dozen hands because of injury and ill-health, but that is a small margin these days.'

'It is indeed. I have known first lieutenants go grey-haired because they could not woo, press or bribe enough hands even to work their ships out of port.'

At the prescribed time the doors were opened and *Trojan*'s officers, excluding the midshipmen and junior warrant officers, filed into the great cabin.

It was a rare event, and took a good deal of time to get them into proper order, and for Foley and Hogg, the captain's coxswain, to find the right number of chairs.

It gave Pears time to watch their varying reactions, to see if their presence in strength would make any sort of difference.

Probyn, relieved from his duties by a master's mate, was flushed and very bright-eyed. Just too steady to be true.

Sparke, prim in his severity, and young Dalyell, were seated beside the sixth and junior lieutentant, Quinn, who just five months ago had been a midshipman.

Then there was Erasmus Bunce, the master. He was called the Sage behind his back, and was certainly impressive. In his special trade, which produced more characters and outstanding seamen than any other, Bunce was one to turn any man's head. He was well over six feet tall, deep-chested, and had long, straggly grey hair. But his eyes, deep-set and clear, were almost as black as the thick brows above them. A sage indeed.

Pears watched the master ducking between the overhead beams and was reassured.

Bunce liked his rum, but he loved the ship like a woman. With him to guide her she had little to fear.

Molesworth, the purser, a pale man with a nervous blink, which Pears suspected was due to some undiscovered guilt. Thorndike, the surgeon, who always seemed to be smiling. More like an actor than a man of blood and bones. Two bright patches of scarlet by the larboard side, the marine officers, D'Esterre and Lieutenant Raye, and of course Cairns, completed the gathering. It did not include all the other warrant officers and specialists. The boatswain, and gunner, the master's mates, and the carpenters, Pears knew them all by sight, sound and quality.

Probyn said in a loud whisper, 'Mr Bolitho doesn't seem to be here yet?'

Pears frowned, despising Probyn's hypocrisy. He was about as subtle as a hammer.

Cairns suggested, 'I'll send someone, sir.'

The door opened and closed swiftly and Pears saw Bolitho sliding into an empty chair beside the two marines.

'Stand up, that officer.' Pears's harsh voice was almost caressing. 'Ah, it is you, sir, at last.'

Bolitho stood quite still, only his shoulders swaying slightly to the ship's slow roll.

'I – I am sorry, sir.' Bolitho saw the grin on Dalyell's face as drops of water trickled from under his coat and on to the black and white checkered canvas which covered the deck.

Pears said mildly, 'Your shirt seems to be rather *wet*, sir.' He turned slightly. 'Foley, some canvas for that chair. It is hard to replace such things out here.'

Bolitho sat down with a thump, not knowing whether to be angry or humiliated.

He forgot Pears's abrasive tone, and the shirt which he had snatched off the wardroom line still wringing wet, as Pears said more evenly, 'We will sail at first light, gentlemen. The Governor of New York has received information that the expected convoy from Halifax is likely to be attacked. It is a large assembly of vessels with an escort of two frigates and a sloop-of-war. But in this weather the ships could become scattered, some might endeavour to close with the land to ascertain their bearings.' His fingers changed to a fist '*That* is when our enemy will strike.'

Bolitho leaned forward, ignoring the sodden discomfort around his waist.

Pears continued, 'I was saying as much to Mr Cairns. You cannot *win* a defensive war. We have the ships, but the enemy has the local knowledge to make use of smaller, faster vessels. To have a chance of success we must command and keep open every trade route, search and detain any suspected craft, make our presence felt. Wars are not finally won with ideals, they are won with powder and shot, and *that* the enemy does not have in quantity. *Yet.*' He looked around their faces, his eyes bleak. 'The Halifax convoy is carrying a great deal of powder and shot, cannon too, which are intended for the military in Philadelphia and here in New York. If just one of those valuable cargoes fell into the wrong hands we would feel the effects for months to come.' He looked round sharply. 'Questions?'

It was Sparke who rose to his feet first.

'Why us, sir? Of course, I am most gratified to be putting to sea in my country's service, to try and rectify some –'

Pears said heavily, '*Please* get on with the bones of the matter.'

Sparke swallowed hard, his scar suddenly very bright on his cheek. 'Why not send frigates, sir?'

'Because there are not enough, there never *are* enough. Also, the admiral feels that a show of strength might be of more value.'

Bolitho stiffened, as if he had missed something. It was in the captain's tone. Just the merest suggestion of doubt. He glanced at his companions but they seemed much as usual. Perhaps he was imagining it, or seeking flaws to cover up his earlier discomfort under Pears's tongue.

Pears added, 'Whatever may happen this time, we must never drop our vigilance. This ship is our first responsibility, our main concern at all times. The war is changing from day to day. Yesterday's traitor is tomorrow's patriot. A man who responded to his country's call,' he shot a wry smile at Sparke, 'is now called a Loyalist, as if he and not the others was some sort of freak and outcast.'

The master, Erasmus Bunce, stood up very slowly, his eyes peering beneath a deckhead beam like twin coals.

'A man must do as he be guided, sir. It is for God to decide who be right in this conflict.'

Pears smiled gravely. Old Bunce was known to be very religious, and had once hurled a sailor into Portsmouth harbour merely for taking the Lord's name into a drunken song.

Bunce was a Devonian, and had gone to sea at the age of nine or ten. He was now said to be over sixty, but Pears could never picture him ever being young at all.

He said, 'Quite so, Mr Bunce. That was well said.'

Cairns cleared his throat and eyed the master patiently. 'Was that all, Mr Bunce?'

The master sat down and folded his arms. 'It be enough.'

The captain gestured to Foley. No words seemed to be required here, Bolitho thought.

Glasses and wine jugs followed, and then Pears said, 'A toast, gentlemen. To the ship, and damnation to the King's enemies!'

Bolitho watched Probyn looking round for the jugs, his glass already emptied.

He thought of Pears's voice when he had spoken of the ship. God help George Probyn if he put her on a lee shore after taking too many glasses.

Soon after that the meeting broke up, and Bolitho realized that he had still got no closer to the captain than by way of a reprimand.

He sighed. When you were a midshipman you thought a lieutenant's life was in some sort of heaven. Maybe even captains were in dread of somebody, although at this moment it was hard to believe.

The next dawn was slightly clearer, but not much. The wind held firm enough from the north-west, and the snow flurries soon gave way to drizzle, which mixed with the blown spray made the decks and rigging shine like dull glass.

Bolitho had watched one ship or another get under way more times than he could remember. But it never failed to move and excite him. The way every man joined into the chain of command to make the ship work as a living, perfect instrument.

Each mast had its own divisions of seamen, from the swift-footed topmen to the older, less agile hands who worked the braces and halliards from the deck. As the calls shrilled, and the men poured up on deck through every hatch and companion, it seemed incredible that *Trojan*'s hull, which from figurehead to taffrail measured two hundred and fifteen feet, could contain so many. Yet within seconds the dashing figures of men and boys, marines and landmen were formed into compact groups, each being checked by leather-lunged petty officers against their various lists and watch-bills.

The great capstan was already turning, as was its twin on the deck below, and under his shoes Bolitho could almost sense the ship stirring, waiting to head towards the open sea.

Like the mass of seamen and marines, the officers too were at their stations. Probyn with Dalyell to assist him on the forecastle, the foremast their responsibility. Sparke commanded the upper gundeck and the ship's mainmast, which was her real strength, with all the spars, cordage, canvas and miles of rigging which gave life to the hull beneath. Lastly, the mizzen mast, handled mostly by the afterguard, where young Quinn waited with the marine lieutenant and his men to obey Cairns' first requirements.

Bolitho looked across at Sparke. Not an easy man to know, but a pleasure to watch at work. He controlled his seamen and every halliard and brace with the practised ease of a dedicated concert conductor.

A hush seemed to fall over the ship, and Bolitho looked aft to see the captain walking to the quarterdeck rail, nodding to old Bunce, the Sage, then speaking quietly with his first lieutenant.

Far above the deck from the mainmast truck the long, scarlet pendant licked and hardened to the wind like bending metal. A good sailing wind, but Bolitho was thankful it was the captain and old Bunce who were taking her through the anchored shipping and not himself.

He glanced over the side and wondered who was watching. Friends, or spies who might already be passing news to Washington's agents. Another man-of-war weighing. Where bound? For what purpose?

He returned his attention inboard. If half what he had heard was true, the enemy probably knew better than they did. There were said to be plenty of loose tongues in New York's civil and military government circles.

Cairns raised his speaking trumpet. 'Get a move on, Mr Tolcher!'

Tolcher, the squat boatswain, raised his cane and bellowed, 'More 'ands to th' capstan! *'Eave*, lads!'

He glared at the shantyman with his fiddle. 'Play up, you bugger, or I'll 'ave you on th' pumps!'

From forward came the cry, 'Anchor's hove short, sir!'

'Hands aloft! Loose tops'ls!' Cairns' voice, magnified by the trumpet, pursued and drove them like a clarion. 'Loose the heads'ls!'

Released to the wind the canvas erupted and flapped in wild confusion, while spread along the swaying yards like monkeys the topmen fought to bring it under control until the right moment.

Sparke called, 'Man your braces! Mr Bolitho, take that man's name!'

'Aye, sir!'

Bolitho smiled into the drizzle. It was always the same with Sparke. *Take that man's name.* There was nobody in particular, but it gave the seamen the idea that Sparke had eyes everywhere.

Again the hoarse voice from the bows, 'Anchor's aweigh, sir!'

Released from the ground, her first anchor already hoisted and catted, *Trojan* side-stepped heavily across the wind, her sails spreading and thundering like a bombardment as the men hauled at the braces, their bodies straining back, angled down almost to the deck.

Round and further still, the yards swinging to hold the wind, the sails freed one by one to harden like steel breastplates until the ship was thrusting her shoulder in foam, her lower gunports awash along the lee side.

Bolitho ran from one section to the next, his hat knocked awry, his ears ringing with the squeal of blocks and the boom of canvas, and above all the groaning and vibrating chorus from every stay and shroud.

When he paused for breath he saw the outline of Sandy Hook sliding abeam, some men waiting in a small yawl to wave as the great ship stood over them.

He heard Cairns' voice again. 'Get the t'gan'sls on her!'

Bolitho peered up the length of the mainmast with its great bending yards. He saw midshipmen in the tops, and seamen racing each other to set more canvas. When he looked aft again he saw Bunce with his hands thrust behind him, his face like carved rock as he watched over his ship. Then he nodded very slowly. That was as near to satisfaction as Bolitho had ever seen him display.

He pictured the ship as she would look from the land, her fierce, glaring figurehead, the Trojan warrior with the red-crested helmet.

Spray bursting up and over the beakhead and bowsprit, the massive black and buff hull glistening and reflecting the cruising whitecaps alongside, as if to wash herself clean from the land.

Probyn's voice sounded raw as he shouted at his men to secure the second anchor. He would need plenty to drink after this, Bolitho thought.

He looked aft, past his own seamen as they slid down stays and vaulted from the gangways to muster again below the mast. Then he saw the captain watching him. Along the ship, over all the bustle and haste their eyes seemed to meet.

Self-consciously, Bolitho reached up and straightened his hat, and he imagined he saw the captain give a small but definite nod.

But the mood was soon broken, for *Trojan* rarely gave much time for personal fancies.

'Man the braces there! Stand by to come about!'

Sparke was shouting, '*Mr Bolitho!*'

Bolitho touched his hat. 'Aye, I know, sir. Take that man's name!'

By the time they had laid the ship on her chosen tack to both the captain's and Bunce's satisfaction the land was swallowed in mist and rain astern.

2

A Wild Plan

Lieutenant Richard Bolitho crossed to the weather side of the quarter-deck and gripped the hammock nettings to hold his balance. Towering above and ahead of him, *Trojan*'s great pyramids of sails were impressive, even to one accustomed to the sight. Especially after all the frustration and pain in the last four and a half days, he thought.

The wind which had followed them with such promise from Sandy Hook had changed within hours, as if driven or inspired by the devil himself. Backing and veering without warning, with all hands required to reef or reset the sails throughout each watch. It had taken one complete, miserable day just to work round and clear of the dreaded Nantucket shoals, with sea boiling beneath the long bowsprit as if heated by some force from hell.

Then after raising their progress to four and even five knots the wind would alter yet again, bellowing with savage triumph while the breathless seamen fought to reef the hard canvas, fisting and grappling while their pitching world high above the decks went mad about them.

But this was different. *Trojan* was standing almost due north, her yards braced round as far as they would to take and hold the wind, and along her lee side the water was creaming past as evidence of real progress.

Bolitho ran his eyes over the upper gundeck. Below the quarterdeck rail he could see the hands resting and chatting, as was the custom while waiting to see what the cook had produced for the midday meal. By the greasy plume which fell downwind from the galley funnel, Bolitho guessed that it was another concoction of boiled beef hacked from salted casks, mixed with a soggy assortment of ship's biscuit, oatmeal and scraps saved from yesterday. George Triphook, the senior cook, was hated by almost everyone but his toadies, but unlike some he enjoyed the hatred, and seemed to relish the groans and curses at his efforts.

Bolitho felt suddenly ravenous, but knew the wardroom fare would be little better when he was relieved to snatch his share of it.

He thought of his mother and the great grey house in Falmouth. He walked away from Couzens, his watchful midshipman, who rarely took his eyes off him. How terrible the blow had been. In the Navy you could risk death a dozen ways in any day. Disease, shipwreck or the cannon's roar, the walls of Falmouth church were covered with memorial plaques. The names and deeds of sea-officers, sons of Falmouth who had left port never to return.

But his mother. Surely not her. Always youthful and vivacious. Ready to stand-in and shoulder the responsibility of house and land when her husband, Captain James Bolitho, was away, which was often.

Bolitho and his brother, Hugh, his two sisters, Felicity and Nancy, had all loved her in their own different and special ways. When he had returned home from the *Destiny*, still shocked and suffering from his wound, he had needed her more than ever. The house had been like a tomb. She was dead. It was impossible to accept even now that she was not back in Falmouth, watching the sea beyond Pendennis Castle, laughing in the manner which was infectious enough to drive all despair aside.

A chill, they had said. Then a sudden fever. It had been over in a matter of weeks.

He could picture his father at this very moment. Captain James, as he was locally known, was well respected as a magistrate since losing his arm and being removed from active duty. The house in winter, the lanes clogged with mud, the news always late, the countryside too worried by pressures of cold and wet, of lost animals and marauding foxes to heed much for this far-off war. But his father would care. Brooding as a ship-of-war anchored or weighed in Carrick Roads. Needing, pining for the life which had rejected him, and now completely alone.

It must be a million times worse for him, Bolitho thought sadly.

Cairns appeared on deck, and after scrutinizing the compass and glancing at the slate on which a master's mate made his half-hourly calculations he crossed to join Bolitho.

Bolitho touched his hat. 'She holds steady, sir. Nor' by east, full and bye.'

Cairns nodded. He had very pale eyes which could look right through a man.

'We may have to reef if the wind gets up any more. We're taking all we can manage, I think.'

He shaded his eyes before he looked to larboard, for although there was no sun the glare was intent and harsh. It was difficult to see an edge between sea and sky, the water was a desert of restless steel fragments. But the rollers were further apart now, cruising down in serried ranks to lift under *Trojan*'s fat quarter to tilt her further and burst occasionally over the weather gangway before rolling on again towards the opposite horizon.

They had the sea to themselves, for after beating clear of Nantucket and pushing on towards the entrance of Massachusetts Bay they were well clear of both land and local shipping. Somewhere, some sixty miles across the weather side, lay Boston. There were quite a few aboard *Trojan* who could remember Boston as it had once been before the bitterness and resentment had flared into anger and blood.

The Bay itself was avoided by all but the foolhardy. It was the home of some of the most able privateers, and Bolitho wondered, not for the first time, if there were any stalking the powerful two-decker at this moment.

Cairns had a muffler around his throat, and asked, 'What make you of the weather, Dick?'

Bolitho watched the men streaming to the hatches on their way to the galley and their cramped messes.

He had taken over the watch as Bunce had been keeping a stern eye on the ritual taking of noon sights, although it was more a routine than to serve any real purpose in this poor visibility. The midshipmen lined up with their sextants, the master's mates watching their progress, or their lack of it.

Bolitho replied calmly, 'Fog.'

Cairns stared at him. 'Is this one of your Celtic fantasies, man?'

Bolitho smiled. 'The master said fog.'

The first lieutenant sighed. 'Then fog it will be. Though in this half gale I see no chance of it!'

'*Deck there!*'

They looked up, caught off guard after so much isolation.

Bolitho saw the shortened figure of the mainmast lookout, a tiny shape against the low clouds. It made him dizzy just to watch.

'Sail on th'weather beam, sir!'

The two lieutenants snatched telescopes and climbed into the shrouds. But there was nothing. Just the wave-crests, angrier and steeper in the searching lens, and the hard, relentless glare.

'Shall I inform the captain, sir?'

Bolitho watched Cairns' face as he returned to the deck. He could almost see his mind working. A sail. What did it mean? Unlikely to be friendly. Even a lost and confused ship's master would not fail to understand the dangers hereabouts.

'Not yet.' Cairns glanced meaningly towards the poop. 'He'll have heard the masthead anyway. He'll not fuss until we're ready.'

Bolitho thought about it. Another view of Captain Pears which he had not considered. But it was true. He never did rush on deck like some captains, afraid for their ships, or impatient for answers to unanswerable questions.

He looked at Cairns' quiet face again. It was also true that Cairns inspired such trust.

Bolitho asked, 'Shall I go aloft and see for myself?'

Cairns shook his head. 'No. I will. The captain will doubtless want a full report.'

Bolitho watched the first lieutenant hurrying up the shrouds, the telescope slung over his shoulders like a musket. Up and up, around the futtock shrouds and past the hooded swivel gun there to the topmast and further still towards the lookout who sat so calmly on the crosstrees, as if he was on a comfortable village bench.

He dragged his eyes away from Cairns' progress. It was something he could never get used to or conquer. His hatred of heights. Each time he had to go aloft, which was mercifully rare, he felt the same nausea, the same dread of falling.

He saw a familiar figure on the gundeck below the quarterdeck rail and felt something like affection for the big, ungainly man in checkered shirt and flapping white trousers. One more link with the little *Destiny*. Stockdale, the muscular prize-fighter he had rescued from a barker outside an inn when he and a dispirited recruiting party had been trying to drum up volunteers for the ship.

Stockdale had taken to the sea in a manner born. As strong as five men, he never abused his power, and was more gentle than many. The angry barker had been hitting Stockdale with a length of chain for losing in a fight with one of Bolitho's men. The man in question must have cheated in some way, for Bolitho had never seen Stockdale beaten since.

He spoke very little, and when he did it was with effort, as his vocal chords had been cruelly damaged in countless barefist fights up and down every fair and pitch in the land.

Seeing him then, stripped to the waist, cut about the back by the barker's chain, had been too much for Bolitho. When he had asked Stockdale to enlist he had said it almost without thinking of the consequences. Stockdale had merely nodded, picked up his things and had followed him to the ship.

And whenever Bolitho needed aid, or was in trouble, Stockdale was always there. Like that last time, when Bolitho had seen the screaming savage rushing at him with a cutlass snatched from a dying seaman. Later he had heard all about it. How Stockdale had rallied the retreating seamen, had picked him up like a child and had carried him to safety.

When Bolitho's appointment to *Trojan* had arrived, he had imagined that would be an end to their strange relationship. But somehow, then as now, Stockdale had managed it.

He had wheezed, 'One day, you'll be a cap'n, sir. Reckon you'll need a coxswain.'

Bolitho smiled down at him. Stockdale could do almost anything. Splice, reef and steer if need be. But he was a gun captain now, on one of

Trojan's upper battery of thirty eighteen-pounders. And naturally he just *happened* to be in Bolitho's own division.

'What d'*you* think, Stockdale?'

The man's battered face split into a wide grin. 'They be watching us, Mr Bolitho.'

Bolitho saw the painful movements of his throat. The sea's bite was making it hard for Stockdale.

'You think so, eh?'

'Aye.' He sounded very confident. 'They'll know what we're about, an' where we're heading. I wager there'll be other craft hull down where we can't see 'em.'

Cairns' feet hit the deck as he slid down a stay with the agility of a midshipman.

He said, 'Schooner by the cut of her. Can barely make her out, it's so damn hazy.' He shivered in a sudden gust. 'Same tack as ourselves.' He saw Bolitho smile at Stockdale, and asked, 'May I share the joke?'

'Stockdale said that the other sail is watching us, sir. Keeping well up to wind'rd.'

Cairns opened his mouth as if to contradict and then said, 'I fear he may be right. Instead of a show of strength, *Trojan* may be leading the pack down on to the very booty we are trying to protect.' He rubbed his chin. 'By God, that is a sour thought. I had expected an attack to be on the convoy's rear, the usual straggler cut out before the escort has had time to intervene.'

'All the same.' He rubbed his chin harder. 'They'll not try to attack with *Trojan*'s broadsides so near.'

Bolitho recalled Pears's voice at the conference. The hint of doubt. His suspicion then had now become more real.

Cairns glanced aft, past the two helmsmen who stood straddle-legged by the great double wheel, their eyes moving from sail to compass.

'It's not much to tell the captain, Dick. He has his orders. *Trojan* is no frigate. If we lost time in some fruitless manoeuvres we might never reach the convoy in time. You have seen the wind's perverse manners hereabouts. It could happen tomorrow. Or now.'

Bolitho said quietly, 'Remember what the Sage said. *Fog*.' He watched the word hitting Cairns like a pistol ball. 'If we have to lie to, we'll be no use to anyone.'

Cairns studied him searchingly. 'I should have seen that. These privateersmen know more about local conditions than any of us.' He gave a wry smile. 'Except the Sage.'

Lieutenant Quinn came on deck and touched his hat.

'I'm to relieve you, sir.'

He looked from Bolitho to the straining masses of canvas. Bolitho would only go for a quick meal, especially as he wanted to know about

Pears's reactions. But to the sixth lieutenant, eighteen years old, it would seem a lifetime of awesome responsibility, for to all intents and purposes he would control *Trojan*'s destiny for as long as he trod the quarterdeck.

Bolitho made to reassure him but checked himself. Quinn must learn to stand on his own. Any officer who depended on help whenever things got awkward would be useless in a real crisis.

He followed Cairns to the companionway, while Quinn made a big display of checking the compass and the notes in the log.

Cairns said softly, 'He'll be fine. Given time.'

Bolitho sat at the wardroom table while Mackenzie and Logan endeavoured to present the meal as best they could. Boiled meat and gruel. Ship's biscuit with black treacle, and as much cheese as anyone could face. But there was a generous supply of red wine which had arrived in New York with the last convoy. From the look on Probyn's face he had made very good use of it.

He peered across at Bolitho and asked thickly, 'What was all that din about a sail? Somebody getting a bit nervous, eh?' He leaned forward to peer at the others. 'God, the Navy's changing!'

Bunce sat at the head of the table and intoned deeply without looking up, 'It is not His doing, Mr Probyn. He has no time for the Godless.'

Sparke said unfeelingly, 'This bloody food is swill. I shall get a new cook at the first chance I can. That rogue should be dancing on a halter instead of poisoning us.'

The deck tilted steeply, and hands reached out to seize plates and glasses until the ship rolled upright again.

Bunce took out a watch and looked at it.

Bolitho asked quietly, 'The fog, Mr Bunce. *Will* it come?'

Thorndike, the surgeon, heard him and laughed. He made a braying sound.

'Really, Erasmus! Fog, when she pitches about in this wind!'

Bunce ignored him and replied, 'Tomorrow. We will have to lie to. There is too great a depth to anchor.' He shook his massive head. 'Time lost. More knots to recover.'

He had spoken enough and stood up from the table. As he passed Probyn's chair he said in his deep voice, 'We will have time to see who is nervous then, I'm thinking.'

Probyn snapped his fingers for some wine and exclaimed angrily, 'He is becoming mad in his old age!' He tried to laugh, but nothing happened.

Captain D'Esterre eyed him calmly. 'At least he seems to have our Lord on his side. What do *you* have, exactly?'

In the cabin above, Captain Pears sat at his large table, a napkin tucked into his neckcloth. He caught the gust of laughter from the wardroom and said to Cairns, 'They seem happier at sea, eh?'

Cairns nodded. 'So it would appear, sir.' He watched Pears's bowed head and waited for his conclusions or ideas.

Pears said, 'Alone or in company the schooner is a menace to us. If only we had been given a brig or a sloop to chase off these wolves. As it is . . .' He shrugged.

'May I suggest something, sir?'

Pears cut a small piece of cheese for himself and examined it doubtfully.

'It is what you came for, surely.' He smiled. 'Speak out.'

Cairns thrust his hands behind him, his eyes very bright.

'You have heard the master's views on the chance of fog, sir?'

Pears nodded. 'I know these waters well. Fog is common enough, though I would not dare to make such a bold prediction this time.' He pushed the cheese aside. 'But if the master says a thing it is usually right.'

'Well, sir, we will have to lie to until it clears.'

'I have already taken that into account, damn it.'

'But so too will our watchdog. Both for his own safety and for fear of losing us. The fog might be an ally to us.' He hesitated, sensing the captain's mood. 'If we could *find* her and take her by boarding – ' He got no further.

'In God's name, Mr Cairns, what are you saying? That I should put boats down, fill them with trained hands and send them off into a damned fog? Hell's teeth, sir, they would be going to certain death!'

'There is a chance there may be another vessel in company.' Cairns spoke with sudden stubbornness. 'They will display lights. With good care and the use of a boat's compass, I think an attack has a good chance.' He waited, seeing the doubts and arguments in Pears's eyes. 'It would give us an extra vessel, and maybe more. Information, news of what the privateers are doing.'

Pears sat back and stared at him grimly. 'You are a man of ideas, I'll give you that.'

Cairns said, 'The fourth lieutenant put the thought in my mind, sir.'

'Might have guessed it.' Pears stood up and walked towards the windows, his thickset frame angled to the deck. 'Damned Cornishmen. Pirates and wreckers for the most part. Did you know that?'

Cairns kept his face stiff. 'I understood that Falmouth, Mr Bolitho's home, was the last place to hold out for King Charles against Cromwell and Parliament, sir?'

Pears gave a tight grin. 'Well said. But this idea is a dangerous thing. We might never find the boats again, and they may not discover the enemy, let alone seize her.'

Cairns insisted, 'The fog will reach the other vessel long before us, sir. I would suggest that as soon as that happens we change tack and close with her with every stitch which will draw.'

'But if the wind goes *against* us.' Pears held up his hand. '*Easy*, Mr Cairns, I can see your disappointment, but it is my responsibility. I must think of everything.'

Overhead, and beyond the cabin doors, life was going on as usual. The clank of a pump, the padding of feet across the poop as the watch hurried to trim a yard or splice a fraying halliard.

Pears said slowly, 'But it does have the stuff of surprise about it.' He made up his mind. 'My compliments to the master and ask him to join us in the chart room.' He chuckled. 'Although, knowing him as I do, I suspect he is already there.'

Out on the windswept quarterdeck, his eyes smarting to salt spray, Bolitho watched the men working overhead, the shivering power of each great sail. Time to reef soon, for the captain to be informed. He had seen the activity beneath the poop, Pears with Cairns entering the small chart room which adjoined Bunce's cabin.

A little later Cairns walked out into the drizzle, and Bolitho noticed that he was without his hat. That was very unusual, for Cairns was always smartly turned out, no matter how bad the circumstances.

'Have you had further reports from the masthead?'

'Aye, sir.'

Bolitho ducked as a sheet of spray burst over the nettings and soaked them both. Cairns barely flinched.

Bolitho said quickly, 'As before, the stranger is holding to wind'rd of us, on the same bearing.'

'I will inform the captain.' Cairns added, 'No matter, he is here.'

Bolitho made to cross to the lee side as was customary when the captain came on deck, but the harsh voice caught him.

'Stay, Mr Bolitho.' Pears strode heavily to the quarterdeck rail, his hat tugged down to his eyes. 'I believe you have been hatching some wild plan with the first lieutenant?'

'Well, sir, I –'

'Madness.' Pears watched the straining main-course as it billowed out from its yard. 'But with a grain, a very *small* grain of value.'

Bolitho stared at him. 'Thank you very much, sir.'

Pears ignored him and said to Cairns, 'The two cutters will have to suffice. I want you to hand-pick each man yourself. You know what we need for this bloody work.' He watched Cairns' face and then said almost gently, 'But you will not be going.' As Cairns made to protest he added, 'I cannot spare you. I could die tomorrow, and with you gone too, what would become of *Trojan*, eh?'

Bolitho watched both of them. It was like being an intruder to see the disappointment showing for the first time on Cairns' face.

Then Cairns replied, 'Aye, sir. I'll attend to it.'

As he strode away, Pears said bluntly, 'But you can send *this* one, he'll not be missed!'

Pears returned to the poop where Bunce was waiting for him, his straggly hair blowing in the wind like spun yarn.

He barked, 'Pass the word to the second lieutenant to lay aft.'

Bolitho considered his feelings. *He was going.* So was Sparke. *Take that man's name.*

He thought of Cairns as his one chance of showing his mettle had been taken from him. It was another measure of the man, Bolitho thought. Some first lieutenants would have kept all the credit for the idea of boarding the other craft, hoarding it for the final reward.

It was getting dark early again, the low cloud and steady drizzle adding to the discomfort both below and on deck.

Cairns met Bolitho as he came off watch, and said simply, 'I have selected some good hands for you, Dick. The second lieutenant will be in command, assisted by Mr Frowd, who is the ablest master's mate we have, and Mr Midshipman Libby. You will be assisted by Mr Quinn and Mr Couzens.'

Bolitho met his even gaze. Apart from Sparke and Frowd, the master's mate, and to a lesser extent himself, the others were children at this sort of thing. He doubted if either the nervous Quinn or the willing Couzens had ever heard a shot fired other than at wildfowl.

But he said, 'Thank you, sir.' He would show the same attitude that Cairns had displayed to the captain.

Cairns touched his arm. 'Go and find some dry clothing, if you can.' As he turned towards his cabin he added, 'You will have the redoubtable Stockdale in your cutter. I would not be so brave as to try and stop him!'

Bolitho walked through the wardroom and entered his little cabin. There he stripped naked and towelled his damp and chilled limbs until he recovered a sensation of warmth.

Then he sat on his swaying cot and listened to the great ship creaking and shuddering beneath him, the occasional splash of spray as high as the nearest gunport.

This time tomorrow he might be on his way to disaster, if not already dead. He shivered, and rubbed his stomach muscles vigorously to quell his sudden uncertainty.

But at least he would be doing something. He pulled a clean shirt over his head and groped for his breeches.

No sooner had he done so than he heard the distant cry getting louder and closer.

'*All hands! All hands! Hands aloft and reef tops'ls!*'

He stood up and banged his head on a ring-bolt.

'*Damnation!*'

Then he was up and hurrying again to that other world of wind and noise, to the *Trojan*'s demands which much always be met.

As he passed Probyn's untidy shape, the lieutenant peered at him and grinned. 'Fog, is it?'

Bolitho grinned back at him. 'Go to hell!'

It took a full two hours to reef to the captain's satisfaction and to prepare the ship for the night. The news of the proposed attack had gone through the ship like fire, and Bolitho heard the many wagers which were being made. The sailor's margin between life and death in this case.

And it would all probably come to nothing. Such things had happened often enough on this commission. Preparation, and then some last-minute hitch.

Bolitho imagined it was going to be an almost impossible thing to find and take the other ship. Equally, he knew he would feel cheated if it was called off.

He returned to the wardroom to discover that most of the officers had turned into their bunks after such a day of wind and bustle.

The surgeon and Captain D'Esterre sat beneath a solitary lantern playing cards, and alone by the streaming stern windows, staring at the vibrating tiller-head, was Lieutenant Quinn.

In the glow of the swaying lantern he looked younger than ever, if that were possible.

Bolitho sat beside him and shook his head as the boy, Logan, appeared with an earthenware wine jug.

'Are you feeling all right, James?'

Quinn looked at him, startled. 'Yes, thank you, sir.'

Bolitho smiled. 'Richard. Dick, if you like.' He watched the other's despair. 'This is not the midshipmen's berth, you know.'

Quinn darted a quick glance at the card players, the mounting pile of coins beside the marine's scarlet sleeve, the dwindling one opposite him.

Then he said quietly, 'You've done this sort of thing before, sir – I mean, Dick.'

Bolitho nodded. 'A few times.'

He did not want to break Quinn's trust now that he had begun.

'I – I thought it would be in the ship when it happened.' Quinn gestured helplessly around the wardroom and the cabin flat beyond. 'You know, all your friends near you, *with* you. I think I could do that. Put up with the first time. The fighting.'

Bolitho said, 'I know. The ship is home. It can help.'

Quinn clasped his hands and said, 'My family are in the leather trade in the City of London. My father did not wish me to enter the Navy.' His chin lifted very slightly. 'But I was determined. I'd often seen a man-o'-war working down river to the sea. I knew what I wanted.'

Bolitho could well understand the shock Quinn must have endured when he was faced with the reality of a King's ship with all the harsh discipline and the feeling that you, as a new midshipman, are the only one aboard who is in total useless ignorance.

Bolitho had grown up with it and to it. The dark portraits which adorned the walls and staircase of the old Bolitho home in Cornwall were a constant reminder of all who had gone before him. Now he and his brother Hugh were carrying on the tradition. Hugh was in a frigate, now probably in the Mediterranean, while he was here, about to embark in the sort of action they often yarned about in the taverns of Falmouth.

He said, 'It will be all right, James. Mr Sparke is leading us.'

For the first time he saw Quinn smile as he said, 'I must admit he frightens me more than the enemy!'

Bolitho laughed, wondering why it was that Quinn's fear had somehow given him strength.

'Turn into your cot while you can. Try to sleep. Tell Mackenzie you'd like a tot of brandy. George Probyn's cure for everything!'

Quinn stood up and almost fell as the ship quivered and lunged across the hidden sea.

'No. I must write a letter.'

As he walked away, D'Esterre left the table, pocketing his winnings, and joined Bolitho by the tiller-head.

The surgeon made to follow, but D'Esterre said, 'No more, Robert. Your poor play might blunt my skill!' He smiled. 'Be off with you to your bottles and pills.'

The surgeon did not give his usual laugh, but walked away, feeling for handholds as he went.

D'Esterre gestured towards the silent cabins. 'Is he worried?'

'A little.'

The marine tugged at his tight neckcloth. 'Wish to God I was coming with you. If I can't put my lads to a fight, they will be as rusty as old pikes!'

Bolitho gave a great yawn. 'I'm for bed.' He shook his head as D'Esterre flicked the cards between his fingers. 'I'd not play with you anyway. You have the uncomfortable knack of winning.'

As he lay in his cot, hands thrust behind his head, Bolitho listened to the ship, identifying each sound as it fitted into the pattern and fabric of the hull.

The watch below, slung in their close-packed hammocks like pods, the air foul around them because of the bilges, and because the gunports had to be tightly sealed against sea and rain. Everything bloomed with damp, the deckheads dripping, the pumps clanking mournfully as *Trojan* worked her massive bulk over a stiff quarter-sea.

On the orlop deck beneath the waterline the surgeon would soon be asleep in his sick-bay. He had only a handful of ill or injured men to deal with. It was to be hoped it remained like that.

Further forward in the midshipmen's berth all would be quiet, although probably a flickering glim would betray somebody trying to read a complicated navigational problem, with a solution expected in the forenoon by Bunce.

Their own world. Seamen and marines. Painters and caulkers, ropemakers and gun captains, coopers and topmen, as mixed a crowd as you could meet in a whole city.

And right aft, doubtless still at his big table, the one who ruled all of them, the captain.

Bolitho looked up at the darkness. Pears was almost directly above him. With the watchful Foley nearby, and a glass at his elbow as he pondered over the day's events and tomorrow's uncertainties.

That was the difference, he decided. We obey and execute his orders as best we can. But he has to give them. And the reward or the blame must be on his shoulders.

Bolitho rolled over and buried his face in the musty pillow.

There were certain advantages in remaining a mere lieutenant.

3

The Faithful

The following day was little different from the preceding ones.
Overnight the wind had backed slightly but had lost much of its
strength, so that the great, dripping sails filled and sagged in noisy
confusion and added in some way to the general air of tension.

Towards noon, with the drizzle as heavy as ever and the sea an
expanse of dirty grey, the pipe echoed around the ship, 'Hands lay aft to
witness punishment!' It was common enough, and under normal
conditions might have excited little comment. In a King's ship discipline
was hard and quickly executed, and the punishment given by members
of the company to one of their own caught stealing from a shipmate's
meagre possessions was far worse.

But today should have been different. After all the weeks and months
of frustration and waiting, of being cooped up in harbour with little
more comfort than a prison hulk, or beating up and down the coastline
on some fruitless mission or other, it had been hoped that this would
bring a change.

The weather did nothing to help. As Bolitho stood with the other
lieutenants, while the marines clattered up and across the poop in two
scarlet lines, the ship's company hurried aft. They had to squint against
the blown spray and rain, and the biting wind which stirred the dripping
canvas with long, uneven gusts. A sullen, unhappy start, Bolitho
thought.

The man to be punished came to the larboard gangway, flanked by
Paget, the swarthy master-at-arms, and Mr Tolcher, the boatswain.
Paget was a tight-lipped, bitter man, and set against him and the squat
boatswain the prisoner looked by far the most innocent.

Bolitho watched him, a young Swede named Carlsson. He had a
clean-cut face with long flaxen hair, and was staring around as if he had
never laid eyes on the ship before. He was typical of the *Trojan*'s
mixture, Bolitho thought. You never knew what sort of man you would
confront from day to day. Many tongues and races had been gathered
up into *Trojan*'s hull in two years, and yet somehow they all seemed to
settle in a very short while of coming aboard.

Bolitho hated floggings, even though they were part of a sailor's life. There still seemed to be no alternative for a captain to maintain discipline when far away from higher authority and the company of other ships.

The grating was rigged by the gangway, and Balleine, a muscular boatswain's mate, stood waiting beside it, the red baize bag dangling at his side.

Cairns crossed the quarterdeck as Pears appeared beneath the poop.

'Company assembled, sir.' His eyes were expressionless.

'Very well.'

Pears glanced at the compass and then walked heavily forward to the quarterdeck rail. There was a hush over the crowded seamen who filled the gundeck and overflowed on to the gangways and into the shrouds themselves.

Bolitho glanced at the midshipmen grouped alongside the older warrant officers. He had been sick at a flogging when he had been a midshipman.

He thought about Carlsson. Found asleep on watch after a whole day of fighting wind and rebellious canvas.

With some officers it might have made a difference. But Lieutenant Sparke had no such weakness as sentiment. Bolitho wondered if he was thinking about it now. How it had cast a blight over the very day he was going to lead a boat attack. He glanced sideways at him but saw nothing but Sparke's usual tight severity.

Pears nodded. 'Uncover.' He removed his hat and tucked it beneath his arm, while the others followed his example.

Bolitho looked to larboard, half expecting to see the sails of their faithful shadow. During the night the schooner had edged closer, and was now visible from the tops of the lower shrouds, but not from the quarterdeck as yet. That made it harder to accept in a sailor's simple reasoning. A Yankee rebel cruising along as safe as you please, and one of their own about to be flogged.

Pears opened the Articles of War and read the relevant numbers with little change from his normal tone. He finished with the words, '. . . he shall be punished according to the Laws and Customs of such cases used at sea.' He replaced his hat, adding, 'Two dozen lashes.'

The rest of the proceedings moved swiftly. Carlsson was stripped to the waist and seized up to the grating, his arms spread up and out as if he was crucified.

Balleine had taken his cat-o'-nine-tails from the red baize bag and was running it through his fingers, his face set in a grim frown. He was to be in Bolitho's boat for the attack. Was he thinking of that?

Pears said in his harsh voice, 'Do your duty.'

Balleine's thick arm came back, over and down, the lash swishing across the man's naked shoulders with a dull crack. Bolitho heard the man gasp as the air was knocked from his lungs.

'One,' counted the master-at-arms.

Nearby, the surgeon and his mates waited to attend the man should he faint.

Bolitho made himself watch the ritual of punishment, his heart like lead. It was unreal. The grey light, the stark clarity of the sailmaker's patches on the heavily flapping main-course. The lash rose and fell, and the scars across the Swede's skin soon changed to overflowing red droplets, which altered into a bloody mess of torn flesh as the flogging continued. Some of the blood had spattered across the man's flaxen hair, the rest eddied and faded in the drizzle across the deck planking.

'*Twenty-one!*'

Bolitho heard a midshipman sobbing quietly, and saw Forbes, the youngest one aboard, gripping his companion's arm to control himself.

Carlsson had not cried out once, but as the final stroke cracked over his mutilated back he broke, and started to weep.

'Cut him down.'

Bolitho looked from the captain's profile to the watching company. Two dozen lashes was nothing to what some captains awarded. But in this case it might destroy the man. Bolitho doubted if Carlsson had understood more than a few words of what had been said to him.

The surgeon's assistants moved in to carry the sobbing man below. Two seamen started to swab up the blood, and others hurried to obey Tolcher's order to unrig the grating and replace it.

The marines trooped down either poop ladder, and Captain D'Esterre sheathed his bright sword as the company broke up and continued about its affairs.

Sparke said to Bolitho, 'We had best go over the raid again, so that we know each other's thinking.'

Bolitho shrugged. 'Aye, sir.'

Maybe Sparke's attitude was the right one. Bolitho liked Carlsson, what he knew of him. Obedient, cheerful and hard-working. But suppose it had been one of the ship's real trouble-makers who had been caught sleeping on watch. Would he still have felt the same dismay?

Sparke leaned his hands on the quarterdeck rail and peered down at the two cutters which had already been manhandled away from the other boats on the tier in readiness for swaying out.

He said, 'I am not too hopeful.' He gestured at the vibrating shrouds and halliards. 'Mr Bunce is usually right, but this time –'

A seaman yelled from the maintop, 'Deck there! T'other vessel's fallin' off, sir!'

Dalyell, who was officer of the watch, snatched a glass and climbed into the weather shrouds.

He exclaimed, 'Right, by God! The schooner's falling down-wind. Not much, but she'll be visible to all hands by the time they've had their spirit ration!' He laughed at Bolitho's face. 'Damme, Dick, that bugger is a saucy one!'

Bolitho shaded his eyes against the strange light and saw a brief blur across the tumbling water. Perhaps the schooner's master believed the same as Bunce and was drawing nearer so as not to lose his large quarry. Or maybe he was merely trying to provoke the captain into doing something foolish. Bolitho pictured Pears' face as he had read from the Articles of War. There was no chance of the latter.

Sparke was saying, 'It will have to be very fast. They might have boarding nets, but I doubt it. It would hamper her people more than ours.'

He was thinking aloud, seeing his name and citation in the *Gazette*, Bolitho guessed. It was clear in his eyes, like fever, or lust.

'I will go and see the master.' Sparke hurried away, his chin thrusting forward like a galley prow.

Stockdale emerged from somewhere and knuckled his forehead.

'I've seen to the weapons, sir. I've put all the cutlasses and boarding axes to the grindstone.' He wheezed painfully. 'We still going, sir?'

Bolitho crossed to the side and took a telescope from the midshipman of the watch.

'I hope so.'

Then he saw that the midshipman was Forbes, the one who had been holding on to his friend during the flogging.

'Are you well, Mr Forbes?'

The boy nodded wretchedly and sniffed. 'Aye, sir.'

'Good.' He trained the glass across the nettings. 'It comes hard to see a man punished. So we must always be on the lookout to remove the cause in the first place.'

He held his breath as the other vessel's topmasts flitted above the heaving water, as if the rest of her were totally submerged. She had a red square stitched against the throat of her mainsail. A makeshift patch, he wondered, or some special form of recognition? He shivered, feeling the rain trickling over his collar, plastering his hair to his forehead. It was uncanny to see the disembodied masts, to know nothing of the vessel and crew.

He turned to speak with Stockdale, but he had vanished as silently as he had appeared.

Dalyell lurched up the sloping deck and said hoarsely, 'It looks as if you'll be staying with us, Dick.' He grinned unfeelingly. 'I'm not sorry. I've no wish to do George Probyn's work when he's in his cups!'

Bolitho grimaced. 'I'm coming round to everyone else's view, Simon. I'll go below now.' He looked up at the flapping masthead pendant. 'It seems I shall have the afternoon watch after all.'

But it appeared that the captain had other ideas and still retained some powerful faith in his sailing master. Bolitho was relieved from his watchkeeping duties, and spent most of the time compiling a letter to his father. He merely added to the same long letter whenever he found the opportunity, and ended it just as abruptly whenever they spoke with a homebound packet. It would be a link with his father. The reverse would also be true as Bolitho described daily events, the sighting of ships and islands, the life which was no more for Captain James.

He sat on his sea chest, squinting his eyes as he tried to think of something new to put in his letter.

A chill seemed to run up his spine. As if a ghost had suddenly entered his tiny cabin. He looked up, startled, and saw the deckhead lantern flickering as before. But was it? He stared, and then peered round at the small hanging space where his other clothing had been swaying and creaking just moments earlier.

Bolitho stood up, but remembered to duck his head as he rushed out and aft into the wardroom. The stern windows were dull grey, streaked with spindrift and caked salt.

He pressed his face against them and exclaimed, 'My God! The Sage was right!'

He hurried up to the quarterdeck, instantly aware of the motionless figures all around him, their eyes peering across the quarter or up at the sails which were lifting and then drooping, shaking against the pressures of rigging and spars.

Cairns had the watch, and looked at him gravely. 'The fog, Dick.' He pointed across the nettings. 'It is coming now.'

Bolitho watched the slow progress, the way it seemed to smooth the turbulence from the waves and flatten the crests as it approached.

'Deck there! Oi've lost sight o' th' schooner, zur!'

Pears' voice cut across the speculation and gossip. 'Bring her up two points, Mr Cairns!' He watched the sudden bustle, the shrill calls between decks.

'Man the braces there!'

Pears said to the deck at large, 'We'll gain a cable or so.'

He looked up as the wheel squeaked and the yards began to swing in response to the braces. With her great spread of canvas still holding the dying wind, *Trojan* heeled obediently and pointed her jib boom further to windward. Flapping canvas, chattering blocks and the yells of petty officers did not cover his voice as he said to the tall sailing master, 'That was *well done*, Mr Bunce.'

Bunce dragged his gaze from the helmsmen and the swaying compass card. In the dull light his eyes and brows stood out from all else.

He replied humbly, 'It is His will, sir.'

Pears turned away as if to hide a smile. He barked, 'Mr Sparke, lay aft. Mr Bolitho, attend the cutters and have them swayed out presently.'

Steel clashed between decks, and more men swarmed up to the boat tier, their arms filled with cutlasses, pikes and muskets.

Bolitho was on the gundeck, watching the second cutter's black painted hull rising on its tackles. Then he turned to look aft and saw that the upper poop and the taffrail were already misty and without substance.

He said, 'Lively, lads, or we'll not find our way over the bulwark!' It brought a few laughs.

Pears heard them and said soberly to Sparke, 'Tend well what the master tells you about the set of the current hereabouts. It will save a mile of unnecessary boat pulling, and not see you arriving on your prize with no breath to lift a blade.' He watched Sparke's eyes as they took it all in. 'And take care. If you cannot board, then stand off and wait for the fog to clear. We'll not drift that much apart.'

He cupped his hands. 'Shorten sail, Mr Cairns! Bring her about and lie to!'

More shouted commands, and moments later as the courses and topsails were brailed up to the yards the two boats detached themselves from the shadowy gundeck and swung up and over the gangway.

Bolitho came aft and touched his hat. 'The people are mustered and armed, sir.'

Sparke handed him a scribbled note. 'Estimated course to steer. Mr Bunce has allowed for the schooner's drift and the strength of the current.' He looked at the captain. 'I'll be away, sir.'

Pears said, 'Carry on, Mr Sparke.' He was going to add good luck, but set against Sparke's severe features it seemed superfluous.

He did say to Bolitho, however, 'Do not get lost, sir. I'll not hunt around Massachusetts Bay for a year!'

Bolitho smiled. 'I will do my best, sir.'

As he ran down to the entry port, Pears said to Cairns, 'Young rascal.'

But Cairns was watching the pitching boats alongside, already filled with men and waiting for Sparke and Bolitho to take them clear of their ship. His heart was with them. It did him no good to realize that the captain's decision had probably been the right one.

Pears watched the black hulls turning end on, the confused splash and thud of oars suddenly picking up the stroke and taking them deeper into the wet, enveloping mist.

'Double the watch on deck, Mr Cairns. Have swivels loaded and set to withstand any boarding attempt on ourselves.'

'What will you do now, sir?'

Pears looked up at his ship's strength. Each sail was either furled or motionless, and *Trojan* herself was paying off to the current, rolling deeply on a steady swell.

'Do?' He yawned. 'I am going to eat.'

Bolitho stood up in the sternsheets and gripped Stockdale's shoulder while he found his balance. Through the man's checkered shirt his muscles felt like warm timber.

The mist swirled into the boat, clinging to their arms and faces, making their hair glisten as if with frost.

Bolitho listened to the steady, unhurried pull of the oars. *No sense in urgency. Save the strength for later.*

He said, 'Hold her nor'-west, Stockdale, I am assured that is the best course to take.'

He thought of Bunce's wild eyes. Could there be any other course indeed!

Then, leaving Stockdale at the tiller, crouching over the boat's compass, Bolitho groped his way slowly towards the bows, climbing over thwarts and grunting seamen, treading on weapons and the feet of the extra passengers.

The twenty-eight-foot cutter had a crew of eight and a coxswain in normal times. Now she held them and an additional party which in total amounted to eighteen officers and men.

He found Balleine, the boatswain's mate, crouching above the stem like a figurehead, peering into the wet mist, a hand cupped around his ear to pick up the slightest sound which might be a ship, or another boat.

Bolitho said quietly, 'I cannot see the second lieutenant's cutter, so we must assume we are dependent on our own resources.'

'Aye, sir.' The reply was blunt.

Bolitho thought Balleine might be brooding over the flogging, or merely resentful in being given a lookout's job while Stockdale took the tiller.

Bolitho said, 'I am depending on your experience today.' He saw the man nod and knew he had found the right spot. 'I fear we are somewhat short of it otherwise.'

The boatswain's mate grinned. 'Mr Quinn and Mr Couzens, sir. I'll see 'em fair.'

'I knew it.'

He touched the man's arm and began to make his way aft again. He picked out individual faces and shapes. Dunwoody, a miller's son from Kent. A dark-skinned Arab named Kutbi who had enlisted in Bristol, although nobody knew much about him even now. Rabbett, a tough little man from the Liverpool waterfront, and Varlo, who had been crossed in love, and had been picked up by the press-gang while he had been drowning his sorrows at his local inn. These and many more he had grown to know. Some he knew very well. Others stayed away, keeping the rigid barrier between forecastle and quarterdeck.

He reached the sternsheets and sat down between Quinn and Couzens. Their three ages added together only came to fifty-two. The ridiculous thought made him chuckle, and he felt the others turning towards him.

They think me already unhinged. I have lost sight of Sparke, and am probably steering in quite the wrong direction.

He explained, 'I am sorry. It was just a thought.' He took a deep breath of the wet salt air. 'But getting away from the ship is reward enough.' He spread his arms and saw Stockdale give his lopsided grin. 'Freedom to do what we want. Right or wrong.'

Quinn nodded. 'I think I understand.'

Bolitho said, 'Your father will be proud of you after this.' *If we live that long.*

Cairns had explained to Bolitho what Quinn had meant about his family being in the leather trade. Bolitho had imagined it to be a tanyard of the kind they had in Falmouth. Bridles and saddles, shoes and straps. Cairns had almost laughed. 'Man, his father belongs to an all-powerful city company. He has contracts with the Army, and influence everywhere else! When I look at young Quinn I sometimes marvel at his audacity to refuse all that power and all that money! He must be either brave or mad to exchange it for *this*!'

A large fish broke surface nearby and flopped back into the water again, making Couzens and some of the others gasp with alarm.

'Easy all!' Bolitho held up his arm to still the oars.

Again he was very conscious of the sea, of their isolation, as the oars rose dripping and motionless along the gunwales. He heard the gurgle of water around the rudder as the boat idled forward into the swell. The splash of another fish, the heavy breathing of the oarsmen.

Then Quinn said in a whisper, 'I hear the other cutter, sir!'

Bolitho nodded, turning his face to starboard, picking up the muffled creak of oars. Sparke was keeping about the same pace and distance. He said, 'Give way all!'

Beside him Couzens gave a nervous cough and asked, 'H-how many of the enemy will there be, sir?'

'Depends. If they've already taken a prize or two, they'll be short of hands. If not, we may be facing twice our number or more.'

'I see, sir.'

Bolitho turned away. Couzens did not see, but he was able to discuss it in a manner which would do justice to a veteran.

He felt the fog against his cheek like a cold breath. Was it moving faster than before? He had a picture of the wind rising and driving the fog away, laying them bare beneath the schooner's guns. Even a swivel could rip his party to shreds before he could get to grips.

He looked slowly along the straining oarsmen and the others waiting to take their turn. How many would change sides if that happened? It had occurred often enough already, when British seamen had been taken by privateers. It was common practice in the Navy, too. *Trojan* had several hands in her company caught or seized in the past two years from both sea and land. It was thought better to fight alongside their old enemy rather than risk disease and possible death in a prison hulk. While there was life there was always hope.

Bolitho reached up and touched his scar; it was throbbing again, and seemed to probe right through his skull.

Stockdale opened the shutter of his lantern very slightly and examined his compass.

He said, 'Steady as she goes, sir.' It seemed to amuse him.

On and on, changing the men at the oars, listening for Sparke's cutter, watching for even a hint of danger.

Bolitho thought that the schooner's master, being a local man, might have made more sail and outpaced the fog, might already be miles away, laughing while they pulled slowly and painfully towards some part of New England.

He allowed his mind to explore what was fast becoming a real possibility.

They might get ashore undetected and try to steal a small vessel and escape under sail. Then what?

Balleine called hoarsely, 'There's a *glow* of sorts, sir!'

Bolitho stumbled forward again, everything else forgotten.

'There, sir.'

Bolitho strained his eyes through the darkness. A glow, that described it exactly, like the window of an alehouse through a waterfront fog. No shape, no centre.

'A lantern.' Balleine licked his lips. 'Hung very high. So there'll be another bugger nearby.'

Bunce had been very accurate. But for his careful calculations they might have passed the other vessel without seeing her or the light. She was standing about a mile away, maybe less.

Bolitho said, 'Easy all!' When he returned to the sternsheets he said, 'She's up ahead, lads. From our drift I'd say she'll be bows on or stern on. We'll take what comes.'

Quinn said in a husky voice, 'Mr Sparke is coming, sir.'

They heard Sparke call, 'Are you ready, Mr Bolitho?' He sounded impatient, even querulous, his earlier doubts forgotten.

'Aye, sir.'

'We will take her from either end.' Sparke's boat loomed through the fog, the lieutenant's white shirt and breeches adding to the ghostlike appearance. 'That way we can divide their people.'

Bolitho said nothing, but his heart sank. Either end, so the boat which pulled the furthest would have a good chance of being seen before she could grapple.

Sparke's oars began to move again and he called, '*I* will take the stern.'

Bolitho waited until the other was clear and then signalled his own men to pull.

'You all know what to do?'

Couzens nodded, his face compressed with concentration. 'I will stay with the boat, sir.'

Quinn added jerkily, 'I'll support you, sir, er, Dick, and take the foredeck.'

Bolitho nodded. 'Balleine will hold *his* men until they are ready to use their muskets.'

Cairns had been insistent about that, and rightly so. Any fool might set off a musket too soon if it was loaded and primed from the start.

Bolitho drew his curved hanger and unclipped the leather scabbard, dropping it to the bottom boards. There it would wait until he needed it. But worn during an attack it might trip and throw him under a cutlass.

He touched the back of the blade, but kept his eyes fixed on the wavering glow beyond the bows. The nearer they got, the smaller it became, as the fog's distortion had less control over it.

From one corner of his eye he thought he saw a series of splashes as Sparke increased his stroke and went in for the attack.

Bolitho watched as with startling suddenness the masts and booms of the drifting schooner broke across the cloudy sky like black bars and the lantern sharpened into one unwinking eye.

Stockdale touched Couzens' arm, making the boy jump as if he had cut him.

'Here, your fist on the tiller-bar, sir.' He guided him as if Couzens had been struck blind. 'Take over from me when I give the word.' With his other hand Stockdale picked up his outdated boarding cutlass which weighed as much as two of the modern ones.

Bolitho held up his arm and the oars rose and remained poised over either beam like featherless wings.

He watched, holding his breath, feeling the drag of current and holding power of the rudder. They would collide with the schooner's raked stem, right beneath her bowsprit with any sort of luck.

'Boat your oars!' He was speaking in a fierce whisper, although surely his heart-beats against his ribs would be heard all the way to Boston. His lips were frozen in a wild grin which he could not control. Madness, desperation, fear. It was all here.

'Ready with the grapnel!'

He watched the slender bowsprit sweeping across them as if the schooner was riding at full power to smash them under her forefoot.

Bolitho saw Balleine rising with his grapnel, gauging the moment, ducking to avoid losing his head on the schooner's bobstay.

There was a sudden bang, followed by a long-drawn-out scream. Bolitho saw and heard it all in a mere second. The flash which seemed to come from the sea itself, the response from the vessel above him, yells and startled movements before more explosions ripped across the water towards the scream.

He jumped to his feet. 'Ready, lads!'

He shut Sparke from his mind. The fool had allowed somebody to load a musket, and it had gone off, hitting one of his men. It was too late now. For any of them.

Bolitho threw up his arm and seized the trailing line as the grapnel thudded into the schooner's bowsprit and slewed the cutter drunkenly around the bows.

'*At 'em, lads!*'

Then he was struggling with feet and hands, the hanger dangling from his wrist as he fought his way up and around the flared hull.

The other end of the vessel was lit by exploding muskets, and as Bolitho's men clambered over the forecastle and cannoned into unfamiliar pieces of gear, more shots hammered into the deck around them or whined above the rocking cutter like maddened spirits.

He heard Quinn gasping and stumbling beside him, Stockdale's heavy frame striding just a bit ahead, the cutlass moving before him as if to sniff out the enemy.

Something flew out of the darkness and a man fell shrieking, a pike driven through his chest. More cracks, and two more of Bolitho's men dropped.

But they were nearer now. Bolitho gripped his hanger and yelled, 'Surrender in the King's name!'

It brought a chorus of curses and derisive shouts, as he knew it would. But it gave him just the few more seconds he needed to get to grips. He hacked out and knocked a sword from somebody's hand. As the man ran to retrieve it, Bolitho heard Stockdale's cutlass smash into his skull, heard the big man grunt as he wrenched it free.

Then they were chest to chest, blade to blade. Behind him Bolitho heard Balleine yelling and blaspheming, the sporadic bang of muskets as he managed to get off a few shots at the shrouds where sharpshooters were trying to find their targets.

A bearded face loomed through the others, and Bolitho felt his blade grate against the man's sword with a clang of steel as they parried, pushed each other clear to find the space to fight. Around them figures staggered and reeled like crazed drunkards, their cutlasses striking sparks, the voices distorted and wild with hate and fear.

Bolitho ducked, slashed the man across the ribs, and as he lurched clear he brought the hanger down on his neck with such force he numbed his wrist.

But they were being pushed back towards the forecastle all the same. Somewhere, a hundred miles away, Bolitho heard a cannon shot, and through his dazed mind he guessed that it was another vessel nearby, trying to show that help was on its way.

His shoes slipped on blood, and a dying sailor, trodden and kicked by the fighting, hacking mass of men above him, tried to seize Bolitho's ankle.

Another man screamed and fell from aloft, dead from a musket ball before he hit the deck. But carried by the desperately fighting seamen he still seemed to cling to life, like a tipsy dancer.

Bolitho saw a pair of white legs against the bulwark and knew it was Quinn. He was being attacked by two men at once, and even as Bolitho slashed one of them across the shoulder and dragged him screaming to one side, Quinn gasped and dropped to his knees, his sword gone, and both hands pressed to his chest.

His attacker was so wild with the lust of battle he did not seem to see Bolitho. He stood above the lieutenant and drew back his arm for the kill. Bolitho caught him by the sleeve, swung him round, using the impetus of the man's sword-thrust to take him off balance. Then he drove the knuckle guard of his hanger into his face, the pain jarring his wrist again like a wound.

The man lurched upright, and seemed to be spitting out teeth as he bore down for another attack.

Then he stopped stock-still, his eyes white in the gloom like pebbles, as he slowly pirouetted around and then fell. Balleine pounced forward and tore his boarding axe from the man's back as he would from a chopping block.

There was a commotion alongside, and moments later the retreating boarders heard Sparke's penetrating voice as he shouted, 'To me, Trojans, to me!'

Attacked from both ends of the schooner, and with the obvious possibility of other boats nearby, the fight ended as swiftly as it had begun.

There were not even any curses thrown at the British seamen this time. *Trojan*'s men were too wild and shocked with the hand-to-hand fighting which had left several of their own dead and badly wounded, to accept insults as well. The schooner's crew seemed to sense this, and allowed themselves to be disarmed, searched and then herded into two manageable groups.

Sparke, a pistol in either hand, strode amongst the corpses and whimpering wounded, and when he saw Bolitho snapped, 'Might have been worse.' He could not control his elation. 'Nice little craft. Very nice.' He saw Quinn and leaned over him. 'Is it bad?'

Balleine, who had torn open the lieutenant's shirt and was trying to stem the blood, said, 'Slit his chest like a peach, sir. But if we can get him to . . .'

But Sparke had already gone elsewhere, bellowing for Frowd, his master's mate, to attend to the business of getting under way at the first breath of a breeze.

Bolitho was on his knees, holding Quinn's hands away from the wound, as Balleine did his best with a makeshift bandage.

'Easy, James.' He saw Quinn's head lolling, his efforts to control his agony. His hands were like ice, and there was blood everywhere. 'You will be all right. I promise.'

Sparke was back again. 'Come, come, Mr Bolitho, there's a lot to do. And I'll wager we'll have company before too long.'

He dropped his voice suddenly, and Bolitho was confronted by a Sparke he had not seen before in the two years he had known him.

'I *know* how you feel about Quinn. *Responsible*. But you must not show it. Not now. In front of the people, d'you see? They're feeling the shock, the fight's going out of them. They'll be looking to us. So we'll save our regrets for later, eh?'

He changed back again. 'Now then. Cutters to be warped aft and secured. Check the armament, or lack of it, and see that it is loaded to repel attack. Canister, grape, anything you can lay hands on.' He looked for somebody in the foggy darkness. 'You! Archer! Train a swivel on the prisoners. One sign that they might try to retake the ship and you know what to do!'

Stockdale was wiping his cutlass on a piece of some luckless man's shirt.

He said, 'I'll watch over Mr Quinn, sir.' He rubbed the cutlass again and then thrust it through his belt. 'A good tot would suit him fine, I'm thinking.'

Bolitho nodded. 'Aye, see to it.'

He walked away, the sobs and groans from the darkened deck painting a better picture than any sight could do.

He saw Dunwoody, the miller's son, groping around an inert shape by the bulwark.

The seaman said brokenly, 'It's me mate, sir, Bill Tyler.'

Bolitho said, 'I know. I saw him fall.' He recalled Sparke's advice and added, 'Get that lantern down from aloft directly. We don't want to invite the moths, do we?'

Dunwoody stood up and wiped his face. 'No, sir. I suppose not.' He hurried away, but glanced back at his dead friend as if to tell himself it was not true.

Sparke was everywhere, and when he rejoined Bolitho by the wheel he said briskly, 'She's the *Faithful*. Owned by the Tracy brothers of Boston. Known privateers, and very efficient at their trade.'

Bolitho waited, feeling his wrists and hands trembling with strain.

Sparke added, 'I have searched the cabin. Quite a haul of information.' He was bubbling with pleasure. 'Captain Tracy was killed just
now.' He gestured to the upturned white eyes of the man killed by
Balleine's boarding axe. 'That's him. The other one, his brother,
commands a fine brig apparently, the *Revenge*, taken from us last year.
She was named *Mischief* then.'

'Aye, sir, I remember. She was taken off Cape May.' It was amazing
that he could speak so calmly. As if they were both out for a stroll
instead of standing amidst carnage and pain.

Sparke eyed him curiously. 'Are you steadier now?' He did not wait
for an answer. 'Good. The only way.'

Bolitho asked, 'Does she have any sort of cargo, sir?'

'None. She was obviously expecting to get *that* from our convoy.' He
looked up at the bare masts. 'Put some hands to work on this deck. It's
like a slaughter-house. Drop the corpses over the side and have the
wounded carried below. There's precious little comfort for them, but
it's a sight warmer than on deck.'

As Bolitho made to hurry away, Sparke added calmly, 'Besides
which, I want them to be as quiet as possible. There may be boats
nearby, and I intend to hold this vessel as our prize.'

Bolitho looked round for his hat which had gone flying in the fight.
That was more like it, he thought grimly. For a brief moment he had
imagined that Sparke's reason for moving the injured was solely for
humanity's sake. He should have known better.

The work to clear up the deck and to search out the vessel's defences
and stores went on without a break. The fit and unwounded men did the
heavy work, the ones with lesser injuries sat with muskets and at the
loaded swivels to watch over the prisoners. The badly wounded, one of
whom was the man who had foolishly fired his musket and had lost half
his face in doing so, managed as best they could.

Sparke had not mentioned the musket incident. But for it the
casualties would have been much reduced, even minimal. The
schooner's crew were brave enough, but without that warning, and
lacking as they did the hardened discipline of *Trojan*'s seamen, it would
likely have ended with little more than a bloody nose or two. Bolitho
knew Sparke must have thought about this. He would doubtless be
hoping that Pears would see only the prize and forget the oversight.

Several times Bolitho climbed down to the master's cabin where the
late Captain Tracy had lived and made his plans. There, Quinn was
lying white-faced on a rough bunk, his bandages soaked in blood, his lip
cut where he had bitten it to stem the anguish.

Bolitho asked Stockdale what he thought and the man answered readily, 'He has a will to live, sir. But he's precious little hope, I'm thinking.'

The first hint of dawn came with the lightening of the surrounding mist.

The schooner's lazaret had been broken open and a generous ration of neat rum issued to all hands, including the two young midshipmen.

Of the attacking force of thirty-six officers and seamen, twelve were already dead, or as near to as made no difference, and several of the survivors had cuts and bruises which had left them too weak and dazed to be of much use for the moment.

Bolitho watched the paling mist, seeing the schooner taking shape around them. He saw Couzens and Midshipman Libby from Sparke's boat staring at the great bloodstains on the planking, perhaps realizing only now what they had seen and done.

Mr Frowd, the master's mate, waited by the wheel, watching the limp sails which Bolitho's men had shaken out in readiness for the first breeze. The only sounds were the clatter of loose gear, the creak of timbers as the vessel rolled uncomfortably on the swell.

With the dawn came the awareness of danger, that which a fox might feel when it crosses open land.

Bolitho looked along the deck. The *Faithful* carried eight six-pounders and four swivel guns, all of which had been made in France. This fact, added to the discovery of some very fine and freshly packed brandy in the captain's lazaret, hinted at a close relationship with the French privateers.

She was a very handy little vessel, of about seventy-five feet. One which would sail to windward better than most and outpace any heavier, square-rigged ship.

Whoever Captain Tracy had once been, he would not have planned to be dead on this new dawn.

The boom of the large gaff-headed mainsail creaked noisily, and the deck gave a resounding tremble.

Sparke shouted, 'Lively there! Here comes the wind!'

Bolitho saw his expression and called, 'Stand by the fores'l!' He waved to Balleine. 'Ready with stays'l and jib!' The schooner's returning life seemed to affect him also. 'A good hand at the wheel, Mr Frowd!'

Frowd showed his teeth. He had picked a helmsman already, but understood Bolitho's mood. He had been in the Navy as long as the fourth lieutenant had been on this earth.

Every man had at least two jobs to do at once, but watched by the silent prisoners, they bustled about the confined deck as if they had been doing it for months.

'Sir! Mastheads to starboard!'

Sparke spun round as Bolitho pointed towards the rolling bank of fog. Two masts were standing through above it, one with a drooping pendant, but enough to show it was a larger vessel than the *Faithful*.

The blocks clattered and squealed as the seamen hauled and panted while the foresail and then the big mainsail with its strange scarlet patch at its throat were set to the wind. The deck tilted, and the helmsman reported gruffly, 'We 'ave steerage way, sir!'

Sparke peered at the misty compass bowl. 'Wind seems as before, Mr Frowd. Let her fall off. We'll try and hold the wind-gage from this other beauty, but we'll run if needs be.'

The two big sails swung out on their booms, shaking away the clinging moisture and yesterday's rain like dogs emerging from a stream.

Bolitho said, 'Mr Couzens! Take three hands and help Balleine with the stays'l!'

As he turned again he saw what Sparke had seen. With the fog rolling and unfolding downwind like smoke, the other vessel seemed to leap bodily from it. She was a brig, with the now-familiar striped Grand Union flag with its circle of stars set against the hoist already lifting and flapping from her peak.

Something like a sigh came from the watching prisoners, and one called, 'Now you'll see some iron, before they bury you!'

Sparke snapped, 'Keep that man silent, or put a ball in his head, I don't care which.' He glanced at Frowd. 'Fall off two points.'

'Steer nor'-east!'

'Will I have the six-pounders run out, sir?'

Sparke had found a telescope and was training it on the brig.

'She's the old *Mischief*.' He steadied the glass. 'Ah. I see her captain. Must be the other Tracy.' He looked at Bolitho. 'No. If we get close enough to use these little guns, the brig will reduce us to toothpicks within half an hour. Agility and speed is all we have.'

He tugged out his watch and studied it. He did not even blink as a gun crashed out and a ball slapped through the foresail like an invisible fist.

Spray lifted over the bows and pattered across the busy seamen there. The wind got stronger as the fog hurried ahead of the little schooner, as if afraid of being impaled on the jib boom.

The brig had set her topsails and forecourse now and was in hot pursuit, trying to beat to windward and outsail the schooner in one unbroken tack. Her two bow-chasers were shooting gun by gun, the air cringing to the wild scream which could only mean chain-shot or langridge. Just one of those around a mast and it would be the start of the end.

Another gun must have been trained round to bear on the elusive *Faithful*, and a moment later a ball ripped low over the poop, cutting rigging, and almost hitting one of the prisoners who had risen to watch.

A seaman snarled at him, 'Y'see, matey? Yankee iron is just as bloody for *you* this time!'

Balleine hurried aft and asked, 'Shall I cut the boats adrift, sir? We might gain half a knot without them.'

Another ball slammed down almost alongside, hurling spray clean over the poop like tropical rain.

A seaman yelled in disbelief, 'The Yankee's goin' about, sir!'

Sparke permitted himself a small smile of satisfaction. With the fog retreating rapidly through her towering masts and rigging like ghostly gunsmoke, the *Trojan* loomed to meet them, her exposed broadside already run out in twin lines of black muzzles.

Sparke said, 'Bless me, Mr Bolitho! They'll have *us* if we're not careful!'

Midshipman Libby ran aft like a rabbit, and seconds later the British ensign broke from the gaff, bright scarlet to match the one above *Trojan*'s gilded poop.

Below, in the tiny cabin, Stockdale wiped Quinn's forehead with a wet rag and looked at the skylight.

Quinn moved his lips very slowly. 'What was that sound?'

Stockdale watched him sadly. 'Cheering, sir. Must've sighted the old *Trojan*.'

He saw Quinn swoon away again on a tide of pain and the brandy which he had been forcing into him. If he lived he might never be the same again. Then he thought of the splashes alongside as the corpses, friends and enemies alike, had been buried at sea. Even so, he'd be better off than them.

4

Rendezvous

Bolitho strode aft and paused beneath the *Trojan*'s poop, conscious of the many watching eyes which followed him along the deck, just as they had greeted his return on board. He was aware too of his dirty and bedraggled appearance, the tear in his coat sleeve, and smears of dried blood across his breeches.

He looked over his shoulder and saw the prize, more graceful than ever at a distance, riding comfortably beneath *Trojan*'s lee. It was hard to picture what had happened aboard her during the night, let alone accept he had managed to survive it.

Sparke had come across to the *Trojan* immediately they had made signal contact, and had left Bolitho to attend to the transfer of wounded and the burial of the man whose musket had exploded in his face.

Before reporting to the captain, Bolitho had hurried down to the orlop, almost dreading what he would find. *Responsible*, that was what Sparke had said. It was how it had felt as he had looked at the spread-eagled body on the surgeon's table, shining like a corpse in the swaying deckhead lanterns. Quinn had been stripped naked, and as Thorndike had slit away the last of the matted bandage, Bolitho had seen the gash for the first time. From the point of Quinn's left shoulder, diagonally across his breast, it opened like an obscene mouth.

Quinn was unconscious, and Thorndike had said curtly, 'Not too bad. But another day,' he shrugged, 'different story.'

Bolitho had asked, 'Can you save him?'

Thorndike had faced him, displaying his bloody apron, as he had snapped, 'I'll do what I can. I have already taken off a man's leg, and another has a splinter in his eye.'

Bolitho had said awkwardly, 'I am sorry. I'll not delay you further.'

Now, as he made his way towards the stern cabin where a scarlet-coated marine stood stiffly on guard, he felt the same dull ache of failure and despair. They had taken a prize, but the cost had been too great.

The marine stamped his boots together, and then Foley, as neat as ever, opened the outer door, his eyes widening as he took in Bolitho's crumpled appearance with obvious disapproval.

In the stern cabin Captain Pears was at his desk, some papers strewn across it, a tall goblet of wine in one hand.

Bolitho stared at Sparke. He was smartly dressed, shaved, and looked as if he had never left the ship.

Pears ordered, 'Wine for the fourth lieutenant.'

He watched Bolitho as he took the goblet from his servant, saw the strain, the dragging weariness of the night's work.

'Mr Sparke has been telling me of your impressive deeds, Mr Bolitho.' Pears' face was devoid of expression. 'The schooner is a good catch.'

Bolitho let the wine warm his stomach, soothe the ache in his mind. Sparke had come straight to the ship, had changed and cleaned himself before presenting his report to the captain. How much had he told him about the first part? The startling crash of the musket which had added so much to the bill.

Pears asked, 'How is Mr Quinn, by the way?'

'The surgeon is hopeful, sir.'

Pears eyes him strangely. 'Good. And I understand both the midshipmen behaved well, too.'

He turned his attention to the littered papers, the rest apparently put aside. Finished.

Pears said, 'These papers were found by Mr Sparke in the *Faithful*'s cabin. They are of even greater value than the prize herself.' He looked at them grimly. 'They give details of the schooner's mission after she had taken on any captured powder and weapons from the convoy. The escorts would have been hard put to protect the whole convoy and keep it intact after the sort of weather we have been experiencing. And I have no doubt it was even worse coming out of Halifax. As it is, the brig will have to manage without her, although I would expect there to be other wolves trailing such rich cargoes even now.'

Bolitho asked, 'When will you expect to sight the ships, sir?'

'Mr Bunce and I believe tomorrow.' He spoke as if it no longer mattered. 'But there is something else which must be done without delay. The *Faithful* was to rendezvous with the enemy near the mouth of Delaware Bay. Our Army in Philadelphia is hard put to force supplies upriver to the garrison. There are patrols and skirmishers every mile of the way to fire on our boats and barges. Just think how much worse it will get if the enemy can lay hands on more arms and powder.'

Bolitho nodded and took another goblet from Foley, his mind seeing it exactly.

Delaware Bay was some four hundred miles south of where he was standing. A fast, lively craft could reach the rendezvous in three days if the weather favoured her.

They had been that confident, he thought. The red patch on the mainsail. The signal to the watchers on the shore. It was just the right place for it, too. Very shallow and treacherous at low tide, where no prowling frigate would dare give chase for fear of tearing out her keel.

He said, 'You will send the *Faithful*, sir?'

'Yes. There will be some risk of course. The passage might take longer than we plan for. The enemy know that *Faithful* has been seized, and will use every ruse to pass the word south without losing a moment. Signals, fast horsemen, it can be done.' He permitted himself a wintry smile. 'Mr Revere has established that point beyond question.'

Sparke drew himself up very stiffly and looked at Bolitho. 'I have been given the honour of commanding this mission.'

Pears said calmly, 'If you wish, Mr Bolitho, you may go with the second lieutenant as before. The choice is yours, this time.'

Bolitho nodded, marvelling that he did not even hesitate. 'Aye, sir. I'd like to go.'

'That is settled then.' Pears dragged out his gold watch. 'I will have your orders written at once, but Mr Sparke already knows the bones of the matter.'

Cairns entered the cabin, his hat tucked under his arm.

'I have sent some hands across to the schooner, sir. The gunner is attending to the armament.' He paused, his eyes on Bolitho. 'Mr Quinn is still unconscious, but the surgeon says his heart and breathing are fair.'

Pears nodded. 'Tell my clerk to come aft at once.'

Cairns hesitated by the door. 'I have brought the prisoners aboard, sir. Shall I swear them in?'

Pears shook his head. 'No. Volunteers I will accept, but this war has taken too firm a hold to expect a change of loyalties as a matter of course. They would be like bad apples in a barrel, and I'll not risk discontent in my ship. We'll hand them to the authorities in New York when we return there.'

Cairns left, and Pears said, 'The written orders will not protect you from the cannon of our patrols in the area. So show them a clean pair of heels. If there are spies about, it will make your guise even more acceptable.'

Teakle, the captain's clerk, scurried into the cabin, and Pears dismissed them. 'Go and prepare yourselves, gentlemen. I want you to keep that rendezvous, and destroy what you discover there. It will be worth a great deal, and may put heart into our troops at Philadelphia.'

The two lieutenants left the cabin, and Sparke said, 'We will be taking some marines this time.' He sounded as if he disliked the idea of sharing his new role. 'But speed is the thing. So go and hurry our people to ferry the rest of the stores and weapons across to the schooner.'

Bolitho touched his hat and replied, 'Aye, sir.'

'And replace Midshipman Couzens with Mr Weston. This is no work for children.'

Bolitho walked out into the chilling air and watched the boats playing back and forth between the unmatched vessels like water-beetles.

Weston was the signals midshipman and, like Libby, who had been in Sparke's boat, would be the next on the list for examination for lieutenant. If Quinn died, the promotion of one of them would be immediate.

He saw Couzens watching from the lee gangway as *Trojan* rolled and complained while she lay hove to for the transfer of men and equipment.

Couzens had obviously already been told of the change, and said breathlessly, 'I'd like to come with you, sir.'

Bolitho eyed him gravely. Couzens at thirteen would be worth two of Weston. He was an overweight, ginger-haired youth of seventeen, and something of a bully when he could get away with it.

He replied, 'Next time, maybe.' He looked away. 'We shall see.'

It was odd that he rarely thought of being replaced himself, of being just another name marked D.D. *Discharged Dead.*

To be killed was one thing. To be *replaced* by someone he actually knew at this moment brought it home like a dash of ice water.

He saw Stockdale, arms folded, on the schooner's little poop as she rolled sickeningly on a procession of troughs. *Waiting.* Knowing with his inner sense that Bolitho would be going across at any moment to join him.

The marines were climbing down into the boats now, pursued by all the usual insults from the watching seamen.

Captain D'Esterre, accompanied by his sergeant, joined Bolitho on the gangway.

'Thanks to you, Dick, my lads will get some exercise, I trust.' He waved to his lieutenant who was remaining aboard with the rest of the marines. 'Take care! I'll outlive you yet!'

The marine lieutenant grinned and touched his hat. 'At least I may have a chance of winning a hand of cards while you're away, sir!'

Then the captain and his sergeant followed the others into the nearest boat.

Bolitho saw Sparke speaking with Cairns and the master, and said impetuously, 'Visit Mr Quinn whenever you can. Will you do that for me?'

Couzens nodded with sudden gravity. It was a special task. Something just for him alone.

'Aye, sir.' He stood back as Sparke came hurrying from the quarterdeck and added quickly, 'I will pray for you, sir.'

Bolitho stared at him with surprise. But he was moved, too. 'Thank you. That was well said.'

Then, touching his hat to the quarterdeck and nodding to the faces along the gangway, he hurried into the boat.

Sparke thumped down beside him, his written orders bulging from an inner pocket. As the boat shoved off Bolitho saw the seamen hurrying along the *Trojan*'s decks and yards getting ready to make sail again once she had retrieved her boats.

Sparke said, 'At last. Something to make them all sit up and take notice.'

D'Esterre was looking at the dizzily swaying schooner with sudden apprehension.

'How the deuce will we all get settled into her, in heaven's name?'

Sparke bared his teeth. 'It will not be for long. Sailors are used to such small hardships.'

Bolitho let his mind drift away, seeing his own hand as he continued with the last letter to his father, as if he were actually writing it at this moment.

Today I had the chance to stay with the ship, but I chose to return to the prize. He watched the masts and booms rising above the labouring oarsmen. *Perhaps I am wrong, but I believe that Sparke is so full of hope for the future he can see nothing else.*

The boat hooked on and the last of the marines clambered and clattered over the bulwark, swaying on the deck like toy soldiers in an unsteady box.

Shears, their sergeant, soon took charge, and within minutes there was not a red coat to be seen as one by one they climbed down into the vessel's main hold.

One of *Trojan*'s nine-pounders had been ferried across, and was now firmly lashed on the deck, with tackles skilfully fitted to the schooner's available ring-bolts and cleats. How William Chimmo, *Trojan*'s gunner, had managed to get it ferried over, remounted and set in its present position was evidence of a real expert, a professional warrant officer. He had sent one of his mates, a taciturn man called Rowhurst, to tend the nine-pounder's needs, and he was looking at the gun, rubbing it with a rag, and probably wondering what would happen to the schooner's deck planking when he had to lay and fire it.

By the time they had sorted out the hands, the new ones and those of the original party who were still aboard, and put them to work, *Trojan* was already standing downwind, with more and more canvas ballooning from her yards. One boat was still being lowered inboard on to the tier, Pears was so eager to make up for lost time.

Bolitho watched her for some minutes, seeing her from a distance, as Quinn had once seen the great ships heading down the Thames. Things of power and beauty, while within their hulls they carried as much hope and pain as any landlocked town. Now Quinn was lying on the orlop. Or perhaps already dead.

Mr Frowd touched his hat. 'Ready to get under way, sir.' He glanced meaningly at Sparke who was peering at his written orders, entirely absorbed.

Bolitho called, 'We are ready, sir.'

Sparke scowled, irritated at the interruption. 'Then please be so good as to turn the hands to.'

Frowd rubbed his hands as he looked at the big boomed sails and the waiting seamen.

'She'll fly, this one.' He became formal again. 'I suggest we take account of the present wind, sir, and steer sou'-east. That'll take us well clear of the bay and prepare us for old Nantucket again.'

Bolitho nodded. 'Very well. Bring her about and lay her on the starboard tack.'

Sparke came out of his trance and crossed the deck as the man ran to bring the schooner under command.

'It is a good plan.' He stuck out his narrow chin. 'The late and unlamented Captain Tracy wrote almost everything about the rendez-vous except the colour of his countrymen's eyes!'

He gripped a stay as the wheel went over and the two great booms swung above the gurgling water alongside and each sail filled until it looked iron-hard.

Bolitho noticed that even the hole in the foresail made by the brig's cannon had been deftly patched during the last few hours. The dexterity of the British sailor when he put his mind to something was beyond measure, he thought.

The *Faithful* was responding well, in spite of her changed ownership. With spray leaping over her stern and sluicing into small rivers along her lee scuppers, she came about like a thoroughbred, the sails filling again and thundering to the wind.

Eventually, leaning over stiffly to take full advantage of the new tack, Frowd was satisfied. After serving under Bunce, he had learned to take nothing for granted.

Sparke watched, unblinking, from right aft by the taffrail.

He said, 'Dismiss the watch below, Mr Bolitho.'

He turned and shaded his eyes to seek out the *Trojan*, but she was hidden in a rain squall, little more than a shadow, or a smudge on an imperfect painting.

Sparke lurched unsteadily to the cabin hatch.

'I will be below if you need me.'

Bolitho breathed out slowly. Sparke was no longer a lieutenant. He had become a captain.

'Mr Bolitho, sir!'

Bolitho rolled over in the unfamiliar bunk and blinked at a shaded lantern. It was Midshipman Weston, leaning over him, his shadow looming across the cabin like a spectre.

'What is it?'

Bolitho dragged his mind reluctantly from the precious sleep. He sat up, massaging his eyes, his throat sore from the stench of the sealed cabin, the damp, and foul air.

Weston watched him. 'The second lieutenant's compliments, sir, and would you join him on deck.'

Bolitho threw his legs over the bunk and tested the schooner's motion. It must be nearly dawn, he thought, and Sparke was already about. That was strange, to say the least, as he usually left the matters of watchkeeping and routine alterations of tack and course to Bolitho or Frowd.

Weston said nothing, and Bolitho was disinclined to ask what was happening. It would show doubt and uncertainty to the midshipman, who had enough of his own already.

He scrambled through the companion hatch and winced to the greeting of needle-sharp spray and wind. The sky was much as he had last seen it. Low scudding clouds, and with no sign of a star.

He listened to the boom of canvas, the creak of spars as the schooner plunged drunkenly across a deep trough with such violence it almost flung him to the deck.

It had been like this for three days. The wind had become their enemy more often than not, and they had been made to change tack again and again, beating back and forth for miles to make an advance of just a few cables, or indeed for a complete loss of progress.

Sparke had been almost desperate as day by day they had driven south and then south-west towards the land and the mouth of the Delaware.

Even the most disciplined seaman aboard had become sullen and resentful at Sparke's attitude. He was intolerant of everyone, and seemed totally obsessed by the task entrusted to him, and now the possibility of failure.

Bolitho crossed the slippery planking and shouted above the wind, 'You sent for me, sir?'

Sparke swung round, retaining his grip on the weather shrouds, his usually immaculate hair streaming in the wind as he replied angrily, 'Of course, damn it! You have taken long enough!'

Bolitho controlled his sudden anger, knowing that Sparke's shouted rebuke must have been heard by most of the men on deck. He waited, sensing the lieutenant's mood, his all-consuming need to drive the ship with every stitch she would carry.

Sparke said abruptly, 'The master's mate has suggested we stay on this tack until noon.'

Bolitho forced his mind to grapple with it, to picture their wavering progress on the chart.

He answered without hesitation, 'Mr Frowd means we are less likely to run foul of local shipping, or worse, one of our own patrols.'

'Mr Frowd is an *idiot*!' He was yelling again. 'And if you agree with him, you are equally so, damn your eyes!'

Bolitho swallowed hard, counting seconds as he would for a fall of shot.

'I have to agree with him, sir. He is a man of much experience.'

'And I am not, I suppose!' He held up his free hand. 'Do not bother to argue with me. My mind is settled on it. We will change tack in one hour and head directly for the rendezvous. It will cut the time considerably. On *this* tack we could be another full day!'

Bolitho tried again. 'The enemy will not know our exact time of arrival, sir, or indeed if we are coming at all. War leaves no room for such planning.'

Sparke had not heard him. 'By the living God, I'll not let them get away now. I've waited long enough, watching others being handed gilt-edged commands because they *know* somebody at the Admiralty or in Court. Well, Mr Bolitho, not me. I've worked all the way. Earned each step up the ladder!'

He seemed to realize what he had said, that he had laid himself wide open before his subordinate, and added, 'Now, call the hands! Tell Mr Frowd to prepare his chart.' He eyed him fixedly, his face very pale in the gloom. 'I'll have no arguments. Tell him that also!'

'Have you discussed it with Captain D'Esterre, sir?'

Sparke laughed. 'Certainly not. He is a marine. A *soldier* as far as I am concerned!'

In the cupboard-like space adjoining the master's cabin which was the *Faithful*'s chart room, Bolitho joined Frowd and peered at the calculations and compass directions which had become their daily fare since leaving *Trojan*'s company.

Frowd said quietly, 'It will get us there more quickly, sir. But . . .'

Bolitho was bent low to avoid the deckhead, conscious of the vessel's violent motion, the nearness of the sea through the side.

'Aye, Mr Frowd, there are always the *buts*. We will just have to hope for some luck.'

Frowd grinned bitterly. 'I've no wish to be killed by my own countrymen, by mistake or otherwise, sir.'

An hour later, with all hands employed on deck, *Faithful* clawed around to starboard, pointing her bowsprit towards the invisible land, a single reef in main and foresail, all that Sparke would tolerate. She was leaning right over to leeward, the sea creaming up and over the bulwark, or sluicing across the tethered nine-pounder like surf around a rock.

It was still extremely cold, and what food the cook managed to produce was soon without warmth, and soggy with spray after its perilous passage along the upper deck.

As the light strengthened, Sparke sent an extra lookout aloft, with orders to report anything he saw. '*Even if it is a floating log.*'

Bolitho watched Sparke's anxiety mount all through the forenoon as the schooner pushed steadily westward. Only once did the lookout sight another sail, but it was lost in spray and distance before he could give either a description or the course she was steering.

Stockdale was rarely out of Bolitho's sight, and was using his strength to great advantage as the seamen were ordered from one mast to the other, or made to climb aloft to repair and splice fraying rigging.

The cry from the masthead when it came was like an unexpected shot. '*Land ho!*'

Men temporarily forgot their discomfort as they squinted through the curtain of rain and spray, searching for the landfall.

Sparke hung on to the shrouds with his telescope, all dignity forgotten as he waited for the schooner to leap on a steep crest and he found the mark he had been hoping for.

He jumped down to the deck and glared triumphantly at Frowd.

'Let her fall off a point. That is Cape Henlopen yonder to the nor'-west of us!' He could not contain himself. 'Now, Mr Frowd, how about your caution, eh?'

The helmsman called, 'West by north, sir! Full an' bye!'

Frowd replied grimly, 'The wind's shifted, sir. Not much as yet, but we're heading for shallows to the south'rd of Delaware Bay.'

Sparke grimaced. '*More* caution!'

'It is my duty to warn you on these matters, sir.' He stood his ground.

Bolitho said, 'Mr Frowd is largely responsible for this final landfall, sir.'

'That I will acknowledge at the right time, provided —'

He stared up the mast as a lookout yelled, 'Deck there! Sail on th' larboard quarter!'

'*God damn!*' Sparke stared up until his eyes brimmed over with water. 'Ask the fool what she is!'

Midshipman Libby was already swarming up the weather shrouds, his feet moving like paddles in his efforts to reach the lookout.

Then he shouted, 'Too small for a frigate, sir! But I think she's sighted us!'

Bolitho watched the tossing grey water. They would all be able to see the newcomer soon. Too small for a frigate, Libby had said. But *like* one in appearance. Three masts, square-rigged. A sloop-of-war. *Faithful*'s slender hull would be no match for a sloop's sixteen or eighteen cannon.

'We had better come about, sir, and hoist our recognition signal.' He saw the uncertainty on Sparke's narrow features, the scar very bright on his cheek, like a red penny.

The other lookout called excitedly, 'Two small craft to loo'rd, sir! Standin' inshore.'

Bolitho bit his lip. Probably local coasting craft, in company for mutual protection, and steering for the bay.

Their presence ruled out the possibility of parleying with the patrolling sloop. If they were nearby, so too might be other, less friendly eyes.

Frowd suggested helpfully, 'If we come about now, sir, we can outsail her, even to wind'rd. I've been in schooners afore, and I know what they can do.'

Sparke's voice rose almost to a scream. 'How dare you question my judgement! I'll have you disrated if you speak like that to me again! Come about, wait and see, run away. God damn it, you're more like an old woman than a master's mate!'

Frowd looked away, angry and hurt.

Bolitho broke in, 'I know what he was trying to say, sir.' He watched Sparke's eyes swivel towards him but did not drop his gaze. 'We can stand off and wait a better chance. If we continue, even with the darkness soon upon us, that sloop-of-war has only to bide her time, to hold us in the shallows until we go aground, or admit defeat. The people we are supposed to meet and capture will not wait to share the same fate, I think.'

When Sparke spoke again he was very composed, even calm. 'I will overlook your anxiety on Mr Frowd's behalf, for I have observed your tendency to become involved in petty matters.' He nodded to Frowd. 'Carry on. Hold this tack as long as the wind favours it. In half an hour send a good leadsman to the chains.' He smiled wryly. 'Will that satisfy you?'

Frowd knuckled his forehead. 'Aye, aye, sir.'

When the half-hour glass was turned beside the compass the other vessel's topgallant sails were in sight from the deck.

D'Esterre, very pale from the hold's discomfort, came up to Bolitho and said hoarsely, 'God, I am so sick, I would wish to die.' He peered at the sloop's straining sails and added, 'Will she catch us?'

'I think not. She's bound to go about soon.' He pointed to the creaming wash alongside. 'There's barely eight fathom under our keel, and it'll soon be half as much.'

The marine stared at the water with amazement. 'You have done nothing to reassure me, Dick!'

Bolitho could imagine the activity aboard the pursuing sloop. She would be almost as big as the *Destiny*, he thought wistfully. Fast, agile, free of the fleet's ponderous authority. Every glass would now be trained on the scurrying *Faithful* and her strange red device. The bow-chasers were probably run out with the hope of a crippling shot. Her captain would be waiting to see what the schooner might do and act accordingly. After months of dreary patrol work, with precious little help from the coastal villages, he would see the schooner as some small reward. When the truth was discovered, and Sparke had to explain what he had been doing, there would be a double-hell to pay.

He could understand Sparke's eagerness to get to grips with the enemy and do what Pears expected of him. But Frowd's advice had been sound, and he should have taken it. Now, they would have the sloop to contend with while they hunted for the Colonists and the craft they would be using to ferry powder and shot to a safe hiding place.

There was a muffled bang, the sound blown away by the wind almost as quickly.

A ball slashed along the nearest wave-crest, and Stockdale said admiringly, 'Not bad shooting.'

A second ball ripped right above the schooner's poop, and then Sparke, who had been standing rigidly like a statue, shouted harshly, '*There!* What did I tell you? She's wearing! Going about, just as I said she would!'

Bolitho watched the angle of the sloop's yards changing, the momentary confusion of her sails before she leaned over on the opposite tack.

Midshipman Weston exclaimed, 'That was most clever of you, sir. I would never have believed . . .'

Bolitho felt his lips crease into a smile, in spite of his anxiety. Sparke, no matter what mood he was in, had little time for crawlers.

'Hold your tongue! When I want praise from you I will ask for it! Now be about your duties, or I'll have Balleine lay his rattan across your fat rump!'

Weston scurried away, his face screwed up with humiliation as he pushed through some grinning seamen.

Sparke said, 'We will shorten sail, Mr Bolitho. Tell Balleine to close up his anchor party in case we have to let go in haste. See that our people are all armed, and that the gunner's mate knows what to do when required.' His eyes fell on Stockdale. 'Get below and put on one of the coats in the cabin. Captain Tracy was about your build, I believe. You'll not be near enough for them to spy the difference.'

Bolitho gave his orders, and felt some relief at Sparke's sudden return to his old self. Right or wrong, successful or not, it was better to be with the devil one knew.

He came out of his thoughts as Sparke snapped, '*Really*, must I do everything?'

As the evening gloom followed them towards the land, *Faithful*'s approach became more stealthy and cautious. The hands waited to take in the sails, or to put the schooner into the wind should they run across some uncharted sandbar or reef, and every few minutes the leadsman's mournful chant from the forecastle reminded anyone who might still be in doubt of their precarious position.

Later, a little before midnight, *Faithful*'s anchor splashed down, and she came to rest once again.

5

The Quality of Courage

'It's getting lighter, sir.' Bolitho stood beside the motionless wheel and watched the water around the anchored schooner until his eyes throbbed with strain.

Sparke grunted but said nothing, his jaw working up and down on a nugget of cheese.

Bolitho could feel the tension, made more extreme by the noises of sea and creaking timbers. They were anchored in a strange, powerful current, so that the *Faithful* repeatedly rode forward until her anchor was almost apeak. If the tide fell sharply, and you could not always trust the navigational instructions, she might become impaled on one of the flukes.

Another difference was the lack of order and discipline about the decks. Uniforms and the familiar blue jackets of the boatswain's and master's mates had been put below, and the men lounged around the bulwarks in varying attitudes of relaxed indifference to their officers.

Only the marines, crammed like fish in a barrel, were still sealed in the hold, awaiting the signal which might never come.

Sparke remarked quietly, 'Even this schooner would make a fine command, a good start for any ambitious officer.'

Bolitho watched him cut another piece of cheese, his hands quite steady as he added, 'She'll go to the prize court, but after that . . .'

Bolitho looked away, but it was another jumping fish which had caught his eye. He must not think about *afterwards*. For Sparke it would mean almost certain promotion, maybe a command of his own, this schooner even. It was obviously uppermost in his mind just now.

And why not? Bolitho pushed his envy aside as best he could. He himself, if he avoided death or serious injury, would soon be back in *Trojan*'s crowded belly. He thought of Quinn as he had last seen him and shivered. Perhaps it was because of the wound he had taken on his skull. He reached up and touched it cautiously, as if expecting the agony to come again. But injury was more on his mind than it had been before he had been slashed down. Seeing Quinn's gaping wound had made it nearer, as if the odds were going against him with each new risk and action.

When you were very young, like Couzens or Midshipman Forbes, the sights were just as terrible. But pain and death only seemed to happen to others, never to you. Now, Bolitho knew differently.

Stockdale trod heavily across the deck, his head lowered as if in deep thought, his hands locked behind him. In a long blue coat, he looked every inch a captain, especially one of a privateer.

Metal rasped in the gloom, and Sparke snapped, 'Take that man's name! I want absolute silence on deck!'

Bolitho peered up at the mainmast, searching for the masthead pendant. The wind had shifted further in the night and had backed almost due south. If that sloop had sailed past their position in the hope of beating back again at first light, she would find it doubly hard, and it would take far longer to achieve.

Another figure was beside the wheel, a seaman named Moffitt. Originally from Devon, he had come to America with his father as a young boy to settle in New Hampshire. But when the revolution had been recognized as something more than some ill-organized uprisings, Moffitt's father had found himself on the wrong side. Labelled a Loyalist, he had fled with his family to Halifax, and his hard-worked farm had been taken by his new enemy. Moffitt had been away from home at the time and had been seized, then forced into a ship of the Revolutionary Navy, one of the first American privateers which had sailed from Newburyport.

Their activities had not lasted for long, and the privateer had been chased and taken by a British frigate. For her company it had meant prison, but for Moffitt it had been a chance to change sides once more, to gain his revenge in his own way against those who had ruined his father.

Now he was beside the wheel, waiting to play his part.

Bolitho heard the approaching hiss of rain as it advanced from the darkness and then fell across the deck and furled sails in a relentless downpour. He tried to keep his hands from getting numb, his body from shivering. It was more than just the discomfort, the anxious misery of waiting. It would make the daylght slow to drive away the night, to give them the vision to know what was happening. Without help they had no chance of finding those they had come to capture. This coastline was riddled with creeks and inlets, bays and the mouths of many rivers, large and small. You could hide a ship of the line here provided you did not mind her going high and dry at low water.

But the land was there, lying across the choppy water like a great black slab. Eventually it would reveal itself. Into coves and trees, hills and undergrowth, where only Indians and animals had ever trod. Around it, and sometimes across it, the two armies manoeuvred, scouted and occasionally clashed in fierce battles of musket and bayonet, hunting-knife and sword.

Whatever the miseries endured by seamen, their life was far the best, Bolitho decided. You carried your home with you. It was up to you what you made of it.

'Boat approaching, sir!'

It was Balleine, a hand cupped round his ear, reminding Bolitho of the last moments before they had boarded this same schooner.

For a moment Sparke did not move or speak, and Bolitho imagined he had not heard.

Then he said softly, 'Pass the word. Be ready for treachery.'

As Balleine loped away along the deck Sparke said, 'I hear it.'

It was a regular splash of oars, the efforts noisy against a powerful current.

Bolitho said, 'Small boat, sir.'

'Yes.'

The boat appeared with startling suddenness, being swirled towards the schooner's bows like a piece of driftwood. A stout fishing dory with about five men aboard.

Then just as quickly it was gone, steered or carried on the current, it was as if they had all imagined it.

Frowd said, 'Not likely to be fishing, sir. Not this time o' day.'

Surprisingly, Sparke was almost jovial as he said, 'They are just testing us. Seeing what we are about. A King's ship would have given them a dose of canister or grape to send them on their way, as would a smuggler. I've no doubt they've been passing here every night and day for a week or more. Just to be on the safe side.' His teeth showed in his shadowy face. 'I'll give them something to remember all their lives!'

The word went along the deck once more and the seamen relaxed slightly, their bodies numbed by the rain and the raw cold.

Overhead the clouds moved swiftly, parting occasionally to allow the colours of dawn to intrude. Grey and blue water, the lush dark green of the land, white crests and the snakelike swirls of an inshore current. They could have been anchored anywhere, but Bolitho knew from his past two years' service that beyond the nearest cape, sheltered by the bay and the entrance to the Delaware River, were towns and settlements, farms and isolated families who had enough to worry about without a war in their midst.

Bolitho's excitement at being at sea again in the calling which had been followed by all his ancestors had soon become soured by his experiences. Many of those he had had to fight had been men like himself, from the West Country, or from Kent, from Newcastle and the Border towns, or from Scotland and Wales. They had chosen this new country, risked much to forge a new life. Because of others in high places, of deep loyalties and deeper mistrusts, the break had come as swiftly as the fall of an axe.

The new Revolutionary government had challenged the King, that should have been enough. But when he thought about it honestly, Bolitho often wished that the men he fought, and those he had seen die, had not called out in the same tongue, and often the same dialect, as himself.

Some gulls circled warily around the schooner's spiralling masts, then allowed themselves to be carried by the wind to more profitable pickings inland.

Sparke said, 'Change the lookouts, and keep one looking to seaward.'

In the strengthening light he looked thinner, his shirt and breeches pressed against his lean body by the rain, shining like snakeskin.

A shaft of watery sunlight probed through the clouds, the first Bolitho had seen for many days.

The telescopes would be watching soon.

He asked, 'Shall I have the mains'l hoisted, sir?'

'Yes.' Sparke fidgeted with his sword-hilt.

The seamen hauled and panted at the rain-swollen halliards until, loosely set, the sail shook and flapped from its boom, the red patch bright in the weak sunlight.

The schooner swung with it, tugging at the cable, coming alive like a horse testing bit and bridle.

'Boat to starboard, sir!'

Bolitho waited, seeing what looked like the same dory pulling strongly from the shore. It was unlikely that anyone would know or recognize any of the *Faithful*'s company, otherwise the recognition patch would be superfluous. Just the sight of the schooner would be enough. Bolitho knew from his childhood how the Cornish smugglers came and went on the tide, within yards of the waiting excisemen, with no more signal than a whistle.

But someone knew. Somewhere between Washington's army and the growing fleet of privateers were the link-men, the ones who fixed a rendezvous here, hanged an informer there.

He looked at Stockdale as he strode to the bulwark, and was impressed. Stockdale gestured forward, and two seamen swung a loaded swivel towards the boat, while he shouted in his hoarse voice, 'Stand off there!'

Moffitt stepped up beside him and cupped his hands. 'What d'you want of us?'

The boat rocked on the choppy water, the oarsmen crouched over with the rain bouncing on their shoulders.

The man at the tiller shouted back, 'That Cap'n Tracy?'

Stockdale shrugged. 'Mebbe.'

Sparke said, 'They're not sure, look at the bloody fools!'

Bolitho turned his back on the shore. He could almost feel the hidden
telescopes searching along the deck, examining them all one at a time.

'Where you from?' The boat idled slowly nearer.

Moffitt glanced at Sparke, who gave a curt nod. He shouted, 'There's
a British man-o'-war to seaward! I'll not wait much longer! Have you
no guts, man?'

Frowd said, 'That's done it. Here they come.'

The open mention of the British sloop, and Moffitt's colonial accent,
seemed to have carried more weight than the scarlet patch.

The dory grated alongside and a seaman caught the line thrown up by
one of the oarsmen.

Stockdale stood looking down at the boat, and then said in an
offhand manner which Bolitho had not heard before, 'Tell the one in
charge to step aboard. I'm not satisfied.'

He turned towards his officers and Bolitho gave a quick nod.

Sparke hissed, 'Keep him away from the nine-pounder, whatever
happens.' He gestured to Balleine. 'Start opening the hold.'

Bolitho watched the man climb up from the boat, trying to picture the
Faithful's deck through his eyes. If anything went wrong now, all they
would have to show for their plans would be five corpses and a dory.

The man who stood on the swaying deck was solidly built but agile
for his age. He had thick grey hair and a matching beard, and his
clothing was roughly stitched, like that of a woodsman.

He faced Stockdale calmly. 'I am Elias Haskett.' He took another half
pace. 'You are not the Tracy I remember.' It was not a challenge but a
statement.

Moffitt said, 'This is Cap'n Stockdale. We took over the *Faithful*
under Cap'n Tracy's orders.' He smiled, letting it sink in. 'He went in
command of a fine brig. Like his brother.'

The man named Elias Haskett seemed convinced. 'We've been
expecting you. It ain't easy. The redcoats have been pushing their
pickets across the territory, and that ship you told of has been up and
down the coast for weeks, like a nervous rabbit.' He glanced at the
others nearby, his eyes resting momentarily on Sparke.

Moffitt said, 'Mostly new hands. British deserters. You know how it
goes, man.'

'I do.' Haskett became businesslike. 'Good cargo for us?'

Balleine and a few hands had removed the covers from the hold, and
Haskett strode to the coaming to peer below.

Bolitho watched the pattern of men changing again, just as they had
practised and rehearsed. The first part was done, or so it appeared. Now
he saw Rowhurst, the gunner's mate, stroll casually to join Haskett, his
hand resting on his dirk. One note of alarm and Haskett would die
before he hit the deck.

Bolitho peered over a seaman's shoulder and tried not to think of the marines who were packed in a hastily constructed and almost airless chamber below a false platform. From the deck it looked as if the hold was full of powder kegs. In fact, there was just one layer, and only two were filled. But it only needed a marine to sneeze and that would be an end to it.

Moffitt clambered down and remarked coolly, 'Good catch. We cut out two from the convoy. We've muskets and bayonets too, and a thousand rounds of nine-pound shot.'

Bolitho wanted to swallow or to clear his parched throat. Moffitt was perfect. He was not acting, he *was* the intelligent mate of a privateer who knew what he was about.

Haskett said to Stockdale, 'I'll hoist the signal. The boats are hid yonder.' He waved vaguely towards some overlapping trees which ran almost to the water's edge. It could be a tiny cove or the entrance of a hitherto unexplored bay.

'What about the British sloop?' Moffitt glanced briefly at Sparke.

'She'll take half a day to claw back here, an' I've put some good look-outs where they can get a first sight of her.'

Bolitho watched Haskett as he bent on a small red pendant and ran it smartly to the foremast truck. He was no stranger to ships and the sea, no matter how he was dressed.

He heard one of the seamen gasp, and saw what looked like part of a tree edging clear of the shore. Then he realized it was a fat, round-bowed cutter, her single mast and yard covered with branches and gorse, while her broad hull was propelled slowly but firmly by long sweeps from either beam. She was followed by her twin. They looked Dutch built, and he guessed they had probably been brought here from the Caribbean, or had made their own way to earn a living from fishing and local trading.

He knew that Sparke had been counting on a single vessel, or several small lighters, even pulling boats. Each of these broad-beamed cutters was almost as large as the *Faithful* and built like a battering-ram.

Moffitt saw his quick nod and said, 'One will be enough. They look as if they could carry a King's arsenal.'

Haskett nodded. 'True. But we have other work after this, south towards the Chesapeake. Our boys captured a British ordnance brigantine a week back. She's aground, but filled to the gills with muskets and powder. We will off-load her cargo into one of the cutters. Enough to supply a whole army!'

Bolitho turned away. He could not bear to look at Sparke's face. He could read his mind, could picture his very plan of attack. With the sloop too far away to be of help, Sparke would seize the whole credit for himself.

The next few moments were the worst Bolitho could recall. The slow business of manoeuvring the two heavy cutters, with their strange disguise and long, galley-like sweeps. They must hold thirty or forty men, he decided. Some seamen, and the rest probably from the local militia, or an independent troop of Washington's scouts.

The *Faithful*'s masthead pendant flapped wetly in the wind, and Bolitho saw the nearest cutter start to swing across the current. Minutes to go. Mere minutes, and it would be too late for her to work clear, or set her sails.

Moffitt murmured, 'Stand by there.' If he was nervous, he was not showing it.

A seaman called, 'Aye, aye, sir!'

Bolitho chilled. It might have been expected. That somebody, even himself who had helped to plan the deception, should overplay his part. The smart acknowledgement to Moffitt's order was not that of a defecting sailor or half-trained privateersman.

Haskett swung round with an oath. 'You dirty scum!'

The crash of a pistol made every man freeze. Voices from the dory alongside mingled with the shrill cries of startled seabirds, but Bolitho could only stare at the grey-haired stranger as he staggered towards the bulwark, blood gushing from his mouth, while his hands clutched at his stomach like scarlet claws.

Sparke lowered his pistol and snapped, 'Swivels! *Open fire!*'

As the four swivels cracked from their mountings, sweeping the side and deck of the nearest cutter with whining canister, Rowhurst's men tore the tarpaulin from the nine-pounder and threw their weight on tackles and handspikes.

A few shots came from the nearest cutter, but the unexpected attack had done what Sparke had intended. The packed canister had swept amongst the men at the long sweeps, cutting them down, and knocking the stroke into chaos. The cutter was broaching to, drifting abeam, while Rowhurst's other crews waited by the stubby six-pounders which would bear, their slow-matches ready, the guns carefully loaded in advance with grapeshot.

'Fire as you bear!' Bolitho drew his hanger and walked amongst his men as they came alive again. '*Steady!*' A ball whined past his face and a seaman fell kicking and screaming beside the dead Elias Haskett.

Sparke took his reloaded pistol from a seaman and remarked absently, 'I hope Rowhurst's aim is as good as his obscenities.'

Even the taciturn Rowhurst seemed shocked out of his usual calm. He was capering from side to side of the nine-pounder's breech, watching as the second cutter managed to set her mainsail and jib, the sweeps discarded and drifting away like bones, the disguise dropping amongst them as the wind ballooned into the canvas.

Rowhurst cursed as one of his men reeled away, a massive hole punched through his forehead. He yelled, 'Ready, sir!' He waited for the *Faithful* to complete another swing on her cable and then thrust his slow-match to the breech.

Double-shotted, and with grape added for good measure, the gun hurled itself back on its makeshift tackles like an enraged beast. The crash of the explosion rolled around the sea like thunder, and the billowing smoke added to the sense of horror as the cutter's mast disintegrated and fell heavily in a tangle of rigging and thrashing canvas.

'Reload! Run out when you're ready and fire at will!'

The shock of Sparke's pistol shot had given way to a wave of wild excitement. This was something they understood. What they had been trained for, day by backbreaking day.

While the swivels and six-pounders kept up their murderous bombardment on the first cutter, Rowhurst's crew maintained a regular attack on the other. With mast and sails gone, she was soon hard aground on a sandbar, and even as someone gave a cheer a savage plume of fire exploded from her stern and spread rapidly with the wind, the rain-soaked timbers spurting steam until the fire took hold and she was ablaze from stem to stern.

Through and above the din of cannon-fire and yelling men Bolitho heard D'Esterre call, 'Lively, Sar'nt Shears, or there'll be little left for us to do!' D'Esterre blinked in the billowing smoke from the cutter and Rowhurst's nine-pounder and said, 'By God, this one will be up to us shortly!'

Bolitho watched the first cutter swinging drunkenly towards the *Faithful*'s bows. There were more men in evidence on her deck now, but there were many who would never move again. Blood ran in bright threads from her scuppers to mark the havoc left by the canister and packed grape.

'Marines, forward!'

Like puppets they stepped up to the bulwark, their long muskets rising as one.

'Present!' The sergeant waited, ignoring the balls which buzzed overhead or thudded into the timbers. '*Fire!*'

Bolitho saw those who had gathered at the point where both vessels would come together stagger and sway like corn in a field as the carefully aimed volley ripped amongst them.

The sergeant showed no emotion as he beat out the time with his handspike while the ramrods rose and fell together as if on a range.

'Take aim! *Fire!*'

The volley was upset by the sudden collision of both hulls, but not enough to save another handful of the yelling, defiant men who started to clamber aboard, cutlasses swinging, or firing at the nine-pounder's crew on the forecastle.

Sparke shouted, 'Strike, damn you!'

'I'll see you in hell!'

Bolitho ran to the bulwark, briefly aware that someone had defied Sparke even in the face of death.

Sergeant Shears shouted, 'Fix bayonets!' He looked at D'Esterre's raised sword. 'Marines, advance!'

Bolitho shouted, 'Tell them again to strike, sir!'

Sparke looked wild as he retorted, 'They had their chance, damn them!'

The marines moved with precision, shoulder to shoulder, a living red wall which cut the boarders off from the gun crews, separated them from their own craft, and from all hope.

Bolitho saw a figure duck past a bayonet and run aft, a cutlass held across his body like a talisman.

Bolitho raised his hanger, seeing the clumsy way he was holding the cutlass. Worse, he was no more than a youth.

'Surrender!'

But the youth came on, whimpering with pain as Bolitho turned his blade aside and with a twist of the wrist sent his cutlass clashing into the scuppers. Even then he tried to get to grips with Bolitho, sobbing and almost blinded with fury and tears.

Stockdale brought the flat of his cutlass down on the youth's head and knocked him senseless.

Sparke exclaimed, 'It's done.'

He walked past D'Esterre and regarded the remaining attackers coldly. There were not many of them. The rest, dead or wounded by the lunging line of bayonets, sprawled like tired onlookers.

Bolitho sheathed his hanger, feeling sick, and the returning ache in his head.

The dead were always without dignity, he thought. No matter the cause, or the value of a victory.

Sparke shouted, 'Secure the cutter! Mr Libby, take charge there! Balleine, put those rebels under guard!'

Frowd came aft and said quietly, 'We lost three men, sir. An' two wounded, but they'll live, with any fortune.'

Sparke handed his pistol to a seaman. 'Damn it, Mr Bolitho, look what we have achieved!'

Bolitho looked. First at the blackened carcass of the second cutter, almost burnt out and smoking furiously above a litter of wreckage and scattered remains. Most of her crew had either died under Rowhurst's solitary bombardment or had been carried away to drown on the swift current. Few sailors could even swim, he thought grimly.

Alongside, and closer to the eye, the other cutter was an even more horrific sight. Corpses and great patterns of blood were everywhere, and he saw Midshipman Libby with his handful of seamen picking his way over the deck, his face screwed up, fearful of what he would see next.

Sparke said, 'But the hull and spars are intact, d'you see, eh? Two prizes within a week! There'll be some envious glances when we reach Sandy Hook again, make no mistake!' He gestured angrily at the wretched Libby. 'For God's sake, sir! Stir yourself and get that mess over the side. I want to make sail within the hour, damn me if I don't!'

Captain D'Esterre said, 'I'll send some marines to help him.'

Sparke glared. 'You will not, sir. That young gentleman wishes to become a lieutenant. And he probably will, shortages in the fleet being what they are. So he must learn that it rates more than the uniform, damn me so it does!' He beckoned to the master's mate. 'Come below, Mr Frowd. I want a course for the Chesapeake. I'll get the exact position of the brigantine at leisure.'

They both vanished below, and D'Esterre said quietly, 'What a nauseating relish he displays!'

Bolitho saw the first of the corpses going over the side, drifting lazily past, as if glad to be free of it all.

He said bitterly, 'I thought you craved action.'

D'Esterre gripped his shoulder. 'Aye, Dick. I do my duty with the best of 'em. But the day you see me gloat like our energetic second lieutenant, you may shoot me down.'

The youth who had been knocked unconscious by Stockdale was being helped to his feet. He was rubbing his head and sobbing quietly. When he saw Stockdale he tried to hit out at him, but Moffitt caught him easily and pinioned him against the bulwark.

Bolitho said, 'He could have killed you, you know.'

Through his sobs the youth exclaimed, 'I wish he had! The British killed my father when they burned Norfolk! I swore to avenge him!'

Moffitt said harshly, 'Your people tarred and feathered my young brother! It blinded him!' He pushed the youth towards a waiting marine. 'So we're equal, eh?'

Bolitho said quietly, 'No, opposite, is how I see it.' He nodded to Moffitt. 'I did not know about your brother.'

Moffitt, shaking violently now that it was over, said, 'Oh, there's more, sir, a whole lot more!'

Frowd reappeared on deck and walked past the sobbing prisoner without a glance.

He said grimly, 'I thought this day's work would be an end to it, sir. For the moment at least.'

He looked up at the pendant and then at the cutter alongside, the hands working with buckets and swabs to clear the bloodstains from the scarred and riddled planking.

'She's named the *Thrush*, I see.' His professional eye confirmed Bolitho's opinion. 'Dutch built. Handy craft, and well able to beat to wind'rd, better even than this one.'

Midshipman Weston hovered nearby, his face as red as his hair. He had shouted a lot during the brief engagement, but had hung back when the Colonials had made their impossible gesture.

Frowd was saying, 'I'd hoped that sloop might have joined us.' He sounded anxious. 'Mr Sparke's got the name of the cove where they beached the brigantine. I know it, but not well.'

'How did he discover that?'

Frowd walked to the rail and spat into the water. 'Money, sir. There's always a traitor in every group. If the price is right.'

Bolitho made himself relax. He could forget Frowd's bitterness. He had been afraid that Sparke, in his desperate eagerness to complete his victory, would use harsher methods of obtaining his information. His face as he had killed Elias Haskett had been almost inhuman.

How many more Sparkes were there still to discover? he pondered.

In a steady wind, both vessels eventually got under way and started to work clear of the sandbars and shoals, the smoke from the burned-out cutter following them like an evil memory.

Charred remains and gaping corpses parted to allow them through, when with all sails set both vessels started the first leg of their long tack to seaward.

Sparke came on deck during the proceedings. He peered through a telescope to see how Midshipman Libby, ably assisted by the boatswain's mate, Balleine, and a handful of seamen, were managing aboard the *Thrush*. Then he sniffed at the air and snapped, 'Run up our proper colours, Mr Bolitho, and see that Mr Libby follows our example.'

Later, with both vessels in close company, heeling steeply on the starboard tack, Bolitho felt the stronger upthrust of deeper water, and not for the first time was glad to be rid of the land.

From the rendezvous point where they had won such a bloody victory, to the next objective, a cove just north of Cape Charles which marked the entrance to Chesapeake Bay, it was approximately one hundred miles.

Sparke had hoped for a change of wind, but on the contrary, it soon became worse and more set against them. Both vessels were able to keep company, but each tack took longer, each mile gained could be quadrupled by the distance sailed to achieve it.

Every time that Sparke went on deck he showed no sign of apprehension or dismay. He usually examined the *Thrush* through his glass and then looked up at his own flag. Bolitho had heard one of the marines whispering to his friend that Sparke had made himself an admiral of his own squadron.

The weather and the constant demands of working the schooner to windward had cleared most of the tension and bitterness from Bolitho's thoughts. On the face of it, it had been a success. A vessel seized, another destroyed, and many of the enemy killed or routed. If the plan had misfired, and the trap laid in reverse, he doubted if the enemy would have showed them any mercy either. Once aboard the schooner, the combined numbers of both cutters would have swamped Sparke's resistance before the nine-pounder could have levelled the balance.

It took three days to reach the place where the brig was supposedly hidden. The rugged coastline which pointed south towards the entrance of Chesapeake Bay was treacherous, even more than that which they had left astern. Many a coasting vessel, and larger ships as well, had come to grief as they had battered through foul weather to find the narrow entrance to the bay. Once within it there was room for a fleet, and then some. But to get there was something else entirely, as Bunce had remarked often enough.

Once again, the sad-faced Moffitt was the one to step forward and offer to go ashore alone and spy out the land.

The *Faithful*'s boat had taken him in, while close to the nearest land both vessels had anchored and mounted guard to ward off any attack.

Bolitho had half expected Moffitt not to return. He had done enough, and might be pining to rejoin his family.

But five hours after being dropped on a tiny beach, while the long-boat laid off to wait for his return, Moffitt appeared, wading through the surf in his eagerness to bring the news.

It was no rumour. The ordnance vessel, a brigantine, was beached inside the cove, exactly as Sparke's informer had described. Moffitt had even discovered her name, the *Minstrel*, and thought her too badly damaged even to be moved by expert salvage parties.

He had seen some lanterns nearby, and had almost trodden on a sleeping sentry.

Sparke said, 'I will see that you are rewarded for this work, Moffitt.' He was almost emotional as he added, 'This is the quality of courage which will always sustain us.'

Ordering that Moffitt be given a large tot of brandy or rum, both if he wished, Sparke gathered his officers and senior rates together. There was barely room to draw breath in the schooner's cabin, but they soon forgot their discomfort when Sparke said bluntly, 'Dawn attack. We will use our own and *Thrush*'s boat. Surprise attack at first light, right?' He eyed them searchingly. 'Captain D'Esterre, you will land with your contingent under cover of darkness, and find some cover above the

cove. Stay there to mark our flank, and our withdrawal if things go
wrong.'

Sparke looked at the rough map which Moffitt had helped to make.
'I will of course take the leading boat. Mr Libby will follow in the
other.' He looked at Bolitho. 'You will assume command of *Thrush* and
bring her into the cove for the transfer of cargo once I have smashed
whatever opposition which may still be near the brigantine. The
marines will then move down and support us from the beach.' He
clapped his hands together. 'Well?'

D'Esterre said, 'I'd like to leave now, if I may, sir.'

'Yes. I shall need the boats very soon.' He looked at Bolitho. 'You
were about to say something?'

'A hundred miles in three days, sir. Another half day by dawn. I doubt
very much if we will surprise them.'

'You're not getting like Mr Frowd, surely? A real Jeremiah indeed.'

Bolitho shut his mouth tightly. It was pointless to argue, and anyway,
with the marines in position to cover them they could fall back if it was a
trap.

Sparke said, 'It is settled then. Good. Mr Frowd will take charge here
in our absence, and the nine-pounder will be more than a match for any
foolhardy attacker, eh?'

Midshipman Weston licked his lips. His face was glistening with
sweat. 'What shall *I* do, sir?'

Sparke smiled thinly. 'You will be with the fourth lieutenant. Do
what he says and you might learn something. Do *not* do what he says
and you may well be dead before you fill yourself with more disgusting
food!'

They trooped up on deck, where a few pale stars had appeared to
greet them.

Moffitt reported to Captain D'Esterre, 'I'm ready, sir. I'll show you
the way.'

The marine nodded. 'You are a glutton for punishment, but lead on,
with my blessing.'

The two boats were already filling with marines and would now be in
continuous use. That left only the captured dory. It was as well
somebody had kept it secured during the fighting.

Stockdale was by the taffrail, his white trousers flapping like
miniature sails.

He wheezed, 'Glad you're not going this time, sir.'

Bolitho stiffened. 'Why did you say that?'

'Feeling, sir. Just a feeling. I'll be happier when we're out of here.
Back with the *real* Navy again.'

Bolitho watched the boats pulling clear, the marines' crossbelts stark
against the black water.

The trouble with Stockdale was that his 'feelings', as he called them, were too often transformed into actual deeds.

Bolitho moved restlessly around the *Thrush*'s tiller, very conscious of the stillness, the air of expectancy which hung over the two vessels.

The wind was from the same direction but was dropping with each passing minute, allowing the warmth to replace the night's chill, the sun to penetrate the full-bellied clouds.

He trained his telescope towards the nearest hillside and saw two tiny scarlet figures just showing above the strange, tangled gorse. D'Esterre's marines were in position, pickets out. They would have a good view of the little cove, although from the *Thrush*'s deck there was nothing to see but fallen, rotting trees by the entrance and the swirl of a cross-current by some scattered rocks.

He heard Midshipman Weston with some seamen sorting out the good sweeps from those broken by the swivels' canister. He could also hear him retching as he found some gruesome fragment which Libby's men had overlooked.

Stockdale joined him by the rail, his face black with stubble and grime.

'Should be there by now, sir. Not heard a shot nor nothin'.'

Bolitho nodded. It was uppermost in his mind. The wind was dropping, and that made movement difficult if urgently required. He would need to move the *Thrush* under sweeps, and the longer it took the more chance of an ambush there was.

He cursed Sparke's eagerness, his blind determination to take all the rewards for himself. At any time of day a frigate might pass nearby and they could depend on support by the boatload, even at the expense of sharing the victory.

He said, 'Get in the dory. I'm going to that little beach yonder.' He pointed to the two scarlet shapes on the hillside. 'I'll be safe enough.'

Midshipman Weston panted along the deck, his ungainly feet catching and jarring on splinters from the raked planking.

Bolitho said, 'You take charge here.' He could almost smell his fear. 'I'll be in view the whole time.'

He saw Stockdale and two seamen climbing down to the dory, eager to be doing something to break the strain of waiting. Or maybe to get away from the scene of such carnage.

When Bolitho stepped on to the firm beach, which was not much bigger than the boat itself, it felt good. To smell the different scents, to hear birds and the vague rustling of small creatures nearby was like a balm.

Then one of the seamen exclaimed, 'There, sir! 'Tis Mr Libby's boat!'

Bolitho saw the midshipman's head and shoulders even before he heard the swish of oars.

'Over here!'

Libby waved his hat and grinned. Relief, and more, was plain on his tanned face.

He shouted, 'The second lieutenant says to bring the cutter, sir! There's no sign of anyone ashore, and Mr Sparke thinks they must have run when they saw the boats!'

Bolitho asked, 'What is he doing now?'

'He is about to board the brigantine, sir. She is a fine little vessel, but is badly holed.'

Sparke probably wanted to make quite sure there was no chance of adding her, as well as her cargo, to his little squadron.

Feet slithered on the hillside, and Bolitho swung round to see Moffitt, followed by a marine, stumbling and falling towards him.

'What is it, Moffitt?' He saw the anguish on his face.

'*Sir!*' He could barely get the words out. 'We tried to signal, but Mr Sparke did not see us!' He gestured wildly. 'Them devils have laid a fuse, I can see the smoke! They're going to blow up the brigantine! They must've been waiting!'

Libby looked appalled. 'Man your oars! We'll go back!'

Bolitho ran into the water to stop him, but even as he spoke the earth and sky seemed to burst apart in one tremendous explosion.

The men in the boat ducked and gasped, while around and across them pieces of splintered wood and rigging rained down, covering the water with leaping feathers of spray.

Then they saw the smoke, lifting and spreading above the cove's shoulder until the sunlight was completely hidden.

Bolitho groped his way to the dory, his ears and mind cringing from the deafening explosion.

Marines blundered down the slope and waited until Libby's oarsmen had recovered sufficiently to bring their boat towards the tiny beach.

But all Bolitho could see was Sparke's face as he had outlined his last plan. *The quality of courage.* It had not sustained *him*.

Bolitho pulled himself together as D'Esterre with his sergeant and two skirmishers walked towards him.

Again he seemed to hear Sparke's crisp voice. Speaking as he had aboard the schooner when the shocked aftermath of battle had begun to take charge.

'*They'll be looking to us. So we'll save our regrets for later.*'

It could have been his epitaph.

Bolitho said huskily, 'Get the marines ferried over as quickly as you can.' He turned away from the stench of burning wood and tar. 'We'll get under way directly.'

D'Esterre eyed him strangely. 'Another few minutes and it could have been Libby's boat. Or yours.'

Bolitho met his gaze and replied, 'There may not be much time. So let's set about it, shall we?'

D'Esterre watched the last squad of marines lining up to await the boat's return. He saw Bolitho and Stockdale climb from the dory to the *Faithful*'s deck, Frowd hurrying across to meet them.

D'Esterre had been in too many fights of one sort or another to be affected for long. But this time had been different. He thought of Bolitho's face, suddenly so pale beneath the black hair with its unruly lock above one eye. Determined, using every ounce of strength to contain his feelings.

Junior he might be in rank, but D'Esterre had felt in those few moments that he was in the presence of his superior.

6

A Lieutenant's Lot

Lieutenant Neil Cairns looked up from the small bulkhead desk in response to a knock on his cabin door.

'Come!'

Bolitho stepped inside, his hat beneath his arm, his features tired.

Cairns gestured to the only other chair. 'Take those books off there and sit yourself down, man.' He groped amongst piles of papers, lists and scribbled messages and added, 'There should be some glasses here, too. You look as if you need a drink. I am certain I do. If anyone advises you to take on the role of first lieutenant, I suggest you tell him to go to hell!'

Bolitho sat and loosened his neckcloth. There was the hint of a cool breeze in the cabin, and after hours of walking around New York, and the long pull across the harbour in *Trojan*'s launch, he was feeling sweaty and weary. He had been sent ashore to try to get some new hands to replace those killed or injured aboard the *Faithful* and later when Sparke's cutter and his men had been blasted to fragments. It all seemed like a vague, distorted dream now. *Three months ago*, and already it was hard to put the order of things together properly. Even the weather made it more obscure. Then it had been miserably cold and bleak, with fierce running seas and the fog which had then seemed like a miracle. Now it was bright sunshine and long periods without any wind at all. The *Trojan*'s hull creaked with dryness and her deck seams shone moistly in the glare, clinging to the shoes and to the seamen's bare feet.

Cairns watched him thoughtfully. Bolitho had changed a great deal, he decided. He had returned to New York with the two prizes a different man. More mature, and lacking the youthful optimism which had marked him out from the others.

The events which had changed him, Sparke's terrible death in particular, had even been noticed by the captain.

Cairns said, 'Red wine, Dick. Warm, but better than anything else to hand. I bought it from a trader ashore.'

He saw Bolitho tilt back his head, the lock of hair clinging to his forehead and hiding the cruel scar. Despite his service in these waters,

Bolitho looked pale, and his grey eyes were like the winter they had long since left behind.

Bolitho knew he was being watched, but he had become used to it. If he had changed, so too had his world. With Sparke dead, the officers had taken another step on promotion's ladder. Bolitho was now the third lieutenant, and the most junior post, then left vacant, had been taken by Midshipman Libby. He was now *Trojan*'s acting sixth lieutenant, whether he was able to take his proper examination or not. The age difference between the captain and his lieutenants was startling. Bolitho would not be twenty-one until October, and his juniors were aged from twenty to Libby's mere seventeen years.

It was a well-used system in the larger ships, but Bolitho could find little comfort in his promotion, even though his new duties had kept him busy enough to hold most of the worst memories to the back of his mind.

Cairns said suddenly, 'The captain wants you to accompany him to the flagship this evening. The admiral is "holding court", and captains will be expected to produce a likely aide or two.' He refilled the glasses, his features impassive. 'I have work to do with the damned victualling yard, so I'll not be able to go. Not that I care much for empty conversation when the whole world is falling apart.'

He said it with such bitterness that Bolitho was moved to ask, 'Is something troubling you?'

Cairns gave a rare smile. 'Just everything. I am heartily sick of inactivity. Of writing down lists of stores, begging for new cordage and spars, when all those rogues ashore want is for you to pass them a few pieces of gold, damn their eyes!'

Bolitho thought of the two prizes he had brought back to New York. They had been whisked away to the prize court, sold and recommissioned into the King's service almost before the new ensigns had been hoisted.

Not one man of the *Trojan*'s company had been appointed to them, and the lieutenant given command of the *Faithful* had barely been out from England more than a few weeks. It was unfair, to say the least, and it was obviously a sore point with Cairns. In about eighteen months he would be thirty. The war could be over, and he might be thrown on the beach as a half-pay lieutenant. It was not a very enjoyable prospect for a man without means beyond his naval pay.

'Anyway,' Cairns leaned back and looked at him, 'the captain has made it plain he'd rather have you with him in his admiral's presence than our tippling second lieutenant!'

Bolitho smiled. It was amazing how Probyn survived. He was fortunate perhaps that after *Trojan*'s return from escorting the convoy from Halifax the ship had barely been to sea at all. Two short patrols in support of the Army and a gunnery exercise with the flagship well within sight of New York was the extent of her efforts. A few more storms and Probyn's weakness might have put an end to him.

Bolitho stood up. 'I'd better get changed then.'

Cairns nodded. 'You're to meet the captain at the end of the first dog-watch. He'll be taking the barge, so make sure the crew are smart and ready. He's in no mood to suffer slackness, I can tell you.'

Sharp at four bells Captain Pears strode on to the quarterdeck, resplendent in his full-dress uniform and carrying his sword at his side like a pointer. If anything, the glittering gold lace set off against the dark blue coat and white breeches made him appear younger and taller.

Bolitho, also dressed in his best clothes, waited by the entry port, a sword, instead of his usual hanger, slung across his waistcoat on a cross-belt.

He had already examined the barge to ensure it was ready and suitable for *Trojan*'s captain. It was a fine-looking boat, with a dark red hull and white painted gunwales. In the stern-sheets there were matching red cushions, while across the transom there was the ship's name in gilt. Swaying against *Trojan*'s side, with the oars tossed in two vertical lines, her crew dressed in red and white checkered shirts and black tarred hats, the barge looked good enough for an emperor, Bolitho thought.

Cairns hurried to the side and murmured something to the captain. Molesworth, the nervous-looking purser, was waiting by the mizzen, and Bolitho guessed that Cairns was going ashore with him to bolster his dealings with the victuallers, who, like ships' chandlers, thought more of personal profit than patriotism.

Captain D'Esterre snapped, 'Marines, present *arms*!'

The bayoneted muskets jerked up almost to the canvas awning overhead, and Bolitho momentarily forgot Pears as he recalled the marines on the *Faithful*'s deck as they had cut down the boarders with the same crisp precision.

Pears seemed to see Bolitho for the first time. 'Ah, it *is* you.' He ran his eye over Bolitho's best cocked hat, his white lapels and freshly pressed waistcoat. 'I thought I had a new officer for a while.'

Bolitho smiled. 'Thank you, sir.'

Pears nodded. 'Carry on.'

Bolitho ran down the ladder to the boat, where Hogg, the burly coxswain, stood in readiness, his hat in his hand like a grim-faced mourner.

The pipes trilled and then the barge tilted to Pears' weight as he stepped down and into the sternsheets.

'Shove off! Out oars!' Hogg was conscious of his captain and watching telescopes from nearby warships. 'Give way *all*!'

Bolitho sat stiffly with his sword between his knees. He found it impossible to relax when he was with the captain. So he watched *Trojan* instead, seeing her curved tumblehome change shape as the boat swung round and beneath her high stern. He saw the red ensign curling listlessly above the taffrail, the glitter of gilt paint and polished fittings.

Every gunport was open to catch the offshore air, and at each one, withdrawn like a resting beast, *Trojan*'s considerable artillery showed a round black muzzle. They too were as clean as D'Esterre's silver buttons.

Bolitho glanced at Pears's grim profile. What news there was of the war was bad. Stalemate at best, real losses too often for comfort. But whatever Pears thought about the situation and the future he was certainly not going to let down his ship by any sign of slackness.

Beneath her furled sails and crossed yards, shimmering in her own haze of black and buff, *Trojan* was a sight to stir even the most doubting heart.

Pears said suddenly, 'Have you heard from your father?'

Bolitho replied, 'Not of late, sir. He is not much for writing.'

Pears looked directly at him. 'I was sorry to learn of your mother's death. I met her just the once at Weymouth. You were at sea, I believe. A gracious lady. It makes me feel old even to remember her.'

Bolitho looked astern at *Trojan*. So that was part of it, and no wonder. Suppose, just suppose, that *Trojan* had to fight. Really fight with ships of her own size and fire power. He thought of the officers Pears would carry into battle. Probyn, getting more difficult and morose every day. Dalyell, cheerful but barely equipped to take over his new role as fourth lieutenant. And poor Quinn, tight-lipped and in constant pain from his wound, and confined to light duties under the surgeon's attention. Now there was Libby, one more boy in a lieutenant's guise. Pears had good cause to worry about it, he thought. It must be like having a shipload of schoolboys.

'How many men did you get today?'

Bolitho stared. Pears knew everything. Even about his trip ashore.

'Four, sir.' It was even worse when you said it aloud.

'Hmm. We may have better luck when the next convoy arrives.' Pears shifted on the red cusion. 'Damned knaves. Prize seamen, protected by the East India Company or some bloody government warrant! Hell's teeth, you'd think it was a crime to fight for your country! But I'll get my hands on a few of 'em, exemptions or not.' He chuckled. 'By the time their lordships hear about it, we'll have changed 'em into King's men!'

Bolitho turned his head as the flagship loomed around another anchored man-of-war.

She was the *Resolute*, a second-rate of some ninety guns, and a veteran of twenty-five years of service. There were several boats at her booms, and Bolitho guessed it was to be quite a gathering. He looked up at the drooping flag at her mizzen and wondered what their host would be like. Rear-Admiral Graham Coutts, in command of the inshore squadron, had controlled *Trojan*'s destiny since her first arrival in New York. Bolitho had never laid eyes on him and was curious to know what he was like. Probably another Pears, he decided. Rocklike, unbreakable.

He shifted his attention to the professional side of their arrival. The marines at the entry port, the gleam of steel, the bustle of blue and white and the faint shout of commands.

Pears was sitting as before, but Bolitho noticed that his strong fingers were opening and closing around the sharkskin grip of his sword, the first sign of agitation he had ever noticed in him.

It was a fine sword and must have cost a small fortune. It was a presentation sword, given to Pears for some past deed of individual courage, or more likely a victory over one of England's enemies.

'Ready to toss yer oars!' Hogg was leaning on the balls of his feet, his fingers caressing the tiller-bar as he gauged the final approach. 'Oars *up*!'

As one the blades rose and remained motionless in paired lines, the sea water trickling unheeded on to the knees of the bargemen.

Pears nodded to his crew and then climbed sedately up the side, doffing his hat to the shrill calls and the usual ceremony which greeted every captain.

Bolitho counted seconds and then followed. He was met by a thin-nosed lieutenant with a telescope jammed beneath his arm who looked at him as if he had just emerged from some stale cheese.

'You are to go aft, sir.' The lieutenant gestured to the poop where Pears, in company with *Resolute*'s flag captain, was hurrying towards the shade.

Bolitho paused to look around the quarterdeck. Very like *Trojan*'s. The lines of tethered guns, their tackles neatly turned on to cleats or flaked down on the snow-white planking. Seamen going about their work, a midshipman studying an incoming brig through the glass, his lips moving silently as he read her flag hoist of numbers which would reveal her name and that of her captain.

Down on the gundeck a seaman was standing beside a corporal of marines, while another midshipman was speaking rapidly to a lieutenant. A crime committed? A man about to be taken aft for punishment? Or he might be up for promotion or discharge. It was a familiar scene which could mean so many things.

He sighed. Like the *Trojan*. And yet again, she was completely different.

Bolitho walked slowly beneath the poop and was startled by the sound of music and the muted laughter of men and women. Every screen had been removed and the admiral's quarters had been opened up into one huge cabin. By the open stern windows some violinists were playing with great concentration, and amongst the jostling crowd of sea officers, civilians and several ladies, servants in red jackets carried trays laden with glasses, while others stood at a long table refilling them as fast as they could.

Pears had been swallowed up, and Bolitho nodded to several lieutenants who, like himself, were only here under sufferance.

A tall figure emerged from the crush, and Bolitho saw it was Lamb, the flagship's captain. He was a steady-eyed man with features which might at first appear to be severe, even hard. But when he smiled, everything changed.

'You are Mr Bolitho, I understand?' He held out his hand. 'Welcome aboard. I heard about your exploits last March and wanted to meet you. We can use men of mettle who have seen what war is all about. It is a hard time, but also one of opportunity for young men such as yourself. If the moment comes, seize your chance. Believe me, Bolitho, they rarely come twice.'

Bolitho thought of the graceful schooner, even the stubby-hulled *Thrush*. His own chance had already come and gone.

'Come and meet the admiral.' He saw Bolitho's expression and laughed. 'He will not eat you!'

More pushing to get through the crowd. Flushed faces, loud voices. It was difficult to imagine that the war was just miles away.

He saw a hunched set of blue shoulders and a gold-laced collar, and groaned inwardly. Ponderous. Slow-moving. A disappointment after all.

But the flag captain pushed the big man aside and revealed a slight figure who barely came up to his shoulder.

Rear-Admiral Graham Coutts looked more like a lieutenant than a flag officer. He had dark brown hair which was tied to the nape of his neck in a casual fashion. He had an equally youthful face, devoid of lines or the usual mask of authority which Bolitho had seen before.

He thrust out his hand. 'Bolitho, is it? Good.' He nodded and smiled impetuously. 'Proud to meet you.' He beckoned to some hidden servant. 'Wine over here!'

Then he said lightly, 'I know all about you. I suspect that if you and not your superior officer had been leading that boat attack you might even have recaptured the brigantine!' He smiled. 'No matter. It showed what can be done, given the will.'

An elegant figure in blue velvet walked from a noisy group by the quarter gallery and the admiral said quietly, 'See that man, Bolitho? That is Sir George Helpman, from London.' His lip curled slightly. 'An "expert" on our malaise here. A very important person. One to be heard and respected at all times.'

The mood changed, and just as swiftly he was the admiral again. 'Be off with you, Bolitho. Enjoy what you wish. The food is palatable today.'

He turned away and Bolitho saw him greeting the man from London. He got the impression that Rear-Admiral Coutts did not like him very much. It had sounded like a warning, although what a lowly lieutenant could do to upset matters was hard to imagine.

He thought about Coutts. Not a bit what he had expected. He shied away from what he felt. Admiration. A strange sense of loyalty for the man he had met for just a few minutes. But it was there. It was useless to deny it.

It was getting dark by the time the guests started to leave. Some were so drunk they had to be carried to their boats, others lurched, glassy-eyed and unsupported, fighting each step of the way for fear of disgracing themselves.

Bolitho waited on the quarterdeck, watching the civilians and the officials, the ladies and a few of the military being helped, pushed or lowered by tackles into the bobbing flotilla of boats alongside.

He had just passed a cabin which he guessed was that of Coutts' flag lieutenant. The door had been slightly ajar, and Bolitho had caught just a brief view before it had swung shut. A woman's body, naked to the waist, her arms wrapped around the officer's head as he tore at her clothing like a madman. And she had been giggling, bubbling with sheer enjoyment.

Her husband or escort was probably lying in one of the boats right now, Bolitho thought. He smiled. Was he shocked or envious again?

A boatswain's mate, harassed by his additional duties, called, 'Yer captain's comin', sir!'

'Aye. Call the barge.' Bolitho adjusted his swordbelt and straightened his hat.

Pears appeared with Captain Lamb. The two men shook hands and then Pears followed Bolitho down into the boat.

As the barge edged clear and swung on a swift-moving current, Pears made one comment. 'Disgusting, was it not?'

He then lapsed into silence and did not move until *Trojan*'s lighted gunports were close by. Then he said curtly, 'If that was diplomacy, then thank God I'm a simple sailor!'

Bolitho stood in the swaying boat beside the coxswain, and as Pears reached out for the ladder his foot slipped. Bolitho thought he heard him swear but was not certain. But he felt vaguely honoured to share the moment. Pears was in perfect control again, but only just. That made him seem more human than Bolitho could remember.

Pears' harsh voice came down from the entry port, 'Don't stand there like a priest, Mr Bolitho! 'Pon my soul, sir, others have work to do, if you do not!'

Bolitho looked at Hogg and grinned. That was more like it.

Amongst other tasks required of ships' lieutenants was the wearying and thankless duty of officer of the guard. In New York, to ease the work of the shorebound authorities, the various ships at anchor were expected to supply a lieutenant for a full twenty-four-hour duty. It entailed checking the various guardboats which pulled around the jetties and moored ships, to make certain they allowed no enemy agents to get near enough to do damage or discover secret information. Equally, they were required to prevent any of the fleet's seamen from deserting to seek shelter and more doubtful pleasures on the waterfront.

Seamen entrusted with work ashore were often tempted, and drunken, wild-eyed sailors had to be sorted out to await an escort back to their rightful ships, and a few lashes for good measure.

Two nights after his visit to the flagship it fell to *Trojan*'s third lieutenant to place himself at the disposal of the port admiral and provost marshal for such duty. New York made him feel uneasy. A city waiting for something to happen, a pattern to settle once and for all. It was a city of constant movement. Refugees arriving from inland, others thronging offices and government buildings in search of relatives lost in the fighting. Some were already leaving for England and for Canada. Others waited to reap rich rewards from the victors, no matter what colour their coats might be. It could be a dangerous place at night, especially along the crowded waterfront with its taverns and brothels, boarding houses and gaming rooms, where anything was available so long as there was gold for the taking.

Bolitho, followed by a file of armed seamen, walked slowly along a line of sun-dried planked buildings, careful to stay close to the wall and avoid any filth which might be thrown or accidentally dropped on to his patrol.

He heard Stockdale's wheezing breath behind him, the occasional clink of weapons as they made their way towards the main jetty. Few people were in view, although behind most of the shuttered windows he could hear music and voices raised in song or blasphemy.

One house stood silhouetted against the swirling water, and he saw the usual marine sentries outside the entrance, a sergeant pacing up and down by a small lantern.

''Alt! 'Oo goes there!'

'Officer of the guard!'

'Advance an' be recognized!'

It was always the same, even though the marines knew most of the fleet's lieutenants by sight, night or day.

The sergeant stamped to attention. 'Two men for the *Vanquisher*, sir. Fightin' drunk they are.'

Bolitho walked through some doors and into a large hall. It had once been a fine house, the home of a tea merchant. Now it served the Navy.

'They seem quiet enough, Sergeant.'

The man grinned unfeelingly. 'Ah, sir, *now* they is!' He gestured to two inert shapes in leg irons. ''Ad to quieten 'em, like.'

Bolitho sat down at a scarred desk, half listening to the noises beyond the doors, the clatter of wheels across the Dutch cobbles, the occasional shriek of some whore.

He looked at the clock. Past midnight. Another four hours to go. At times like this he longed for the *Trojan*, when hours earlier he had pined to be free from her regulated routine.

When the fleet had first arrived off Staten Island, someone had described it as being like London afloat. It had become too much of a reality to be mentioned nowadays. Bolitho had seen two lieutenants from one of the frigates as they had gone into a gaming house. He knew both by sight but little more. In those few moments he had caught a snatch of their conversation. *Sailing on the tide. Going to Antigua with despatches.* What it was to be free. Able to get clear away from this floating muddle of ships.

The sergeant reappeared and regarded him doubtfully.

'I got a crimp outside, sir.' He jerked his thumb towards the door. 'I know 'im of old, a rogue but reliable. 'E says there are some 'ands from the brig *Diamond*. Jumped ship afore she weighed three days back.'

Bolitho stood up, reaching for his hanger. 'What was she?'

The sergeant grinned hugely. 'No bother, sir. She weren't under no warrant, she was with general cargo from an English port.'

Bolitho nodded. A brig from England. That implied trained seamen, deserters or not.

He said, 'Bring the, er, crimp inside.'

The man was typical of his trade. Small, greasy, furtive. They were common enough in any seaport. Boarding-house runners who sold information about likely hands to officers of the Press.

'Well?'

The man whined, 'It be my duty, sir. To 'elp the King's Navy.'

Bolitho eyed him coldly. The man still retained the accent of the London slums.

'How many?'

'Six, sir!' His eyes glittered. 'Fine strong lads they be.'

The sergeant said offhandedly, 'They're in Lucy's place.' He grimaced. 'Poxed to the eyebrows, I shouldn't wonder.'

'Tell my men to fall in, Sergeant.' Bolitho tried not to think of the delay this would cause. He would probably miss his sleep altogether.

The crimp said, 'Could we come to an agreement nah, sir?'

'No. You wait here. If I get the men, you'll get paid. If not. . .' He winked at the grinning marines. 'We'll have you seized up and flogged.'

He strode out into the night, hating the crimp, these detestable methods of getting enough men. Despite the hardships of naval life, there were plenty of volunteers. But there were never enough. Death by many means, and injury by many more, saw to that.

Stockdale asked, 'Where, sir?'

'A place called Lucy's.'

One of the seamen chuckled. 'Oi bin there, zur.'

Bolitho groaned. 'Then you lead. Carry on.'

Once in the narrow, sloping street which stank like an open sewer, Bolitho split his men into two groups. Most of the trusted hands had done it before several times. Even pressed men, once settled in their new life, were ready enough to bring the Navy's rough justice to the fore. *If we have to go, why not you!* seemed to be their only yardstick.

Stockdale had vanished to the rear of the building, his cutlass in his belt and carrying instead a cudgel as big as a leg of pork.

Bolitho stood for a few more seconds, taking deep breaths while he stared at the sealed door, beyond which he could hear someone crooning quietly like a sick dog. They were probably sleeping it off, he thought grimly. If they were there at all.

He drew his hanger and smashed the pommel against the door several times, shouting, 'Open, in the King's name!'

The response was immediate. Shuffles and startled cries, the muffled tinkle of breaking glass followed by a thud as a would-be escaper fell victim to Stockdale's cudgel.

Then the door was flung open, but instead of a rush of figures Bolitho was confronted by a giant of a woman, whom he guessed to be the notorious Lucy. She was as tall and as broad as any sailorman, and had the language to match as she screamed abuse and waved her fists in his face.

Lanterns were appearing on every hand, and from windows across the street heads were peering down to enjoy the spectacle of Lucy routing the Navy.

'Why, you poxy young bugger!' She placed her hands on her hips and glowered at Bolitho. ''Ow dare you come accusin' me of 'arbouring deserters!'

Other women, some half-naked, were creeping down a rickety stairway at the back of the hallway, their painted faces excited and eager to see what would happen.

'I have my duty.' Bolitho listened to his own voice, disgusted with the jeering woman, humiliated by her contempt.

Stockdale appeared behind her, his face unsmiling as he wheezed, 'Got 'em, sir. Six, like 'e said.'

Bolitho nodded. Stockdale must have found his own way through the rear.

'Well done.' He felt sudden anger running through him. 'While we're here we shall take a look for more *innocent* citizens.'

She reached out and seized his lapels, and pursed her lips to spit into his face.

Bolitho got a brief view of bare, kicking legs and thighs as Stockdale gathered her up in his arms and carried her screaming and cursing down the steps to the street. Without further ado he dropped her face down in a horse trough and held her head under the water for several seconds.

Then he released her, and as she staggered, retching and gasping for breath, he said, 'If you talks to the lieutenant like that again, my beauty, I'll take my snickersnee to yer gizzard, see?'

He nodded to Bolitho. 'All right now, sir.'

Bolitho swallowed hard. He had never seen Stockdale behave like it before.

'Er, thank you.'

He saw his men nudging each other and grinning, and tried to assert himself. 'Get on with the search.' He watched the six deserters lurching past, one holding his head.

From one of the other houses an anonymous voice yelled, 'Leave 'em be, you varmints!'

Bolitho entered the door and looked at the upended chairs, empty bottles and scraps of clothing. It was more like a prison than a place for pleasure, he thought.

Two additional men were brought down the stairs, one a lobster fisherman, the other protesting that he was not a sailor at all. Bolitho looked at the tattoos on his arms and said softly, 'I suggest you hold your tongue. If, as I suspect, you are from a King's ship, it were better to say nothing.' He saw the man pale under his sunburn, as if he had already seen the noose.

A seaman clattered down the stairs and said, 'That's the lot, sir. 'Cept for this youngster.'

Bolitho saw the youth being pushed through the watching girls and decided against it. Probably someone's young son, out on an errand, seeking a first thrill in this foul place.

'Very well. Call the others.'

He looked at the youth, slim-shouldered, eyes downcast and in shadow.

'This is no place for you, boy. Be off, before something worse happens. Where do you live?'

When there was no reply, Bolitho reached out and lifted the other's chin, allowing the lantern light to spill over the frightened face.

He seemed to stand locked in the same position for an age, and yet he was aware of other things happening elsewhere. The feet shuffling on the cobbles as his men sorted their new hands into file, and the distant shout of orders as a military patrol approached from the end of the street.

Then events moved swiftly. The figure twisted away and was out and through the door before anyone could move.

A seaman bellowed, '*Stop that man!*' And along the street Bolitho heard a challenge from the soldiers.

Bolitho ran out shouting, '*Wait!*' But it was too late, and the crash of the musket seemed like a cannon in the narrow street.

He walked past his men and stood over the sprawled figure as a corporal of infantry ran forward and rolled the body on to its back.

'Thought 'e was escapin' from you, sir!'

Bolitho got down and unbuttoned the youth's rough jerkin and shirt. He could feel the skin, still hot and inflamed, and very smooth like the chin had been. There was blood too, glittering in the lantern light as if still alive.

Bolitho ran his hand over the breast. There was no heart-beat, and he could feel the dead eyes staring at him in the darkness. Hostile and accusing.

He stood up, sickened. 'It's a girl.'

Then he turned and added, 'That woman, bring her here.'

The woman called Lucy edged closer, gripping her hands together as she saw the sprawled corpse.

Gone was the bluster and coarse arrogance. Bolitho could almost smell her terror.

He asked, 'Who was she?' He was surprised at the sound of his own voice. Flat and unemotional. A stranger's. 'I'll not ask a second time, woman.'

More noises echoed along the street, and then two mounted figures cantered through the army patrol, and a voice barked, 'What the *hell* is going on here?'

Bolitho touched his hat. 'Officer of the guard, sir.'

It was a major, who wore the same insignia as the man who had shot the unknown girl.

'Oh, I see. Well then.' The major dismounted and stooped over the body. 'Bring that lantern, Corporal!' He put his hand under the girl's head, letting it roll stiffly towards the beam.

Bolitho watched, unable to take his eyes from the girl's face.

The major stood up and said quietly, 'Fine kettle of fish, Lieutenant.' He rubbed his chin. 'I'd better rouse the governor. He'll not take kindly to it.'

'What is it, sir?'

The major shook his head. 'What you don't know will do you no harm.' He became businesslike as he snapped to the other mounted soldier, 'Corporal Fisher! Ride to the post and rouse the adjutant, I want him and a full platoon here on the double.' He watched the man gallop away and then added, 'This damned house will be closed and under guard, and *you*,' his white-gloved finger shot out towards the shivering Lucy, 'are under arrest!'

She almost fell as she pleaded, 'Why *me*, sir? What have *I* done?'

The major stood aside as two soldiers ran to seize her arms. 'Treason, *madam*. That's what!'

He turned more calmly to Bolitho. 'I suggest you go about your affairs, sir. I have no doubt you will hear more of this.' Surprisingly, he gave a quick smile. 'But if it's a consolation, you may have stumbled on something of real value. Too many good men have fallen to treachery. Here's one who will betray no more.'

Bolitho walked back towards the waterfront in silence. The major had recognized the dead girl, and from the fineness of her bones, the smoothness of her skin, she came from a good family.

He tried to guess what had been happening before he and his men had burst in, but all he could remember were her eyes as she had looked at his face, when they had both known the truth.

7

Hopes and Fears

Bolitho moved a few paces across the quarterdeck in an attempt to stay in the shadow of *Trojan*'s great spanker. It was oppressively hot, and despite a steady wind across the quarter it was impossible to draw comfort from it.

Bolitho turned as a ship's boy reversed the half-hour glass and six bells chimed out from the forecastle. An hour of the forenoon still to run.

He winced as the sun smashed down between the sails' shadows and seared his shoulders like a blacksmith's forge. He took a telescope from its rack and trained it ahead, seeing the flagship *Resolute* leap to meet him. How quickly things had changed, he thought. Just the day after the mystery of the dead girl orders had been received to weigh and put to sea with the first favourable wind. No mention was made of the destination or the purpose, and up to the last some of the wardroom cynics had expected it to turn into another exercise, a brief display of strength for the Army's moral support.

That had been four days ago. Four long days of crawling south with barely a ripple around the rudder to show some progress. It had taken them four days to make good four hundred miles.

Bolitho swung the glass slowly across the quarter and saw the sun shimmering on the topgallant sails of the frigate *Vanquisher*, well out to windward, ready to dash down to assist her ponderous consorts if she were needed. He returned to study the flagship again. Just occasionally, as she pitched heavily in a deep swell, he caught sight of another, smaller set of sails, far ahead of the squadron, the admiral's 'eyes'.

As *Trojan* had weighed anchor and prepared to leave Sandy Hook, Bolitho had watched the sloop-of-war *Spite* spreading her sails and speeding out of harbour with the minimum of fuss. She was up there now, ready to pass back her signals if she sighted anything which might interest the admiral.

She was a lovely little vessel of eighteen guns, and Bolitho had discovered her to be the one which had fired on the *Faithful* before Sparke's attempt to seize the ordnance brigantine. Her commander was only twenty-four years old, and, like the three other captains here today, knew exactly what he was doing and where he was ordered to go.

Secrecy seemed to have crept into their world like the first touch of a disease.

The deck trembled, and he heard the port-lids on the lower battery's starboard side being opened, and after a pause the squeak of gun trucks as thirty of *Trojan*'s thirty-two-pounders were run out as if to give battle. If he looked over the side he would be able to see them easily. Just the thought of it was enough. Even the touch of the tinder-dry bulwark or quarterdeck rail was like a burn. What Dalyell, now appointed in charge of the lower gundeck, was suffering, he could barely imagine.

The sails clapped and rustled overhead, and he glanced up at the trailing pendant, looking for a shift of wind. It seemed steady enough from the north-west, but without the strength they needed to drive the humidity and discomfort from between decks.

Rumble, rumble, rumble, the thirty-two pounders were being run in again, and no doubt Dalyell was peering at his watch and consulting with his midshipmen and petty officers. It was taking too long, and Captain Pears had made his requirements plain from the start of the commission. Clear for action in ten minutes or less, and when firing, three rounds every two minutes. This last exercise had sounded twice as long.

He could picture the stripped and sweating gun crews, struggling to run out those massive cannon. With the ship leaning over on the starboard tack, the guns, each weighing over three tons, had to be hauled bodily up the sloping deck to the ports. This was not the weather for it, but then, it never was, as Cairns had often remarked.

Bolitho stared across the nettings, picturing the invisible land as he had studied it on the chart during each watch. Cape Hatteras and its shoals lay some twenty miles abeam, and beyond, Pamlico Sound and the rivers of North Carolina.

But as far as Bolitho and the lookouts were concerned the sea was theirs. Four ships, spread out to obtain best advantage of wind and visibility, moving slowly towards a secret destination. Bolitho thought about their combined companies, which must amount to close on eighteen hundred officers and men.

Just a few moments earlier he had seen the purser with his clerk hurrying down the main companion, Molesworth carrying his ledger, his clerk with a box of tools which he used for opening casks and checking the quality of their contents.

It was Monday, and Bolitho could imagine the scribbled instructions in Molesworth's ledger. Per man this day, one pound of biscuit, one gallon of small beer, one pint of oatmeal, two ounces of butter and four ounces of cheese.

After that, it was up to Triphook and his mates to do what they could with it.

No wonder pursers were always worried or dishonest. Sometimes both. Multiply a man's daily ration by the whole company, and by the long days and weeks at sea, and you got some idea of his problems.

Midshipman Couzens, standing discreetly by the lee rail with his telescope ready to train on the flagship, hissed, '*Captain*, sir!'

Bolitho turned swiftly, the effort making the sweat run between his shoulder blades and gather at his waistband like hot rain.

He touched his hat. 'Sou'-sou'-west, sir. Full and bye.'

Pears glanced at him impassively. 'The wind appears to have veered in the last hour. But not enough to make any difference.'

He said nothing further, and Bolitho crossed to the lee side to allow his captain the freedom of the deck.

Pears paced slowly up and down, his face totally absorbed.

What was he thinking about, Bolitho wondered? His orders, or his wife and family in England?

Pears paused and swivelled his head towards him. 'Pipe some hands forrard, Mr Bolitho. The weather forebrace is as slack as this watch, dammit! 'Pon my soul, sir, you'll have to do better!'

Bolitho nodded. 'Aye, sir. At once.'

He gestured to Couzens, and a moment later some seamen were hauling lustily, each knowing he was under the captain's scrutiny.

Bolitho found himself pondering over Pears's behaviour. The fore-brace had seemed no slacker than you might expect in the rising and falling gusts of wind. Was it just to keep him on his toes? He thought suddenly of Sparke and his, *take that man's name*.

The memory saddened him.

He saw Quinn coming up the ladder from the gundeck and nodded to him, adding a quick shake of the head to warn him of Pears's presence.

Quinn was doing far better than Bolitho had dared hope. He had got his colour back, and could walk upright without twisting his face in readiness for the pain.

Bolitho had seen the great scar on Quinn's breast. If his attacker had not been startled and taken off guard, his blade would have sliced through bone and muscle to the heart itself.

The voice settled on the young fifth lieutenant like a mesh.

'Mr Quinn!'

'Sir!' He hurried across the deck, his face working anxiously as to what he had done wrong.

Pears studied him grimly. 'I am indeed glad to see you are up and about.'

Quinn smiled gratefully. 'Thank you, sir.'

'Quite so.' Pears continued with his daily walk. 'You will exercise your men at repelling boarders this afternoon. *Then*, if we remain on this tack, you will put the new hands aloft for sail drill.' He nodded curtly. 'That should restore your well-being better than any pills, eh?'

Couzens yelled excitedly, 'Signal from Flag, sir!' He was peering through his big telescope, his forehead wrinkled like that of an old man as he read the hoist of coloured bunting at *Resolute*'s yard. '*Make more sail*, sir!'

Pears growled, 'Call the hands. Get the royals on her. Stuns'ls too if she can take them.' He strode aft as the master appeared beneath the poop, and Bolitho heard him say in his harsh tone, 'More sail, that is all *he* can think of, damn it!'

Cairns hurried up as the calls trilled between decks and brought the watch below scampering to their stations.

'Hands aloft! Set the royals!'

Cairns saw Bolitho and shrugged. 'The captain is in a foul mood, Dick. We lay each course a day ahead, but I am as wise as you as to where we are bound.' He looked to see that Pears was not close by. 'It has always been *his* way to explain, to share his views with us. But now, it seems our admiral has other ideas.'

Bolitho thought of the admiral's youthful enthusiasm. Maybe Pears had become staid, out of touch with things.

But there was nothing wrong with his eyes as he yelled, 'Mr Cairns, sir! Get those topmen aloft, flog them if you must! I'll not be goaded again by the flagship!'

It was noon by the time the royals and then the great, batlike studding sails had been set on either beam. The flagship had also made as much sail as she could carry, and appeared to be buried under the towering pyramids of pale canvas.

Lieutenant Probyn relieved Bolitho without his usual sarcasm or complaint, but remarked, 'I see no gain in this at all. Day after day, with ne'er a word of explanation. It makes me uneasy, and that's no lie!'

But two more days were to pass before anyone had settled on the truth of the matter.

Rear-Admiral Coutts's little squadron continued on its southerly course and then swung south-east, skirting Cape Fear, so aptly named, to take advantage of the wind's sudden eagerness to help them.

Bolitho was about to go off watch when he was unexpectedly summoned aft to the great cabin.

But it was not a conference, and he found the captain alone at his desk. His coat was hanging across his chairback, and he had loosened his neckcloth and shirt.

Bolitho waited. The captain looked very calm, so it seemed unlikely there was to be a reprimand for something he had done, or not done.

Pears glanced up at him. 'The master, and now the first lieutenant, know the extent of my orders. You may think it strange for me to confide in you before the rest of my officers, but under the circumstances I think it is fair.' He bobbed his head. '*Do sit down.*'

Bolitho sat, sensing the sudden irritation which was never far from Pears's manner.

'There was some trouble at New York. You played no small part in it.' Pears smiled wryly. 'Which did *not* surprise me, of course.'

Bolitho pricked up his ears. Somehow he had known that the matter of the dead girl would come up again. Even that it might be connected in some small way with the squadron's unexpected departure from Sandy Hook.

'I will not go into full detail, but the girl you discovered in that brothel was the daughter of a New York government official, a very important one to boot. It could not have come at a worse time. Sir George Helpman is out from England under the direct instructions of both Parliament and Admiralty to discover what is being done to pursue the war, to prevent the whole campaign being bogged down in a stalemate. If, or rather when, the French come into the open to fight in strength, we will be hard put to hold what we have, let alone make any gains.'

'I thought we were doing all we could, sir.'

Pears looked at him pityingly. 'When you are more experienced, Bolitho . . .' He looked away, frowning angrily. 'Helpman will see it for himself. The corrupt officials, the dandies of the military government who dance and drink while our soldiers in the field pay the price. And now this. An important official's daughter is discovered to be working hand-in-glove with the rebels. She has been leaving her home in a carriage and changing into boy's clothes just so that she can meet one of Washington's agents and pass him any titbit of secret information she could lay her hands on.'

Bolitho could well imagine the fury and consternation it must have caused. He could find pity for the blowzy whore who had tried to spit in his face. With so much at stake, and with important heads on the block, her interrogators would have few scruples in the manner of gaining information.

Pears said, 'Due to her treachery, the Tracy brothers were able to plot our every move, and but for our taking the *Faithful*, and Mr Bunce's liaison with the Almighty on matters concerning the weather, we might never have known anything. Links in a chain. And now we have one more scrap to play with. That damned whore had her ear to the keyhole more often than not. The Colonials have a new stronghold, constructed with the express purpose of receiving and transporting powder and weapons to their ships and soldiers.'

Bolitho licked his lips. 'And we are heading there now, sir?'

'That's the strength of it, yes. Fort Exeter, in South Carolina, about thirty miles north of Charles Town.'

Bolitho nodded, remembering clearly what happened near there about a year ago, at another rebel fort, only that had been to the south of Charles Town. A large squadron, with troops as well as marines embarked, had sailed to seize the fort which commanded the inshore waters, and would thus interdict all trade and privateer traffic to and from Charles Town, the busiest port south of Philadelphia. Instead of victory, it had ended in humiliating defeat. Some of the ships had gone aground because of wrongly marked charts, while elsewhere the water had been too deep for the soldiers to wade ashore as had been intended. And all the time the Colonials, snug behind their fortress walls, had kept up a steady bombardment on the largest British vessels, until Commodore Parker, whose flagship had taken the worst of it, had ordered a complete withdrawal. *Trojan* had been on her way to offer support when she had met the returning ships.

In the Navy, unused to either defeat or failure, it had seemed like an overwhelming disaster.

Pears had been watching his face. 'I see you have not forgotten either, Bolitho. I only hope we all live to remember this new venture.'

With a start Bolitho realized the interview was over. As he made to leave, Pears said quietly, 'I told you all this because of your part in it. But for your actions, we might not have found out about that girl. But for her, Sir George Helpman would not be raising hell in New York.' He leaned back and smiled. 'And but for *him*, our admiral would not now be trying to prove he can do what others cannot. Links in a chain, Bolitho, as I said earlier. Think about it.'

Bolitho walked out and cannoned into Captain D'Esterre.

The marine said, 'Why, Dick, you look as if you have seen a ghost!'

Bolitho forced a smile. 'I have. Mine.'

When the time came for Lieutenant Cairns to share Pears's orders with the lieutenants and warrant officers, even the most unimaginative one present could not fail to marvel at their admiral's impudence.

While out of sight of land, and with the frigate patrolling to ensure they were left undisturbed, the sloop *Spite* was to embark all of the flagship's and *Trojan*'s marines, and with boats under tow would head inshore under cover of darkness. The two-deckers, in company with *Vanquisher*, would then continue along the coast towards the same fort which had routed Commodore Parker's squadron the previous year.

To any watchers along the coast, and to the officers of the fort and the Charles Town garrison, it would not seem an unlikely thing for the British to attempt. Hurt pride, and the fact that the fort was still performing a useful protection for privateers and the landing of stores and powder, were two very good reasons for a second attempt.

Fort Exeter, on the other hand, was easier to defend to seaward, and would feel quite safe when the small squadron had sailed past in full view of the Colonial pickets.

Bolitho, when he had listened to Cairns's level, unemotional voice as he explained the extent of their orders, had imagined he could detect Rear-Admiral Coutts speaking directly to him.

Spite would land the marines, a party of seamen and all the necessary tackle and ladders for scaling walls, and then stand out to sea again before dawn. The rest, an attack from inland towards the rear of the fort, would be left to the discretion of the senior officer. In this case he was Major Samuel Paget, commanding officer of the flagship's marines.

D'Esterre had said of him in confidence, 'A very hard man. Once he has made up his mind nothing will shift him, and no argument is tolerated.'

Bolitho could well believe it. He had seen Paget a few times. Very erect and conscious of the figure he made in his scarlet coat and matching sash, impeccable white lapels and collar, he was nevertheless having difficulty in concealing his growing corpulence. His face had once been handsome, but now, in his middle thirties, the major had all the signs of a heavy drinker, and one who enjoyed a good table.

D'Esterre had also said, 'This little jaunt might take some of the fat off him.'

But he had not smiled, and Bolitho had guessed that he had wished he and not the major was to command.

Once their mission was out in the open the ship's company got down to work and preparation with the usual mixture of attitudes. Grim resignation for those who would be taking part, cheerful optimism from those who would not.

At the chosen time the work of ferrying the marines and seamen to the little sloop-of-war was begun without delay. After the blazing heat of a July day the evening brought little respite, and the gruelling, irksome work soon roused tempers and on-the-spot justice from fist and rope's end.

Bolitho was counting the last group of seamen and making sure they were all armed, as well as being equipped with flasks of water and not hoarded rum, when Cairns strode up to him and snapped, 'There has been another change.'

'How so?'

Bolitho waited, expecting to hear that the raid was being delayed.

Cairns said bitterly, 'I am remaining aboard.' He looked away, hiding his hurt. '*Again*.'

Bolitho did not know what to say. Cairns had obviously set his heart on going with the attack as senior lieutenant. Having missed the chance of being a prize-master, or even of taking part in the *Faithful*'s capture, he must have seen the landing as his rightful reward, although by going he stood as much chance of being killed as anyone else.

'Someone from the flagship, sir?'

Cairns faced him. 'No. Probyn is to lead, God help you!'

Bolitho examined his feelings. 'And young James Quinn is to go with us also.'

Quinn had said nothing when he had been told, but he had looked as if someone had struck him.

Cairns seemed to read his thoughts. 'Aye, Dick. So it may fall to you to look after our people.'

'But why not the flagship? Surely they have a lieutenant and more to spare?'

Cairns regarded him curiously. 'You don't understand admirals, Dick. They never let go of their own. They must always show a perfect front, a well ordered world of officers and men. Coutts will be no exception. He'll want perfection, not a rabble of old men and boys like we are fast becoming.'

He could have said more, Bolitho thought. That Quinn was being sent to prove that his wound had not destroyed his resolution and courage, and Probyn because he would not be missed. He thought of his own position and almost smiled. Pears was only doing what the admiral had done. Keeping the best for himself. Anyone below Cairns in rank and quality would be sacrificed first.

Cairns said, 'I am glad you can still discover humour in this affair, Dick. For myself, I find it intolerable.'

Midshipman Couzens, hung about with telescope, dirk, pistols and a bulging sack of food, called breathlessly, '*Spite* has signalled, sir! Last party to go across now.'

Bolitho nodded. 'Very well. Man your boats.'

He watched a second midshipman, a serious-faced sixteen-year-old named Huyghue, climbing down into the cutter to sit beside the coxswain, who was probably twice his age.

'I see you are ready, Mr Bolitho.'

Probyn's thick voice made him turn towards the quarterdeck. The second lieutenant could only just have been told of Pears's change of plans, but he looked remarkably unworried. He was very flushed, but that was quite usual, and as he leaned on the quarterdeck rail to peer at the boats alongside he seemed calm to the point of indifference.

Cairns straightened his back as the captain's heavy tread came across the deck. 'Good luck. Both of you.' He glanced at the dizzily swaying sloop. 'By God, I wish I was coming with you.'

Probyn said nothing but touched his hat to the quarterdeck before following the others down into a crowded boat.

Bolitho saw Stockdale in one of the other boats and nodded to him. If for some reason he had not been taking part, it would have been like an ill-omen, something final. Seeing him there, big and quiet-faced, made up for many of the other, nagging doubts.

Probyn said, 'Shove off, cox'n. I don't want to fry in this damn heat!'

As they drew closer to the sloop, her commanding officer hurried to the side and cupped his hands. 'Move yourselves, damn you! This is a King's ship, not a bloody lobster boat!'

Only then did Probyn show some mettle. 'Hear that? Impudent young chicken! God, how command changes a man!'

Bolitho shot him a quick glance. In just those few angry words Probyn had revealed a lot. Bolitho knew he had been beached on half-pay before the war. Whether it was because of his drinking, or he had simply become a hardened drinker because of his ill-luck, he was not sure. But he had certainly been passed over for promotion, and to be shouted at by the *Spite*'s youthful commander would not make it any easier.

As they clambered up on to the sloop's busy deck, he wondered where all the marines had gone. As in the *Faithful*, they had been swallowed up within minutes of boarding. Aft by the taffrail he saw Major Paget speaking with D'Esterre and the two marine lieutenants.

The sloop's commander walked across to meet the last arrivals.

He nodded curtly and then shouted, '*Mr Walker!* Get the ship under way, if you please!'

To Bolitho he added, 'I suggest you go below. My people have enough to contend with at present, without being faced by unknown officers from every hand!'

Bolitho touched his hat. Unlike Probyn, he could understand the young man's sharpness. He was very conscious of his command and the mission suddenly thrust upon him. Close by, two ships of the line, his admiral and some senior post captains would be watching, waiting to find fault, to compare his efficiency with others.

The commander swung on his heel. 'I understand that you were the officer *involved* with my ship two weeks back, eh?'

He had a sharp, incisive tone, and Bolitho guessed he would be a difficult man to get on with. Twenty-four years old. What had Probyn said? *How command changes a man.*

'Well?'

'Aye, sir. I was second-in-command of the raid. My senior was killed.'

'I see.' He nodded. 'My gunner nearly did that to you earlier.' He walked away.

Bolitho made his way aft, pushing through the bustling seamen as they ran to braces and halliards, oblivious to everyone but their own officers.

The pulling boats were already falling obediently astern on their lines, and almost before Bolitho's head had passed into the shadow of the companionway the *Spite* was heeling over to the wind and presenting her counter to the big two-deckers.

The wardroom was crowded with officers, and *Spite*'s purser soon produced bottles and glasses for all the additional guests.

When it came to Probyn he shook his head and said abruptly, 'Not for me, but thankee. Later maybe.'

Bolitho looked away, unable to bear the sight of the man's battle. Probyn had never refused a drink before. And it had cost him a great deal to do it now.

He thought of Probyn's bitterness about the sloop's commander and what lay ahead of them tomorrow.

It was of paramount importance to Probyn that he should succeed, and for that he would give up a lot more than brandy.

During the night and through the following day, *Spite* tacked back and forth, biding her time while she continued a slow approach towards the land.

Fort Exeter stood on a sandy four-mile-long island which was shaped rather like an axe-head. At low water it was connected to the mainland by an unreliable causeway of sand and shingle, and the entrance to a lagoon-like anchorage was easily protected by the fort's carefully sited artillery.

As soon as the landing party was ashore, *Spite* would withdraw and be out of sight of land by the following dawn. If the wind died, the attack would be postponed until it returned. Whatever happened, it would not be abandoned unless the enemy were ready and waiting.

When Bolitho thought of Major Samuel Paget, the man who would be leading the attack, he doubted if it would be cancelled even then.

8

Fort Exeter

The landing, which took place at one in the morning, was carried out with unexpected ease. A favourable wind carried the sloop close inshore, where she dropped anchor and started to ferry the marines ashore as if it were part of a peacetime manoeuvre.

Major Samuel Paget went with the first boat, and when Bolitho eventually stepped on to glistening wet sand and squelched after a hurrying file of marines, he found time to admire the man's sense of planning. He had brought two Canadians with him, and had explained they were better at scouting 'than any damn dogs'. They were both fierce-looking men with beards and rough trapper's clothing, and a smell to match any pelt.

One, a sad-eyed Scot named Macdonald, had originally lived for some years in South Carolina, and had been driven from his land when the main Loyalist force in the area had been beaten in a pitched battle by the Patriot militia. His hate reminded Bolitho of the resourceful Moffitt.

Paget greeted Bolitho with his usual abruptness. 'All quiet. I want our men positioned before first light. We'll issue rations and water.' He scanned the starry sky and grunted, 'Too bloody hot for my liking.'

Stockdale said hoarsely, 'Mr Couzens is comin' with the last lot, sir.'

'Very well.' Bolitho watched as Probyn blundered out of some dark scrub, sniffing around him like a fox. 'Everyone's ashore, sir.'

Probyn watched the marines plodding past, their weapons and equipment carefully muffled, like silent ghosts from some forgotten battle.

'God, it makes you think. Here we are, bloody miles from anywhere, marching into heaven knows what, and to what purpose, eh?'

Bolitho smiled. He had been thinking much the same. The marines seemed quite at home on land as they did at sea, but he could sense the wary caution of the seamen, the way they tended to bunch together, no matter what they were threatened with.

D'Esterre appeared from somewhere and showed his teeth. 'Come along, Dick, join the marines and see the world!' He went off to find his lieutenant, swinging his sword like a cane.

Bolitho looked at the beach, shining faintly in the darkness. The boats had already gone, and he imagined he could hear the sounds of sails being shaken out above the murmur of breakers. Then it really hit home. They were to all intents and purposes abandoned on this unknown shore, with just the skill of two Canadian scouts whom Paget had 'borrowed from the Army'.

Suppose that even now they were being trailed, their stumbling progress marked as they approached some terrible ambush. The night was still but for the wind in the trees and the occasional cry of a startled bird. Even the wind sounded different here, which was not surprising, Bolitho thought, as he peered at the strange palms which ran almost to the water's edge. They gave the land a tropical touch, something alien.

Lieutenant Raye of *Trojan*'s marines marched out of the darkness and exclaimed cheerfully, 'Ah, here you are. The major says you are to follow with the rearguard, Mr Bolitho. Make certain the men do not crash into each other with their ladders and suchlike.' He touched his hat to Probyn. 'He sends his compliments, sir, and would you join him with the main party.'

Probyn nodded, muttering, 'Bloody soldiers, that's what we are!'

Bolitho stood aside to allow the seamen to lurch past, some with ladders and heavy tackles, others carrying muskets, powder and shot. The remainder were loaded down with food and water.

Lieutenant Quinn was right at the rear, with only the blurred shapes on either side to reveal some of the marine skirmishers who were covering their advance.

Bolitho fell in step beside him and asked quietly, 'How is the wound, James?'

'I don't feel it much.' Quinn sounded as if he were shivering. 'But I wish we were afloat, instead of here.'

Bolitho recalled him saying much the same before the last fight. D'Esterre and Thorndike, the surgeon, playing cards under a lantern, the ship sleeping around them.

Quinn said, 'I'm afraid of what I might *do*.' He was almost pleading. 'If I have to face another hand-to-hand, I think I shall break.'

'Easy, man. Don't start meeting trouble before you must.'

He knew exactly how Quinn felt. He had not been in action before that last time.

Quinn did not seem to hear.

'I think of Sparke a lot. How he used to rant and rave. I never really liked him, but I admired his courage, his, his,' he groped for words, 'his *style*.'

Bolitho reached out to steady a seaman as he almost tripped over a root with his load of muskets.

Style. Yes, it described Sparke better than anything else.

Quinn sighed. 'I could never do what he did. Never in a thousand years.'

There was a thud, and a marine raised his musket and brought down the butt a second time on some coarse grass beside the file of seamen. 'Snake!' He mopped his face. 'Cor, that's the bloody potful as far as I'm concerned!'

Bolitho thought suddenly of Cornwall. In July. At this very moment. Hedgerows and lush fields, sheep and cows dotted on the hillsides like scattered flowers. He could almost smell it, hear the bees, the swish of hooks as the farm workers cleared some new land to grow more food. To feed the country, the Army.

Midshipman Couzens said between gasps for breath, 'Sky's brighter, sir.'

Bolitho replied, 'We must be near the place then.'

What would happen if instead of a suitable hideout for the landing party, as remembered by the Canadian, Macdonald, they found an enemy encampment?

Sure enough, the rearguard was already catching up with the main party, where Paget's sergeants and corporals waited like the keepers of invisible gates to guide and push the men into smaller sections. Bolitho watched the white cross-belts and the checkered shirts fading away obediently to the preselected sites.

In the centre of what felt like a shallow, wooded basin, the officers grouped together and waited to receive their orders.

Bolitho felt unusually tired and wanted to keep yawning. And yet his mind was very clear, and he guessed that the yawning might also betray his fear. He had known it before. Too often.

Major Paget, still erect and showing no trace of weariness, said, 'Stay with your people. Issue the rations. But mind they waste nothing and leave no trace of their rubbish.' He looked at D'Esterre meaningly. 'You know what to do. Take control of the perimeter. Double the pickets, and tell them to keep *down*.' To Probyn he said, 'You are in charge here, of course. I shall need an officer with me in a moment.'

Probyn sighed. 'You go, Bolitho. If I send Quinn, the major will eat him for breakfast!'

Bolitho reported to Paget after the others had vanished into the gloom to seek out their men. He took Couzens with him, and answered Stockdale's plea to go too by saying firmly, 'Save your strength for when it is needed, as needed it will be!'

In a fight, or in a raging storm at sea, Stockdale was unbeatable. Creeping through unfamiliar territory, when at any second they might stumble on an enemy look-out patrol, was not his place. His big frame and powerful limbs were enough to wake an army. But it was painful to sense his hurt all the same.

Couzens, on the other hand, was bubbling with excitement. Bolitho had never known anything like it. He seemed to put the awful sights and sounds behind him, dropping them with the tough resilience of youth in war.

Major Paget was drinking from a silver flask while his orderly checked a brace of pistols for him.

He held out the flask. 'Here. Have some.' He leaned forward, his polished boots squeaking. 'Oh, it's you, Bolitho. I've heard about *you*.' He did not elaborate.

Bolitho gasped as the hot brandy trickled over his tongue.

Paget nodded to the midshipman. 'Him, too. Man's drink for a man's work, eh?' He chuckled, the sound like two dry sticks rubbing together.

Couzens smacked his lips. 'Thank you, sir. That was lovely!'

Paget looked at Bolitho and exclaimed, '*Lovely!* In hell's name, what sort of a navy is this?'

With the orderly following respectfully at their heels, they set off in a south-westerly direction, the sea to their left, out of sight but comfortingly close.

Bolitho sensed some of D'Esterre's scouts nearby, flitting through the scrub and trees like forest animals as they protected their commanding officer from attack.

They walked on in silence, aware of the lightening sky, the stars fading obediently as the land took shape from the shadows.

They seemed to be moving up a gentle slope now, weaving occasionally to avoid sprawling clumps of prickly bushes and fallen trees.

A dark figure rose out of the shadows, and Paget said, 'Ah, the Canadian *gentleman!*'

The scout greeted them with a lazy wave. 'This is far enough, Major. The rest o' th' way you gets down on yer belly!'

Paget snapped his fingers, and like a footman serving his master a picnic, the marine orderly brought out with a flourish something like a short green cape.

Paget removed his hat and his sword, then slipped the cape over his head. It completely hid his uniform down as far as his waist.

Bolitho could feel the scout and Couzens staring open-mouthed, but when he glanced at the orderly he saw only stiff indifference, and guessed that Paget's own men knew better than to show amusement.

Paget muttered, 'Had the thing made last year. No sense in getting your head blown off by some backwoodsman, what?'

Bolitho grinned. 'Good idea, sir. I've seen poachers use them, too.'

'Huh.' The major lowered himself carefully on to his hands and knees. 'Well, let's get on with it. We'll be pestered by flies and a million sorts of beetles before another hour. I want to be back at the camp by then.'

It took all of half an hour to discover a suitable observation point, and by that time the sky was considerably brighter, and when Bolitho propped himself on his elbows he saw the sea, the horizon like a thin gold thread. He craned forward, the sharp-pointed grass pricking his face and hands, the soil alive with minute insects. With the sun still below the horizon, the lagoon-shaped bay was in darkness, but against the shimmering water, with the restless procession of white horses further to seaward, he could see the fort clearly. A black, untidy shape perched on the end of the low island. He saw two lanterns, and what appeared to be a sheltered fire outside the wall, but little else.

Paget was breathing heavily as he trained a telescope through the grass and rough scrub.

He seemed to be thinking aloud as he muttered, 'Got to be careful at this angle. If the sun comes up suddenly, some fellow down there might see it reflected in this damn glass.'

Couzens whispered to Bolitho, 'Can you see the guns, sir?'

Bolitho shook his head, picturing the marines charging across the alleged causeway into a hail of canister or worse. 'Not yet.' He strained his eyes again. 'The fort is not square, or even rectangular. Six, maybe seven sides. Perhaps one gun per wall.'

The scout wriggled nearer and said, 'They're supposed to have a flat pontoon, Major.' He raised an arm, releasing an even sourer smell. 'When they get supplies sent by land they put th' wagons an' horses on th' pontoon an' haul the thing across.'

Paget nodded. 'As I thought. Well, that's how we'll go. This time tomorrow. While the devils are still asleep.'

The scout sucked his teeth. 'Night-time'd be better.'

Paget replied scornfully, 'The dark is damn useless to everybody, man! No, we'll watch today. Tomorrow we attack.'

'As you say, Major.'

Paget rolled over heavily and peered at Bolitho. 'You take the first watch, eh? Send the boy to me if you sight anything useful.' Then, with remarkable stealth, he was gone.

Couzens smiled tightly. 'Are we alone, sir?' For the first time he sounded nervous.

Bolitho replied, 'It would seem so. But you saw where the last picket was. If you go back with a message, put yourself in his hands. I don't want you wandering off.'

He drew a pistol from his belt and felt it carefully. Then he unsheathed his hanger and laid it beside him, thrusting the blade into the sand to hide any reflection.

It was going to be very hot before long. Bolitho tried not to think of fresh drinking water.

Couzens said, 'I feel I'm doing something, sir. Something *useful* at last.'

Bolitho sighed. 'I hope you're right.'

By the time the sun's rim had broken above the horizon and come spilling down towards the fort and its protected anchorage, Bolitho had learned a lot more about his companion. Couzens was the fifth son of a Norfolk clergyman, had a sister called Beth who intended to marry the squire's son if she got half a chance, and whose mother made the best apple pie in the county.

They both fell silent as they peered at the newly revealed fort and its immediate surroundings. Bolitho had been right about its shape. It was hexagonal, and the walls, which were of double thickness and constructed of stout palmetto wood, had their inner sections filled with rocks and packed earth. Both inner and outer wall was covered by a parapet, and Bolitho guessed that even the heaviest ball would find it hard to penetrate such a barrier.

He saw a squat tower on the seaward side, with a flagpole, and a drifting smear of smoke which suggested a galley somewhere below in the central courtyard.

There were the usual loopholes, and as the light strengthened Bolitho saw two gun embrasures pointing towards the mainland and the causeway, and he could also see the shadow of a gateway between them.

Two small boats were pulled up on to the nearest beach, and the skeleton of another, probably the only remains of some skirmish a year or more ago.

Couzens whispered excitedly, 'There, sir! The pontoon!'

Bolitho lowered his eye to the telescope and scanned first the fort and then the moored pontoon. It was a crude affair, with trailing ropes, and slatted ramps for horses and wagons. The sand on both mainland and beach was churned up to mark the many comings and goings.

He moved the glass carefully towards the anchorage. Small, but good enough for two vessels. Brigs and schooners most likely, he thought.

A trumpet echoed over the swirling water, and moments later a flag jerked up to the top of the pole and broke dejectedly towards them. A few heads moved on the parapet, and then Bolitho saw a solitary figure appear from the pontoon's inner ramp, a musket over his shoulder, gripped casually by the muzzle. Bolitho held his breath. That was worth knowing. He had had no idea there was a space there for a sentry.

With daylight spreading inland, and his companions on the move again, the sentry's night vigil was done. If Paget's scheme was going to work, that sentry would have to be despatched first.

As the first hour dragged by, Bolitho studied the fort carefully and methodically, as much to take his mind off the mounting glare and heat as with any purpose in mind.

There did not appear to be many men in the garrison, and the amount of horse tracks by the pontoon suggested that quite a number had left very recently. Probably in response to the news of the British squadron which had been sighted heading further south.

Bolitho thought of Rear-Admiral Coutts's plan, the simplicity of it. He would like to be here now, he thought. Seeing his ideas taking shape.

The Canadian, Macdonald, slid up beside him without a sound and showed his stained teeth.

'It'd bin no use you reachin' fer yer blade, mister!' His grin widened. 'I could'a slit yer throat easy-like!'

Bolitho swallowed hard. 'Most probably.' He saw Quinn and Midshipman Huyghue crawling through the scrub towards him and said, 'We are relieved, it seems.'

Later, when they reached Paget's command post, Bolitho described what he had seen.

Paget said, 'We must get that pontoon.' He looked meaningly at Probyn. 'Job for seamen, eh?'

Probyn shrugged. 'Of course, sir.'

Bolitho sat with his back to a palm and drank some water from a flask.

Stockdale squatted nearby and asked, 'Is it a bad one, sir?'

'I'm not sure yet.'

He saw the pontoon, the sentry stretching as he had emerged from his hiding place. He'd quite likely been asleep. It would not be difficult for such an easily defended fort to become over-confident.

Stockdale watched him worriedly. 'I've made a place for you to lie, sir.' He pointed to a rough cover of brush and fronds. 'Can't fight without sleep.'

Bolitho crawled under the tiny piece of cover, the freshness of the water already gone from his mouth.

It was going to be the longest day of all, he thought grimly, and the waiting unbearable.

He turned his head as he heard someone snoring. It was Couzens, lying on his back, his freckled features burned painfully by the sun.

The sight of such apparent confidence and trust helped to steady Bolitho. Couzens was probably dreaming of his mother's pies, or the sleepy Norfolk village where something or somebody had put the idea in his mind to be a sea officer and leave the land.

Stockdale leaned back against a tree and watched Bolitho fall asleep.

He was still watching when one of D'Esterre's marines crawled through the scrub and hissed, 'Where is the lieutenant?'

Bolitho awoke reluctantly, his mind trying to grapple with where he was and what he was doing.

The marine explained wearily, 'The major's compliments, sir, and would you join 'im where you was this mornin'.'

Bolitho stood up, each muscle protesting violently.

'Why?'

'Mr Quinn sighted a strange sail, sir.'

Bolitho looked at Stockdale and grimaced. 'What timing! It couldn't be at a worse moment!'

It took longer to reach the lookout the second time. The sun was much higher in the sky and the air so humid it was hard to draw breath.

Paget, complete with green cape, was lying with his telescope carefully shaded by some leaves. Probyn sprawled beside him, and further down the slope, trying to find some shade, Quinn and his midshipman looked like survivors from a desert trek.

Paget snapped, 'So here you are.' He relented slightly and added, 'Look for yourself.'

Bolitho took the glass and trained it on the approaching craft. She was broad in the beam, and from her low freeboard he guessed her to be fully laden. She was moving at a snail's pace, her tan-coloured sails flapping uncomfortably as she tacked towards the fort. Three masts on a small, sturdy hull, she was obviously a coasting lugger. There were plenty of such craft along the east coast, as they were good sea-boats, but equally at home in shallow water.

Bolitho wiped the sweat from his eyes and moved the lens on to the fort's square tower. There were quite a lot of heads there now, watching the approaching lugger, and Bolitho saw that the gates were wide open, and some more men were walking unhurriedly below the walls and making for the beach on the far side of the island.

None of the fort's cannon was run out or even manned.

He said, 'Must be expecting her.'

Paget grunted. 'Obviously.'

Probyn complained, 'It'll make our task damn near impossible. We'll have the enemy on two sides of us.' He swore crudely and added, 'Just our luck!'

'I intend to attack *as planned*.' Paget watched the lugger bleakly. 'I can't waste another full day. A patrol might stumble on our people at any moment. Or the *Spite* may return ahead of time to see what we are about.' He thrust out his heavy jaw. 'No. We attack.'

He crawled awkwardly across some sharp stones and snapped, 'I'm going back. Keep watch and tell me what you think later.'

Probyn glared after him. 'He makes me sick!'

Bolitho lay on his back and covered his face with his arms. He was being stung and bitten by tiny, unseen attackers, but he barely noticed. He thought of the lugger and how the unexpected could rearrange a puzzle in seconds.

Probyn said grudgingly, 'Still, he may be right about another delay. And I can't see him calling off the attack altogether.'

Bolitho knew he was watching him and smiled. 'What about you?'

'Me?' Probyn grabbed the telescope again. 'Who cares what I think?'

It was well into the afternoon before the lugger had worked around the end of the island and into the anchorage. As her sails were carelessly brailed up and her anchor dropped, Bolitho saw a boat pulling from the beach towards her.

Probyn looked and sounded tired out. He asked irritably, 'Well, what d'you see?'

Bolitho levelled the glass on the man who was climbing down into the boat. Bravado, conceit, or was it just to display his confidence? But his uniform, so bright against the lugger's untidiness, was clearer than any message.

Bolitho said quietly, 'That's a French officer down there.' He looked sideways at Probyn's features. 'So now we know.'

9

Probyn's Choice

Mishipman Couzens crawled on his hands and knees until he had reached Bolitho at the top of the rise.

'All accounted for, sir.' He peered down the slope towards the sea and the fort's uncompromising outline.

Bolitho nodded. There were a dozen questions at the back of his mind. Had the seamen's weapons been checked to make sure that some nervous soul had not loaded his pistol despite the threats of what would happen to him? Had Couzens impressed on them the vital importance of silence from now on? But it was too late now. He had to trust every man jack of them. Bolitho could sense them at his back, crouching in their unfamiliar surroundings, gripping their weapons, worrying.

At least there was no moon, but against that, the wind had dropped away, and the slow, regular hiss of surf made the only sound. To get the men down to the beach and across to the island without raising an alarm would be doubly difficult without some noise to cover their approach.

He thought of D'Esterre's cool appraisal of the island and its defences. He had studied it through his telescope from three different angles. The fort had at least eight heavy cannon, and several smaller pieces. The garrison, although depleted, appeared to number about forty. Just a dozen men could hold the fort and sweep away a frontal attack without effort. It was a miracle that some hunter or scout had not stumbled on the hidden marines. But this place was like an abandoned coast. They had seen nothing but a few men around the island and the occasional comings and goings from the anchored lugger.

The French officer was thought to be in the fort, although his purpose for being there was still a mystery.

Stockdale hissed, 'Mr Quinn's party is 'ere, sir.'

'Good.' Poor Quinn, he looked like death, and they had not even begun yet. 'Tell him to get ready.'

Bolitho peered through his glass towards the lugger, but saw nothing but her shadow. No riding light to betray her presence, and even some drunken singing had stopped hours ago.

A hand touched his shoulder, and he heard the Canadian scout say, '*Now!*'

Bolitho stood up and followed him down the steep side of the hill towards the water. His shoes loosened stones and sand, and he could feel the sweat running down his chest. It was like being naked, walking towards levelled muskets which at any moment would cut him down.

Too late now. Too late now.

He walked steadily behind the other man's shadow, knowing the rest of his party were close on his heels. He could even picture their faces. Men like Rowhurst, the gunner's mate, Kutbi, the staring-eyed Arab, Rabbett, the little thief from Liverpool who had escaped the rope by volunteering for the Navy.

The sea's noises came to meet them, giving them confidence like an old friend.

They paused by some sun-dried bushes while Bolitho took stock of his position. The bushes had looked much larger from the hilltop. Now the seamen crowded behind and amongst them, peering across the rippling water towards the fort, and probably thinking that they were the last cover until they reached those walls.

The Canadian whispered, 'Them there are th' guide ropes fer th' pontoon.'

He was chewing methodically, his body hunched forward as he studied the shelving strip of beach.

Bolitho saw the great timbers which had been raised to carry the ropes, and found himself praying that their calculations on tide and distance were right. If the pontoon was hard aground it would take an army to move it. He thought of the two big muzzles he had seen pointing towards the mainland and the hidden causeway. He doubted if the garrison would give them time for regrets.

He wondered if Paget was watching their progress from some vantage point, seething with impatience.

Bolitho took a grip on his racing thoughts. This was no moment to get flustered.

The scout was stripping off his jerkin as he said, 'I'll be goin' over then.' He could have been remarking on the weather. 'If you hear nothin', you'd better follow.'

Bolitho reached out and touched the man's shoulder. It was covered in grease.

He forced himself to say, 'Good luck.'

The scout left the bushes and walked unhurriedly to the water's edge. Bolitho counted the paces, four, five, six, but already the Canadian was merging with the water, then he was gone altogether.

The sentries around the fort stood three-hour watches. Probably because they were short-handed. It would, with luck, make them extra weary.

The minutes dragged past, and several times Bolitho thought he heard something, and waited for the alarm to be raised.

Rowhurst muttered, 'Should be long enough, sir.' He had a bared cutlass in his fist. '*Must* be all right.'

Bolitho looked at the gunner's mate in the darkness. Was he that confident? Or did he think his lieutenant had lost his nerve and was merely trying to jolt him into action?

'One more minute.' He beckoned to Couzens. 'Go and tell Mr Quinn to prepare his men.'

Again he had to check himself. Make sure the ladders were muffled. Quinn would have seen to that. He must have.

He nodded to Rowhurst. 'You take the left rope.' He beckoned to Stockdale. 'We'll take the right one.'

The seamen had split into two groups, and he saw them crossing the open beach towards the massive timbers, then up and out on the sagging ropes. Dangling at first, and then lower until their legs and then their bodies were pushed and buffeted by the swirling current.

After the heat of the day and the discomfort of waiting, the water was like cool silk.

Bolitho dragged himself along the rope. It felt greasy, like the scout's shoulder.

Every man in the party was hand-picked. Even so, he could hear a few grunts and gasps, and felt his own arms throbbing with strain.

Then, all of a sudden, they were there, dropping silently on to the pontoon's crude deck, peering round with white eyes, waiting for a challenge.

Instead, the scout moved out of the shadows and drawled, 'All done. 'E never even woke up.'

Bolitho swallowed. He did not need to be told anything more. The luckless sentry must have fallen asleep, to awake with the scout's double-edged hunting knife already sawing into his throat.

He said, 'Rowhurst, you know what to do. Carry on and collect the others. Let the current move the thing.'

Rowhurst nodded patiently. 'Aye, sir. I'll do that.'

Bolitho stepped carefully off the ramp, his foot brushing against an outflung arm where the dead sentry lay at the water's edge. He shut him from his mind as he tried to remember all he had seen here. The fort was on the other side of the narrow island. About half a mile. Less. The sentries would be watching to seaward, if they were watching at all. They had plenty of reason for confidence, he thought. The lugger had taken an age to work around the point, so even firing blindly the fort could cripple a large man-of-war in no time at all.

Nobody in his right mind would anticipate an attack from inland, without even boats provided for the crossing.

Stockdale whispered huskily, 'She's movin', sir.'

The pontoon was slipping away, merging with the shadows and the black mainland beyond.

Bolitho walked towards the fort, his little group of men spreading out on either side. Now he felt really alone, and completely cut off from aid if things went wrong.

After groping their way towards the fort for some while, they discovered a shallow gully and gratefully clambered into it.

Bolitho lay with his telescope propped over the lip of coarse sand and tried to discover some sign of life. But, like the island itself, the fort seemed dead. The original building, long since destroyed by fire and battle, had been constructed to defend the early settlers from attack by Indians. Those hardy adventurers would be laughing now if they could see us, Bolitho thought grimly.

After what seemed like a lifetime a seaman whispered, 'Mr Couzens is comin', sir.'

Led by the Canadian scout, out of breath and grateful to have discovered his companions, Couzens fell into the gully.

He said, 'Mr Quinn is over here now, sir. And Captain D'Esterre with his first section of marines.'

Bolitho let his breath exhale very slowly. Whatever happened now, he was not alone and unsupported. The pontoon would be on its way back, and with any sort of luck more marines would soon be landing.

He whispered, 'Take two men and feel your way along the beach to those boats. I want them guarded, in case we have to leave with sudden haste.' He could sense the youth's concentration. 'So be off with you.'

He watched him crawl over the lip of the gully with two armed seamen. One less to worry about. There was no sense in Couzens getting killed for such a hazy plan.

It was easy to picture the marines spreading out in two sections, making their way towards the fort's gates while the next to land took station to cover the eventual attack, or retreat.

Bolitho guessed that Probyn would be with the major, if only to make certain he was not forgotten after the excitement was over.

Another figure slithered amongst the tense seamen. It was Quinn's midshipman, out of breath, and quivering with exertion.

'Well, Mr Huyghue?' Bolitho thought suddenly of Sparke in the heat of a fight. Cool, detached. It was easier said than done. 'Is your party ready?'

Huyghue bobbed his head. 'Aye, sir. Ladders and grapnels'. He licked his lips noisily. 'Mr Quinn says it will be light very soon now.'

Bolitho looked at the sky. Quinn must be ill at ease to mention the obvious to his midshipman.

He said, 'We'd best begin, in that case.'

He stood up and loosened his shirt. How many more times like this? When would it be his turn to fall and never get up again?

Bolitho said harshly, 'Follow me.' The unnatural sound of his own voice made him feel slightly unsteady, light-headed. 'Mr Huyghue, remain here and keep a good watch. If we are repulsed, you will join Mr Couzens at the boats.'

Huyghue was shifting from foot to foot, as if he were standing on hot coals.

'And then, sir?'

Bolitho looked at him. 'You will have to decide on that. For I fear there will be none left to advise you!'

He heard Rabbett's little titter, and wondered how anyone could laugh at such a feeble, gruesome joke.

He felt the breeze on his face, soft and coolly caressing, as he strode towards the corner of the fort. It was still a cable away, and yet he felt starkly visible as he made his way towards Quinn's hiding place.

Someone rose to his knees with an aimed musket, but fell prone again as he recognized Bolitho's party.

Quinn was with his men by the ladders, edgy and nervous as he waited for Bolitho to use his telescope.

Bolitho said, 'Nothing. It looks quiet. Very quiet. I think they must place a lot of trust in the seaward entry and the one we left by the beach.' He saw Quinn flinch and added softly, 'Get a *grip*, James. Our people have nothing but us to judge their chances by.' He forced a grin, feeling his lips tighten as if freezing. 'So let us earn our pay, eh?'

Rowhurst strode from the shadows. 'Ready, sir.' He glanced quickly at Quinn. 'No sign of the buggers on this parapet.'

Bolitho turned his back towards the fort and raised his arm. He saw the crouching figures breaking from cover and knew he had committed all of them. There was no turning back.

The ladders were carried swiftly towards the chosen wall, and on either side of them the first party of seamen loped forward, their cutlasses and boarding axes making them look like figures from an old Norman tapestry Bolitho had once seen at Bodmin.

Bolitho gripped Quinn's wrist, squeezing it until he winced with pain.

'We don't know what we'll find, James. But the gates *must* be opened, do you hear me?' He spoke slowly, despite his tumbling thoughts. It was essential for Quinn to hold out now.

Quinn nodded. 'Yes. I – I'll be all right, sir.'

Bolitho released him. 'Dick.'

Quinn stared at him dazedly. 'Dick!'

The first ladder was already rising against the pale stars, up and up, and the second following even as the waiting seamen hurried to steady them.

Bolitho made sure that his hanger was looped around his wrist and then ran lightly to the nearest ladder, knowing that Stockdale was following.

Rowhurst watched Quinn and then tapped his arm, seeing him jump as he hissed, 'Come along, sir!'

With a gasp Quinn ran to the other ladder, scrambling and panting as he pulled himself towards the hard black edge below the stars.

Bolitho hoisted himself over the rough planking and dropped on to the wooden rampart. It was little different from a ship, he thought vaguely, except for the terrible stillness.

He felt his way along a handrail, past a mounted swivel gun and towards where he thought the gates would be. He sucked breath to his aching lungs, seeing the rounded hump on the wall which he knew was directly above the entrance. He could smell the embers of a wood fire, cooking, horses, and men. The smell of a tightly packed garrison almost anywhere in the world.

He twisted round as the seaman Rabbett slid forward and brought down the side of his boarding axe on what Bolitho had thought to be a pile of sacks. It was another sentry, or perhaps just a man who had come up to the parapet to find some cool air. It was such a swift and savage blow that Bolitho thought it doubtful if he would draw breath again.

The shock of it helped to tighten his reactions, to compress every ounce of concentration in what he was doing. He found the top of a ladder and knew the gates were just yards away.

Stockdale moved beside him. 'I'll do it, sir.'

Bolitho tried to see his face but there was only shadow.

'We'll do it together.'

With the remainder of the men kneeling or lying on the parapet, Bolitho and Stockdale stepped very slowly down the uneven wooden stairs.

At the other end of that same wall Quinn and his party would be making towards the watch-tower to protect Bolitho from the rear if the guard turned out.

It had all begun in Rear-Admiral Coutts's mind, many miles from this sinister place. Now they were here, when previously Bolitho had thought they would be attacked and beaten back before they had even found a refuge to hide. It had been so ridiculously easy that it was unnerving at the same time.

He felt the ground under his shoes and knew he had reached the courtyard. He could sense rather than discern the low buildings and stables which lined the inner walls, but when he looked at the tower he discovered he could see the flagpole and the paling sky above.

Stockdale touched his arm and pointed towards a small out-thrust hut beyond the gates. There was a soft glow of light through some shutters, and Bolitho guessed it was where the guard took its rest between watches.

He whispered, 'Come.'

It took only seven paces to reach the centre of the gates. Bolitho found he was counting each one as if his life depended on it. There was a long beam resting on iron slots to secure the gates, and nothing more. Stockdale laid down his cutlass and took the weight of the bar at one end while Bolitho watched the hut.

It was just as Stockdale put his great strength under the beam that it happened. A terrified shout, rising to a shrill scream, before being cut off instantly as if slammed behind a massive door.

For an instant longer nobody moved or spoke, and then as startled voices and padding feet echoed around the courtyard Bolitho yelled, 'Open it! Fast as you can!'

Shots cracked and banged haphazardly, and he heard them slamming into the timber or whistling harmlessly towards the water. He could imagine the confusion and pandemonium it was causing, and plenty of the garrison must still be thinking the attack was coming from outside the defences.

Light spilled from the guard hut, and Bolitho saw figures running towards him, one firing his musket and then being knocked down by more men who were charging out, palely naked against the shadows.

He heard someone yell, 'Load and fire at will, lads!'

Then steel grated on steel, and more shouts changed to screams and desperate cries before anyone from Bolitho's party could fire.

A man lunged at him with a bayoneted musket, but he parried it away, letting the charge carry his attacker past, gasping with terror, until the hanger slashed him down at Stockdale's feet.

Bolitho yelled, 'To me, Trojans!'

There were more cries and then cheers as the first gate began to move and Stockdale heaved the great beam aside, hurling it amongst the confused figures by the hut like a giant's lance.

But others were appearing from across the courtyard, and some semblance of order came with shouted commands, a responding rattle of musket-fire which hurled two seamen from the parapet like rag dolls.

Stockdale snatched up his cutlass and slashed a man across the chest, turning just enough to take a second in the stomach as he tried to stab under Bolitho's guard.

Kutbi, the Arab, screamed shrilly and ran forward, whirling his axe like a madman, oblivious to everything but the urge to kill.

Another seaman fell coughing blood by Bolitho's feet, and he heard Quinn's men clashing blades with the guards from the tower, getting nearer and louder as they were driven back towards the gates.

Clang, clang, clang. Bolitho thought his arm would break as he hacked and parried at a uniformed figure which had seemingly risen from the ground beneath him. He could feel the man's strength, his determination, as step by step he drove him back, and further still.

Bolitho felt strangely clear-headed, devoid of fear or any recognizable sensation. This must be the moment. What it was like. The end of luck. Of everything.

Clang, clang, clang.

He locked his hilt with the other man's, sensing his power against his own fading strength. Vaguely he heard Stockdale bellowing, trying to cut his way through to help him.

Instinct told him there was no help this time, and as the other man swung him round, using the locked hilts like a hinge, he saw a pistol protruding from his belt. With one last agonizing effort he flung himself forward, letting his sword-arm drop while he snatched for the trigger, cocking the weapon and firing even as he tore it free.

The explosion threw it from his hand, and he saw the man double over, his agony too terrible even for screams as the heavy ball ripped through his groin like molten lead.

Bolitho raised his hanger, swayed over the writhing man and then lowered it again. It would be kinder to free him from his agony forever, but he could not do it.

The next moment the other gate was being thrust aside, and through the drifting smoke of musket and pistol fire Bolitho saw the white cross-belts and the faintly glittering bayonets as the marines surged through.

There were a few last pockets of resistance. Handfuls of men, fighting and dying in a cellar and on the parapet. Some tried to surrender, but were shot down in a wave of madness by the victorious marines. Others burst through the gates and ran for the sea, only to be trapped by Paget's next cordon of muskets.

Probyn limped through the chaos of dying men and prisoners with their hands in the air. He saw Bolitho and grunted, 'That was close.'

Bolitho nodded, leaning against a horse-rail, sucking air into his aching body. He looked at Probyn's limp and managed to gasp, 'Are you wounded?'

Probyn replied hotly, 'Got tripped by some fools with a ladder! Might have broken my damn leg!'

It was so absurd in the midst of all the pain and death that Bolitho wanted to laugh. But he knew if he did he would not be able to stop or control it.

D'Esterre came from beneath the stable roof and said, 'The fort is taken. It's done.' He turned to receive his hat from a marine and brushed it against his leg before adding, 'The devils had a gun already loaded and trained on the causeway. If they had been warned, we would have been cut down completely, attacking *or* running away!'

Rowhurst waited until Bolitho had seen him and then said heavily, 'We lost three men, sir.' He gestured with his thumb towards the tower. 'An' two badly wounded.'

Bolitho asked quietly, 'And Mr Quinn?'

Rowhurst replied gruffly, ''E's all right, sir.'

What did that mean? Bolitho saw Paget and more marines coming through the open gates and decided not to press further. Not yet.

Paget looked at the hurrying marines and seamen and snapped, 'Where is the fort's commanding officer?'

D'Esterre said, 'He was absent, sir. But we have taken his second-in-command.'

Paget snorted. 'He'll do. Show me to his quarters.' He looked at Probyn. 'Have your people lay a couple of heavy cannon on that lugger. If she tries to make sail, dissuade her, what?'

Probyn touched his hat and muttered sourly, 'He's having a fine time, and no mistake!'

Rowhurst was already looking up at the gun embrasures with a professional eye. 'I'll attend to the lugger, sir.' He strode off, yelling names, glad to be doing something he understood.

The man whose pistol Bolitho had used just minutes earlier gave a single cry and then died. Bolitho stood looking at him, trying to discover his feelings towards someone who had tried to kill him.

A marine from the *Trojan* marched across the courtyard and could barely stop himself from grinning as he reported, 'Beg pardon, sir, but one of your young gennlemen 'as caught a prisoner!'

At that moment Couzens and two seamen came through the gates. Leading them, for that was how it looked, was the French officer, his coat over one arm and carrying his cocked hat as if going for a stroll.

Couzens exclaimed, 'He was making for the boats, sir. Ran right into us!' He was glowing with pride at his capture.

The Frenchman glanced from Bolitho to Probyn and said calmly, 'Not *running*, I assure you! Merely taking advantage of circumstances.' He bowed his head. 'I am Lieutenant Yves Contenay. At your service.'

Probyn glared at him. 'You are under arrest, damn you!'

The Frenchman gave a gentle smile. 'I think not. I command yonder vessel. I put in for . . .' He shrugged. 'The reason is unimportant.'

He looked up as some seamen used handspikes to train one of the cannon further round towards the anchorage. For the first time he showed alarm, even fear.

Probyn said, 'I see. Unimportant. Well, I shall expect you to tell your people not to attempt to leave, or to damage the vessel in any way. If they do, I will have them fired upon without quarter.'

'I believe that.' Contenay turned to Bolitho and spread his hands. 'I have my orders also, you know.'

Bolitho watched him, the strain dragging at his body like claws. 'Your lugger is carrying gunpowder, is she not?'

The Frenchman frowned. 'Lug-ger?' Then he nodded. 'Ah, yes, *lougre*, I understand.' He shrugged again. 'Yes. If you put one shot into her, *pouf*!'

Probyn snapped, 'Stay with him. I must go and tell the major.'

Bolitho looked at Couzens. 'Well done.'

The French officer smiled. 'Indeed, yes.'

Bolitho watched the bodies being dragged from the gates and the guard hut. Two of the prisoners in their blue and white uniforms were already being put to work with brooms and buckets to clear away the blood.

He said quietly, 'You will be *asked* about your cargo, *m'sieu*. But you know that.'

'Yes. I am under official orders. There is no law to stop me. My country respects the revolution. It does not respect your oppression.'

Bolitho asked dryly, 'And France hopes to gain nothing, of course?'

They both grinned at each other like conspirators, while Couzens, robbed of some of his glory, watched in confusion.

Two lieutenants, Bolitho thought. Caught up in a tidal wave of rebellion and war. It would be hard to dislike this French officer.

But he said, 'I suggest you do nothing to rouse Major Paget.'

'Just so.' Contenay tapped the side of his nose. 'You have officers like that too, do you?'

As Probyn returned with a marine escort, Bolitho asked, 'Where did you learn such good English, *m'sieu*?'

'I lived in England for a long time.' His smile widened. 'It will be useful one day, *oui*?'

Probyn snapped, 'Take him to Major Paget.' He watched the man go with his escort and added angrily, 'You should have shot him, Mr Couzens, dammit! He'll be exchanged for one of our officers, don't doubt it. Bloody privateers, I'd hang the lot of 'em, theirs and ours!'

Stockdale called, 'See the flag, sir!'

Bolitho looked up at the garrison flag which Paget had sensibly ordered to be hoisted in the usual way. There was no sense in drawing suspicion from sea or land until they had finished what they had begun.

But he knew what Stockdale meant. Instead of flapping lazily towards the land, it was lifting and falling towards the brightening horizon. The wind had completely changed direction overnight. Up to now, everyone had been too busy and apprehensive to notice.

He said quietly, '*Spite* will not be able to stand inshore.'

Probyn's palm rasped across his bristles as he replied anxiously, 'But it'll shift back again. You see if it don't!'

Bolitho turned his back on the sea and studied the hillside where he and Couzens had baked in the sun. From the fort it looked different again. Dark and brooding.

'But until it does, *we* are the defenders here!'

Major Paget squatted on the corner of a sturdy table and eyed his weary officers grimly.

Sunlight streamed through the windows of the garrison commander's room, and through a weapon slit Bolitho could see the trees along the shore and a small sliver of beach.

It was halfway into the morning, and still without a sight of friend or enemy.

That did not mean they had not kept busy. On the contrary, with the captured French lieutenant as hostage, Probyn and an escort of armed marines had been pulled across to the lugger.

When he had eventually returned he had described the vessel's cargo for Paget's benefit. She was full to the deck seams with West Indian gunpowder, several stands of French muskets, pistols and numerous pieces of military equipment.

Paget said, 'She is a very valuable capture. Denying the enemy her cargo will do Washington's campaign some damage, I can assure you, gentlemen. If we are attacked here before help comes for us, it seems very likely that the enemy will destroy the lugger if they cannot recapture her. I intend that she should not fall into their hands again.'

Bolitho heard the tramp of marching feet and the hoarse cries of the marine sergeants. Paget's assessment made very good sense. Fort Exeter had to be destroyed, and with it all the defences, weapons and equipment which had been gathered over the months.

But it would take time, and it seemed unlikely that it could be long before the enemy counter-attacked.

'I am in command of this operation.' Paget ran his eyes over them as if expecting an argument. 'It falls to me to appoint a prize crew for the lugger, to sail her without delay to New York, or to report to any King's ship whilst on passage there.'

Bolitho tried to contain his sudden excitement. The lugger had a crew of natives which had been recruited by the French authorities in Martinique. No wonder a man like Lieutenant Contenay had been picked for such a small and lonely command. He was a cut above many officers Bolitho had met, and well suited for such arduous work. It was no mean task to sail the lugger from Martinique in the Caribbean all the way to this poorly charted anchorage.

Even with such a devastating and lethal cargo she would make a pleasant change from this, he thought. And once in New York, anything might happen before *Trojan*'s authority caught up with him again. A frigate perhaps? Going back to the most junior aboard a frigate would be reward enough.

He thought he had misheard as Paget continued, 'Mr Probyn is to command. He will take some of the lesser wounded men to watch over the native crew.'

Bolitho turned, expecting Probyn to explode in protest. Then it came to him. After all, why should not Probyn feel as he did? Go with the prize and present himself to the commander-in-chief in the hopes of getting a better appointment, and promotion to boot.

Probyn was so obsessed with the idea he had not touched a drop of wine or brandy, even after taking the fort. He was not shrewd enough to see beyond the new prize and his eventual entrance to Sandy Hook, not the sort of man to consider that others might think it strange for so senior a lieutenant to take so small a command.

Probyn stood up, his features showing satisfaction better than any speech.

Paget added, 'I will write the necessary orders, unless . . .' he glanced at Bolitho, 'you intend to change your mind?'

Probyn's jaw lifted firmly. 'No, sir. It is my right.'

The major glared at him. 'Only if I say so.' He shrugged. 'But so be it.'

D'Esterre murmured, 'I am sorry for your missed chance, Dick, but I cannot say the same of your remaining with us.'

Bolitho tried to smile. 'Thank you. But I think poor George Probyn may soon be back in *Trojan*. He is likely to run into a senior ship on his journey whose captain may have other ideas about the lugger's cargo.'

Paget's eyebrows knitted together. 'When you have quite *finished*, gentlemen!'

D'Esterre asked politely, 'What of the French lieutenant, sir?'

'He will remain with us. Rear-Admiral Coutts will be interested to meet him before the authorities in New York get the chance.' He gave a stiff smile. 'If you can see my point?'

The major stood up and flicked some sand from his sleeve. 'Be about your affairs, and see that your men are on the alert.'

Probyn waited by the door for Bolitho and said curtly, 'You are the senior here now.' His eyes glittered through his tiredness. 'And I wish you luck with this rabble!'

Bolitho watched him impassively. Probyn was not that much senior in years, but looked almost as old as Pears.

He asked, 'Why all this bitterness?'

Probyn sniffed. 'I have never had any real luck, or the background of your family to support me.' He raised his fist to Bolitho's sudden anger. 'I came from nothing, and had to drag myself up every rung by my fingernails! You think I should have asked for you to be sent with the lugger, eh? What's a damned Frenchie blockade-runner to a senior lieutenant like me, that's what you're thinking!'

Bolitho sighed. Probyn was deeper than he had imagined.

'It did cross my thoughts.'

'When Sparke was killed, the next chance fell to me. I took it, and I intend to exploit it to the fullest range, d'you see?'

'I think so.' Bolitho looked away, unable to watch Probyn's torment.

'You can wait for the relief to arrive, then you can tell Mr bloody Cairns, and anyone else who might be interested, that I'm not coming back to *Trojan*. But if I ever do have to visit the ship, I will be piped aboard as a captain in my own right!'

He swung on his heel and walked off. Whatever pity or understanding Bolitho might have felt melted when he realized that Probyn had no intention of speaking with the men he was leaving behind, or visiting those who would die from their wounds before the lugger had tacked clear of the anchorage.

D'Esterre joined him on the parapet and watched Probyn as he marched purposefully along the beach towards one of the long-boats.

'I hope to God he stays out of his cups, Dick. With a hull full of powder, and a crew of frightened natives, it could be a rare voyage if George returns to his favourite pastime!' He saw his sergeant waiting for him and hurried away.

Bolitho went down one of the stairways and found Quinn leaning against a wall. He was supposed to be supervising the collection of side-arms and powder flasks, but was letting his men do as they pleased.

Bolitho said, 'Well, you heard what the major had to say, and what Probyn said to me just now. I have a few ideas of my own, but first I want to know what happened at dawn when we attacked.' He waited, remembering the awful cry, the bark of musket fire.

Quinn said huskily, 'A man came out of the watch-tower. We were all so busy, looking at the gates and trying to mark down the sentries. He just seemed to come from nowhere.' He added wretchedly, 'I was the nearest. I could have cut him down easily.' He shuddered. 'He was just a youngster, stripped to the waist and carrying a bucket. I think he was going down to get some water for the galley. He was unarmed.'

'What then?'

'We stood looking at each other. I am not sure who was the more surprised. I had my blade to his neck. One blow, but I couldn't do it.' He looked desperately at Bolitho. 'He knew it, too. We just stood there until . . .'

'Rowhurst, was it?'

'Yes. With his dirk. But he was too late.'

Bolitho nodded. 'I thought we were done for.' He recalled his own feelings as he had stood over the man he had shot to save himself.

Quinn said, 'I saw the look in the gunner's mate's eyes. He despises me. It will go through the ship like fire. I'll never be able to hold their respect after this.'

Bolitho ran his fingers through his hair. 'You'll have to try and earn it, James.' He felt the sand and grit in his fingers and longed for a bath or a swim. 'But we've work here now.' He saw Stockdale and some seamen watching him. 'Take those hands to the pontoon directly. It is to be warped into deep water and broken up.' He gripped his arm and added, 'Think of them, James. *Tell* them what you want done.'

Quinn turned and walked dejectedly towards the waiting men. At least with Stockdale in charge he should be all right, Bolitho thought.

A petty officer knuckled his forehead and asked, 'We've broached the main magazine, zur?' He waited patiently, his eyes like those of a sheepdog.

Bolitho collected his thoughts, while his mind and body still tried to detain him. But it had to be faced. He *was* in charge of the seamen, just as Probyn had said.

He said, 'Very well, I'll come and see what you've found.'

Cannon had to be spiked and made useless, stores to be set alight before the fort itself was blasted to fragments with its own magazine. Bolitho glanced at the empty stables as he followed the petty officer into the shade. He was thankful there were no horses left in the fort. The thought of having to slaughter them to deny them to the enemy was bad enough. What it might have done to the battle-wearied seamen was even worse. Death, injury or punishment under the lash, the average sailor seemed to accept as his lot. But Bolitho had seen a boatswain's mate split open a man's head in Plymouth, merely for kicking a stray dog.

Marines bustled everywhere, in their element as they prepared long fuses, stowed casks of powder and trundled the smaller field-pieces towards the gates.

By the time the work was half completed, the pontoon had been warped into deep water, and from a parapet Bolitho saw the seamen hacking away the ropes and destroying the ramp with their axes. Small in the distance, Quinn stood watching them. The next time he was thrown into a fight he would not be so lucky, Bolitho decided sadly.

He saw Midshipman Couzens in the watch-tower, a telescope trained towards the anchorage. When he turned, Bolitho saw the lugger making sail, her anchor swinging and dripping as it was hoisted to the cathead.

The same wind which would delay *Spite* should carry Probyn and his little command well clear of the land by nightfall. Pity was never a good reason for making friends, Bolitho thought. But it had been a bad parting, and if they ever met again, it would be between them, of that he was certain.

'So there you are, Bolitho!' Paget peered down from his crude window. 'Come up here and I will give you your instructions.'

In the room once again, Bolitho felt the weariness, the aftermath of destruction and fear, pulling him down.

Paget said, 'Another piece of intelligence. We now know where the enemy are getting some of their armaments and powder, eh?' He watched Bolitho narrowly. 'It's up to the admiral now.'

There was a rap at the door, and Bolitho heard someone whispering urgently outside.

'*Wait!*' Paget said calmly, 'I had no choice over the lugger. She was yours by right, in my view, because of the manner in which you opened the fort for us.' He shrugged heavily. 'But the Navy's ways are not mine, and so . . .'

'I *understand*, sir.'

'Good.' Paget moved across the room with remarkable speed and flung open the door. '*Well*, man?'

It was Lieutenant FitzHerbert of the flagship's marines.

He stammered, 'We have sighted the enemy, sir! Coming up the coast!'

Together they walked into the blinding sunlight, and Paget calmly took a telescope from one of the sentries. Then after a full minute he handed it to Bolitho.

'There's a sight for you. I reckon your Mr Probyn will be sorry to miss it.'

Bolitho soon forgot his disappointment and the major's sarcasm as he trained the glass towards the shore. There must be a track there, following the sea's edge, probably all the way to Charles Town.

Weaving along it was a slow-moving ribbon of blue and white. It was broken here and there by horses, and shining black shapes which could only be artillery.

Paget folded his arms and rocked back on his heels. 'So here they come. No use trying any more deceptions, I think.' He looked up at the pole, his eyes red-rimmed with strain.

'Run up the colours, Sergeant! It'll give 'em something to rant about!'

Bolitho lowered the glass. Quinn was still down by the partly wrecked pontoon, oblivious to the threatening column coming up the road. Probyn was too involved in working his vessel clear of the sand-spit to notice it, or care much if he did.

He swung the glass towards the horizon, his eyes stinging in the fierce glare. Nothing broke the sharp blue line to betray the presence of a friendly sail.

He thought of the captured French officer. With any luck, his captivity would be one of the shortest on record.

Paget barked, 'Stir yourself, sir! Main battery to be manhandled towards the causeway. You have a good runner with you, I believe? Tell him I want a full charge in each weapon. This is going to be hot work, dammit!'

Bolitho made to hurry away, but Paget added firmly, 'I don't care what they promise or offer. We came to destroy this place, and we will, so help me God!'

When Bolitho reached the courtyard he turned and looked again at the tower. Paget was standing bareheaded in the sun, staring at the newly hoisted Jack which the marines had brought with them.

Then he heard a seaman say quietly to his friend, 'Mister Bolitho don't look too troubled, Bill. Can't be anythin' we won't be able to tackle.'

Bolitho glanced at them as he passed, his heart both heavy and proud. They did not question why they were here, or even where they were. Obedience, trust, hope, they were as much a part of these men as their cursing and brawling.

He met Rowhurst by the gate. 'You have heard, no doubt?'

Rowhurst grinned. 'Seen 'em too, sir. Like a whole bloody army on the march! Just for us!'

Bolitho smiled gravely. 'We've plenty of time to get ready.'

'Aye, sir.' Rowhurst looked meaningly at the mounting pile of powder casks and fuses. 'One thing, they won't have to bury us. They'll just 'ave to pick up the bits!'

10

Night Action

Bolitho entered the room at the top of the tower, where the former garrison commander had lived out his spartan days, and found Paget discussing a map with D'Esterre.

Bolitho asked, 'You sent for me, sir?'

He barely recognized his own voice. He had got past tiredness, almost to a point of exhaustion. All through the day he had hurried from one task to another, conscious the whole time of that far-off blue and white column as it weaved in and out of sight along the coast. Now it had vanished altogether, and it seemed likely that the road turned sharply inland before dividing opposite the island.

Paget glanced up sharply. He had shaved, and looked as if he had been freshly pressed with his uniform.

'Yes. Won't be long now, what?' He gestured to a chair. 'All done?'

Bolitho sat down stiffly. *All done*. Like an endless muddle of jobs. Dead had been buried, prisoners moved to a place where they could be guarded by the minimum of men. Stores and water checked, powder stacked in the deep magazine to create one devastating explosion once the fuses were set and fired. The heavy field-pieces manhandled to the landward side to be trained on the causeway and the opposite stretch of shoreline.

He replied, 'Aye, sir. And I've brought all the seamen inside the fort as you ordered.'

'Good.' Paget poured some wine and pushed the goblet across the table. 'Have some. Not too bad, considering.'

The major continued, 'You see, it's mostly a matter of bluff. We know quite a lot about these fellows, but they'll not know much about us. Yet. They'll see my marines, but one redcoat looks much like another. Anyway, why *should* the enemy think we are marines, eh? Could just as easily be a strong force of skirmishers who have cut through their lines. That'll give 'em something to worry about.'

Bolitho glanced at D'Esterre, but his normally agile face was expressionless, so Bolitho guessed he and not Paget had thought up the idea of concealing the presence of his sailors.

It made sense, too. After all, there were no boats, and who better than the returning garrison commander would know the impossibility of getting a man-of-war into the anchorage without passing those heavy cannon?

The wind showed no sign of changing direction, and in fact had gained in strength. All afternoon it had driven a pall of dust from the distant marching column out across the sea like gunsmoke.

Paget said, 'Hour or so to sunset. But they'll make themselves felt before dark. That's my wager.'

Bolitho looked across the room and through a narrow window. He could just see part of the hillside where he had lain with young Couzens, a million years ago. The sun-scorched bushes and scrub were moving in the wind like coarse fur, and everything was painted in fiery hues by the evening light.

The marines were down by the uprooted timbers where the pontoon had been moored. Dug into little gullies, they were invisible to eyes across the restless strip of water.

D'Esterre had done a good job of it. Now they all had to sit and wait.

Bolitho said wearily, 'Water is the problem, sir. They always brought it from a stream further down the coast. There's not much left. If they guess we're waiting for a ship to take us off the island, they will know exactly how much time they have. And us, too.'

Paget sniffed. 'I'd thought of that, naturally. They'll try to bombard us out, but there *we* have the advantage. That beach is too soft to support artillery, and it will take another day at least for them to move their heavier pieces up the hill to hit us from there. As for the causeway, I'd not fancy a frontal attack along it, even at low water!'

Bolitho saw D'Esterre give a small smile. He was probably thinking it was exactly what would have been expected of him and his men if Bolitho had failed to open the gates.

The door banged open and the marine lieutenant from the flagship said excitedly, 'Enemy in sight, sir!'

Paget glared. 'Really, Mr FitzHerbert, this is a garrison, not a scene from Drury Lane, dammit!'

Nevertheless, he got up and walked into the hot glare, reaching for a telescope as he strode to the parapet.

Bolitho rested his hands on the sun-dried wood and stared at the land. Two horsemen, five or six foot soldiers and a large black dog. He had not expected to see the whole enemy column crammed on to the narrow beach, but the little group was a complete anticlimax.

Paget said, 'They're looking at the pontoon ramps. I can almost hear their brains rattling!'

Bolitho glanced at him. Paget really was enjoying it.

One of the horsemen dismounted and the dog ran across to him, waiting for something to happen. His master, obviously the senior officer present, reached down to fondle his head, the movement familiar, without conscious thought.

FitzHerbert asked cautiously, 'What will they do, sir?'

Paget did not answer immediately. He said, 'Look at those horses, D'Esterre. See how their hooves are digging into the sand. The only piece of supported road led to the pontoon loading point.' He lowered the glass and chuckled dryly. 'Never thought *they'd* have to attack, I imagine!'

Sergeant Shears called, 'Saw some more of 'em on the hillside, sir!'

'Can't hit us with a musket from there, thank God.' Paget rubbed his hands. 'Tell your gunner to put a ball down on the end of the causeway.' He looked at Bolitho sharply. '*Now.*'

Rowhurst listened to Paget's order with obvious enthusiasm. 'Good as done, sir.'

With some of his men at their handspikes, and others slackening or tightening the tackles, he soon trained the cannon towards the wet bank of sand nearest the land.

'Stand clear, lads!'

Bolitho yelled, 'Keep out of sight, you men! Stockdale, see that our people stay down!'

The crash of the single shot echoed around the fort and across the water like thunder. Scores of birds rose screaming from the trees, and Bolitho was just in time to see a tall spurt of sand as it received the heavy ball like a fist. The horses shied violently and the dog ran round and round, his bark carrying excitedly across the water.

Bolitho grinned and touched Rowhurst's arm. 'Reload.' He strode back to the tower and saw Quinn watching him from the other parapet.

Paget said, 'Good. Fine shot. Just close enough for them to know we're ready and able.'

A few moments later Sergeant Shears called, 'Flag o' truce, sir!'

One horseman was cantering towards the causeway where a tendril of smoke still drifted to mark the fall of shot.

Paget snapped, 'Ready with another ball, Mr Bolitho.'

'It's a flag of truce, sir.' Bolitho forgot his tiredness and met Paget's glare stubbornly. 'I cannot tell Rowhurst to fire on it.'

Paget's eyebrows rose with astonishment. 'What is this? A spark of honour?' He turned to D'Esterre. 'Explain it to him.'

D'Esterre said quietly, 'They'll want to sound us out, discover our strength. They are not fools. One sight of a marine's coat and they'll know how we came, and what for.'

FitzHerbert said unhelpfully, 'The horseman is an officer, sir.'

Bolitho shaded his eyes to follow the distant horse and rider. How was it possible to argue over honour and scruples at such a moment?

Today or tomorrow he would be expected to cut down that same man if need be, without question or thought. And yet . . .

He said bluntly, 'I'll put a ball in the centre of the causeway.'

Paget turned from studying the little group on the beach. 'Oh, very well. But do get *on* with it!'

The second shot was equally well aimed, and threw spray and sand high into the air while the horseman struggled to regain control of his startled mount.

Then he turned and trotted back along the beach.

'Now they know.' Paget seemed satisfied. 'I think I'd like a glass of wine.' He left them and re-entered his room.

D'Esterre smiled grimly. 'I suspect Emperor Nero was something of a Paget, Dick!'

Bolitho nodded and moved to the seaward side of the tower. Of Probyn's new command there was no trace, and he pictured her gaining more and more distance in the favourable off-shore wind. If the enemy column had seen the vessel leave, they would assume she had turned away at the sight of the redcoats. Otherwise, why should not the fort's new occupiers go with her?

Bluff, stalemate, guessing, it all added up to one thing. What would they do if the sloop did not or could not come to take them off the island? If the water ran out, would Paget surrender? It seemed unlikely the enemy commander would be eager to be lenient after they had blown up his fort and every weapon with it.

He leaned over the parapet and looked at the seamen who were sitting in the shadows waiting for something to do. If the water ran out, could these same men be expected to obey, or keep their hands off the plentiful supply of rum they had unearthed by the stables?

Bolitho recalled Paget's words. He knew where the enemy were getting much of their powder and shot. The information would be little help to Rear-Admiral Coutts if their brave escapade ended here.

Just to be back in *Trojan*, he thought suddenly. After this he would never complain again. Even if he remained one of her lieutenants for the rest of his service.

The very thought made him smile in spite of his uncertainty. He knew in his heart that if he survived this time he would be as eager as ever to make his own way.

He heard Lieutenant Raye of *Trojan*'s marines clattering up the ladder and reporting to D'Esterre.

To Bolitho it was another sort of life. Tactics and strategy which moved at the speed of a man's feet or a horseman's gallop. No majesty of sail, no matter how frail when the guns roared. Just men, and uniforms, dropping into the earth when their time came. Forgotten.

He felt a chill at the nape of his neck as D'Esterre said to the two lieutenants, 'I feel certain they will attack tonight. An assault to test us out, to be followed up if we are caught unawares. I want two platoons on immediate readiness. The guns will have to fire over their heads, so keep 'em down in their gullies until I give the word.' He turned and looked meaningly at Bolitho. 'I'll want two guns by the causeway as soon as it gets dark. We might lose them if we fall back, but we stand no chance unless we can give them bloody noses at the first grapple.'

Bolitho nodded. 'I'll see to it.' How calm he sounded. A stranger.

He remembered his feelings as he had stood facing the fort with the pontoon moving away in the darkness. If the enemy broke through the causeway pickets, it was a long way to the gates for those in retreat.

D'Esterre was watching him gravely. 'It sounds worse than it is. We must be ready. Keep our men on the alert and together. We might find ourselves with visitors after dark.' He gestured to the roughly dressed Canadian scouts. 'Two can play their game.'

As shadows deepened between island and mainland, the marines and seamen settled down to wait. The beach was empty once more, and only the churned-up sand betrayed where the horses and men had stood to watch the fort.

Paget said, 'Clear night, but no moon.' He wiped one eye and swore. 'Bloody wind! Constant reminder of our one weakness!'

Bolitho, with Stockdale close by his side, left the fort and went to watch the two guns being hauled down to the causeway. It was hard, back-breaking work, and there were no laughs or jests now.

It seemed cold after the day's heat, and Bolitho wondered how he could go through another night without sleep. How any of them could. He passed little gullies, their occupants revealed only by their white cross-belts as they crouched and cradled their muskets and watched the glitter of water.

He found Quinn with Rowhurst, siting the second cannon, arranging powder and shot so that it would be easily found and used in total darkness.

Stockdale wheezed, 'Who'd be a soldier, eh, sir?'

Bolitho thought of the soldiers he had known in England. The local garrison at Falmouth, the dragoons at Bodmin. Wheeling and stamping to the delight of churchgoers on a Sunday, and little boys at any time.

This was entirely different. Brute force, and a determination to match anything which came their way. On desert or muddy field, the soldier's lot was perhaps the worst of all. He wondered briefly how the marines saw it? The best or the worst of their two worlds?

Quinn hurried across to him, speaking fast and almost incoherent. 'They say it will be tonight. Why can't we fall back to the fort? When we attacked it they said the cannon commanded the causeway and the pontoon. So why not the same for the enemy?'

'Easy, James. Keep your voice low. We must hold them off the island. They know this place. We only think we know it. Just a handful of them around the fort and who knows what could happen.'

Quinn dropped his head. 'I've heard talk. They don't want to die for a miserable little island which none of them had ever heard of before.'

'You know why we came.' He was surprised yet again by the tone of his own voice. It seemed harder. Colder. But Quinn must understand. If he broke now, it would not be a mere setback, it would be a headlong rout.

Quinn replied, 'The magazine. The fort. But what will it matter, really count for, after we're dead? It's a pin-prick, a gesture.'

Bolitho said quietly, 'You wanted to be a sea officer, more than anything. Your father wanted differently, for you to stay with him in the City of London.' He watched Quinn's face, pale in the darkness, hating himself for speaking as he was, as he must. 'Well, I think he was right. More than you knew. He realized you would never make a King's officer. Not now. Not ever.' He swung away, shaking off Quinn's hand and saying, 'Take the first watch here. I will relieve you directly.'

He knew Quinn was staring after him, wretched and hurt.

Stockdale said, 'That took a lot to speak like so, sir. I know 'ow you cares for the young gentleman, but there's others wot depends on 'im.'

Bolitho paused and looked at him. Stockdale understood. Was always there when he needed him.

'Thank you for that.'

Stockdale shrugged his massive shoulders and said, 'It's nothing. But I thinks about it sometimes.'

Bolitho touched his arm, warmed and moved by his ungainly companion. 'I'm sure you do, Stockdale.'

Two hours dragged past. The night got colder, or seemed to, and the first stiffening tension was giving way to fatigue and aching discomfort.

Bolitho was between the fort and the causeway when he stopped dead and turned his face towards the mainland.

Stockdale stared at him and then nodded heavily. '*Smoke.*'

It was getting thicker by the second, acrid and rasping to eyes and throat as it was urged across the island by the wind. There were flames too, dotted about like malicious orange feathers, changing shape through the smoke, spreading and then linking in serried lines of fires.

Midshipman Couzens, who had been walking behind them, asleep on his feet, gasped, 'What does it mean?'

Bolitho broke into a run. 'They've fired the hillside. They'll attack under the smoke.'

He forced his way through groups of startled, retching marines until he found the cannon.

'Get ready to fire!' He picked out FitzHerbert with one of his corporals, a handkerchief wrapped around his mouth and nose. 'Will you tell the major?'

FitzHerbert shook his head, his eyes streaming. 'No time. He'll know anyway.' He dragged out his sword and yelled, '*Stand to! Face your front!* Pass the word to the other section!'

He was groping about, coughing and peering for his men, as more marines ran through the smoke, D'Esterre's voice controlling them, demanding silence, restoring some sort of order.

Couzens forgot himself enough to seize Bolitho's sleeve and murmur, 'Listen! Swimming!'

Bolitho pulled out his hanger and felt for his pistol. Near his home in Cornwall there was a ford across a small river. But sometimes, especially in the winter, it flooded and became impassable to wagons and coaches. But he had seen and heard horses often enough to know what was happening now.

'They're swimming their mounts across!'

He swung round as above the sounds of water and hissing fires he heard a long-drawn-out cheer.

D'Esterre shouted, 'They're coming from the causeway as well!' He pushed through his men and added, 'Keep 'em down, Sarn't! Let the cannon have their word first!'

Some armed seamen amongst them blundered out of the darkness and slithered to a halt as Bolitho called, 'Keep with me! Follow the beach!' His mind was reeling, grappling with the swiftness of events, the closeness of disaster.

A cannon roared out, and from somewhere across the water he heard the cheers falter, broken by a chorus of cries and screams.

The second cannon blasted the darkness apart with its long orange tongue, and Bolitho heard the ball smashing into men and sand, and pictured Quinn stricken with fear as the defiant cheers welled back as strong as before.

Stockdale growled, 'There's one of 'em!'

Bolitho balanced himself on the balls of his feet, watching the hurtling shadow charging from the darkness.

Someone fired a pistol, and he saw the horse's eyes, huge and terrified, as it pounded towards the seamen, and then swerved away as another horseman lurched from the water and loomed above them like an avenging beast.

He thought Stockdale was saying to Couzens, 'Easy, son! Keep with me! Stand yer ground!'

Or he may have been speaking to me, he thought.

Then he forgot everything as he felt his hanger jerk against steel and he threw himself to the attack.

*

Lieutenant James Quinn ducked as musket-fire clattered along the causeway and some of the shots clanged and ricocheted from the two cannon. He was almost blinded by smoke, from the burning hillside and now with additional fog of gun-fire.

Out in the open it seemed far worse than any gundeck. Metal shrieked overhead, and through the smoke men stumbled and cursed as they rammed home fresh charges and grapeshot to try and hold off the attack.

'*Fire!*'

Quinn winced as the nearest cannon belched flame and smoke. In the swift glare he saw running figures and a gleam of weapons before darkness closed in again and the air was rent by terrible screams as the murderous grape found a target.

A marine was yelling in his ear, 'The devils are on the island, sir!' He was almost screaming. 'Cavalry!'

Lieutenant FitzHerbert ran through the smoke. 'Silence, that man!' He fired his pistol along the causeway and added savagely, 'You'll start a panic!'

Quinn gasped, '*Cavalry*, he said!'

FitzHerbert glared at him, his eyes shining above the handkerchief like stones.

'We'd all be corpses if there was, man! A few riders, no doubt!'

Rowhurst shouted hoarsely, 'Gettin' short of powder!' He blundered towards Quinn. 'Damn yer eyes, sir! Do somethin', fer Christ's sake!'

Quinn nodded, his mind empty of everything but fear. He saw Midshipman Huyghue crouching on one knee as he tried to level a pistol above a hastily prepared earthwork.

'Tell Mr Bolitho what is happening!'

The youth stood up, uncertain which way to go. Quinn gripped his arm. 'Along the beach! Fast as you can!'

A shrill voice shouted, ''Ere the buggers come!'

FitzHerbert threw his handkerchief away and waved his sword. 'Sar'nt Triggs!'

A corporal said, 'He's dead, sir.'

The marine lieutenant looked away. 'God Almighty!' Then as the shouts and whooping cheers echoed across the water he added, '*Forward*, marines!'

Stumbling and choking in the smoke, the marines emerged from their gullies and ditches, their bayonets rising in obedience to the order, their feet searching for firm ground as they peered with stinging eyes for a sign of their enemy.

A hail of musket-fire came from the causeway, and a third of the marines fell dead or wounded.

Quinn stared with disbelief as the marines fired, started to reload and then crumpled to another well-timed volley.

FitzHerbert yelled, 'I suggest you spike those guns! Or get your seamen to reload our muskets!'

He gave a choking cry and pitched through his dwindling line of marines, his jaw completely shot away.

Quinn shouted, 'Rowhurst! Fall back!'

Rowhurst thrust past him, his eyes wild. 'Most of the lads 'ave gone already!' Even in the face of such danger he could not hide his contempt. 'You might as well run, too!'

From over his shoulder Quinn heard the sudden blare of a trumpet. It seemed to grip the remaining marines like a steel hand.

The corporal, earlier on the edge of terror, called, 'Retreat! Easy, lads! Reload, take aim!' He waited for some of the wounded to hop or crawl through the line. '*Fire!*'

Quinn could not grasp what was happening. He heard the snap of commands, the click of weapons, and somehow knew that D'Esterre was coming to cover the withdrawal. The enemy were barely yards away, he could hear their feet slipping and squelching on the wet sand, sense their combined anger and madness as they surged forward to retake the landing-place. Yet all he could think of was Rowhurst's disgust, the need to win his respect in these last minutes.

He gasped, 'Which gun is loaded?'

He staggered down the slope, his pistol still unloaded, and the hanger which his father had had specially made by the best City sword cutler firmly in its scabbard.

Rowhurst, dazed and bewildered by the change of events, paused and stared at the groping lieutenant. Like a blind man.

It was stupid to go back with him. What safety remained was a long run to the fort's gates. Every moment here cut away a hope of survival.

Rowhurst was a volunteer, and prided himself on being as good a gunner's mate as any in the fleet. In a month or so, if fate was kind, he might gain promotion, proper warrant rank in another ship somewhere.

He watched Quinn's pathetic efforts to find the gun, which because of the marines leaving cover was still unfired. Either way it was over. If he waited, he would die with Quinn. If he escaped, Quinn would charge him with disobeying orders, insolence to an officer. Something like that.

Rowhurst gave a great sigh and made up his mind.

''Ere, this is the one.' He forced a grin. '*Sir!*'

A corpse propped against one of the wheels gave a little jerk as more random shots slammed into it. It was as if the dead were returning to life to witness their last madness.

The crash of the explosion as the slow-match found its mark, and the whole double-shotted charge swept through the packed ranks of attackers, seemed to bring some small control to Quinn's cringing mind. He groped for the finely made hanger, his eyes streaming, his ears deafened by that final explosion.

All he could say was, 'Thank you, Rowhurst! Thank you!'

But Rowhurst had been right about one thing. He lay staring angrily at the smoke, a hole placed dead centre through his forehead. No gunner's mate could have laid a better shot.

Quinn walked dazedly away from the guns, his sword-arm at his side. The white breeches of dead marines shone in the darkness, staring eyes and fallen weapons marked each moment of sacrifice.

But Quinn was also aware that the din of shouting had gone from the causeway. They too had taken enough.

He stopped, suddenly tense and ready as figures came down towards him. Two marines, the big gun captain called Stockdale. And a lieutenant with a drawn blade in his hand.

Quinn looked at the ground, wanting to speak, to explain what Rowhurst had done, had made him do.

But Bolitho took his arm and said quietly, 'The Corporal told me. But for your example, no one outside the fort would be alive now.'

They waited as the first line of marines came down from the fort, letting the battered and bleeding survivors from the causeway pass through them to safety.

Bolitho ached all over, and his sword-arm felt as heavy as iron. He could still feel the fear and desperation of the past hour. The thundering horses, the swords cutting out of the darkness, and then the sudden rallying of his own mixed collection of seamen.

Couzens had been stunned after being knocked over by a horse, and three seamen were dead. He himself had been struck from behind, and the edge of the sabre had touched his shoulder like a red-hot knife.

Now the horses had gone, swimming or drifting with the current, but gone from here. Several of their riders had stayed behind. For ever.

D'Esterre found them as he came through the thinning smoke and said, 'We held them. It was costly, Dick, but it could save us.' He held up his hat and fanned his streaming face. 'See? The wind is going about at last. If there is a ship for us, then she can come.'

He watched a marine being carried past, his leg smashed out of recognition. In the darkness the blood looked like fresh tar.

'We must get replacements to the causeway. I've sent for a new gun crew.' He saw Couzens walking very slowly towards them, rubbing his head and groaning. 'I'm glad he's all right.' D'Esterre replaced his hat as he saw the sergeant hurrying towards him. 'I'm afraid they took the other midshipman, Huyghue, prisoner.'

Quinn said brokenly, 'I sent him to look for you. It was my fault.'

Bolitho shook his head. 'No. Some of the enemy got amongst us.

They'd allowed for failure, I expect, and wanted to seize a few prisoners just in case.'

Bolitho made to thrust his hanger into its scabbard and discovered that the hilt was sticky with blood. He let out a long sigh, trying to fit his thoughts in order. But, as usual, nothing came, as if his mind was trying to protect him, to cushion him from the horror and frantic savagery of hand-to-hand fighting. Sounds, brief faces and shapes, terror and wild hate. But nothing real. It might come later, when his mind was able to accept it.

Had it all been worthwhile? Was liberty that precious?

And tomorrow, no, *today*, it would all begin again.

He heard Quinn call, 'They will need more powder for those guns! See to it, will you!'

An anonymous figure in checkered shirt and white trousers hurried away to do his bidding. An ordinary sailor. He could be every sailor, Bolitho thought.

Quinn faced him. 'If you want to report to Major Paget, I can take charge here.' He waited, watching Bolitho's strained features as if searching for something. 'I can, really.'

Bolitho nodded. 'I'd be grateful, James. I shall be back directly.'

Stockdale said roughly, 'With Rowhurst gone, you'll need a fair 'and at the guns, sir.' He grinned at Quinn's face. 'Keep up the good work, eh, sir?'

Bolitho made his way into the fort, weaving through groups of wounded, each one a small island of pain in the glow of a lantern. Daylight would reveal the real extent of what they had endured.

Paget was in his room, and although Bolitho knew he had been controlling the defences from the first minutes, he looked as if he had never left the place.

Paget said, 'We will hold the causeway tonight, of course.' He gestured to a bottle of wine. 'But tomorrow we will prepare for evacuation. When the ship comes, we will send the wounded and those who have stood guard tonight, *first*. No time for any bluff. If they've got prisoners, they know what we're up to.'

Bolitho let the wine run over his tongue. God, it tasted good. Better than anything.

'What if the ship does not come, sir?'

'Well, that simplifies things.' Paget watched him coldly. 'We'll blow the magazine, and fight our way out.' He smiled very briefly. 'It won't come to that.'

'I see, sir.' In fact, he did not.

Paget ruffled some papers. 'I want you to sleep. For an hour or so.' He held up his hand. 'That is an order. You've done fine work here, and now I thank God that fool Probyn made the decision he did.'

'I'd like to report on Mr Quinn's part, sir.' The major was getting misty in Bolitho's aching vision. 'And the two midshipmen. They are all very young.'

Paget pressed his fingertips together and regarded him unsmilingly. 'Not like you, of course, an ancient warrior, what?'

Bolitho picked up his hat and made for the door. With Paget you knew exactly where you were. He had selected him for some precious sleep. The very thought made him want to lie down immediately and close his eyes.

Equally, he knew the true reason for Paget's concern. Someone would have to stay behind and light the fuses. You needed a measure of alertness for that!

Bolitho walked past D'Esterre without even seeing him.

The marine captain picked up the wine bottle and said, 'You told him, sir? About tomorrow?'

Paget shrugged. 'No. He is like I was at his age. Didn't need to be *told* everything.' He glared at his subordinate. 'Unlike some.'

D'Esterre smiled and walked to the window. Somewhere across the water a telescope might be trained on the fort, on this lighted window.

Like Bolitho, he knew he should be snatching an hour's rest. But out there, still hidden in darkness, were many of his men, sprawled in the careless attitudes of death. He could not find it in his heart to leave them now. It would be like a betrayal.

A gentle snore made him turn. Paget was fast asleep in the chair, his face completely devoid of anxiety.

Better to be like him, D'Esterre thought bitterly. Then he downed the drink in one swallow and strode out into the darkness.

11

Rear-guard

When the sun eventually showed itself above the horizon and felt its way carefully inland, it revealed not only the horror of the night's work, but to those who had survived it also brought new hope.

Hull down with the early sunlight were two ships, and at first it seemed likely that the enemy had somehow found the means to frustrate any attempt of evacuation. But as the vessels tacked this way and that, drawing nearer and nearer to land with each change of course, they were both identified and cheered. Not only had the sloop-of-war, *Spite*, come for them, but also the thirty-two-gun frigate *Vanquisher*, sent, it seemed, by Rear-Admiral Coutts himself.

As soon as it was light enough the work of collecting and burying the dead got under way. Across the causeway, now partially submerged, a few corpses rolled and moved with the current. Most had been carried away to deeper water during the night, or retrieved perhaps by their comrades.

Paget was everywhere. Bullying, suggesting, threatening, and occasionally tossing a word of encouragement as well.

The sight of the two ships put fresh life into his men, and even though neither of them was a match for well-sited shore batteries, they would shorten the work of evacuation. More pulling boats, fresh, rested seamen to work them, officers to take over the strain of command.

Bolitho was in the deep magazine with Stockdale and a marine corporal for much of the morning. The place had a dreadful stillness about it, a quality of death which he could feel like a chill breeze. Keg upon keg of gunpowder, boxes of equipment, and many unpacked cases of new French muskets and side-arms. Fort Exeter had a lot to answer for in past dealings with England's old enemy.

Stockdale hummed to himself as he attached the fuses to the foot of the first mound of explosives, entirely engrossed and glad to be out of the bustle in the fort above.

Boots tramped in the courtyard, and there were sounds of grating metal as the cannons were spiked and then moved to a point above where the explosion would be.

Bolitho sat on an empty keg, his cheeks stinging from the shave which Stockdale had given him when he had awakened from his deep, exhausted sleep. He remembered his father telling him when he had been a small boy, 'If you've not had to shave with salt water, you never know how soft is the life of a landsman by comparison.'

He could have had all the fresh water he wanted. But even now, with the ships so near, you could not be complacent, or certain.

He watched Stockdale's big hands, so deft and gentle as he worked with the fuses.

It was a gamble, always. Light the fuses. Head for safety. Minutes to get clear.

A seaman appeared on the sunlit ladder.

'Beg pardon, sir, but the major would like you with 'im.' He looked at Stockdale and at the fuses ad paled. 'Gawd!'

Bolitho ran up the ladder and across the courtyard. The gates were open, and he looked across the trampled ground, the dried blood-stains, the pathetic mounds which marked the hasty graves.

Paget said slowly, 'Another flag of truce, dammit.'

Bolitho shaded his eyes and saw the white flag, some figures standing on the far end of the causeway, their feet touching the water.

D'Esterre came hurrying from the stables where some marines were piling up papers and maps and all the contents of the tower and quartermaster's stores.

He took a telescope from Paget's orderly and then said grimly, 'They've got young Huyghue with them.'

Paget said calmly, 'Go and speak with them. You know what I said this morning.' He nodded to Bolitho. 'You, too. It might help Huyghue.'

Bolitho and the marine walked towards the causeway, Stockdale just behind them with an old shirt tied to a pike. How he had heard what was happening and been here in time to keep Bolitho company was a mystery.

It seemed to take an age to reach the causeway. The whole time the little group at the far end never moved. Just the white flag streaming over a soldier's head to display the wind's impartial presence.

Bolitho felt his shoes sinking into sand and mud the further they walked towards the waiting group. Here and there were signs of battle. A broken sword, a man's hat and a pouch of musket balls. In deep water he saw a pair of legs swaying gently, as if the corpse was merely resting and about to surface again at any moment.

D'Esterre said, 'Can't get any closer.'

The two groups stood facing each other, and although the man who waited by the flag was without his coat, Bolitho knew it was the senior officer from yesterday. As if to prove it, his black dog sat on the wet sand at his side, a red tongue lolling with weariness.

A little to the rear was Midshipman Huyghue. Small, seemingly frail against the tall, sunburned soldiers.

The officer cupped his hands. He had a deep, resonant voice which carried without effort.

'I am Colonel Brown of the Charles Town Militia. Who have I the honour of addressing?'

D'Esterre shouted, 'Captain D'Esterre of His Britannic Majesty's Marines!'

Brown nodded slowly. 'Very well. I have come to parley with you. I will allow your men to leave the fort unharmed, provided you lay down your weapons and make no attempt to destroy the supplies and the arms.' He paused and then added, 'Otherwise my artillery will open fire and prevent evacuation, even at the risk of blowing up the magazine ourselves.'

D'Esterre called, 'I see.' To Bolitho he whispered, 'He is trying to drag out the time. If he can get cannon on the hilltop he can certainly throw some long shots at the ships when they anchor. It only needs a lucky ball, just one in the right place.' He shouted again, 'And what does the midshipman have to do with all this?'

Brown shrugged. 'I will exchange him here and now for the French officer you are holding prisoner.'

Bolitho said softly, 'I see it. He is going to open fire anyway, but wants the Frenchman in safety first. He fears we might kill him, or that he would be cut down in a bombardment.'

'I agree.' D'Esterre said loudly, 'I cannot agree to the exchange!'

Bolitho saw the midshipman take a pace forward, his hands half raised as if pleading.

Brown called, 'You will regret it.'

Bolitho wanted to turn his head and look for the ships, to see how near they had managed to tack. But any sign of uncertainty now might bring disaster. Another frontal attack perhaps. If the enemy knew about the guns being spiked they would be halfway across the island by now. He felt suddenly vulnerable. But how much worse for Huyghue. Sixteen years old. To be left out here amongst enemies in a strange land where his death or disappearance would excite very little comment.

D'Esterre said, 'I might exchange your second-in-command instead.'

'No.' Colonel Brown's hand was rubbing the dog's head as he spoke, as if to calm his own thoughts.

He obviously had his orders, Bolitho decided. As we all do.

The mention of the second-in-command had changed little, except to prove that Paget still had his prisoners guarded and alive. That knowledge might help Huyghue to survive.

A gun banged out suddenly, the sound hollow and muffled. Bolitho thought the militia had got their guns into position already, and felt the disappointment tug at his heart until he heard distant cheering.

Stockdale wheezed, 'One o' the ships 'as dropped anchor, sir!'

D'Esterre looked at Bolitho and said simply, 'We must go. I'll not prolong the boy's misery.'

Bolitho shouted, 'Take care, Mr Huyghue! All will be well! You will be exchanged soon, I've no doubt!'

Huyghue must have believed up to the last second that he was going to be released. His experiences during the bloody fighting had been enough in his eyes perhaps. Being taken prisoner was beyond his understanding.

He tried to run into the water, and when a soldier seized his arm he fell on his knees, calling and sobbing, '*Help me!* Don't leave me! Please help!'

Even the militia colonel was moved by the boy's despair, and he gestured for him to be taken up the beach again.

Bolitho and his companions turned their backs and started back towards the fort, Huyghue's pathetic cries following them like a curse.

The frigate was anchored well out from the land, but her sails were brailed up and there were boats in the water already, pulling strongly towards the island.

The *Spite*, being smaller, was still working her way inshore, leadsmen busy in the chains to seek out any uncharted reef or bar.

They looked so clean, so efficiently remote, that Bolitho felt suddenly sick of the land. The heavy smell of death which seemed to overpower even that of the night's fires.

Quinn was by the gates, watching his face as he strode into the shade. 'You left him?'

'Yes.' Bolitho looked at him gravely. 'I'd no choice. If all we had to do was exchange our victims, there'd be no point in coming here.' He sighed. 'But I'll not forget his face in a hurry.'

Paget examined his watch. 'First wounded men to the beach.' He glanced at Bolitho. 'Do you think they might try and rush us, eh?'

Bolitho shrugged. 'The smaller swivels could deal with them in daylight, sir. It'd make our work harder though.'

Paget turned to listen as more cheers echoed around the fort. 'Simple fools.' He looked away. 'Bless 'em!'

A marine ran down a ladder from the parapet. 'Mr Raye's respects, and he's sighted soldiers on the hill. Artillery too, he thinks, sir.'

Paget nodded. 'Right. We must make haste. Signal *Spite* to anchor and lower boats as fast as she can.' As Quinn hurried away with the marine, Paget added, 'Warm work for you, Bolitho, I'm afraid. But whatever happens, see that the magazine *goes up*.'

'What about the prisoners, sir?'

'If there's room enough, and time to spare, I'll have them shipped to the frigate.' He smiled wryly. 'If I was left as rear-guard, I'd see they went up with the magazine, damned bloody rebels. But as you will be in charge, you may use your discretion. On your head be it.'

The *Vanquisher*'s boats were being beached, and seamen were already hoisting wounded marines aboard, their faces shocked at the small number of survivors.

Then the sloop's boats pulled ashore, and more men started on their way to safety and medical care.

Bolitho stood on the parapet above the gates, where he and Stockdale had crouched on that first terrible night when Quinn had lost his nerve.

The fort already felt emptier, and as marines hurried through the gates towards the rear Bolitho watched the little scarlet figures down by the causeway and the two remaining cannon. Once he gave the order for final withdrawal, Sergeant Shears and his handful of pickets would light the fuses which were attached to both guns. Two tightly packed charges would blow off the trunnions and render them as useless as those in the fort.

He wondered if anyone would ever hear about it in England. The small but deadly actions which made up the whole. Few ever wrote of the real heroes, he thought. The lonely men on the prongs of an attack, or those left behind to cover a retreat. Sergeant Shears was probably thinking about it just now. Of the distance to the fort. Of the marines under his charge.

There was a loud bang, followed by a whimpering drone, as a heavy ball passed low overhead and slammed hard into the sand.

Midshipman Couzens pointed at the hillside. 'See, sir? The smoke! They've got one gun at least in position!'

Bolitho watched him. Couzens looked pale and sick. It would take time to recover from the night's fighting, the rearing horses and sabres.

'Go and tell the major. He'll know, but tell him anyway.' As Couzens made for the ladder he added quietly, 'Then report to the senior officer with the boats. Don't come back here.' He saw the emotions flooding across the boy's face. Relief, concern, finally stubbornness. Bolitho added firmly, 'I am not asking. It is an order.'

'But, sir. I want to stay with you.'

Bolitho turned as another bang echoed from the hillside. This time the ball hit the sea and ricocheted over the wavecrests like a maddened dolphin.

'I know. But how will I explain to your father if anything happens to you, eh? Who'd eat your mother's pies?'

He heard what sounded like a sob, and when he turned again the parapet was empty. Time enough for you, Bolitho thought sadly. Three years younger than Huyghue. A child.

He saw the brilliant flash of a cannon, and felt the ball tear above the fort with the sound of ripping canvas. They had the range now. The shot fell directly in line with the anchored frigate, throwing spray over one of her boats as it pulled back to the island for more men.

D'Esterre came up the ladder and looked at him. 'Last section moving out now. They're taking most of the prisoners, too. Major Paget's sent the Frenchman, Contenay, over with the first boat. Taking no chances.' He removed his hat and stared at the causeway. 'Damnable place.'

A voice called from the courtyard, '*Vanquisher*'s shortenin' 'er cable, sir!'

'Getting clear before she gets a piece of Colonel Brown's iron on her quarterdeck.' D'Esterre looked anxious. 'It might spark off an attack, now that they think we're on the run, Dick.'

Bolitho nodded. 'I'll get ready. I hope they've got a fast boat for us.'

It was meant to sound amusing. Relaxed. But it merely added to the strain, the tension which was making it difficult to breathe evenly.

D'Esterre said, '*Spite*'s jolly boat, it's there waiting. Just for you.'

Bolitho said, 'Go now. I'll be all right.'

He watched a small squad of marines scurrying through the courtyard, one pausing to hurl a torch into the pile of papers and stores inside the stables.

D'Esterre watched him walking towards the magazine, and then just as quickly turned and followed his men through the gates.

A ball shrieked above the squat tower, but D'Esterre did not even look up. It seemed to have no menace. All danger and death was here. Like a foul memory.

He saw the frigate's outline shortening as she tacked steeply away from the land, her forecourse filling and flapping even as one of her boats pulled frantically alongside. For the other boats it would be a long hard pull to reach her. But her captain would know the danger of well-hidden artillery. To lose a frigate was bad enough, to allow her to be added to the Revolutionary Navy was even worse.

Bolitho forgot D'Esterre and everything else as he found Stockdale with his slow-match, a solitary marine corporal and a seaman he recognized through the grime and stubble as Rabbett, the thief from Liverpool.

'Light the fuses.'

He winced as a heavy ball crashed through a parapet and came splintering amongst the stables which were now well alight.

He said, 'Get to the gates, Corporal, call back your pickets. Fast as you can.'

The fuses hissed into life, somehow obscene in the gloom, like serpents.

They seemed to be burning at a terrible speed, he thought.

He clapped Stockdale on the shoulder. 'Time for us.'

Another ball smashed into the fort and hurled a swivel gun into the air like a stick.

Two more sharp explosions came from the causeway, and he knew the cannon had been destroyed.

Musket-fire, too, remote and without effect at this range. But they would be coming soon.

They ran out into the blinding sunlight, past discarded boxes and blazing stores.

Two loud bangs and then splintering woodwork flying above the parapet told Bolitho that Brown's men must have worked like demons to get their guns up the hill.

The corporal yelled, 'Sergeant Shears is comin' at th' double, sir! The whole bloody rebel army's on their 'eels!'

Bolitho saw the running marines even as one fell headlong and stayed down.

Soldiers were wading and struggling across the causeway too, firing and reloading as they came.

Bolitho measured the distance. It was taking too long.

Round one wall of the fort, along the sloping beach where the jolly boat was waiting. Bolitho noticed that the crew had their oars out, backing water, watching the land, mesmerized.

Sergeant Shears panted down the beach, his men behind him.

'Into the boat!' Bolitho looked up at the tower, their flag still above it.

Then he realized he was alone on the beach, that Stockdale had his arm and was hauling him over the gunwale as a nervous-looking lieutenant ordered, '*Give way all!*'

Minutes later, as the jolly-boat bounded over the first lazy roller, some soldiers appeared below the fort, firing at the boat, the shots going everywhere. One hit the side and threw droplets of water across the panting marines.

Shears muttered, 'I'd get the hell out of here, if I was them, sir!'

They were midway between the beach and the sloop when the explosion blasted the day apart. It was not the sound, but the sight of the complete fort being hurled skywards in thousands of shattered fragments which remained fixed in Bolitho's reeling mind, long after the last piece had fallen. As the smoke continued to billow across the island, Bolitho saw there was nothing there but one huge, black wilderness.

All the prisoners had been taken off after all, and he wondered what they must be thinking at this moment. And young Huyghue, too. Would he remember the part he had played, or would he think only of his own plight?

When he turned his head he saw the sloop's masts and yards swaying above him, willing hands waiting to assist them on board.

He looked at Stockdale, and their eyes met. As if to say, once again, we survived. Once more fate stayed her hand.

He heard the sloop's young commander, Cunningham, shouting irritably, 'Lively there! We've not got all damn day!'

Bolitho smiled wearily. He was back.

Captain Gilbert Brice Pears sat at his table, his strong fingers interlaced in front of him, while his clerk arranged five beautifully written copies of the Fort Exeter raid for his signature.

Around him *Trojan*'s great hull creaked and clattered to a stiff quarter sea, but Pears barely noticed. He had read the original report most carefully, missing nothing, and had questioned D'Esterre on the more complex details of the attack and withdrawal.

Nearby, his lean body angled to the deck, and silhouetted against the spray-dappled windows, Cairns waited patiently for some comment.

Pears had fretted at the delay in reaching the rendezvous after their feint attack towards Charles Town. The wind's sudden change, a total absence of news and the general lack of faith he held in Coutts's plan added to his worst fears. Even Coutts must have sensed his uneasiness, and had despatched the frigate to assist *Spite*'s recovery of the landing party. Pears had watched *Trojan*'s seamen and marines climbing back aboard after they had eventually regained contact. The tired, haggard, yet somehow defiant marines, what was left of them, and the filthy seamen. D'Esterre and Bolitho, with young Couzens waving to his fellow midshipmen, half laughing, partly weeping.

Fort Exeter was no more. He hoped it had all been worthwhile, but secretly doubted it.

He nodded grimly to his clerk. 'Very well, Teakle. I'll sign the damn things.' He glanced at Cairns. 'Must have been a bloody business. Our people did well, it seems.'

Pears glared through the dripping windows at the blurred shape of the flagship, close-hauled on the same tack, her courses and topsails filling to the wind.

'Now *this*, blast his eyes!'

Cairns followed his glance, knowing better than most how his captain felt.

It had taken six days for the ponderous ships of the line to rendezvous with *Vanquisher* and *Spite*. Then a further two while their admiral had interviewed the senior officers of his little squadron, watched an interrogation of the disarmingly cheerful French prisoner and had considered the information which Paget had gleaned at the fort.

Now, instead of returning to New York for further orders, and to obtain replacements for the dead and wounded, *Trojan* was to proceed further south. Pears's orders were to seek out and finally destroy an island base which, if half of the intelligence gathered from the prisoners was to be trusted, was the most important link in the supply chain for arms and powder for Washington's armies.

At any other time Pears would have welcomed it as the chance to use his ship as he had always wanted. To make up for the humiliating setbacks and delays, the months of patrol duty or the boredom of being at anchor in harbour.

The flagship *Resolute* would be leaving them shortly and would return to Sandy Hook, taking Coutts's impressive reports to the commander-in-chief, along with the prisoners and most of the badly wounded seamen and marines.

The youthful rear-admiral had taken the unprecedented step, in Pears's view, of appointing his flag captain, Lamb, as acting officer-in-charge of the inshore squadron, while he, Coutts, transferred his flag to *Trojan* to pursue the attack in the south.

Coutts probably guessed that if he returned with his own flagship the commander-in-chief, in connivance with or under direct orders from the government 'expert', Sir George Helpman, would be ordered elsewhere before he could see his strategy brought to a successful end.

There was a tap at the door.

'Enter.'

Pears looked up, watching Bolitho's face from the moment he walked into the great cabin, his cocked hat tucked under one arm.

He looked older, Pears decided. Strained, but more confident in some way. There were lines at the corners of his mouth, but the grey eyes were steady enough. Like those battered marines. Defiant.

Pears noticed how he was holding his shoulder. It was probably stinging badly from that sabre's quick touch, more so from the surgeon's attentions. But in his change of clothing Bolitho appeared restored.

Pears said, 'Good to see you in one piece.' He waved to a chair and waited for his clerk to leave. 'You'll hear soon enough. We're to stand further south, to seek out and destroy an enemy supply headquarters there.' He grimaced. 'French, to all accounts.'

Bolitho sat down carefully. His body clean, his clothes fresh and strangely unfamiliar, he was just beginning to feel the slackening of tension.

They had been good to him. Cairns, the Sage, Dalyell. All of them. And it felt free to be here, in this groaning, overcrowded hull.

He had no idea what was happening, until now. After the swift passage aboard the sloop, the sadness of seeing more survivors die and be buried over the side, he had found little time, other than to scribble his own version of what had happened. Apart from a few quiet words with Pears as he and the others had been helped aboard, he had not spoken with him at all.

Pears said, 'The war makes great demands. We were short of experienced officers, now we are even shorter.' He stared at the empty table where the report had been lying. 'Good men killed, others maimed for life. Half my marines gone in the blink of an eye, and now, with two officers taken prisoner to boot, I am feeling like a clergyman with an empty church.'

Bolitho glanced at Cairns, but his face gave nothing away. He had seen a brig speaking with the flagship that morning, but he knew nothing further.

He asked, '*Two* officers, sir?' He must have missed something.

Pears sighed. 'Young Huyghue, and now the flagship has told me about Probyn. He was apparently run down by a privateer, one day after leaving you at Fort Exeter.' He watched Bolitho's face. 'Shortest command in naval history, I'd imagine.'

Bolitho thought of the last time he had seen Probyn. Angry, triumphant, bitter. Now it had all been taken away. His hopes dashed.

All he could find in his heart was pity.

'*So*,' Pears's voice brought him back with a jerk, 'you are hereby appointed as second lieutenant of this ship, *my* ship.'

Bolitho stared at him dazedly. From fourth to second. He had heard of it happening, but had never expected it like this.

'I – that is, thank you, sir.'

Pears eyed him flatly. 'I am glad you did not crow over Probyn's fate. But I think I could have understood even that.'

Cairns nodded, his lips parted in a rare smile. 'Congratulations.'

Pears waved his large hands. 'Save them for later and spare me, Mr Cairns. Be about your affairs. Appoint another midshipman to Huyghue's duties, and I suggest you consider the master's mate, Frowd, as acting lieutenant. A promising fellow, I think.'

The marine sentry opened the door gingerly. 'Beg pardon, sir, midshipman o' th' watch is 'ere.'

It was little Forbes, somehow grown in stature to his title.

'S-sir. Mr Dalyell's respects, and the flagship has just signalled us to heave to.'

Pears glanced at Cairns. 'See to it. I'll be up presently.'

As the two lieutenants hurried after the midshipman, Bolitho asked, 'Why is this?'

Cairns stared at him. 'You *are* out of touch, Dick!' He pointed to a petty officer with a flag neatly rolled under his arm. 'Today we will hoist the flag to our mizzen. Rear-Admiral Coutts is to be our very present help in trouble!'

'*Flagship?*'

'Acting.' Cairns straightened his hat as they strode forward to the quarterdeck rail. 'Until Coutts reaps his reward, or lays his head on the block.'

Seamen were already running to their stations, and Bolitho had to make himself look at the massive trunk of the mainmast, where he had once taken so many orders and goads from Lieutenant Sparke.

Now he was second lieutenant. With still two months between him and twenty-one years.

He saw Stockdale watching him and nodding. It was thanks to Stockdale, and some missing faces, that he was here at all.

'All hands! Stand by to wear ship!'

Cairns's voice found him with the speaking trumpet. 'Mr Bolitho, sir! Hurry those men at the braces! They are like old cripples today!'

Bolitho touched his hat and kept his face straight.

Across the scrambling seamen he saw Quinn staring at him, still uncertain at his new station. He smiled at him, trying to break the strain that was still there.

'Lively, Mr Quinn!' He hesitated, holding another memory. 'Take that man's name!'

12

Rivals

The day after Rear-Admiral Coutts had shifted his flag to *Trojan* found
Bolitho pacing the quarterdeck, keeping an eye on the forenoon watch
and enjoying a fresh north-west breeze. During the night the big
ninety-gun *Resolute* with the frigate in company had vanished astern,
and would now be beating back towards New York, the wind making
every mile a battle of its own.

For the *Trojan* things were different, as if Coutts's unexpected arrival
had brought a change of circumstances. She must make a fine sight,
Bolitho thought as his feet took him up and down the windward side
without conscious effort. In her fair-weather canvas, and under courses,
topsails and topgallants, she was leaning her shoulder into the blue
water, throwing curtains of spray high above her beakhead.

The compass held steady at south, south-east, taking the powerful
two-decker well away from the land, down towards the long chain of
islands which separated the Atlantic from the Caribbean.

The wind held back the heat, and allowed the less badly wounded and
injured men to move about the decks, to find themselves again in their
own way. The remainder, some of whom might die before they reached
Sandy Hook, had gone with the flagship, as had the prisoners, and
Coutts's report of the attack.

Only one captive remained aboard, the Frenchman, Contenay. He
took regular walks on deck without an escort, and seemed completely at
home in a King's ship.

Bolitho had discovered that he still knew little about his own captain.
The brief moments of contact, even warmth, upon his return to the ship
had been replaced by Pears's usual stern, remote demeanour. Bolitho
thought that the admiral's presence had a lot to do with it.

Coutts had appeared on deck this morning. Youthful, relaxed and
apparently interested, he had strolled along the weather gangway,
pausing to watch the bare-backed seamen at their work, the carpenter
with his crew, the sailmaker and the cooper, the ship's tradesmen who
daily changed a man-of-war into a busy street.

He had spoken to the officers and some of the senior hands. The Sage had been impressed by his knowledge of Arctic exploration, and Midshipman Forbes reduced to blushing incoherence by a few well-aimed questions.

If he was troubled at the doubtful prospect of running another enemy supply cache to earth, or at what the commander-in-chief might say at his behaviour, he certainly did not show it. His plans he kept to himself, and only Ackerman, his urbane flag lieutenant, the one Bolitho had seen in a cabin with a half-naked woman, and his personal clerk shared his confidences.

Bolitho decided that would also irritate Pears beyond measure.

A step fell on the deck nearby and Cairns joined him at the rail, his eyes taking in the working parties and the set of each sail with practised authority.

He said, 'The admiral is with our captain. I sense an air of grapeshot close by.' He turned and glanced meaningly at the poop skylight. 'I was glad to leave the great men.'

'No news yet?'

'Not much. Like D'Esterre, the admiral plays a taut hand. He will rise like a comet.' He gestured at the deck. 'Or fall like one.'

With Coutts aboard, Cairns also faced changes. The main result was that he shared more of his thoughts with his second lieutenant.

He added slowly, 'The captain was wanting to know why this ship and not *Resolute* was selected for the mission.' He smiled grimly. 'The admiral explained, as cool as you please, that *Trojan* is the faster vessel, and her company deserving of reward for their work.'

Bolitho nodded. 'I suppose so. *Resolute* has been out here far longer and has had few refits, I believe. She must be foul with weed.'

Cairns eyed him admiringly. 'We'll make a politician of you yet.' He waved Bolitho's confusion aside. 'You see, the back-handed compliment. Coutts lays on treacle with talk of reward and the better ship for the task, then in the next breath he gently reminds Captain Pears that his own flagship is in truth the more deserving.'

Bolitho pursed his lips. 'That is clever.'

'It takes a rogue to recognize one, Dick.'

'In that case, what *is* the real reason?'

Cairns frowned. 'I suspect because he wants the flagship on her proper station. That would make sense. Also, he despatched *Vanquisher* as escort, and because *she* will be sorely needed elsewhere with the growth of privateers everywhere.'

He dropped his voice as Sambell, master's mate of the watch, strolled past with elaborate indifference on his tanned face.

'He will want to follow this plan to the end. Reap the reward, or cover the flaws as best he can. He would not trust our captain to act alone. And if things go disastrously badly, then he will need a scapegoat other than his own flag captain.' Cairns watched Bolitho's eyes. 'I see that *you* see.'

'I'll never understand this kind of reasoning.'

Cairns winked. 'One day, you'll be teaching it!'

More feet thudded on the sun-dried planking, and Bolitho saw Pears and the sailing master leaving the chart room, the latter carrying his leather satchel which he used to stow his navigational notes and instruments.

He looked much as usual, turning briefly to examine the compass and the two helmsmen, his eyes glittering in the sunlight beneath the great black brows.

Pears, by comparison, appeared tired and in ill humour, impatient to get whatever it was over and done with.

'We'll soon know where this blessed spot is to be, Dick.' Cairns loosened his neckcloth and sighed. 'I hope it is not another Fort Exeter.'

Bolitho watched the first lieutenant continue on his daily rounds, wondering if Cairns was still brooding over the chances of leaving *Trojan* and getting a ship of his own.

So far, *Trojan*'s lieutenants had not fared very well away from her protection. Sparke killed, Probyn a prisoner of war, while Bolitho had returned each time like a wayward son.

He saw Quinn without his coat, his shirt sticking to his back like another skin, stepping between the busy sailmaker and his mates, his face still pale and strained. Eighteen years old, he looked far more, Bolitho thought. The savage slash across his chest still troubled him. You could see it in his walk and the tightness of his mouth. A constant reminder of other things, too. That moment at the fort when his nerve had failed, and by the guns when he had almost gone mad because of Rowhurst's scorn.

Midshipman Weston shouted suddenly, '*Spite*'s signalling, sir!'

Bolitho snatched a telescope from its rack and climbed swiftly into the weather shrouds. It took a few moments to find the little sloop-of-war, their only companion on this 'adventure', as Cairns had described it. The glass steadied on *Spite*'s pale topgallant sails and the bright hoist of flags at her yards.

Weston was saying, 'From *Spite*. Sail in sight to the south'rd.'

Bolitho turned and looked at him. Weston was now the senior midshipman, and probably smarting at Pears's advice to promote Mr Frowd to acting lieutenant instead of him. Advice from a captain was as good as a command.

Bolitho felt almost sorry for Weston. Almost. Ungainly, overweight, belligerent. He would be a bad officer if he lived long enough.

'Very well. Keep watching *Spite*. I'll not inform the captain yet.'

Bolitho continued his measured pacing. The air seemed fresh, but when you paused for too long you felt the sun's power right enough. His own shirt was sodden with sweat, and the scar across his shoulder stung like a snakebite.

The sloop's captain would be fretting and eager to be off on his own, he thought. Right now he would be watching the unknown sail, considering, translating details into facts to relay as well as he could with his signal book for his admiral's decision.

Half an hour passed. Smoke gushed from the galley funnel, and Molesworth, the purser, and his clerk appeared en route for the spirit store to check the daily issue of rum or brandy.

Some marines, who had been drilling on the forecastle, holding off imaginary boarders, marched aft and returned their pikes. There was also a small contingent of marines from the flagship to help fill the gaps until proper replacements could be obtained. Bolitho thought of all the little mounds on the island. Who would care?

Weston called, 'From *Spite*, sir. Disregard.'

Another small encounter. Most likely a Dutchman on her lawful occasions. Anyway, Cunningham of the *Spite* was satisfied. In fact, the strange sail had probably made off at full speed at the first sign of the sloop's topsails. It paid to be careful these days. The margin between friend and foe changed too often for over-confidence.

Stockdale crossed the quarterdeck on his way aft to the starboard battery.

As he passed he whispered, 'Admiral, sir.'

Bolitho stiffened and turned as Coutts walked out of the poop and into the glare.

Bolitho touched his hat, wondering briefly if Weston had deliberately failed to warn him.

Coutts smiled easily. ''Morning, Bolitho. Still on watch, I see.' He had a pleasant, even voice, unaffected.

Bolitho replied, 'A moment more, sir.'

Coutts took a glass and studied the far-off *Spite* for several minutes. 'Good man, Cunningham. Should be posted soon with any luck.'

Bolitho said nothing, but thought of Cunningham's youth. His *luck*. With Coutts's blessing he would be made a full captain, and with the war going as it was he would make post rank within three years. Safe from demotion, on the road to higher things.

'I can hear your mind at work, Bolitho.' Coutts tossed the glass to Weston. Again, the action was casual, yet timed to the second. 'Do not fret. When your time arrives you will discover that a captain's life is not all claret and prize-money.' Just for a moment his eyes hardened. 'But the opportunities are there. For those who will dare, and who do not use their orders as substitutes for initiative.'

Bolitho said, 'Yes, sir.'

He did not know what Coutts was implying. That there was hope for him? Or that he was merely revealing his feelings for Pears?

Coutts shrugged his shoulders and added, 'Dine with me tonight. I will have Ackerman invite a few others.'

Once more, Bolitho discerned the youthful devilment and touch of steel.

'In my quarters of course. I feel certain the captain will not object.'

He strolled away, nodding to Sambell and Weston as if they were yokels on the village green.

The hands were already gathering on the upper gundeck for the afternoon watch, and Bolitho knew that Dalyell would soon be here to relieve him. Unlike George Probyn, he was never late.

Bolitho was confused by what he had heard. He felt excited at Coutts's interest, yet uneasy because of it. It was like disloyalty to Pears. He smiled at his confusion. Pears probably didn't even like him, so what was the matter?

Dalyell appeared, blinking in the sunlight, some crumbs sticking to his coat.

'The watch is aft, sir.'

Bolitho eyed him gravely. 'Very well, Mr Dalyell.'

They both winked, their faces hidden from the men, their good spirits masked by the formality.

Quinn, on the larboard gangway, watched the two lieutenants as they supervised the usual milling confusion of changing watches. He had seen, and had felt, the ache of longing rising to match the pain of his wound. Bolitho had come out of it, or if not, had managed to put his memories behind him. While all he could do was to measure each step, calculate every action as he went along. He kept telling himself that his momentary defiance, his stand at the causeway had not been a fluke. That he had failed once, but had fought to retrieve and hold on to his pride again.

He felt that the ship's company were watching him, rating his confidence. It was why he was lingering on the gangway, waiting for Bolitho before he went below for the noon meal. Bolitho was his strength. His only chance, if chance there was.

Bolitho beckoned to him. 'Not hungry, James? And I am told that we have some fine beef today, barely a year or so in the cask!' He clapped Quinn on the shoulder. 'Make the best of it, eh?'

When Quinn faced him he saw the sudden gravity in Bolitho's eyes and knew the words had nothing to do with food.

With her yards re-trimmed and her great spread of canvas filling and banging in the wind, *Trojan* settled down on her new tack.

Bolitho looked at Cairns and touched his hat. 'Steady as she goes, sir.'

Cairns nodded. 'Dismiss the watch below, if you please.'

As the seamen and the afterguard hurried thankfully below, Bolitho glanced quickly at Pears, who was with the admiral on the weather side of the quarterdeck.

It was another fiery sunset, and against it the two men were in silhouette, their faces hidden. But there was no mistaking Coutts's irritation, Pears's dogged stubbornness.

It all seemed a long, long way from the relaxed supper in the great cabin. Coutts had kept the wit and conversation going with little pause, except to recharge the glasses. He had enthralled the young lieutenants with stories of intrigue and corruption in the New York military government. Of the grand houses in London, the men, and in many cases the ladies who held the reins of power.

Once Pears and the sailing master had concluded their calculations, the ship's destination and purpose had gone through each deck like a bolt of lightning.

There was a small island, one of a group, which lay in the passage between Santa Domingo and Puerto Rico. Avoided by all but the most experienced navigators, it would seem to be the ideal place for transferring arms and powder to Washington's growing fleet of supply vessels.

As Coutts had discussed his hopes for a swift ending of the mission, Bolitho and most of the others had sensed his eagerness, his excitement at the prospect of a quick victory. He had known that nothing could outpace him with a warning, no horseman to carry the word that the British were coming. Not this time. With the vast Atlantic at his back, the keen-eyed *Spite* sweeping well ahead, Coutts had had good reason for confidence.

But that had been fifteen days ago. The delays had been unavoidable, but nevertheless had put a marked strain on Coutts and his officers. Several times *Trojan* had been forced to lie to while *Spite* made off under full sail to investigate a strange vessel and then beat the weary miles round again and make her report. The wind too had backed and veered as Bunce had predicted, but had on the whole favoured their slow advance.

Now, with another sunset closing over the ship, Bolitho could sense a growing impatience, even anger in Coutts's quick movements with head and hands.

Once more *Spite* had been sent ahead to discover if the tiny island was in fact the one described in Paget's documents. If it was, Cunningham was to put a boat ashore and if possible discover the strength of the enemy there. If there was nothing at all, he was to report back instantly. Either way, he should have returned by now. With darkness closing in with its usual swiftness, it was very unlikely they would make contact until tomorrow. Another day. More anxiety.

He stiffened and touched his hat as Pears strode past, his feet thudding loudly on the planking. The slam of the chart-room door was further evidence of his mood.

Bolitho waited, knowing Coutts was going to speak with him.

'A long day, Bolitho.'

'Aye, sir.' Bolitho faced him, trying to discover the man's feelings. 'But the glass is steady. We should be able to maintain our tack during the night.'

Coutts had not heard. He rested his hands on the quarterdeck rail and stared down intently at the larboard battery of eighteen-pounders. He was without his hat, and his hair was blowing across his forehead to make him appear even younger.

He asked quietly, 'Are you like the others? Do you think me a fool to press on with this mission, a task which has no more substance than a scrap of paper?'

'I am only a lieutenant, sir. I was not aware of any doubt.'

Coutts laughed bitterly. 'Doubt? God, man, there's a mountain of it!'

Bolitho waited, feeling the admiral's urgency, his frustration.

Coutts said, 'When you reach flag rank you believe the world is yours. You are only partly right. I was a frigate captain, and good at my work.'

'I know, sir.'

'Thank you.' Coutts seemed surprised. 'Most people look at an admiral and seem to think he has never been anything else, not an ordinary man at all.' He pointed vaguely through *Trojan*'s black web of shrouds and stays. 'But I believe the information is true. Otherwise I would not have risked my ships and my reputation. I do not care what some soft-spoken official from London thinks of me. I want to get this war over, with more cards on our side than across the enemy's table.' He was speaking quickly, his hands moving eloquently to describe his feelings, his fears. 'Each extra day brings more enemies against us. Ships to seek out and bring to battle. We have no squadrons to spare, but the enemy's agility is such that we must match his every move. No merchantman is safe without escort. We have even been forced to send armed vessels to the Davis Strait to protect our whaling ships! It is no time for the timid, or the one who waits for the enemy to act first.'

His terse, emphatic manner of speaking, of sharing his thoughts, was something new to Bolitho. It was like seeing the world, his world, opening up to reach far beyond the ship's hull, and further still to every sea where Britain's authority was being challenged.

'I was wondering, sir.' Bolitho hesitated and then added, 'Why did you not request ships to be sent from Antigua? We have sailed four times the distance it would have taken the vessels which patrol from there.'

Coutts watched him, his face in shadow, saying nothing, as if he were seeking some criticism in Bolitho's question.

Then he said, 'I could have sent *Spite* to the admiral at Antigua. It would have been faster certainly.' He turned away. 'But would they have acted? I think not. The affairs in New York and the threat of Washington's armies seem a long way off in the Caribbean. Only the commander-in-chief could have made a request, and with Sir George Helpman at his elbow, I doubt he would have done more than enter it in his report for the Admiralty.'

Bolitho understood. It was one thing to hear of a victorious sea fight, but nothing to match the sight of a beaten enemy being brought into port, her flag beneath the British ensign.

Coutts had evidence, but that was insufficient. Too many men had died so far to warrant another haphazard scheme. And with Probyn's prize being re-taken by the enemy, even the destruction of Fort Exeter might appear unimportant in far-off London.

But a sharp, determined attack on a supply base, right under the noses of the French who were flaunting their neutrality like a false flag, might sway the balance. Especially if successfully completed before anyone could say no.

Coutts seemed to read his thoughts. 'Remember this, Bolitho. When you attain high rank, never ask what you shall do. The superior minds of Admiralty tend to say no, rather than encourage risk, which might disturb their rarefied existence. Even if you put your career and your life in jeopardy, do as you believe is right, and in the manner best for your country. Acting merely to placate your superiors is living a lie.'

Pears loomed through the dimming light and said harshly, 'We will shorten sail in one hour, Mr Bolitho. But I'll not lie to. There's too much current for comfort hereabouts.' He looked at the admiral and added curtly, 'We shall need to be on station for *Spite*'s return.'

Coutts took Pears's arm and guided him away, but not far enough for Bolitho to miss the anger in his voice as he snapped, 'By God, you drive me too hard, Captain! I'll brook no insolence from you, or anyone else, d'you hear?'

Pears rumbled something, but they were out of earshot.

Bolitho saw Couzens, his face glowing in the compass light as he wrote his entry on the master's mate's slate. He seemed to symbolize something. Youth, innocence or ignorance, whichever way you looked at it. They were all being carried forward to what might easily turn into a disaster. Coutts's determination to win might soon give way to grasping straws. Pears's mistrust of his superior could do for all of them just as easily.

Bolitho was torn betweeen them. He admired Coutts more than he could say. Yet he could understand Pears's more cautious approach. The old and the new. One man at the peak of his career, whereas the admiral saw himself in a far greater role in the not too distant future.

He heard Cairns on the upper gundeck speaking with Tolcher, the boatswain.

Discussing tomorrow's routine which could never be allowed to falter. Not in war or peace, and no matter what kind of man walked the poop in lordly silence. The ship came first. Tomorrow, and all the other tomorrows. Painting to be done, a man to be flogged, another to be promoted, rigging and spars to be overhauled. It never ceased.

He remembered suddenly what Probyn had said about taking full advantage of any chance which offered itself. It was as if he had heard him speak aloud.

Well, Cairns would be off the ship soon. Even Pears could not refuse the next time. Bolitho sighed, finding no comfort in the fact that in a matter of weeks or days he might be doing Cairns's work until Pears could find himself a more experienced replacement.

Cairns would make a good commander. Fair, firm and intelligent. A few more like him and there would be victories enough to satisfy everyone, he thought bitterly.

Midshipman Couzens crossed the deck and asked, 'Will we see any more action, sir?'

Bolitho considered it.

'You know as much as I.'

Couzens stepped back to hide his expression. He had seen Bolitho discussing important matters with the admiral. Naturally he would not allow himself to share such privileged information with a mere midshipman. But that Bolitho knew that *he* knew was almost as good as sharing it, he thought.

To everyone's relief, and no little surprise, the *Spite*'s topsails were reported by the masthead lookout within minutes of the first dawn light. A tiny, pale pyramid of sails, drawing nearer and nearer with such maddening slowness that Bolitho could sense the mood around him like a threat.

The decks were holystoned, and the hands had their breakfast washed down with beer. Then they mustered for the many tasks throughout the ship, and more than one petty officer had to use threats and brute force to stop his men from peering outboard to see how much nearer the sloop had come.

When she had beaten as close as she could manage, she went about and lay hove to under *Trojan*'s lee, and a boat was dropped smartly in the water to carry Cunningham in person to make his report.

Bolitho stood with the side party to receive the youthful commander, and did not envy him at all. He had seen Coutts pacing the poop and staring at the *Spite*, and had also felt Pears's harsh reprimands more than once during the morning about matters which at any other time he would have thought too trivial for comment.

But Cunningham showed no anxiety as he climbed through the entry port and doffed his hat to the quarterdeck and saluting marines. His eyes passed over Bolitho without even a blink of recognition and then he strode aft to meet the captain.

Later, Bolitho was summoned to the great cabin, where he found Cairns already waiting with the flag lieutenant.

He was not really surprised at being called aft. It was customary for the first lieutenant and his immediate subordinate to be invited, if only to listen, when some important manoeuvre was to be undertaken.

They could hear Pears's voice from the dining cabin, loud and angry, and Cunningham's clipped, almost matter-of-fact tone as he explained something.

Cairns looked at Lieutenant Ackerman. 'They seem to be in a sour mood today.'

Ackerman kept his face blank. 'The admiral will have his way.'

A screen door was thrust open and the three other men entered the cabin abruptly, like late arrivals in a theatre.

Bolitho looked at Coutts. Gone was the uncertainty.

He said lightly, 'Well, gentlemen, Major Paget's piece of intelligence has proved its worth.' He nodded to Cunningham. 'Tell them.'

Cunningham explained how he had discovered the little island, and under cover of darkness had put a landing party ashore. It had taken longer than expected, but after sighting wood-smoke he had guessed there were people there and every care had to be taken to avoid detection.

Bolitho guessed he had been rehearsing that part on his way over in the boat. To forestall any criticism which, once made, might damage his chances of reward.

He said, 'There is a good anchorage, not large, but well concealed from seaward. There are several huts, and plenty of evidence that ships put in to load and unload cargo, even to refit if need be.'

Pears asked, 'Who did you send?'

Bolitho waited, seeing Coutts's brief smile as the sloop's commander replied just as sharply, 'I went myself, sir. I was not mistaken about what I saw.'

Coutts asked, 'What else?'

Cunningham was still glaring at Pears. 'A sizeable schooner is anchored there. Privateer. No doubt of it.'

They exchanged glances, and Coutts said, 'She'll be waiting for another vessel. I'll lay odds that there are enough weapons to supply two regiments!'

Pears persisted, 'But suppose there's nothing but the schooner.' He looked round the cabin with something like dismay. 'Like taking a cudgel to crack a small egg!'

'The first part of the information is correct, Captain Pears.' Coutts was watching him. Compelling, insisting. 'Why do you still doubt the rest? This island is obviously chosen for its access. From the Leeward or Windward Islands, from as far south as the Spanish Main, it would present an excellent place for exchange, even for rearming a merchant vessel and changing her to a privateer.' He did not conceal his impatience. 'This time we'll cut them off at the roots. For good.'

He started to move around the cabin, as if unable to hold his excitement in check.

'Think of it. All we have to do is trap them in their anchorage and seize whatever vessel tries to enter. The French will think again about allowing their people to be laid so low. A setback like that would also give their Spanish friends something to ponder on before they run like jackals to sample the spoils.'

Bolitho tried to see it like an outsider. To avoid considering Coutts as his superior, someone he had shared a few weeks of his life with.

Was this discovery really that important? Or was Coutts merely blowing it up like a bladder to *make* it appear so?

A few huts and a schooner did not sound very promising, and it was obvious from Pears's resentful expression that he thought much the same.

When he looked again the mood had changed once more. Foley, the cabin servant, was here, and glasses of wine were already being handed round as if to celebrate Cunningham's news.

Coutts raised his glass. 'I'll give you a sentiment.' He was smiling broadly. 'To a victory, gentlemen. And let us make it as painless as we can!'

He had turned to look through the stern windows and did not see Pears place his glass on the tray, untouched.

Bolitho tasted the wine, but like the mood it was suddenly bitter.

13

No More Pretence

'Captain's a'comin', sir!' The boatswain's mate's whisper seemed unnaturally loud in the dawn stillness.

Bolitho turned, seeking out Pears's heavy figure as he moved to the compass, murmured something to Sambell, the master's mate, and then walked forward to the quarterdeck rail.

Bolitho knew better than to say anything at this point. It was early in the morning, and as *Trojan* ploughed a steady southerly course under her topsails and jib, it was as if they were in the middle of a tropical downpour. The rain had burst over the slow-moving ship with the fierceness of a storm, advancing out of the darkness to thunder across canvas and decks and pass just as quickly across the opposite beam. But now, an hour later, the water still trickled and thudded from sails and rigging, from the tops and down through the scuppers in miniature cascades. When the sun rose there would be so much steam it would be like a fire-ship, Bolitho thought.

But Pears knew all this, and required no telling. He had watched too many dawns on so many seas to need some lieutenant to remind him.

It was still quite dark on the upper gundeck, but Bolitho knew that every cannon was manned and cleared for action within minutes of the galley fires being doused. It was an uncanny, sinister feeling. This great ship, moving like a shadow into deeper darkness, the sails shaking occasionally to a tired wind, the wheel creaking as the helmsmen sought to hold her on course.

Somewhere, up ahead, lay Coutts's objective. The tiny, remote island where he hoped, no, intended to find so much. Isla San Bernardo, little more than a dot on Erasmus Bunce's chart. It was said to have been the last resting place of some exclusive order of friars who had landed there over a hundred years ago. Bunce had remarked scathingly that they had probably arrived there by accident, imagining it to be one of the mainlands. That seemed likely, Bolitho thought. The passage between Santo Domingo and Puerto Rico was some ninety miles wide, a veritable ocean for some tiny, inexperienced boat. The friars had long passed into history, massacred it was said by pirates, by marooned captives, by one of a dozen scourges which still ravaged the length and breadth of the rich Caribbean.

Spite was there now, in position and ready to seal the anchorage. Cunningham must be rubbing his hands, seeing the citation in the *Gazette* as if it were already written.

Bolitho heard Pears moving towards him. It was time. He said, 'Wind holding steady, sir, nor' by west.' He waited, sensing the man's responsibility, his doubt.

Pears muttered, 'Very well, Mr Bolitho. We shall get light to see our way before long.' He raised his eyes to the mastheads, to the great rectangles of pale canvas and the fading stars beyond.

Bolitho followed his glance, wondering how it must feel. To command, to carry the final reward, or blame. Cairns seemed exactly ready for it, whereas he felt unsure, too far removed to understand what Pears must be feeling. Cairns would be leaving soon, he thought. Would that bring him closer to Pears? He doubted it.

Cairns came now out of the darkness without causing a stir, as he always did.

He touched his hat to Pears's bulky shape and to Bolitho said, 'I've just been round the lower gundeck. Not enough hands there, but I doubt we'll be fighting a fleet today!'

Bolitho recalled Coutts's excitement over a single schooner and smiled.

'With *Spite*'s aid, I expect we'll give a good account of ourselves!'

Pears turned with sudden anger. 'Get aloft, Mr Bolitho! Use some of your wit on the masthead lookout and report what you see.' He swung away. 'Unless your sickness at heights still prevails!'

His sarcasm was clearly heard by the helmsmen and the quarterdeck gun crews. Bolitho felt both surprised and embarrassed by the outburst, and saw a marine turning away to hide a broad grin.

Cairns said quietly, 'Which gives you some idea of his own anxiety, Dick.'

That simple comment helped to steady Bolitho as he climbed up the mainmast ratlines, purposefully disdaining the lubber's hole at the maintop to climb out and cling with fingers and toes to the futtock shrouds, his body arched above the deck far below. His resentment at Pears's words enabled him to reach the topgallant mast without even a stab of nausea, and when at last, breathless and sweating, he clambered on to the crosstrees beside the lookout, he realized he had climbed that far with more haste than his usual caution.

The seaman said, 'It be lightenin' now, zur. Be a fine old day, I'm thinkin'.'

Bolitho looked at him, drawing deep breaths to recover himself. He recognized the man, an elderly topman named Buller. Elderly by naval standards, but he was probably no more than thirty. Worn out by the endless demands of wind and sea, of fighting maddened canvas in the teeth of a gale, fisting and kicking until every nail was almost torn from his hands, and his muscles strained and ruptured beyond treatment, he would soon be relegated to safer work on the forecastle or with the afterguard.

But the important thing to Bolitho was that the man was untroubled. Not merely by height and discomfort, but by the unexpected appearance of his second lieutenant.

Bolitho thought of the marine's grin. That too was suddenly important. There had been no malice, no pleasure at seeing him trodden on by the captain.

He replied, 'It will be hot anyway.' He pointed past the foremast, strangely bare without its topgallant set at the yard. 'D'you know these waters, Buller?'

The man considered it. 'Can't say I do, zur. But then, can't say I don't. One place is like another to a sailorman.' He chuckled. 'Less 'e's let ashore, o' course.'

Bolitho thought of the brothel in New York, the woman screaming obscenities in his face, the dead girl's breast still warm under his palm.

One place like another. That was true enough, he thought. Even the merchant seamen were the same. Every ship was the last. One more voyage, just enough pay and bounty saved, and it would be used to buy a little alehouse, a chandlery, a smallholding from some country squire. But it never seemed to happen, unless the man was thrown on the beach in peacetime, or rejected as a useless cripple. The sea always won in the end.

The outboard end of the fore-topsail yard paled slightly, and when he twisted round Bolitho saw the first hint of dawn. He peered down and swallowed hard. The deck, darkly ribbed around by the upper batteries of guns, seemed a mile beneath his dangling legs. He would just have to put up with it. If the hatred of heights had plagued him since his first ship when he had been twelve years old, it was not likely to relent now.

Bolitho felt the mast and its spars trembling and swaying beneath him. He had gone to sea as a midshipman in 1768. The year *Trojan* had been launched. He had thought of it before, but this morning, up here and strangely isolated, it seemed like an omen, a warning. He shivered. He was getting as bad as Quinn.

On the quarterdeck, unaware or indifferent to his second lieutenant's fancies, Pears paced back and forth across the damp planking.

Cairns watched him, and aft on the raised poop D'Esterre stood with his arms crossed, thinking of Fort Exeter, of Bolitho, and of his dead marines.

A door opened and slammed, and voices floated around the

quarterdeck to announce the admiral's arrival. He was followed by his aide, Ackerman, and even in the poor light looked alert and wide awake.

He paused near the wheel and spoke to Bunce, then with a nod to Cairns said, "Morning, Captain. Is everything ready?'

Cairns winced. Where Pears was concerned, things were always *ready*.

But Pears sounded unruffled. 'Aye, sir. Cleared for action, but guns not loaded,' the slightest hint of dryness, 'or run out.'

Coutts glanced at him. 'I can see that.' He turned away. '*Spite* must be in position now. I suggest you set more sail, Captain. The time for guessing is done.'

Cairns relayed the order and seconds later, with the topmen rushing out along the upper yards and the wet canvas falling and then billowing sluggishly to the wind, *Trojan* tilted more steeply to the extra pressure.

'I've been looking at the chart again.' Coutts was half watching the activity above the deck. 'There seems to be no other anchorage. Deep water to the south'rd and a shoal or two against the shore. Cunningham put his landing party to the south'rd. A clever move. He thinks things out, that one.'

Pears dragged his eyes from the lithe topmen as they slithered down to the deck again.

He said, 'It was the *only* place, I'd have thought, sir.'

'Really?'

Coutts moved away with his flag lieutenant, the cut well and truly driven home.

A few gulls dipped out of the darkness and circled the ship like pieces of spindrift. They seemed to tell of the land's nearness, and their almost disinterested attitude implied they had other sources of food close by.

From his dizzy perch Bolitho watched the birds as they floated past him. They reminded him of all those other times, different landfalls, but mostly of Falmouth. The little fishing villages which nestled in rocky clefts along the Cornish coast, the boats coming home, the gulls screaming and mewing above them.

He came out of his thoughts as Buller said, "Ell, zur, *Spite*'s well off station!' He showed some excitement for the first time. 'There'll be the devil to pay now!'

Bolitho found time to marvel that the seaman should care and be so accurate in his opinions. Coutts would be furious, and it might take *Trojan* a whole day to beat back to her original station and allow Cunningham a second chance.

'I'd better get down and tell the captain.' He was thinking aloud.

Why had he mentioned it? Even thought of it? Had it been to stop another wave of frustration throughout the ship, or merely to protect Coutts's credibility?

Buller grunted. 'She probably lost a man over the side.'

Bolitho did not answer. He hoped Cunningham was the kind of man who would waste valuable time to look for a man overboard. But that was as far as it went. He swung the telescope over his arm and pressed his shoulders against the shivering mast.

'I'll leave this with you, Buller. When I go down, give us a hail as soon as you can make out what she's up to.'

He tried not to think of the drop to the deck, how long it would take if the ship gave a lurch before he could use both hands to hold on again.

It was like looking through a dark bottle. A few hints of whitecaps, a glassiness on the sea's face to show that dawn was nearby. Then he saw the pale squares of canvas, barely clear as yet, but rising from the darkness like a broken iceberg.

Spite must have changed tack considerably, he thought. She was standing in well towards the hidden anchorage, but she should have been miles nearer by now. Buller was right, but there would be more than the devil to pay after this. There would be . . . he stiffened, momentarily forgetting his precarious position.

'Wot is it, zur?' Buller had sensed something.

Bolitho did not know what to say. He was wrong of course. Had to be.

He held the swaying blur of sails in his lens and then, straining every nerve until the wound on his forehead began to throb in time with his heart-beats, he lowered the glass just a fraction.

Still deep in shadow, but it was there right enough. He wanted it to be a dream, a fault in the telescope. But instead of *Spite*'s rakish single deck there was something more solid, deep and hard like a double reflection.

He thrust the glass at the seaman and then cupped his hands to his mouth.

'Deck there! Sail on the starboard bow!' He hesitated a few moments longer, imagining the sudden tension and astonishment below him. Then, '*Ship of the line!*'

Buller exclaimed slowly, 'You done it proper now, zur!'

Bolitho was already slithering downwards, groping for a backstay, his eyes still holding that menacing outline.

Coutts was waiting for him, his head thrust forward as he asked, 'Are you certain?'

Pears strode past them, his eyes everywhere as he prepared himself for the next vital hours.

Only once did he glance at Bolitho. Then to Coutts he snapped, 'He's *certain*, sir.'

Cairns said quietly, 'Now here's a fine thing, Dick. She'll not be one of ours.'

The admiral heard him and said curtly, 'I don't care what she is, Mr

Cairns. If she stands against us, then damn your eyes, she's an enemy in my book!' He peered after the captain and raised his voice. 'Have the guns loaded, if you please!' He seemed to sense Pears's arguments from the opposite side of the deck. 'And let me see what this ship of yours can do today!'

Along either side of the upper gundeck the crews threw themselves on their tackles and handspikes and manhandled their heavy cannon up to the closed ports.

Bolitho stood by the boat-tier, straining his eyes through the gloom as he watched one gun captain after another raise his fist to signify he was loaded and ready.

Midshipman Huss peered over the main hatch and yelled, 'Lower gundeck *ready*, sir!'

Bolitho pictured Dalyell down there with thirty great thirty-two-pounders. Like everyone else in the wardroom, he had risen in rank, but his experience had altered little. Bolitho knew that if and when *Trojan* was required to give battle it would test everyone to the limit.

Quinn crossed from the opposite side and asked, 'What *is* going on, Dick?' He was almost knocked from his feet as some ship's boys hurried aft with carriers of shot for the quarterdeck nine-pounders.

Bolitho looked up at the mainmast, through the shaking rigging and spread canvas, recalling his feelings such a short while back when he had watched the other ship through the telescope. It had been fifteen minutes ago, but the daylight seemed reluctant to reveal the newcomer, and only the lookouts, and perhaps the marines in the tops, could see the ship properly.

He replied, 'Maybe that ship is here on passage for another port in the Caribbean.'

As he said it he knew he was deluding himself, or perhaps trying to ease Quinn's anxiety. The ship was no English man-of-war. Every large vessel was being held within a squadron, just in case France openly joined in the fight. Unlikely to be a Spaniard either. They usually used their larger men-of-war to escort the rich treasure ships from the Main, through the pirate-infested waters and all the way to Santa Cruz and safety. No, it had to be a Frenchman.

Bolitho chilled with excitement. He had seen French ships in plenty. Well designed and built, they were said to be equally well manned.

He looked around the tiered boats and saw Coutts, hands behind his back, speaking with Pears and old Bunce. They all appeared calm enough, although with Pears you could never be sure. It was strange to see the quarterdeck so busy in the first light. Crouching gun crews on either side, and further aft, standing against the hammock nettings, D'Esterre's depleted ranks of marines. Near one battery of nine-pounders he could see Libby, one-time signals midshipman, now acting fifth lieutenant. What must he be thinking, Bolitho wondered? Seventeen years old, and yet if a blast of canister and grape raked the quarterdeck with its bloody furrows he might find himself in temporary command until someone else could reach him. Frowd was there, too. From master's mate to acting sixth lieutenant. It was mad when you considered it, he was even older than Cairns by a year or two. He was standing quite near Sambell, the other master's mate. But that was all. Before Sparke had been killed and Probyn captured it had been Jack and Arthur. Now it was sir and Mr Sambell.

He heard Cairns call, 'Let her fall off a point!'

Then later the helmsman's cry, 'Steady as she goes, sir! Sou'-east by sou'!'

The braces were manned, the yards trimmed for the slight alteration of course. Apart from the rustle and grumble of the sails, the ship's own private sounds, there was silence.

Bolitho pictured the chart, and beyond the bows the island as it must appear to those who could see. A headland sliding out towards the starboard bow, around which lay the entrance to the anchorage. Where *Spite*, presumably, was on station after all. God, she would get a surprise when the newcomer showed herself around the shoulder of land. Cunningham's lookouts would probably mistake her for the *Trojan*.

'Deck there!' Buller's hoarse voice. 'T'other ship's shortenin' sail, zur!'

Someone said, 'She's sighted *Spite*, 'tis my guess.'

The larboard battery dipped over slightly to the pressure of wind in the sails, and Bolitho saw the tethered guns glint suddenly as the daylight lanced through the shrouds and halliards.

Colour was returning to familiar things. Faces emerged as people, features became expressions again. Here and there a man moved, to adjust a gun tackle, or push loose equipment away from a carriage or breech, to brush hair from eyes, to make sure a cutlass or boarding axe was within reach.

The petty officers and midshipmen stood out at intervals, little blue and white markers in the chain of command.

Far above the deck, at the highest point, the long masthead pendant licked out ahead like a scarlet serpent. Wind was holding steady, Bolitho thought. Even so, there was no chance of heading off the other ship.

Quinn whispered, 'What will the admiral do? What can he do? We're not at war with France.'

Midshipman Forbes scurried along the deck, skipping over tackles and flaked halliards like a rabbit.

He touched his hat and said breathlessly, 'Captain's compliments, sir, and would you bring the French lieutenant aft?'

Bolitho nodded. 'Very well.'

Forbes was really enjoying himself. Aft with the mighty, too excited and too young to see the teeth of danger.

Quinn said, 'I'll fetch him.'

Bolitho shook his head, smiling at the absurdity of it. He had to bring the French officer because Cairns was busy on the quarterdeck and everyone else was too junior. Etiquette would be observed even at the gates of hell, he thought.

He found the Frenchman on the orlop deck, sitting with the surgeon outside the sick-bay while Thorndike's assistants laid out the makeshift table with his instruments.

Thorndike asked irritably, 'What the hell are we doing now?' He glared at his helpers. 'Wasting time and dirtying my things. They must be short of work to do!'

Bolitho said to Contenay, 'The captain wishes to see you.'

Together they climbed up through the lower gundeck, a place in almost complete darkness with every port shut and only the slow-matches glowing slightly in the tubs by each division of cannon.

Contenay said, 'There is trouble, my friend?'

'A ship. One of yours.'

It was strange, Bolitho thought, it was easier to speak with the Frenchman than the surgeon.

'*Mon Dieu.*' Contenay nodded to a marine sentry at the next hatchway and added, 'I will have to watch my words, I think.'

On deck it was much brighter. It seemed impossible that it had changed so much in the time to go to the orlop and back again.

On the quarterdeck Bolitho announced, '*M'sieu* Contenay, sir.'

Pears glared at him. 'Over here.' He strode across to the nettings where Coutts and the flag lieutenant were training telescopes towards the other ship.

Bolitho stole a quick glance at her. He had not been mistaken. She made a proud sight, leaning over, close-hauled on the starboard tack, her topgallant sails and maincourse already brailed up to the yards, her bilge clearly visible as she tacked towards the entrance.

'The prisoner, sir.' Pears too was looking at the other vessel.

Coutts lowered his glass and regarded the Frenchman calmly. 'Ah yes. The ship yonder, *m'sieu*, do you know her?'

Contenay's mouth turned down, as if he was about to refuse an answer. Then he shrugged and replied, 'She is the *Argonaute.*'

Ackerman nodded. 'Thought as much, sir. I saw her once off Guadeloupe. A seventy-four. Fine-looking ship.'

Pears said heavily, 'She too wears a rear-admiral's flag.' He glanced questioningly at Contenay.

He said, 'It is true. *Contre-Admiral* André Lemercier.'

Coutts eyed him searchingly. 'You were one of his officers, am I right?'

'I *am* one of his officers, *m'sieu.*' He looked towards the other two-decker. 'It is all I am prepared or required to say.'

Pears exploded, 'You mind your manners, sir! We don't need to be told more. You were aiding the King's enemies, abetting an unlawful rebellion, and now you expect to be treated as an innocent bystander!'

Coutts seemed surprised at the outburst. 'Well said, Captain. But I think the lieutenant is well aware of what he has done, and where he stands.'

Bolitho watched, fascinated, hoping Pears would not notice him and order him down to the gundeck.

A private drama which excluded everyone else, and yet which could decide their future.

Cairns said quietly, 'Here is a problem for the admiral, Dick. Is it a real stalemate? Or shall we force our views on the Frenchman?'

Bolitho watched Coutts's youthful profile. He was no doubt regretting his shift of flag now. His ninety-gun *Resolute* would be more than a match for the French seventy-four. *Trojan* had no such advantage. About the same size, and with just two more guns than the *Argonaute*, she was undermanned and lacking experienced officers.

If Contenay was typical of *Argonaute*'s wardroom, she would be an adversary to reckon with. What the hell was Cunningham doing? A sloop-of-war was far too frail to match iron with the line of battle, but an extra show of strength, no matter how small, would be doubly welcome.

'Take the prisoner down. I may require him presently.' Coutts beckoned to D'Esterre. 'Attend to it.' To Bolitho he said, 'Warn the masthead to report what *Spite* is doing the instant he sights her.'

Bolitho hurried to the quarterdeck ladder. The masthead lookout, like everyone else above deck, was probably more interested in the French two-decker than in *Spite.*

Trojan maintained her set course, every telescope trained on the other ship as she moved at right angles across the bows, nearer and nearer to the headland.

Coutts must be worried. He could not anchor, and if he continued past the entrance he would lose the wind-gage and it might take hours to beat back again. If he stood out to sea, the same must apply. His only course was to follow the Frenchman, who obviously intended to ignore *Trojan*'s intentions, to treat her as if she did not exist.

The headland was sloping more quickly now, to reveal the one on the opposite side of the entrance. Two green arms reaching out to receive them.

Bolitho felt the mounting glare from the sun, the sudden dryness in his throat as the lookout yelled, 'Deck there! *Spite*'s aground, zur!'

Something like a sigh ran along the *Trojan*'s decks.

Of all the bad luck, this was it. Cunningham must have misjudged his entrance, or had been deceived by the currents. It was humiliating enough for Coutts. For Cunningham it must be the end of the world, Bolitho thought.

Stockdale whispered, 'The Frenchie can do as 'e pleases now, sir.'

The anchorage was opening up with every dragging minute. Bolitho could see the sheltered water beyond the turbulence at the entrance. *Spite*'s three masts, slightly angled and stiffly unmoving. Beyond her the deeper shadows, and a schooner at anchor, close inshore.

The lookout shouted, 'They're tryin' to tow 'er off, zur!'

Bolitho could not see without a telescope, and like the seamen around him, fretted and waited for more news from aloft. Cunningham had boats down and would probably lay out an anchor to kedge his ship free from the ground.

Quinn asked, 'What is the Frenchman doing?' He sounded beside himself with worry.

'He'll no doubt anchor, James. He has beaten us to the island. To attack him there would be a sure way of starting a war.'

He looked away, confused and bitter. Whatever they did, no matter how right the cause, fate seemed to be against them.

The *Argonaute* was quite likely bringing another great cargo of ordnance and powder. Some to be loaded into the schooner, more to be stacked in a safe hiding place to await the next privateer or transport. Contenay must have sailed from here more than a few times. No wonder he found Fort Exeter without any trouble.

As if to bear out his ideas, another lookout shouted wildly, 'Sail on the starboard quarter, sir!'

Figures bustled across the quarterdeck, sunlight glinting on raised telescopes, as the lookout continued, 'Brig, sir! She's goin' about!'

Bolitho looked at Quinn's pale features. 'I'll bet she is, James! Just the sight of us will be enough. She must have been coming here to collect her cargo from the French!'

'Is there nothing we can do?'

Quinn looked up, startled, as Buller yelled again, 'Deck there! *Spite*'s come off, zur! She's shakin' out 'er tops'ls!'

Quinn gripped Bolitho's arm as the news brought a wild burst of cheering from the watching seamen and marines.

They looked aft as Midshipman Weston's signals party burst into life and sent a hoist of bright flags flying to the yards.

Bolitho nodded. In the nick of time. Coutts had signalled *Spite* to leave the anchorage and give chase. Even the delay at hoisting her boats would not mean much to Cunningham. With a following wind, and his honour very much at stake, he would overhaul and take the brig before noon.

And there was still the schooner. If she was a privateer, the French could not prevent Coutts taking action against her if she attempted to leave.

He shaded his eyes, seeing more sails breaking out from the sloop's yards, imagining the excitement and relief pushing all disappointment aside.

'*Spite*'s acknowledged, sir!'

Midshipman Couzens bounded past on some mission or other, his freckled face alive with anticipation.

'Now it's the Frenchman's turn to be an onlooker, sir!'

Bolitho turned sharply as the anchorage echoed violently to the crash of cannon fire. He saw the gunsmoke hit the calm water and burst skyward, eddying across the pale sunlight like a cloud.

Everyone was yelling and shouting at once, stricken by the unexpected turn of events. *Spite* was turning to one side, still reeling from a savage broadside at extreme range. Like a hurricane the *Argonaute*'s iron had ripped through her masts and rigging, reducing her to an unmanageable wreck in seconds. Her foremast had gone, and while they watched, her maintopmast fell alongside in a welter of spray and tangled cordage. *Spite* stopped moving, and Bolitho guessed she had run aground again on an extension of the same sandbar. Seeing her go from movement to sudden stillness was like watching something beautiful die.

The *Argonaute* had made certain the brig would not be captured, and even now was coming about, her long jib boom swinging through the smoke of her one, murderous broadside.

Quinn said in a choking voice, 'God, they're coming out!'

Bolitho looked aft as Cairns's voice boomed through his speaking trumpet.

'Hands aloft and shorten sail! Mr Tolcher, rig your nets!'

A bright scarlet ensign rose to the gaff, and Stockdale spat on his hands. Coutts had shown his colours. He was going to fight.

Nets were already being spread above the gundeck, the men working without thought, as they had so often at their drills.

Bolitho watched the *Argonaute*'s shape shortening as she completed her turn towards the entrance.

She too had run up her colours. The white flag of France. No more pretence or bluff.

Later, higher authorities might argue over excuses and deceptions.

But now, today, each captain had his own clear reason to engage an enemy.

'*Open your ports!*'

Tackles squeaked, and along either side a double line of port lids lifted in time with the lesser quarterdeck batteries.

'*Run out!*'

Bolitho drew a deep breath, forcing himself to watch as his own guns trundled noisily to their ports, thrusting out their black muzzles like snouts in the strengthening sunlight.

Two ships of the line, without aid, not even a spectator to watch their ponderous strength as they manoeuvred towards each other, in no haste, and in total silence.

Another glance aft and he saw Coutts lifting his arms to allow the captain's coxswain to buckle on his sword for him.

Bolitho realized that Coutts would never give in. He dare not. It must be victory today. Or nothing.

'Starboard battery, *stand by!*'

Bolitho tugged out his hanger and pulled his hat over his eyes.

'Ready, lads!'

He glanced to left and right, the familiar faces passing his vision, merging, then disappearing as he faced the enemy.

'On the uproll!'

Somewhere, a man started to cough violently, another was pounding a slow, desperate tattoo on the deck beside his gun.

'*Fire!*'

14

A Very High Price

As the upper battery, followed instantly by the thirty-two-pounders on the lower gundeck, roared out in a full broadside, *Trojan* gave a tremendous shudder, as if she would wrench herself apart.

Even though every man had been expecting it, the deafening crash of gun-fire was beyond imagination, the sound going on and on as each cannon hurled itself inboard on its tackles.

Bolitho watched the dense smoke being forced downwind from the starboard bow and stared towards the French ship as the sea around her became a mass of leaping white feathers. The *Argonaute* was steering on a converging tack, her yards braced hard round to carry her away from the nearest spit of land. Without a telescope it was impossible to see if they had hit her, although with such a massive broadside they should have found some targets. But *Trojan* had fired at the first possible moment, and Bolitho estimated the range to be at least eight cables.

On either side of him the gun captains were yelling like demons, the crews ramming home charges and fresh balls, while others stood with handspikes in readiness to control their ponderous weapons.

It sounded blurred, unreal, and Bolitho rubbed his ears rapidly to restore his hearing. The deck tilted very slightly as Pears ordered an alteration of course towards the other ship. How invulnerable she looked. With topsails and forecourse flapping to retain the wind, the French captain was trying to gain sea-room, to escape the blanketing shelter of the land across his quarter.

What was he up to, he wondered? What motive did Coutts's opposite number have in mind? Perhaps he wished to draw *Trojan* away from the island to allow the schooner time to escape. Or maybe, having put the *Spite* out of action, all he wanted to do was slip away himself and avoid further conflict. Perhaps he had other orders, to find a second rendezvous and unload his cargo without delay.

It was incredible that he could think at all. He peered along the deck, seeing the captains raise their fists, their faces masked in concentration.

He looked aft. 'Ready, sir!'

Again, the senior midshipman of the lower gundeck bobbed through the hatch and yelled, 'Ready, sir!'

Couzens went past at the run, carrying a message from the forecastle to Cairns on the quarterdeck.

As he passed Midshipman Huss he shouted, 'You were slow that time!' They grinned at one another as if it were a huge game.

Bolitho turned towards the enemy again. Nearer now, her deck angled over to the wind, the lines of guns shining in the sunlight like teeth.

He knew in his heart that the French admiral had no intention of telling his captain to haul off. He was going to fight. What the world said later mattered little out here. Justification would be sought and found by both sides, but the winner would have the real say in things.

The side of the French ship vanished in a writhing bank of smoke, broken by darting orange tongues, as she delivered her reply to *Trojan*'s challenge.

Bolitho gritted his teeth, expecting to feel the hull quiver to the crash of the broadside. But only a few balls hit the tumblehome, while above the decks the air became alive with screaming, shrieking chain-shot.

Bolitho saw the boatswain's hastily spread nets jumping with fallen blocks and severed rigging, and then a marine fell headlong from the maintop, struck the gangway and vanished over the side without even a cry.

Bolitho swallowed hard. *First blood.* He looked aft, seeing Pears watching the enemy while his hand rose level with his shoulder.

Bolitho said quickly, 'Ready, lads!'

The captain's arm fell, and once more the air was blasted by the thunder of guns.

'Stop your vents! Sponge out! *Load!*'

The seamen, who had cursed their captain and officers as they had drilled again and again in every kind of condition, went through the motions without even pausing to watch some of their companions hurrying aloft to make repairs.

Bolitho saw the great rent in the main-topsail spreading and ripping as it was pushed by the wind, and knew that the enemy was following a regular French tactic. To cripple the adversary first, render her useless and impossible to handle so that she would fall downwind and present her stern to another murderous broadside. Cleared for action, a ship of the line was open from bow to stern, and a well-timed bombardment through the poop and counter could change the gundecks into a slaughterhouse.

The *Argonaute* was showing some signs of damage, too. Shot-holes in her canvas, and a savage gash in her larboard gangway where two balls had struck home together.

Five cables. Just half a mile between them, and both ships gathering speed as they thrust clear of the land.

Again the writhing bank of smoke, and once more the shriek of chain-shot overhead. It was unbelievable that no spar was hit, but the terrible sound made more than one man gasp with alarm as he worked at his gun.

Stockdale paused at his efforts and shouted, 'We're holdin' the wind, sir!' His battered features were stained with smoke, but he looked unbreakable.

'On the uproll!'

Bolitho heard Midshipman Huss repeating the order to Dalyell below.

'*Fire!*'

The deck rebounded as if the ship was driving ashore, and then there was a ragged cheer as the enemy's main-topgallant mast swung wildly on its stays before breaking away and plunging down like a lance.

A lucky shot, and nobody would ever know who had aimed it.

Pears's harsh voice carried easily above the squeak of gun trucks and the clatter of rammers.

'Well done, Trojans! Hit 'em again!'

More cheers, quenched by the enemy's return fire, the terrifying crash of iron smashing into the hull and through some of the gunports below.

Bolitho winced, wondering why the Frenchman had changed his tactics. He heard the rumble of a cannon careering across the lower deck, the sudden lurch as it hit something solid. Men were yelling down there, their voices strangely muffled, like souls in torment.

The *Argonaute* seemed to be gaining, drawing slightly ahead, so that her jib boom appeared to be touching *Trojan*'s bowsprit. With the advantage of wind and position, Pears would probably let his ship fall off, then spread more sail and try to cross the enemy's stern.

He heard Cairns's voice through his speaking trumpet. 'Hands aloft! Loose t'gan'sls!'

Bolitho found himself nodding as if in agreement. The ship was turning again, just a few points, while her topgallant sails flapped and then hardened at their yards.

He watched the other ship, his eyes smarting in the smoke. One giant arrowhead of blue water, and both vessels aiming for some invisible mark which would bring them together.

'*Fire!*'

The seamen leapt aside as their guns crashed inboard, groping in the funnelling smoke to sponge out the muzzles before a packed charge was rammed home.

Bolitho felt the hull quiver and realized the enemy had fired again, and saw part of a gangway splinter apart as if under an invisible axe. A seaman ran screaming and stumbling past his companion, his hands clawing at his face.

A marine seized him and pushed him to a hatchway, and others reached up to drag him below.

Bolitho glanced at Quinn and saw him retching. The seaman had taken a giant wood splinter in his eye as big as a marline-spike.

The sharper crack of the quarterdeck nine-pounders told him that their crews had at last been able to bring them to bear on the enemy.

The noise was growing and spreading as the two ships moved inexorably towards each other. Wood splinters, fragments of cordage and yet another corpse joined the tangle on the nets, and from below Bolitho heard a man screaming like a tortured hare.

A quick glance aft again. Pears still there, unmoving and grim-faced as he studied the enemy. Coutts, apparently untroubled by the din of battle, one foot on a bollard as he pointed to something on the Frenchman's deck for Ackerman's benefit.

'*Fire!*'

The guns were recoiling more unevenly now. The crews were getting tired, stunned by the constant thunder and crash of explosions.

Bolitho made himself walk along the deck, ducking to peer through each port as the men hauled their guns back in readiness to fire. A small world, a square of hazy sunlight in which each crew saw just a portion of the enemy.

He felt unsteady, his gait jerky as he moved behind them. His face was stiff with strain, and he imagined he must look halfway between laughing and squinting from shock.

Stockdale glanced round at him and nodded. Another man, Bolitho recognized him as Moffitt, waved his hand and shouted, 'Hot work, sir!'

More powerful thuds into the lower hull, and then a column of black smoke through an open hatch to bring a chorus of shouts and cries of alarm. But the smoke was quickly brought under control, and Bolitho guessed that Dalyell's men had been ready for such an emergency.

'Cease firing!'

As the men stood back from their smoking guns, Bolitho thought the silence almost as painful as the noise. The enemy had moved further across the bows, so that it was pointless to try to hit her.

Cairns shouted, 'Put some men to larboard!' He gestured with his trumpet. 'We will engage him as we cross his stern!'

Bolitho saw petty officers pushing dazed men across to the opposite side to help the depleted crews there. Pears had timed it well. With the slight change of tack, and extra canvas to give her more speed, *Trojan* would sweep across the enemy's wake and pour a broadside, gun by gun, the length of her hull. Even if she were not dismasted, she would be too crippled to withstand the next encounter.

He shouted, 'Ready, James!' Again he felt his jaw locked in a wild grin. 'Yours is the honour this time!'

A gun captain touched Quinn's arm as he hurried past. 'We'll show 'em, sir!'

'Hands to the braces there!'

Bolitho swung round as Cairns's voice echoed from the quarterdeck.

Stockdale gasped, 'The Frenchie's luffed, by God!'

Bolitho watched, his body like ice, seeing the *Argonaute* swinging steadily up into the wind, her reduced sails almost aback as she turned to face her enemy.

It was all happening in minutes, yet Bolitho could still find time for admiration at the superb seamanship and timing. Round and further still, so that when she had finished her manoeuvre she would be on the reverse tack, while *Trojan* was still struggling to slow her advance.

'Hands aloft! Take in the t'gan'sls!'

Masts and spars shook and creaked violently as the helm was put over, but it was all taking too long.

As men ran wildly back to the starboard battery, Bolitho saw the enemy's side belch smoke and fire, felt the ship stagger as a carefully timed broadside smashed into the side from bowsprit to quarterdeck. Because of the angle, many of the shots did little damage, but others, which burst through the gunports or smashed through the flimsy defences of gangways and nettings, caused terrible havoc. Three guns were upended, their crews either crushed or hurled aside like rubbish, and Bolitho heard the splintering bang of more balls ripping through the boat-tier and sending a wave of splinters across the opposite side like tiny arrows. Men were falling and stumbling everywhere, and when Bolitho glanced at his legs he saw they were bloody from the carnage at the nearest gun.

A great chorus of voices made him turn in time to see the fore-topgallant mast fall across the bows and plunge over the side, taking with it a writhing trail of rigging like maddened snakes, spar and canvas, and two screaming seamen.

Momentarily out of control, *Trojan* swung drunkenly away from her enemy, while all the time, as her jubilant crews reloaded, *Argonaute* continued to go about until she had completed one great circle. Then as she settled down on a parallel course, but slightly ahead of the *Trojan*, she opened fire with her sternmost guns.

Blinded by smoke, and fighting to free themselves from the mass of tangled rigging, the forward gun crews aboard the *Trojan* were able to return only half their shots.

Bolitho found himself striding up and down yelling meaningless words until he was hoarse, raw with the stench of battle.

Around him men were fighting back, dying, or sprawled in the bloody attitudes of death.

Others hurried past, following the boatswain and his mates, axes shining in the smoky glare, to hack the wreckage away before it swung the ship stern on towards those merciless guns.

And aft, his face like stone, Pears watched all of it, giving his orders, not even flinching as splinters whipped past him to bring down more of the crouching gun crews.

Midshipman Huss appeared on deck, his eyes white with fear. He saw Bolitho and shouted frantically, 'Mr Dalyell's fallen, sir! I – I can't find . . .' He spun round, his face gaping with astonishment and freezing there as he pitched forward at Bolitho's feet.

Bolitho shouted, 'Get below, James! Take command of the lower gundeck!'

But Quinn was staring transfixed at the midshipman. Blood was pouring from a great hole in his back, but one hand still moved, as if it and nothing else was holding on to life.

A seaman turned the boy over and rasped, 'Done for, sir.'

'Did you hear?' Bolitho gripped Quinn's arm, Huss and all else forgotten. '*Get below!*'

Quinn half turned, his eyes widening as more cries and screams came up from the other gundeck.

He stammered, 'Can't. Can't . . . do . . . it.'

His head fell forward, and Bolitho saw tears running down his face, cutting pale furrows through the grime of gunsmoke.

An unfamiliar voice snapped, 'I'll go.' It was Ackerman, the immaculate flag lieutenant. 'I can manage.' He stared at Quinn as if he could not believe what he saw. 'The admiral sent me.'

Bolitho peered aft, shocked by Quinn's collapse, stunned by the horror and bloody shambles all around him.

Through the drifting smoke and dangling creeper of severed rigging their eyes met. Then Coutts gave a slight wave and what could have been a shrug.

The deck shivered, and Bolitho knew that the broken mast had been hacked free.

Trojan was turning to windward, laying her enemy in the sights again, seemingly unreachable and beyond hurt.

'*Fire!*'

The men sprang back, groping for their rammers and spikes, cursing and cheering like mad things from bedlam.

Quinn stood as before, oblivious to the hiss of iron overhead, to the crawling wounded, to the danger of his position as the enemy's mizzen and then mainmast towered high above the nettings.

Fifty yards, certainly no more, Bolitho thought wildly. Both ships were firing blindly through the churning smoke which was trapped between them as if to cushion the hammer blows.

A seaman ran from his gun, crazed by the din and slaughter, trying to reach a hatchway. To go deeper and deeper until he found the keel, like a terrified animal going to ground. A marine sentry raised his musket as if to club him down, but let it fall, as if he too was past reason and hope.

Couzens was tugging Bolitho's sleeve, his round face screwed up as if to shut out the awful sights.

'Yes?' Bolitho had no idea how long he had been there. 'What is it?'

The midshipman tore his eyes from Huss's corpse. 'The captain says that the enemy intends to board us!' He stared at Quinn. 'You are to take charge forrard.' He showed his old stubbornness. 'I will assist.'

Bolitho gripped his shoulder. Through the thin blue coat the boy's body was hot, as if burning with fever.

'Go and get some men from below.' As the boy made to run he called, '*Walk*, Mr Couzens. Show the people how calm you are.' He forced a grin. 'No matter how you may feel.'

He turned back to the guns, astounded he could speak like that when at any second he would be dead. Worse, he might be lying pinned on the surgeon's table, waiting for the first touch of his knife.

He watched the set of the enemy's yards, the way the angle was more acute as both ships idled closer together. The guns showed no sign of lessening, even though they were firing at point-blank range, some hurling blazing wads through the smoke which were almost as much danger as the balls.

There were new sounds now. The distant crack of muskets, the thuds of shots hitting deck and gangway, or ripping harmlessly into the packed hammock nettings.

From the maintop he heard the bark of a swivel and saw a cluster of marksmen drop from the enemy's mizzen-top, swept aside like dead fruit by a hail of canister.

Individual faces stood out on the *Argonaute*'s decks, and he saw a petty officer pointing him out to another sharpshooter on the gangway. But he was felled by one of D'Esterre's marines even as he raised his musket to shoot.

He heard men scrambling up from the lower gundeck, the rasp of steel as they seized their cutlasses. Balleine, the boatswain's mate, stood by the mainmast rack, issuing the boarding pikes to anyone who came near him.

'We will touch bow to bow.' Bolitho had spoken aloud without knowing it. 'Not much time.' He drew his curved hanger and waved it over his head. 'Clear the larboard battery! Come with me!'

A single ball crashed through an open port and beheaded a seaman even as he ran to obey. For a few moments the headless corpse stood stock-still, as if undecided what to do. Then it fell, and was forgotten as swearing and cheering the seamen dashed towards the forecastle, nothing in their minds but the towering bank of pockmarked sails alongside, the crimson stab of musket-fire.

Bolitho stared, watching the other ship's great bowsprit and jib boom poking through the smoke, thrusting above the forecastle and beakhead as if nothing could stop it. There were men already there, firing down at *Trojan*'s deck, brandishing their weapons, while beneath them their fierce-eyed figurehead watched the scene with incredible menace.

Then with a violent shudder both hulls ground together. Hacking and stabbing, *Trojan*'s men swarmed to repel boarders, and from aft D'Esterre's men kept up a withering fire on the enemy's quarterdeck and poop.

Bolitho jumped over a fallen seaman and yelled, 'Here they come!'

A French seaman tried to scramble on to the cathead, but a blow with a belaying pin knocked him aside, and a lunge from a pike sent him down between the hulls.

Bolitho found himself face to face with a young lieutenant. His sword-arm came up, the two blades circled warily and with care, despite the surging press of fighting figures all around.

The French officer lunged, his eyes widening with fear as Bolitho side-stepped and knocked his arm aside with his hanger, seeing the sleeve open up, the blood spurting out like paint.

Bolitho hesitated and then hacked him across the collar-bone, seeing him die before he hit the water alongside.

More men were hurrying to his aid, but when he twisted his head he saw Quinn standing by his guns as before, as if he would never move again.

Smoke swirled and then enveloped the gasping and struggling men, and Bolitho realized that the wind was strengthening, pushing the ships along in a terrible embrace.

Another figure blocked his path, and again the clang of steel dominated everything else.

He watched the man's face, detached, without feeling, meeting each thrust, testing his strength, expecting an agonizing blade through his stomach if he lost his balance.

There were others beside him. Raye of the marines, Joby Scales, the carpenter, wielding a great hammer, Varlo, the seaman who had been crossed in love, Dunwoody, the miller's son, and of course Stockdale, whose cutlass was taking a terrible toll.

Something struck him on the head and he felt blood running down his neck. But the pain only helped to tighten his guard, to make him examine his enemy's moves like an onlooker.

A dying seaman fell whimpering against the other man, making him dart a quick glance to his right. Just a second, no more than a flash of his eyes in the misty sunlight. It was enough, and Bolitho leapt over the corpse, his hanger still red as he rallied his men around the forecastle. He could not even remember driving the blade into flesh and bone.

Somebody slipped in a pool of blood and crashed into his spine. He fell sprawling, only retaining his hanger because of the lanyard around his wrist.

As he struggled to rise he saw with amazement that there was a glint of water below him, and as he stared down he could see it was widening. The ships were drifting apart.

The French boarders had realized it too, and while some tried to climb back on to the overlapping bowsprit, others made to jump, only to fall headlong into the sea to join the bobbing litter of corpses and frantic swimmers.

A few threw up their hands in surrender, but when a marine was shot dead by an enemy marksman, they too were driven bodily over the side.

Bolitho felt the strength ebbing out of him, and he had to hold on to the bulwark for support. A few guns were still firing haphazardly through the smoke, but it was over. The *Argonaute*'s sails were coming about, and very slowly she began to stand away, her stern turning towards *Trojan*'s poop like the hinges of a gate.

Bolitho realized that he was on his back, looking at the sky, which seemed unnaturally clear and blue. So clean, too. Far away. His thoughts were drifting like the smoke and the two badly mauled ships.

A shadow loomed over him and he realized that Stockdale was kneeling beside him, his battered face lined with anxiety.

He tried to tell him he was all right. That he was resting.

A voice shouted, 'Take Mr Bolitho to the orlop at once!'

Then he did try to protest, but the effort was too much and with it came the darkness.

Bolitho opened his eyes and blinked rapidly to clear his vision. As the pain returned to his head he realized he was down on the orlop deck, a place of semi-darkness at the best of times. Now, with deckhead lanterns swinging to the ship's heavy motion, and others being carried this way and that, it was like looking at hell.

He was propped against *Trojan*'s great timbers, and through his shirt he could feel the hull working through a deep swell. As his eyes grew used to the gloom he saw that the whole area from the sick-bay to the hanging magazine was filled with men. Some lay quite still and were probably dead, others rocked back and forth, crouching like terrified animals as they nursed their private pain.

In the centre of the deck, directly below the largest number of lanterns, Thorndike and his assistants worked in grim silence on an unconscious seaman, while one of the surgeon's loblolly boys dashed away with a bucket from which protruded an amputated arm.

Bolitho reached up and felt his head. It was crusted in blood, and there was a lump like an egg. He felt the relief welling from his taut stomach muscles like a flood, stinging the back of his eyes so that he could feel tears running down his face. As another figure was carried to the table and stripped of his blackened clothing, Bolitho felt ashamed. He had been terrified of what would happen, but compared with the man who was whimpering and pleading with the surgeon he was unhurt.

'*Please*, sir!' The man was sobbing uncontrollably, so that even some of the other wounded forgot their pain and watched.

Thorndike turned from a locker, wiping his mouth. He looked like a stranger, and his hands, like his long apron, were red with blood.

'I am *sorry*.'

Thorndike nodded to his assistant, and Bolitho saw the injured man's shattered leg for the first time and realized it was one of his own gun crews who had been pinned under a cannon.

He was still pleading, 'Not me leg, sir!'

A bottle was thrust to his lips, and as he let his head fall back, choking and gasping on neat rum, a leather strap was put between his teeth.

Bolitho saw the glitter of the knife and turned his face away. It was wrong for a man to suffer like this, to scream and choke on his own vomit while his stricken messmates watched in silence.

Thorndike snapped, 'Too late. Take him on deck.' He reached out for his bottle again. 'Next!'

A seaman was kneeling beside Bolitho while some wood splinters were plucked from his back.

It was the masthead lookout, Buller.

He winced and then said, 'Reckon I'm a lucky one today, zur.' That was all he said, but it spoke volumes.

'You all right, sir?' It was Midshipman Couzens. 'I was sent by the first lieutenant.' He flinched as someone started to scream. 'Oh God, sir!'

Bolitho reached out. 'Help me up. Must get out of here.' He staggered to his feet and clung to the boy's shoulder like a drunken sailor. 'I'll not forget this, ever.'

Stockdale strode to meet them, ducking beneath the deckhead beams, his face creased with worry.

'Let me take him!'

The journey to the upper deck was in itself another part of the nightmare. The lower gundeck was still wreathed in trapped smoke, the red-painted sides only hiding some of the battle's agony.

He saw Lieutenant Dalyell with his two remaining midshipmen,

Lunn and Burslem, discussing with the gun captains what had to be done.

Dalyell saw Bolitho and hurried over, his open face filled with obvious pleasure.

'Thank God, Dick! I had heard you were done for!'

Bolitho tried to smile, but the pain in his skull stopped it.

'I heard much the same about you!'

'Aye. A gun exploded. I was stunned by the blast. But for the men nearby, I would be dead.' He shook his head. 'Poor Huss. He was a brave lad.'

Bolitho nodded slowly. They had begun with nine midshipmen. One promoted, one taken prisoner, and now one killed. The midshipmen's berth would be a sad place after this.

Dalyell looked away. 'So much for the admiral's strategy. A very high price for what we have done.'

Bolitho continued with his two helpers to the upper gundeck, and stood for several moments sucking in the air and looking up at the clear sky above the severed topgallant mast.

Men were being carried below, and Bolitho wondered how Thorndike could go on. Cutting, sawing and stitching. He shuddered violently. Others were being dragged beneath the gangways, limp and without identity, to await the sailmaker and his mates, who would sew them up in their hammocks for the last journey. How far had Bunce said it was? One thousand five hundred fathoms hereabouts. A long, dark passage. Perhaps there was peace there.

He shook himself and winced at the stabbing pain. He was getting hazy again. It had to stop.

Cairns said, 'Good to see you, Dick.' He looked tired and drained. 'I could do with some help,' he hesitated, 'if you feel up to it?'

Bolitho nodded, moved that this man who carried so much had found time to ask about him and how he was faring on the orlop.

'It will be good for me.'

He made himself look along the torn and splintered deck where he had been such a short while ago. Upended guns, great coils of fallen cordage and ripped canvas. Men picking their way amongst it like survivors from a shipwreck. How could any man have lived through it? To see such chaos made it seem impossible.

He asked, 'How is James?'

Cairns's eyes were bleak. 'The *fourth lieutenant* is alive, I believe.' He patted Bolitho's arm. 'I must be off. You remain here and assist the boatswain.'

Bolitho crossed to the first division of eighteen-pounders, where he had been for most of the battle. He could see the *Argonaute*, stern on and a good three miles downwind. Even if they could complete some temporary repairs in time, they would not catch the Frenchman now.

Stockdale spoke for both of them. 'Anyways, we beat 'em off. Short-handed though we was, sir, we gave as good as we got.'

Couzens said huskily, 'But the brig got away.'

The sailing master towered above the quarterdeck rail and boomed, 'Come now, Mr Bolitho, this will not do! I have a ship to steer, a course to lay! To do that I need sails and more halliards than I can see at present!' His black brows descended over his deepset eyes and he added, 'You did well today. I saw.' He nodded firmly, as if he had said far too much.

For the rest of the day the ship's company went about the work of putting *Trojan* to rights as best they could. The dead were buried and the wounded made as comfortable as possible. Samuel Pinhorn, the sailmaker, had kept plenty of spare canvas on deck, knowing that more would die before reaching port.

It was amazing that men could work after what they had been through. Perhaps it was work which saved them, for no ship can sail without care and constant attention.

A jury-mast was hoisted to replace the topgallant, and as the seamen bustled far above the deck the cordage dangled down on either side like weed.

Hammers and saws, tar and paint, needles and twine.

The only thing which happened to make them stop, to stare abeam and remember, was the sudden appearance of the schooner from the anchorage at Isla San Bernardo. *Spite* had been abandoned as a hopeless wreck, then set alight to make sure no pirate or privateer would lay hands on her.

In a short and savage boat action, Cunningham attacked and took the schooner. The one reward of the whole operation.

But Bolitho was certain of one thing. The prize, no matter what secrets she disclosed, would not remove the ache from Cunningham's heart as he had ordered his men to abandon his own command.

At sunset, Cairns ordered a halt. A double ration of spirits was issued to all hands, and after shortening sail for the night *Trojan* was content to reflect and lick her wounds.

Bolitho received a summons to the great cabin without curiosity. Like most of the company, he was drained, and too shocked to care.

But as he made his way aft, ducking his head beneath the poop, he heard Pears's voice, clearly audible through two sets of screen doors.

'I know your father, otherwise I would have you stripped of your appointment *at this very moment!*'

Bolitho hesitated outside the door, feeling the sentry's eyes watching him.

It was Quinn of course. Poor, broken Quinn. He could still see him, standing on the gundeck amongst the litter of dead and dying. Stricken, unable to think or move.

The sentry looked at him. 'Sir?'

Bolitho nodded wearily, and the marine banged his musket on the deck and called, 'Second lieutenant, *sir!*'

The door opened and Teakle, the clerk, ushered Bolitho inside. He had a bandage on his wrist and looked very shaken. Bolitho wondered why he had never thought of a clerk being in as much danger as any of them.

Quinn came from the cabin, his face as white as a sheet. He saw Bolitho and looked as if he were about to speak. Then with a gasp he blundered past him into the shadows.

Pears strode to meet Bolitho. 'Ah, not too knocked about, eh?' He was restless, off balance.

Bolitho replied, 'I was fortunate, sir.'

'Indeed you were.'

Pears looked round as Coutts came from the adjoining cabin.

The admiral said, 'I will be leaving at daylight and transferring to the prize, Bolitho. I intend to head for Antigua and take passage from there in a courier brig, or one of the frigates.'

Bolitho looked at him, trying to guess where it was leading. He could feel the tension between the two men, see the bitterness in Pears's eyes. Like physical pain.

Coutts added calmly, '*Trojan* will follow, of course. Full repairs can be carried out there before she returns to the squadron. I will ensure that the people at Antigua give full attention to it, and to obtaining replacements for –'

Pears interrupted bluntly. 'For all the poor devils who died today!'

Coutts flushed, but turned to Bolitho again.

'I have watched you. You are the right stuff, with the ability and the steel to lead men.'

Bolitho glanced at Pears's grim features and was shocked to see his expression. Like a man under sentence.

'Thank you, sir.'

'Therefore . . .' the word hung in the damp air, 'I am offering you a new appointment as soon as you reach Antigua. With me.'

Bolitho stared, realizing what it would do to Pears. With Coutts back in Antigua, or probably in New York before *Trojan* reached harbour, Pears would have nobody to speak for him but Cairns. A scapegoat. Someone to use to cover Coutts's costly exercise.

He was surprised that he could answer without hesitation. It was all he wanted, the one opportunity to transfer to another ship, smaller, faster, like *Vanquisher* or one of the other frigates. With Coutts's patronage it would be the best chance he would ever get.

'I thank you, sir.' He looked at Pears. 'But my appointment is under Captain Pears. I would wish it to remain so.'

Coutts regarded him curiously. 'What an odd fellow you are, Bolitho. Your sentimentality will do for you one day.' He nodded, curt, final. 'Good evening.'

In a daze Bolitho went down a ladder and found himself in the wardroom, remarkably untouched by the battle.

Cairns followed him a few moments later and took his arm, beckoning to the wardroom servant as he did so.

'Mackenzie, you rogue! Some good brandy for this officer!'

D'Esterre appeared with his lieutenant and asked, 'What is happening?'

Cairns sat down opposite Bolitho and watched him intently.

'It *has* happened, gentlemen. I have just witnessed a misguided but *honest* man doing something which was right.'

Bolitho flushed. 'I – I didn't know . . .'

Cairns took a bottle from Mackenzie and smiled sadly.

'I was outside. Peering through a crack like a schoolboy.' He became suddenly serious. 'That was a fine thing you did just now. He'll never thank you for it, in as many words.' Cairns raised his glass. 'But I know him better than most. You gave him something to make up for what Coutts did to his ship!'

Bolitho thought of the schooner steering somewhere under *Trojan*'s lee. Tomorrow she would leave them and take with her his chance of promotion.

He got another surprise. He no longer cared.

15

Another Chance

Bolitho stood in the shadow of the mainmast's massive trunk and watched the busy activity around the ship. It was October, and for two months *Trojan* had been here in English Harbour, Antigua, head-quarters of the Caribbean squadrons. There were plenty of ships needing repairs and overhaul, but mostly because of the wear and tear of storms or old age. *Trojan*'s arrival had aroused plenty of excitement and curiosity as Captain Pears had brought her to rest, with the ensign at half-mast for her many dead.

Now, looking around the taut rigging and shrouds, the neatly furled sails and skilfully repaired decks, it was hard to picture the battle which had raged here.

He shaded his eyes to look at the shore. Scattered white buildings, the familiar landfall of Monk's Hill. A busy procession of boats, yard hoys, water lighters and the inevitable traders offering doubtful wares to the inexperienced and the foolish.

There had been a lot of changes, not only to the ship herself. New faces from other vessels from England, from ports up and down the Caribbean. All to be tested and worked into the rest of the company.

A Lieutenant John Pointer had arrived aboard, and because of his seniority had been made fourth lieutenant, as Bolitho had once been. A cheeerful young man with a round Yorkshire dialect, he seemed competent and willing to learn.

Young Midshipman Libby, stripped of his acting rank, had gone to the flagship on one fine morning to face his examination for lieutenant. He had passed with honour, although he was the only one to show surprise at the verdict. Now he had gone, appointed to another two-decker without delay. But his parting had been a sad occasion, both for him and the other midshipmen. There were two more of those as well. Fresh from England, and in Bunce's view, 'Less than useless!'

Of Coutts they had heard nothing, other than he had returned to New York. Promotion or disgrace seemed unimportant in the face of the latest news which even now seemed impossible to grasp.

In America, General Burgoyne, who had been operating with some success from Canada in the earlier stages of the revolution, had been directed to take control of the Hudson River. He had advanced with his usual determination with some seven thousand troops, expecting to be reinforced by the New York regiments. Someone had decided that there were insufficient soldiers in New York and barely enough to defend the city.

General Burgoyne had waited in vain, and this month had surrendered with all his men at Saratoga.

There had been news of greater activity by French privateers, encouraged, and with good cause, by the military defeat.

Trojan would soon be ready to rejoin the fight, but Bolitho could see no way of retaining a grasp of a rebellious colony even if Britain commanded the sea-lanes. And with more French involvement, that was no certainty either.

Bolitho moved restlessly to the nettings to watch another trading boat passing *Trojan*'s glittering reflection. It was hot, but after the earlier months, and the torrential tropical downpours, it seemed almost cool.

He glanced aft, at the flag which hung so limp and still. It would be even hotter in the great cabin.

He tried to see Quinn as a stranger, someone he had just met. But he kept recalling him as the most junior lieutenant, when he had just come aboard. Eighteen years old and straight from the midshipmen's berth, beginning as Libby was now for himself. Then again, gasping in agony from the great slash across his chest. After all his quiet confidence, his determination to be a sea-officer when his wealthy father wished otherwise.

These last weeks must have been hell for him. He had been released from his duties, and even if he retained his appointment would now be junior to the new officer, Pointer.

Because of the activity within the local squadrons, and the general air of expectancy of a French intervention in strength, Quinn's troubles had taken a low position in priorities.

Now, in this October of 1777, he was being examined by a board of inquiry in Pears's cabin. Just one short step from a court martial.

Bolitho looked at the other ships, so still in the sheltered harbour, each paired above her image in the water, awnings spread, ports open to catch the slightest breeze. Very soon these vessels and more beside would endure what *Trojan* had suffered under *Argonaute*'s guns. They would not be fighting brave but untrained rebels, but the flower of France. Discipline would be tightened, failure not tolerated. It made Quinn's chances seem very slim.

He turned as Lieutenant Arthur Frowd, officer of the watch, crossed the deck to join him. Like Libby, he had gained his coveted promotion, and now awaited an appointment to a more suitable ship. The most junior lieutenant, he was still the oldest in years. In his bright new uniform, with his hair neatly tied to the nape of his neck, he looked as good as any captain, Bolitho thought admiringly.

Frowd said uneasily, 'What d'you reckon about him?' He did not even mention Quinn by name. Like a lot of other people he was probably afraid of being connected with him in any way.

'I'm not certain.'

Bolitho fidgeted with his sword hilt, wondering why it was taking so long. Cairns had gone aft, as had D'Esterre and Bunce. It was a hateful business, like seeing the court martial Jack on a man-of-war, the ritualistic procession of boats for a flogging around the fleet, or a hanging.

He said, '*I* was afraid. So it must have been a lot worse for him. But —'

Frowd said vehemently, '*But*, aye, sir, that small word makes a world of difference. Any common seaman would have been run up to the mainyard by now!'

Bolitho said nothing and waited for Frowd to walk away to speak with the guard-boat alongside. Frowd did not understand. How could he? To reach a lieutenant's rank was hard enough for any youth. By way of the lower deck it was much, much harder. And Frowd had done it with his own sweat and little education. He would see Quinn's failure as a betrayal rather than a weakness.

Sergeant Shears marched across the quarterdeck and touched his hat smartly.

Bolitho looked at him. 'Me?'

'Yessir.' Shears glanced quickly at the men on watch, the sideboys and the sentry. 'Not doin' very well, sir.' He dropped his voice to a whisper. 'My captain give 'is evidence, and one of the board says, all 'aughty-like, "Wot does a marine know about sea officers!"' Shears sounded outraged. 'Never 'eard the like, sir!'

Bolitho walked quickly aft, gripping his sword tightly to prepare himself.

Pears' day cabin had been cleared, the furniture replaced by a bare table at which were seated three captains.

There were others present too, seated on chairs to either side, mostly strangers to Bolitho, but he saw the earlier witnesses, Cairns, D'Esterre, and alone, with his hands folded in his lap, Captain Pears.

The senior captain looked at him coolly. 'Mr Bolitho?'

Bolitho tucked his hat under his arm and said, 'Aye, sir. Second lieutenant.'

The captain to the right, a sharp-faced man with very thin lips, asked, 'Were you present on deck when the events which led to this investigation took place?'

Bolitho saw the clerk's pen poised above his pile of papers. Then for the first time he looked at Quinn.

He was standing very stiffly by the door of the dining cabin. He looked as if he was finding it hard to breathe.

'I was, sir.' How absurd, he thought. They all knew exactly where everyone was. Probably right down to the ship's cook. 'I was in charge of the upper gundeck when we engaged the enemy to starboard.'

The president of the court, a captain Bolitho remembered seeing in New York, said dryly, 'Forget the formality, if you can. You are not on trial here.' He glanced at the captain with the thin lips. 'It would do well to remember that.' His level gaze returned to Bolitho. 'What did you see?'

Bolitho could feel those behind him, watching and waiting. If only he knew what had been said already, especially by the captain.

He cleared his throat. 'We'd not been expecting to fight, sir. But the *Argonaute* had dismasted *Spite* without any challenge or warning. We had no option.'

'We?' The question was mild.

Bolitho flushed and felt clumsy under the three pairs of eyes. 'I heard the admiral express the view that we should fight if need be, sir.'

'Ah.' A small smile. 'Continue.'

'It was a bloody battle, sir, and we were sorely short of good hands even before it began.' He sensed the scorn in the thin-lipped captain's eyes and added quietly, 'That was not meant as an excuse, sir. Had you seen the way our people fought and died that day, you would have known my meaning.'

He could sense the silence, like the terrible calm before a hurricane. But he could not stop now. What did they know about it? They had probably never had to fight with such inexperienced officers and so few seasoned hands. He thought of the man on the surgeon's table pleading for his leg, the marine who had been the first to die, falling from the top to drift in the sea alone. There were so many of them. Too many.

He said, 'The Frenchman came up to us and drove hard alongside. They boarded, or tried to . . .' He faltered, seeing the French lieutenant falling between the grinding hulls, his own sword red with blood. 'But we fought them off.' He turned and looked directly at Quinn's stricken face. 'Mr Quinn was assisting me up to that moment, and stood under the enemy's fire until action was broken off.'

The president added, 'Then *you* were taken below. Correct?'

He looked at Bolitho's tense features and asked, 'How old are you?'

'Twenty-one, sir. This month.' He thought he heard someone snigger behind him.

'And you entered the Navy at the age of twelve, I understand. As did most of us. In addition, you come from a distinguished seafaring family.' His voice hardened suddenly. 'In your *experience* as a King's officer, Mr Bolitho, did you at any time during this series of unfortunate events consider that Mr Quinn's behaviour was lacking in skill or courage?'

Bolitho replied quietly, 'In my opinion, sir –' He got no further.

The president persisted, 'In your *experience*.'

Bolitho felt desperate, trapped. 'I do not know how to answer, sir.'

He expected to be rebuked, even dismissed from the court, but the president merely asked, 'He was your friend, is that it?'

Bolitho looked across at Quinn, suddenly hating the three captains, the gaping spectators, everything.

He said firmly, 'He *is* my friend, sir.' He heard the murmur of surprise and expectancy but added, 'Maybe he was afraid, but so was I, as were many more. To deny it would be foolish.'

Before he turned back to the table he saw Quinn lift his chin with pathetic defiance.

Bolitho said, 'His record has been a good one. And I have had him with me on several difficult missions. He has been badly wounded and –'

The thin-lipped captain leaned over to look at his companions. 'I think we have heard enough. This witness has little to add.' He glanced at Bolitho. 'I understand that you declined a new appointment which Rear-Admiral Coutts was prepared to offer? Tell me, was that lack of ambition on your part?'

The president frowned, and then turned as feet moved heavily on the deck.

Without looking, Bolitho knew it was Pears.

The president asked, 'You wished to say something, Captain Pears?'

The familiar harsh voice was remarkably calm. 'The last question. I feel I should answer. It was not lack of ambition, sir. In my family we call it *loyalty*, dammit!'

The president held up his hand to still the sudden excitement. 'Quite so.' He looked sadly at Bolitho. 'However, I am afraid that in the case of Lieutenant Quinn loyalty is not enough.' He stood up, and throughout the cabin the spectators and witnesses lurched to their feet. 'The inquiry is adjourned.'

Outside, on the sunlit quarterdeck, Bolitho waited for the visitors to leave.

Dalyell and the new lieutenant, Pointer, were with him when Quinn appeared on deck.

He crossed over to him and murmured, 'Thank you for what you said, Dick.'

Bolitho shrugged. 'It didn't seem to help much.'

Dalyell said quietly, 'You have more courage than I, Dick. That cold-eyed captain scared hell out of me, just looking at him!'

Quinn said, 'Anyway, the president was right. I could not move. It was like being dead, unable to help.'

He saw Cairns approaching and added quickly, 'I shall go to my cabin.'

The first lieutenant leaned over the rail and watched the boats alongside.

Then he said, 'I hope we can get back to sea soon.'

The others moved away and Bolitho asked, 'Did the captain kill Quinn's chances, Neil?'

Cairns eyed him thoughtfully. 'No. I did. I witnessed it, but was less involved than you. Suppose you had been marked down by one of the Frenchman's sharpshooters, or broken by chain-shot. Do you think Quinn could have held the fo'c'sle and driven off the boarders?' He smiled gravely and gripped Bolitho's arm. 'I'll not ask you to betray a friendship. But you know, as well as I, that we would have been made to strike to the *Argonaute* if Quinn had been left in charge forrard.' He looked along the deck, probably remembering it, as Bolitho was. He said, 'There are more lives at stake than the honour of one man.'

Bolitho felt sick. Knowing Cairns was right, but feeling only pity for Quinn.

'What will they decide?'

Cairns replied, 'The admiral who commands here will be aware of this. It has taken long enough to come to light. He will also know of Quinn's father, his power in the City.'

Bolitho could feel the man's bitterness as he added, 'He'll not hang.'

After lunch the court was recalled, and Cairns was proved correct.

The court of inquiry had decided that Lieutenant James Quinn had been rendered unfit by cause of injury in the King's service to continue with active duty. Upon confirmation from the commander-in-chief, he would be sent ashore to await passage home to England. After that he would be discharged from the Navy.

Nobody outside would know of his disgrace. Except the one man who really cared, and Bolitho doubted very much if Quinn could carry that final burden for long.

Two days later, with Quinn's fate still unconfirmed, *Trojan* weighed, and put to sea.

It would, it appeared, take a little longer.

Two and a half days after leaving English Harbour *Trojan* was steering due west, under reefed topsails and forecourse in a stiff following wind. It was a good opportunity to exercise the old and new hands together in sail drill, as with spray bursting over the poop and quarterdeck the two-decker pointed her jib at the misty horizon.

Apart from a few tiny islands far away on the starboard bow, the sea was empty. An endless deep blue desert, with long cruising rollers and white crests to display the power of the wind.

Bolitho waited on the larboard gangway, the taste of strong coffee warming his stomach, while he prepared to take over the afternoon watch in fifteen minutes' time. With so many new faces and names to grapple with, the constant efforts to discover the skilled hands from the clumsy ones, all of whom seemed to have five thumbs on each fist, Bolitho had been kept very busy. But he could sense the atmosphere in the ship all the same. Confused acceptance by the lower deck and an air of bitterness from aft.

Trojan was ordered to Jamaica, her lower decks crammed with a contingent of marines which the admiral was sending to enforce law and order at the governor's urgent request. Bad weather had wrecked many of Jamaica's local trading vessels, and to make matters worse there had been news of another slave uprising on two of the larger plantations. Rebellion seemed to be in the air everywhere. If Britain was to hold on to her Caribbean possessions she must act now and not wait for the French and possibly the Spanish to blockade and occupy some of the many islands there.

But Bolitho guessed that Pears saw his role through different eyes. While the fleet was preparing for the inevitable spread of war, when every ship of the line would be desperately needed, he was being ordered to Jamaica. His *Trojan* had taken on the task of transport and little more.

Even the admiral's explanation, that *Trojan* needed no escort, and was therefore releasing other vessels for work elsewhere, had had no effect. Daily Pears walked his quarterdeck, still watchful for his ship and the routine which ran her, but alone and quite removed from everyone else.

It could not be helping him now, Bolitho thought, to realize that hidden just below the horizon was the south-eastern shore of Puerto Rico, so near to where Coutts had committed all of them to a hopeless battle. In some ways it would have been better if the *Argonaute* had not broken off the fight. At least there would be a total victory to hold on to. Maybe the French had used their captain as a scapegoat, too?

But, as Cairns had said, it was better to be at sea and be kept busy than to swing at anchor, moping over what might have happened.

He looked down at the gundeck, at the milling scarlet uniforms and piled weapons as D'Esterre and the captain in charge of the marine contingent inspected and checked everything for the hundredth time.

'Deck there!'

Bolitho looked up, the sun searing his face like sand.

'Sail, sir! On the starboard bow!'

Dalyell had the watch, and it was at moments such as this that his inexperience showed through.

'*What? Where?*' He snatched a telescope from Midshipman Pullen and rushed to the starboard shrouds.

The lookout's voice was drifting with the wind. 'Small sail, sir! Fisherman, mebbee!'

Sambell, who was master's mate of the watch, remarked sourly, 'Lucky Admiral Coutts ain't here. He'd have us chasin' the bugger!'

Dalyell glared at him. 'Get aloft, Mr Sambell. Tell me what you see.' He saw Bolitho and smiled awkwardly. 'So long without sighting anything, I was off guard.'

'So it would appear, sir.' Pears strode on to the quarterdeck, his shoes squeaking on the seams. He glanced at the set of the sails and then moved to the compass. 'Hmm.'

Dalyell peered up at the master's mate, who seemed to be taking an age to make the long climb.

Pears walked to the rail and watched the marines. 'Fisherman. Maybe so. There are plenty of small islets there. Good places for water and firewood. Not too dangerous if you keep one eye open.'

He frowned as Sambell yelled, 'She's sheered off! Makin' for one of the islands!'

Dalyell licked his lips and watched the captain. 'Sighted us, d'you suppose, sir?'

Pears shrugged. 'Unlikely. Our masthead has a far greater vision than some low-lying hull.'

He rubbed his chin, and Bolitho thought he saw a sudden gleam in his eyes.

Then Pears said harshly, 'Hands to the braces, Mr Dalyell. We will alter course three points. Steer nor'-west by north.' He banged his big hands together. 'Well, *jump* to it, sir! 'Pon my soul, you'll have to do better than this!'

The shrill of calls and the immediate rush of seamen brought Cairns on deck, his eyes everywhere as he looked for a ship.

Pears said, 'Vessel on starboard bow, Mr Cairns. Could be a fisherman, but unlikely. They usually keep in company in these hard times.'

'Another privateer, sir?'

Cairns was speaking very carefully, and Bolitho guessed he had taken much from Pears's tongue in the past few weeks.

'Possibly.'

Pears beckoned to D'Esterre, who was being pushed and jostled by the extra marines as they sought to avoid the seamen at the braces and halliards.

'Captain D'Esterre!' Pears peered aloft as the yards squeaked round

and the deck heeled over to the change of course. 'How d'you propose
to land your men at Jamaica if there has been a further uprising?'

D'Esterre replied, 'In boats, sir. Land by sections above the port and
take the high ground before seeking the local commander.'

Pears almost smiled. 'I agree.' He pointed at the boat-tier. 'We will
exercise landing the contingent at dusk.' He ignored D'Esterre's
astonished stare. 'On one of those islands yonder.'

Bolitho heard him say to Cairns, 'If there is some damned pirate
there, we will swamp him with marines. Anyway, it will be good
practice for them. If *Trojan* is to act as a troop transport, then she will
do it well. No, better than well.'

Cairns smiled, grateful to see a return of Pears's old enthusiasm. 'Aye,
sir.'

The helmsman shouted, 'Nor'-west be north, zur!'

'Steady as you go, man.' Cairns waited impatiently for Bolitho's
watch to relieve Dalyell and then said, 'I wish to God we could catch one
of them again. Just to show Rear-Admiral bloody Coutts a thing or
two!'

Pears heard him and murmured, 'Now, now, Mr Cairns. That will
do.' But that was all he said.

Bolitho watched his men settling down to their duties while the rest
went below to eat. He still believed that what Coutts had tried to do had
been right. But his reasons were less certain.

Why was Pears taking the trouble to land marines for so trivial a
sighting? Hurt pride, or did he expect to face an eventual court martial
at Coutts's instigation over the *Argonaute* encounter?

He heard Pears say to Bunce, 'I intend to stand off as soon as we have
landed the marines. I know these waters very well. I've an idea or two of
my own.'

Bunce gave a rough chuckle. 'That you do know 'em, Cap'n. I think it
may be God's will that we are here today.'

Pears grimaced. 'Most probably, Mr Bunce. We shall have to see.' He
turned away. 'And pray.'

Bolitho looked at Cairns. 'What does he mean?'

Cairns shrugged. 'He certainly knows this part of the world, as much
as the Sage, I would think. I have studied the chart, but apart from reefs
and currents, I see no cause for excitement.'

They both faced Pears as he strode across the quarterdeck.

He said, 'I am going aft to take lunch. This afternoon we will muster
all hands and prepare the boats. Swivels in the bows of cutters and
launches. Only hand-picked men will go.' He glanced at Bolitho. 'You
can supervise the landing arrangements, and will take Mr Frowd as
your second. Captain D'Esterre will command the land force.' He
nodded and strode aft, hands behind his back.

Cairns said softly, 'I'm glad for him. But I'm not so sure he is acting wisely.'

Bunce muttered, 'My mother used to 'ave a saying, zur, about too wise 'eads on too young shoulders. Not good for 'em, she'd say.' He went to the chart room chuckling to himself.

Cairns shook his head. 'Didn't know the old bugger ever *had* a mother!'

Trojan closed to within a mile of the nearest island and then lay hove to while the business of lowering boats and filling them with marines was begun.

Most of the marines had been in Antigua for a long time and had only heard about the war in America from visiting ships. Although few of them knew why they were being sent across to the island, and those who did regarded it as something of a joke, they carried out their part willingly and in good humour.

The cheerful atmosphere made Sergeant Shears exclaim angrily, 'My Gawd, sir, you'd think it was a bloody 'oliday, an' no mistake!'

The sea was still very choppy and lively, and it took more time than calculated to get the boats fully loaded and headed for the shore. It was growing dark, and the sunset painted the wave crests amber and dull gold.

Bolitho stood in the sternsheets of the leading cutter, one hand on Stockdale's shoulder as he controlled the tiller-bar. It was difficult to see the cove where they were supposed to land, although it had looked clear enough on the chart. The grim truth was that nobody really knew the exact position of every reef and sandbar. Already they had seen several jagged rocks, shining in the strange light and bringing a few anxious remarks from the crowded marines. In their heavy boots and hung about with weapons and pouches, they would go to the bottom before anything else if the boats were capsized.

D'Esterre was saying, 'Fact is, Dick, we may have been sighted already. They'll not stop to fight all these marines, but we'll not find them either!'

Another seething rock passed down the starboard oar blades, and Bolitho signalled with a white flag to the boat astern, and so on down the line. *Trojan* was only a blurred shadow now, and she had been making more sail even as the boats had pulled clear. She would use the prevailing wind to ride in the island's lee for some sign of results.

'Land ahead, sir!'

That was Buller in the bows. A good hand, as he had shown, his wood splinters apparently forgotten. He was lucky to be able to forget so easily, Bolitho thought.

Like darkly hooded monks some tall rocks rose on either side of the boat, while directly across the bows and the loaded swivel gun lay a bright strip of sand.

'Easy all! Boat yer oars!'

Seamen were already leaping and splashing into the surf on either beam to steady the boat as she drove ashore.

D'Esterre was out, waist-deep in water and calling his sergeant to lead the first pickets to the higher ground.

It was a tiny island, no more than a mile long. Most of the others were even smaller. But there were rock pools for gathering fresh water and shellfish, and wood to burn for any small and self-sufficient vessel.

Bolitho waded ashore, thinking suddenly of Quinn. He had heard him asking, pleading with Cairns to be allowed to come with the landing party.

Cairns had been coldly formal, almost brutal. 'We want experienced, picked men, Mr Quinn.' The last part had been like a slap in the face. 'Reliable, too.'

Midshipman Couzens was arriving with the next cutter, and the *Trojan*'s red-painted barge was following her. Bolitho smiled tightly. Frowd and the other marine captain were in her. Being held back in case the first boats had fallen under a deluge of shot and fire.

'Take your positions! Boat-handling parties stand fast!'

Stockdale strode from the shallows, his cutlass across one shoulder like a broadsword.

From tumbling confusion and whispered threats from the sergeants and corporals, the marines formed into neat little sections. At a further command they moved up the slope, boots squelching on sand and then on rough, sun-hardened earth.

An hour later it was dark and the air was heavy with damp smells, of rotten vegetation and seabird droppings.

While the marine skirmishers hurried away on either side, Bolitho and D'Esterre stood on a narrow ridge-backed hill, the sea ahead and behind them, invisible but for an occasional gleam of surf.

It seemed deserted. Dead. The unknown vessel had gone to another island, or had sailed north-west towards the Bahamas. If Sambell had not seen her for himself, Bolitho might have thought the lookout mistaken by a trick of light and haze.

'This is no Fort Exeter, Dick.' D'Esterre was leaning on his sword, his head cocked to listen to the hiss of wind through fronds and bushes.

'I wish we had those Canadian scouts with us.' Bolitho saw some seamen lying on their backs, staring at the sky. They were quite content to leave it to others. They merely had to obey. To die if need be.

They heard a nervous challenge and then Shears strode up the hill towards them. He carried a clump of grass or creeper to cover his uniform, which was why the sentry had been so startled. It reminded Bolitho of Major Paget's little cape.

'Well?' D'Esterre leaned forward.

Shears sucked in gulps of air. 'She's there, right enough, sir. Anchored close in. Small vessel, yawl by the looks of 'er.'

D'Esterre asked, 'Any signs of life?'

'There's a watch on deck, an' no lights, sir. Up to no good, if you ask me.' He saw D'Esterre's smile and added firmly, 'One of the marines from Antigua says they'd have lights lit and lines down right now, sir. There's a special sort of fish they goes after. No *real* fisherman would lie an' sleep!'

D'Esterre nodded. 'That was well said, Sergeant Shears. I'll see that the man has a guinea when we get back aboard. And you, too. You must have something about you to inspire an unknown marine to offer his confidences!' He became crisp and formal. 'Fetch Mr Frowd. We will decide what to do. Pass the word to watch out for anyone coming ashore from the yawl.'

Shears said cheerfully, 'They got no boats in the water, sir.'

'Well, watch anyway.'

As the sergeant hurried away D'Esterre said, 'Well, Dick, are you thinking as I am? A surprise attack on them?'

'Aye.' He tried to picture the anchored vessel. 'The sight of all your marines should do it. But two armed cutters would be safer. In case they are unimpressed by your little army.'

'I agree. You and Mr Frowd take the cutters. I'll keep the midshipman with me and send him with a message if things go wrong. So work your way round. No risks, mind. Not for a damned yawl!'

Bolitho waited for Frowd to join him, thinking back to Pears's casual reference to these small islands. It had all been clear to him. If the vessel was an enemy, or up to no good, she would run at the first hint of trouble. Towards the land and the marines, or more likely use the prevailing wind and put to sea again or hide amongst the islands. Either way she would find *Trojan* lying there, using the offshore current and wind. Waiting like a great beast to overwhelm her in a matter of minutes.

At sea, in open waters, there was hardly a vessel afloat which could not outsail the slow-moving *Trojan*. But in confined space, where one false turn of the helm could mean a grounding at best, *Trojan*'s massive artillery would make escape impossible.

Frowd remarked dourly, 'Boat action then.'

Bolitho watched him curiously. Frowd could probably think of nothing but his next appointment, getting away from the ship where so many had been his equals and were now expected to knuckle their foreheads to him.

'Yes. Pick your men, and let's be about it.'

He noticed the sharpness in his own voice, too. Why was that? Did he see Frowd's attitude as a challenge, as Rowhurst had once vied with Quinn?

With muffled oars the two cutters pulled away from the other moored boats and turned east towards the far end of the island, the wind making each stroke of the oars harder and more tiring.

But Bolitho knew his men by now. They would rally when the time came. They had done it before. It was strange to be pushing through the choppy water without doubts of these silent, straining men. He hoped they held some trust in him also.

It would be funny if, after all this stealth, they found only terrified traders or fishermen rising to the marines' rough awakening. It would not seem so amusing when they had to tell the captain about it.

'Somebody must be comin', sir!'

Bolitho scrambled through the cutter to join the lookout in the bows. He could see the two seamen he had put ashore, framed against the sky, one moving his arm above his head very slowly.

How loud everything sounded. The water sluicing around the two moored boats, the distant boom of surf and the hissing roar as it receded from some hidden beach.

They had reached this tiny inlet several hours ago and had made fast to get as much rest as possible. Most of the seamen appeared to have no trouble. They could sleep anywhere, indifferent to the rocking boats, the spray which occasionally spattered across their already damp clothing.

Frowd, in the boat alongside, said, 'It's gone wrong, I expect.'

Bolitho waited, realizing that the men on the shore were easier to see, more sharply defined against the dull sky. It would be dawn soon.

Stockdale said feelingly, 'It's Mr Couzens, not the enemy!'

Couzens came slithering down the slope and then waded and floundered towards the cutters.

He saw Bolitho and gasped, 'Captain D'Esterre says to start the attack in half an hour.'

He sounded so relieved that Bolitho guessed he had got lost on his way here.

'Very well.' *Attack*. That sounded definite enough. 'What is the signal?'

Stockdale hoisted the midshipman unceremoniously over the gunwale.

'One pistol shot, sir.' Couzens sank down on a thwart, his legs dripping on the bottom boards.

'Good. Recall those men.' Bolitho made his way aft again and held his watch against a shaded horn lantern. There was not much time. 'Rouse the hands. Make ready to cast off.'

Men stirred and coughed, groping around to get their bearings.

From the set of the current Bolitho could picture how the yawl would be swinging to her cable. He thought suddenly of Sparke, deciding on his attack. Pushing sentiment aside after the bloody fighting was over.

'Load your pistols. Take your time.'

If he hurried them, or shared his own anxiety over the brightening sky, somebody was bound to get muddled and loose off a ball. It only took one.

Stockdale swayed through the boat and then returned. 'All done, sir.'

'Mr Frowd?'

The lieutenant waved to him. 'Ready, sir!'

In spite of his tense nerves Bolitho felt he wanted to smile. *Sir*. Frowd would never call him by his first name in a hundred years.

'Out oars.' He raised his arm. '*Easy*, lads. Like field mice!'

Stockdale sounded approving. 'Shove off forrard! Give way larboard!'

Very slowly, with one set of oars pulling the boat round like a crab, they moved away from their tiny haven.

Frowd was following, and Bolitho saw the bowman training the swivel from side to side as if to sniff the way.

Couzens whispered, 'There's the corner, sir!'

Bolitho watched the jutting spur of rock, Couzens's 'corner'. Once round it, they would be on exposed water and visible to any vigilant sentry.

It was brightening so rapidly that he could see a touch of green on the land, the glitter of spray over some fallen stones. Weapons too, and in the bows, leaning forward like a figurehead, the topman, Buller.

'Christ, there she be, sir!'

Bolitho saw the swaying mainmast and the smaller one right aft on the anchored yawl, stark against the sky, even though the hull was still in shadow.

A yawl, or dandy, as they were usually termed, would be just the thing for using amongst the islands.

He heard the gurgle of water around the stem, and from astern the regular, muffled beat of Frowd's oars.

Stockdale eased the tiller over, allowing the cutter to move away from the island to lay the yawl between him and D'Esterre's marines.

Soon now. It had to be. Bolitho held his breath, drawing his hanger carefully, although he knew from past experience that a tired look-out would hear little but his own shipboard noises. An anchored vessel was always alive with sound and movement.

But there was a long way to go yet. He said, 'Roundly, lads! Put your backs into it!'

The cutter was moving swiftly and firmly towards the yawl's larboard bow. Bolitho saw the anchor cable beneath the pole-like bowsprit, the casual way the sails were furled and brailed up.

The crack of a pistol shot was like a twelve-pounder on the morning air, and as somebody gave a startled cry aboard the yawl, an undulating line of heads, closely linked with muskets and fixed bayonets, appeared along the top of the island, then touches of scarlet as the marines continued to march in a long, single rank up and then down towards the water.

'*Pull!* All you've got!' Bolitho leaned forward as if to add weight to the fast-moving cutter.

Figures had appeared on the yawl's deck, and a solitary shot lit up the mainmast like a flare.

Across the water they all heard D'Esterre shouting for the yawl to surrender, and more confused cries, followed by the sound of cordage being hauled madly through blocks.

Bolitho momentarily forgot his own part in it, as with unhurried precision the line of shadowy marines halted and then fired a volley across the vessel's deck.

There was no movement aboard after that, and Bolitho shouted, 'Stand by to board! Grapnel ready there!' From a corner of his eye his saw Frowd's boat surging past, a grapnel already streaking towards the yawl's bulwark, while the selected men charged up with drawn cutlasses.

Yelling and cheering, the seamen clambered on either side of the bowsprit, seeing the crew crowding together near the mainmast, too shocked by what had happened to move, let alone resist. A few muskets had been thrown down on the deck, and Bolitho ran aft with Stockdale to ensure that no more men were hiding below and even now attempting to scuttle their vessel.

Not a man lost, and across the water he saw the marines waving their hats and cheering.

Frowd snapped, 'Privateers, right enough!' He dragged a man from the crowd. He had thrown his weapons away, but was so loaded with pouches of shot and cartridges that he looked like a pirate.

Bolitho sheathed his hanger. 'Well done, lads. I'll send word across to the marines and –'

It was Couzens who had shouted with alarm. He was pointing across the bows, his voice breaking, 'Ship, sir! Coming round the point!'

He heard D'Esterre calling through his speaking trumpet, his voice urgent and desperate. 'Abandon her! Man your boats!'

Frowd was still staring at the neat array of braced yards and sails as the approaching vessel tilted suddenly to a change of tack.

He asked, 'What the *hell* is she?'

Bolitho felt fingers tugging his sleeve, and he saw Buller, his eyes on the newcomer.

'It's 'er! Th' one I saw, zur! Th' brig which went about when *Spite* were dismasted!'

It was all tumbling through Bolitho's mind like a tide in a mill-race. The brig, the yawl waiting to load or unload more weapons and powder, D'Esterre's last order, his own decision which lay frozen in his reeling thoughts.

There was a flash, followed by a dull bang, and a ball whipped overhead and smashed down hard on the island. The marines were falling back in good order, and Bolitho could sense the change in the yawl's crew. Fear to hope, and then to jubilation at their unexpected rescue.

'What'll we do?' Frowd was standing by the capstan, his sword still in his hand. 'She'll rake her as she passes with every gun she's got!'

Bolitho thought of Pears, of Coutts's disappointment, of Quinn's face at the court of inquiry.

He yelled, 'Cut the cable! Stand by to break out the mains'l! Mr Frowd, take charge there! Stockdale, man the helm!'

Another ball came out of the misty light and smashed into one of the cutters which was bobbing beneath the stem. Before it heeled over and sank, its loaded swivel gun exploded, and a blast of canister cut down a seaman even as he ran to sever the cable.

With only one boat there was no chance to obey D'Esterre's order. Bolitho stared at the brig, his heart chilling with anger and unexpected hatred.

And he knew, deep down, that he had had no intention of obeying.

The great mainsail swung outboard on its boom, thundering wildly as the anchor cable was hacked away to allow the yawl to fall downwind, out of command.

'Put up your helm!'

Men were slipping and stumbling at the halliards, ignoring the dumbfounded crew as they fought to bring the yawl under control.

Bolitho heard a ragged crash of gun-fire, and turned in time to see the small after mast pitch over the rail, missing Stockdale by a few feet.

'Hack that adrift!'

Another crash shook the hull, and Bolitho heard the ball slamming through the deck below. She could not take much of this.

'Put those men on the pumps!' He thrust his pistol into Couzens's hand. 'Shoot if they try to rush you!'

'I've got 'er, sir!' Stockdale stood, legs wide apart, peering at the sails and the freshly set jib as the land swam round beneath the bowsprit. He looked like an oak.

But the brig was gaining, her deck tilting as she tacked round to hold the wind and overreach her adversary.

The yawl had two swivels, but they were useless. Like a pike against a charge of cavalry. And all the hands were better employed at sheets and braces than wasting their strength on empty gestures.

A bright ripple of flashes again, and this time the balls battered into the lower hull like a fall of rock.

Bolitho saw the flag at the brig's gaff, the one he had been hearing about. Red and white stripes, with a circle of stars on a blue ground. She looked very new, and was being handled by a real professional.

'We'm makin' water fast, sir!'

Bolitho wiped his face and listened to the creak of the pumps. It was no use. They could never outreach her.

Small, vicious sounds sang past the helm, and he knew they were in musket range.

Somebody screamed, and then he saw Frowd stagger and fall against the bulwark, both hands clutching a shattered knee.

Couzens appeared at the hatch, his back towards the deck as he trained the pistol down the companion ladder.

'We're sinking, sir! There's water bursting into the hold!'

A ball burst through the mainsail and parted shrouds and stays like an invisible sabre.

Frowd was gasping, 'Run her ashore! It's our only chance!'

Bolitho shook his head. Once on firm sand, the yawl's cargo, and he had no doubt now that she was loaded with arms for the brig, would still be intact.

With sudden fury he climbed on to the shrouds and shook his fist at the other vessel.

His voice was lost on the wind and the answering crash of cannon-fire, but he found some satisfaction as he yelled, 'I'll sink her first, *damn you!*'

Stockdale watched him, while beyond the bows and the sea which was being churned by falling shot he saw the headland sliding away.

Please God she'll be there, he thought despairingly. Too late for us, but they'll not live neither.

16

Orders

As she floundered further from the island's shelter and into open water, the yawl rapidly became unmanageable. With so much damage below, and the dead-weight of weapons and iron shot, she was destroying herself on every wave.

The brig had changed tack again, sweeping away sharply to run almost parallel, while her gun crews settled down to pound the smaller craft into submission. There was no thought left of saving anything or anybody, and even the terrified prisoners were falling under the murderous cannon-fire.

Bolitho found time to notice that the brig, obviously new from some master-builder's yard, was not fully armed. Otherwise the fight would have been over long since. Only half her ports were firing, and he guessed the remainder were supposed to have been filled from the yawl's cargo. And this was her master's second attempt. The first had cost many lives, and the loss of the *Spite*. It seemed as if the brig had a charmed life and would escape yet again.

The deck gave a tremendous lurch and the topmast and upper yard fell in a mess of rigging and flapping canvas. Immediately the deck began to lean over, throwing men from their feet and bringing down more severed rigging.

From the open hatch Bolitho heard the violent inrush of water, the cries of the prisoners as the sea pushed through the frail timbers into the hold.

Bolitho clung to the bulwark and shouted, 'Release those men, Mr Couzens! The rest of you help the wounded!' He stared at Stockdale as he released the useless tiller. 'Lend a hand.' He winced as more shots whistled low overhead. 'We must abandon!'

Stockdale threw an unconscious seaman over his shoulder and strode to the side, peering down to make sure the remaining cutter was still afloat. 'Into the boat! Pass the wounded down.'

Bolitho felt the deck tilt and begin to settle more steeply. She was going by the stern, and the taffrail, with the stump of the after mast, was already awash.

If only the brig would cease firing. It needed just one ball to fall amongst the wounded and they would sink with the cutter. He looked at the swirling water and lively white crests. They would have a poor chance of survival in any case. On the island, which seemed to have moved a mile astern, he could see a few red coats, and guessed that the majority of the marines were running back to man the other boats. But marines were not seamen. By the time they managed to draw near, it would be over.

Couzens staggered towards him and gasped. 'The bows are out of the water, sir!' He ducked as another shot ripped through the mainsail and tore it away to rags.

Stockdale was trying to climb back on deck, but Bolitho shouted, 'Stand away! She's going down fast!'

With his face like a mask, Stockdale cast off the painter and allowed the current to carry him clear. Bolitho saw Frowd struggling aft to watch the sinking yawl, his fingers bloody as he waved his sword above his head.

The brig was shortening sail, the forecourse vanishing to reveal the rest of her neat hull.

Will they try to save us or kill us?

Bolitho said, 'We will swim for it, Mr Couzens.'

The boy nodded jerkily, unable to speak, as he kicked off his shoes and tore frantically at his shirt.

A shadow moved below the open hatch, and for a moment Bolitho imagined a wounded or trapped man was still down there. But it was a corpse, drifting forward as the water pounded between the decks. It was as high as that.

Couzens stared at the water and murmured, 'I'm not much of a swimmer, s-sir!' His teeth were chattering in spite of the sunlight.

Bolitho looked at him. 'Why in hell's name didn't you leave with the cutter then?' He realized the answer just as quickly and said quietly, 'We will keep together. I see a likely spar yonder . . .'

The brig fired again, the ball skipping over the wave-crests, past the swaying cutter and between some floundering swimmers like an attacking swordfish.

So that was why they had shortened sail. To make sure the British force was totally destroyed. So that every officer would think again if in the future he saw a chance of seizing much-needed supplies.

The yawl lurched over, tipping loose gear and corpses into the scuppers.

Bolitho watched the brig. But for Couzens he would have stayed and died here, he knew it. If he had to die anyway, it were better to let them see his face. But Couzens did not deserve such a death. For him there must always seem a chance.

The brig was putting her helm over, her yards in confusion as she swung away from the drifting wreck. He could even see her name on the broad counter, *White Hills*, and a startled face peering at him from the stern windows.

'He's going about!' Bolitho spoke aloud without knowing it. 'What is he thinking of? He'll be in irons in a minute!'

The wind was too strong and the brig's sails too few. In no time she was rendered helpless, her sails all aback in flapping, disordered revolt.

There was a muffled bang, and for an instant Bolitho thought she had sprung a mast or large yard. With disbelief he saw a great gaping hole torn in the brig's main-topsail, the wind slashing it to ribbons against the mast even as he watched.

He felt Couzens clutching his arm and shouting, 'It's *Trojan*, sir! She *is* here!'

Bolitho turned and saw the two-decker, standing as if motionless in the haze, like an extension to the next pair of islets.

Pears must have judged it to the second, biding his time while the same wind which was hampering the brig carried him slowly across the one safe channel of escape.

Two bright tongues stabbed from the forecastle, and Bolitho could see the gun captains as if he were there with them. Probably Bill Chimmo, *Trojan*'s gunner, would personally be supervising each careful shot.

He heard the splintering crash as an eighteen-pound ball blasted its way into the brig.

Then, below his feet the deck started to slide away, and with Couzens clinging to him like a limpet he plunged over the bulwark. But not before he had heard a wild cheer, or before he had seen the bright new flag being hauled down from the brig's gaff.

Even at that range *Trojan*'s starboard broadside could have smashed the brig to pieces in minutes, and her master knew it. A bitter moment for him, but many would thank him all the same.

Gasping and spluttering they reached the drifting spar and clung on to it.

Bolitho managed to say, 'I think you saved *me*.' For, unlike Couzens, he had forgotten to remove his clothes or even his hanger, and he was grateful for the spar's support.

As he tried to hold his head above the choppy wave-crests he saw the cutter turning towards him, the oarsmen leaning outboard to pull some of the swimmers to safety, or allow them to hang along either side of the hull. Further beyond them the other boats were coming too, the marines and the small party of seamen left to guard them doing better than Bolitho had expected.

He called, 'How is the brig?'

Couzens stared across the spar and answered, 'She's hove to, sir! They're not going to make a run for it!'

Bolitho nodded, unable to say anything more. The *White Hills* had no choice, especially as D'Esterre's boats were being careful not to lay themselves between him and *Trojan*'s formidable artillery.

The brig's capture might not make up for all those who had died, but it would show *Trojan*'s company what they could do, and give them back some pride.

Trojan's remaining boats had been lowered and were coming to join in the rescue. Bolitho could see the two jolly-boats and even the gig bouncing over the water. It took a full hour before he and Midshipman Couzens were hauled aboard the gig by a grinning Midshipman Pullen.

Bolitho could well imagine what the delay had done to Stockdale. But Stockdale knew him well enough to stand off with his overloaded boat of wounded and half-drowned men, rather than to show preference for a lieutenant who was to all intents safe and unhurt.

The eventual return aboard the *Trojan* was one of mixed feelings. Sadness that some of the older and more experienced hands had died or suffered wounds, but riding with it a kind of wild jubilation that they had acted alone, and had won.

When the smartly painted brig was put under the command of a boarding party, and the seamen lining the *Trojan*'s gangway cheered the returning victors, it felt like the greatest triumph of all time.

Small moments stood out, as they always did.

A seaman shaking his friend to tell him they were alongside their ship again, the stunned disbelief when he discovered he had died.

The cheers giving way to laughter as Couzens, as naked as the day he was born, climbed through the entry port with all the dignity he could manage, while two grinning marines presented arms for his benefit.

And Stockdale striding to meet Bolitho, his slow, lopsided smile of welcome better than any words.

Yet somehow it was Pears who held the day. Tall, massive like his beloved *Trojan*, he stood watching in silence.

As Couzens tried to hide himself Pears called harshly, 'That is no way for a King's officer to disport himself, sir! 'Pon my soul, Mr Couzens, I don't know what you are thinking about, and that's the truth!' Then as the boy ran, flushing, for the nearest companionway, he added, 'Proud of you, all the same.'

Bolitho crossed the quarterdeck, his feet squelching noisily.

Pears eyed him grimly. 'Lost the yawl, I see? Loaded, was she?'

'Aye, sir. I believe she was to arm the brig.' He saw his men limping past, tarred hands reaching out to slap their shoulders. He said softly, 'Our people did well, sir.'

He watched the brig spreading her sails again, the torn one little more

than rags. He guessed that Pears had sent a master's mate across, while
the marines searched and sorted out the captured crew. Frowd might be
made prize-master, it might make up for his badly shattered knee.
Whatever Thorndike did for him now, or some hospital later on, he
would have a bad limp for the rest of his life. He had reached the rank of
lieutenant. Frowd would know better than anyone that his wound
would prevent his getting any further.

It was late afternoon by the time both vessels had cleared the islands
and had sea-room again. It was no small relief to see the reefs and
swirling currents left far astern.

When D'Esterre returned to the *Trojan* he had another interesting
find to report.

The *White Hills'* captain was none other than Jonas Tracy, the
brother of the man killed when they had seized the schooner *Faithful*.
He had had every intention of fighting his way from under *Trojan*'s
guns, hopeless or not. But the odds had been against him. His company
were for the most part new to the trade of a fighting ship, which was the
reason for a seasoned privateersman like Tracy being given command in
the first place. His reputation, and list of successes against the British,
made him an obvious choice. Tracy had ordered his men to put the
White Hills about, to try and discover another, narrow passage through
the islands. His men, already cowed by the *Trojan*'s unexpected
challenge, were completely beaten when that second, carefully aimed
ball had smashed into the brig's side. It had shattered to fragments on
the breech of a gun on the opposite bulwark, and one splinter, the size of
a block, had taken Tracy's arm off at the shoulder. The sight of their
tough, hard-swearing captain cut down before their eyes had been more
than enough, and they had hauled down their flag.

Bolitho did not know if Tracy was still alive. It was an ironic twist
that he had been firing on the man who was responsible for his brother's
death without knowing it.

Bolitho was washing himself in his small cabin when he heard a
commotion on deck, the distant cry that a sail was in sight.

The other vessel soon showed herself to be a frigate under full sail.
She bore down on *Trojan* and with little fuss dropped a boat in the
water to carry her captain across.

Bolitho threw on his shirt and breeches and ran on deck. The frigate
was called *Kittiwake*, and Bolitho knew she was one of those he had
seen at Antigua.

With as much ceremony as if they were safely anchored in Plymouth
Sound, *Trojan* received her visitor. As the guard presented muskets, and
calls shrilled, Pears stepped forward to greet him. Bolitho realized it was
the post-captain who had been on Quinn's court of inquiry. Not the
president, nor the one with the thin lips and vindictive manner, but the

third officer who had, as far as Bolitho recalled, said nothing at all.

Sunset was closing in rapidly when the *Kittiwake*'s lord and master took his leave, his step less firm than when he had come aboard.

Bolitho watched the frigate make sail again, her canvas like gold silk in the dying sunlight. She would soon be out of sight, her captain free of admirals and ponderous authority. He sighed.

Cairns joined him, his eyes on the duty watch who were preparing to get the ship under way again.

He said quietly, 'She was from Antigua with despatches. She has been released from her squadron to go ahead of us to Jamaica. We are not outcasts after all.'

He sounded different. Remote.

'Is something wrong?'

Cairns looked at him, his face glowing in the sunset.

'Captain Pears thinks that the sea war will end in the Caribbean.'

'Not America?' Bolitho did not understand this mood.

'Like me, I think he believes that the war is already finished. Victories we will have, *must* have if we are to meet the French when they come out. But to win a war takes more than that, Dick.' He touched his shoulder and smiled sadly. 'I am detaining you. The captain wants you aft.' He walked away, calling sharply, 'Now then, Mr Dalyell, what is this shambles? Send the topmen aloft and pipe the hands to the braces! It is like a fish market here!'

Bolitho groped through the shadowed passageway to Pears's cabin.

Pears was sitting at his table, studying a bottle of wine with grim concentration.

He said, 'Sit down.'

Bolitho heard the pad of bare feet overhead, and wondered how they were managing with the captain away from his familiar place by the rail.

He sat.

The cabin looked comfortable and content. Bolitho felt suddenly tired, as if all the strength had drained out of him like sand from an hour-glass.

Pears announced slowly, 'We shall have some claret presently.'

Bolitho licked his lips. 'Thank you, sir.' He waited, completely lost. First Cairns, now Pears.

'Captain Viney of the *Kittiwake* brought orders from the flagship at Antigua. Mr Frowd is appointed into the *Maid of Norfolk*, armed transport. With all despatch.'

'But, sir, his leg?'

'I know. The surgeon has patched him as best he can.' His eyes came up and settled firmly on Bolitho's face. 'What does he want most in the world?'

'A ship, sir. Perhaps one day, a command of his own.'

He recalled Frowd's face aboard the yawl. Perhaps even then he had been thinking of it. A ship, any ship, like the armed transport written in his appointment, would have done.

'I agree. If he languishes here it will be too late. If he returns to Antigua,' he shrugged, 'his luck may have changed by then.'

Bolitho watched him, fascinated by Pears's authority. He had fought in battles, and was now taking his command to deal with God alone knew what in Jamaica, and yet he had time to think about Frowd.

'Then there is Mr Quinn.' Pears opened the bottle, his head to one side as the hull shivered and rolled before settling down on a new tack. 'He was not forgotten.'

Bolitho waited, trying to discover Pears's true feelings.

'He is to be returned to Antigua for passage to England. The rest we already know. I have written a letter for his father. It won't help much. But I want him to understand that his son only had so much courage. When it left him he was as helpless as Frowd with his leg.' Pears nudged a heavy envelope with the bottle. 'But he *tried*, and if more young men were doing that, instead of living in comfort at home, we might be better placed than we are.'

Bolitho looked at the bulky envelope. Quinn's life.

Pears became almost brisk. 'But enough of that. I have things to do, orders to dictate.'

He poured two large glasses of claret and held them on the table until Bolitho took one. The ship was leaning so steeply that both would have slithered to the deck otherwise.

It was strange that no one else was here. He had expected D'Esterre, or perhaps Cairns, once he had completed his duties with the watch on deck.

Pears raised his glass and said, 'I expect this will be a long night for you. But there will be longer ones, believe me.'

He raised his glass, like a thimble in his massive fist.

'I wish you luck, Mr Bolitho, and as our redoubtable sailing master would say, God's speed.'

Bolitho stared at him, the claret untouched.

'I am putting you in command of the *White Hills*. We will part company tomorrow when it is light enough to ferry the wounded over to her.'

Bolitho tried to think, to clear the astonishment from his mind.

Then he said, 'The first lieutenant, sir, with all respect . . .'

Pears held up his glass. It was empty. Like Probyn's had once been.

'I was going to send him. I *need* him here, now more than ever, but he deserves an appointment, even as a prize-master.' He eyed him steadily. 'As you did to Rear-Admiral Coutts, so did he refuse my suggestion.' He smiled gravely. 'So there we are.'

Bolitho saw his glass being refilled and said dazedly, 'Thank you very much, sir.'

Pears grimaced. 'So get the claret down you, and say your farewells. You can bother the life out of someone else after this!'

Bolitho found himself outside beside the motionless sentry again, as if it had all been a dream.

He found Cairns still on deck, leaning against the weather nettings and staring across at the brig's lights.

Before Bolitho could speak Cairns said firmly, 'You are going as prize-master tomorrow. It is settled, if I have to send you across in irons.'

Bolitho stood beside him, conscious of the movements behind him, the creak of the wheel, the slap of rigging against spars and canvas.

I expect this will be a long night for you.

'What has happened, Neil?'

He felt very close to this quiet, soft-spoken Scot.

'The captain also received a letter. I don't know who from. It is not his style to whimper. It was a *friendly* piece of information, if you can call it that. To tell Captain Pears he has been passed over for promotion to flag rank. A captain he will remain.' He looked up at the stars beyond the black rigging and yards. 'And when *Trojan* eventually pays-off, that will be the end for him. Coutts has been ordered to England under a cloud.' He could not hide his anger, his hurt. 'But he has wealth, and position.' He turned and gestured towards the poop. '*He* only has his ship!'

'Thank you for telling me.'

Cairns's teeth were very white in the gloom. 'Away with you, man. Go and pack your chest.'

As Bolitho was about to leave him he added softly, 'But you do understand, my friend? I couldn't desert him now, could I?'

The next morning, bright and early, with both vessels hove to, *Trojan*'s boats started to ferry the wounded seamen across to the brig. On their return trips they carried the *White Hills*'s crew into captivity. It must have been one of the shortest commissions in sea history, Bolitho thought.

Nothing seemed exactly real to him, and he found himself forgetting certain tasks, and checking to discover if he had completed others more than once.

Each time he went on deck he had to look across at the brig, rolling uncomfortably in steep troughs. But once under sail again she could fly if need be. It was too close a memory to forget how she had been handled.

Cairns had already told him that Pears was allowing him to select his own prize-crew. Just enough to work the brig in safety, or run before a storm or powerful enemy.

He did not have to ask Stockdale. He was there, a small bag already packed. His worldly possessions. Pears had also instructed him to take the badly wounded Captain Jonas Tracy to Antigua. He was too severely injured to be moved with the other prisoners, and should be little trouble.

As the time drew near for him to leave, Bolitho was very aware of his own torn emotions. Small incidents from the past stood out to remind him of his two and a half years in the *Trojan*. It seemed quite unbelievable that he was leaving her, to place himself at the disposal of the admiral commanding in Antigua. It was like starting life all over again. New faces, fresh surroundings.

He had been surprised and not a little moved by some of the men who had actually volunteered to go with him.

Carlsson, the Swede who had been flogged. Dunwoody, the miller's son, Moffitt, the American, Rabbett, the ex-thief, and old Buller, the topman, the man who had recognized the brig from the start. He had been promoted to petty officer and had shaken his head in astonishment at the news.

There were others too, as much a part of the big two-decker as her figurehead or her captain.

He watched Frowd being swayed down to the cutter in a bosun's chair, his bandaged and splinted leg sticking out like a tusk, and hating it all, the indignity of leaving his ship in this fashion.

Quinn had already gone across. It would be difficult to stand between those two, Bolitho thought. Bolitho had already seen Frowd looking bitterly at Quinn. He was probably questioning the fairness of it. Why should Quinn, who was being rejected by the Navy, be spared, while he was a cripple?

Most of the goodbyes had been said already. Last night, and through the morning. Rough handshakes from gunner and boatswain, grins from others he had watched change from boys to men. Like himself.

D'Esterre had sent some of his own stock of wine across to the brig, and Sergeant Shears had given him a tiny cannon which he had fashioned from odd fragments of silver.

Cairns found him checking over his list of things which he was required to do and said, 'The Sage says that we're in for a blow, Dick. You'd better be going now.' He thrust out his hand. 'I'll say my farewells here.' He glanced around the deserted wardroom where they had shared so much. 'It will seem emptier with you gone.'

'I'll not forget you.' Bolitho gripped his hand hard. 'Ever!'

They walked forward to the companion ladder, and Cairns said suddenly, 'One thing. Captain Pears thinks you should take another officer to stand watches with you. We cannot spare a master's mate, and lieutenants are as rare as charity until our replacements arrive. So it will have to be a midshipman.'

Bolitho thought about it.

Cairns added, 'Weston will be acting-lieutenant as of now, and both Lunn and Burslem are better left here to finish their training. That leaves Forbes and Couzens who are young enough to begin again anywhere.'

Bolitho smiled. 'I will put it to them.'

Watched by the lieutenants and marine officers, Erasmus Bunce, the master, beckoned to the two thirteen-year-old midshipmen.

'A volunteer is needed, young gentlemen.' Bunce glared at them disdainfully. 'Though what use either o' you will be to Mr Bolitho, I can't say.'

They both stepped forward, Couzens with such a look of pleading on his round face that Bunce asked, 'Is your gear packed?'

Couzens nodded excitedly, and Forbes looked near to tears as he shook his head.

Bunce said, 'Mr Couzens, off you go, and lively. It must be the Lord's blessing to clear the ship of your high spirits and skylarking!' He looked at Bolitho and dropped one eyelid like a gunport. 'Satisfied?'

'Aye.'

Bolitho shook their hands, trying to hold back his emotion.

D'Esterre was the last. 'Good luck, Dick. We'll meet again. I shall miss you.'

Bolitho looked across at the *White Hills*, seeing the wave-crests rolling along her hull, making her sway more and more steeply.

His orders were in his pocket, in a heavily sealed envelope. He waited to go, but the ship held on to him.

He walked towards the entry port, seeing the gig rising and falling alongside. In for a blow, Bunce had said. Perhaps it was just as well. To hasten the break and keep him too busy for regrets.

Cairns said quietly, 'Here is the captain.'

Pears strolled across the quarterdeck, his coat-tails flapping out like studding sails, while he held on to his gold-laced hat with one hand.

'Prepare to get under way, Mr Cairns. I'll not lose this wind.' He seemed to see Bolitho for the first time. 'Still here, sir?' His eyebrows went up. ''Pon my soul . . .' For once he did not finish. Instead he walked across and held out his big hand.

'Be off with you now. My regards to your father when next you see him.' He turned away and moved aft towards the compass.

Bolitho touched his hat to the quarterdeck, and clutching his hanger to his hip hurried down into the boat.

The oars dipped into the water, and immediately *Trojan* fell away, the men on the gangways turning to continue with their work while others ran up the ratlines to loose the topsails again.

Couzens stared back at the ship, his eyes watering in the wind. It looked as if he was crying. Unknown to Bolitho, it was the happiest day in the midshipman's short life.

Bolitho raised his hand, and saw Cairns doing the same. Of Pears there was no sign. Like the *Trojan*, he was letting go.

Bolitho turned his back and studied the *White Hills*. His for so short a time. But *his*.

As Bunce had predicted, the wind rose rapidly to gale force, and with it the sea changed its face from cruising white horses to long, violent troughs with ragged yellow crests.

The prize-crew got down to work in grim earnest, bringing the ship's head to the south as the wind backed and pushed them hard over, the yards braced round until they would not shift another inch.

Bolitho discarded his hat and coat and stood beside the unprotected wheel, his ears ringing to the roar of wind and sea, his whole body soaking with spray.

It was lucky the *White Hills* carried a spare main-topsail, he thought. The one which had been torn apart by *Trojan*'s first shot had been saved for patching but was useless for anything more.

Under reefed topsails and jib, the *White Hills* ran close-hauled to the south, away from the islands and danger.

Quinn, stiff-faced and barely speaking, worked with the hands on deck, and without him Bolitho wondered what he would have done. Couzens had the determination and loyalty of ten men, but experience in handling rigging and sails in a full gale he had not.

Stockdale came aft and joined the two hands at the wheel. Like Bolitho he was drenched to the skin, his clothing stained by tar and salt. He grinned through the drifting streamers of spindrift and bobbed his head at Bolitho.

'Real little lady, ain't she?'

For most of the day they ran with the wind, but towards sunset the strength fell away, and later still the bruised and breathless seamen managed to get aloft and set both mainsail and forecourse. The additional bulging area of canvas pushed the hull over further still, but held her steadier, and more firmly on course.

Bolitho shouted to Quinn, 'Take over! I'm going below!'

After the noise and confusion on deck it seemed almost quiet once he had lowered himself through the companionway.

How small she seemed after *Trojan*'s great girth. He groped his way aft to the cabin, a miniature of Pears's quarters. It was barely large enough to contain Pears's table, he thought. But it looked inviting, and too new to show signs of a previous owner.

He reeled as the sea boiled and thundered along the quarter, and then managed to reach the stern windows. There was nowhere in the cabin, apart from a battened-down skylight, where he could stand upright. What it was like in the messes, he could well imagine. As a midshipman he had once served in a brig very similar to this one. Fast, lively, and never still.

He wondered what had happened to Tracy's other command, the captured brig which he had renamed *Revenge*. Still attacking British convoys and stalking rich cargoes for ready prize-money.

The cabin door banged open and Moffitt lurched through it carrying a jug of rum.

He said, 'Mr Frowd thought you might like a drop, sir.'

Bolitho disliked rum, but he needed something. He swallowed it in a gulp, almost choking.

'Mr Frowd, is he all right?' He must visit him soon, but now he was needed and would have to return to the deck.

Moffitt took the empty goblet and grinned at it admiringly. 'Aye, sir. I've got him propped in a cot in his cabin. He'll be safe enough.'

'Good. Get Buller for me.'

Bolitho lay back, feeling the stern rising and then sliding down beneath him, the sea shaking the rudder like a piece of driftwood.

Buller came into the cabin, his head lowered to avoid the beams. 'Zur?'

'You take charge of the victuals. Find someone who can cook. If the wind drops some more we'll get the galley fire re-lit and put something hot into our bellies.'

Buller showed his strong teeth. 'Right away, zur.' Then he too was gone.

Bolitho sighed, the aroma of rum around him like a drug. Chain of command. And he must begin it. No one else was here to goad or encourage his efforts.

His head lolled and he jerked it up with sudden disgust. Like George Probyn. That was a fine beginning. He jumped up and gasped as his head crashed against a beam. But it sobered him even more quickly.

He made his way forward, swaying and feeling his balance with each jubilant lunge of the brig's bowsprit.

Tiny cabins on either side of a small, square space. The wardroom. Stores, and shot garlands, swaying ranks of pod-like hammocks. The ship smelt new, right down to her mess tables, her great coils of stout cable in the tier forward.

He found the wounded Tracy in a cot, swinging in a tiny cabin which was still unfinished. A red-eyed seaman sat in one corner, a pistol between his feet.

Bolitho peered at the figure in the cot. About thirty, a powerful, hardfaced man, who despite his terrible wound and loss of blood still looked very much alive. But with his arm torn off at the point of the shoulder he would not be much trouble.

He glanced at the sentry and said, 'Watch him, all the same.'

The other wounded men were quiet enough, bandaged, and cushioned from the fierce motion by spare hammocks, blankets and clothing from the brig's store.

He paused by a wildly swinging lantern, feeling their pain, their lack of understanding. Again, he was ashamed for thinking of his own reward. They on the other hand knew only that they were being carried away from their ship which, good or bad, had been their home. And to where? Some home-bound vessel, and then what? Put ashore, just another cluster of crippled sailors. Heroes to some, figures of fun to others.

'There'll be some hot food along soon, lads.'

A few heads turned to look at him. One man he recognized as Gallimore, a seaman employed as a painter aboard the *Trojan*. He had been badly injured by canister during the attack on the yawl. He had lost most of his right hand, and had been hit in the face by wood splinters.

He managed to whisper, 'Where we goin', sir?'

Bolitho knelt down on the deck beside him. The man was dying. He did not know how he knew, or why. Others nearby were more badly hurt, yet bore their pain with defiant, even surly resignation. They would survive.

He said, 'English Harbour. The surgeons there will help you. You'll see.'

The man reached out, seeking Bolitho's hand. 'Oi don't want to die, sir. Oi got a wife an' children in Plymouth.' He tried to shake his head. 'Oi mustn't die, sir.'

Bolitho felt a catch in his throat. Plymouth. It might just as well be Russia.

'Rest easy, Gallimore.' He withdrew his hand carefully. 'You are with your friends.'

He walked aft again to the companionway, bent almost double in the space between decks.

The wind and spray were almost welcome. He found Couzens with Stockdale by the wheel, while Quinn was groping along the forecastle with two seamen.

Stockdale said gruffly, 'All 'oldin' firm, sir. Mr Quinn is lookin' at the weather braces.' He peered up at the dark sky. 'Wind's backed a piece more. Fallin' off, too.'

The bows lifted towards the sky, then came down in a trough with a shuddering lurch. It was enough to hurl a man from the yards, had there been one up there.

Stockdale muttered, 'Must be bad for the lads below, sir.'

Bolitho nodded. 'Gallimore's dying, I think.'

'I know, sir.'

Stockdale eased the spokes and studied the quivering maintopsail, the canvas ballooning out as if to tear itself from the yard.

Bolitho glanced at him. Of course, Stockdale would have known. He had lived with suffering for most of his life. Death would seem familiar, recognizable.

Quinn came aft along the pale deck, staggering to each swooping dip across the troughs.

He shouted, 'The larboard anchor was working free, but we've catted it home again!'

Bolitho replied, 'Get below. Work out two watches for me, and I'll discuss it with you later.'

Quinn shook his head. 'I don't want to be on my own. I must do something.'

Bolitho thought of the man from Plymouth. 'Go to the wounded, James. Take some rum, or anything you can find in the cabin, and issue it to those poor devils.'

There was no sense in telling him about Gallimore. Let the dying man join his companions in a last escape. The sailor's balm for everything.

A seaman, accompanied by Buller, ducked down the companion ladder, and Bolitho saw it was a swarthy Italian named Borga. It seemed as if Buller had already chosen a cook, and Bolitho hoped it was a wise decision. Hot food in a seaman's belly after fisting canvas and trying to stay inboard was one thing, but some foreign concoction might spark off a brawl. He glanced at Stockdale and smiled to himself. If so, it would soon be dealt with.

Another hour, and the stars appeared, the scudding clouds driven off like fleeing vagrants.

Bolitho felt the deck becoming steadier, and wondered what tomorrow would be like, how Bunce would have predicted it.

As promised, a hot meal was produced and issued first to the wounded, and then to the seamen as they were relieved from watch in small groups.

Bolitho ate his with relish, although what he was having he did not know. Boiled meat, oatmeal, ground biscuit, it was also laced with rum. It was like nothing he had ever had, but at that moment would have graced any admiral's table.

To Couzens he said, 'Are you sorry for your eagerness to join the *White Hills*?'

Couzens shook his head, his stomach creaking with Borga's first meal.

'Wait till I get home, sir. They'll never believe it.'

Bolitho pictured Quinn, sitting below with the wounded, and thought of Pears writing a letter to his father. *He tried.*

He thought too of the despatches he was carrying from Captain Pears to the admiral at Antigua. It was probably safer not to know what Pears had said about him, although it would certainly affect his immediate future. But he still did not really understand Pears, only that under his command he had learned more than he had first realized.

Bolitho stared up at the sky. 'I think we've seen the worst of it. Better fetch Mr Quinn on deck.'

Couzens watched him and blurted out, 'I can stand watch, sir.'

Stockdale grinned lazily. 'Aye, sir, he can at that. I'll be on deck, too.' He hid his grin from the midshipman. 'Though I'll not be needed, I'm thinkin'.'

'Very well.' Bolitho smiled. 'Call me if you're in any doubt.'

He lowered himself through the companionway, glad he had given Couzens the opportunity to face responsibility, surprised too that he had been able to trust him without hesitation.

As he found his way to his small cabin, he heard Frowd snoring loudly and the clatter of a goblet rolling back and forth across the deck.

Tomorrow would be a lot of hard work. First to try to estimate their position and drift, then to set a new course which with luck would carry them to the Leeward Islands and Antigua.

On the chart it did not seem so far, but the prevailing winds would be against them for much of the passage, and it could take days to make good the loss of being driven south.

And once in Antigua, what then? Would the French lieutenant still be there, taking lonely walks in the sun, on his honour not to try and escape?

He lay down on the bench beneath the stern windows, ready to run on deck at the first unusual sound. But Bolitho was fast asleep in a matter of seconds.

It was noon, two days after leaving the *Trojan*, but a lifetime of new experiences and problems.

The weather was less demanding now, and the *White Hills* was leaning over on the larboard tack, with even her big spanker set and filled by the wind. The vessel felt clean and dry after the storm, and the makeshift routine which Bolitho had worked out with Quinn and Frowd was performing well.

Frowd was on deck, seated on a hatch cover, his leg propped before him as a constant reminder.

Couzens stood by the wheel, while Bolitho and Quinn checked their sextants and compared calculations.

He saw the seaman Dunwoody walk to the lee bulwark and hurl a bucket of slops over the side. He had just emerged from the forecastle, so had probably been with Gallimore. He had still not died, but had been moved to the cable tier, the only place where the stench of the great slimy rope was matched by his own. His wound had gone gangrenous, and it seemed impossible for any man to stand the misery of it.

Quinn said wearily, 'I think we are both right, sir. With the wind staying as it is, we should make a landfall the day after tomorrow.'

Bolitho handed his instrument to Couzens. So it was *sir* again. The last link broken.

He said, 'I agree. We may sight the island of Nevis tomorrow, and after that it will be a hard beat all the way across to Antigua.'

He felt a sharp sense of loss. The thought of losing the *White Hills* seemed unbearable. It was ridiculous of course. Just a few days, but what confidence she had given him, or had discovered in him.

Bolitho glanced along the sunlit deck. Even that no longer seemed so narrow and confined after *Trojan*'s spacious gundeck.

Some of the wounded were resting in the shade, chatting quietly, or watching the other hands at work with professional interest.

Bolitho asked quietly, 'What will you do, James?'

Quinn looked away. 'As my father pleases, I expect. I seem to have the knack of obeying orders.' He faced Bolitho suddenly. 'One day. If you want to, I – I mean, if you have nowhere to go, would you care to see me?'

Bolitho nodded, wanting to strip away his despair. It was killing him with no less mercy than Gallimore's wounds.

'I will be happy to, James.' He smiled. 'Although I've no doubt your father will think badly of a mere lieutenant in his house. I expect you'll be a rich merchant by the time I get to London.'

Quinn studied him anxiously. Something in Bolitho's tone seemed to comfort him and he said, 'I thank you for that. And much more.'

'Deck there! Sail on the weather bow!'

Bolitho stared up at the lookout. He tried to see the *White Hills* like a cross on a chart. There were so many islands, French, British, Dutch. This sail could be any kind of ship.

Since the *Kittiwake* had left Antigua anything might have happened. Peace with the American rebels, war with France.

With a start he realized they were all looking at him.

He said, 'Get aloft, Mr Quinn. Take a glass and tell me what you see.'

Frowd groaned as Quinn hurried past. 'God damn this leg! I should be up there, not, not . . .' By the time he had thought of a suitable insult Quinn was already hurrying up the shrouds.

Bolitho paced rapidly back and forth, trying to stay calm and unmoved. She was quite likely a Spaniard, southward bound for the Main and all its treasures. If so, she would soon haul off. She might think *White Hills* to be a pirate. In these waters you could choose from a dozen sorts of enemy.

'Deck, sir! She's a brig!'

One of the wounded men gave a thin cheer. 'She'll be one of ours, lads!'

But Frowd rasped painfully, 'You know what I'm thinking, don't you?'

Bolitho looked at him, his brain suddenly ice-cold.

Of course, it made sense. Cruel sense. And they had got so far. This time, he had believed, with success.

There was still a chance.

He held his voice steady as he called, 'Keep watching her!' To Couzens he added more quietly, 'We shall have a closer look at her soon enough, I imagine.' He saw the understanding clouding Couzens' eyes. 'Clear for action, if you please. Then load, but do not run out.'

He glanced along the deck, at the brig's small defences. Enough guns to rake the defenceless yawl, but if the oncoming vessel was Captain Tracy's previous command, they would be all but useless.

17

None so Gallant

Bolitho waited for the deck to steady again and then trained his telescope across the larboard bow. He could see the other brig's topsails and topgallants sharply etched against the blue sky, but the rest of the vessel was lost in distance and haze.

If the vessel was the *Revenge*, her master would recognize the *White Hills* as soon as she was within reasonable distance. He might have done so already. To alter course away, to wear completely and fly with the wind would tell him what had happened quicker than any challenge.

Bolitho looked up at the masthead pendant. The wind had backed a point or so further. It was tempting to turn and run, but if the wind went against them again, and they were repeatedly made to change tack, the other brig would soon overhaul them. With only a small prize-crew to work the ship, Bolitho knew it would be asking too much of any man.

He said, 'Let her fall off a point, Stockdale.'

From the mainmast he heard Quinn call, 'I can see her better now! She's the old *Mischief*! I'm almost certain!'

Frowd swore. 'Bloody hell! We'd better show her a clean pair of heels!'

Stockdale said, 'Nor'-east by east, sir.'

Bolitho cupped his hands. 'Man the braces! You, Buller, put more men on the weather forebrace!'

He watched narrowly as the yards moved slightly to allow each sail to fill to capacity. But not enough to betray an attempt to escape.

Couzens came running aft, his hands filthy, his shirt torn in several places.

'Cleared for action, sir. All guns loaded.'

Bolitho smiled tightly. By *all guns*, Couzens meant the *White Hills*'s eight six-pounders. She was designed to carry fourteen, and some swivels, but the sinking of the yawl had put paid to that. Eight guns, and only four on either beam. To try and shift a full battery to one side would certainly be seen by the other brig. She was growing in size at a surprising speed, and Bolitho could see the sun reflecting on metal, or perhaps the glass of several telescopes.

She was closing with the *White Hills* on a converging tack, bowsprit to bowsprit.

The *White Hills'* original crew had been new and raw, but the *Revenge*'s master would certainly know Tracy by sight. They must try and stand off. Keep up some sort of bluff until dusk.

'Land on the lee bow, sir!' The lookout had been keeping his eyes open too while Quinn watched the other brig.

Bolitho looked at Frowd, seeing his despair. The land was most likely to be one or more of the tiny islands which marked their course past Nevis and then fifty miles on to Antigua. It made it seem much worse. So near, yet so far.

'Brig's altered course, sir!' Then another cry, 'She's run up her flag!'

Bolitho nodded grimly. 'Hoist the same one, Mr Couzens.' He watched as the red and white striped flag ran up to the gaff and broke to the wind.

Frowd was straining up on the hatch cover. 'No use, blast his eyes! He's closing, and making sure he can keep the wind-gage!'

'He'll want to speak with us. To find out if we got the guns and powder. This brig was probably meant to join with him at some point.' Bolitho was thinking aloud and saw Frowd nod in agreement.

Stockdale pulled at Couzens's sleeve. 'Get the *real* flag ready, Mr Couzens. I can't see our lieutenant fighting under false colours. Not today.'

Frowd said despairingly, 'How can we fight, you fool! These privateers are always armed to the gills! They need to smash an enemy into submission as fast as they can, and before help can be sent to drive 'em off!' He groaned. 'Fight? You must be mad!'

Bolitho made up his mind. 'We will begin to shorten sail directly, as if we are about to speak with him. If we can get near enough without rousing suspicion, we'll rake his poop, do for as many of the after-guard as possible and then run for it.'

Stockdale nodded. 'Later we could shift two guns aft, sir. A stern chase is better'n nothin'.'

Bolitho made himself stand quite still, to give his mind time to work. He had no other choice, and this was not much of one. But it was either a sudden act of daring, or surrender.

'Take in the mains'l.'

Bolitho watched the few spare hands swarming up the ratlines. The other master would see the depleted crew, and might imagine they had been in a battle. The gash through the bulwark made by *Trojan*'s eighteen-pounder must be plain enough to see.

He levelled his glass on the other vessel, ignoring the shouts and curses as his men fought with the rebellious canvas. Frowd was right. She was heavily armed, and there were plenty of men about her deck, too.

He wondered what had happened to her original captain when she had been captured from under him. Fourteen guns and a determined company would make her a formidable enemy. Bolitho watched her tilting towards him, revealing her maindeck, the line of guns on the opposite side. None was manned, but on this side he could see a few heads peering over the sealed gunports, and guessed they were probably loaded and ready.

Moffitt crossed the deck and said dourly, 'You'll be needin' me, sir? I know how to speak to them bastards!'

'Be ready.'

He studied the set of each sail, the lively froth around the privateer's stem as she edged over even further, her yards moving as if controlled by one hand.

Half a mile. Not long now.

He shifted his glance inboard, seeing the quick, anxious gestures of his small company, even the wounded were craning their heads and trying to see above the weather bulwark.

'Come down, Mr Quinn!' Bolitho looked at Stockdale and Buller. 'See that our people keep their weapons out of sight. When I give the word, I want those four guns run out as smartly as you like and fire at will. If we can mark down her officers we may use the surprise to fight clear.'

Quinn arrived beside him, breathing fast, his eyes towards the enemy. 'D'you think they are on to us?'

'No.' Bolitho folded his arms, hoping that across the glittering pattern of waves and spray he would appear more relaxed than he felt. 'They would have run down on us before now. They have all the advantage.'

If the wind chose this moment to change . . . He shut his mind to the possibility and concentrated on the sails and masthead pendant. The wind, which was fresh and steady, came from the north-west. The *White Hills* had her yards well braced, heeling on the larboard tack, the wind across her quarter. If they could just delay the other captain's suspicions, and then hold him off until dark, they might well lose him amongst the islands when daylight returned.

And even then, if the privateer's captain was so set on another victory and made further contact, they might be able to give him the slip further north, or in the narrows between Nevis and St Christophers. In those treacherous waters, off some deadly place like the Scotch Bonnet, they might even tempt their pursuer aground.

The only ally at this precarious stage was the wind. Both brigs were carrying the bulk of their sails, so either could tack or come about with agility if need be.

Stockdale observed, 'She must be steerin' almost sou'-east, sir. The wind right astern of 'er.'

Bolitho nodded, knowing Stockdale wanted to help, if only by making a professional comment.

The range had dropped to a mere quarter-mile, and it was possible to see the watching figures on the other vessel's poop and forecastle.

'When she tries to hail us, Moffitt, tell her captain that Tracy is sick, badly wounded after a brush with the British.' He saw the man tighten his lips. 'It's no lie, so keep it simple, eh?'

Moffitt said coldly, 'I'll see that he don't recover if them buggers board us, sir!'

Along the weather side the seamen were crawling on their hands and knees, like strange worshippers around the four small cannon. Ball and grape to each gun. It would not even be felt by a stately two-decker like *Trojan*. But one good blast across the enemy's quarterdeck might do the trick. Time, time, time. It was like a hammer on an anvil.

Two small shadows moved on the *Revenge*'s side, and Bolitho heard a murmur of anxiety from some of the wounded seamen. *Revenge* had raised two of her forward port lids, and as he watched he saw the sunlight touch a pair of black muzzles as she ran out the guns.

Frowd muttered uneasily, 'He *knows*, the bugger!'

Bolitho shook his head. 'I think not. He would run out a broadside if he was sure of an enemy, and maybe tack across our stern.' Again, it was like sharing his thoughts with those around him. 'He'll have been watching us all this time, as we have him. Tracy's absence from the deck will have been noted. If *Revenge*'s captain is newly appointed, he'll be wary of taking a chance, but unwilling to show fear or uncertainty to his men. Following a man like Tracy must be quite a task.'

He saw some of his seamen glance at each other, for support, to discover a new confidence. But he knew he was only guessing out of sheer hope.

Revenge's captain might be even more experienced than Tracy. And at this very moment was using the *White Hills*'s unchanged tack for one terrible bombardment, his guns already manned and ready to fire.

Moffitt took a speaking trumpet and climbed casually into the weather shrouds. It was far too early, but it might lull the enemy's caution.

If not, the fight would explode across this deck within fifteen minutes.

Bolitho said evenly, 'You men, carry Mr Frowd and the other wounded below. If we have to abandon, the quarter boat will be used for them only.'

Frowd swivelled round on his hatch cover like an enraged terrier.

'Damn your eyes, I'll not die like a sick woman!' He grimaced as the pain stabbed through him, and he continued in a more controlled tone, 'I meant no disrespect, sir, but try and see it my way.'

'And which way is that?'

Frowd swayed about like a bush in a wind as the hull lifted and sliced through the choppy water.

'If your plan works, sir, and I pray to God it does, it will be a chase which only luck and superior seamanship can win.'

Bolitho smiled. 'Perhaps.'

'But, as I suspect, we may have to fight, for God's sake let me play my part. I have been in the Navy all my remembered years. To end my time cowering below when the metal flies overhead would make my life as worthless as that of any gallows-bird.'

'Very well.' Bolitho looked at Couzens. 'Help the lieutenant aft and see that he is supplied with enough powder and shot to reload the pistols and muskets to give an impression of strength and greater numbers.'

Frowd exclaimed, 'That's it, sir. I ask for nothing more. Those devils will outnumber us four to one, maybe more. We can take a few with us if we can maintain rapid fire.'

It was incredible, Bolitho thought. The prospect of sudden death had been made suddenly stark and inevitable by Frowd's words, and yet the previous apprehension seemed to have gone. The waiting had been the worst part, the simple task of fighting and dying was something they all understood. It was like hearing Sparke all over again. Keep them busy. No time to moan and weaken.

He turned to watch as the *Revenge*'s jib and staysails quivered and flapped like tapered wings, and knew she was falling off a little more to run even closer to the *White Hills*. Nearer, she looked impressive and well armed.

Her hull was weatherbeaten and the sails stained and patched in several places. She must have been made to work and fight hard against her previous owners, Bolitho thought grimly.

'We will give her a few more minutes, Stockdale, and then you can bring her round to steer due east. It will be the obvious thing to do if we are to draw close enough to speak.'

He winced as a handspike clattered across the deck and a man retrieved it under a stream of threats and curses from Buller.

He saw the cutlasses and pistols by each man, the way they kept tensing their muscles as if carrying some great load while they waited and lived out each agonizing minute.

'Man the braces. Stand by!' Bolitho strode to the side and added sharply, 'Be easy, lads! Take your time.' He saw some of them pause to stare. After serving in a King's ship it was like a blasphemy to be told to take your time. He added, 'You are *landmen*, remember?' It was unbelievable that some of them could grin and chuckle at such a stupid joke. 'So forget you are prime seamen.'

Buller called, 'But not for long, eh, zur?' Even he was laughing.

'*Now*, Stockdale.'

With yards and rudder moving in clumsy unison, the little brig fell three points downwind, the *Revenge*'s masts appearing to slide astern until she was running on a parallel course, her bowsprit and jib boom just overlapping the *White Hills*'s taffrail, and half a cable away.

Obediently, or so it appeared, the other vessel followed suit, dropping even further with the wind and leaning over on the larboard tack. Fifty yards separated the two brigs now, with the *Revenge* still slightly astern. Each alteration of tack had given *White Hills* a few more precious minutes and a tiny lead on her unwanted companion.

Frowd said between his clenched teeth, 'Thank the good Lord they have no prepared signals this time.'

'You sound like the Sage.'

But Frowd was right. The enemy could have examined them at leisure had they had the time to create an efficient form of signalling as in more professional navies.

Apart from the creaming water alongside, the resonant slap and boom of canvas, it was very quiet on deck.

Moffitt remarked, 'I can see one of 'em with a trumpet, sir.'

He looked at Bolitho, his eyes calm. 'I know what to say. I'll not let you down.'

Rabbett said, 'You'd better not, matey. I've been in too many jails to rot in one o' theirs!'

Moffitt grinned and then waved his speaking trumpet towards the other vessel. Both brigs were moving swiftly on the same tack, and at any other time would have made a fine sight. Now, in their controlled advance, they each had a quality of menace. Like two wary beasts, the one unwilling to fall into a trap, the other afraid of showing weakness to her enemy.

It was then, even as someone waved back from the *Revenge*'s quarterdeck, that the tension was shattered by a terrible scream. It was like something inhuman, a soul in hideous torment.

The seamen at the braces, or hiding beside their guns, peered round, horrified and then angry as the sound got louder and wilder.

Quinn gasped, 'What is it, in the name of God?'

Stockdale said, 'Gallimore, sir. His wound must 'ave burst.'

Bolitho nodded, tasting the bile in his throat, as he pictured the awful gangrenous, rotting flesh which had given off such a stench that he had had to move Gallimore to the cable tier.

'Tell Borga to silence him.'

He tried to shut out the screams, to exclude the picture of the tortured man below.

A voice came across the water, bringing Bolitho back to danger and reality.

'*White Hills* ahoy! What in hell's name was that?'

Bolitho swallowed hard. Poor Gallimore's last moments of terror had unnerved the enemy as much as his own prize-crew.

Moffitt yelled, 'Wounded man!' He staggered as the brig pitched through a steep-sided wave, but Bolitho knew it was an act. Moffitt was as nimble as a cat. But it gave more time. 'Had a brush with the English! Lost some good hands!'

The scream stopped with dramatic suddenness, as if the man had been beheaded.

Across the water the other voice asked, 'An' Captain Tracy? Is he safe? I've orders for him, y'see!'

'He's wounded right enough.' Moffitt gripped the shrouds with his free hand, then relaxed his fingers as he whispered over his shoulder, 'Them two guns, sir. Their crews have stood down.'

Bolitho wanted to lick his lips, to wipe the sweat from his eyes, anything to break the strain of waiting and watching the other vessel. Moffitt had seen what he had not even dared to hope for. Maybe it was Gallimore's screams which, added to Moffitt's outward confidence and the fact that the *White Hills* was the right vessel in almost the right place, had convinced *Revenge*'s captain that all was well.

But there was still the matter of Tracy's new orders. Probably details of the next rendezvous, or news of a supply convoy left open to attack.

In a few moments *Revenge*'s captain would have to face the fact he was now in the senior position. He was the one who would have to decide what to do.

Bolitho said quietly, 'He'll suggest we both heave to so that he can come over to us and speak with Tracy and see how he is.'

Quinn stared at him, his face like a mask. 'Will we go about then, sir?'

'Aye.' Bolitho stole a quick glance at the masthead pendant. 'The moment he decides to shorten sail and head into the wind, we'll use our chance.' He called to the nearest gun crew, 'Be ready, lads!' He saw an over-eager seaman struggling off his knees and reaching for a slow-match. 'Belay that! Wait for the word!'

The *Revenge*'s captain called, 'We'll heave to. I'll be over to you as soon as –'

He got no further. Like some terrifying creature emerging from a tomb, Captain Jonas Tracy lurched through the forehatch, his eyes bulging from his head with agony and fury.

He carried a pistol which he fired at a seaman who ran to restrain him, the ball smashing the man in the forehead and hurling him on his back in a welter of blood.

And all the time he was bellowing, his voice stronger than most of the men around him.

'*Rake the bastard! It's a trick, you damn fool!*'

From the other brig came a series of shouts and confused orders, and then like bewildered hogs the guns began to run out through the ports along her side.

Another seaman hurried towards the swaying figure by the hatch, only to be clubbed senseless by the pistol. That last effort was more than enough. Blood was spurting through the wad of bandages around his armpit, and his stubbled face seemed to be whitening even as he tried to drag himself to the nearest gun, as if the life was flooding out of him.

Bolitho saw it all as in a wild dream, with events and sequences overlapping, yet totally separate. Gallimore's sudden cries had lured Tracy's guard from his post. And who could blame him? Tracy's terrible wound should have been enough to kill almost anyone.

And *Revenge*'s captain's voice calling across to Moffitt must have somehow dragged Tracy from his unconscious state to sudden, violent action.

Whatever had begun it, Bolitho knew there was no chance at all of completing his flimsy plan.

He yelled, '*Run out!*'

He watched his men hurling themselves on their tackles, the four guns squeaking to the open ports with desperation matched only by despair.

'*Fire!*'

As the guns crashed out in a ragged salvo, Bolitho shouted, 'Stockdale! Put the helm down!'

As Stockdale and a helmsman spun the spokes, Bolitho dragged out his hanger, knowing that nothing, nothing on earth could change this moment.

He heard startled shouts from his own men and musket shots from the *Revenge* as like a wild animal the *White Hills* responded to the helm and swung up into the wind, sails shaking and convulsing, as the other vessel appeared to charge right across her bowsprit.

There were several isolated shots, his or theirs, Bolitho did not know. He was running forward, his feet slipping on blood as he tore past the dying Tracy towards the point of impact.

Like a great tusk the jib boom smashed through *Revenge*'s rigging and stays, the impact shaking the hull and deck with the force of going aground.

And still the wind, and the *White Hills*'s impetus, drove them harder and faster together, until with a tremendous crash, followed by the sounds of spars splintering in half, the two brigs came together in a brutal embrace.

Bolitho's ears were ringing to the sounds of falling rigging and thrashing sails, of *Revenge*'s topmast, complete with topgallant and a mountain of uncontrollable canvas, plunging down through the drifting gunsmoke to add to the destruction.

But he was angry, wildly so, and could not control himself as he waved his hanger and shouted, 'Come on, lads! *At 'em!*'

He saw the dazed faces change to maddened excitement as they responded. In a small tide they charged towards the bows, while from aft Bolitho could hear Frowd and his collection of cripples firing across the arrowhead of water with every weapon they could lay hands on.

And here was the enemy's deck right beneath his legs. Staring eyes and wild shouts, while others struggled and kicked beneath the severed rigging and splintered woodwork.

A bayonet lunged out and sent a seaman screaming down into the smoke, but Bolitho let himself drop, felt his feet find their balance on the other deck, while on either side of him his boarding party surged forward to the attack. The man with the bayoneted musket swung wildly to face him, but Stockdale seized him and smashed the cutlass-guard in his mouth. As the man toppled away, Stockdale hacked him across the neck and finished it.

The first shocked surprise at seeing the *White Hills* turn towards them and deliberately force herself into a collision would soon give way to a rage and determination to overwhelm that of the boarders. This, Bolitho knew, but at a distance, as if it were already beyond his reach.

Once, as he ducked beneath a fallen yard to slash a man across the arm who was aiming a pistol at somebody, Bolitho caught a glimpse of his brief command. With her big mainyard sprung in two like a giant's longbow, and with the canvas and rigging piled over her forecastle like so much rubbish, she looked almost a wreck.

Beyond the debris, and licking above the thinning smoke, he saw a patch of scarlet, and realized that despite everything which had happened he had given the order to run up the colours, and yet could remember nothing about it.

'This way, lads!' It was Buller, brandishing a boarding axe and a pistol. 'Fight yer way aft!' Then he fell, his face set in an expression of complete surprise.

Bolitho gritted his teeth. Time, which they had won with such care, had run out.

From the *Revenge*'s quarterdeck came the crash of a swivel gun, and Bolitho realized that someone was still firing at the *White Hills*. Above the din of clashing steel, screams and curses, he heard answering shots, and could picture Frowd yelling defiance, and waiting to die.

Somehow they had fought their way to the midships part of the deck, where the piled debris of cordage and broken spars made every move doubly hard, but where, if you hesitated, it was asking to be killed.

He saw Dunwoody rolling over and over on the bloodied deck, struggling with one of the *Revenge*'s seamen, one hand cut to shreds as he tried to hold off the man's dirk while he groped for his fallen cutlass.

Another man ran from the smoke, raised a boarding pike and drove it through Dunwoody's neck, pinioning his kicking body to the planking until the dirk stabbed him into stillness.

Bolitho saw it all, and as he struggled over an upended gig he found himself face to face with the *Revenge*'s captain. Beyond him he could see the abandoned wheel and the torn splinters standing up from the quarterdeck like quills, the sprawled bodies and crawling wounded who had fallen to the four doubly loaded six-pounders.

Bolitho ducked as the man's blade sliced above his head, caught his foot in a trailing rope and fell heavily on his side. He watched the blade rise and plunge towards him again, and held up his hanger to take the brunt of the blow. The numbing shock jarred his shoulder like a kick, and he saw the other officer turn and run aft, leaving Bolitho rather than face a sudden rally of the boarding party. Rabbett, his cutlass bloody to the hilt, Carlsson, the Swede, with a bayoneted musket he must have snatched from one of the brig's men, even Borga, the Roman cook, who held a dirk in either hand like one of his ancestors in the gladiators' arena, were still here and ready to fight.

On the far side of the deck he saw Quinn with the rest of the boarders, white-faced and with blood running from his forehead, locked in combat with twice his own number.

Bolitho saw Couzens and yelled hoarsely, 'Get back aboard! I told you to stay with Mr Frowd!'

He gasped and ducked as a shadow passed in front of him. Then with a sharp twist of his arm he brought the hanger round to lock with his attacker's cutlass.

The man was a petty officer of sorts and, he guessed, as English as himself.

'You've bitten off too much this time, *sir*!'

Bolitho felt the man's strength forcing him back, the blade inches from his chest. It was not that he was a better swordsman, but his voice, if not Cornish, was certainly from Bolitho's own West Country.

Moffitt rose shaking his head like a prize-fighter, the blood of another victim glittering on his cutlass.

'And *you*!'

Bolitho fell back with the petty officer on top of him. Moffitt's blade had been driven into his spine with such force it was a wonder it had not pinioned both of them.

Couzens was ducking and side-stepping wildly as figures staggered and kicked around him like madmen. Steel on steel, and from right aft a chorus of screams as a swivel exploded and burst apart amongst its own crew.

But he managed to shout, 'I came to help!'

Bolitho shook his arm, feeling him cringe, as he said, 'Take two men and get below! Tell them I want this brig set alight!' He knew the boy was terrified of him, his wildness, and his despair. '*Do it!*'

Shots were hitting the deck around him and making the corpses jerk to their impact. The *Revenge*'s captain had sent marksmen aloft to mark down Frowd's puny challenge and to kill any of the boarders who looked like an officer or a leader.

Stockdale bellowed, 'Watch out, sir!' He lunged forward as a man rushed at Bolitho with a cutlass, but was not quick enough.

Bolitho saw the fury on the seaman's contorted features and wondered if he himself looked like that, if that was why Couzens had seemed so frightened of him.

The heavy cutlass grated across Bolitho's sword-belt, scoring the brass plate like a musket-ball.

Bolitho saw the man's expression change to fear, then to nothing as the hanger opened his face from eye to jaw and threw him screaming into the men behind him.

Bolitho felt sick, worn out and stunned by the savagery of battle. Couzens would not be able to fire the brig, and in any case they had started to cheer. The battle was nearly done. Like Quinn, he had tried.

There it was again, wild and uncontrolled. '*Huzza! Huzza!*'

Bolitho stared at Stockdale. 'That was no enemy!'

He swung round, dropping his guard for the first time, as through the fore-hatch came a sudden rush of dirty, unshaven figures.

Couzens was running with them, beside himself with ecstasy as he shouted, 'Prisoners, sir!'

He was pushed away by the released men as they snatched up fallen cutlasses, belaying pins, anything which could hit or maim their old captors.

Bolitho thought he must be going mad, and yet it was happening. They were obviously seamen captured in previous battles, maybe some from this very brig. But they charged through the dwindling boarding party like an avenging tidal wave, beating down the privateer's crew and hurling some of them over the side in their determination to seize the poop.

Bolitho shouted, 'Come on, lads! One last effort!'

Then, cheering and yelling meaningless words he ran with the rest, his arm like lead as he hacked and parried, cut and pushed his way aft.

A few shots were still hitting the deck nearby, and without warning a seaman slithered down a stay and snatched a pistol from his belt, his face frozen in concentration as he stared at the onrushing figures.

He must have known that nothing could save him, and yet some last spark of anger or pride held him there.

Couzens found himself face to face with him. Bolitho saw what was happening, but was several paces away, and Stockdale further still.

Bolitho shouted hoarsely, 'You shoot and I will kill you!'

The man's eyes did not even flicker, and Bolitho knew he was going to fire, he could even see the trigger starting to give under his finger.

A figure bounded over a pile of tangled sails and threw himself between the pistol and the stricken Couzens, so that the shot was almost muffled.

Bolitho ran and caught Quinn as he fell. He did not see Stockdale's big cutlass swing, but heard just a sharp grunt as the other man died.

Bolitho held Quinn and lowered him to the deck. He knew he was dying and there was nothing he could do. The ball had entered his stomach and there was blood everywhere.

Quinn gasped, 'Sorry . . . to . . . leave . . . you . . . sir.'

Bolitho held him firmly, knowing Stockdale was guarding his back and that Couzens was kneeling on the deck beside him sobbing uncontrollably.

'*Dick*,' he said. 'Remember, eh?'

He felt near to tears himself. What made it worse, if that were possible, was the cheering. Aft, in another world, his jubilant sailors and the released captives were hauling down the flag, watched by the *Revenge*'s captain who had been badly wounded in the last charge.

Bolitho said quietly, 'We won, James. It's done.'

Quinn smiled, his eyes looking up through the torn rigging and sails. '*You* did.'

He was finding it difficult to speak and his skin looked like damp wax. Bolitho unbuttoned his shirt, seeing the great, cruel scar from Quinn's first battle.

With his free hand he loosened his cross-belt and said gently, 'And you were supposed to be a passenger. But for you, young Couzens would be dead. I'll see they know about it in England. About your courage.'

Quinn's eyes shifted to Bolitho's face. 'I'm not afraid any more,' he coughed and some blood ran down his chin, 'Dick.'

Bolitho was about to speak when he saw the light go from Quinn's eyes. Like a candle being snuffed out.

Very carefully he lowered Quinn's shoulders to the deck and then stood up.

Stockdale touched his elbow. 'Be easy, sir. The people are watchin'.'

Bolitho nodded, his eyes almost blind with strain and emotion. 'Thank you. Yes.'

He faced the weary but triumphant seamen. It had been a near thing. But these men had done as well as anyone could. They deserved every last effort, no matter how he was feeling.

He said quietly, 'That was well done. For a company so small, there could be none so gallant.'

*

Three days later the two prizes sailed into English Harbour under the eyes of the whole squadron.

It had been a hard three days. Repairing damage just enough to carry them to Antigua, selecting the released prisoners and sharing them between the two brigs.

It should have been a proud moment for Bolitho, but the sadness of Quinn's death was still with him when the lookout reported land in sight.

He had taken command of the *Revenge*, and one of the first jobs he had ordered after rigging the jury-mast, and burying the dead of both sides, had been the removal of her new name, beneath which Jonas Tracy had painted the favoured motto, DON'T TREAD ON ME, with the serpent insignia for good measure.

As the land had grown out of the sea haze, and the two brigs had tacked carefully towards the harbour, a patrolling frigate had run down on them to investigate.

Couzens had called, 'What shall I tell them, sir?'

Stockdale had looked at Bolitho's features and had thought he had understood.

He had said, 'I'll do it, Mr Couzens.'

Then he had cupped his big hands and had shouted across for all to hear.

'His Majesty's brig *Mischief* is rejoining the fleet!' It had been a very special moment for him as he had added, 'Lieutenant Richard Bolitho, *in command*!'

SLOOP
OF
WAR

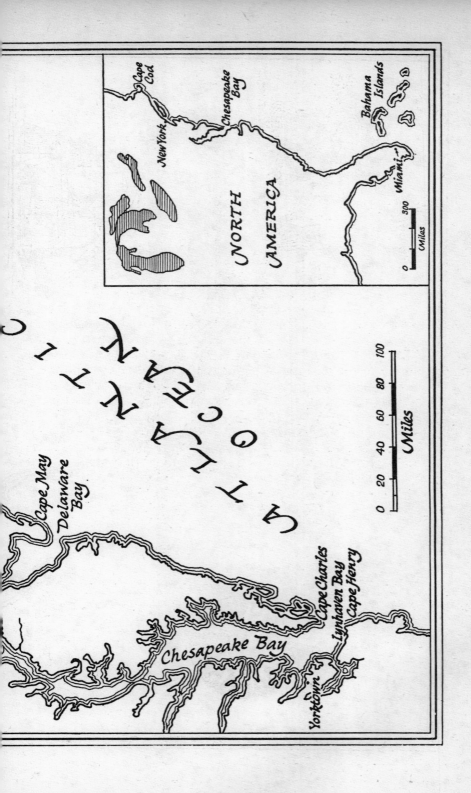

Part One
1778

I

The Most Coveted Gift

It was a little more than a hundred yards' walk from the busy foreshore to the elegant white building at the top of the coast road, but within a minute of leaving the launch Richard Bolitho was damp with sweat. In the broad expanse of English Harbour there had been an illusion of a breeze, but here, as the noon sun stood high above Monk's Hill and bathed the island of Antigua in a shimmering haze, there was no such comfort.

Nevertheless, Bolitho quickened his pace, conscious of his rising excitement and a sense of unreality which had been with him since his arrival just a week earlier. Events had moved so fast that he felt unable to keep a grip on them, as if he was a spectator watching somebody else, a being quite alien to his own resources.

Through wide gates, the sand and dust covering his new shoes with a pale layer, and across some well-tended gardens towards the building itself. But for the flag which hung limply from its staff it could have been the residence of some rich merchant or shipowner. From the number of Negro servants who were working amidst the flowers and shrubs he guessed that the previous occupant had probably been a dealer in African slaves.

Within the deep porch it felt almost cold after the sun's fierce glare, and he found himself confronted by a red-faced sergeant of marines who, after a cursory glance which covered Bolitho from top to toe, said, 'If you will step into this room, sir.' His tone, if not offhand, was that of a man so used to dealing with the comings and goings of sea-officers that he could no longer be excited by anything or anyone.

Bolitho entered the small room and heard the door slam behind him. For the first time since he could recall he was quite alone. Alone, and poised on what might be the most important step in his life.

He made himself walk very slowly to the window and stood looking down at the harbour spread below him like some great painting. English Harbour. The headquarters and linchpin of England's sea power in the Indies and Caribbean. Every type of ship seemed to be here. Stately two-deckers in the deep anchorage, their awnings spread and every gun port open to catch the merest breath of air. Lithe frigates and supply vessels, and a whole collection of smaller craft from brigs to schooners, between which countless oared boats plied back and forth like water-beetles.

Somewhere in the building a man shouted loudly and feet clattered in a passageway. Bolitho tore his eyes from the anchored ships and crossed to a wall mirror, his mind suddenly very aware of what the next minutes might bring or take away.

He still could not get used to his change of appearance. He had never imagined that a uniform would alter a man's outward image so much yet leave him inwardly the same. Just weeks ago he had been second lieutenant in the *Trojan*, an eighty-gun ship-of-the-line. For three years he had lived, worked and nearly died within her crowded hull, rising from his original position of fourth lieutenant by way of one man's death and the promotion of another. He had become used to the *Trojan*, even though he had to fight off the yearning to free himself from her ponderous authority to find more individual scope for his ideas.

Like everyone aboard he had been kept busy enough. With the rebellion in America every ship-of-war was needed as never before. As the rebellion grew and spread and some real hint of its purpose filtered through to the fleet the *Trojan* was called from one crisis to another.

It seemed incredible that disorganized bands of men could be welded into armies. Armies strong and agile enough to outmanoeuvre some of the best troops from England. But like most of his companions Bolitho had firmly believed that some sort of compromise would still present itself. That was until six months ago in October 1777, when the news of Burgoyne's surrender had burst upon them. Overnight, or so it seemed, the rebellion had developed into a new and bitter conflict. On the one hand the British with their overstretched resources, and on the other the armies of the American Revolution backed as they were by a whole fleet of privateers from France and Spain. No supply ship could sail alone without the real risk of being taken by such privateers. Even troop convoys were not immune from attack.

It was in the middle of this new hit-and-run war that Bolitho's own life had changed. *Trojan* had run down and boarded a prize, a handsome brig, off the coast of Puerto Rico, her holds jammed with contraband goods and powder for the Americans. Caught between two sets of shoals, and confronted by the *Trojan*'s impressive artillery, her master decided to surrender without fuss.

Trojan's first lieutenant was badly needed in his own ship as most of the officers were newly appointed and without much experience. To Bolitho fell the lot of prize-master, with orders to take her to Antigua and await further instructions. It was like the beginning to some impossible dream. Freedom, excitement, the room to move and act without his captain's eye upon him, the little brig seemed to offer unlimited possiblities, even though he knew it would not last.

But fate had other ideas. Within a few days they had sighted another, larger brig, well handled, and displaying a heavier armament than was usual for such a craft. There had been no doubt that she was a privateer, and further, it had seemed likely she was approaching to make a rendezvous with the prize.

There was little time to think, let alone plan. The other ship would outsail and outshoot anything Bolitho's small prize-crew could offer. To fight and die to no purpose was unthinkable, and to surrender without doing so was equally so.

It had turned out to be so simple that looking back it too seemed like part of the dream. Closing the unsuspecting privateer, apparently to pass despatches, they had run alongside and grappled her, both vessels being buried under a mass of fallen spars and canvas in the collision. A volley of musket fire, a wildly yelling rush of boarders, and the other ship was taken, even though her company outnumbered Bolitho's party by four to one. *Trojan*'s seamen were well used to this sort of game. The privateer's crew were not. In fact, it was her captain's first voyage in that capacity.

So instead of one prize Bolitho entered harbour with a pair. With the war going badly on land, and affairs at sea so confused as to be equally disheartening, his arrival under the guns of the harbour's battery was like a tonic. Handshakes from a rear-admiral, smiling greetings from senior captains, Bolitho had been staggered by the welcome.

With the prizes handed over to the dockyard he had been found accommodation in an old hulk called *Octavia*. Originally a two-decker, she had been all but sunk in a hurricane the previous year, and now served as accommodation ship. Junior officers whiled away the time gambling, sleeping or drinking to excess as they awaited their next appointments. Promotion and transfers, courts martial or passage home as a crippled victim of some encounter with the enemy, the old *Octavia* had seen them all.

As the days passed, Bolitho began to imagine he had been forgotten. Soon the *Trojan* would arrive and he would find himself back again in her tight community. Living from day to day. Hoping, yet not daring to hope for too much.

The orders, when they were delivered by an immaculate flag lieutenant, were as brief as they were astounding. By consent of the Commander-in-Chief, Richard Bolitho would take upon himself the appointment of commander with the rank and benefits attached. The appointment would take effect forthwith. He would furnish himself with all necessary vestments and report to the newly acquired headquarters building in two days' time.

He stared at himself in the glass. *Today*.

It seemed that in Antigua you could obtain everything even at such short notice, for a price. And now, instead of his faded lieutenant's uniform, he was looking at the broad blue lapels of commander, the single gold stripe on each sleeve which showed him to be what was to all intent a junior captain. Behind him on the chair a gold-laced cocked hat shone in the filtered sunlight, and like everything else about him, his white waistcoat and breeches, a tight neckcloth and his dusty shoes, even the handsome basket-hilted sword which he had chosen with such care, were so new that they felt like borrowed finery. He had not dared to contemplate the cost, the bribes required to obtain everything within the allotted time. An advance on his well-earned prize money had sufficed for the present.

He touched the lock of black hair which hung rebelliously above his right eye. Beneath it the deep, savage scar which ran to his hairline felt hot, as if it had been a matter of weeks rather than years when he had been struck down by a cutlass.

In spite of his inner tension he grinned at himself. Junior or not, he had taken the first real step. One which would bring him either fame or disgrace, but which like all his family before him he had awaited with both anxiety and eagerness.

More footsteps sounded in the passageway and he adjusted his neckcloth and settled the new sword more comfortably on his hip. Once again his image in the mirror was like a stranger's. The uniform, the tense way he was holding his slim figure as if on parade, displayed more apprehension than he had believed he harboured.

The footsteps halted outside the door, and in one movement Bolitho swept up the cocked hat and jammed it beneath one arm, trying to ignore his heart pounding against his ribs like a hammer. His mouth was bone dry, yet he could feel the sweat running between his shoulder-blades like warm rain.

Richard Bolitho was twenty-two years old and had been in the King's Navy since the age of twelve. But as he stared fixedly at the gilt door handle he felt more like a frightened midshipman than the man who was about to receive the most coveted gift to be bestowed on any living creature. A command of his own.

The marine sergeant stared at him woodenly. 'When you're ready, sir. Cap'n Colquhoun will see you now.'

'I'm ready, thank you.'

The marine eyed him with the merest hint of a smile. 'He'll be glad to know that, I'm sure, sir.'

Bolitho did not hear a word. Following the sergeant he strode out into the passageway, and another world.

*

Captain Vere Colquhoun rose briefly from behind a large desk, made as if to offer his hand, and then sank back into his chair.

'Pray be seated, Bolitho.'

He had his back to a window and it was impossible to see his expression. But as Bolitho arranged himself into a narrow, high-backed chair he was well aware of the other man's scrutiny.

Colquhoun said, 'You have a good report.' He opened a canvas folder and ran his eyes across the attached papers. 'I see that you were commissioned lieutenant in 'seventy-four.' He glanced up sharply. 'Well?'

Bolitho replied, 'Yes, sir. The *Destiny*, frigate.'

He had been long enough in the Navy to realize that interviews with superior officers took time. Each had his own way, but all seemed to result in being kept hanging on a thread of uneasy expectation. He tried to ignore Colquhoun's bowed head and made himself look instead at the room. White walls and a colourful tiled floor. Some pieces of dark, heavy furniture and one table which was almost covered with handsome decanters. Colquhoun, it appeared, enjoyed life. He shifted his gaze to his new superior. At a guess he was about thirty, and from what he could see from the sunlit window he had finely cut features with a small, aggressive chin. He had fair hair, pulled back to the nape of his neck like his own, in the current fashion, and Bolitho noticed that in spite of his service on the station his skin was remarkably pale.

Colquhoun said, 'Your captain speaks well of you.' He rustled his papers. 'Quite well.'

Bolitho tried not to swallow and display the dryness in his throat. Captain Pears of the *Trojan* had sent a report with him aboard the prize. Had he been aware of Bolitho's later luck with the privateer his report might have been even better. It was strange, he thought. In the three years aboard Pears's ship he had never really understood the man. Sometimes he had imagined his captain disliked him, and at best only tolerated his efforts. Yet now, on his desk, under the eyes of a new superior, Pears's words were showing him in a different light.

'Thank you, sir.'

'Hmph.' Colquhoun stood up and walked towards the table and then changed his mind. Instead he moved to the window and stared absently at the anchorage. 'I am commanded to give you your new appointment. It will be up to you to prove your worth, an ability to carry out orders rather than to make play with them for your own advantage.'

Bolitho waited. It was impossible to follow this man.

Colquhoun added, 'Since the military disaster at Saratoga last year we have seen all the signs of the French increasing their aid to the Americans. Originally they sent supplies and military advisers. Then privateers and soldiers-of-fortune, mercenaries.' He spat out the words.

'Now they are more open in their efforts to use the Americans to further their own ends and regain territory lost to us in the Seven Years War.'

Bolitho gripped the hilt of his new sword and tried to remain outwardly calm. Somewhere outside this room was a ship awaiting her new captain. Old or new, large or insignificant as a fighting unit, she was to be all his own. And he had to remain quite still, listening to Captain Colquhoun's observations on the war. Bolitho had been involved in the war since its beginning, and he had already learned from a fellow officer in the *Octavia* that Colquhoun had arrived from England just six months ago.

Colquhoun was saying in the same dry tone, 'But while we command the sea-lanes and supply routes neither the French nor the damned Pope can stop us regaining overall control of the mainland.' He turned slightly, the sun glinting across the gold lace of his coat. 'Don't you agree?'

Bolitho shifted in his chair. 'Up to a point, sir. But . . .'

Colquhoun snapped, '*But* is not a word which appeals to me. Either you agree or you disagree.'

'I think more should be done to seek out the privateers and destroy them in their bases, sir.' He paused, anticipating some caustic remark. Then he continued, 'We have too few ships to spare for convoy work. Any attack on merchantmen, pressed home by two or more vessels at once, can play the devil with a solitary escort.'

'Really. You surprise me.'

Bolitho bit his lip. He had allowed himself to be drawn. Perhaps Colquhoun had been hoping that one of his friends or protégés would be given the new appointment, and saw Bolitho as an intruder. Whatever it was, there seemed to be no doubting his hostility.

'I have, of course, heard of your family, Bolitho. Seafaring stock. None of 'em ever afraid to risk his neck. And out here at this moment we need the best fighting officers we can get.'

He turned abruptly to the window. 'Come over here.'

Bolitho crossed to his side and followed his glance towards the ships at anchor.

'Look impressive, don't they?' Colquhoun gave what might have been a sigh. 'But once at sea, scattered to the winds, they are just a handful. With the Frogs at our backs and threatening England once more we are stretched beyond any safety limit.' He gestured across the harbour. A frigate was being careened, heeled right over on her beam, her bilges covered with busy figures, their naked backs shining in the glare like polished mahogany. Colquhoun said, quietly, '*Bacchante*, thirty-six.' He tightened his jaw. '*My* ship. First time I've been able to get her underwater repairs done since I assumed command.'

Bolitho darted a quick glance at him. He had always dreamed of commanding a frigate since his first and only experience in the little twenty-eight-gun *Destiny*. Freedom to move and hit hard at anything but a ship-of-the-line, with all the dash and agility that any young captain could ask for. But Colquhoun did not seem to fit the role. Slightly built, with the pale, petulant good looks of a true aristocrat. His clothes were beautifully made, and the sword at his hip must be worth two hundred guineas.

Colquhoun raised his arm. 'Look yonder. Beyond my ship you will see the rest of our flotilla. With these and nothing more I am expected to patrol and seek out the enemy, run errands for the fleet, dab away the tears of rich merchantmen whenever they sight an unfamiliar sail. It would need a force five times as large, and even then I would hope for more.'

He turned to watch Bolitho's expression as he stared across the shimmering water.

Bolitho said slowly, 'Three sloops-of-war.' He saw a tiny armed schooner anchored beyond the others. Was she to be his? He swallowed hard. 'And a schooner.'

'Correct.' Colquhoun moved to his table and picked up a heavy decanter. As he held it against the sunlight he said, 'You are being given the *Sparrow*, Bolitho. Eighteen guns and only two years old.' He eyed him flatly. 'Next to my frigate, she is the best under my command.'

Bolitho could only stare at him.

'I do not know what to say, sir.'

The other man grimaced. 'Then say nought.' He poured two glasses of brandy.

'I have no doubt of your ability as a sea-officer, Bolitho. Your past record is proof of that. To obey and carry out orders without question is one thing, however. To lead others, to hold their skills and lives in your hands without ever losing grip, is something else entirely.' He offered him a glass. 'To your first command, Bolitho. I wish you more of the luck which has guided your feet to this year of 'seventy-eight, for I *promise* you will need it!'

The brandy was like fire, but Bolitho's head was still reeling and he hardly noticed it. A new sloop. The best under Colquhoun's command. In a moment he would awake aboard *Octavia* to find today just beginning.

Colquhoun said calmly, 'Your predecessor in *Sparrow* died recently.'

'I am sorry to hear it, sir.'

'Hmm.' Colquhoun studied him thoughtfully. 'Fever. His first lieutenant is too junior even for temporary command.' He shrugged. 'Your timely arrival, the blessing of our devoted admiral, and, of course, Bolitho, your obvious qualities for the appointment, made you an immediate choice, eh?' He was not smiling.

Bolitho looked away. It would be safer to assume from the beginning that Colquhoun had no sense of humour.

He said, 'I will do my best, sir.'

'Be sure of that.' Colquhoun took out his watch and flicked it open. '*Sparrow* is at full complement. For seamen, that is. I will have to send your prize-crew to other vessels in greater need. Unless you have any particular fellow you wish to keep?'

'Yes, sir. Just one. I appreciate that.'

Colquhoun sighed. 'You are a curious mixture. A Cornishman, I believe?'

'Aye, sir.'

'Ah well . . .' He did not continue. Instead he said, 'I have made arrangements for a boat to collect you in a half-hour. Your documents will be ready by then.'

Bolitho waited, half expecting some fresh advice.

Colquhoun seemed to read his thoughts and said quietly, 'From time to time you will receive written instructions. But you will only be told *what* to do. How you achieve success and carry them out will be your burden alone.' He turned back to the window, his eyes on the careened frigate. 'I have held four different commands. The first was, of course, the most exciting. But also, as I recall, the loneliest. No more could I ask for help from my companions in the wardroom. Nor could I seek freedom outside my hours of duty. In earlier days I always imagined a captain to be a kind of god, put on earth to command and to leave all worry of execution to mere subordinates. Now, I know different, as you will.'

Bolitho picked up his hat. 'I shall try and remember that, sir.'

Colquhoun did not face him. 'You will not. You will think you know better than everyone else, which is as it should be. But somewhere along the way, in the teeth of a gale, or facing an enemy broadside, or becalmed perhaps with the ship's people near mad with thirst, you will know the true meaning of command. When you need help and advice most, and there is none. When all others are looking aft at you, and you have the power of life and death in your fingers. *Then* you will know, believe me.'

He added shortly, 'You may wait in the room by the entrance.'

The interview was ended.

Bolitho crossed to the door, his eyes on the silhouette against the bright window. It was such an important moment that he wanted to hold on to every part of it. Even the furniture and the well-stocked decanters.

Then he closed the door behind him and returned to the waiting room. When he looked at his watch he saw he had been just twenty minutes in the building.

At the window he stood staring at the small ships on the far side of the anchorage, trying to distinguish one from the other, wondering what she would be like. What his company would think of him.

Eventually the door opened and an elderly lieutenant peered into the room.

'*Sparrow*, sir?'

Bolitho saw the sealed envelope in the man's hands and took a deep breath.

He nodded. 'Yes.'

The lieutenant bobbed his head and smiled. 'Your orders, sir. The boat has been sighted approaching the jetty. I will arrange for your gear to be collected from *Trojan* when she reaches here.' He shrugged. 'I am not so sure it will ever catch up with you, however.'

Bolitho grinned, unable to maintain his outward calm.

'Have it sold for me, eh? Put it towards helping some of those wounded seamen awaiting passage to England.'

As he strode towards the sunlight the lieutenant took out a pair of steel-rimmed glasses and peered after him. Then he shook his head very slowly. A remarkable young man, he thought. It was to be hoped he would remain so.

After the shadowy cool of the building Bolitho found the sun's glare harsher than before. As he strode down the coast road, his mind half dwelling on the interview with Colquhoun, he was already wondering what his new command would offer. With, but not *of* the fleet, there should at least be room to move, freedom from the daily flow of signals and requirements which had been his lot in the powerful *Trojan*.

He paused at a curve in the road and shaded his eyes to watch the boat which was already drawing near to the jetty. He shivered in spite of the heat and started to walk more quickly towards the sea. To anybody else it was just one more boat going about its ship's affairs, but to him it represented far more. A first contact. Some of his men. *His* men.

He saw the familiar shape of Stockdale standing beside some of his newly bought belongings and felt a sudden touch of warmth. Even if Colquhoun had said that not one single man of Bolitho's prize-crew could be spared for his first command he felt sure Stockdale would have arrived aboard in his own way. Thickset and muscular, in his broad white trousers and blue jacket, he reminded him of some indestructible oak. He, too, was watching the approaching boat, his eyes slitted against the light with critical interest.

Bolitho had been junior lieutenant in the frigate *Destiny* when their paths had first crossed. Sent ashore on the thankless task of drumming up recruits for the ship, and with little hope of much success, he had arrived at a small inn with his party of seamen to set up headquarters and, more to the point, to find some peace and a moment to refresh himself for the next attempt to obtain volunteers. Tramping from village to village, inn to inn, the system rarely changed. It usually resulted in a collection of those who were either too young for the harsh demands of a frigate or old sailors who had failed to find fortune or success ashore and merely wanted to return and end their days in surroundings they had originally sworn to forsake forever.

Stockdale had been none of these. He had been a prize-fighter, and stripped to the waist had been standing like a patient ox outside the inn while his sharp-faced barker had called upon all and sundry to risk a battering and win a guinea.

Tired and thirsty, Bolitho had entered the inn, momentarily leaving his small party to their own devices. Exactly what had happened next was not quite clear, but on hearing a string of curses, mingled with the loud laughter of the sailors, he had hurried outside to find one of his men pocketing the guinea and the enraged barker beating Stockdale round the head and shoulders with a length of chain. Whether the victorious seaman, a powerful gunner's mate well used to enforcing authority with brute force, had tripped Stockdale or gained a lucky blow was never discovered. Certainly, Bolitho had never seen Stockdale beaten in any fight, fair or otherwise, since that day. As he had shouted at his men to fall in line again he had realized that Stockdale had been standing as before, taking the unjust punishment, when with one stroke he could have killed the barker who was tormenting him.

Sickened by the spectacle, and angry with himself at the same time, he had asked Stockdale to volunteer for the King's service. The man's dumb gratitude had been almost as embarrassing as the grins on the sailors' faces, but he had found some comfort in the barker's stunned disbelief as without a word Stockdale had picked up his shirt and followed the party away from the inn.

If he had imagined that was the end of the matter he was soon to discover otherwise. Stockdale took to a life at sea in a manner born. As strong as two men, he was gentle and patient, and whenever Bolitho was in danger he always seemed to be there. When a cutlass had hacked Bolitho to the ground and his boat's crew had retreated in panic, it had been Stockdale who had rallied them, had fought off the attackers and carried his unconscious lieutenant to safety. When Bolitho had left the frigate for the *Trojan* Stockdale had somehow contrived to transfer also. Never far away, he had been his servant as well as gun captain, and when aboard the prize ship he had merely to glare at the captured crew to obtain instant respect. He spoke very little, and then only with a husky whisper. His vocal cords had been maimed over the years of fighting for others in booths and fairgrounds up and down the country.

But when Bolitho's promotion had been delivered he had said simply,

'You'll be needing a good cox'n, sir.' He had given his lazy, lopsided grin. 'Whatever sort of ship they gives you.'

And so it was settled. Not that there would have been any doubt in Bolitho's mind either.

He turned as Bolitho strode down the jetty and touched his hat.

'All ready.' He ran his eyes over Bolitho's new uniform and nodded with obvious approval. 'No more'n you deserve, sir.'

Bolitho smiled. 'We shall have to see about that.'

With oars tossed, and a seaman already scrambling ashore with a line, the cutter eased gently against the piles.

Stockdale stooped and steadied the gunwale with his fist, his eyes on the motionless oarsmen as he said hoarsely, 'A fine day for it, sir.'

A slim midshipman leapt from the boat and removed his hat with a flourish. About eighteen, he was a pleasant-looking youth, and as tanned as a native.

'I'm Heyward, sir.' He shifted under Bolitho's impassive gaze. 'I—I've been sent to collect you, sir.'

Bolitho nodded. 'Thank you, Mr Heyward. You can tell me about the ship as we go.'

He waited for the midshipman and Stockdale to follow his sea-chest and bags into the boat and then stepped after them.

'Shove off forrard! Out oars!' Heyward seemed very conscious of Bolitho's nearness. 'Give way all!'

Like pale bones the oars rose and fell in regular precision. Bolitho glanced swiftly at the two lines of oarsmen. Neatly dressed in check shirts and white trousers, they looked fit and healthy enough. A ship could always be judged by her boats, some people contended. Bolitho knew otherwise. Some captains kept their boats as outward show-pieces, while within their own ships the people lived little better than animals. Their expressions gave nothing away. The usual, homely faces of British sailors, set in careful masks to avoid his scrutiny. Each man was probably wondering about the new captain. To any seaman his captain was not much junior to God. He could lead, and use his skills on their behalf in battle. He might just as easily turn their lives into a daily hell with no one to whom they could protest or plead their cause.

The midshipman said haltingly, 'We have been at anchor for three days, sir.'

'Before that?'

'Patrol duty off Guadeloupe. We did sight a French brig but lost her, sir.'

'How long have you been in *Sparrow*?'

'Two years, sir. Since she commissioned on the Thames at Greenwich.'

Stockdale craned round. 'There she is, sir. Fine on the larboard bow.'

Bolitho sat upright in the sternsheets, knowing that as soon as his eyes left the boat every man would be staring at him. He could barely contain his excitement as he peered towards the anchored sloop which was now fully in view beyond a heavy transport. She was riding almost motionless above the twin of her own reflection, her ensign making a scarlet patch of colour against the haze-shrouded hills beyond.

Bolitho had seen sloops in plenty during his service. Like frigates, they were everywhere and always in demand. Maids of all work, the eyes of the fleet, they were familiar in most naval harbours. But right at this moment in time he also knew that the *Sparrow* was going to be different from all those others. From her gently spiralling mastheads to the single line of open gun ports she was a thing of beauty. A thoroughbred, a miniature frigate, a vessel which seemed eager to be free of the land. She was all and none of these things.

He heard himself say, 'Steer round her bows.'

As the tiller went over he was conscious of the silence, broken only by the sluice of water around the cutter's stern and the rhythmic creak of oars. As if he was sharing this moment with nobody. Like a raked black finger the sloop's long jib-boom swept out and over his head, and for a few more moments he stared up at the figurehead below the bowsprit. A man-sized sparrow, beak wide in fury and wings spread as if to fight, its curved claws firmly gripping a gilded cluster of oak leaves and acorns. Bolitho watched until the boat had moved around and under the starboard cathead. He had never thought a mere sparrow could be depicted as being so warlike.

He started with surprise as his eyes fell on a gun muzzle in the first port.

Heyward said respectfully, 'We have a thirty-two-pounder on either bow, sir. The rest of the gundeck is made up of sixteen twelve-pounders.' He flinched as Bolitho turned to look at him. 'I beg your pardon, sir, I did not mean to intrude.'

Bolitho smiled and touched his arm. 'I was merely surprised. She seems to have very heavy artillery for such a small ship.' He shook his head. 'Those two bow-chasers must have brought many an enemy aback with shock. Nine-pounders are more common in sloops, I believe.'

The midshipman nodded, but his eyes were on the ship's side, his lips in an anxious line as he gauged the moment.

'Put her about!'

The cutter swung in a tight arc and headed for the main chains. There were many heads lining the gangway, and Bolitho saw the blue and white of an officer's uniform by the entry port, a press of more figures by the mainmast.

'Toss your oars!'

The boat idled towards the chains where the bowman brought down his boathook with a well-timed slash.

Bolitho stood up in the sternsheets, conscious of all the eyes above and around him. Of Stockdale's hand, half-raised, ready to steady him if he lost his balance. Of the new sword at his hip and not wanting to look down to make sure it would not tangle with his legs as he climbed up the sleek tumblehome.

With a quick breath he reached out and hauled himself from the boat. He had been prepared for almost everything but was still taken totally off guard by the piercing shrill of pipes as his head and shoulders rose through the port. Perhaps, more than anything else, the time-honoured salute from a ship to her captain made him realize just how great was the step from lieutenant's berth to command.

It was all too much to take in and comprehend in this small cameo. The drawn swords, the boatswain's mates with their silver calls to their lips, the bare-backed seamen on the gangways and high in the shrouds. Below his feet he felt the deck lift easily, and once more was aware of the change this ship had brought him. After the *Trojan's* fat bulk, her massive weight of guns and spars, this sloop even *felt* alive.

One officer stepped forward as Bolitho removed his hat to the quarterdeck and said, 'Welcome aboard, sir. I am Graves, second lieutenant.'

Bolitho regarded him searchingly. The lieutenant was young and alert, but had the controlled caution on his dark features of a man much older.

He half turned and added, 'The others are awaiting your pleasure, sir.'

Bolitho asked, 'And the first lieutenant?'

Graves looked away. 'In the flagship, sir. He had an appointment.' He faced him quickly. 'He meant no disrespect, sir, I am quite sure of that.'

Bolitho nodded. Graves's explanation was too swift, too glib. Or that of a man who wished to draw attention to the absent officer's behaviour by excusing it.

Graves hurried on, 'This is Mr Buckle, the sailing master, sir. Mr Dalkeith, surgeon.' His voice followed Bolitho down the small line of senior warrant officers.

Bolitho marked each face but checked himself from further contact. That would come soon enough, but now his own impression on them was far more vital.

He stood by the quarterdeck rail and stared down at the gundeck. The *Sparrow* was one hundred and ten feet long on that deck, but had a broad beam of thirty feet, almost that of a frigate. No wonder she could contain such powerful armament for her size.

He said, 'Have the hands lay aft, Mr Graves.'

As the order was passed and the men came pressing down on those already assembled, he drew his commission from his pocket and spread it on the rail. How hot the wood felt beneath his hands.

Again he darted a glance at the faces beneath him. In so small a ship how did they all manage to exist? There were one hundred and fifteen souls crammed aboard *Sparrow*, and as they jostled together below the quarterdeck there appeared to be twice that number.

Graves touched his hat. 'All present, sir.'

Bolitho replied with equal formality, 'Thank you.' Then in a steady voice he began to read himself in.

He had heard other captains do it often enough, but as he read the beautifully penned words he felt once more like a spectator.

It was addressed to Richard Bolitho, Esquire, and required him forthwith to go on board and take upon him the charge and command of captain in His Britannic Majesty's Sloop-of-War *Sparrow*.

Once or twice as his voice carried along the deck he heard a man cough or move his feet, and aboard another sloop close by he saw an officer watching the proceedings through a telescope.

He put the commission in his coat and said, 'I will go to my quarters, Mr Graves.'

He replaced his hat and walked slowly towards a covered hatch just forward of the mizzen mast. He noticed that the ship's wheel was completely unsheltered. A bad place in a storm, he thought, or when the balls begin to fly.

At his back he heard the rising murmur of voices as the men were dismissed, and noticed, too, the heavy smell of cooking in the listless air. He was glad he had restrained himself from making a speech. It would have been vanity, and he knew it. All the same, it was so precious a day that he wanted to share it with all of them in some way.

In his excitement he had forgotten about the time. Now as he made his way down a ladder to the gundeck and aft behind Graves's crouched figure he was more than glad he had restricted himself to the formal reading of his appointment. Men kept standing in the sun to hear a pompous speech were one thing. Men kept also from their well-earned meal were something else entirely.

He gasped as his head crashed against a deck beam.

Graves spun round. 'I beg your pardon, sir!' He seemed terrified Bolitho should blame him for the lack of headroom.

'I will remember next time.'

He reached the stern cabin and stepped inside. For an instant he stood motionless, taking in the graceful sloping stern windows which spread from quarter to quarter, displaying the anchorage and the headland like some glistening panorama. The cabin was beautifully painted in pale green, the panels picked out with gold leaf. The deck was concealed with a black and white checked canvas covering, and arranged on either side was a selection of well-made furniture. Gingerly he raised his head and found he could just stand upright between the beams above.

Graves was watching him worriedly. 'I am afraid that after a ship-of-the-line, sir, you'll find this somewhat cramped.'

Bolitho smiled. 'Have the ship's books brought to me after you have dined, Mr Graves. I will also want to meet the other officers informally sometime today.' He paused, seeing again the caution in his eyes. '*Including* the first lieutenant.'

Graves bowed himself out and Bolitho turned his back to the closed door.

Cramped, after a ship-of-the-line, Graves had said. He hurled his hat across the cabin on to the bench seat below the windows. His sword he unbuckled and dropped in a green velvet chair. He was laughing aloud, and the effort to restrain it was almost painful.

Cramped. He walked, ducking between the beams. It was a *palace* after the *Trojan*'s wardroom.

He sat down beside his hat and stared around the neat, cheerful-looking cabin.

And it was his own.

2

Freedom

It was late afternoon when Bolitho finally decided he had read all that there was available about the ship around him. Muster and punishment books, watch-bills and ledgers of stores and victualling returns, the list seemed endless. But at no time was he bored. With his new coat hanging on a chair-back, his neckcloth loosened and shirt unbuttoned, he found each item fascinating.

His predecessor, Captain Ransome, had kept a smart and well-run ship on the face of things. The punishment book had all the usual culprits and awards for minor misdemeanours. A few for drunkenness, even less for insolence and insubordination, and the worst recorded crime was that of a seaman who had struck a petty officer during gun drill.

Ransome had been extremely lucky in one thing. With the ship being commissioned on the Thames he had been able to secure the cream of the press. Men off incoming merchant ships, transfers from vessels laid up in ordinary, he had been in a position to complete his company with far less difficulty than most captains.

Against the apparent taut atmosphere in the ship was a rather negative list of reports in the log books. Only once had *Sparrow* been called to action in the two years since leaving England, and then as secondary reinforcement to a frigate attacking a blockade runner. It was little wonder that Midshipman Heyward had showed some concern at his remarks about the big bow-chasers. He had probably imagined his words to be some sort of criticism at their lack of use.

There were the usual lists of men transferred to other ships because of promotion and the like. Their places had been filled by what Ransome had termed 'local colonist volunteers' in his personal log. Bolitho had lingered a good deal on the previous captain's daily records. His comments were extremely brief and it was impossible to get even a feel of the man. As he paused to glance around the cabin from time to time Bolitho found himself wondering about Ransome. An experienced and competent officer, obviously a man of good breeding and therefore influence, the cabin seemed at odds with his mental portrait. Extremely attractive, comfortable, yet just that too much removed from what you might expect in a ship-of-war.

He sighed and leaned back in the chair as his cabin servant, Fitch, padded into the shafted sunlight to remove the remains of his meal.

Fitch was tiny. A miserable scrap of a man, who had already confessed to having been a petty thief in his unfortunate past. Saved from transportation or worse by the timely arrival of a King's ship as he awaited sentence at the Assizes, he had accepted life at sea more as an extension to his punishment than from any love of service. But he seemed a capable servant, and was probably well pleased with his work. It kept him from the heavier tasks on deck, and provided his current master was a humane man he had little to fear.

Bolitho watched him as he collected the crockery on to a tray. It had been an excellent meal. Cold tongue and fresh vegetables from ashore, and the claret which Fitch had mournfully observed was 'the last of Cap'n Ransome's stock' had been a touch of perfection.

'Your late captain.' Bolitho saw the small man stiffen. 'Did he leave any instruction as to his property aboard?'

Fitch dropped his eyes. 'Mr Tyrell 'as attended to it, sir. It's been sent to a transport for passage 'ome.'

'He must have been an officer of some consequence.'

Bolitho hated this form of questioning, but he felt he needed some link, no matter how small, with the man who had controlled this ship from the day she had slid into the water.

Fitch bit his lip. ' 'E were a strict cap'n, sir. 'E saw that the 'ands took fairly to their work. If they obeyed, 'e was 'appy. If not . . .' he shrugged his frail shoulders, 'then 'e tended to swear a piece.'

Bolitho nodded. 'You may leave.'

It was useless to proceed with Fitch. His life concerned only the comings and goings. Food and drink, a warm cot, or a swift curse if things were not to his master's liking.

Feet padded overhead and he had to restrain himself from running to the stern windows or standing on a chair to peer through the skylight above the table. He thought of his old companions in the *Trojan*'s wardroom and wondered if they were missing him. Probably not. His promotion would mean a gap, and therefore a step up the ladder for another. He smiled to himself. It would take time to fit himself into this new role. Time and vigilance.

There was a tap at the door and Mathias Buckle, the sailing master, stepped inside.

'Do you have a moment, sir?'

Bolitho gestured to a chair. Again this was so unlike a bigger ship-of-war. There were no marines in the company, and visitors to the captain's quarters seemed free to come and go almost as they pleased. Perhaps Ransome had encouraged such informality.

He watched Buckle fitting himself into the chair. He was a short, square-built man, with steady eyes and hair almost as dark as his own. Aged forty, he was the oldest man in the ship.

Buckle said, 'I'd not trouble you, sir, but as the first lieutenant's away, I thought . . .' He shifted in the chair. 'I thought I should settle the matter of promotion for one of the hands.'

Bolitho listened in silence as Buckle ran through the points which concerned a man named Raven. It was an internal matter, but he was conscious of the importance it represented. The very first time as captain he was being confronted with the affairs of one of his own company.

Buckle was saying, 'I thought, begging your pardon, sir, that we might advance him to master's mate for a trial period.'

Bolitho asked, 'How long have you been master?'

'Just in this ship, sir.' Buckle's clear eyes were distant. 'Before that I was master's mate in the old *Warrior*, seventy-four.'

'You've done well, Mr Buckle.' He was trying to place the dialect. London, or further east. Kent.

'How does she handle?'

Buckle seemed to consider it. 'She's heavy for her size, sir. All of four hundred and thirty tons. But the better the wind, the livelier she goes. You can even get the stunsails and royals on her in anything but a true blow.' He frowned. 'In a calm she can be the devil's daughter.' He gestured vaguely. 'You've probably seen the little port alongside each gun port, sir?'

Bolitho had not. He said slowly, 'I am not too sure.'

Buckle smiled for the first time. 'If you gets becalmed you may run a sweep through each o' those ports, sir. Clear lower deck and get every man-jack on the sweeps and you can still get a knot or two out of her.'

Bolitho looked away. Reading the ship's books and correspondence had not even told him the half of it. He felt vaguely angry that his first lieutenant was still not present. Normally the departing captain would have been aboard to tell him the ship's behaviour and failings, or at least the senior lieutenant.

Buckle said, 'You'll soon get the better of her, sir. She's the best yet.'

Bolitho eyed him thoughtfully. The master was nobody's fool, and yet, like Graves, he seemed to be holding back. Maybe waiting for him to display his strength or weakness to them.

He made himself reply coldly, 'We shall see about that, Mr Buckle.'

When he glanced up he saw the man watching him with sudden anxiety. He added, 'Any other matter?'

Buckle rose to his feet. 'No, sir.'

'Good. I anticipate that sailing orders will be arriving shortly. I will expect the ship to be ready.'

Buckle nodded. 'Aye, sir. Have no fear.'

Bolitho relented slightly. It was just possible his own uncertainty was making him unnecessarily harsh towards his sailing master. And it was equally likely he would need Buckle's guiding hand very much until he got the feel of his new command.

He said, 'I have no doubt that I will be as satisfied with your appointment as Captain Ransome was.'

Buckle swallowed hard. 'Yes, sir.' He stared round the low cabin. 'Thank you, sir.'

The door closed behind him and Bolitho ran his fingers through his hair. Just a few hours since he had climbed aboard to the squeal of pipes and already he was beginning to *feel* different.

It was all so alien to his past life when you could argue and compete with your companions, curse your captain behind his back or reveal his weakness which only you really understood. As from today a mere word could bring a shutter across a man's eyes or make him fear for his own safety. Buckle was eighteen years his senior, yet at the first hint of Bolitho's displeasure had almost cringed.

He closed his eyes and tried to fathom out how he should proceed. To try to be too popular was to be a fool. To hold unswervingly to matters of discipline and order was to be a tyrant. He recalled Colquhoun's words and grinned ruefully. Until you reached Colquhoun's lofty post-rank you could never be certain of anything.

Somewhere beyond the bulkhead he heard a challenge and a shouted reply from a boat. Then the squeak of a hull alongside, the patter of feet on a gangway. It seemed unreal and incredible that the ship, his ship, was running her affairs while he just sat here at the table. He sighed again and stared at the pile of papers and books. It would take longer than he had imagined to adjust.

There was another rap at the door and Graves ducked inside removing his hat and jamming it under his arm as he announced, 'The guardboat has just been alongside, sir.' He held out a heavily sealed canvas envelope. 'From the flag, sir.'

Bolitho took it and laid it carelessly on the table. His sailing orders without doubt, and he had to restrain himself from acting as he truly felt. He wanted to rip them open, to know and understand what was required of him.

He saw Graves looking round the cabin, his eyes passing swiftly over the discarded dress coat, the hat lying on the bench seat, and finally on Bolitho's unbuttoned shirt.

Graves said quickly, 'Will you wish me to stay, sir?'

'No. I will inform you of their content when I have had time to study them.'

Graves nodded. 'I am waiting for the last water-lighter to come out to us, sir. I have sent the cooper ashore to speed them up, but . . .'

Bolitho smiled. 'Then attend to it, if you please.'

Bolitho watched him leave and then slit open the envelope. He was still reading the neatly worded orders when he heard voices in the passageway beyond the door. Graves first, curt and resentful, then another, calm to begin with and then loud with anger. The latter finished with, 'Well, how in God's name was I to know? You could have made a signal, you bloody fool!'

There was a sudden silence and then a further tap on the door.

The lieutenant who stepped into the cabin was not at all what Bolitho had been expecting. Too junior for temporary command, Colquhoun had said, and yet this man was probably two years older than himself. He was tall, broad-shouldered, and deeply tanned. His thick auburn hair brushed the deckhead between the beams so that he seemed to fill the cabin.

Bolitho glanced up at him calmly. 'Mr Tyrrell?'

The lieutenant nodded briefly. 'Sir.' He took a quick breath. 'I must apologize for my late arrival aboard. I have been in th' flagship.'

Bolitho looked down at the table. Tyrrell had an easy drawl, the mark of a man born and bred in the American colony. He was like a half-tamed animal, and the quickness of his breathing betrayed the anger which he still harboured.

Bolitho added, 'Our sailing orders have just arrived.'

Tyrrell did not seem to hear. 'It was personal business, sir, I hadn't th'time to arrange otherwise.'

'I see.'

He waited, watching the man as he stared restlessly towards the stern windows. He had a strange way of standing, with one arm hanging down his side, the other inclined towards his sword. Relaxed, but wary. Like someone expecting an attack.

He continued, 'I would have preferred to meet my first lieutenant on board when I arrived.'

'I have sent Cap'n Ransome's remains ashore to be conveyed home with his possessions, sir. As you were not yet in command I felt personally free to act as I thought fit.' He looked at Bolitho evenly. 'I was aboard th' flagship to ask, plead if required, for a transfer to another ship. It was refused.'

'You felt that by being passed over for command that your talents would be better suited elsewhere, is that it?'

Tyrrell gave a slow smile. It changed him instantly from an angry man to one of obvious charm, with the inbuilt recklessness of a fighter.

'I am really sorry, sir. But no, it was not that. As you no doubt know, I am what th' late Cap'n Ransome would term a "local colonist".' He added bitterly, 'Although when I came aboard a year back it appeared we were all on th' same side against th' rebels.'

Bolitho stiffened. It was strange he had never considered the feelings of those like Tyrrell before. Good American families, loyal to the Crown, the first to stand together against the sudden revolution in their midst. But as the war had spread, and Britain had fought to retain a grip, then a foothold in the colony, the loyal ones like Tyrrell had all at once become the outsiders.

He asked quietly, 'Where is your home?'

'Virginia. Gloucester County. My father came out from England to found a coastal shipping trade. I was master of one of his schooners when th' war began. I have been in th' King's service since that time.'

'And your family?'

Tyrrell looked away. 'God knows. I have heard nothing of them.'

'And you wished to transfer to a ship nearer home? To take yourself back to what you now consider your own people?' Bolitho did not conceal the bite in his tone.

'No, sir. That ain't it.' He raised one arm and dropped it again, his voice angry. 'I am a King's officer, no matter what Ransome chose to believe, damn his eyes!'

Bolitho stood up. 'I will not have talk of your late captain!'

Tyrrell replied stubbornly, 'Cap'n Ransome is safe now in his cask of spirits in th' hold of a transport. His widow at his great London residence will weep for him, his service which cost him his life.' He laughed shortly. '*Fever*, they said.' He looked round the cabin. 'See all this, sir? A woman's hand. We barely logged a mile in *Sparrow* without him having some damned doxy aboard for company!' He seemed unable to stop himself. 'That's th' sort of *fever* which killed him in th' end, and damned good riddance, if you ask me.'

Bolitho sat down. Once again the ground had been cut from under him. Women, here in his cabin. He had heard of such things in grander ships, but only occasionally. But in *Sparrow*, where there could be little safety if called to do battle, it was unthinkable.

Tyrrell was studying him grimly. 'I had to tell you, sir. It's my way. But I'll say this one thing more. If disease hadn't taken him, I'd have killed him myself.'

Bolitho looked up sharply. 'Then you're a fool! If you have no more strength than in your bare hands then *I* will ask for your transfer, and make no mistake about it!'

Tyrrell stared at a point beyond Bolitho's shoulder.

'Would you behave so calmly, sir, if one of th' women had been *your* sister?'

The door opened a bare inch and Stockdale's battered face peered in at them. In his hand was balanced a small silver tray, two glasses and a decanter.

He wheezed, 'Thought you might want a bit o' refreshment, sir.' He watched the two men and added, 'Sort o' celebration like.'

Bolitho gestured to the table and waited until Stockdale had left. Still without speaking he filled the glasses, conscious of Tyrrell's eyes following every movement. A bad start. For both of them. If there was still time to make amends it was now. This minute. If Tyrrell took advantage of his surrender, there was no saying where it would lead.

He handed him a glass and said gravely, 'I have two sisters, Mr Tyrrell. In answer to your question, I daresay that I would not.' He smiled, seeing the sudden surprise in the lieutenant's eyes. 'I suggest you propose a toast for the pair of us, eh?'

Tyrrell reached out and held his glass against Bolitho's.

'Then let's drink to a new beginning, sir.'

Bolitho held his glass steady. 'No transfer?'

He shook his head. 'None'.

Bolitho raised the glass. 'Then, to a new beginning.' He took a sip and added quietly, 'Which is well for you, Mr Tyrrell. We are sailing tomorrow to join the inshore squadron.' He paused, seeing the sudden desperation on the other man's features. 'Not so very far from the coast of Maryland.'

Tyrrell said, 'Thank God. I know I'm being stupid, but just being off that shoreline again will make th' world of difference.'

Bolitho put down his glass. 'Then I will meet our officers informally at the close of the first dog watch.' He was careful to make his tone formal again. Each of them had shown enough of his inner reserves for the present. 'In the meantime you can take me on an inspection around the ship. And I will want to see everything, good and bad.'

Tyrrell nodded. 'So you shall, sir.' A slow grin spread across his face. 'I have a shrewd feeling that *Sparrow* is going to fly like she's never done before.' He stood aside as Bolitho threw on his coat and buttoned his shirt. 'Now if you will follow me, sir.'

Bolitho looked at Tyrrell's broad shoulders as they walked towards the sunlight on the gundeck and held down a sigh. If each day was going to present a battle of wills, it would make the privilege of command a testing experience.

He said, 'We will begin with the starboard battery, Mr Tyrrell.'

The first lieutenant paused below the break in the quarterdeck. 'As you said, sir. Everything.' He grinned again. 'Good and bad.'

Stockdale picked up Bolitho's shaving bowl and peered at the untouched breakfast on the cabin table. Overhead and throughout the ship the air was alive with noise and bustle. To a landsman the activity of preparing to get under way would appear haphazard and disorganized, but to the practised eye each man had his place, and his reason for being there. The miles of cordage and rigging, each scrap of sail had a vital part to play if a ship was to move and act to perfection.

Bolitho crossed to the stern windows and stared at the nearest strip of land. It was a bright morning, with the sky above the hills very pale, washed-out and clean. He could just see the staff above the headland battery, its flag no longer listless but lifting and curling to a fair north-easterly. It was almost physical pain to stay sealed in the cabin, waiting and fretting for the exact moment to show himself.

Voices pealed along the upper deck and shadows flitted busily across the skylight. Occasionally he could hear the plaintive squeak of a fiddle, the distorted rumble of a shanty as the men tramped around the capstan.

In the past hours and for most of the night he had tossed and turned in his cot, listening to the sea noises, the creak of timbers and rigging, his mind exploring every contingency, his brain bursting to the mental picture of his chart. Every unemployed eye would be watching him this morning. From the flagship's quarterdeck to some unknown lieutenant who probably hated Bolitho for getting the golden chance which he considered should have been his.

'The coffee, sir.' Stockdale hovered by the table. 'While it's still 'ot.'

Bolitho swung round to curse him for breaking his racing thoughts, but the sight of his anxious face was too much for him. As was so often the case.

He sat down at the table and tried to relax. Stockdale was right. If he had forgotten anything it was already too late. You could cram your head just so much. After that the mind became awash and confused beyond reason.

He sipped his coffee and stared at the cold meat. He could not touch that. His stomach was already twisting with apprehension, the lean slices of pork would be just enough to tip the balance.

Stockdale peered through the windows. 'It will be a good passage, sir. Long enough to get the measure of these fellows.'

Bolitho glanced up at him. He must be a mind-reader. In company with another sloop they were to escort two fat transports with supplies for the troops at Philadelphia once a rendezvous with the inshore squadron had been made. Two thousand miles, mostly in open waters, would certainly allow him time to test himself and his company. He had met his officers in the small wardroom the previous evening. With the exception of Tyrrell, all had been aboard since commissioning at Greenwich. He felt vaguely jealous of their obvious familiarity with the *Sparrow*. The two midshipmen, each eighteen years old, had joined as untrained novices. They had grown up in the *Sparrow*, and were now hopefully awaiting promotion. It was a pity they were only midshipmen, he thought. They might vie too much for their captain's approval, where in a larger ship and with more competition amongst the 'young gentlemen' it would be less direct.

Buckle had said little during their informal meeting. Reserved, and no doubt waiting to see how his captain would behave under sail, he had restricted himself to matters of navigation.

Robert Dalkeith, the surgeon, was an odd one. Young, but already too plump for his own good, he was also completely bald, and wore a bright red wig. But he appeared more skilled in his trade than was usual in a King's ship, as well as cultivated, and Bolitho imagined there was more to him than he showed at face value.

Lock, the purser, a bobbing, genial stick of a man, completed the gathering.

Graves had joined them later, making a good deal of noise about his trouble with the water-lighters, the difficulties in obtaining help ashore for loading boats, in fact the list had been formidable.

Tyrrell had interrupted cheerfully, 'It ain't fair, Hector. Your being singled out to be a bloody martyr like this!'

Graves had frowned and then forced a smile when the others had joined Tyrrell in the laughter.

Bolitho leaned back and stared at the skylight. He was not sure of Graves either. A hard worker. Ransome's toady? It was hard to see where the latent bad feeling had started between him and Tyrrell. But it *was* there right enough.

'Captain, sir?'

Bolitho started and looked at the door. Midshipman Bethune was standing with his hat under his arm, his free hand grasping the hilt of his dirk. He was a round-faced, sturdy youth, and his face was a mass of dark freckles.

'Well?'

Bethune swallowed. 'Mr Tyrrell's respects, sir, and the transports have weighed. *Fawn* has her preparative hoisted, sir.' He glanced curiously round the cabin.

Bolitho nodded gravely. 'I will be up directly.'

With elaborate care he forced himself to take another sip of coffee. It almost choked him. *Fawn* was the other sloop for the escort and would be carrying Colquhoun, in addition to her commander, as senior officer.

The midshipman was still inside the cabin. He added awkwardly, 'I am from Cornwall, too, sir.'

Bolitho smiled in spite of his tension. The competition had begun already.

He replied, 'I will try not to hold it against you, Mr Bethune.' He dropped his eyes as the boy fled from the cabin.

He stood up and took his hat from Stockdale. Then with a brief nod he strode out towards the waiting sunlight.

The gangways and decks seemed more crowded than ever as seamen ran this way and that, pursued by the hoarse shouts of their petty officers. As he reached the quarterdeck he saw two heavy transports idling towards the headland, their tan sails flapping and billowing in the breeze.

Tyrrell touched his hat. 'Anchor's hove short, sir.'

'Thank you.'

Bolitho strode to the larboard side and stared towards the anchored *Fawn*. He could see the muddle of men at her capstan, the scurrying preparations as the cable became bar-taut beneath her beakhead.

He crossed to the opposite side, trying to ignore the seamen who were poised at their stations on every hand. Beyond the nearest headland towards the hard blue horizon he saw a lively pattern of small white horses. Once outside this sheltered anchorage it would be good sailing weather. He glanced at the sluggish swirl of currents around a nearby storeship and bit his lip. He had to get free of all the shipping first.

'*Fawn*'s signal is close up, sir!' Bethune was clinging to the shrouds with his telescope, although Colquhoun's signal was clear enough to be seen without any glass.

'Stand by on the capstan!'

Tyrrell ran to the rail and cupped his big hands. 'Loose th' head'ls!'

Beside the wheel Buckle stood near the two helmsmen, his eyes watching Bolitho.

'Breeze is freshening a mite, sir.'

'Yes.'

Bolitho walked to the rail and stared along his command. He saw Graves watching over the anchor party, Midshipman Heyward at the foot of the mainmast with his division of seamen.

'Signal, sir! *Up anchor!*'

'Hands aloft and loose tops'ls!'

He stood back to watch the seamen surging up the shrouds and out along the swaying yards, their bodies black against the sky. Tyrrell said very little, and Bolitho observed that the topmen were well able to manage without added inducement from the deck. As canvas thundered loosely from the yards and the ship gave a long-drawn shudder, he saw the *Fawn*'s masts already swinging across the stern, her foretopsail filling to the wind as she heeled over.

Bethune called, 'Signal! *Make haste*, sir!' He lowered his glass, trying to avoid Bolitho's eye.

'Man the braces!'

He tried to shut out Colquhoun's last signal. Maybe he was endeavouring to goad him into doing something foolish. Perhaps he was always the same. But nothing must or would spoil this moment.

From forward came the cry, 'Anchor's aweigh, sir!'

Free of the land the *Sparrow* tilted deeply to the wind, the headland sliding across her jib-boom as with more and more canvas thundering and hardening from her yards she paid off into the wind.

Blocks clattered and whined, and high above the decks the seamen sprang about like monkeys.

Bolitho looked at Buckle. 'Lay her on the larboard tack. Then set a course to weather the headland.' He held the master's gaze and added, 'We will get the courses on her directly and see if we can take the edge off *Fawn's* lead.'

Moments later, with her courses and topsails filling to the morning breeze, the *Sparrow* glided swiftly past an anchored two-decker which wore a vice-admiral's flag at the fore.

Bolitho glanced at Tyrrell and saw him give a quick grimace. He might have cause to regret his application for transfer, Bolitho thought. And so, if his trust in Tyrrell proved false, would he.

Between two anchored Indiamen and on down the fairway towards that beckoning headland. Small craft bobbed astern in the frothing wake, and when Bolitho moved from studying the compass he saw they had already cut *Fawn's* lead by half a cable.

Buckle glanced at the surgeon who was clinging to the mizzen shrouds with one hand and holding on to his outrageous wig with the other.

He winked. 'We have a rare one here, Mr Dalkeith.'

Dalkeith kept his face immobile as Bolitho glanced aft towards him before replying, 'Poor Captain Ransome would never have left port with such dash, eh?' He gave a sly grin. 'But then, at this time o' the morning he would have been somewhat *tired*!'

They both laughed.

Bolitho's voice brought them up with a jerk.

'There is a yawl on the larboard bow, *Mr* Buckle. Laugh later with my blessing, but run her down within sight of the flagship and you will laugh to another tune!'

He turned back to the rail as Buckle hurled himself towards his helmsman.

The tip of the headland was already dropping abeam, and he felt the *Sparrow's* stem bite into the first gentle roller, her deck tilting still further under her press of canvas.

Tyrrell shouted, 'Anchor's secured, sir!' Spray had soaked his face and shirt but he was grinning broadly.

Bolitho nodded. 'Good. Now get the forecourse trimmed. It looks like a piece of untidy linen.' But he could not hold his severity. 'By God, she *flies*, does she not?'

He looked aloft at the squared sails and braced yards, the masthead pendant which flicked out like a coachman's whip. He had seen it all before so many times, but now it felt as if it was unique.

Bethune called, 'From *Fawn*, sir. *Take station to wind'rd!*'

Bolitho smiled at him. 'Acknowledge.'

To the quarterdeck at large he added, 'A *fine* morning.'

By the hatchway Stockdale watched Bolitho's pleasure and felt inwardly happy. He ran his eye over the hurrying seamen as they slithered down once more to the deck. Tanned and healthy, what did they know about anything? He picked his uneven teeth with an ivory pin. The captain had seen more action in the past years than they knew about. He watched Bolitho's squared shoulders as he paced restlessly on the weather side. Given time, they'd come to find out, he decided.

3

The Privateer

Bolitho opened his eyes and stared for several seconds at the unlit lantern spiralling above his cot. Despite the weariness in his limbs and the fact he had been on deck repeatedly during the night he found it hard to sleep. Beyond the screen which partitioned his sleeping quarters from the cabin he could see the pale light of dawn, and knew from the lantern's sluggish movement and the uneasy creak of timbers that the wind was little more than a breeze. He tried to relax, wondering how long it would take to break the habit of awakening with each dawn, to enjoy his new-found privacy.

Feet thudded on the quarterdeck above, and he guessed that soon now the seamen would be turning to for another day. It had been two weeks since the little convoy had sailed from Antigua, and in that time they had covered only half their set distance. One thousand miles in open waters, and each mile marked by perverse winds and no winds at all. Barely an hour passed without the need to call the hands to make or shorten sail, to trim yards in the hope of catching a dying breeze, or to reef against one violent and taunting squall.

Buckle's gloomy prediction about *Sparrow*'s sailing qualities in a poor wind had proved only too true. Time and time again she had paid off, her canvas flapping in confusion as yet one more wind had died and left them almost becalmed. Hard work and angry words had eventually brought her back on station again, only to have the whole thing repeated before the end of a watch.

Patrol and scouting duty had been the lot of *Sparrow*'s company for most of their commission and they had yet to learn the true misery of convoy over long passages. The two transports had not helped. They appeared totally unwilling to realize the importance of staying in close company, so that if they became scattered by a swift squall it took many hours to urge, threaten and finally drive them back into formation. Colquhoun's curt signals had only succeeded in antagonizing the master of one of them, a big transport named *Golden Fleece*. On more than one occasion he had ignored the signals altogether or had caused the *Fawn* to withdraw from her proper station at the head of the convoy in order to commence a verbal exchange which could be heard by everyone else nearby.

Bolitho climbed from the cot and walked slowly into the cabin, feeling the deck lifting gently beneath his bare feet before slipping away in a trough, the motion bringing the usual clatter of blocks, the drawn-out groan of the rudder as the helmsman brought the sloop back under command.

He leaned his hands on the sill of the stern windows and stared out at the empty sea. The two transports, if they were still together, would be somewhere on *Sparrow*'s starboard bow. Bolitho's orders were to stay to windward of the well-laden ships so as to be ready to run down on any suspicious vessel and hold the maximum advantage until she was proved friend or foe.

In fact they had sighted an unknown sail on three separate occasions. Far astern, it had been impossible to know if it was the same on each sighting or three individual vessels. Either way, Colquhoun had refused to be drawn to investigate. Bolitho could sympathize with his un-willingness to leave the valuable transports, especially as the wind might choose the very moment when his sparse forces were scattered to play a new trick or bring some real enemy amongst them. On the other hand, he was very conscious of a sense of uneasiness after each call from the masthead. The strange sail was like a will-o'-the-wisp, and if it was hostile could be methodically following the little convoy, awaiting exactly the right moment to attack.

The door opened and Fitch padded into the cabin carrying two jugs. One was coffee, and the other contained water from the galley for Bolitho's shave. In the pale light from the windows he looked smaller and scrawnier than ever, and as usual kept his eyes averted while he prepared the necessary cup of Bolitho's first coffee of the day.

'How is it on deck?'

Fitch raised his eyes only slightly. 'Mr Tilby reckons it'll be another roastin' day, sir.'

Tilby was the boatswain, a great untidy hulk of a man who was given to some of the most profane language Bolitho had heard in ten years at sea. But his knowledge of weather, his forecast of what each dawn might bring, had been only too accurate.

And under a blazing sun, with little space to find shade or comfort, the *Sparrow*'s seamen had more torment to face before night found them again. It was amazing how they all managed to survive in such a small hull. What with extra stores and spare spars, powder and shot, and countless other requirements for keeping a ship at sea, some of the men were hard put to find space for a hammock. In addition the *Sparrow* had all the great lengths of anchor cable to be neatly stowed when she was under way. Several hundred fathoms of thirteen-inch hemp for the main anchors and another hundred of eight-inch for the kedge took up more space than fifty human beings required for even the most basic needs.

But if this or any other ship was to survive and live from her own resources then such discomforts had to be endured.

He sipped the coffee. If only the wind would freshen and stay with them. It would help drive away the weariness and drudgery of work aloft, and also give him time to drill the guns' crews to better advantage. They had had few such drills during the first days out of harbour, and once more he had been made aware of the strange attitude of acceptance he had originally noticed. Perhaps they had been so long without actually being called to do battle they had taken the drills as merely something to be tolerated, even expected from a new captain. Their timing had been good enough, if somewhat rigid, they had gone through all the motions of running out, traversing and pointing, but again and again he had felt something was badly lacking. As the crews had faced outboard through their open ports he had sensed their indifference. There was nothing to fight, so what was the point of it all, their relaxed bodies seemed to indicate.

He had tackled Tyrrell about it but the first lieutenant had said cheerfully, 'Hell, sir, it don't signify they won't be able to fight if th' time calls for it.'

Bolitho's sharp reply brought a new barrier between them, and for the moment he was prepared to let it remain.

Captain Ransome must have used the sloop like a personal possession, a yacht, he thought. Sometimes during the night when Bolitho had come down to the cabin after a frustrating hour on deck watching the hands shortening sail yet again he had pictured Ransome with some woman or other. Or Tyrrell pacing the quarterdeck, tearing himself apart as he imagined his sister just a few feet below him. He had not mentioned the matter to Tyrrell since his first outburst, but had found himself wondering about the real story, and what had happened to the girl after Ransome's sudden death.

Stockdale came into the cabin with the shaving bowl. He glared at Fitch and wheezed, 'Get the cap'n's breakfast!'

To Bolitho he added, ' 'Nother clear mornin', sir.' He waited until Bolitho was in his chair and then held the razor against the window. He seemed content with its edge. 'Wot we need is a real good blow.' He showed his uneven teeth. 'Make some o' these young puppies jump about!'

Bolitho relaxed as the razor moved precisely over his chin. Stockdale said very little but he always seemed to hit the exact point.

In between strokes he replied, 'In another month we'll be in the hurricane season again, Stockdale. I hope *that* will satisfy you.'

The big coxswain grunted. 'Seen 'em afore. Us'll see 'em again an' live to tell of it.'

Bolitho gave up. Nothing, it seemed, could break the man's supreme confidence in his ability to produce a miracle, even in the face of a hurricane.

Voices rang out overhead, and then he heard feet dashing down the companion ladder from the quarterdeck.

It was Midshipman Heyward, impeccable as ever in spite of being on his feet for much of the night.

'Captain, sir.' He watched Stockdale's razor poised in mid-air. 'Mr Graves's respects and *Fawn* has just signalled. Sail to the nor'-east.'

Bolitho snatched the towel. 'Very well. I will come up.'

Stockdale laid down the bowl. 'That same one, sir?'

Bolitho shook his head. 'Unlikely. She'd never overreach us in one night, even if she was after our blood.' He rubbed his face vigorously. 'But in this empty sea a sight of anything is welcome.'

When he reached the quarterdeck he found Tyrrell and most of the others already there. Below the mainmast the hands had just been mustered in readiness for the morning assault on the decks with holystones and swabs, while others were waiting by the pumps or just staring up at the barely filled sails. Graves touched his hat.

'Masthead lookout has not yet sighted anything, sir.'

Bolitho nodded and strode to the compass. North-west by north. It seemed as if it had been riveted in that direction since time began. It was hardly surprising *Fawn* had sighted the newcomer first. In her position ahead and slightly to starboard of the transports she was better placed. All the same, he would have wished otherwise. *Fawn*'s signals and execution of Colquhoun's orders always seemed to be that much quicker than his.

Through the criss-cross of rigging and shrouds and slightly to starboard of the rearmost transport he saw the other sloop tacking awkwardly in the gentle westerly breeze. With every stitch of canvas on her braced yards she was barely making headway.

From aloft came the sudden cry, 'Deck there! Sail on the starboard beam!'

Tyrrell crossed to Bolitho's side.

'What d'you think? One of our own?'

Graves said swiftly, 'Or a damned Yankee, eh?'

Bolitho saw the exchange of glances, the sudden hostility between them like something physical.

He said calmly, 'We will know directly, *gentlemen*.'

Midshipman Bethune called, 'From *Fawn*, sir. *Remain on station*.'

Graves said complacently, 'There goes *Fawn*. She's going about to take a soldier's wind under her tail.'

Bolitho said, 'Get aloft, Mr Graves. I want to know everything you can discover about that sail.'

Graves stared at him. 'I've a good hand aloft, sir.'

Bolitho met his resentment gravely. 'And now I require a good officer there, too, Mr Graves. An experienced eye and not just a clear one.'

Graves moved stiffly to the weather shrouds and after the merest hesitation began to climb.

Tyrrell said quietly, 'Do him good, that one!'

Bolitho glanced around the crowded quarterdeck.

'Maybe, Mr Tyrrell. But if you imagine I am using my authority to foster some petty spite between you then I must assure you otherwise.' He lowered his voice. 'It is an enemy we are fighting, not each other!'

Then he took a telescope from the rack and walked to the foot of the mizzen mast. Steadying his legs against the uncomfortable motion he trained the glass on the *Fawn* and then very slowly beyond her. Minutes passed, and then as the distant ship lifted on some large roller he saw her topgallant sails shining in the first sunlight like matched pink shells. She was clawing her way close-hauled on a converging course, her yards braced so tightly they were almost fore-and-aft.

Graves yelled down, 'Frigate, sir!' A pause as every man looked up at his tiny silhouette against the sky. 'English built!'

Bolitho stayed silent. English built perhaps. But who now stood behind her guns? He watched *Fawn* edging round, her masthead pendant lifting and curling listlessly. More flags shot up her yards and Bethune yelled, 'From *Fawn*, sir. Recognition signal.' A further pause as he groped through his grubby book. 'She's the *Miranda*, thirty-two, Captain Selby, sir.'

Buckle said to the deck at large, 'From England most likely.'

The light was already stronger, and as he stared across the brightening water Bolitho could feel the first warm rays against his face. From England. Every man aboard was probably thinking of those words. Except for Tyrrell and the colonists in the company. But all the rest would be picturing his own past way of life. Village or farm, some ale house outside a harbour or fishing port. A woman's face, a child's last grip before the harder hands of the pressgang.

He found himself thinking of his own home in Falmouth. The great stone house below Pendennis Castle where his father would be waiting and wondering about him and his brother Hugh, while he remained in Cornwall. Like all the Bolitho ancestors, his father had been a sea-officer, but having lost an arm and his health was now confined to a landbound existence, always within sight of the ships and the sea which had forsaken him.

'From *Fawn*, sir. *General. Heave to.*'

Colquhoun, it seemed, was quite satisfied with the other ship's identity. For once the two transports needed no extra goading to obey the signal. Perhaps like the rest they, too, were eager for news from the other world.

Bolitho closed the glass and handed it to a boatswain's mate.

'Shorten sail, Mr Tyrrell, and heave to as ordered.' He waited until the lieutenant had shouted for the topmen to get aloft and then added, 'That frigate has been hard worked so her mission must be important.'

He had watched the newcomer while she had forged towards the uneven cluster of ships, had seen the great scars on her hull where the sea had pared away the paintwork like a giant knife. Her sails, too, looked much repaired, evidence of a rapid voyage.

Bethune shouted, '*Miranda*'s hoisted another signal, sir!' He swayed in the shrouds as he tried to level his big telescope. 'To *Fawn*. *Captain repair on board*.'

Once again *Fawn*'s response was swift, her big gig being swayed out within minutes of the signal. Bolitho could imagine Colquhoun hurrying to the other ship and the *Miranda*'s consternation when they discovered that he was senior to their own captain.

Whatever it entailed, the matter was obviously urgent, and not merely an exchange of gossip at this chance encounter in open waters.

Bolitho rubbed his chin and said, 'I'm going below. Call me if anything happens.'

In the cabin he found Stockdale waiting with his coat and sword, his lopsided grin very broad as he muttered, 'Thought you'd be wantin' these, sir.'

Fitch was gripping the table, his legs spread apart as the sloop rolled and staggered in the uncomfortable troughs, the power gone from her sails. He was staring at the breakfast he had just brought, his narrow features resigned.

Bolitho smiled. 'Never fear, I'll find time to eat it later.'

It was strange that the mere sight of another ship, the obscure hint of excitement, had given him an appetite at last. He gulped down some coffee as Stockdale adjusted his sword-belt before handing him the coat.

Perhaps *Miranda* had discovered an enemy and needed help to attack them. Maybe the war was over, or another had broken out elsewhere. The possiblities seemed endless.

He looked up and saw Tyrrell peering through the open skylight.

'Cap'n, sir! The *Fawn*'s gig is shoving off from th' frigate.'

Bolitho replied, 'Thank you.' He forcibly disguised his disappointment. 'That was quick.'

Tyrrell vanished and he added quietly, 'There'll be time for breakfast after all.'

He was mistaken. Even as he began to unfasten his sword-belt

Tyrrell's face reappeared at the skylight, his words filling the cabin as he shouted, 'From *Fawn*, sir. *Repair on board forthwith*.'

Stockdale bounded from the cabin, his hoarse voice bellowing for the gig's crew which the boatswain had already thought prudent to muster.

With frantic haste the boat was swung outboard and dropped alongside, where with little thought for dignity or safety, Bolitho hurled himself into the sternsheets, his sword clattering against the gunwale and almost tripping him on top of the oarsmen.

Stockdale bawled, 'Give way all!' In a lower but no less menacing tone he added, 'An' remember, my beauties, if one o' you misses a stroke you'll 'ave me to answer!'

The gig seemed to fly across the water, and when at last Bolitho regained his composure and looked astern he saw the *Sparrow* was already a cable clear. She was pitching steeply in the swell, her sails rippling and flashing in disorder while she lay hove to in the pale sunlight. In spite of his own busy thoughts and anxiety he could still find time to admire her. In the past he had often watched the stern cabin of a passing man-of-war and pondered about her captain, what sort of person, his qualities or lack of them. It was very hard to accept that the *Sparrow*'s cabin was his own and that others might be wondering about him.

He turned and saw *Fawn*'s outline overlapping that of the idling frigate, figures moving round her entry port to receive him with all formality. He smiled to himself. In the face of hell it seemed likely that no captain, no matter how junior, was expected to go without his proper acknowledgement.

Bolitho was met at the entry port by Maulby, *Fawn*'s commander. He was very thin, and but for a pronounced stoop would have stood well over six feet. Life between a sloop's decks must be uncomfortable for such a man, Bolitho thought.

He appeared a few years older than himself and had a drawling, bored manner of speaking. But he seemed pleasant enough and made him welcome.

As they ducked beneath the quarterdeck Maulby said, 'The little admiral is excited, it would seem.'

Bolitho paused and stared at him. 'Who?'

Maulby shrugged loosely. 'In the flotilla we *always* refer to Colquhoun as our little admiral. He has a way of inserting himself in the role without actually holding the necessary rank!' He laughed, his bent shoulders touching a deckhead beam so that he appeared to be supporting it with his own frame. 'You look shocked, my friend?'

Bolitho grinned. Maulby, he decided, was a man you could like and trust on sight. But he had never before heard such comments made about a superior by two subordinates meeting for the first time. In some ships it would be inviting disaster and oblivion.

He replied, 'No, but I am refreshed!'

The stern cabin was much the same size as his own. There was no other similarity. Plain, even spartan, he was reminded of Tyrrell's anger, his bitter attack on the *woman's touch*. He saw Colquhoun sitting at a table, his chin in his hands as he stared at some newly opened despatches.

Without pausing he said, 'Sit down, both of you. I must give this matter my attention.'

Maulby looked gravely at Bolitho and dropped one eyelid in a quick wink.

Bolitho glanced away, Maulby's easy acceptance of their superior was daunting. *The little admiral.* It suited Colquhoun very well.

Maulby seemed well able to remain relaxed, yet he was nobody's fool. Bolitho had noted the smart way his men had moved about the gundeck, the crisp passing and execution of orders. Bolitho had not met the other captains of Colquhoun's flotilla. If they were all such odd birds as Maulby it was hardly surprising that Colquhoun was showing signs of strain. Or maybe in such small ships individual characters were more noticeable. He thought of Pears in the old *Trojan*, his rugged features which had never seemed to alter under any circumstances. In a gale, close to a lee shore, or under enemy fire, witnessing a flogging, or commending some sailor on promotion, he had always seemed remote and beyond personal contact. It was hard to imagine Maulby, he paused, or himself either, with such aloof and godlike powers.

Colquhoun's voice broke across his thoughts, sharp and incisive. '*Miranda*'s captain has brought serious news.' He still did not lift his head. 'France has signed an alliance with the Americans. It means that General Washington will have the full support of the French regular troops *and* a powerful fleet.'

Bolitho shifted in his chair, his mind grappling with Colquhoun's announcment. The French had already done much to help their new ally, but this would mean that the war was now firmly in the open. It also implied that the French were showing fresh confidence in the Americans' chance of victory.

Colquhoun stood up quickly and stared through the stern windows. 'The *Miranda* is carrying despatches and intelligence for the Commander-in-Chief at New York. When he left Plymouth he had a brig in company with duplicate information for Antigua. The ships were caught in a storm shortly after clearing the Channel and the brig was not seen again.'

Maulby asked quietly, 'Taken by the French, sir?'

Colquhoun swung on him with unexpected anger. 'What the hell does it matter? Taken or wrecked, dismasted or bloody well eaten by worms, it makes no difference to us, does it!'

Suddenly Bolitho realized the cause of his attack. Had Colquhoun remained at Antigua until his own ship had refitted, Maulby would have been in charge of the convoy's escort. *Miranda*'s captain, desperate to carry his news to New York, and senior to Maulby, would have ordered him to make arrangements for the information to be taken without delay to Antigua. Nobody could rely on the brig's survival as an excuse for doing nothing. By a mere twist of fate, or Colquhoun's determination to keep control of his ships at sea, *Miranda*'s captain had been able to pass on the decision to him.

In a calmer tone Colquhoun continued, 'It has been reported that the French have been preparing ships for months. From Toulon a whole squadron set sail weeks ago and slipped through the Gilbraltar patrols without so much as a squeak of news getting out.' He looked at each of them in turn. 'They could be on their way here, to the American coast, anywhere, for all we know, damn their eyes!'

The *Fawn* had swung slightly in the slow procession of troughs, and through the swaying windows Bolitho could see the two transports, huge and ungainly, their yards askew as they awaited the next signal. Each transport was filled to the deck seams with much needed supplies for the army in Philadelphia. In the wrong hands they would represent a tremendous prize, and the realization must be foremost in Colquhoun's mind.

Colquhoun said, '*Miranda* has agreed to stand by the convoy until we contact the inshore squadron. But in this damned weather it might take weeks.'

Bolitho imagined Colquhoun was picturing the distance like a mental chart. All those miles, with the knowledge that he must eventually make the long passage back to Antigua to resume control of his small force.

Maulby drawled, 'May I suggest that I continue with the transports, sir? With *Miranda* in company we will be safe enough.' He glanced at Bolitho. 'You could then return in *Sparrow* to English Harbour, pass the news to the admiral and prepare our own ships for further work.'

Colquhoun stared at him, his eyes unseeing.

'God damn the complacency of our precious Government! For years this has been brewing, and while the French have been building new ships, ours have been allowed to go rotten for want of money. If the Channel Fleet were to be ordered to sea tomorrow I doubt that more than twenty sail of the line would be capable!' He saw their surprise and nodded vehemently. 'Oh yes, gentlemen, while you have been out here imagining that all would be ready if once the call came, I have been made to stay silent and watch it happening.' He struck the table with his fist. 'Some flag officers are too concerned with political power and gracious living to care for the wants of the fleet!'

He sat down heavily. 'I must decide . . .'

The door opened slightly and a frightened-looking midshipman said, 'From *Miranda*, sir. She requests instructions . . .' He got no further.

'Tell him to mind his manners!' Colquhoun glared at him hotly. 'It is *my* decision!'

Bolitho glanced at Maulby. For the first time in his life he was beginning to realize the meaning of command. Whatever Colquhoun decided could be equally right or wrong. Bolitho had learned one thing well. If you made a right decision, others often received the credit. But make a wrong one and you were in no doubt where the blame would lie.

Colquhoun said suddenly, 'Send for your clerk, Maulby. I will dictate new orders for . . .' he looked at Bolitho, 'for *Sparrow*.'

He seemed to be speaking his thoughts aloud. 'I do not doubt your ability, Bolitho, but you lack experience. I will need Maulby's *Fawn* with me until I know what is to happen next.' He gestured to the table as the ship's clerk entered the cabin. 'You must remain with the transports. *Miranda*'s captain will give you guidance, and you will obey him to the best of your skill. Your orders will allow you to return to the flotilla when the transports have been delivered.' He paused and added softly, 'Delivered.'

Bolitho rose to his feet. 'Aye, sir.'

'Now get out and leave me to draft these orders.'

Maulby took Bolitho's elbow and guided him towards the gundeck.

'I think the little admiral is worried, my friend.' He sighed. 'I was hoping to rid my ship of his presence and pass him on to you.' He turned and gave a quick grin. 'There is no justice in this world!'

Bolitho saw his gig falling and rising in the swell, Stockdale shading his eyes as he watched the sloop for a recall.

He said, 'The news is bad, but not unexpected. At least the pretence is done with.'

Maulby nodded gravely. 'No comfort, I fear, to the lamb about to be devoured.'

Bolitho stared at him. 'Not that serious surely?'

'I am not certain. What the Frogs do today the damned Spaniards will copy tomorrow. Soon we will have the whole world at our throats.' He frowned. 'The little admiral is right on one score. It seems that our Government is run by demons, most of whom appear determined to drive the rest of us to madness.'

The first lieutenant hurried into view and proffered a freshly sealed envelope.

Maulby clapped Bolitho on the shoulder and said cheerfully, 'Think of us sometimes. While you enjoy your leisurely voyage, I will be forced to share my table with *him*.' He rubbed his hands. 'But with any luck he may get promotion and vanish forever.'

The lieutenant said urgently, 'Captain Colquhoun's compliments, and will you join him immediately?'

Maulby nodded and held out his hand.

'Until we meet again, Bolitho.' He seemed unwilling to let him leave. Then he said awkwardly, 'Be warned, my friend. You have a fine command, but you also have a large number of colonists in your company.' He tried to smile. 'If the war goes badly, there are some who might be tempted to change allegiance. In their shoes I could perhaps feel the same.'

Bolitho met his gaze and nodded. 'Thank you. I will remember it.'

Maulby did not hide his relief. 'There, I knew you were a good fellow! Not one to treat my clumsy advice as patronage.'

Bolitho grinned. 'You took a risk. I might have gone to Colquhoun and told him of your name for him.'

'I would have denied it!'

'Naturally!'

They both laughed.

Then as the gig hooked on to the chains they became formal again. Even before Bolitho had reached the boat flags were soaring up the *Fawn*'s yards, and an acknowledgement appeared above the frigate with equal speed.

Bolitho settled himself in the sternsheets and stared towards his ship. Colquhoun had taken the responsibility and made a decision. His own responsibility was just beginning.

Lieutenant Tyrrell turned as Bolitho's head and shoulders rose through the quarterdeck hatch and waited until he had made his usual inspection of the sails and compass before remarking, 'She's running well, sir.'

Bolitho walked across the tilting deck and rested his hands on the rail, feeling the hull quivering beneath him like a living creature. The noon sun stood high over the ship, but he was able to ignore it, conscious only of the well-filled sails, the leap of spray up and over the bowsprit. It had been five days since *Fawn* had turned back for Antigua, and it seemed as if Colquhoun's disappearance from their midst had brought a change of luck and weather. Perverse as ever, but for once on their side, the wind had backed suddenly to south-south-west and had freshened into a lively blow which had hardly dropped during the whole time. Under bulging canvas the ships had driven on towards the American coast, which according to the most recent calculations now lay some two hundred and fifty miles away. The heavy merchantmen had maintained a good five knots, satisfied perhaps that *Miranda*'s captain was content to leave them to their own devices. The frigate's signals had been confined for the most part to *Sparrow*. For within twenty-four hours of leaving *Fawn* the masthead lookout had sighted a solitary sail once again, far astern of the convoy, a tiny white flaw on the horizon.

Bolitho had sent Graves aloft with a telescope, but even he had been unable to identify the mysterious follower. Next he signalled to the frigate, requesting permission to investigate. He had been refused. *Miranda*'s captain was probably regretting his meeting with the convoy. But for their dragging weight he would have reached his objective by now and would have borne no blame for failing to pass his news to Antigua. But once in contact with the slower vessels he had no choice but to act as he had. Also, he would be fully aware that once beyond his control *Sparrow* might become too involved with a separate situation to return, and thus leave him with total responsibility for the transports.

The unknown sail had not been sighted again, and Bolitho had accepted that *Miranda*'s captain had been right, if over cautious, to restrain his efforts.

He looked at Tyrrell's bronzed features and nodded. 'I am well satisfied.'

He watched some foretopmen sliding down the backstays, racing each other to the deck after their work aloft. Buckle was right. She moved like a bird with any sort of wind. He watched the *Bear*, the transport closest to his own ship, and wished they were free of the convoy. Then he could really put *Sparrow* to the test. Royals, even studding sails could be rigged, if only to find out what she could accomplish under every stitch of canvas.

Most of the unemployed officers were on deck enjoying their usual gossip before the midday meal, careful to stay on the lee side and as much out of his way as possible.

He saw Dalkeith, the surgeon, laughing with Buckle, his head very white in its baldness under the harsh light. The red wig was being vigorously shaken by the wardroom servant, and Bolitho guessed it had been given some sort of a wash. Lock, the purser, was in a more serious conversation with young Heyward, opening and ruffling a big ledger in the wind as he explained some point of victualling which might place the midshipman's knowledge above that of his friend Bethune. The latter, being on watch, stood untidily by the quarterdeck rail, his shirt open to his waist and massaging his stomach with one hand. Bolitho smiled. The boy was no doubt hungry. Midshipmen like Bethune usually were.

Down on the gundeck many of the seamen were lounging beneath the sails' great shadows or passing the time like their officers. The boatswain was with his own friend Yule, the gunner, and together they would have made a frightening pair of highwaymen, Bolitho thought. Whereas Tilby was vast and ungainly, his heavy features seamed with too much drink, Yule was swarthy and lithe, like a stoat, with darting, flinty eyes which were forever on the move.

As he glanced from group to group he was again reminded of his new-found isolation. Privacy which could lead to loneliness. Privilege which might become a burden.

He thrust his hands behind him and began to pace slowly along the weather side, letting the warm wind ruffle his hair and play with his open shirt. Somewhere out there beyond the hammock nettings was the coast of America. It would be strange to drop anchor only to find the war had finished, that blood had proved too strong in the face of France's new challenge. If England were to admit to America's independence then perhaps both nations would unite against France and settle her ambitions once and for all. He glanced at Tyrrell's profile and wondered if he was thinking the same.

He shut Tyrrell's personal problems from his mind and tried to concentrate on the string of affairs which daily needed his attention. The water supply should replenish as soon as possible. The casks were poor, and water soon became rancid in this climate. And he would purchase fresh fruit whenever they contacted the land or some supply vessel. It was amazing that the ship's company had stayed so healthy when Ransome had failed to take such simple precautions. Aboard the old *Trojan* he had not seen one case of scurvy in the three years he had been in her, evidence of Captain Pears's concern for his men and a valuable lesson to all his subordinates. He had already spoken about it to Lock, and after some hesitation the purser had muttered, 'A *costly* affair, sir.'

'Costlier if our people go down with disease, Mr Lock. I have known a whole squadron rendered useless because of such skinflint methods.'

Then there was the matter of a flogging, his first as captain. He had always disliked unnecessary use of punishment even though he knew it to be necessary on occasions. In the Navy discipline was harsh and instant, and when a ship was miles from home and other authority, it was a captain's deterrent to insubordination and final confusion. Some captains used it without thought. Brutal and inhuman floggings were commonplace in many ships, and as a young midshipman Bolitho had nearly fainted after one such spectacle. Other captains, weak and inefficient, left authority to subordinates and shut their ears to its misuse.

But for the most part the English seaman knew the measure of his service, and if he took chances was prepared to accept the consequences. And if one man thieved or cheated another of his messmates he had no mercy at all. The justice of the lower deck was equally feared to that of a captain.

But this case was different, or could be from what he knew of it. A seaman had defied Lieutenant Graves during a night watch when the hands had been called to reef topsails in an unexpected squall. He had shouted at the officer and called him a 'heartless bugger' within earshot of some twenty other people.

In confidence Tyrrell had asked Bolitho to accept the seaman's explanation. He was a good hand, and Graves had provoked him in a fit of anger when he had failed to reach his station on the mainyard with his companions.

A *dirty Yankee bastard*. They were the words Graves had used. Too lazy to do his proper duty, and no doubt too gutless to fight when the time came.

All this and Tyrrell's heated attack on Graves's handling of the matter were fresh proof of the latent tension amongst the company under his command.

Graves had been adamant. The man had insulted him in front of his watch and must be punished.

He was right in one respect. His authority had to be upheld or he would never be able to regain control again.

Bolitho blamed himself. If he had had more time to consider this unusual situation, or had taken less comfort from his own new position, he could have prevented it. By example or by forcing his will on his officers he might have made them realize that such behaviour would not be tolerated. But that was all too late now. It had happened.

He had compromised by standing the man over, knowing then as at this moment that he was merely postponing the inevitable.

He glanced up towards the mainyard, braced hard round as the ship heeled close-hauled on a larboard tack. He could see the man now, naked but for a scrap of canvas, working with some others on the endless business of re-splicing and repairs high above the deck. Did Tyrrell really think the man was provoked? he wondered. Or was he standing up for him because he imagined Graves was getting at him by punishing another colonist?

'Deck there!' The masthead lookout's cry was muffled by the wind and the lively crack of sails. '*Miranda*'s signallin'!'

Bolitho swung round. 'Jump to it, Mr Bethune! You are half asleep today!'

Tyrrell stood aside as the midshipman ran to the lee shrouds with his telescope.

'Thinking of his next meal!' He was smiling at the boy's confusion.

'It seems that the masthead lookout was the only one in *this* watch thinking of his duty, Mr Tyrrell!'

The edge of his voice brought a flush to the lieutenant's face and he turned away without answering.

Bethune called, 'From *Miranda*, sir! *Sail to the nor'-west!*'

'Acknowledge.'

Bolitho was angry with Tyrrell's careless attitude, angrier still more with his own unfair outburst.

Some two miles ahead of the *Golden Fleece*, her patched sails hard-bellied and drawing well, the *Miranda* was already setting her topgallants in readiness to investigate. The unknown ship, whatever she was, lay somewhere across the larboard bow, and as she had not been seen before it seemed likely she was on a converging course.

'Deck there! Sail in sight! Fine on th' weather bow!'

Bolitho looked around at the intent faces. For an instant he toyed with the idea of making his way to the dizzy mainmast crosstrees himself, in spite of his fear of heights which he had never been able to overcome. The long climb up those shivering, vibrating shrouds might drive his anger away and leave his mind clear once again.

He saw Raven, the newly appointed master's mate, and said, 'Go aloft. Take a glass and tell me what you see.'

Buckle had told him that the man was an experienced sailor, one who had already served in King's ships and would not be easily fooled by first appearances.

Before Raven had even reached the mainyard the lookout called again, 'Two ships! Close in company!'

Every eye was on Raven's body as he swarmed out and around the futtock shrouds and up towards the topmast head.

Bethune, still smarting over his failure to see *Miranda*'s signal, suddenly stiffened and called, 'Gunfire, sir!' He had his hands cupped round his ears, giving his round face the appearance of a freckled goblin.

Bolitho looked down at him. Then as his hearing adjusted itself beyond the crack of sails and the plunging sweep of spray around the hull, he, too, heard the deeper, discordant thud of cannon fire. He was almost beside himself with impatience, but he knew if he hurried Raven he might become too confused to make a proper assessment.

'Deck there!' It was Raven at last. 'First ship's a merchantman! She's under attack from a brig!'

Buckle exclaimed thickly, 'Privateer, by God!'

Bolitho snatched a telescope and trained it through the dark mass of rigging and beyond some men who were grouped on the forecastle. A trick of the light. He blinked and tried again. No, there it was, a tiny white speck which seemed to mingle with the unending pattern of crisp wave-crests. The lonely merchantman had been unlucky, but now with any sort of good fortune they might turn the tables on her attacker.

The *Miranda* was already tacking violently, her sails in confusion as she headed away from her original station. Even as her sails refilled and hardened on the new tack Bolitho saw her signal flags breaking to the wind.

Bethune said quickly, 'General signal, sir. *Remain on station.*'

Buckle swore. 'After the bloody prize money himself, the greedy bugger!'

The gunfire was clearer now, and as he raised the glass again Bolitho saw smoke drifting down-wind from the two ships, the lithe shape of the attacking brig as she endeavoured to close the range still further.

He shut the glass with a snap, aware of the muttering behind him, disappointment which matched his own. *Miranda*'s captain was probably making the attack more to break the frustration of a slow passage than to humiliate the *Sparrow*.

He looked at Tyrrell's broad shoulders and said, 'Signal the *Bear* to make more sail. She's dropping astern badly.'

Then he turned back to watch the frigate. She was moving fast in spite of the wind being almost abeam of her sails, and he could see her port lids opening, the single line of muzzles catching the sunlight as they were run out in readiness to fight.

The brig's captain must have realized what was happening. Even so, he was probably unwilling to lose his prize with victory almost in his grasp.

On the gangways and gun deck his own seamen were chattering and waving their arms about, and he guessed they were discussing how they would have acted had they been given the chance to go for the privateer.

Bolitho recalled Raven to the deck and said, 'You did well.'

The man grinned uncomfortably. 'Thank you, sir. The brig's a Yankee right enough. Seen many like her in me time. T'other one's an Indiaman by her looks, 'though her gunnery ain't so good as some on 'em. There's never a mark on the Yankee's canvas.'

Tyrrell shouted, 'Th' brig's broken off the action! He's going to make a run for it!'

Bolitho sighed. The merchantman was already turning steadily towards the little convoy while the *Miranda* under full sail charged towards her attacker. The brig, if well handled, stood a fair chance against a frigate in matters of speed and manoeuvrability. But this one had waited just that much too long. Converging like prongs of a trap the three vessels would pass beam to beam, the frigate shielding the merchantman and well able to rake the brig from stem to stern as they passed.

Provided the brig was not too badly damaged she might be useful to the fleet. Either way, *Miranda*'s captain would gain a nice purse of prize money.

He tore his eyes away as sounds of angry voices came up the quarterdeck ladder at his side.

It was Tilby, flushed from some secret hoard of rum, his face heavy with rage as he said, 'Beg pardon, sir, but this 'ere man says 'e wants to speak to 'ee.' He glared severely at the seaman in question. 'I told 'im that no man under punishment can speak to an officer without permission.'

Bolitho saw that the seaman behind Tilby was the one waiting to be flogged. He was a young, well-made man and was dragging at the boatswain's arm with frantic determination.

'What is it, Yelverton?' Bolitho nodded to Tilby. 'Is it *so* important?'

The seaman reached the quarterdeck and swallowed hard. 'That ship, sir! She ain't no Indiaman! She's a damned Frenchie! I seen her in Boston some years back!'

Bolitho swung round. 'God in heaven!'

It was at that moment the oncoming merchantman fired a full broadside into the *Miranda*'s unmanned side as she passed, the sound going on and on until it reached the heart of every man in the convoy.

4

A Total Responsibility

Even at two miles' range Bolitho saw the *Miranda* give a violent shiver as the broadside swept across her. It must have been aimed high, for as the smoke fanned away he saw the havoc left by the sudden onslaught, maintopmast gone, and most of her sails ripped and punctured like rags in a gale.

He thrust himself from the nettings and noticed that the men near him were still standing like groups of statues, or people so stricken they were unable to think or respond.

He shouted, 'Mr Tyrrell! Beat to quarters and clear for action!' He gripped Bethune's arm, seeing his dazed expression as he added, 'Run up the colours!'

A ship's boy seized his drum and began to beat out the staccato tattoo. The men on deck, and poised in the bows where they had waited to watch *Miranda*'s swift victory, came alive and began to run to their stations. But gone was the automatic movement of men at drill, or the grim silence of old hands facing one more battle. They hurried like those already too confused to act for a set purpose. Some cannoned into one another, others stood momentarily at the wrong gun, or groping with unfamiliar equipment until a petty officer kicked them away.

Bolitho looked at Buckle, trying to keep his tone level amidst the din around him. 'Get the courses off her and set the t'gallants. There'll be enough risk of fire without having the canvas burn around our ears.'

Below the quarterdeck he heard the thud and bang of screens being torn down, a patter of feet as the boys dashed from the magazine with powder for each waiting gun.

He made himself face the approaching ships, knowing it was taking far too long to prepare for action. How near they looked. There was more gunfire, and he saw smoke lifting and writhing between the vessels making it impossible to know what was happening.

He held his breath as he saw the *Miranda*'s yards swinging above the smoke, and knew her captain was trying to go about and run parallel with his attacker. Guns roared through the drifting fog, their long orange tongues flashing above the churned water, some of the balls whipping away over open sea, leaving vicious spurts of spray to mark their progress.

Miranda was still edging round, her pockmarked sails flapping weakly as she began to swing past the wind's eye. Her captain was either going to fight the bigger ship gun to gun, or intended to slip past her stern and rake her with a broadside as he did so.

Bolitho heard someone groan as the enemy fired into the smoke. Gun by gun down her hidden side, the balls could almost be felt across the tumbling white-horses.

It was superbly timed, catching the frigate even as she was beginning to pass across the wind. The enemy was using langridge or chain-shot, for as the slow broadside smashed home Bolitho saw the *Miranda*'s fore and mainmasts stagger and then begin to topple sideways into the smoke, the sails jerking to the bombardment. From a lithe and beautiful ship to a crippled wreck, the *Miranda* was still trying to turn, her bow-chaser firing blindly, the ensign showing scarlet from her mizzen.

Tyrrell shouted wildly, 'Cleared for action!'

Bolitho looked at him. 'Load and run out, if you please.'

The lieutenant stayed facing him, his eyes very bright in the sunlight. 'You ain't going to fight *both* of 'em, surely?'

'If necessary.'

Bolitho turned as more shots echoed and murmured across the shortening distance. He saw the brig clawing away from the two larger ships, her maintopgallant leaning at a dangerous angle where *Miranda*'s first balls had found their mark.

The planks vibrated under his shoes, and as the port lids opened the *Sparrow*'s eighteen guns squeaked and rumbled towards the sunlight, the bare-backed seamen slipping on sanded decks as they tried to keep in time to the shouted commands from their captains.

Bolitho stared along the length of his ship with something like despair. In moments now, all would be finished. His ship, his precious *Sparrow*, would be sharing the frigate's fate.

And it had all been so easy. It had happened so often in the past that the sight of a helpless merchantman being harried by a well-armed privateer had not even aroused the faintest suspicion. No wonder the privateer's sails had been unmarked in their carefully staged battle. How the two American captains must have laughed when *Miranda* had swept in to defend her own murderer.

He felt Stockdale breathing noisily beside him, the sudden grip of the swordbelt around his waist.

He said huskily, 'By God, sir, them's bad odds!'

'Deck there!' The masthead lookout had been forgotten in the sight of disaster. '*Miranda*'s goin' to grapple!' The unseen lookout gave a cracked cheer. 'She's goin' to close with the bugger!'

Bolitho ran to the rail. The frigate was almost hidden by the heavier shape of the enemy ship, but he could tell from the set of her mizzen that she was indeed lurching towards her attacker. Another crash of gunfire made the smoke spout upwards between them, and the frigate's remaining mast vanished in a welter of rigging and ripped canvas. But Bolitho could see the sudden activity on the enemy's gangways, the surge of figures by her foremast, and pictured the battered frigate heading her bows straight for the forecastle. Muskets cracked feebly across the water and he saw the telltale flash of steel as the two vessels grounded momentarily together and the fight became hand to hand.

He grasped Tyrrell's arm and shouted, '*Miranda*'s given us time!' He saw no understanding in his eyes, only disbelief. 'If she can hold on, we will close with the brig!'

He shaded his face against the glare and watched the brig as she swept down towards the two transports.

'She'll cross *Golden Fleece*'s bows, and rake her as she passes.' He was shouting his thoughts aloud. 'We will wear ship directly, pass between the transports, and return the compliment!'

Tyrrell bit his lip. 'But we might collide with th' privateer, sir!'

Bolitho swung him round, pointing him at the embattled ships.

'Do you want those lads to die for nothing, man?' He pushed him to the rail. 'Now get ready to wear when I give the order!'

The brig was already dead ahead of *Sparrow*'s raked jib-boom, no more than a mile away. Aboard the leading transport Bolitho could see smoke from a solitary gun, although he saw no sign of a ball.

'Signal the transports to keep station, Mr Bethune!' He repeated the order to break the midshipman from his unmoving stance. '*Lively!*'

If either of the transports' captains lost his head now all would fail. The enemy would destroy or capture at leisure. Even now there was little room for hope of any kind.

And all of it, from the first hint of surprise to this moment, had been merely minutes.

He made himself walk aft towards the taffrail, his eyes passing over the crouching swivel gunners, the two helmsmen at their unprotected wheel, Buckle grim-faced and staring at the sails above. All of them.

He saw Raven, the new master's mate, watching him wretchedly, and paused to say, 'You weren't to know. She *was* an Indiaman after all, but not, I fear, as she was intended.'

Raven shook his head, so concerned with his failure to recognize the enemy that he seemed oblivious to the sporadic crash of cannon fire.

'I should've *seen* 'er, sir. But I saw what I *expected* to see, an' I'm powerful sorry on it after you givin' me a chance to better meself.'

Bolitho smiled, feeling his lips cracking with the effort.

'And I will expect you to do even better this day, Mr Raven!'

He strode aft, hands behind his back, the new sword flapping against his thigh.

Buckle pursed his lips in a silent whisper. 'He's a calm one. Death coming up the hawse an' he just walks about like he was enjoying himself.'

Behind the fixed smile Bolitho continued to pace the deck, his ears pitched above the gunfire to catch the news that the brig had reached the first transport. If her captain saw through his frail plan it would be pointless to continue with it. He would either have to run away from the fight and carry *Miranda*'s important news to the admiral, or stay and await the final meeting with the converted Indiaman. A few of the *Miranda*'s guns were still firing here and there, their muzzles almost overlapping those of the other ship. Between decks it must be a slaughterhouse, he thought despairingly.

Tyrrell shouted, 'Brig's crossing her bows!'

Sharper explosions echoed over the water, and Bolitho knew the brig was firing her starboard battery as she ran easily across the transport's bowsprit. Before she had vanished beyond *Golden Fleece*'s great bulk he saw the American flag whipping jauntily from her gaff, the sudden stab of musket fire from her low deck as sharpshooters practised their aim.

'*Now!*' Bolitho sliced the air. 'Wear ship!'

As the helm went over and along the *Sparrow*'s crowded decks the men threw themselves on the braces, the hull seemed to stagger violently under the shock. Blocks screamed, and above the decks the great yards creaked round with such speed that Bolitho could feel the whole fabric shaking in protest. But nothing carried away, as she heeled steeply to take the wind under her stern the sails lifted then filled to its thrust.

Bolitho cupped his hands. 'Mr Graves! Engage with the larboard guns first! You will point the thirty-two-pounder yourself!' He saw Graves nod before vanishing beneath the forecastle in the direction of the bow-chaser.

How fast she was moving, despite both her courses being brailed up to the yards for fear of fire when the guns started to engage. The main-topgallant seemed to bend forward, the masthead pendant flicking straight out towards the bows as if to point the way.

Already the jib-boom must be crossing the leading transport's quarter, and to starboard Bolitho saw the second one, *Bear*, altering course slightly as if fearful of a collision with the sloop which was dashing across her path. More shots came from beyond the first transport, and he saw smoke funnelling down her hull to mark the brig's progress.

From forward came the cry, 'Thar she be! On th' larboard bow!'

The *Sparrow*'s unexpected appearance between the two transports seemed to have caught the brig's captain totally by surprise. The privateer was passing down the transport's side, about a cable clear, her yards braced round to hold her on a starboard tack.

Bolitho yelled, 'We'll cross the enemy's hawse and rake him as we go!' He saw some of his men staring at him from their guns, faces strained and confused. He drew his sword and held it over his head. 'As you bear, lads! Make each ball strike home!'

The brig was barely half a cable away, her bowsprit pointing at right angles towards *Sparrow*'s figurehead. The distance seemed to be falling away at a tremendous speed, and Bolitho knew that if he had misjudged it, or if the wind chose this instant to drop, the enemy would drive into the sloop's side like a battering ram and split her seams wide open.

The big thirty-two-pounder in the bows broke the spell, the crash of the explosion transmitting itself through the deck until it reached Bolitho's feet. He saw the brig's shrouds slashed open, the whirl of bright wood splinters as the ball ploughed into her tiered boats. Then gun by gun down *Sparrow*'s side the broadside continued, with Graves bursting into the smoky sunlight, waving his sword and yelling orders to each crew in succession.

Frantically the enemy captain tried to wear ship and follow *Sparrow*'s onrushing charge. Unable to get her own guns to bear, and with most of the forward shrouds and rigging hanging like black weed above her deck, the brig was staggering drunkenly under the well-aimed barrage.

Then with the helm over and some wind still alive in the torn sails the brig finally came under command. Here and there a gun banged out, but in their haste the privateers were firing haphazardly into the whirling smoke.

'Load and run out!' Tyrrell was yelling above the din. 'Roundly!'

Bolitho shouted. 'Don't wait for a broadside! Let each captain fire whenever he was loaded!' It was useless to expect these men to keep on firing as a team once they, too, were under the enemy's metal.

Graves rasped, 'Sponge out, you stupid bugger!' He had to drag a dazed man to the rear of his gun. 'Are you mad?' He pushed the luckless seaman towards the gun captain. 'I'll put you in irons if I see you . . .'

Bolitho did not hear the rest of it. The brig was slowly edging round until she was lying almost diagonally across the larboard quarter. Smoke fanned down around him and he felt musket balls thudding into the deck planks, the maniac whine as one ricocheted from a swivel gun just feet away.

Stockdale said desperately, 'Keep on the move, sir! Them buggers'll mark you down else!'

Bolitho stared at him, knowing his own face was set in a wild grin. It never failed to amaze him that it was so easy to lose control and reason once a battle had begun. Later perhaps . . . He shook himself. There would be no later when they closed with the bigger ship.

He yelled, 'They are shooting blind, Stockdale!' He waved his sword around the quarterdeck. None of the officers had found time to get their uniform coats or hats and like himself were dressed only in shirts and breeches, and those were already grimy with drifting powder-smoke. 'See? They can take their pick of us today!'

A seaman at the mizzen braces gave a terrible scream and was hurled on to his side by the force of a musket ball. Blood spurted from his chest, and as he rolled about in agony Bolitho called, 'See to that man, Mr Bethune!' When the midshipman hesitated, his face like chalk under the freckles, he added harshly, 'Your mother is at home, boy, so you can weep alone *after* you have done your duty!'

Bethune dropped to his knees, his breeches spattered with the blood, but his face suddenly determined as the dying sailor groped for his hand.

Buckle yelled, 'The Yankee will try to work across our stern, sir!'

Bolitho nodded. There was nothing else the enemy could do. With most of his sails damaged by cannon fire, and already overreached by *Sparrow*'s maddened attack through the transports, the brig's captain must either try to cross astern or tack and risk his own poop coming under fire.

He snapped, 'We will wear ship, Mr Buckle. Lay her to the larboard tack and follow the brig round, nose to tail!'

He was still grinning, but could feel his mouth raw with tension as once again the men hurled themselves on the braces, their smoke-grimed bodies glistening in the glare as they angled back above the deck, their eyes on the yards above them.

'Helm a'lee!' Buckle was adding his own weight to the wheel.

Bolitho watched the bowsprit swinging, heard the immediate crash of guns as Graves directed his newly loaded battery towards the other ship.

Through the dense gunsmoke Bolitho saw the murky shape of the leading transport, now some two cables away.

'Steady as you go, Mr Buckle!' A ball whimpered overhead, and when he glanced up he saw a neat hole in the centre of the big spanker. 'Keep station on *Golden Fleece*, she is better than any compass today!'

He winced as the hull jumped once, twice and yet again, as some enemy shots smashed into it. But the brig was in a bad way, and she was drifting stern-first, her complete foremast dragging over the side like a fallen tree. Men were working in the wreckage, axes flashing, while others continued to fire and reload the guns as before.

'Steady, sir! Nor'-west by north!'

Bolitho raised his sword, his eyes narrowed against the reflected sunlight as he watched the brig swinging drunkenly on the tow of fallen spars.

'Easy!' The sword held the sunlight. '*Easy*, lads!' Not a gun fired, and along the deck only at the weapons not yet reloaded was there any sort of movement.

Another ball slammed into the lower hull, and somewhere a man screamed in torment as he was clawed down by flying splinters.

The sun was shining into his eyes now, and through the drifting smoke he saw the outline of the brig's tattered maintopsail, the glint of glass as she helplessly presented her stern.

'Fire as you bear!'

Driven by the wind, the smoke came funnelling inboard through port after port as Graves ran along the gundeck, his voice cracking from the strain of shouting directions.

A shadow passed briefly above the smoke, and through the din Bolitho heard the splintering crash of a complete mast falling, and guessed it had been sheared off between decks by the *Sparrow*'s merciless bombardment.

Then as the *Sparrow* forged ahead once more he heard cheering and knew it was from the *Golden Fleece*. As wind drove the smoke apart he saw the brig very clearly and someone on her splintered deck waving the flag in surrender. Mastless, and with her stern gouged open by the slow broadside, she was little better than a hulk. Within her small hull her company must have been savagely mauled.

Tyrrell was staring at it, his eyes bright with concentration, and by his side Heyward was almost jumping up and down, his voice half choked by smoke.

Then, almost before the *Sparrow*'s dazed company could feel the taste of their conquest, the air was blasted apart with one deafening explosion. Spars, complete sections of timber and deck planking, all whirled above an angry scarlet core, and across the water a shock wave rolled towards the sloop like a miniature typhoon. When the smoke and flying fragments subsided there was nothing to show of the privateer but for a few pieces of charred flotsam and an upended jolly-boat which was miraculously undamaged. A sudden spark, an upended lantern, or someone so crazed in the horror between the shattered decks that he had ignited a fuse, the brig's end was terrible in its completeness.

Bolitho said, 'Get the maincourse on her, Mr Tyrrell! We must make haste to assist *Miranda*.' He waited until Tyrrell had brought the stunned seamen to their senses, his voice hoarse through his speaking trumpet, and then added. 'They will know that we can still sell our lives dearly.'

It took little time to overhaul the *Golden Fleece* and to see the two embattled ships about a mile distant. They had drifted in the fury of combat, their hulls masked in smoke, through which the flash of musket fire, the occasional glare of a swivel, were clear to see.

The frigate was listing against her heavier adversary, like a hulk already dead, and without using a glass Bolitho could see that the fighting had spread down across the fore deck as more boarders hacked their way between the grappled ships.

'We will go about, Mr Tyrrell. Lay her on the starboard tack once we have gained some room and prepare to engage with the other battery.'

He bit his lip to steady his racing thoughts. A quick glance aloft told him that the masthead pendant was lifting as firmly as ever. The wind was steady from south-south-west.

'Pass the word for Mr Graves to lay aft.'

When the lieutenant arrived, his face gaunt with fatigue, Bolitho said, 'I want the starboard bow-chaser to keep firing at the enemy. As soon as we have gone about I'll expect it to concentrate on that ship, no matter what.'

Buckle called, 'Ready on th' quarterdeck, sir.'

Bolitho nodded. 'Put the helm down, if you please.'

'Helm a'lee, sir!'

Tyrrell was already bellowing through his trumpet, and forward the seamen were leaping like demons at the headsail sheets, and with canvas flapping the *Sparrow* started to swing into the wind.

'Man the braces!'

Bolitho gripped the rail, his eyes smarting as the sun lanced between the shrouds.

'Heave there! With all your weight!'

Across the wind and still further round, the yards groaning in unison. Then as the sails refilled and laid the deck over in the opposite angle he watched the distant ships edging very slowly between the foremast shrouds as if caught in a giant web.

'Steady, Mr Buckle! Hold her!'

He paced a few steps this way and that, aware that Tyrrell was urging the men at the braces to trim the yards still further, that the dead seaman had gone from the quarterdeck, and that Ben Garby, the carpenter, with his mates, was slithering through the after hatch to inspect the damage there. Aware of all this and more, yet not a part of it as he had once been.

'Steady, sir! Full an' bye!'

He nodded, his mind busy with the two ships. Close-hauled it would take thirty minutes to reach them, maybe more. *Miranda* was almost overrun by enemy boarders. Outnumbered from the start, she would have lost many good men in that first savage broadside.

'*Fire!*'

As the muffled cry came from forward he saw the puff of smoke beneath the starboard cathead, felt the sharp convulsion as the thirty-two-pounder crashed inboard on its tackles. He snatched up a glass and saw the ball plunge close to the enemy's hull throwing up a tall waterspout.

Heyward muttered hoarsely, 'Near!'

Bolitho looked away. The big ex-Indiaman mounted anything up to forty guns, at a guess. She could finish *Sparrow*, if ever she could bring her artillery to bear, with even a badly aimed broadside. Less.

Bang. Another ball crashed away from the bow-chaser, and he watched the feathers of spray lifting from wave to wave until it plunged hard alongside the other ship.

They should hear us and see we are coming. He tried to clear his brain. What should he do? Signal the transports to run? No. They were helplessly overladen and slow. It would merely prolong their agony.

Overhead, the spanker cracked noisily, and Buckle cursed it before allowing the helm to be eased still further.

Bolitho knew without looking that sailing so close to the wind was cutting away his chances of reaching the ships in time to help.

Someone walked past him. It was Bethune, his arms hanging at his sides, his breeches covered with dark blood blotches and a smear where the seaman's fingers had made their last agonized grip on this earth. Bolitho stared at him.

'Mr Bethune!' He saw the youth jump. 'Come here!'

He walked to the rail and back again. It was worth an attempt. Anything was now. If they arrived alongside after *Miranda* had struck to the enemy, *Sparrow*'s decks would be as red as the flag above his head.

The midshipman waited. 'Sir?'

'Make this signal at once.' He rested his hand on Bethune's plump shoulder. He could feel the skin through his shirt. Like ice, in spite of the sun.

'*Signal,* sir?' He stared up at him as if he had misheard. Or his captain had gone mad.

'Yes. To *Miranda*. Sail in sight to the nor'-east!' He tightened his grip. 'Then *move* yourself!'

Bethune fled, calling shrilly for his assistants, and within a minute the bright signal flags broke to the wind, while Tyrrell stared from them to Bolitho, first with incredulity and then with slow understanding.

Buckle said, 'There's few poor devils'll see that aboard *Miranda*.'

Tyrrell was studying Bolitho. 'No. But th' privateer will. He might just think that a patrol from th' squadron has come to join th' fight!'

Bolitho waited until Graves' bow-chaser had fired yet again and said, 'It is all we can do at present.'

Minutes dragged by like hours, and then as a freak down-draught of wind swept across the two snared ships Bolitho caught his breath. A thin shaft of light where there had been none. Then a glint of water. Wider still, as the ships drifted apart and the big privateer set her foresail and jib to work clear. Then *Miranda* was quite separate, the water between her and the other ship dotted with wreckage and torn canvas, where here and there a man thrashed to stay afloat amidst a litter of bobbing corpses.

A ragged cheer came up from *Sparrow*'s gundeck, and several ran to the gangways to watch while the enemy spread more canvas and lengthened her outline against the wind.

Tyrrell's grin froze as Bolitho snapped, 'Keep those men *silent*!' He realized he was still holding his sword, that his hand was aching with the force of his grip. 'Look yonder, Mr Tyrrell. There's no call for cheers this day.'

Tyrrell turned to stare at the *Miranda*'s dark shape. The rising clouds of smoke as her remaining hands quenched fires and groped amidst the wreckage of their ship. As *Sparrow* drew closer they could all see the thin tendrils of scarlet which ran from her scuppers, the great pitted holes along every part of her hull.

'Pass the word for Mr Tilby to prepare boats for lowering. Call the surgeon and send him with them.' Bolitho hardly recognized his own voice. Clipped, dull, inhuman. 'Then shorten sail and get the t'gallants off her. We will stand under *Miranda*'s lee for the present.'

He ignored the rush of feet as Tilby's men dashed to the boat shackles. He saw Graves walking aft towards the quarterdeck, wiping his face and chest with a wet rag. Above the activity the sails were still drawing well, but there were plenty of holes which would need attention before nightfall. A few stays and halyards were broken, and he knew the hull had been hit several times on or near the waterline. But the pumps sounded normal enough. She was taking it like a veteran.

Dalkeith came hurrying up the ladder, his heavy bag gripped against his chest, face streaming with exertion.

'How many, Mr Dalkeith?' Again he heard his own voice as a stranger's.

The plump surgeon was staring at the frigate, his eyes dull. 'Two killed, sir. Five wounded by splinters.'

Bolitho tried to recall the man who was killed by his side. Manners. That was his name.

He said, 'Manners. Who was the other?'

'Yelverton, sir. He was killed by a ball at the foremast.' He looked down. 'Took his head off.'

Graves was halfway up the ladder but recoiled as Bolitho said, 'Yelverton. Did you hear that, Mr Graves? The one man who kept his senses when all others were too blind to see the truth. The one you wanted to flog?' He turned away. 'Well, he'll not trouble you further, Mr Graves. Nor we him.'

Blindly he saw Stockdale watching from the foot of the mizzen mast. 'Call away the gig. I will visit Captain Selby and see what must be done.'

'Aye, sir.'

Stockdale glanced back at him as he hurried to the boat tier. He had never seen Bolitho so stricken or so moved before. And for once he did not know what to do to help.

Bolitho entered his cabin and unbuckled his sword before throwing it on to the bench seat below the windows. Fitch and a young seaman were busy replacing the furniture, and another was mopping away smoke stains from the low deckhead. For in action even the captain's quarters were not spared. With the hasty removal of screens the cabin became an extension of the gundeck, and on either side of it was a squat twelve-pounder, now once again hidden by discreet chintz covers.

He stared at the nearest gun, his eyes blurred with strain. *A woman's touch.* Then he turned abruptly to face Tyrrell and Graves who had followed him into the cabin upon his return from the crippled *Miranda*.

His mind was so filled with questions and suppositions, his brain so racked by the sights and sounds aboard the frigate, that for a moment he was unable to speak at all.

Beyond the bulkhead he could hear the steady thud of hammers, the rasp of saws as the ship's company continued work on repairs. After a full hour aboard the *Miranda* he had returned to find his own command settling down to the task of making good the damage from their encounter with the privateer with such orderly dedication that he had been unable to compare the scene with what he had just left. The sailmaker and his mates had already replaced the punctured canvas, and with their needles and palms flashing in the sunlight covered every foot of deck space as they patched the others sent down from the yards.

Garby, the carpenter, had greeted him at the entry port and had told him that the brig's gunnery had not been too damaging. Two shot holes below the waterline which his men were already plugging, and several others which he would repair before sunset. Garby had spoken quickly, professionally, as if like the rest he was unwilling to think about the *Miranda* and the fate which could have been theirs.

Graves was the first to break the silence.

'All guns secured, sir. No damage to tackles or ports.' He dropped his eyes under Bolitho's unmoving stare. 'Better'n we could have hoped.'

Tyrrell asked quietly, 'How was it, sir?'

Bolitho let himself drop into a chair and thrust out his legs in front of him. The breeches were black with powder stains and his climb up the frigate's side. *How was it?* Once again he saw the pictures of death and horror, the few uninjured men who were trying even now to put the frigate to rights. Smoke stains and great patches of drying blood, gaping corpses littered amongst the fallen spars and broken planking. It was a miracle that *Miranda* was still able to keep afloat.

He said, 'They hope to get a jury rig hoisted by sometime tomorrow.

Provided the wind doesn't get up, or the pumps foul, they will obtain steerage way.' He rubbed his eyes with his knuckles, feeling the weariness enclosing him like a vice. 'Some of the wounded will be transferred to the transports directly. There they will have more room to recover.'

He tried again to shut the agony from his mind. Men so badly mutilated by splinters that they should be dead already. Midshipmen and even seamen in charge of repairs because of the carnage on the quarterdeck. He had found the frigate's first lieutenant supervising the recovery of the mizzen topmast when he had climbed aboard. The man had had one arm in a sling and his forehead had looked as if it had been laid open by a hot iron.

Graves breathed out very slowly. 'They did well against such odds.'

'Yes.'

Bolitho wanted to get them out of the cabin. Seal the door and shut them away from his uncertainty.

Tyrrell said, 'I've passed th' word around th' ship, sir. I think our people know how satisfied you . . .'

Bolitho's tone made him fall back. '*Satisfied?*' He lurched to his feet. 'If you feel cause for complacency, Mr Tyrrell, then please contain it!' He moved to the windows and back again. 'I have seen it for myself. Our people are not moved by a sense of victory. They are *relieved*, and nothing deeper than that! Thankful to be spared a similar mauling, and all too eager to overlook their own shortcomings!'

Tyrrell said quickly, 'But that's a mite unfair, surely.'

'You think so?' He sank down at the table, his anger spent. 'Raven had the measure of it. He saw what he expected to see, as did Captain Selby in *Miranda*. And like you, Mr Tyrrell, our people thought that fighting an enemy was just an extension of drill, a few cuts and a few curses, and all would be well. Perhaps we have been too victorious in the past and have been overreached by this newer kind of warfare.'

There was another silence, so that the hammering somewhere deep in the hull became insistent, and to Bolitho suddenly urgent.

Graves asked, 'What will we do now, sir?' He sounded wary.

Bolitho faced them gravely. 'Captain Selby is dead. Killed in the first broadside.'

He walked to the quarter windows and stared towards the drifting frigate. Without effort he could picture the wounded first lieutenant, the man who had somehow fought his ship alongside the enemy. Knowing it was all he could do despite the crippling losses and damage already suffered. Now, without a single lieutenant, aided by a mere handful of junior warrant officers, he was doing his utmost to repair the ship. To get her to safety before the sea or an enemy found him again.

In the shattered chaos of Selby's cabin he had unlocked the safe and handed Bolitho the despatches without hesitation. Even now that he was back in his own cabin he found it hard to believe. Junior command, and then, almost in the twinkling of an eye, he was to shoulder the total responsibility for them all. Colquhoun and Maulby were beyond reach. And Selby was dead. He had seen his corpse on the splintered quarterdeck, pinned beneath an upended nine-pounder, one hand still clutching his sword like a useless talisman.

Tyrrell's voice made him turn towards them again.

'Then *you* are in command, sir?'

The lieutenants were watching him intently, their faces showing both doubt and apprehension.

Bolitho nodded slowly. 'We will continue with the transports before dusk. After we have ferried the *Miranda*'s wounded across to them and done what we can for their own ship.' He tried not to think of the endless problems which lay ahead. 'When we have made contact with the squadron as ordered we will proceed with the despatches to the Commander-in-Chief.'

He let his eyes stray around the cabin. All at once it was smaller, the sloop more vulnerable.

'And *Miranda*, sir?' Tyrrell's tone was hushed.

Bolitho kept his voice level and without emotion, knowing that if he showed them even for an instant, his true feelings, they would lose what small faith they still retained.

'Her people will do what they must. We cannot stay with her, nor would they wish it.'

Spray pattered against the thick windows. The wind was already freshening slightly.

Tyrrell licked his lips, his eyes distant as he stared towards the dismasted frigate.

Bolitho added, 'That will be all. Keep the hands working until the last minute.'

The two lieutenants, in their filthy shirts and breeches, turned and left the cabin without another word.

Bolitho looked at Fitch and said, 'You may go, too. I wish to think.'

When Fitch and his helpers had gone he rested his head in his hands and allowed his body to sway with the ship's uncomfortable motion.

Tyrrell probably thought him heartless for leaving the other ship without company or aid. Graves too, would no doubt be finding plenty of fuel for his own personal fires.

He stood up, fighting back the tiredness and strain, knowing he must not heed nor care about their considerations. They were in a war which for too long they had only skirted like spectators. If learn they must, it were better to be done at once.

Then he recalled the *Miranda*'s lieutenant, the bitterness in his voice as he had described the action. He was able to add little to what Bolitho already knew and guessed. But for one thing, the name of the big privateer. *Bonaventure*. It was a name he would not forget.

There was a tap at the door. It was Lock, his face dark with gloom as he began to recount a list of stores damaged in the brief fight with the brig.

Bolitho faced him and said quietly, 'Now let me have a full list, Mr Lock, and I will give you my opinion.'

It was useless to think of what had passed. He was alone now, and only the future, like the next horizon, had any true meaning for him.

5

All the Luck . . .

'Guardboat approaching, sir!'

Bolitho nodded. 'Very well.'

He had already seen it, but was concentrating instead on the overlapping lines of anchored ships, the nearest of which, a two-decker, wore a rear-admiral's flag at her mizzen.

Then he took a quick glance along the busy gundeck, the preparations to drop anchor for the first time since leaving Antigua. It was ten days since they had watched the *Miranda*'s battered outline fall further and furthern astern until they had lost it altogether. Days of fretting impatience as they repeatedly shortened sail to keep station on the two transports. And when at last they had found a frigate of the inshore squadron they had received not freedom but yet another unexplained leg to the journey. *Sparrow* would not hand over her charge of the transports, nor would she close with the shore to supervise their unloading. Instead she was to proceed with all despatch to New York. The frigate's captain had been impatient to be away and merely sent a midshipman across to *Sparrow* with his orders. From what little he had discovered, Bolitho gathered the frigate had been waiting and patrolling for three weeks in order that his message could be passed on to the convoy and had no wish to be involved further.

He shifted his gaze to the guardboat, rocking gently in the offshore swell, a large blue flag lifting and curling from her bows to mark where the sloop should anchor.

The wheel creaked as Buckle passed his directions to the helmsmen, and forward on the beakhead, framed against the glittering water, he saw Graves waiting for the command to anchor. He heard someone laugh and saw the two transports idling awkwardly towards another anchorage, their yards alive with men as they shortened sail.

Dalkeith saw him turn and remarked, 'Glad to see the back of 'em, eh, sir?' He mopped his face with a handkerchief. 'They've been with us so long I felt we were towing the beasts.'

The gunner climbed halfway up the ladder and called, 'Permission to begin the salute, sir?'

Bolitho nodded. 'If you please, Mr Yule.' He turned away, knowing that but for the gunner's request he would have forgotten all about it in his concern for what would happen next.

While the *Sparrow* continued easily towards the guardboat, her canvas clewed up but for topsails and jib, the air shook to the regular bang of cannon fire as she paid her respects to the rear-admiral's flag.

Bolitho wanted to take Bethune's big telescope and study the other ships, but guessed too many glasses would now be on him. His natural curiosity might be seen as uncertainty, or the apprehension of a young commander approaching an unfamiliar anchorage. Instead he made himself walk a few paces along the weather side, noting with satisfaction that the nettings were neatly filled with hammocks and every unused line and halliard was either belayed or flaked down on the decks. Of their clash with the brig there was little or no visible sign. The ten days had been well used to replace woodwork and apply fresh paint.

Tyrrell was standing at the rail, a speaking trumpet under one arm. In his blue coat and cocked hat he seemed unfamiliar again, a stranger, like the day he had come into the cabin after his visit to the flagship.

The last wisp of gunsmoke drifted forward above the anchor party, and he concentrated his attention on the last half cable of distance. The other ships were spread out on either bow and looked impressive, indestructible.

He raised one hand slowly. 'Lee braces, Mr Tyrrell. Hands wear ship!'

Why then was he so apprehensive? Perhaps the frigate's curt orders had hidden something deeper? He tried to disregard it. After all, he had been sick to death of the slow passage with the transports, so how much worse it must have been for the solitary frigate.

Tyrrell's voice brought a screaming chorus from the circling gulls which had been with them for several days.

'Tops'l sheets!' He was squinting into the sunlight, watching the darting figures high above the deck. 'Tops'l clew lines! Roundly does it, lads!'

Bethune's voice cut across the shouted orders and the flapping crack of canvas.

'From *Flag* to *Sparrow*, sir. *Repair on board.*'

Bolitho nodded. 'Acknowledge.' The admiral did not believe in wasting time.

'Helm a'lee!'

Gently, easily, the *Sparrow* turned her jib-boom into the wind, her sails vanishing as the topmen vied with each other to fist the unruly canvas under control.

'Let go!'

From forward came a brief splash as the anchor plunged to the bottom, and before Graves had turned to signal the quarterdeck Tilby, the boatswain, was already urging the boat-lowerers to sway out the gig.

Tyrrell came aft and touched his hat. 'I hope you get good news, sir.'
'Thank you.'

Bolitho wondered what it must be like for Tyrrell. He was back off his own coastline. Sandy Hook. He must have sailed this way many times in his father's schooner. But there was nothing on his features to betray whatever he was thinking. The usual controlled respect which he had shown since the battle.

Tyrrell had not spared himself in his efforts to get the damage repaired. He had a manner which at first glance seemed easy going, even casual, but there was no doubting his ability, or the edge of his tongue if someone was foolish enough to mistake his attitude for weakness.

'I doubt that I will be long in the flagship.' Bolitho watched the gig's crew tumbling down the side.

'Th' admiral may ask you to take lunch, sir.' Tyrrell's eyes crinkled in a rare smile. 'I gather th' old *Parthian* is known for a good table.'

Stockdale called, 'Gig's ready, sir.'

Bolitho looked at Tyrrell. 'Make arrangements for taking in fresh water and casks. I have told Mr Lock to see what he can do about fruit.'

Tyrrell followed him to the entry port where the side party were assembled.

He hesitated and then asked quietly, 'If you could find out anything about . . .' he shrugged. 'But then I guess you'll be too busy, sir.'

Bolitho ran his eye over the nearby seamen. Had he learned anything about them since he had taken command? Did he even know what they thought of him?

He replied, 'I will do what I can. Perhaps your father has sent some message for you.'

Tyrrell was still staring after him as he clambered into the boat, his ears ringing to the squeal of pipes.

When Bolitho climbed up through the *Parthian*'s gilded entry port and doffed his hat to the quarterdeck he was immediately reminded of the *Trojan*, the life he had so recently left behind. All the old smells and sights came crowding back, and he marvelled that he had forgotten so much in so brief a time.

A lieutenant guided him to the flag captain's cabin and relieved him of the despatches and a bag of letters which *Miranda* had brought from England.

He said, 'The admiral will read these first, sir.' His eyes moved swiftly over Bolitho's new uniform coat. Searching perhaps for the same old answer. *Why him and not me?*

The admiral did not send for him for a full hour, although it felt twice as long. To avoid repeatedly examining his watch he made himself listen to the sounds around and above him. The old, familiar noises of a teeming community encased in one great hull. It took little imagination to hear Captain Pears's harsh voice complaining, 'Mr Bolitho! Are you aware that the weather forebrace is as slack as a sow's tail? 'Pon my soul, sir, you'll have to do better if you wish to make something of yourself!'

He was smiling ruefully when the lieutenant returned and without further ceremony led him aft to the great cabin.

Sir Evelyn Christie, Rear-Admiral of the Red, and commanding the Inshore Squadron, was fanning his face with a napkin, and after a searching examination of Bolitho's general appearance said, 'A glass of claret, Commander.' He did not wait for an answer but gestured to his servant, a splendid-looking man in scarlet jacket and brilliant yellow breeches.

'I was somewhat surprised to see *your* name affixed to the report.' The admiral's eyes were fastened on the claret, as if daring the servant to spill even a drip. 'You say in it that Ransome died of fever.' He took a glass and examined it critically. 'Damn good job, if you ask me. Young popinjay. Too much money and no damn integrity.' Ransome disposed of he continued calmly, 'I expect you're concerned about the change of plans, eh?'

Bolitho felt a chair nudge the back of his legs and realized the silent servant had somehow managed to arrange a glass of claret on a small table, fetch a chair, and all without apparently moving or uttering a sound.

The admiral scowled. 'Take no notice. The man's a fool.' He added sharply, '*Well?*'

Bolitho replied, 'I was expecting to . . .'

Rear-Admiral Christie interrupted, 'Yes, I imagine you were.' He paused, his head on one side like an irritable bird. 'The claret. Well?'

'Very good, Sir Evelyn.'

'Hmm.' The admiral seated himself carefully on a gilt chair. 'Took it off a blockade runner last month. Palatable.'

Something metallic crashed across a deck beyond the bulkhead and he snapped savagely, 'Go and tell the officer of the watch, with my *compliments*, that if I hear one more unseemly sound during this interview I will personally take him to task!'

The servant fled from the cabin and the admiral gave a slow smile.

'Keep them jumping. That's the answer. Don't give 'em too much time to think.'

In the very next breath he changed the tack yet again.

'Fact is, Bolitho, things are not going too well. Thank God you at least are a man who knows how to abide by the letter of his orders. In your place I might have said to hell with waiting around for some damn patrol to find out what was happening. I might even have gone so far as to take those transports direct to the army.'

Bolitho stiffened. It sounded genuine enough, but perhaps the admiral was merely hinting at criticism. Maybe he thought he should have made straight for the exact rendezvous, used his initiative instead of acting as he had.

The admiral's next words changed that.

'You were not to know, of course, but the army is in the process of evacuating Philadelphia. Falling back.' He looked down at the empty glass. 'Sounds better than a retreat, but it amounts to the same.'

Bolitho was stunned. Reverses he could accept. This war was so extended, the areas so vast and little known, that no plan of battle of the old style could be expected. But to quit Philadelphia, the vital command garrison of the Delaware, was unthinkable. In spite of his caution he said, 'Surely that was unnecessary, sir? I thought we had destroyed all the American forts and outposts on the Delaware last year.'

The admiral eyed him shrewdly. 'That was *last* year, before Burgoyne surrendered at Saratoga. The whole of this area is overrun with bands of raiders and enemy informers.' He threw open the chart. 'With my squadron I must patrol and keep watch over the whole three hundred miles of coastline, from New York down to Cape Henry on Chesapeake Bay. It is a labyrinth. Inlets and rivers, coves and hiding places where you could fail to sight a three-decker at a mile's range. And every day the sea teems with shipping. From the north, and as far south as the Spanish Main and Carribean. Dutch, Portuguese, Spanish, and most of 'em intent on slipping past my patrols with stores and guns for the enemy.'

He poured two more glasses of claret.

'However, now that you have brought these despatches we are aware of the extent of our dangers. The French are out in the open at last. I have already sent word to the Commander-in-Chief and all senior officers here.'

He smiled. 'You did well, Bolitho. No one could have expected so newly appointed a commander to act as you did.'

'Thank you, sir.'

Bolitho thrust away the opposite side of the picture. If he had sailed with the rich transports into an enemy trap, the admiral would have spoken very differently.

'Pity about *Miranda*. We are cruelly short of frigates.'

'About the *Bonaventure*, sir. I was wondering . . .'

'You are a man who does a lot of wondering.' The admiral continued to smile. 'Not too bad a fault in some. I knew your father. I hope he is well?' He did not wait for or expect an answer. He hurried on, 'I am drafting fresh orders for you. The military, in their haste, unfortunately allowed an headquarters company to become lost.' He added dryly, 'Between ourselves, I, too, have done a certain amount of *wondering*. About some of our military colleagues ashore. Some, or so it would appear, did not obtain the necessary brains to match their appointments.'

He gave an elaborate sigh. 'But then, who am I to judge? We are fortunate. We carry our homes, our manner of existence, around with us like sea-turtles. It is hard to compare that with some wretched infantryman, loaded down with pack and musket, footsore and half starved. He has to contend with living off the land, fighting shadows, being shot at by American woodsmen as well as coming to grips with well-trained troops.'

Bolitho watched him curiously. On the face of it the admiral was nothing out of the ordinary, no more than you would expect of one backed up by his power and authority. But his features certainly hid a razor-sharp mind, the way he could throw it around from one aspect to the next without losing sight of anything.

'What about the *Bonaventure*, by the way?'

'She's big and fast, sir.' Bolitho readjusted his mind again. 'At least forty guns and well handled. I am sure she was the one which followed us, yet was well able to outsail us when the time came.' He waited, but the admiral's face was a mask. 'A match for any frigate.'

'Point taken. I will make inquiries about her pedigree.' He opened his watch. 'I want you to sail today and find that missing company of foot-soldiers before they are captured.'

Bolitho stared at him. 'But, sir, I have my orders.'

'Ah, yes.' He bobbed his head. 'Now you have *mine*, eh?'

Bolitho sank back in the chair, 'Yes, sir.'

'I neglected to mention that the soldiers are transporting gold bullion. God knows the exact amount, I find it difficult on occasions to crack the military mind into precise details. But it is a great deal. Fortunes of war, army pay, booty, whatever it is, you may be sure it is valuable.' He smiled. 'It has a complete general with it!'

Bolitho swallowed the claret in one gulp.

'A general, sir?'

'No less. Take care, he is well connected, and not given to much tolerance.' He continued evenly, 'Your arrival is a godsend. I have only one small brig available, and I was loath to send her.'

Bolitho stayed silent. *Lose* her, was probably what he really meant.

'Arrangements have been made for some army scouts to accompany you, and a small detachment is already trying to make contact with the missing company.' He paused before saying quietly, 'You will be under the instruction of one, Colonel Foley. He knows the area well, so you must abide by his experience.'

'I understand, sir.'

'Good. I will have your written orders sent to you without delay.' Another glance at the watch. 'I will expect you to be ready to weigh before dusk.'

'May I ask where I am to go, sir?'

'You may not. It will be clear in your orders. I do not want the whole of New York to learn of it yet. General Washington has many friends here, just as we have many who are waiting to change sides if things go badly for us.'

He held out his hand. It was over.

'Take care, Bolitho, England will need all her sons if she is to survive, let alone win this damn war. But if you succeed in this venture you will be more than able to face whatever lies ahead. You can rejoin your own squadron with much more than seniority to your credit.'

In something like a daze Bolitho found his way to the entry port, his mind grappling with the admiral's words.

This time he was greeted by the flag captain in person who asked quickly, 'Has he told you what he wants of you?'

'Yes.'

The captain studied Bolitho thoughtfully. 'The general's brother is a member of the Government. I thought I should tell you.'

Bolitho tugged his hat down on his forehead. 'Thank you, sir. I will try to remember.'

The captain grinned at his grave expression. 'You youngsters have all the luck!' His laughter was drowned by the trilling pipes as Bolitho climbed once more into his gig.

It was towards the end of the last dog watch when Bolitho's passenger, Colonel Hector Foley, climbed aboard from the guardboat. In his early thirties, he had the dark, even swarthy good looks of a Spaniard, set off with a hooked nose and deepset brown eyes. The appearance seemed totally at odds with the impeccable scarlet coat and close-fitting white breeches of an infantry officer. He glanced around the stern cabin, and accepted Bolitho's offer of the sleeping compartment and cot with little more than a nod, before seating himself in one of the chairs. He was tall and straight-backed, and like Bolitho had to be careful when moving between the deckhead beams.

He took out his watch and said calmly, 'I suggest you read your orders, Captain. Given luck, your part of the game should be no more than transport.'

He did not smile or show any emotion which Bolitho could recognize. His contained, aloof manner was vaguely disturbing. Irritating. It made Bolitho feel cut off from the more vital aspects of his strange mission.

The orders took little time to read. He was to proceed with as much despatch as possible, some one hundred and fifty miles southward along the coastline of New Jersey. Under cover of darkness, if considered possible and prudent, he would then enter Delaware Bay to such distance and position as would be directed by Colonel Foley. He re-read the orders more slowly, conscious the whole time of Foley's polished boots tapping gently on the deck beside the table.

If considered possible and prudent. That passage seemed to stand out more than all the rest, and he was again reminded of Colquhoun's prophecy. It meant simply that it was his responsibility. Foley could suggest what he liked, pick any landing place or rendezvous with equal indifference to the problems of sailing the ship close inshore through badly charted channels where in places the sea-bed was visible even to a man nearly blind.

He looked up. 'Can you tell me nothing more, sir?'

Foley shrugged. 'I have twenty scouts aboard. They will have to make the first contact.'

The scouts had arrived some time before the colonel. They were Canadians, and in their buckskin clothing and fur caps, their outward appearance of slovenly ease, gave little hint of being soldiers. Bolitho had seen them sprawled around the gundeck, cleaning their assortment of weapons or idly watching the busy seamen with amused contempt.

Foley seemed to read his mind. 'They are good soldiers, Captain. Well used to this sort of warfare.'

'I should have thought you could have obtained similar assistance locally, sir?'

Foley regarded him coldly. 'An American is an American. I do not choose to trust any of them if I can obtain an alternative.'

'Then there seems little point in continuing the war, sir.'

For the first time Foley smiled. 'I need to have perfect trust in my men. Idealists I do *not* need at present.'

Stockdale opened the door and asked huskily, 'Are you ready for the officers, sir?' He glanced at Foley. 'Eight bells 'ave just struck.'

'Yes.'

Bolitho pulled at his neckcloth, angry that he could rise so easily to Foley's arrogance.

Fitch hurried into the cabin and lit two lanterns, for although it was early evening the sky was unusually overcast and the wind veered to the west with a hint of rain in it. It was also hot and stuffy, and when the other officers had somehow crammed themselves into the cabin it was almost unbearable.

He waited, watching Foley's gently tapping boots as there were more delays while chairs were brought from the wardroom and in awkward, shuffling silence they got themselves sorted out.

Then he said, 'We will weigh as soon as this meeting is over. Is everything prepared, Mr Tyrrell?'

Tyrrell had his eyes fixed on the colonel. 'Aye, sir.'

'Mr Buckle?'

'Ready, sir.'

Bolitho looked at the carefully worded orders, recalling Tyrrell's astonishment when he had returned from the flagship.

He had blurted out, 'But we ain't had time to take on water, sir.'

The admiral had kept to his word on the matter of secrecy. He was not even going to allow the *Sparrow*'s boats in contact with the shore, no matter for what purpose.

What he would have said if he had learned that Lock had begged a trip ashore in a passing lighter, Bolitho could not imagine. Lock had returned just as secretly with several large casks of lemons, and a more mournful face than usual as he had told of their cost.

He said, 'We will proceed to the south'rd and enter Delaware Bay. There we will act in co-operation with the army and take aboard . . .'

Foley interrupted calmly, 'I think that will suffice for the present, Captain.' Without looking at Bolitho he added, 'So, gentlemen, your duty is to ensure that this vessel is in the right place at the right time, and ready to fight if necessary to complete the mission.'

The others shifted in their seats, and Bolitho saw the two midshipmen staring at him with surprise. To them, Foley's obvious control must seem strange.

Buckle muttered, 'Bad bit o' coast down there, sir. Shoals and sandbars a'plenty.' He sucked his teeth noisily. 'Bad.'

Foley glanced at Bolitho, his deepset eyes showing annoyance. 'We are not here to discuss the competence or otherwise of your officers, surely?'

Bolitho met his gaze steadily, suddenly very calm. 'Indeed not, sir. I will vouch for my people.' He paused. 'Just as I am sure you will vouch for yours when the time comes.'

In the stiff silence Bolitho heard Tilby's booming voice along the upper deck, driving some unfortunate man about his work. Again, he had made a bad start, but he was unrepentant.

Foley nodded slowly. 'We shall see.'

Graves asked, 'May I speak, sir?'

Bolitho nodded.

'Why cannot one of the inshore squadron do this mission, sir?'

Foley stood up, his head lowered between the beams. 'Because your vessel is more suitable, Lieutenant. Not, I assure you, because you are in any way outstanding in such work.'

Bolitho looked at their faces. Resentment, surprise, even hurt. It was all there.

He said slowly, 'Carry on, gentlemen. Call all hands in ten minutes.'

When they had filed out he said, 'You have said that my duty is to act as your transport. How I do it is my responsibility, and I am not required to remain quiet while you insult my officers.'

When the soldier stayed silent he continued, 'These same men helped to save two transports which are needed so badly for the military. They fought and sank a privateer and helped to drive away another, more powerful ship.'

'For which you will receive the credit, no doubt?'

Bolitho faced him quickly, his voice low with anger. 'Thank you, Colonel. I had no doubt you expected me to say that in front of the others, just so you could make such a suggestion.' He picked up his hat. 'Had I known that the army was already quitting Philadelphia, I might have spent more time in harrying that privateer than dragging my heels with your transports!'

Foley smiled. 'Well said, Captain. I like a man who can still show some feeling.'

Bolitho slammed out of the cabin and strode unseeingly to the companion ladder. He could tell from the way some seamen avoided his eye, the alert manner with which young Bethune was studying the flagship, that they could all recognize his fury.

Had he changed so much? Before he would have laughed or cursed at Foley's rudeness once his back was turned. Now, at the mention of some criticism, the merest hint of an attack on his subordinates, and therefore his ship, was enough to drive away control and reason.

Tyrrell came aft and said quietly, 'I know those waters well enough, sir. Mr Buckle is a mite bothered, but I can stand by him.'

'I know. Thank you.'

He had seen Tyrrell's expression when Buckle had voiced his concern at the meeting. He had been about to make the same suggestion. Perhaps that was why he had rushed in to defend the master against Foley's sarcasm. Foley had already made it clear what he thought of Americans. Rebels, colonists, or those unwillingly caught between the crossfire of different factions and divided families, any of them.

Tyrrell turned to watch the gig being swayed up and over the starboard gangway.

'Bit of a bastard, that one, sir.' He shrugged. 'I've met 'em before.'

Bolitho bit back the reproof he should have given. But what was the use? Even Bethune must have seen the antagonism between himself and Foley.

'Let us hope he knows what he is doing, Mr Tyrrell. For all our sakes.'

The boatswain's mates charged along the gundeck and hovered over hatchways as they bawled, 'All hands! All hands! Clear lower deck!'

Bolitho said, 'I did not get time to discover any news of your family.'

'Ah well.' Tyrrell tilted his hat to shade his eyes in a shaft of dying sunlight. 'Maybe later.'

The hatch casing slid open and Foley appeared at the top of the companion.

Bolitho said evenly, 'I must ask you to leave the quarterdeck, sir.' He saw him start angrily and added, 'Or cover your red coat. It will not help if we are seen to be carrying even one soldier with us.'

Foley withdrew and Tyrrell said cheerfully, 'One to you, sir!'

'It was unintended.' Bolitho took a telescope and trained it beyond the anchored shipping. 'Our sailing must be seen as normal. Spies will have reported our arrival and no doubt will think only of our despatches. I don't intend to have the news abroad that we are going on some special mission. The world may soon know of it, but the later the better.'

He walked to the quarterdeck rail, watching the seamen being mustered at their stations by the petty officers, but wondering at the truth of his words. Could a man like Foley really make him so quick to hit back as Tyrrell believed?

'Man the capstan!' Tilby was clinging to the foremast shrouds, his mottled face shining with sweat as he yelled at the scurrying seamen. 'Jump to it, you idle buggers, or I'll be amongst you with my starter!' Caught off guard by the unexpected sailing orders, he was showing signs of a recent drinking bout.

Bolitho looked at Buckle. 'Once we have worked clear of the land we will get the t'gallants on her. The wind seems steady enough, but we'll have rain before nightfall, I'm thinking.'

Buckle tugged his hat. 'Aye, sir.' He hesitated. 'I'm sorry I spoke out as I did. I should have known different.'

Bolitho smiled. 'Better to speak your doubts before you meet trouble. It is too late when you are hard aground, eh?' He touched his arm lightly. 'But before we draw that close to land we will see what *Sparrow* can do under full canvas.'

He walked away, hoping Buckle felt less worried. It could not be easy for him either. His first ship as master, and about to plunge into dangerous waters he had never seen before.

'Anchor's hove short, sir!' Graves's voice was loud on the blustery wind.

Bolitho looked at Tyrrell. 'Get the ship under way, if you please.'

He swung round as a chorus of derisive laughter burst from the deck below. A seaman had caught his foot on one of the army scout's muskets and gone sprawling into the scuppers. It seemed to amuse the soldiers greatly.

Bolitho added coldly, 'With this fresh wind you'll need plenty of weight on the capstan bars.' He let his eyes rest on the Canadians.

Tyrrell grinned. 'Right away, sir!' He cupped his hands. 'Bosun! Put those men on th' capstan!' He silenced the immediate protests by adding, 'Don't hesitate to start 'em if you find 'em slacking!'

Bolitho thrust his hands beneath his coat tails and walked away from the rail so that he could watch the topmen more easily. He had taken enough insults from Foley. There was no good reason for his own seamen to suffer also.

'Anchor's aweigh, sir!'

He stared up at the thundering pattern of canvas as the ship heeled over, free to the wind.

Once clear of the land's sheltering arm the motion became more violent, the waves shorter and the colour of straw in the dull light. Spray lifted and dashed over the busy seamen and pattered across the quarterdeck like heavy rain. Bolitho felt it on his lips and wet against his shirt, sensing the released power as the courses and then the topgallant sails filled and bellied to the wind.

He watched the jib-boom rise towards the scudding clouds, stagger and then plunge forward and down over the next line of crests, the stays and shrouds gleaming like wet ebony. He pictured the angry sparrow beneath the beakhead clutching its oak leaves and acorns, and wondered if the *Bonaventure*'s captain had seen it when he had broken off the action, and would remember it.

Tyrrell lurched aft, his body angled steeply to the deck. He yelled to the mizzen topmen before pausing to check those working at the weather braces. Fitch scurried past carrying a bucket and Tyrrell called after him.

Bolitho shouted above the thunder of canvas, 'What is it?'

Tyrrell laughed. 'Th' colonel's being sick, sir! A shame, ain't it?'

'Terrible.' Bolitho turned to hide a grin. 'Especially as it seems to be blowing harder now!'

Buckle clung to the binnacle and yelled, 'Steady she goes, sir! Sou'-east by south!'

'Hold her so!' Bolitho removed his hat and let the wind press the hair against his forehead. 'We will wear ship soon.' He walked up the deck and rapped the half-hour glass beside the compass. 'I am going below to inform the colonel.'

As he swung down the ladder he heard Tyrrell laughing and Buckle's equally cheerful chuckle. It was a small thing. But it was a beginning.

6

Scarlet and Gold

Bolitho entered his cabin and was surprised to see Foley seated at the table studying a chart. He was fully dressed, and his features had regained most of their colour. After leaving Sandy Hook he had spent most of the passage sprawled on the bench seat, unable or unwilling to climb into the cot, eyes half closed and his face like a wax mask.

He glanced up and grimaced. 'The motion feels easier.'

Bolitho nodded. 'We are standing into the bay. Cape May lies about five miles off the starboard beam.'

'I see.' Foley peered at the chart for several seconds, his fingers drumming a little tattoo across Bolitho's calculations and bearings. 'What is your opinion, Captain?'

Bolitho looked at his lowered head. It was the first fime he had asked him for his views on anything. Under full canvas the *Sparrow* had lived up to her name, so that on the passage southward Bolitho had been able to put aside his apprehensions, if not forget them, while he had enjoyed the sloop's vitality and freedom of movement. Then as they had closed the land to fix their position a great squall had risen, bleating and moaning with such violence that it had taken all hands to reef down and gain more sea room. After the untroubled sailing with even the royals set to catch the wind it was a severe disappointment. They had arrived off Cape May at the entrance to Delaware Bay precisely as Bolitho had planned, one full day after weighing anchor. Yet even as Buckle had been taking his bearings the squall had swept offshore, flattening the wavecrests and cloaking the distant land more effectively than night itself. It had taken another day, beating and clawing round in a great circle, the land hidden to all but the masthead lookout by rainsqualls and low cloud.

He heard himself answer, 'The wind has backed again, sir. To the sou'-west, and it is dropping.'

He listened to the groan of yoke lines as the rudder went over beneath the transom, and thought of Tyrrell and Buckle beside the wheel. He could also imagine the chart, the great bay opening up on either beam as the *Sparrow*, under close-reefed topsails, headed further and further away from the sea. Tyrrell was a tower of strength, and seemed to remember these waters as if every sandbar and current was imprinted on his brain.

Foley looked up, his face grim. 'It has already taken too long. I must know if you think we can proceed.' He laid one finger on the chart. 'Here, directly north of where you say we are now. I estimate it to be about six leagues. There is a cove.' He was speaking quickly and Bolitho could feel his agitation.

Bolitho leaned over the table. 'To the west of Maurice River?' He paused, visualizing the set of the yards, the weakening wind across the quarter. 'It will take at least four hours. More if the wind goes.'

He stood back and tugged his neckcloth. With the shutters tightly closed to mask the chance of showing even a glimmer of light, the cabin was like a small oven. On deck, as he had been for much of the passage, he had not felt either fatigue or strain. Now, he was not so sure, and could even pity Foley's misery during the journey. Outside the hull it was pitch-black, and once the ship had slipped past the protective headland he had felt the same sensation as a man striding blindly into an unlit cave.

He asked, 'How long will your scouts need?'

'Six hours maybe.' Foley stretched his arms and yawned. He was giving little away.

Bolitho made up his mind. 'In that case we will have to anchor and wait for tomorrow night before we can leave the bay. There may be enemy ships nearby, and I can't risk a conflict in these confined waters. Especially if your scouts fail to find our missing soldiers and need one more day.'

'Handling the ship is *your* concern.' Foley regarded him evenly. 'Well?'

'The tide is right and if we wait further we might lose the wind altogether.' He nodded. 'I am ready.'

Foley stood up and massaged his stomach. 'Good. By God, I think I have recovered my appetite.'

'I am sorry, sir.' Bolitho smiled. 'For the galley fire has been doused.' He added, 'Unless you would care for some salt beef from the cask?'

Foley eyed him ruefully. 'You have a cruel streak. One sight of that muck would render me as weak as a rat.'

Bolitho made for the door. 'In a King's ship the rats are rarely that!'

On deck he had to wait several seconds before he could see further than the rail. Below on the gundeck he could just make out the waiting seamen, their bodies etched against the darker shapes of the nearest guns. He walked aft and held his hand above the shaded compass light.

Buckle said, 'Due north, sir. Full an' bye.'

'Good.' He beckoned to Tyrrell. 'I want our two best leadsmen in the chains.'

'Already done, sir.' Tyrrell shrugged. 'Seemed th' thing to do.'

'When we draw closer to the northern shore we will slip the gig.' Bolitho sought out Stockdale's thick outline by the hammock nettings. 'You will take the gig and a boat's lead and line. The waters hereabouts are so shallow and treacherous that you must keep ahead of the ship, sounding all the while. Understood?'

Stockdale said stubbornly, 'I should be 'ere, sir. Just in case.'

'Your place is where I *say*, Stockdale.' He relented immediately. 'Do as I ask, and keep a shaded lantern with you. You may need to signal us.' He glanced towards Tyrrell. 'If that happens we will drop the kedge anchor and pray.'

The sails flapped loosely above the deck, and Bolitho knew the wind was still dropping, its touch clammy across his face. He pushed the nightmare of *Sparrow* grinding aground from his mind. He was committed. No, he had committed all of them.

'When we reach our destination, Mr Tyrrell, you may have the starboard cutter lowered. Mr Heyward will convey our passengers ashore and return when all is well.'

Tyrrell said, 'They'll have to wade th' last few yards, I'm thinking. It's shallow up there.'

'You've guessed the place then?'

He grinned, his teeth white in the gloom. 'There ain't no other suitable for this sort of game, sir.'

From forward, hollow-toned like a lost spirit's, came the leadsman's cry, 'By th' mark five!'

Tyrrell muttered, 'Bring her up a point, Mr Buckle.' His palm rasped over his chin. 'We must have drifted a piece.'

Bolitho remained silent. They were doing all they could. Thank God *Sparrow* had such shallow draught. Otherwise . . .

'Deep six!'

Tyrrell grunted. 'Fair enough. In bad times I've seen a tide race turn a schooner round like a bit o' flotsam.'

'Thank you.' Bolitho watched the faint splash beyond the bows as another lead went down. 'That is a comfort.'

'By th' mark five.'

'Trust a soldier to choose such a place.' Tyrrell leaned over the compass. 'To th' west still further and in th' main Delaware channel there's depth to spare for us, even if th' tide's wrong.'

'A quarter less five!'

Buckle whispered, 'Hell's teeth!'

Boots scraped on the planking and Foley asked crisply, 'How are we getting along, Captain?'

'By th' mark three!'

'Is it necessary for that man to make so much noise?' Foley stared round at the figures grouped by the wheel.

Tyrrell drawled calmly, 'It's either that, Colonel, or we rip our keel out.'

Bolitho said, 'A man as tall as yourself, sir, could just about walk twixt the keel and the ground below if he had a mind to.'

Foley did not speak for a full minute. Then he said, 'I'm sorry. It was a foolish thing to say.'

'Deep four!'

Buckle breathed out slowly. 'Better.'

Bolitho felt Tyrrell's fingers on his arm as he said, 'If we can keep her steady we should rest easy, with some room to swing at anchor. The bottom's safe and we might touch without too much danger.'

'Captain!' Foley's tone was as before. Sharp and impatient. He waited by the nettings and then said, 'Tyrrell. Is he an American?'

'A colonist, sir. Like a good many of the hands.'

'God damn!'

Bolitho added, 'He is also a King's officer, sir. I hope you will remember that.'

Foley's white breeches vanished into the hatchway, and Tyrrell said bitterly, 'Thinks I'm running th' ship aground just to spite him, I suppose.'

'That will be enough.' Bolitho stared past him at the dancing phosphorescence below the closed gun ports. Like magic weed, changing shape and vanishing only to reappear elsewhere along the slow-moving hull. 'I do not envy him his work.' Surprisingly, he found that he meant it.

Somewhere out there in the darkness was the great mass of land. Hills and rivers, forest and scrub which could tear out a man's eye if he was careless. There had been many stories of attacks and ambushes in this area, and even allowing for their being magnified in the telling, they were enough to chill even a seasoned fighter. Indians who were used to scout for Washington's army, who moved as silently as foxes and struck with the savagery of tigers. A world of shadows and strange noises, cries which would bring a drowsy sentry wide awake in a cold sweat, if he was lucky. If not, he would be found dead, his weapons gone.

'Deep eight!'

Tyrrell moved restlessly. 'We can leave th' channel now. I suggest we steer nor'-east.'

'Very well. Man the braces and bring her round.'

And so it went on, hour by hour, with the leads going and the reefed topsails being trimmed and re-trimmed to hold the fading wind like something precious. Occasionally Tyrrell would hurry forward to feel the tallow in one of the leads, rubbing particles from it between his fingers or sniffing it like a hunting-dog.

Without his uncanny knowledge of the sea bottom, his complete confidence despite the shallow water beneath the keel, Bolitho knew he would have anchored long ago and waited for the dawn.

Foley came and went several times but said nothing more about Tyrrell. He mustered the Canadian scouts and spoke for several minutes with their sergeant. Later he remarked, 'Good men. If I had a regiment of them I could retake half of America.'

Bolitho let him talk without interruption. It broke the tension of waiting. It also helped to discover the man behind the disciplined arrogance which Foley wore like a shield.

'I have fought the Americans in many places, Captain. They learn quickly and know how to use their knowledge.' He added with sudden bitterness, 'So they should, they have a hard core of English deserters and soldiers-of-fortune. Whereas I have had to manage with dregs. In one battle most of my men spoke only a few words of English. Imagine it, Captain, in the King's uniform, yet their tongues were more used to German dialect than ours!'

'I did not know there were so many English deserters, sir?'

'Some were stationed here before the rebellion. Their families are with them. They have found roots in this country. Others pin their hopes on rich pickings later, land, maybe, or some abandoned farmstead.' Again the harsh bitterness. 'But they will fight dearly, no matter what their conviction. For if they are taken and are found to be deserters, they will leave this world on a noose and with Jack Ketch to speed their passing!'

Tyrrell loomed out of the darkness, his voice hushed. 'Ready to slip th' gig, sir. Th' cove will be fine on th' larboard bow, by my reckoning.'

The tension was momentarily removed as with whispered commands and groping fingers the waiting seamen hoisted the gig over the gangway to tow jerkily alongside.

Midshipman Heyward was standing nearby as the gig idled clear, and Bolitho said quietly, 'Take good care when you land with the cutter. Keep your wits about you, and no heroics.' He gripped his arm, feeling the tension like the spring of a cocked pistol. 'I want to see you leave *Sparrow* as a lieutenant and in one piece.'

Heyward nodded. 'Thank you, sir.'

Graves climbed lightly up the ladder. 'Cutter's hoisted out and ready.' He glanced at the midshipman. 'Send me, sir. He's no match for this sort of thing.'

Bolitho tried to see Graves' expression but it was impossible. Maybe he really cared about the midshipman. Or perhaps he saw the prospect of action as his first chance of quick promotion. Bolitho could sympathize with him on either count.

But he replied, 'When I was his age I was already commissioned lieutenant. It was not easy then, and it will not be so for him until he has learned to accept all that goes with his authority.'

Bethune said quickly, 'Signal from gig, sir! Three flashes!'

Tyrrell snapped, 'Th' bottom has changed, most likely.' He became calm again. 'I suggest you anchor, sir.'

'Very well.' Bolitho saw the black outline of the gig bobbing slowly off the larboard bow. 'Back the mizzen tops'l. Prepare to go about. We will let go the anchor and then take the kedge away in the other cutter. Lively there, or we'll be joining Stockdale in the gig!'

Feet thudded on the gangways, and somewhere above the deck a man yelped with pain as he almost fell headlong. The mizzen topsail was flapping and cracking in spite of the wind's weak pressure, and the noise seemed loud enough to wake the dead. On darkened decks the men ran to braces and halliards, each so familiar that there was hardly any more delay than if they had been in bright sunlight.

Unsteadily, drunkenly, the sloop rode into her cable, the water beneath the stem alive with swirling phosphorescence. Both cutters were already swaying up and over the gangways, their crews tumbling into them, groping for oars and each other in the rush to get clear.

Then, and it all seemed to happen in a matter of minutes, everything was quiet again. Sails furled, and the hull rocking gently to a pair of anchors, while close by the boats moved warily, like predators around a tethered whale.

Foley stood beside the nettings and said, 'Send my scouts ashore, Captain. You have done your part.'

Then he strode to the larboard gangway to watch Heyward's cutter hooking on to the chains where the army scouts were already clinging like so many untidy bundles.

Bolitho asked softly, 'What is this cove like, Mr Tyrrell? Describe it.'

The lieutenant ran his fingers through his thick hair. 'It's well sheltered, 'less some other vessel comes close by. Inland it's heavily wooded, and as I recall, there's two rivers running down towards us.' He peered over the side. 'Th' cutter's nearly there. If we hear shooting we'll know we're in for a spell of bother.' He forced a grin. 'One thing. We don't need no wind to work clear. We can run out th' sweeps and *pull* her to safety.'

Bolitho nodded. In almost any other vessel this mission would have been madness. Close inshore and with little chance of beating clear into the centre of the bay, they would have been as good as wrecked.

He said, 'Get Tilby to grease the sweeps while we are waiting. If go we must, then I think we had best do it silently.'

Tyrrell strode away, his head jutting forward to seek out the boatswain.

Foley reappeared and remarked, 'I think I will get some sleep. There is nothing more we can do but wait.'

Bolitho watched him go. You will not sleep, Colonel. For now it is your turn to bear the load.

Bethune said excitedly, 'Cutter's returning, sir. All's well.'

Bolitho smiled. 'Pass the word that our people will remain at quarters during the night, but may sleep watch by watch. Then find the cook and see what he can produce without relighting his fires.'

The midshipman hurried away and Graves said sourly, 'He'd eat anything. Even if he cannot see the damn maggots in the dark.'

Bolitho sat down on the hatch casing and loosened his shirt. As his head lolled in a doze he heard a heavy body lower itself to the deck nearby. Stockdale had returned. Waiting. *Just in case*, as he always put it.

The very next instant Bolitho fell into a dreamless sleep.

'Where th' *hell* are they?' Tyrrell trained a glass over the nettings and moved it slowly from side to side.

It was approaching noon, and lying at two anchors the *Sparrow* held the heat like a kiln. The cloud, like the wind, had gone overnight, and beneath an empty sky and dazzling sunlight it was impossible to move without sweating badly.

Bolitho plucked his shirt away from his waist. He had been on deck since awakening at dawn, and like Tyrrell was uneasy about the lack of results. How different it was in daylight. At the first glimmer of sunrise he had watched the nearby land growing from the shadows, the rounded hills and thick green trees beyond. Pleasant crescents of beach, shaded by thick foliage which ran almost to the water's edge. It had all seemed quiet and harmless. Perhaps too quiet.

He made himself walk to the opposite side of the quarterdeck, wincing as the sun burned his shoulders like fire. The bay looked vast. The water was unbroken by crests, and but for a swirling uneasiness of currents it could have been one large lake. It measured about twenty miles across and as much from the headland to the north, where the great Delaware River gave it its substance. Beyond the jutting point which made the cove and protected *Sparrow* from any passing vessel, the river curved and twisted in an ever-changing concourse, with a full seventy miles before you could sight the outskirts of Philadelphia.

He looked along the gundeck, seeing the men on watch, some protruding legs to mark where others lay resting beneath the gangways to escape the merciless glare. He let his gaze move upwards, where the yards were now festooned with branches and leaves brought aboard soon after first light. They might help disguise her outline and deceive all but the professional observer.

Between the ship and the nearest beach a cutter pulled slowly and painfully back and forth, Midshipman Bethune squatting in the sternsheets watching the shore. Foolishly he had stripped to the waist, and despite his tan would suffer for it later.

Tyrrell followed him as he returned to the shelter of the hammock nettings.

'I'd like to go ashore, sir.' He waited until Bolitho faced him. 'I could take a small party of men. Try and find out what's happening.' He opened the front of his soiled shirt and sucked in a lungful of air. 'Better'n waiting like bloody cattle for slaughter.'

'I'm not sure.' Bolitho shaded his eyes as a movement made the trees shimmer by the beach. But it was only a large bird.

Tyrrell persisted, 'Look sir, I guess th' orders are supposed to be secret, but th' whole ship knows why we're here. Them scouts spoke freely enough with a tot of rum under their belts.'

Bolitho smiled wryly. 'I thought as much.'

'Yes. An' it seems we're expected to rescue a whole crowd of soldiers who've got lost coming overland.' He grimaced. 'I can well believe it, too. It ain't no barrack square.'

Bolitho studied his strong profile and pondered over the suggestion. He had not mentioned the gold bullion, so that was obviously a secret which Foley had not even shared with his own men. And it was just as well. Some might be tempted to try for it rather than any kind of rescue.

'Very well. Pick your men quietly and take the gig. You will need arms and provisions, too, otherwise . . .'

Tyrrell smiled. 'Otherwise it might be too bad for us if *Sparrow* sails without waiting, eh?'

'It is a risk. Do you want to reconsider?'

He shook his head. 'I'll start now.'

Bolitho said, 'I'll make a report of this in the log.'

'No need, sir. If I come to grief it'd be best left unwritten.' He smiled sadly. 'I'd not want for you to face a court martial on my account.'

'I will make it, none the less.' Bolitho forced a grin. 'So be off with you.'

The gig had covered less than a cable from the side when Foley burst on deck, his face screwed up in the glare.

'Where is he going?' He clung to the nettings, staring after the small boat which was almost shapeless in a drifting haze. 'Did you give him permission?'

'I did.'

'Then you are a bigger fool than I imagined!' Foley's anxiety was pushing aside his self-control. 'How dare you take it on yourself?'

'Colonel Foley, I have no doubt you are an excellent field officer. Experienced enough to realize that if your scouts have failed to make contact with those landed here earlier they must either be dead or taken.' He kept his voice level. 'You will also appreciate that I am not going to risk my ship and company to comply with a plan already misfired.'

Foley opened his mouth and then shut it again. He said flatly, 'I have my orders. The general must be rescued.'

'And the gold.' Bolitho could not hide the bitterness. 'That, too, surely?'

Foley rubbed his eyes, his face suddenly showing the strain. 'You'd need a regiment to search this area. Even then . . .' His voice trailed away.

Bolitho took a glass and swung it over the rail. There was no sign of the gig now.

He said, 'Mr Tyrrell has my confidence. At least *he* might discover something.'

Foley glanced around the sunlit deck. 'I hope so, Captain. Otherwise you will lose this ship, and that will be the very least of your worries.'

Graves appeared on the ladder, saw them together and walked away. Bolitho frowned. So he had been the one to inform Foley of Tyrrell's expedition.

He asked, 'This general. Who is he, sir?'

Foley dragged himself from his brooding thoughts. 'Sir James Blundell. He came out here on a tour of inspection!' He laughed shortly. 'By the time he reached New York there was less to inspect than he had anticipated. He owned a great deal of property in Pennsylvania, enough to buy a thousand ships like this one.'

Bolitho turned away. He had never heard of the man, but this was more than he wanted to know. Foley would never speak his mind more clearly than he had already done. But it was enough. Blundell had obviously been caught in the middle of retrieving some of his personal wealth by the sudden military evacuation. Worse, he had been using his role of an inspector-general for his own ends and had involved a company of desperately needed soldiers.

Foley looked at him for several seconds. 'The men with him are mine. All that are left from the whole battalion. So you see why I must do this thing.'

Bolitho replied quietly, 'Had you told me that from the beginning, Colonel, it might have been better for both of us.'

Foley did not seem to hear. 'They were the best men I have commanded here and we've seen a dozen skirmishes together. By God, when it comes to the line of battle there is nothing to beat the English foot soldier. Even a small square of them will withstand the cream of French cavalry.' He spread his hands. 'But out here, they are like lost children. They cannot compete with men who have lived all their lives in the woods and plains, who have known times when one musket ball was the margin between survival and starvation!'

Bolitho did not know how to phrase the next question. He said slowly, 'But you were not with your men when it all happened?'

'No.' Foley stared at two gulls diving and screaming around the topgallant yards. 'I had been sent to New York with a convoy. Mostly it consisted of unwanted supplies and the soldiers' women.' He looked hard at him. 'And the general's niece, I should not forget to mention *her*.' He was speaking quickly. 'Even on a safe trail we were dogged by enemy skirmishers, and there was never a day without some poor devil being brought down by one of their long muskets. By God, I think some of them can knock the eye out of a fly at fifty paces!'

The deck moved very slightly, and when he looked aloft Bolitho saw the masthead pendant flicking out feebly before falling lifeless once more. But it was the first hint of a breeze so far.

He said, 'I suggest you get some rest while you can, Colonel. I will inform you when I hear anything.'

Foley said heavily, '*If* your Mr Tyrrell returns.' In the same breath he added, 'That was unfair. I have been so unbalanced by all this I am not myself.'

Bolitho watched him walk to the hatchway and then seated himself on a bollard. If nothing happened soon Foley would have to make a fresh decision. With Tyrrell out of the ship and the mission a failure, there would be little hope for his own future once they returned to Sandy Hook.

All afternoon and into the evening the *Sparrow* lay pinned down by the unwavering glare. Deck seams were so sticky that they gripped a man's foot, and the gun barrels were as hot as if they had been in action for many hours. The watches changed and sentries came and went, hearing and seeing nothing.

The first rosy glow of sunset had settled over the cove, and the hillside beyond was deep in purple when Foley came on deck again.

He said, 'There is nothing more we can do.'

Bolitho bit his lip. Tyrrell had not returned. Perhaps he was already on his way south overland. Or even now guiding American scouts towards the cove. He shook himself like a dog. His tiredness and disappointment were tearing down his reserves. His trust.

Midshipman Heyward was standing by the starboard gangway, his body limp against the rail like a man half asleep. Suddenly he jerked upright, his voice hoarse as he called, 'Gig, sir! Coming from the point!'

Bolitho ran to his side, caring nothing for what Tyrrell may or may not have discovered. He had come back. That was more than enough.

When the gig ground alongside he saw the oarsmen lolling on the thwarts like puppets, faces and arms raw from the harsh sunlight of the day. Tyrrell climbed to the quarterdeck, his legs and feet filthy, his clothing torn.

He said thickly, 'Your scouts couldn't find th' ones sent on ahead,

Colonel. But we did.' He took a mug of water and gulped it down gratefully. 'They're all dead. Up river in a burned-out fort.'

Foley stared at the dark trees beyond the cove. 'So my men are still out searching.'

Tyrrell ignored him. 'We pulled th' gig into th' inlet and tumbled on this old fort by accident.' He looked away. 'An' that ain't all, by a potful.'

Bolitho waited, seeing the tension, the pain of what he had found.

Tyrrell said slowly, 'Just up th' channel, sitting as bold as you please, is a bloody frigate!'

Foley swung round. 'American?'

'No, Colonel, not American.' He looked at Bolitho gravely. 'A Frenchie by th' cut of her. No colours, so I guess she's a privateer.'

Bolitho steadied his racing thoughts. But for their stealthy entry into the bay under Tyrrell's guidance, they would have run under the frigate's guns, or at best been attacked when they had anchored.

Tyrrell was saying, 'So it looks as if your general has been took, Colonel. Not much use in us staying here to follow his example, eh?'

'Did you see what they were doing?' Bolitho tried to picture the great river sweeping around the point. The frigate anchored in the safe knowledge she could fight off an attacker from either direction.

Tyrrell shrugged. 'There were marks on th' beach. I guess they'd had boats ashore getting fresh water. But no sign of prisoners.'

'Then it would appear that the missing soldiers are *still* missing.' Bolitho glanced at the colonel. 'If the wind gets up it is my guess that the frigate will weigh. She'd not risk a night passage, so we're safe here 'til dawn at least. After that . . .' He did not have to explain further.

Heyward called, 'Cutter's signalling, sir!'

They all turned and stared at the darkening beach as the oars came to life and the cutter started towards the shore. A solitary figure was just visible waving his musket back and forth towards Bethune. It was one of Foley's scouts.

Foley snapped, 'I must go ashore at once.' He ran towards the entry port. 'They have found the general!'

Bolitho hurried after him, and with Stockdale on his heels plunged into the waiting gig.

When the boat had grounded in the shallows Bolitho leapt over the gunwale and waded the last yards through clear water, vaguely aware that it was the first time he had been on land, apart from a few occasions in Antigua, for months. He stood beneath a tree as Foley questioned the scout, knowing the man would probably become flustered with both of them present.

Foley walked towards him, his boots squeaking in the sand. 'They found them.' He gestured to the wall of trees. 'The first party will arrive in about an hour.'

'First party?' Bolitho saw the despair in Foley's eyes.

'The general is coming with my scouts and all the fit men.' He took a deep breath. 'But there are some sixty sick and wounded following behind at a slower pace. They've been on the move for days. They ran into an ambush in a gully the night before last but fought their attackers off. The general says they were French.'

'Off that frigate most likely.' Bolitho tried to imagine what it must be like for the sick and injured soldiers. Not knowing where they were. How they would survive.

He said, 'The cat is out of the bag now. That ship will be expecting some rescue attempt. *I* would be in their shoes.'

Foley sighed. 'I agree. What will you do?'

Bolitho did not reply directly. He beckoned to Bethune who was giving the weary scout some water from his flask.

'Return to the ship at once. My compliments to Mr Tyrrell. Tell him to stand by to receive the first party in an hour. I want one watch of the hands ashore and all the boats. It must be well handled and these men fitted into the ship if we have to jettison the stores to do it.'

He watched the youth running to the cutter, his shoulder glowing like a ripe fruit.

Foley said quietly, 'It'll be a miracle if we can get them off in time.'

Bolitho smiled. 'Miracles do happen, Colonel. Just occasionally.'

He walked towards the gig, his tiredness forgotten. Then he realized that Foley had not followed but was standing with his scout.

The colonel called after him, 'I'm going inland.' He looked away. 'To meet my men. Or what is left of them.'

His scarlet coat faded between the trees and was gone.

General Sir James Blundell lay back in one of Bolitho's chairs and thrust a leg towards his orderly.

'For God's sake get these damn boots off!' He stared up at a deckhead lantern and added, 'I could relish a glass of something. I am as dry as dust!' He cursed the orderly and pushed him in the shoulder with his boot. '*Easy*, you damn fool!'

Foley turned and looked at Bolitho by the door, his eyes showing anger and embarrassment.

'Could you arrange something for the general?'

Bolitho nodded, and saw Fitch scurrying away for some wine. It was all like a part of a dream. A nightmare.

As the last of the daylight had begun to fade the soldiers who had accompanied the general had appeared along the beach. Even *Sparrow*'s seamen, who moments before had been skylarking and chattering while they enjoyed their unusual freedom of dry land, had fallen still and silent.

Torn and bedraggled, red coats filthy from forced marches and sleeping when they could in the undergrowth, they had shuffled into lines like obedient animals. Others had followed with pack mules, so loaded that it was a wonder they had survived.

Bolitho had been on the beach with Dalkeith, explaining the needs and preparations for this mass of passengers, and had watched in silence as Foley had stood with his face like stone while a solitary lieutenant had lurched towards him, the regimental colours across one shoulder, his sword dangling from his wrist on a lanyard. Foley had been unable to speak. He had merely touched the lieutenant's shoulder and nodded towards the dull-eyed soldiers along the edge of the trees before saying to Bolitho, 'For God's sake, do what you can for these fellows.'

As the seamen had hurried forward to help the soldiers into the waiting boats the last reserve had cracked. Along the swaying lines of red coats men had dropped like corpses, while others had merely stared speechlessly at the bronzed sailors, their filthy faces running with tears, hands outstretched like men seeing messengers of salvation itself.

It had been pitiful and moving just to watch while they had lurched into the shallows and the boats. The lieutenant carrying his regiment's colours, as he must have done all the way south from Philadelphia, trying to show some last control but his face reversing the lie, the despair and the disbelief.

Now, as he stood watching the general it was hard to connect the two scenes together. Blundell was a rotund but powerfully built man, and apart from dirt on his boots, his uniform looked as if it had been only recently pressed. His iron-grey hair was neat, and his heavy, florid features must have been shaved within the day.

So far, he had given Bolitho little more than a cursory glance, and was content to make his needs known through Foley.

He touched the glass of wine with his tongue and grimaced. 'I suppose one cannot hope for too much in a craft of this size, what?'

Foley looked again at Bolitho, his expression one of physical pain.

Overhead and deep in the hull the timbers were alive with thudding boots, the occasional bellow of orders and the squeak of tackles above the boats.

The general said, 'You should have put those men to work, Foley. No sense in letting 'em lie about like squires of the manor.'

Bolitho said, 'My people can manage the loading, sir.'

'Hmm.' The general seemed to consider him for the first time. 'Well, make sure that every mule is properly checked. Some careless or greedy fool might be thinking of stealing their loads. There's a king's ransom in those packs. So think on these things when you report you're ready for sea.'

Graves appeared in the door. 'All the soldiers are on board, sir. Some of them are in a poor way.'

Bolitho tore his eyes from the general, the droplets of wine on his lips.

'Have the cook light the galley fire, Mr Graves. That French frigate will not attempt to weigh in the dark, even if the wind gets up. I want those men to get something hot to eat. Rum, too, while they are waiting. Tell Mr Lock to arrange it.'

He thought of the staggering men, the fallen redcoats by the trees. And this was the party of *fit* men.

Foley asked quietly, 'When will you be raising anchor, Captain?'

Bolitho saw the anguish in his eyes, the way he lingered on his question.

'An hour after dawn the tide will be right, as will the current hereabouts, according to my information.'

The general's glass hovered in mid-air, so that his orderly allowed the wine to pour from the decanter and across the deck.

'What the hell are you talking about?' He struggled up in the chair. 'You can sail *now*. I heard your men saying the time was as good as any for it.'

Bolitho faced him coldly. 'That is true only up to a point, sir. But if I am to wait for the sick and wounded to reach the cove, I must prepare for the next tide.' He hardened his tone. 'I have sent my first lieutenant and forty seamen to aid their passage here. I pray to God we can save them from more suffering.'

The general lurched to his feet, his eyes flashing angrily. 'Tell this young upstart, Foley! There is an enemy ship up-channel and no time to be wasted. I have gone through enough in the last few days, and I command you to . . .'

Bolitho said, 'My orders say that I am in command of *transportation* for this mission, sir. They make no distinction between gold bullion or men.' He paused, the anger churning his stomach like brandy. 'Even those too weak and sick to fend for themselves. Is that not so, Colonel?'

Foley was staring at him, his eyes in dark shadow. When he spoke his voice was different, husky. 'It is true, Captain. You are in command.' He swung round and faced his astonished superior. '*We*, Sir James, are just so much cargo.'

Bolitho turned and walked from the cabin. On deck the air seemed cleaner, and he made himself stand quite still by the rail above the nearest twelve-pounders for several minutes.

Below he could see figures moving in all directions, and from the galley funnel he caught the aroma of meat stew. Even Lock must have been too overcome by the tattered, starving soldiers to restrain the cook.

He heard Foley's boots beside him but did not turn.

'Thank you, Captain. From me and my men. And those who will owe their lives to your humanity. And courage.' He held up his hand as Bolitho turned to reply. 'You could risk your very future because of this action, as well you know.'

Bolitho shrugged. 'Rather that than live with a foul memory.'

Someone called in the darkness and a nearby cutter began to pull inshore.

'I'd not leave those men behind.' He walked towards the gangway. 'If needs be, I'll drop the gold overboard first!'

'Yes. I believe you would, Captain.'

But Foley was speaking to the darkness. And when he reached the side he saw the gig already on its way to the beach, Bolitho sitting beside Stockdale at the tiller. He peered down at the gundeck. Where would Bolitho put all these men? He heard the creak of oars as the first boat thrust off from the beach. One thing was certain. He would find the space somehow, if it cost him his commission.

7

To Dare or to Die

Bolitho opened his eyes and stared at the mug of steaming coffee which Stockdale was holding above the side of the cot. He struggled upright, his mind and vision readjusting to the unfamiliar surroundings, the awareness that it must already be dawn. He was in Tyrrell's small screened cabin adjoining the wardroom, and as he held the mug to his lips he realized he could not remember how he came to be there.

Stockdale wheezed, 'You've 'ad a good hour's sleep, sir. I was fair loath to wake you.' He shrugged heavily. 'But your last orders was to rouse all 'ands afore dawn.'

Bolitho's aching mind suddenly cleared. He could feel the uneven motion around him, the creak of the stays and shrouds.

'The wind? How is it?' He threw his legs over the side of the cot, feeling crumpled and unclean.

'Risin', sir.' Stockdale sounded unhappy. 'From the west'rd.'

Bolitho looked at him. '*Damn!*'

With the mug still in his hand he hurried from the cabin and almost fell across a line of sleeping soldiers. Despite the need to know what was happening he stood motionless looking at them. Remembering the long night, the stream of sick and wounded men he had watched brought aboard by his sailors. Some would not see another day pass, others were like skeletons, racked with fever or the agony of wounds gone rotten. He still felt that same cold anger and shame which he had endured then. The realization that most of the men could have been carried on the mules instead of being left to stagger further and still further in the rear of their comrades. And the general.

He stepped over the inert shapes and continued to the quarterdeck.

Tyrrell saw him and said, 'You know about th' wind?'

Bolitho nodded and walked to the nettings, seeing the bay opening up in the pale early light like ruffled steel, the dancing cat's-paws against the hull, pushing it gently but insistently on the taut anchor cables.

Buckle came to his side, his face grey with fatigue.

'We can't set even a scrap o' canvas, sir. We're on a lee shore an' no mistake.'

Bolitho was staring along the larboard gangway and away towards the dark slab of land emerging from the shadows. The point, around which lay the river and the deep channel.

Graves said, 'We will have to stay where we are and hope that Frog has a mind to do likewise.' He sounded doubtful.

Bolitho shook his head, thinking aloud. 'No. The Frenchman will have guessed we are about, even if he does not realize our exact strength. Either way he will up anchor soon and make for open water. If he sees us in passing he will have little difficulty in aiming his broadsides.'

He peered up at the yards where some topmen were casting away the last of their leafy camouflage. Above their heads the masthead pendant was whipping towards the cove, and he saw the beach regaining shape in the light, the marks of many feet, the small humps to show where some of the soldiers had been buried within sight of rescue. *Rescue*. He rubbed his chin and tried to think more logically.

Once out in the bay they could make sail and tack towards the entrance and open sea. The Frenchman, on the other hand, already had the advantage of the wind. Could even anchor if desired and pound *Sparrow* to fragments while she lay helpless in the cove. She would sink with her masts above water. It was a cruel picture.

He said, 'Break out the kedge anchor, Mr Tyrrell, and then hoist all boats.' He looked at the long racks of sweeps. 'We will have to see what those will achieve this morning.'

Once free of the kedge the hull swung sternwards towards the beach, the current swirling around her stem as if she was already under way.

The gundeck and gangways were crowded with men, and he knew that below every space was filled with exhausted soldiers. He watched the gig rising above the gangway before dropping neatly on its chocks between the cutters, the seamen working in unusual silence, glancing occasionally towards him by the rail as if to see his intentions.

He was able to pick out individual faces in the strengthening light, and realized he now knew most of them by name. The reliable and the lazy, the malcontents and those who were able to accept their calling, enforced or otherwise, with varying degrees of trust. He remembered that first day, the sea of unknown men, with Graves excusing Tyrrell's absence. It seemed so long ago.

Tyrrell reported, 'Boats secured, sir!'

Bolitho walked to the rail and leaned on it. The wood was moist and clammy, but within a few hours would be like a furnace bar. If it was still above water.

He said, 'You all know of that frigate, lads. She's up there now, taking her time, as Frogs do in such matters.' He paused, seeing some of the older men nudging each other and grinning at his feeble wit. 'You can also see that we are unable to loose tops'ls without driving ashore. But if soldiers can march all the way across country to us, I reckon we should be able to get 'em home again, what d'you say?'

For a long moment nobody moved or spoke and he felt despair rising as if to mock him. Why should they care? After his displeasure following the fight with the privateers they might simply see it as a just rebuff.

Surprisingly, it was the boatswain who was the first to break the silence. Bursting from the larboard gangway, his face glowing like a grotesque heated shot, he bellowed, 'What are we waiting for, my lovelies? A huzza for the cap'n! An' another for *Sparrow*!'

The cheering spread along the decks and up to the topmen on the yards. To the dazed soldiers below and in the cramped holds, and wherever a foot or so had been found for them.

Tilby yelled, 'An' to 'ell with them bloody Frogs!' He was already cutting the lashings on the nearest sweeps, pushing men towards them while others scampered to open the small ports on either beam.

Bolitho turned away, seeing Tyrrell's great grin and Buckle nodding his head and beaming as if they were already at sea and away under full sail. Even Graves was smiling, his tired face both dazed and pleased by the din.

He said, 'Man the capstan.' He wished they would stop cheering. That Tyrrell would obey and leave him to his thoughts. 'Run out the sweeps, if you please.'

Tyrrell shouted the order, and as the helmsmen stood to the wheel and the capstan took the first slow strain, he turned and said, 'They'll not let you down. Not after what you've done for these poor redcoats. Not now. Not ever, Cap'n.'

Bolitho could not face him. Instead he stared along the larboard side at the wavering line of sweeps poised above the swirling water like the oars of some ancient galley. It would take a great deal of effort to move her into the bay. With the wind against her and the dead weight of all her guns and extra passengers it might prove impossible.

'Stand by!'

The sweeps swung gingerly forward, the seamen clinging to the long looms and gripping the deck with their bare toes.

'Anchor's aweigh!' Graves came running aft above the seamen and yelled, 'She's paying off, sir!'

'Give way all!' Tilby threw his own weight on the aftermost sweep, his bulging muscles showing evidence of strain. ''*Eave!* Come on, boyos, 'eave! Agin now!'

Rising and falling, the lines of sweeps thrust and slashed at the water to hold the *Sparrow*'s drift towards the beach, and then very slowly, painfully brought her under command and towards the bay.

Bolitho called, 'Mr Buckle, take the wheel!' To Tyrrell he added, 'Every officer and man on the sweeps! *Everyone!*'

As the anchor was catted home and Graves led his own party to the sweeps others slithered down backstays or ran from their stations elsewhere to give weight to the stroke.

Bolitho tried not to watch the point, green and brown now in the light. It was stationary and the sloop was hardly making headway. Yet already the men were gasping for breath, and only Buckle and himself were not helping. The wind was too strong, the current too insistent.

Tyrrell's voice carried like a trumpet. 'Heave! Heave! An' one more, lads!' But it was no use.

Buckle called softly, 'We'll have to anchor again, sir! They'll be beat in a moment!'

Several seamen missed their grip and almost fell as a voice shouted above the plunge and creak of sweeps.

'Quickly there! Spread yourselves out with the seamen!'

Bolitho stared with disbelief as Foley emerged below the quarterdeck, and following him, two by two, some limping, others blinded by bandages, came the remnants of his company.

Foley looked up. 'The 51st have never been known to fail in showing up the Navy, Captain!' He steadied one of his men who was groping past him before adding, 'You spoke earlier of miracles. But sometimes they, too, need a little help.' He turned away and put himself beside a master's mate on the end of a sweep.

Bolitho gripped the rail, wanting to hide his face from them, but unable to tear his eyes from their combined efforts.

Buckle called huskily, 'I've got steerage way, sir. She's answering now!'

Bolitho said softly, 'The colonel told me he could take half the continent with the right men. With men such as these he could conquer the world.'

When he looked again he saw that the point was slipping across the starboard quarter as with great care Buckle eased the helm over and watched the jib-boom pointing towards deeper water.

Here and there a man fell exhausted from a sweep, but the stroke barely faltered.

When the full rim of sunlight eventually broke above the distant hills, *Sparrow* was well out of the bay.

Bolitho shouted, 'Topmen aloft! Stand by to make sail!'

The jib cracked and flapped angrily, then hardened into a firm crescent, and as the long sweeps were withdrawn from their ports the deck tilted to a small but satisfying angle.

'Lay her on the starboard tack, Mr Buckle. As close to the wind as you can. We will need all the room possible to weather Cape May.'

Tyrrell came aft and stood beside the compass, his eyes fixed on the hazy shoreline. He looked strangely contented. Reassured.

He saw Bolitho watching him and remarked, 'It was a good feeling to get ashore again. But then I guess you feel th' same about England.'

Bolitho nodded gravely. Maybe Tyrrell had been tempted after all. But he had come back, and that was what counted.

He said, 'You did well, Mr Tyrrell. You all did.'

Tyrrell gave his lazy grin. 'If you'll pardon th' liberty, sir, you ain't no hoof-dragger yourself.'

'Deck there! Sail on th' starboard quarter!'

Bolitho looked at Buckle. 'The Frenchman is after us sooner than I thought. Get the t'gallants on her, if you please.' He walked up the slanting deck and shaded his eyes. 'We'll give him a run for his money.'

Tyrrell was grinning. 'For th' *general's* money, you mean!'

Bolitho glanced down at his stained breeches. 'I'm going to shave.' But the mood persisted for him also. 'In case we have visitors this morning, eh?'

Buckle watched him go and then said, 'Nothing ever seems to worry that one.'

Tyrrell was peering up at the topmen, his eyes critical. He recalled Bolitho's face when the wounded soldiers had staggered on deck to help man the sweeps. For just those few moments he had seen beyond the brittle composure, the mantle of command, to the real man beneath.

Half to himself he murmured, 'Don't be too sure of that, Mr Buckle. He *feels* it right enough. Just like th' rest of us.'

Bolitho closed the telescope with a snap and steadied himself against a belaying-pin rack.

'Alter course two points, Mr Buckle. Steer due east.'

It had taken another two hours from sighting the French frigate to tacking dangerously close around Cape May. With the nearest spur of that untidy headland barely two cables under the lee side they had surged towards the open sea, close enough to see smoke from some inland fire and the morning sunlight flashing on a hidden window or an unseen watcher's telescope.

It had been harder than he could have imagined to remain in a wardroom chair while Stockdale shaved him and laid out a clean shirt. Now, as he watched the men running to the braces, the lifting, dipping bowsprit beyond that taut rigging, he wondered why he had made himself waste time below. Pride or conceit, the need to relax even for minutes, or a greater need that his seamen should think him so calm he could concentrate on his own comfort?

As the sloop plunged round still further until she had the wind directly astern, he could feel every spar and timber quaking to the motion. Above the quarterdeck rail he saw the mainyard bending like one huge bow, the splayed legs of the topmen denoting the savage vibration aloft, the need for care when one false step could mean instant death. Or the longer agony of watching the ship ploughing away to leave the fallen man to drown alone.

'Steady she be, sir! Due east!'

He walked to the compass and then took a careful glance at the set of the sails. Every inch of canvas was fully drawn, the bellies so rounded and hard they looked about to burst.

He gestured with the telescope. 'Another pull on the larboard forebrace, Mr Tyrrell, and then belay.'

As the men ran to obey he took one more glance astern. The enemy had gained on them during the dash from the bay, had cut away their early advantage while *Sparrow* had lost valuable time clawing around the last headland. Now, as he steadied the glass across the taffrail he could see their pursuer rising and driving over the lively white-horses, her hull bathed in spray, the gun ports awash as she surged on a starboard tack, showing her sleek hull and full pyramids of canvas. She had set her royals once away from the headland and was heading into deeper water before continuing the chase.

Tyrrell came aft, wiping droplets of salt from his arms and face.

'We're standing well afore th' wind, sir. There's nought else we can do at present.'

Bolitho did not reply. At the quarterdeck rail he leaned over and saw the uneven lines of wounded soldiers, and others less handicapped, helping with food and bandages. Two of Dalkeith's assistants came on deck and hurled a bundle over the gangway and vanished down a hatchway with hardly a glance. Bolitho watched the bundle bobbing away on *Sparrow*'s creamy wake and felt his stomach contract violently. Some bloodied bandages, but most likely the amputated limb of one more luckless soldier. Dalkeith was in his makeshift sick-bay, as he had been since the sloop had weighed anchor, working in almost total darkness with saw and swabs while the ship yawed and staggered around him.

Graves called above the boom of canvas, 'The Frenchman's wore, sir!'

The frigate was now about eight cables off the starboard quarter. Certainly no more, and steering a parallel course, her royals fully squared and straining at their bolts like pale breastplates.

Bolitho said, 'She's pulling up, Mr Tyrrell. Not a great deal, but enough to worry about.'

Tyrrell rested at the rail and kept his eyes forward, away from the enemy frigate.

'Will I clear for action?'

He shook his head. 'We cannot. Every bit of space is packed with soldiers. There is barely room on the gundeck for a twelve-pounder to recoil.'

He thought of the thirty-two-pounders pointing from either bow. With the enemy astern they were impotent. Just so much extra weight. Had the enemy been in their line of fire they might have been able to cripple her, if only temporarily, or until some ship of the inshore squadron could give them support.

Tyrrell looked at him worriedly. 'You have a choice, sir. You close th' shore now and risk losing th' wind altogether. Or you alter course to seaward with th' hour.' He angled his thigh against the rail as *Sparrow* plunged heavily, the spray dashing aft over the decks, rattling against the courses like lead pellets. 'There's a long ridge of sandbars running north to south. You take one side or t'other. But in an hour you'll have to decide which.'

Bolitho nodded. Even with the barest information he had discovered on his charts he knew Tyrrell's estimate was only too true. The sandbars, like uneven humps, ran for over twenty miles across their line of advance. To wear ship north or south to avoid them would mean loss of time, and with the enemy so near, it could represent the measure of disaster.

Tyrrell said, 'We could wait and see what th' Frenchie intends.' He rubbed his chin. 'But it would be too late for us by then.' He shrugged helplessly. 'I'm sorry, sir. I ain't much help.'

Bolitho stared past him towards the land. As the coast turned northeast it was falling away. Ten, fifteen miles, it was hard to gauge in the bright sunlight and low sea haze.

'You have been helpful.'

He walked aft to the compass and saw Buckle watching him grimly. The earlier laughter, the sudden relaxation of clearing the land, had all gone now. From a rumour to the sight of a sail. From a distant ship to real, deadly menace in the frigate's line of gun ports. It had all changed against them so quickly.

'Deck there! Sail fine on th' starboard bow!'

Graves said excitedly, 'The squadron! By God, that's better!'

Moments later, 'Deck! She's a lugger, sir! Headin' away!'

Bolitho clasped his hands behind his back. Some frightened trader, no doubt. If still within sight she might witness a swift one-sided fight within the hour.

'The Frenchman's altered course apiece!' Buckle was peering astern through a telescope. 'His yards are coming back!'

Bolitho waited, counting seconds. The frigate had swung off her original course, her speed and drive taking her away slightly further off *Sparrow*'s quarter. He tensed, seeing the telltale puff of brown smoke, driven away instantly by the following wind.

The heavy ball plunged short by a cable, the waterspout rising violently as if to mark a spouting whale.

Bolitho shut the seamen's jeers from his thoughts. No matter what they believed, it was a fair shot. She had fired nearly two miles with what must be a powerful bow-chaser like his own.

Foley appeared at his side. 'I heard the cannon.' He shaded his eyes to peer over the nettings. 'He means to unnerve you.'

Bolitho smiled gravely. 'He intends much more than that, Colonel.'

He heard more footfalls on the quarterdeck and saw Dalkeith blinking in the sunlight, wiping his face on his big handkerchief. He had removed his heavy apron, but there were dark stains on his legs and shoes, not yet dry.

He saw Bolitho and reported, 'That is all for now, sir. Ten have died. More will follow, I fear.'

Foley said admiringly, 'Thank you, Mr Dalkeith. It is better than I dared hope.'

They all looked round as another dull bang echoed across the cruising white-caps. It was nearer, and level with the starboard quarter.

Dalkeith shrugged. 'On dry land I might have saved more, Colonel.' He walked away towards the taffrail, his brilliant wig askew, his shoulders sagging as if from a great weight.

Bolitho said, 'A good surgeon. Usually the calling attracts the failure or the drunkard. He is neither.'

Foley was studying the frigate with a telescope. 'A woman drove him to sea maybe.' He ducked involuntarily as the other ship fired and the ball whimpered high overhead before throwing up a shark's fin of spray on the opposite side.

Bolitho said, 'Hoist the colours, Mr Tyrrell. He has the feel of us now.' He watched the scarlet flag break from the gaff. 'Mr Dalkeith! Have your helpers move those wounded men to the larboard side.' He silenced his unspoken protest with, 'Better now than when we are in real trouble.'

Graves came running aft along a gangway. 'Run out, sir?'

'No.' He looked up as another ball fanned above the deck. 'Load the starboard battery. Double-shotted and with grape for good measure.' He ignored Graves's puzzled expression and added to Foley, 'If we must fire it will have to be the one broadside. You have been below yourself. You know we cannot indulge in close action with the hull filled to its brim with sick men.'

Foley looked away. 'I am sorry, Captain.'

Bolitho studied him gravely. 'Do not be. My orders said little of fighting. Transportation was the ideal arrangement.' He forced a smile. 'Unfortunately, the Frenchman has not read them also!'

He turned to watch the wounded being carried to the opposite side, while Graves and Yule, the gunner, supervised the slow loading of every starboard gun which was not impeded by either passenger or cargo.

Graves came to the ladder eventually and called, 'All but four guns loaded and ready, sir.' He broke off with a gasp as the air overhead came alive with a long-drawn-out shriek, as if a thousand devils had been freed from the sea itself.

Rigging and shrouds jerked savagely, and men ducked holding their hands above them as torn cordage and several severed blocks hurtled amongst them.

Bolitho gripped his hands together behind him still tighter until the pain helped to steady him. Langridge shot, as used by the big *Bonaventure*. It was vicious and very dangerous. Consisting of fragments of iron bound together, it could cut away rigging and tear down spars with ease. But unlike chain-shot, which was more generally used, it could also do terrible damage to men otherwise hidden by gangway or bulwark. The Frenchman obviously wanted to dismast *Sparrow* and take her and cargo intact. The gold would pay for many requirements in the future, and *Sparrow* would make a valuable addition to the enemy's fleet. It had happened before. Within the hour he might see it happen again. To him.

The bow-chaser threw out a spurt of smoke and the *Sparrow*'s main course burst open with a searing explosion, the great sail ripping itself to a hundred fragments in the wind even before the enemy's iron had finished falling alongside.

Bolitho could feel the difference instantly, the heavier motion between each lift and plunge, the increase of turns on the wheel as Buckle's helmsmen fought to hold her on course.

Yet again that demoniac scream of whirling fragments, the thud and clatter of falling rope and halliards. Men were working feverishly far above the decks to make good the severed rigging, but the frigate was much nearer, and as Bolitho swung round he saw three of her foremost guns belching fire and smoke, proof that she was overhauling rapidly to bring more of her armament to bear.

Balls shrieked and whimpered overhead and one ripped through the mizzen topsail with the slap of a whip against wood. Men yelled and cursed to control it as once again the wind explored the damage, tearing the shot-hole in an uneven gash from head to foot.

Bolitho gripped the rail hard. If only there was sight of a friendly sail, anything which might make the frigate lose heart or change tack even for a few moments.

He saw a ball skipping across the wave-crests, its progress clearly marked by the leaping feathers of spray; winced as the deck jumped beneath him as the shot slammed into the lower hull.

From below the gundeck he heard muffled cries, and pictured the sick and wounded, some with limbs only just cut away by Dalkeith, enduring the menacing roar of gunfire, the increasing accuracy of each successive shot.

Bethune came running from the ladder. 'Captain, sir! The general wishes to be kept informed . . .' He ducked as a ball burst through the taffrail and hurled two seamen in a tangle of writhing limbs and horrifying spurts of blood.

Bolitho turned from the sight. He had been speaking to one of them just minutes ago. Now he was less than a man. Nothing.

'Tell the general to stay below and . . .'

He broke off as with a splintering crash the maintopgallant canted over, the sail whipping madly in a web of parted rigging, while the yard itself snapped into equal halves before pitching towards the deck. Men ran in confusion until the avalanche of wood and cordage had draped itself over the larboard gangway to trail alongside in a maelstrom of spray. A man, it must have been the lookout, was hurled bodily to the topsail yard, and even above the din Bolitho heard his shrill scream, saw him roll over and fall the rest of the way to the gundeck.

Another ragged burst of cannon fire, and Tilby dashed amongst the struggling seamen, his arms flailing as he pushed and drove them with their axes to free the ship from its torn rigging.

Tyrrell shouted, 'We will have to alter course, sir!' He was yelling to make himself heard as men rushed past him, faces screwed into tight masks, their eyes blind even to the butchered corpses beside the nettings.

Bolitho stared at him. 'How much water is there over those bars?'

Tyrrell seemed to think he had misheard. 'At *this* time? Next to nothing!' He peered wildly at the sails as more jagged iron screamed amongst them.

A topman had slipped and was being suspended by his hands by two of his companions while his legs kicked helplessly in the air. Sweat, fear or a flying splinter cut the contact, and with a brief cry the man fell head over heels, seemingly very slowly, until he hit the sea by the hull. Bolitho saw him passing below the quarterdeck, arms outspread, his eyes very white as the water closed over them.

'I must risk it!' He was shouting aloud without realizing it was more than a murmur. 'Tack either way and that frigate will rake us!'

Tyrrell nodded jerkily. 'As you say! I'll get a leadsman in th' chains and . . .'

Bolitho seized his arm. '*No!* Do that, or shorten sail, and that bastard will know what we're about!' He shook him violently. 'If I fall, you must try to take her through.'

A ball crashed into the nettings and sliced behind him. Splinters and fragments filled the air, and he saw Foley throw one hand to his shoulder where the epaulette had been torn cleanly away.

He faced Bolitho and said, 'Warm work, Captain.'

Bolitho stared at him, feeling that same fixed grin on his mouth and jaw like a cruel vice. Like him, the ship was acting like something beyond control, the remaining sails driving her onwards towards the hidden menace of those hard sandbars. He was banking everything on Tyrrell's knowledge, and the hope that the Frenchman was ignorant of his danger, or so blinded by all else but *Sparrow*'s closeness to defeat that he was totally absorbed.

Yet in spite of the intermittent gunfire, the responding crashes and thuds of balls striking home, he was able to see small but important details on every side.

A badly wounded seaman, his shoulder mashed to bloody pulp, was being held in the arms of a wounded soldier. The latter was blinded from some previous fight and his face covered by bandages. But his hands seemed to stand out even in all the confusion around him. Moving and calming, shielding the sailor and groping for a flask of water to ease his suffering. And Dalkeith, his wig screwed into one pocket while he knelt beside another injured man, his fingers like scarlet claws as he felt the extent of the wound, while his eyes rested on the next victim, and the one after that.

And through it all Graves walking behind the loaded guns, chin on chest, pausing only to check a particular crew or to step astride a corpse or fallen rigging.

From forward came the frightened cry, 'I kin see th' bottom!'

Bolitho ran to the netting and pulled himself above the tightly stowed hammocks. In the bright sunlight he saw the spray bursting from the rounded bilge, trailing ropes and a complete section of a broken cutter dragging alongside. Then he saw the darting, shadowy shapes gliding deeper still, weed and rock clusters, some of which seemed to be rising towards the keel like disturbed monsters.

If she struck now the mast would be ripped out of her and she would plough forward, grinding and breaking open to the waiting sea.

He turned to seek out the enemy. How near she looked. Less than three cables off the quarter, her complete battery run out in readiness to finish the contest.

Buckle muttered hoarsely, 'By the living God, the Frenchie's in a safe channel!' There was a break in his voice. 'The bastards have done for us!'

Bolitho looked at Tyrrell. 'Get the t'gallants off her.' He could not hide the despair this time.

As the men swarmed aloft to shorten sail, Tyrrell shouted, 'There was nothing else you could do . . .'

He broke off as Buckle and Midshipman Heyward yelled together, '*She's struck!*'

Bolitho pushed between them and stared with sick disbelief at the other ship. She had been changing tack, either because her captain had at last seen his danger or was about to rake the sloop with his first full broadside, and had struck one of the bars at full speed. Across the strip of water they could hear the jarring crashes, the awful rumble of her hull pounding aground. And as she began to slew round her foremast, followed and entangled with her main mizzen topmasts, came down in one mighty curtain of leaping spray.

Bolitho had to yell several times to stop his men from shouting and cheering, to make them understand that their own danger was just as real.

'Alter course five points to starboard!' He dashed the sweat from his eyes to peer at the compass, his mind dulled by the crash of spars and groaning timbers. 'Steer sou' sou'-east!'

With only her torn course and topsails set, the *Sparrow* came round sluggishly, as if she, too, was beyond reason.

Gear flapped and banged, and men clambered over the scattered debris like dazed animals in their efforts to obey the shouts from aft.

Bolitho cupped his hands and yelled, 'Mr Graves! Run out!'

The ports squeaked open, and on their trucks the guns which could be manned trundled into the sunlight. With the sloop leaning over on her new tack each cannon moved quickly down the deck until with a shout of, 'All run out!' Graves stared once again towards Bolitho.

Bolitho watched narrowly, his hand lifting while he forced himself to see the other ship as a target and not a once living creature writhing in agony.

'As you bear, Mr Graves! Full elevation!'

He saw the listing, dismasted frigate falling past *Sparrow*'s starboard bow, the churned sand around her beakhead to mark the extent of her charge on to the bar.

His hand came down. '*Fire!*'

The hull jerked and bucked as gun by gun the double-shotted charges ripped over the wave-crests to smash into the helpless enemy. A few shots from swivel guns answered the first onslaught, but as the heavy balls, coupled with a full load of grape, swept into her side and decks those, too, fell silent.

Bolitho held up his hand. 'Cease firing! Secure guns!' To Buckle he added, 'We will wear ship directly. Nor'-east by north.' He glanced astern at the smoking wreck. 'She will rest there until someone comes, friend or foe, it makes little difference for her.'

Tyrrell watched him gravely. 'Aye, aye, sir.'

He appeared to be waiting for something more.

Bolitho walked to the rail and studied the men below him. Restoring lashings on the guns, working to repair damage and sort out the tangle of rigging, everywhere something was happening to prepare *Sparrow* for her next challenge. There was no cheering, in fact little sound of voices at all. Just a few grins as seamen discovered good friends still alive. A nod here, a casual thump on the shoulder there. Together they told him more than words.

'They've learned well, Mr Tyrrell.' He saw Dalkeith coming aft again, and steeled himself for the list of dead and dying. 'After this they will be ready for anything.'

He handed his sword to Stockdale, who had been near him the whole time although he could not recall seeing him.

'As *I* will.'

8

A Captain's Decision

The *Sparrow*'s stay at New York proved to be the most frustrating and testing time Bolitho could remember. Instead of weeks, as he had hoped, to carry out his repairs and replace stores, he was forced to wait and watch with mounting impatience while every other ship, or so it appeared, took precedence.

As the time dragged into one and then a second month, he found himself ready to plead rather than demand, beg instead of awaiting his rightful aid from the shore authorities, and from what he could gather elsewhere, it seemed that most other junior vessels were in the same situation.

Work aboard continued without pause, and already *Sparrow* had taken on the appearance of a tried veteran. Sails were carefully patched rather than being replaced without thought of cost. Nobody seemed to know when more replenishments were arriving from England, and those already in New York were jealously guarded or, he suspected, hoarded for some suitable bribe. The maintopgallant yard had been fished, and from the deck appeared as good as new. How it would withstand a real storm, or a chase after some blockade runner, was often in Bolitho's mind, along with the endless stream of reports to be made, requisition and victualling lists to be checked and argued over with the supply yard, until he began to think neither he nor his ship would ever move again.

Most of the pride and excitement at running the French frigate aground, or seeing the rescued soldiers safely landed, had given way to resigned gloom. Day after day, the ship's company endured the heat and the work, knowing there was no chance of setting foot on land unless under close supervision and then only on matters of duty. Bolitho knew the reasons for this rule were sound up to a point. Every vessel which came and went from Sandy Hook was shorthanded, and unscrupulous captains had been known to steal seamen from other ships if offered half a chance.

Since assuming command he, too, was short of fifteen men, those killed or so badly injured as to be unfit for further service.

And the news was not encouraging. Everywhere on the mainland the British forces were in trouble. In June a complete army was forced to retreat from General Washington's attacks at the battle of Monmouth, and the reports which filtered to the anchored ships showed little hope of improvement.

To add to the fleet's troubles had come the first hurricane of the season. Sweeping up from the Caribbean like a scythe through corn it had destroyed several ships in its path, and so damaged others they were out of commission when most needed. Bolitho was able to appreciate the admiral's concern for his patrols and prowling frigates, for the whole management of strategy along the American coast depended on their vigilance, their ability to act like his eyes and an extension to his brain.

He was thankful for one thing only. That his ship had not been so seriously damaged below the waterline as he had first feared. As Garby, the carpenter, had said, 'She's like a little fortress, sir.'

On his regular inspections below decks to watch the work's progress Bolitho had understood the carpenter's pride. For *Sparrow* had been built as a sloop of war, quite unlike most of her contemporaries which had been purchased for the Navy from the less demanding tasks of merchant service. Even her stout frames had been grown to the right proportions and not cut with a saw, so that the hull had all the added security of natural strength. The fact that but for a few ragged shot-holes below the quarter which needed the aid and tools of the New York shipwrights his ship could sail and fight as before, made the delay all the more unbearable.

He had been to see Rear-Admiral Christie aboard his flagship, but had gained little idea of when he could complete repairs. The admiral had said wryly, 'If you had been less, er, difficult with General Blundell, things might be different.'

When Bolitho had tried to draw him further he had snapped, 'I know the general was wrong to act as he did. The whole of New York knows it by now. He may even be censured when he returns to England, although knowing his influence in certain regions, I doubt that.' He had shrugged wearily. '*You*, Bolitho, had to be the one to humble him. You did right, and I have already written a report to show my confidence in you. However, the *right* way is not always the most popular.'

One item of news hung over Bolitho like a cloud and seemed to torment him as day by day he tried to prepare his ship for sea. An incoming brig had brought news of the privateer *Bonaventure*. She had fought several actions against supply vessels and ships-of-war alike. She had seized two prizes and destroyed an escorting sloop. Just as he had predicted, as he had feared. But to him the worst part was that the privateer had returned to the same area where they had exchanged shots, and had found the crippled frigate *Miranda*.

A handful of survivors had been discovered drifting in a small boat, some wounded or half-mad with thirst, the rest stunned by the suddenness of their ship's end, when they had done so much to repair and save her.

Over and over again Bolitho searched his mind to examine his actions, to discover what else he might or should have done. By carrying out his orders, by putting duty before the true desire to help the damaged frigate, he had left her like a helpless animal before the tiger.

In his heart he believed he could have made no other decision. But if he had realized that the two transports were no longer so desperately needed, he also knew he would have acted differently. When he had admitted as much to the brig's captain he had replied, 'Then your *Sparrow*, too, would be at the bottom, for *Bonaventure* is more than a match for anything but a ship of the line!'

Apart from matters of duty, errands to use his presence or his purse on shipyard clerks, Bolitho refrained from going ashore. Partly because he thought it unfair when his men were penned in their ship, the size of which seemed to shrink with each passing day, and partly because of what he saw there. The military preparations were usual enough. Artillery wheeling and exercising, the horse-drawn limbers charging at full tilt, to the delight of idlers and yelling children. Foot soldiers drilling and sweating in the grinding heat, he had even seen cavalry on several occasions.

No, it went far deeper. The worsening news from inland seemed to reach just so far and then stop. In the great houses, rarely a night passed without some fine ball or reception being held. Staff officers and rich traders, ladies in full gowns and glittering jewels, it was hard to realize they were so close to a full-scale war. Equally, he knew his disgust came from his own inability to mix in such circles. In his home town of Falmouth his family had always been respected, but more as seafarers than local residents. He had gone to sea at the age of twelve, and his education had been more concerned with navigation and learning the mysteries of every eye and cleat, each foot of cordage required to sail a ship under all conditions, than the art of making small-talk and mingling with some of the bewigged jackadandies he had seen in New York. The women, too, seemed different. Beyond reach. Unlike the outspoken countrywomen in Cornwall or the wives and daughters of fellow sea-officers, they appeared to give off a power all of their own. A boldness, a certain amused contempt which both irritated and confused him whenever he came in contact with their perfumed, privileged world.

He had allowed Tyrrell to go ashore whenever possible, and had been surprised to see the change in him. Instead of showing excitement or relief at being amongst men like himself, places he had often visited in his father's schooner, he withdrew still further, until eventually he avoided leaving the ship unless on some particular duty. Bolitho knew he had been making enquiries about his family's whereabouts, anything which might give him some hint of their safety or otherwise. Also, he believed that Tyrrell would tell him in his own good time, if that was what he wished.

And then, three months almost to the exact day after watching the French frigate pounding herself to fragments on the hidden bar, *Sparrow* was once more ready for sea. When the last shipwright had been escorted ashore, each watched to make certain he took no more than he had brought with him, and the water-lighters and yard hoys had pulled clear of the side, Bolitho wrote his report for the admiral. Another special mission, to carry despatches, or merely to return to Captain Colquhoun's command, he now cared very little which it was to be. Just to be under sail again, free of urbane flag officers and inscrutable clerks, it was all he wanted.

When Tyrrell came aft to report the ship cleared of shore workers Bolitho asked, 'Will you dine with me this evening? We may be too occupied in the near future.'

Tyrrell looked at him dully. 'My pleasure, sir.' He sounded worn out. Spent.

Bolitho stared through the open stern windows towards the anchored ships and the pale houses beyond.

'You may share your worries with me, Mr Tyrrell, if you wish.' He had not meant to say what he did. But the look of despair on the lieutenant's face had pushed all caution aside.

Tyrrell watched him by the windows, his eyes in shadow. 'I did get news. My father lost his schooners, but that was expected. They went to one side or t'other. Makes no difference. My father also owned a small farmstead. Always said it was like th' one he had once in England.'

Bolitho turned slowly. 'Is that gone, too?'

Tyrrell shrugged. 'Th' war reached th' territory some months back.' His voice became distant, toneless. 'We had a neighbour, called Luke Mason. He an' I grew up together. Like brothers. When th' rebellion began Luke was up north selling cattle an' I was at sea. Luke was always a bit wild, an' I guess he got carried along by all the excitement. Anyway, he joined up to fight th' English. But things got bad for his company, they were almost wiped out in some battle or t'other. Luke decided to go home. He had had enough of war, I guess.'

Bolitho bit his lip. 'He went to your father?'

'Aye. Trouble was, my father was apparently helping th' English soldiers with fodder an' remounts. But he was fond of Luke. He was like family.' He gave a long sigh. 'Th' local colonel heard about it from some goddamn informer. He had my father hanged on a tree and burned th' house down for good measure.'

Bolitho exclaimed, 'My God, I'm sorry!'

Tyrrell did not seem to hear. 'Then th' Americans attacked an' th' redcoats retreated.' He looked up at the deckhead and added fiercely, 'But Luke was safe. He got out of th' house before it burned around him. An' you know what? Th' American colonel hanged Luke as a deserter!'

He dropped on a chair and fell against the table. 'In th' name of hell, where's the goddamn sense in it all?'

'And your mother?' He watched Tyrrell's lowered head. His anguish was breaking him apart.

'She died two years back, so she was spared all this. There's just me now, an' my sister Jane.' He looked up, his eyes reflecting the sunlight like fires. 'After Cap'n Ransome had done with her she disappeared. Christ alone knows where she is!'

In the sudden silence Bolitho tried to discover how he would feel if, like Tyrrell, he was faced with such an appalling discovery. Ever since he could remember he had been taught to accept the possibility of death and not shirk from it. Most of his ancestors had died at sea in one manner or another. It was an easy thing to do. Quite apart from a brutal end under cannon fire or the plunge of an enemy's sword, there were countless traps for the unwary. A fall from aloft, drowning, fever, men died as much from these as anything fired from a gun. His brother Hugh had been a lieutenant in the Channel Fleet when he had last seen him. He could be commanding a ship against the French, or at this very moment lying many fathoms down with his men. But the roots would still be there. The house in Falmouth, his father and married sisters. What would he be suffering if, like Tyrrell, he knew all that was broken and trodden down in a country where brother fought brother and men cursed each other in the same language as they struggled and died?

Now Tyrrell, and many more besides, had nothing left. Not even a country.

There was a rap on the door and Graves stepped into the cabin.

'This was delivered by the guardboat, sir.' He held out a canvas envelope.

Bolitho walked to the windows again and slit it open with a knife. He hoped Graves would not notice Tyrrell's misery, that the time taken to read the message would give him a moment to recover.

It was very brief.

He said quietly, 'We are ordered to weigh at first light tomorrow. We will be carrying important despatches to the admiral in Antigua.'

He had a mental picture of the endless sea miles, the long passage back to English Harbour and Colquhoun. It was a pity they had ever left in the first place.

Graves said, 'I'm not sorry. We'll have something to boast about this time.'

Bolitho studied him gravely. What an unimaginative man he is.

'My compliments to the master. Tell him to make preparations at once.'

When Graves had gone Bolitho added, 'Maybe you'll wish to postpone dining with me?'

Tyrrell stood up, his fingers touching the table as if to test his balance.

'No, sir. I'd like to come.' He looked round the cabin. 'This was th' last place I saw Jane. It helps a bit now.'

Bolitho watched him leave and heard the slam of a cabin door. Then with a sigh he sat down at the table and began to write in his log.

For seven untroubled days the *Sparrow* pushed her bowsprit southwards, taking full advantage of a fresh wind which hardly varied in bearing or substance throughout that time. The regrets and brooding despondency which most of the company had felt at New York seemed to have blown away on the wind, and their new freedom shone in the straining canvas which gleamed beneath a cloudless sky. Even the memory of the last fight, the faces of those killed or left behind crippled to await passage home had become part of the past, like old scars which took just so much time to heal.

As Bolitho studied his chart and checked the daily sunsights he felt cause for satisfaction in *Sparrow*'s performance. She had already logged over a thousand miles, and like himself seemed eager to leave the land as far away as possible. They had not sighted even a solitary sail, and the last hopeful gulls had left them two days earlier.

The routine aboard such a small ship-of-war was regular and carefully planned, so that the overcrowded conditions could be made as comfortable as possible. When not working aloft on sails and rigging the hands spent their time at gun drill or in harmless contests of wrestling and fighting with staves under Stockdale's professional eye.

On the quarterdeck, too, there was usually some diversion to break the monotony of empty horizons, and Bolitho came to know even more about his officers. Midshipman Heyward had proved himself to be an excellent and skilful swordsman, and spent several of the dog watches instructing Bethune and the master's mate in the art of fencing. The biggest surprise was Robert Dalkeith. The plump surgeon had come on deck with the finest pair of pistols Bolitho had ever seen. Perfectly matched and made by Dodson of London, they must have cost a small fortune. While one of the ship's boys had thrown pieces of wood chippings from a gangway, Dalkeith had waited by the nettings and when they had bobbed past on the wash had despatched them without seeming to take aim. Such marksmanship was rare for any ship's surgeon, and added to the price of the pistols made Bolitho think more deeply about Dalkeith's past.

Towards the end of the seventh day Bolitho received the first warning that the weather was changing. The sky, clear and pale blue for so long, became smeared by long tongues of cloud, and the ship reeled more heavily in a deep swell. The glass was unsteady, but it was more the feel of things which told him they were in for a real blow. The wind had backed to the north-west and showed every sign of strengthening, and as he faced it across the taffrail he could sense the mounting power, its clamminess on his skin.

Buckle observed, 'Another hurricane, I wonder?'

'Maybe.' Bolitho walked to the compass. 'Let her fall off a point.' He left Buckle to his helmsmen and joined Tyrrell by the quarterdeck rail. 'The fringe of a storm perhaps. Either way we will have to reef down before dark, maybe much sooner.'

Tyrrell nodded, his eyes on the bulging canvas. 'Th' mainto'gan'sl seems to be drawing well. They did good work aloft while we were in port.' He watched the masthead pendant as it twisted and then flapped out more firmly towards the larboard bow. 'Goddamn th' wind. It backs still further by th' looks of it.'

Buckle smiled glumly. 'Course sou' sou'-east, sir.' He cursed as the deck tilted steeply and a tall spectre of spray burst above the nettings.

Bolitho considered the matter. They had made a good passage so far. There was no point in tearing the sails off her just to spite the wind. He sighed. Perhaps it would ease again soon.

'Get the t'gallants off her, Mr Tyrrell. It's coming down on us now.'

He stood aside as Tyrrell ran for his trumpet. Out from the swaying hull he saw the telltale haze of rain advancing across the uneven swell and blotting out the horizon like a fence of chain-mail.

Within an hour the wind had backed even further and had risen to gale force, with the sea and sky joined together in a torment of bursting wave-crests and torrential rain. It was useless to fight it, and as the clouds gathered and entwined above the swooping mastheads *Sparrow* turned and ran before it, her topmen fighting and fisting the sodden canvas as yet another reef was made fast. Half-blinded by rain and spray, their feet groping for toeholds, while with curses and yells they used brute strength to bring the sails under control.

Night came prematurely, and under close-reefed topsails they drove on into the darkness, their world surrounded by huge wave-crests, their lives menaced at every step by the sea as it surged over the gangways and boiled along the decks like a river in flood. Even when the hands were dismissed in watches to find a moment of rest and shelter below there was little to sustain them. Everything was dripping or damp, and the cook had long since given up any idea of producing a hot meal.

Bolitho remained on the quarterdeck, his tarpaulin coat plastered to his body like a shroud while the wind howled and screamed around him. Shrouds and rigging whined like the strings of some mad orchestra, and above the deck, hidden in darkness, the crack and boom of canvas told its own story. In brief lulls the wind seemed to drop, holding its breath as if to consider its efforts against the embattled sloop. In those small moments Bolitho could feel the salt warming on his face, raw to the touch. He could hear the clank of pumps, the muffled shouts from below and on the hidden forecastle as unseen men fought to make fast lashings, seek out severed cordage, or merely to reassure each other they were alive.

All night the wind battered against them, driving them further and still further to the south-east. Hour by hour, as Bolitho peered at the compass or reeled below to examine his chart, there was neither rest nor relief from its pounding. Bolitho felt bruised and sick, as if he had been fighting a physical battle, or dragged half-drowned from the sea itself. Despite his reeling mind he thanked God he had not tried to lie to and ride out the storm under a solitary reefed topsail. With this strength of wind and sea *Sparrow* would never have recovered, could have been all aback and dismasted before anyone had realized what they were truly against.

He could even find a moment to marvel at *Sparrow*'s behaviour. Uncomfortable she was to every man aboard. Fighting the jerking canvas or working on the pumps with sea and bilge water swirling amongst them like rats in a sewer, their lives were made worse by the motion. Up, higher still, and then down with the sound of thunder across a great crest, every spar and timber shaking as if to rip free of the hull. Food, a few precious possessions, clothing, all surged about the decks in wild abandon, but not a gun tore away from its lashings, not a bolt snapped, nor was any hatch stove in by the attacking sea. *Sparrow* took it all, rode each assault with the unsteady belligerence of a drunken marine.

By the time they sighted a first hint of grey in the sky the sea had begun to ease, and when the sun peeped languidly above the horizon it was hard to believe they were in the same ocean.

The wind had veered again to the north-west and as they stared with salt-caked eyes at the patches of blue between the clouds they knew they were being left in comparative peace.

Bolitho realized that if he allowed the hands to rest now they would not be able to move again for hours. He looked down at the gundeck and gangways, seeing their tired faces and torn clothing, the way the topmen's tarred hands were held like claws after their repeated journeys to those treacherous yards to battle with the sails.

He said, 'Pass the word for the galley fire to be lit. We must get some food into them directly.' He looked up as a shaft of sunlight touched the upper yards so that they shone above the retreating darkness like a triple crucifix. 'It will be warm enough soon, Mr Tyrrell. Rig wind-sails above each hatch and open the weather gun ports.' He let his salt-stiffened lips crack into a smile. 'I suggest you forget your usual concern for the ship's looks and have the hands run their spare clothing aloft to dry out.'

Graves came aft and touched his hat. 'Able Seaman Marsh is missing.' He swayed and added wearily, 'Foretopman, sir.'

Bolitho let his eyes stray over the starboard quarter. The seaman must have been hurled overboard during the night, and they had not even heard a cry. Which was just as well. They could have done nothing to save him.

'Thank you, Mr Graves. Note it in the log, if you please.'

He was still watching the sea, the way the night appeared to withdraw itself before the first gold rays, like some retreating assassin. The seaman was out there somewhere, dead and remembered by just a few. His shipmates, and those at home he had left so long ago.

He shook himself and turned to the master. 'Mr Buckle, I hope we can fix our position today. Somewhere to the sou'-west of the Bermudas, I have no doubt.' He smiled gently at Buckle's gloomy expression. 'But fifty miles or five hundred, I am not sure.'

Bolitho waited another hour until the ship had been laid on a new tack, her jib-boom prodding towards the southern horizon, her decks and upperworks steaming in the early sunlight as if she was smouldering.

Then he nodded to Tyrrell. 'I will take some breakfast.' He sniffed the greasy aroma from the galley funnel. 'Even that smell has given me an appetite.'

With the cabin door firmly closed and Stockdale padding around the table with fresh coffee and a pewter plate of fried pork, Bolitho was able to relax, to weigh the value and cost of the night's work. He had faced his first storm in command. A man had died, but many others had stayed alive. And the *Sparrow* was once again dipping and creaking around him as if nothing out of the ordinary had happened at all.

Stockdale put a plate with half a loaf of stale bread on it beside a crock of yellow butter. The bread was the last of that brought aboard at New York, the butter probably rancid from the cask. But as Bolitho leaned back in his chair he felt like a king, and the meagre breakfast seemed no less than a banquet.

He stared idly around the cabin. He had survived much in so short a time. It was luck, more than he deserved.

He asked, 'Where is Fitch?'

Stockdale showed his teeth, 'Dryin' your sleepin' gear, sir.' He rarely spoke when Bolitho was eating and thinking. He had learned all about Bolitho's odd habits long back. He added, 'Woman's work.'

Bolitho laughed, the sound carrying up through the open skylight where Tyrrell had the watch and Buckle was scribbling on his slate beside the binnacle.

Buckle shook his head. 'What did I tell you? No worries, that one!'

'Deck there!' Tyrrell stared up at the masthead as the cry came. 'Sail! Fine on th' starboard quarter!'

Feet clattered on the ladder and Bolitho appeared beside him, his jaw still working on some buttered bread.

He said, 'I have a feeling about this morning.' He saw a master's mate by the mainmast trunk and called, 'Mr Raven! Aloft with you!' He held up his hand, halting the man as he ran to the shrouds. 'Remember your lesson, as I will.'

Graves had also come on deck, partly shaved and naked to the waist. Bolitho looked around the waiting men, studying each in turn if only to contain his impatience while Raven clawed his way to the masthead. Changed. They were all different in some way. Toughened, more confident perhaps. Like bronzed pirates, held together by their trade – he hesitated – their loyalty.

'Deck there!' Another maddening wait and then Raven yelled down, 'It's her right enough! The *Bonaventure*!'

Something like a growl came from the watching seamen.

One man shouted, 'The bloody *Bonaventure*, is it? Us'll give that bugger a quiltin' today an' that's for sure!'

Several others cheered, and even Bethune called excitedly, 'Huzza, lads!'

Bolitho turned to look at them again, his heart suddenly heavy, the promise of the morning sour and spoiled.

'Get the t'gallants on her, Mr Tyrrell. The royals, too, if the wind stays friendly.'

He saw Tyrrell's eyes, worried, even sad, and snapped, 'We have orders. To carry despatches to our admiral.' He gestured angrily towards the taffrail. 'Do you want to match guns with her?' He turned away, adding vehemently, 'By God, I'd like nothing better than to see her strike!'

Tyrrell took his trumpet and shouted, 'Call th' hands! All hands make sail!'

He glanced quickly at Bolitho who was staring astern. The privateer was not visible from anywhere but the masthead. Not would she be now. But Bolitho was staring fixedly, as if he could see every gun, each gaping muzzle, like the day she had swept *Miranda*'s defences aside like so much rubbish.

Graves moved to his side, his eyes on the seamen as they hurried to their various stations, some still puzzled by their orders.

Tyrrell said quietly, 'It ain't easy to run before an enemy.'

Graves shrugged. 'How about you? I'd have thought you should be somewhat comforted by the fact.' He fell back before Tyrrell's cold stare but added smoothly, 'It would have been less easy for you to fight a Yankee, eh?' Then he hurried down the ladder towards his men at the foremast.

Tyrrell followed him with his eyes. 'Bastard.' He spoke only to himself and was surprised to find he was so calm. '*Bastard*.'

When he turned his head he saw that Bolitho had left the deck.

Buckle dipped his thumb to the skylight. 'He's not laughing now, Mr Tyrrell.' He sounded grim. 'I'd not have his rank for all the whores in Plymouth!'

Tyrrell tapped the half-hour glass and said nothing.

How different from Captain Ransome, he thought. He would have shared neither hopes nor fears with any of them. And these same seamen who were already swarming up the ratlines on either beam would have shown no surprise if he made a similar decision to Bolitho. It was because they seemed to think Bolitho could lead them anywhere, and with all odds against them, that they were puzzled by his action. The sudden realization troubled him. Partly because Bolitho did not understand, but mainly because he should have been the one to make Bolitho realize how they all felt for him.

Ransome had always used and never led them. Instead of example he had laid down rules. Whereas he . . . Tyrrell glanced at the cabin skylight now shut, and imagined he could hear a girl's voice again.

Graves strode aft and touched his hat, his tone formal in front of the watching eyes.

'Permission to dismiss the watch below, sir?'

'Aye. Carry on, Mr Graves.' They held each other's gaze, then Tyrrell turned his back.

He walked to the rail and stared up at the freshly trimmed sails, the seamen on the upper yards, their skins brown in the sunlight.

The privateer would never catch them now, even if she so intended. It would be another ship, a fat merchantman, or some unsuspecting trader from the Bahamas.

He saw the captain's coxswain beside the nettings and asked, 'How is he, Stockdale?'

Stockdale regarded him warily, like a watchdog examining a possible intruder.

Then he relaxed slightly, his big hands loose at his sides. ''E's in irons at th' moment, sir.' He stared angrily at the blue water. 'But we've come through worse afore. A whole lot worse.'

Tyrrell nodded, seeing the certainty in Stockdale's eyes like something written.

'He has a good friend in you, Stockdale.'

The coxswain turned his broken face away. 'Aye. I could tell you things I seen 'im do that'd make some of these Jacks run to their mothers and pray.'

Tyrrell kept quiet and very still, watching the man's profile as he relived some memory, an incident so vivid it was like yesterday.

Stockdale said in his wheezing voice, 'I've carried 'im like a child, seen 'im so beside hisself with anger there's not a man-jack'd draw near. Other times I've seen 'im 'old a man in 'is arms until 'e died, even though there were nought anyone could do for th' poor bugger.' He swung round, his eyes fierce. 'I ain't got the words for it, else I'd make 'em all listen.'

Tyrrell reached out and touched his massive arm.

'You're wrong. You've got th' words right enough. And thanks for telling *me*.'

Stockdale grunted and walked heavily towards the hatch. He had never spoken like that before, but somehow he trusted Tyrrell. Like Bolitho, he was a man, not just an officer, and for him that was more than enough.

All that day the *Sparrow* ran freely towards an empty horizon. The watches changed, drills were carried out, and one man was flogged for drawing his knife against a messmate after an argument. But there were no contests on deck, and when Heyward appeared with his swords to begin another period of instruction he found no takers, nor did Dalkeith leave his sick-bay for a pistol shoot.

In his cabin Bolitho remained with his thoughts, wondering why a simple action was so hard to bear, merely because he had been the one to dictate it. Command, leadership, authority, they were mere words. At no time could they explain his true feelings, or wipe away inner misgivings.

As Rear-Admiral Christie had said, the right way was not always the most popular, or the easiest to accept.

When the bell chimed out for the first dog watch he heard another cry from the masthead.

'Deck there! Sail on the lee bow!'

He made himself remain seated at the table until Midshipman Bethune came down to report that the sail was barely moving and was perhaps hove-to.

Even then he delayed before going on deck. Another disappointment, a fresh need to take avoiding action from one more enemy, only time and distance would tell him these things.

Graves, who had the watch, said, 'If it's one of our frigates we could turn and close with the *Bonaventure*, sir.'

Heyward added, 'Maybe we could take her as a prize.'

Bolitho faced them coldly. 'And if she's a *French* frigate, what then?' He saw them stiffen under his stare. 'I suggest you hold your suppositions until later.'

But it was neither privateer nor patrolling ship-of-war. As *Sparrow* sped down towards her Bolitho watched the stranger through his glass, seeing the gap in her outline where her main topmast had been torn away like a branch from a tree, and the huge scars along her tumblehome to show the battering she had received from sea and wind.

Buckle said quietly, 'By God, she must have taken the storm full on herself. She's in a poor way, I'm thinking.'

Tyrrell, who had climbed to the main topmast yard, shinned down a backstay and reported, 'I know her, sir. She's th' *Royal Anne*, West Indiaman.'

Buckle agreed. 'Aye, that's so. She set sail from Sandy Hook three days afore us. Bound for Bristol, I heard.'

'Run up the colours.'

Bolitho shifted the glass carefully, watching the tiny figures swarming along the other ship's decks, the broken gangway where a great sea had thundered inboard like a falling cliff. She made a pitiful sight. Spars missing, sails in ribbons. She must have ridden out the same storm which they had skirted just a night ago.

Bethune exclaimed, 'I have her here in my book, sir. She is under warrant to the Commander-in-Chief.'

But Bolitho barely heard him. He saw the figures along the vessel's upper deck pausing to stare at the approaching sloop, while here and there a man was waving, perhaps cheering to see a friendly flag.

He stiffened and then said, 'There are women aboard that ship.' He lowered the glass and looked at Tyrrell questioningly. 'Under warrant, is she?'

Tyrrell nodded slowly. 'Indiamen do take a government charter when it suits, sir.' He glanced away. 'Th' *Royal Anne*'ll be carrying folk from New York to England. And away from th'war, no doubt.'

Bolitho raised the glass again, his mind working on Tyrrell's words.

He said, 'We will close her now, Mr Tyrrell, and keep her under our lee. Have the starboard cutter cleared for lowering. The surgeon will accompany me on board.' He glanced at Bethune. 'Signal her to that effect. If she fails to understand, then hail her when we draw nearer.'

He walked away from the rail as the flags soared aloft on their halliards.

Tyrrell followed and said gravely, 'She'll not be able to outsail th' *Bonaventure*, sir. Even if she was without damage.'

Bolitho faced him. 'I know.'

He tried to sound composed even though his mind was screaming. Turn after all and face the big privateer. The facts had not altered.

Sparrow would still be outgunned and sunk without too much diffculty. The *Royal Anne* was so badly damaged that a respite brought about by sacrificing this ship and all her company would make no difference. But to run once more, to leave her helpless and allow the enemy to take her at leisure was too cruel even to contemplate.

He *must* contemplate it. It was his decision. *His*.

Buckle called, 'She's standing by, sir! We'd best take the way off us.'

'Very well.' Bolitho walked slowly along the side. 'Get the royals and t'gallants off her, Mr Tyrrell. We will heave-to directly.'

He saw Stockdale hurrying towards him with his coat and sword. It would be dark in five hours. If they were to do anything, they would need haste and luck. Especially the latter.

He slipped into his coat and said, 'Mr Tyrrell, you will come with me.'

Then as the boat was hoisted over the gangway and lowered alongside he looked astern, almost expecting to see a sliver of sail, or hear the masthead's call.

'Cutter alongside, sir!'

He nodded and strode towards the gangway.

'Let us be about it then.'

And without a glance at the others he followed Tyrrell down into the boat.

9

'Boarders Away!'

As he pulled himself up a dangling rope ladder to the *Royal Anne*'s thick bulwark Bolitho was conscious of the tension which awaited him. There were many people on the upper and poop decks, passengers and sailors, singly and in large groups, but all joined together in some way as they stared at him, then at the seamen who followed him up from the cutter.

Bolitho paused to collect his thoughts, and while he adjusted the sword on his hip and Tyrrell mustered the boarding party into line, he took a slow appraisal of the ship around him. Fallen rigging and broken spars, whole strips of torn canvas and cordage littered the decks in profusion, and he could tell by the heavy motion that she had taken a good deal of water in the bilges.

A tall, gangling man in a blue coat stepped forward and touched his forehead.

'I'm Jennis, sir.' He swallowed hard. 'Mate and senior officer.'

'Where is the Master?'

Jennis gestured wearily towards the rail. 'He went overboard in the storm. Him and twenty more besides.'

Boots thudded on a companion ladder and Bolitho stiffened as a familiar figure thrust the others aside and strode towards him. It was General Blundell, impeccable as ever, but with two pistols at his belt.

Bolitho touched his hat. 'I am surprised to see you, Sir James.' He tried to mask his dislike. 'You appear to be in some trouble.'

The general glared around him, then across at the *Sparrow* as she swayed easily in the swell, her sails flapping loosely as if resting.

He barked, 'And about time, too! This damn ship should never have been allowed out of harbour!' He pointed at the mate. 'That fool cannot even keep order!'

Bolitho looked at Tyrrell. 'Take your men and examine the hull and other damage. Quick as you can.' He glanced narrowly at a group of sailors lolling by the forward hatch, noticing how they swayed out of time with the deck, their eyes devoid of interest in his arrival or the disorder which lay on every hand.

The mate explained hurriedly, 'We've had to use pistols, sir. Some men ran wild when the storm broke. We've a full cargo of rum and other spirits, as well as molasses and coffee. While the rest of us were working the ship they and a few passengers broached holds and began drinking.' He shuddered. 'What with women crying an' screaming, the ship falling about us, an' Cap'n Harper lost overboard, I was hard put to watch everything at once.'

Blundell snapped, 'You're bloody useless! I'd have you shot for your incompetence!'

As the first of *Sparrow*'s seamen approached the fore hatch the drunken figures seemed to come to life. With jeers and taunts they blocked the way across the deck, and from right forward an unseen hand hurled a bottle which shattered against a ring bolt, bringing bright droplets of blood down a sailor's chest.

Bolitho said sharply, 'Carry on, Mr Tyrrell!'

The lieutenant nodded. 'Party! Draw cutlasses!' He took his pistol and pointed it at the line of swaying figures. 'Kill anyone who interferes! Bosun's mate, take 'em below and put 'em on the pumps!'

One made as if to run amongst the small party, but fell senseless as the boatswain's mate brought the flat of his blade hard down on the side of his head.

Bolitho said, 'There is much to do. Mr Jennis, turn the hands to and replace your fores'l. Have all this clutter cut adrift so that the injured may be laid on deck where my surgeon can attend them.' He waited until the mate had shouted his instructions before adding, 'How are you armed?'

Jennis waved vaguely around him. 'Not much sir. Twenty six-pounders and some swivels. We aim to steer clear of trouble. These guns are all we need for fighting off the *boucanier* or would-be pirate.' He looked up, startled. 'Why do you ask?'

General Blundell interrupted, 'Hell's teeth, must I stand here while you people discuss the fittings of this wretched ship? I have had all I can tolerate and . . .'

Bolitho said abruptly, 'Sir James, there is an enemy privateer to the north. She is probably still following us. The *fittings*, as you call them, will be very useful if that enemy comes our way.'

He turned, cocking his head, as the clank of pumps told him Tyrrell had the mutinous seamen in hand.

To Stockdale he said, 'Go aft, see what you can discover.'

Blundell sounded less confident. 'Privateer? Attack us?'

Bolitho replied, 'The *Sparrow* is very small, sir. The enemy more than twice our strength.'

The general grunted. 'Well, better than nothing. If fight you must, it will be for the finest reasons.'

Bolitho ignored him as Tyrrell came on deck again.

'I have sounded th' well. Th' hull is taking water steadily, but th' pumps seem to be containing it. It's all hell below. Cabins broken open, drunks, and two dead from knife wounds.' He frowned towards the mate who was urging his men to clear away fallen spars. 'He must have been mad with worry.' He saw Bolitho's expression. 'What'll we do?'

Blundell said, 'Your captain will do his duty. If we are attacked he will defend this ship and passengers. Do you need telling, man?'

Tyrrell eyed him coolly. 'Not by *you*, General.'

Bolitho snapped, 'How many women are there?' He was watching Stockdale ushering them from the poop, his voice barely audible as he tried to placate them.

There were children, too. More than he had realized.

'For God's sake, how much longer are you going to stand like this?' The general was shouting, his face almost as red as his tunic. 'What does it matter how many this or that we have on board, or what colour their eyes are?' He got no further.

Tyrrell stepped between them, his head lowered so that their faces were nearly touching.

'Look here, General, what th' cap'n says is right. Th' enemy can outshoot anything we have to offer, an' this Indiaman is a damn sight worse off.'

'Not my concern, and I'll tell you once more to mind your manners!'

'Warn me, General?' Tyrrell laughed silently. 'But for you meddling with us at Sandy Hook th' *Sparrow* would have completed repairs an' been away at sea a month back. So but for that you would be alone out here, sitting like a fat duck waiting to be shot for th' pot.' His tone hardened. 'So mind *your* damn manners, *sir*!'

Bolitho was standing apart from them, only half listening to their hushed anger. Once again Blundell's interference was to put him and the ship in real jeopardy. But the facts were unchanged. He turned to conceal his despair. All he had was the hope that *Bonaventure* would not find them. That he could set sail on the battered Indiaman and leave the area with all possible haste.

The mate, Jennis, came aft again. 'I've got the hands bending on a new fores'l, sir. Apart from that we've little spare canvas aboard, not made up that is. This is a Company ship, and we were expecting to have a complete overhaul once we reached Bristol. That's why we sailed short-handed and one officer under strength.' He wiped his hand across his lined face. 'If you hadn't found us I think more of the men might have gone mad and mutinied. We've a fair sprinkling of rogues amongst the passengers as well as honest ones.'

Bolitho looked up as a block swayed and clattered against the mizzen topmast. He saw the torn sails stirring like ragged banners, the sudden movement in the bright Company flag. He frowned. The wind was freshening. Very slightly, but it made things harder if he was to face the decision which had to be made.

And yet, there was still a chance he might be wrong. If so, all this would do nothing but harm and cause more suffering to the passengers.

He pulled out his watch and flipped open the cover. Less than four hours of visibility left.

'Mr Tyrrell, have the *Royal Anne*'s boats lowered at once. Send a message to Graves and tell him I want our boats and fifty seamen here without delay. We must work like the devil if we are to get this ship fit to make sail again.' He waited until Tyrrell and the Indiaman's mate had hurried away before saying, 'Well, Sir James, I must see what needs to be done.'

The general called after him, 'And if as you fear the enemy appears, do you intend to steal away and leave us?' He sounded hoarse with suppressed anger. 'Will written orders save your disgrace after taking such a course?'

Bolitho stopped and faced him again. 'No, Sir James, to both questions. If we are allowed time I will transfer all *Royal Anne*'s passengers and additional hands to my own ship.'

The general's eyes were bulging. '*What?* Leave the cargo and sail away without it?' He seemed stunned in disbelief.

Bolitho shifted his gaze outboard, watching the boats alongside, the slow return of order as his own men took control.

Of course, he should have realized. The general's booty was on board, too. Surprisingly, the thought helped to steady him. He could even smile as he said, 'You can appreciate the need for haste, sir. For both our reasons!'

Tyrrell fell in step beside him. 'That took th' wind from his sails!'

Bolitho said, 'It is no joke. If we can get under way in company at dawn we will have a fair chance. It may be that the *Bonaventure* changed tack altogether when we lost her. She could be many leagues away by now.'

Tyrrell glanced at him. 'But you don't think so?'

'No.' He stepped aside as broken rigging was dragged like black snakes from an upended boat. 'It is the *when* rather than the *if* which troubles me.'

Tyrrell pointed across the bulwark. 'Graves is sending th' first of th' men over.' He grimaced. 'It'll leave him short-handed in *Sparrow*. Barely enough to work ship.'

Bolitho shruggged. 'If the company was halved by fever the rest would *have* to manage.'

He added, 'Now let us meet the ladies. They will be more worried than the general, I should imagine.'

There were about fifty of them. Crowded together below the high poop, but separated by their rank and station in that other world outside the ship. Old and young, plain and beautiful, they watched Bolitho in silence, as if he had risen from the sea like a messenger from Neptune.

'Ladies.' He licked his lips as a strikingly beautiful girl in a gown of yellow silk smiled at him. He tried again. 'I must regret the inconvenience, but there is much to do before we can see you safely on your voyage.' She was still smiling. Direct. Amused. Just the way which always reduced him to confusion. 'If anyone is injured my surgeon will do his best for her. A meal is being prepared, and my own men will stand guard over your quarters.'

The girl asked, 'Do you think the enemy will come, Captain?' She had a cool, confident voice which spoke of education and breeding.

He hesitated. 'It is always possible.'

She showed her even teeth. 'There now. What profound words from so young a King's officer!' Several of the others smiled. Some even laughed aloud.

Bolitho said stiffly, 'If you will excuse me, ladies.' He shot the girl a fierce stare. 'I have work to do.'

Tyrrell hid a smile as he strode past him, recalling Stockdale's words. *So angry that not a man-jack would draw near.* He was angry now. Blazing. It was good, Tyrrell concluded. It might take his mind off the real danger.

A servant girl touched his arm. 'Beggin' yer pardon, sir, but there's a lady below in a poor way. Very feverish.'

Bolitho stopped and looked at them. 'Fetch the surgeon.'

He tensed as the other girl came towards him, her face suddenly grave.

'I am sorry I made you angry, Captain. It was unforgivable.'

'Angry?' Bolitho plucked at his swordbelt. 'I do not recollect . . .'

She touched his hand. 'Now that is beneath you, Captain. Unsure maybe, but never pompous. I see you quite differently.'

'When you have *quite* finished . . .'

Again she stopped him without even raising her voice. 'The other women were close on hysteria, Captain. One minute the storm was throwing us about like rag dolls, the very next instant there is the cry of mutiny and riot. Men fighting each other, for the drink and for what they might take from us when they were too crazed to know otherwise.' She dropped her eyes. 'It was horrible. Terrifying.' The eyes came up again and levelled on his face. They were the colour of violets. 'Then all at once there was a shout. Someone called, "A ship! A King's ship!", and we ran on deck despite the dangers.'

She turned to look across the bulwark. 'And there you were. Little *Sparrow*. It was almost too much for most of us. Had I not made that jest at your expense, I think some might have broken down.'

Bolitho's defence wavered. 'Er, yes. Quite so.' He toyed with his sword-hilt, seeing Dalkeith hurry past and giving him a curious glance as he went. 'You thought quickly, ma'am.'

'I know about some things, Captain. I saw your eyes when you spoke to your lieutenant and Sir James. There is worse to come, is there not?'

Bolitho shrugged. 'In truth I do not know.'

He heard the general shouting angrily at a seaman and said, 'That man is bad enough for me!'

She gave a mock curtsy, smiling again. 'Sir James? He can be difficult, I agree.'

'You know him?'

She moved back towards the other women. 'My uncle, Captain.' She laughed. 'Really you must try to hide your emotions better! Or else you will never be an admiral!'

Tyrrell came on deck and said, 'That woman in th' cabin is ill. But Dalkeith is managing well enough.' He frowned. 'Are you all right, sir?'

Bolitho rasped, 'In God's name stop asking me stupid questions!'

'Aye, sir.' He grinned, seeing the girl by the rail and far more beside. 'I understand, sir.'

There was a dull bang, and as they all turned Bolitho saw a puff of smoke drifting from one of *Sparrow*'s larboard batteries.

The general came panting up a ladder and shouted, 'What was that?'

Bolitho replied quietly, 'The signal, sir. My lookout has sighted the enemy.'

He ignored the general and those near him as his mind accepted the one important fact. In a way it was almost a relief to meet it. Recognize what must be done.

'Mr Tyrrell, *Bonaventure* will take several hours to show her intentions. By then it will be too dark for her captain to attack. Why should he? He merely has to await the dawn and then pounce.'

Tyrrell watched him, fascinated by his even tone.

Bolitho continued, 'If the wind does not act against us, we will be able to transfer the passengers to *Sparrow*. I want every boat working, and all who are neither sick nor injured to take fairly to their tasks.'

'I understand.' Tyrrell studied him impassively. 'There's nothing else you could do. Many would leave 'em to their own devices.'

Bolitho shook his head. 'You have *not* understood. I am not going to abandon the *Royal Anne* or scuttle her to avoid capture as a prize.' He saw Tyrrell's jaw tighten, the quick anxiety in his eyes. 'I intend to stay with her with sixty volunteers. What happens later will depend very much on *Bonaventure*'s captain.'

He had not noticed that the others had crowded round him, but turned as the general exclaimed, 'You cannot! You dare not risk this ship and cargo! I'll see you damned first!'

Silk rustled against Bolitho's arm and he heard the girl say calmly, 'Be still, Uncle. The captain intends to do more than dare.' She did not turn her face. 'He intends to *die* for us. Is that not enough, even for you?'

Bolitho nodded curtly and strode aft, hearing Stockdale's voice as he hurried to cover his retreat. He had to think. Plan every last moment until the actual second of death. He paused and leaned against the ornate taffrail. Death. Was it so soon upon him?

He turned angrily and said, 'Pass the word for those boats to begin loading immediately! Women and children, then the injured.' He glanced past the ship's mate and saw the girl staring after him. 'And no arguments from anyone!'

He walked to the opposite side and looked at his own command. How beautiful she was as she edged carefully across the Indiaman's quarter. Soon now he would be able to see the enemy's sails on the horizon. Closing, like the hunter, for his kill. There was so much to do. Orders for *Sparrow* to carry to Antigua. Perhaps even a quick letter to his father. But not just yet. He must stand quite still a little longer to watch his ship. Hold her in his memory before she was taken from him.

Bolitho was still staring across the water when Tyrrell came aft to report that all available boats were working, carrying the passengers and Indiaman's company over to the waiting sloop.

He added, 'She'll be a mite more crowded than when we rescued th' redcoats.' He hesitated and then said, 'I'd like to stay with you, sir.'

Bolitho did not look at him. 'You realize what you are saying? There is more at stake than your life.'

Tyrrell tried to grin. 'Hector Graves will make a better commander, sir.'

Bolitho faced him. 'You will be called on to fight some of your own people.'

Tyrrell smiled. 'I knew that was what you were thinking.' He gestured towards some of *Sparrow*'s seamen as they carried an elderly woman towards the boat tackles. 'These are my people. Then can I stay?'

Bolitho nodded. 'Gladly.' He removed his hat and ran his fingers through his hair. 'Now I'll go and write Graves's orders.'

'Deck there! Sail on th' larboard quarter!'

They looked at each other and then Bolitho said quietly. 'Hurry our people along. I do not want the enemy to see what we are about.'

As he strode away Tyrrell stared at him and then murmured, 'So be it, Cap'n.'

He heard a sudden cry and saw the girl who had made Bolitho angry struggling to push her way through a cordon of seamen.

A boatswain's mate bellowed, 'She don't want to go, sir!'

The girl punched the sailor's arm but he did not seem to feel it.

Then she shouted at Tyrrell, 'Let me stay! I want to be here!'

He grinned down at her and then pointed at the boat alongside. Kicking and protesting she was picked up bodily and carried to the rail, where with little ceremony she was passed down the side like a bright silk parcel.

The sky was much darker when Bolitho came on deck with a sealed envelope for the boat still hooked on to the chains. All other boats were hoisted, and the ship around him seemed very quiet and empty.

He raised a telescope and trained it over the quarter. The *Bonaventure* was visible now, some six miles distant. But she had already shortened sail, waiting, as he had expected, for the new day.

Tyrrell touched his hat. 'Our men are aboard, sir.' He gestured to the main deck where Midshipman Heyward was speaking to a petty officer. 'I picked 'em myself, but you could have had volunteers a'plenty.'

Bolitho handed the envelope to a seaman. 'Pass this to the boat.' To Tyrrell he added slowly, 'Go and take some rest. I shall think awhile.'

Later as Tyrrell lay in an abandoned cabin, the deck of which was littered with open chests and discarded clothing, he heard Bolitho's shoes on the planking overhead. Back and forth, up and down. Thinking. Eventually the sound of his pacing made Tyrrell's eyelids droop, and he fell into a dreamless sleep.

Bolitho stood straddle-legged on the *Royal Anne*'s poop, seeing his own shadow for the first time across the taffrail. How long the night had been, but at the hint of dawn everything seemed to begin at once, like the start of some ill-rehearsed drama. Away on the larboard quarter he saw the hardening pyramid of sails where the big privateer moved purposefully before the wind. Strangely, her hull was still lost in shadow, with only a bone of white around her stem to reveal her growing speed. About three miles distant. He turned his glass to the opposite quarter, to the little sloop. *Sparrow* was much closer, yet in spite of this seemed even smaller.

Tyrrell joined him and said, 'Th' wind seems steady enough, sir. Nor'-west by north, by my reckoning.' He was speaking in a hushed voice, as if afraid to disturb the ships and their deliberate preparations to fight.

Bolitho nodded. 'We will steer sou'-east. It is what the enemy will expect.'

He tore his eyes from the privateer and turned to look along the Indiaman's deck. The new foresail was drawing well, as were spanker and jib. The rest were little better than shreds, and to try to tack more than a point or so would be a waste of time.

Tyrrell sighed. 'I've checked th' guns myself. Loaded as ordered.' He scratched his stomach. 'Some of 'em look so old they'd split if we double-shotted 'em.'

Bolitho faced aft again to watch the other ships. Raising his glass he moved it slowly over *Sparrow*'s deck, seeing the figures on the gangways, a solitary seaman at her mainmast crosstrees. Then aft, as a freak gust lifted the foot of the maincourse like a miller's apron, he saw Graves. He was standing beside the wheel, arms folded, looking every inch a captain. Bolitho breathed out very slowly. So much depended on Graves. If he lost his head, or misinterpreted his carefully worded instructions, the enemy would still catch two for the price of one. But Graves had got the first part right. He was wearing Bolitho's new uniform, the gold lace showing clearly in spite of the feeble light. The enemy captain would be wary, watchful. Nothing must go wrong at the beginning. Heaven alone knew how all the extra passengers had been crammed below and out of sight. It would be like a sealed tomb, a nightmare for the women and children once the gunfire began.

Midshipman Heyward came to the poop and said, 'All our boarding party are ready, sir.' Like Bolitho and Tyrrell he had discarded his uniform and looked even younger in his open shirt and breeches.

'Thank you.' Bolitho noticed that instead of a midshipman's dirk Heyward had thought fit to wear one of his precious swords.

There was a bang, and he saw a ball ricocheting across the lively wave-crests before throwing up a quill of spray between him and the *Sparrow*'s bows. A sighting shot, a declaration of intent, probably both, he thought grimly.

Over the water, and audible above the rustle of torn canvas, he heard the staccato beat of drums, and pictured the scene aboard *Sparrow* as her men ran to quarters. Phase two. He saw the patch of scarlet as the ensign broke jauntily from her gaff, felt a catch in his throat as the ports opened to reveal her line of guns. With less than half a company available, Graves must have pressed some of the Indiamen's crew into service to get the guns out so smartly. But it had to look exactly right. As if the sloop was preparing to show defiance and trying to defend her heavy consort.

Another bang, and the ball ploughed into the sea about a cable clear of *Sparrow*'s stem.

Bolitho clenched his jaw. Graves was cutting it fine. If the wind chose this moment to veer he would be unable to go about, would be in irons if he tried to fall back and try again.

Tyrrell said hoarsely, 'There she goes!'

The sloop's yards were swinging and as her lee gangway dipped heavily into the swell she began to tack close-hauled to larboard, crossing *Royal Anne*'s stern like a small protective terrier. Flags broke from her yards, and Bolitho imagined Bethune yelling at his party to make haste and hoist the meaningless signal. The enemy would think *Sparrow* was preparing to fight to the death and was ordering the Indiaman to make a run for it.

Cannon fire ripped along the *Bonaventure*'s foremost battery and more splashes leapt closer to the heeling sloop. Graves was shortening sail, clearing away the hampering canvas from his guns, even though it was unlikely he had more than a quarter of them manned.

Tyrrell spoke between his teeth. 'That's close enough, Hector! For God's sake don't make a meal of it!'

One heavy bang rolled across the shark-blue water, and even though the flash was hidden by *Sparrow*'s hull, Bolitho knew it was one of her bow-chasers. He saw the ball slap hard into the spray by the other ship's forecastle, the immediate spurt of orange tongues as she fired back in earnest.

The *Sparrow*'s foretopgallant mast quivered and then seemed to curtsy downwards into the swirling brown smoke, the furled sail marking its progress as it caught and swung in the criss-cross of rigging before plunging into the sea alongside. Holes appeared in several of her sails, and Bolitho caught his breath as the hammock nettings below the quarterdeck bucked and burst apart from a direct hit.

The enemy was much nearer now, her foretopsail bulging as she stood before the wind, charging down on the sloop which was now less than two cables from her starboard bow.

Tyrrell exclaimed, 'He's done it! Blast th' man, he's going about!'

The *Sparrow* was wearing, her masts swinging upright as she came round violently, the growing light making her sails shine as they flapped and puckered to the strain.

The gunfire had stopped, for with her stern towards the enemy *Sparrow* presented no target at all. Her forecourse was already being unleashed, and as she gathered way through the water Bolitho saw the topmen running out along the yards like black insects until more and still more canvas bellied to the wind. He could see Buckle by the quarterdeck rail, too intent on his work even to watch the labouring Indiaman as she surged past. *Sparrow* was abeam, and then in minutes was well beyond the Indiaman's bows, heading towards the first rays of sunlight from the placid horizon.

Bolitho felt suddenly dry, his limbs very loose, as if belonging to someone else. He watched the *Bonaventure*'s forecourse being brailed up to reveal her great span of poop, the men on her gangways who were waving and gesturing after the retreating sloop. Jeering no doubt. All the madness of intended battle now lost in the confused actions of an unfought victory.

Bolitho walked to the rail and said quietly, 'Remember, Mr Tyrrell, and remember it well. We have to cripple her if we can. Then if a patrolling frigate finds her she can finish what we started.' He gripped his wrist. 'But make sure our people play their parts. If *Bonaventure* hauls off now, she can pound us to pieces without losing a breath!'

The privateer had edged closer, running down towards the quarter so that she would eventually overhaul *Royal Anne* along her larboard side. Her captain was a superb seaman. With all but his topsails clewed up he was handling the heavy vessel with both confidence and skill, and would certainly hold the wind-gage no matter what Bolitho tried to do.

A gun flashed out its long tongue, and Bolitho felt the ball smack into the lower hull, jerking the planks at his feet with savage violence.

He saw bunched figures in the other ship's poop, the wink of sunlight on raised telescopes, and guessed they were examining their victim. It looked much as it had when he had come aboard. Damaged bulwarks and broken rigging. One hatch had been purposefully left open, and several of his men were running about in apparent confusion while Heyward directed their performance from beneath the forecastle.

'Now!' Bolitho waved his hand, and from the main deck one then another of the six-pounders hurled its challenge across the narrowing strip of water.

From aft a swivel banged sharply, the canister probably falling harmlessly long before it reached the enemy's side.

The response was immediate. Gun by gun, the *Bonaventure*'s broadside sent ball after ball crashing into the hull. Bolitho was thankful he had sent most of his men below, otherwise they would have been cut down by the fierceness of the onslaught. Timber and planks flew in all directions, and he saw a seaman hurled like a bloody rag to the opposite side, his limbs kicking as he died.

Stockdale looked at Bolitho and saw him nod. With a grunt he dashed along the deck waving a cutlass, while Bolitho drew his pistol and yelled after him. When Stockdale ran on towards the halliards he fired, praying that his hand was steady as the shot whined clear above the coxswain's head. Stockdale reached his goal, and with one slash severed the halliards, bringing the big Company flag tumbling down like some bright shroud across the weather rail.

In a lull of noise and gunfire Bolitho heard a voice across the water, magnified and unreal in a speaking trumpet.

'Heave to or I'll sink you!'

From forward he heard Heyward urging his men to obey the call, the sudden groan of timber as the ship lurched drunkenly into the wind, her remaining sails flapping and banging in disorder.

Tyrrell said, 'He's going to grapple!'

There were men on the *Bonaventure*'s yards, and as the big hull surged carefully and then more insistently against the side Bolitho saw grapnels flying from a dozen points at once. The men on the yards were busily making fast their lines to *Royal Anne*'s shrouds and spars, so that as both ships drifted and swayed together Bolitho knew the moment to act had arrived.

'Now! Boarders away!'

With a wild chorus of yells the hidden seamen surged up from both hatches and on to the bulwarks, their cutlasses and boarding pikes marking down several enemy hands before they realized what was happening. Moments, seconds earlier, they had seen *Royal Anne* as one more helpless prize, a ship which had struck them, her flag hacked down by one of her own crew. Then, as if from nowhere, the bulk of Bolitho's seamen came surging up and over the side, their steel bright in the sun, their voices hoarse and wild with the madness of combat.

Bolitho ran to the rail and jerked the lanyard of another swivel, seeing the packed canister scything through a bunch of men on *Bonaventure*'s gangway and blasting them aside in its murderous hail.

Then he was running with the second party and pulling himself on to the shrouds, slashing with his sword at a man's arm on the chains below. Screams and curses, the bang of pistols and rasp of steel, he was dazed by the noise. A man plummeted past him to be held like a tortured animal between the two grinding hulls, his blood running pink in the leaping feathers of foam.

He was on the enemy's deck, his arm jarring as he struck down a man's guard and drove the hilt against his jaw, throwing him back into the struggling figures beyond. Another charged forward with a levelled bayonet, slipped on a smear of blood and took Stockdale's blade across his neck. It sounded like an axe biting into a log.

He yelled wildly, 'Cut the rigging, lads! Cripple the bastard!'

He felt a ball fan hotly past his face, and ducked as another smacked into a seaman's chest right beside him, his cry lost in the other din of battle.

Now he was on a ladder, shoes sliding in blood, his fingers feeling up a rail, conscious of the torn wood where one of the swivels had made its mark. Two officers were parrying aside pikes and swords as they tried to rally their men from the opposite side. Bolitho saw one of them drive his sword into a boatswain's mate, saw the eyes roll with agony as he pitched to the deck below, then he was up and facing the privateer's officer, their swords clashing as they struck and explored their strength and weakness.

'Damn you!' The man ducked and thrust up at Bolitho's throat. 'Strike while you are still alive, you mad bugger!'

Bolitho caught the blade across his basket hilt and levered the man clear, feeling the warmth of his body, the fierceness of his breathing.

He yelled back, 'Strike be damned!'

A pistol exploded and the officer dropped his arm, staring blankly at the blood which pumped through his shirt in a bright red stain.

Tyrrell strode past and fired a second pistol into the man's chest. When he turned Bolitho saw that Tyrrell's face was like stone.

He shouted, 'I knew that bastard, Cap'n! A bloody slaver afore th' war!'

Then with a gasp he dropped on one knee, blood running from his thigh. Bolitho dragged him aside, cutting down a screaming seaman and thrusting the blade through his chest in two swift movements.

'*Easy!*'

He stared desperately above the nearest men. Much of the enemy's rigging had been slashed, but the attack had made little impression after all. And his men were falling back around him, the lust to fight and win dwindling to match their numbers.

On every hand, or so it appeared, muskets and pistols were firing down into the retreating English seamen, and he saw Heyward standing astride a wounded man and screaming like a madman as he fought off two attackers at once.

As if from a great distance he saw the American captain watching from his poop, a tall, handsome man who was standing quite motionless, either so confident in his men's efforts or so appalled by his attackers' sacrifice that he was unable to tear his eyes away.

Bolitho hacked a cutlass aside and sobbed aloud as his blade broke within inches of the hilt. He hurled the remains at the man's head and saw him fall kicking, impaled on a pike. In a half daze he recalled the glib trader at English Harbour who had sold him the sword. He would not get his money now, damn his eyes.

To Stockdale he croaked, 'You know what to do!' He had to push him away, and even as he ran from the fighting he was still peering back, his eyes filled with anxiety.

Then there was the distorted voice again, and when he looked up he saw the American captain using his trumpet.

'Strike now! You have done more than enough! Strike or die!'

Bolitho swung round, his heart bursting, his mind sick as he saw a young seaman fall to the deck, his face opened by a cutlass from ear to chin.

Tyrrell was struggling on his injured knee and pointing wildly, 'Look! Stockdale's done it!'

From the main hatch on the Indiaman's deck came a growing plume of dark smoke, spreading and thickening until it seemed to spurt up through the seams like steam under pressure.

Bolitho yelled, 'Fall back, lads! *Back!*'

Then they were limping and staggering across the bulwarks, dragging their wounded, carrying others too crippled to move. There were not many of them, wounded or otherwise.

Bolitho wiped his streaming eyes, hearing Tyrrell gasp with agony as he half carried, half dragged him to the opposite bulwark. Behind him he could hear frenzied shouts, the sudden click of steel as the *Bonaventure*'s men tried to cut away the lashings which they themselves had so skilfully used to hold both ships together. But it was too late. It had been from the instant Stockdale had begun the last and most dangerous act. A short fuse, and then the fire had burst amongst the cargo of rum and the massive barrels of spirits, spreading through the hull at a terrible rate.

Flames licked out of open ports and ran along the *Bonaventure*'s tarred rigging like angry tongues, sails vanished into ashes, and then with a bellow one great sheet of flame leapt between the two hulls, joining them finally in a single pyre.

Bolitho peered down at the one remaining boat tethered to the ship's quarter, riding where it had been since taking his orders across to Graves.

'Abandon ship, lads!'

Some clambered down, while others fell headlong, splashing and yelling until they were helped inboard by their companions. Blazing canvas, ashes and gusts of sparks rained across their heads, but as a seaman severed the bow rope and they groped half blinded for the oars Bolitho heard another great explosion, as if from the sea itself.

The Indiaman began to settle down immediately, her masts and spars interlocking with her attacker's to throw flames and sparks hundreds of feet into the air.

He watched his small handful of fit men pulling at the oars, feeling the heat searing his back as he steered the boat away from the blazing ships. Exploding powder and toppling masts, a ship's hold splitting wide open in an inferno of noise and shooting flames, and later the engulfing sounds of inrushing water. He heard it all, even pictured the general's gold bullion, which someone might discover one day on the sea bottom.

But it was all beyond him now. They had done the impossible. *Miranda* was avenged.

He looked sadly at his men, at their faces which now meant so much to him. At young Heyward, filthy and exhausted, a wounded seaman propped across his lap. Tyrrell, a bloody bandage around his thigh, eyes closed with pain, but holding back his head as if to seek the first yellow bars of warmth from the sun. And Stockdale, who was everywhere. Bandaging and bailing, lending weight to an oar, or helping to heave a dead man over the gunwale. He was tireless. Indestructible.

He held out his hand and studied it. It was quite steady, even though every nerve and muscle seemed to be quivering. He glanced at his empty scabbard and gave a rueful smile. No matter. Nothing mattered now.

How long they pulled the oars, the time it took for the two blazing hulks finally to sink, Bolitho did not remember. The sun beat down on their aching, exhausted limbs, the stroke became slower and more hesitant. Once, when Bolitho peered astern he saw the sea's face covered by a great spread of drifting remains from the ships and the men who had fought across them. But the privateer had managed to launch at least one boat, and before it was blotted out in haze he saw it was crammed with survivors. Perhaps, they, too, would know the same despair as *Miranda*'s men.

Then a shadow fitted across his face and he stared round, caught off guard as *Sparrow*'s topsails flashed gaily across the sun's path.

The men in the boat watched silently, unable to speak even to each other. Unable yet to realize they had survived.

Bolitho stood by the tiller, his eyes stinging as he watched her careful approach, the lines of heads along her decks and gangways. She had come for him. Despite the danger, the unlikelihood of his plan succeeding, she had returned to make sure.

Across the water a voice hailed, 'Boat ahoy?'

It sounded like Buckle, anxious maybe to know who had survived.

Stockdale looked at him, his battered face questioning. When Bolitho said nothing he stood up and cupped his big hands.

'*Sparrow*! Stand by for th' captain!'

Bolitho sank down, the last reserve draining from him. He was back.

Part Two
1781

10

Sea Change

Captain Richard Bolitho stared at the partly written letter he had been composing to his father, and then with a sigh carried his chair to the opposite end of the table. It was stiflingly hot, and as the *Sparrow* idled sluggishly on a flat calm she swung her stern very slightly allowing the hard sunlight to reach him and require him to move still further away from the windows.

Becalmed. How used he had grown to this situation. He rubbed his eyes and held his pen above the paper again. It was difficult to know what to write, especially as he never knew when this or any letter might find its way aboard a home-bound vessel. It was harder still to feel involved with that other world in England which he had left in *Trojan* nearly six years back. And yet . . . the pen hovered uncertainly, his own world, so close and so vital in colour and smell in the bright sunlight, and that word *becalmed* would still be too painful, too harsh a reminder for his father of the Navy which he had been forced to leave.

But Bolitho wanted to tell him so desperately, put his thoughts and memories into perspective, to share his own life and thereby fill the one remaining gap in it.

Overhead, blocks clattered and feet thudded on the quarterdeck. Someone laughed, and he heard a faint splash as one of the hands cast a fishing line outboard to try his luck.

His eyes moved from the letter to his open log which lay across the chart nearby. The log had changed as much as himself. Worn around the edges, matured perhaps. He stared at the date on the open page. April 10th 1781. Three years, almost to the day, since he had first stepped aboard this ship in English Harbour to assume command. Without moving it was possible to glance back through the bulky log book, and even though he did not even touch a page he could recall so many of the things which had happened, faces and events, the demands made upon him and his varying successes in dealing with them.

Often, during moments of quiet in the cabin, he had tried to fathom out some set thread in his life beyond the narrower explanations of luck or circumstance. So far it had defied him. And now as he sat in the familiar cabin where so much had happened he could accept that fate had had much to do with his being here. If, when he had left the *Trojan* he had failed to take a prize *en route* for Antigua, or upon arrival there had been no opportunity for immediate promotion, he might still be a lieutenant in the old ship-of-the-line. And on that very first convoy, if Colquhoun had sent him back to English Harbour instead of going himself, would he have ever succeeded in proving to be more than average in either skill or luck?

Perhaps Colquhoun's fateful decision on that far-off day had been the chance, the offering which had set his feet on the final path.

Bolitho had returned to Antigua not merely as just one more officer rejoining his rightful squadron, but, to his astonishment, as some sort of hero. In his absence the stories of his rescuing the soldiers from Delaware Bay, his running a frigate aground, had been well spread. Then, with the news of *Bonaventure*'s end and his arrival with the rescued passengers, it seemed that every man wanted to see him and shake his hand.

The *Bonaventure* had been even more deadly than Bolitho had realized at the time, and her successes formidable. Her loss to the enemy might mean little, but to the British it was a tremendous lift to their battered pride and morale.

The admiral had received him in Antigua with controlled pleasure, and had made no bones about his hopes for the future. Colquhoun, on the other hand, had been the one man to offer Bolitho neither encouragement nor praise for his achievements in so short a time.

Whenever Bolitho recalled their first meeting, Colquhoun's warnings about the lot of any sea captain, he was reminded of the thinness of margin between fame and oblivion. Had Colquhoun stayed with that first convoy it was unlikely he would have shared *Miranda*'s fate, for he was too shrewd and cautious to take anything for granted. Had he been lucky enough to meet and destroy *Bonaventure* he would have gained the one thing he cared about, just as Commander Maulby had suggested, the unshakable power of flag rank, or at very least the coveted broad-pendant of commodore. Instead he had stayed where he was, frigate captain, and, with the war changing so rapidly, now likely to lose even control of the small flotilla. Maulby no longer called him *little admiral*. Today it seemed too cruel, too unjust even for him.

Eight bells chimed out from the forecastle, and without effort he pictured the hands preparing for the midday meal, the welcome ration of rum. Above his head Tyrrell and the master would be taking their noon sights, comparing their findings before bringing them down to the chart.

The year after Bolitho's destruction of the big privateer he had received his next surprise. The admiral had sent for him and had calmly announced that their lordships of Admiralty, like himself, believed in offering *Sparrow*'s commander a chance of exploiting his experience and skill. Promotion to full captain. Even now, after eighteen months of it, he found it hard to accept and believe.

Within the flotilla the unexpected rise up the ladder had caused a great stir. Genuine pleasure from some, open resentment from others. Maulby had taken the news better than Bolitho had dared to hope, for he had come to like the *Fawn*'s laconic commander too much to have their friendship broken. Maulby was senior to him, but had merely remarked, 'I'd like to see the rank go to no other man, so let's drink to it!'

Aboard *Sparrow* the news had had no division at all. They all seemed to share the same pride, the same sense of achievement, which could not have come at a better time for them. For the war had changed greatly even in the past year. No longer was it a matter of patrol or convoy for the army. The great powers had taken their stand, and Spain and Holland had joined France against England in their support of the American Revolution. The French had mustered a well-matched and powerful fleet in the West Indies under the Comte de Grasse, the most effective and talented admiral available. Admiral Rodney commanded the British squadrons, but with the pressures mounting daily he was hard put to spread the resources where they were most needed.

And the Americans were not content to leave affairs to their seasoned allies. They continued to use privateers whenever possible, and a year after *Bonaventure*'s destruction yet another challenger emerged to shake British morale to its foundation. The privateer and ex-slaver Paul Jones, in his *Bonhomme Richard*, defeated the frigate *Seraphis* off the coast of England itself. The fact that the privateer, like the *Seraphis*, was reduced to a battered wreck in the hotly contested battle made no difference. British captains were expected to take on odds and win, and the defeat so close to home did more than many Americans believed possible to take the war and its reasons into English homes as well as their own.

In the West Indies and along the American coast the work of patrolling took on new importance. As Bolitho had always thought, it was far better for the eyes of the fleet to be left unhampered by close authority. True to his word, the admiral had offered him almost total independence, and had given him scope to patrol and seek out the enemy in his own way, provided, of course, his efforts were rewarded with some success.

Bolitho leaned back in his chair and stared at the deckhead. Again the word luck seemed to hover in his mind.

Maulby had scoffed at the explanation. He had once said, 'You are successful because you have trained yourself to think like the enemy!

God damn it, Dick, I caught a lugger loaded with contraband which had come from as far south as Trinidad, and even that wretched fellow had heard of you and *Sparrow*!'

It was certainly true about one thing, Bolitho decided, they had been successful. In the past eighteen months alone they had taken twelve prizes and despatched two small privateers with the loss of twenty killed and wounded and very little damage to the ship.

He let his eyes wander round the cabin, less elegantly painted now, even shabby after ceaseless service in all weathers. It was strange to realize that apart from the unexpected promotion, symbolized by the dress coat with white lapels and bright gold facings which swung gently inside the sleeping compartment, there was outwardly little to show for it. And yet he was a rich man, and, for the first time in his life, independent of the home and estate in Falmouth. He smiled ruefully. It seemed almost shameful to become moderately wealthy merely because he was doing the one thing he enjoyed.

He frowned, trying to think of something to purchase if and when they were allowed a stay in port. And they were well overdue for that. Despite her coppered hull, *Sparrow*'s speed had been reduced by a full knot in otherwise perfect sailing conditions by long clinging weed which defied the copper and their efforts to move it. He would buy some wine perhaps. Good wine, not the bitter-tasting muck which was normally used as the only alternative for foul drinking water. A dozen shirts or more. His mind played with the idea of such luxury. At the present moment he had only two shirts which would bear close inspection.

It might be possible to find a good sword somewhere. Not like the one which had shattered aboard the privateer, nor the curved hanger which he had used since, but something better. Lasting.

He heard footsteps beyond the door and knew it was Tyrrell. He would have known it even if it had been another time, a different watch. For since being wounded Tyrrell had been unable to rid himself of a limp and not a little pain.

The first lieutenant had otherwise not changed very much, he thought. Or maybe the three years had drawn them so close he had not noticed it. Unlike Graves, who seemed to have withdrawn even further and had grown noticeably more nervous after each action or skirmish. Upon his promotion to captain, Bolitho had become entitled to an extra lieutenant, and the appointment fell vacant on the very day the two midshipmen went aboard the flagship to sit for their commissions. Heyward had passed with flying colours, and now, looking back, it was hard to recall him as a midshipman at all. Bethune had unfortunately failed his exams, not once, but three times, and Bolitho repeatedly wondered how best to get rid of him. He had grown very fond of

Bethune, but knew that being retained in *Sparrow*'s confined community was only acting against his remaining, if dwindling, chances. His navigation was hopeless, his ability to take charge of the quarter-deck and set the hands to making or shortening sail was dismal to behold. As a marine officer, or even a foot soldier, he would have been adequate. He could obey orders, even if he found them hard to formulate. Under fire he had shown plenty of courage, and a boyish stoicism which was rarely matched even by a seasoned sailor. Now, aged twenty, and with no hope of gaining the commission he so obviously desired, he stood out like a sore thumb. Heyward had tried to help him, more so than Bolitho had imagined he would. But it was no use. The ship's company treated him with cheerful acceptance, as they would a child. His burden had not been eased by the appointment of a new midshipman to take Heyward's place.

Roger Augustus Fowler, sixteen years of age, and with the pouting features of a petulant pig, had soon learned to add to rather than detract from Bethune's misery.

Fowler's arrival had further enlarged the rift between Bolitho and Colquhoun. The boy was the son of the admiral's best friend, and so his appointment to this or any ship was very close to a royal command. The offspring of some influential person could be a great handicap to a young and busy captain, but equally he could open doors otherwise denied by the chain of command. Colquhoun had probably seen the boy's arrival from England as an opportunity in the latter category, and had been outraged when the admiral had chosen *Sparrow* rather than his frigate *Bacchante*.

Fowler had been aboard for eight months and was not popular. It was nothing you could put a name to. Obedient and attentive in the presence of his superiors, he could be equally sharp and sarcastic with seamen old enough to be his father. He had a way of shutting off his expression, using his pale eyes and pouting lips like the extensions of a mask. If he ever reached command rank he would be a tyrant to serve, Bolitho thought.

There was a tap at the door and Bolitho swept his musings into the background.

Tyrrell limped into the cabin and sat down at the table. Against his open shirt his skin was burned almost to mahogany, and his hair had become a shade lighter under forgotten suns. He pushed the calculations across the chart and together they looked at *Sparrow*'s approximate position.

To the south lay the nearest extensions of the Bahama Islands, the countless spans of cays and reefs, treacherous sandbars and islets. Some eighty miles to the west lay the coast of Florida, and to the east the main routes used by ships going to and from the Indies and New York. It

was a veritable warren of islands and narrow channels, although to the
untried eve of a landsman the sea might appear at peace, broken here
and there by restful purple humps of land shrouded in low haze. But to
the mariner the chart showed much more, and that was less than he
required to know the true margin of safety. The occasional dab of white
betrayed a reef, the duller patch on the sea's face might represent a cloak
of weed across some vast pinnacle lurking beneath the surface, the
spines of which could tear the keel from a ship like the string from an
orange.

Tyrrell said at length, 'I reckon we've lost th' bugger.'

'Maybe.' Bolitho opened a drawer in the table and took out two long
clay pipes. Handing one to Tyrrell he groped for a tobacco bowl and
then said, 'Is *Fawn* still in sight?'

Tyrrell grinned. 'Sure enough. 'Bout three miles to th' east'rd.' He
tamped down the tobacco in his pipe and added, 'Our masthead
lookout thought he saw breakers to th' sou'-west. If so, that would be
the Mantanilla Shoal, which fixes our calculations, so to speak.'

Bolitho lit his pipe from the hanging smoking-lantern and then
walked restlessly to the windows. Once near the sill he felt the slow
breeze across his face and chest like air fanned from a blacksmith's
forge. When eventually the wind returned to give life to the sails it was
to be hoped it came from the south-east as before. It was no time to be
driven closer to those deadly shoals. But they had to stay near enough to
be able to watch at least three channels while *Fawn* patrolled further to
the east. For six weeks, in company with the other sloop, they had been
searching for a big blockade runner, a French *flute* which had been
reported out of Martinique and heading north, most likely for the
enemy base of naval operations in Newport, Rhode Island. The
information from spies, or those merely after recognition or reward,
was always open to doubt. But a *flute*, which was a large man-of-war
with some of her armament removed to facilitate the fast passage of
men or stores, was too important to be ignored.

The flotilla's third sloop, *Heron*, was sweeping somewhere to the
south, off the Andros Islands, and Colquhoun's *Bacchante* had, as far as
he knew, remained in more open waters to the west, between the
Bahamas and the American mainland.

Once away from Colquhoun's supervision, Bolitho had taken the
sloops to their present position. On the chart the chance of making contact
with a solitary enemy seemed impossible, but he knew by now that if the
sea appeared empty, it was in fact divided into channels by sprawling reefs
and cays, and was just as much a hazard to enemy as to friend.

'If we take her, it'll be another feather for us.' Tyrrell watched his
pipe-smoke drifting through the skylight above him. 'I often wonder if it
makes all that difference to th' war.'

'It *all* helps, Jethro.'

Bolitho studied him gravely. How close they had become. Like the use of first names, the ritual pipe-smoking for as long as the tobacco stock lasted, it all seemed to symbolize what the ship had made them.

Time and distance, hours and days spent in every sort of condition, they had all left their mark on *Sparrow*'s company. Even the necessary changes brought about by death and injury, transfer and discharge had seemed unable to break the little ship's hold on their destiny. Over a third of the company were replacements made since he had taken command, and apart from colonists, included a sprinkling of Negroes, some merchant seamen pressed from a home-bound ship, and a solitary Greek who had deserted his own vessel only to be taken aboard a French brig as captive. The brig, seized as a prize by *Sparrow*, had yielded several new hands, and the Greek had proved to be an excellent assistant cook.

'How long will you give her?'

Bolitho considered the question. 'Another week maybe. If she doesn't show herself, I think we can assume she's slipped past us, or turned back somewhere. She might have run into one of the patrols further south.'

'Aye.' Tyrrell yawned. 'An' then *we* can get some time in port.'

Feet pounded overhead and they heard Buckle shout, 'Call all hands! Th' wind's a'coming back!'

Then there was a rap on the door and Bethune peered in at them, his round face sweating badly.

'Mr Buckle's respects, sir. The wind is freshening from the sou'-east. *Fawn*'s tops'ls are already filling.'

'I'll come up.' Bolitho waited until the midshipman had withdrawn before asking quietly, 'What am I to do about him?'

Tyrrell shrugged. 'He'll not get promoted unless by a miracle. Maybe if we put him in charge of our next prize?' He shook his head before Bolitho could comment. 'Almighty God, the lad'd lose his way *an*' th' prize!'

On deck they found the hands already being mustered while overhead the sails were stirring uneasily, the masthead pendant lifting as the first breeze reached it.

'Man th'braces!' Tyrrell strode to the rail and squinted into the glare. 'It'll be up to us soon, lads.'

Bolitho shaded his eyes to stare at the other sloop as her sails suddenly filled and brought her round in a slow pirouette. Across the sea's glittering face he saw the first ruffle of wind, then felt the sun-dried planking lift under his shoes, the immediate response of blocks and halliards.

The *Sparrow*'s decks were like tinder and it made no difference how many times they were doused down. Paintwork was blistered by the

heat, and as he turned to watch the busy seamen he realized it was hard
to tell the Negroes from his original company. Lean and sun-dried
maybe, he thought, but they looked healthy and bright-eyed, ready for
anything.

Tyrrell called, 'Shall I have th' larboard cutter towed astern now, sir?'

Bolitho nodded. Only by towing them alternately could they hope to
keep them from drying out and opening their seams. Even half-filling
them with water on board seemed to have small effect.

'Yes. Tell Mr Tilby to . . .' He checked himself and added, 'Pass the
word to the boatswain, if you please.'

After six months, it was still difficult not to speak his name, or expect
to see his sweating features peering aft at the quarterdeck.

They had run down a Spanish schooner off the Great Bahama Bank,
but had been forced to fire on her when she refused to yield. Then, with
grapnels flying like snakes, *Sparrow* had surged alongside in the manner
so well practised that it was accepted without comment even by the new
men. A few pistol shots, the sight of the half-naked boarders with drawn
cutlasses had been enough to quench the Spaniard's resistance and it
was all over almost before it had begun. Sometime in the middle of it,
while men had dashed to shorten sail and prepare for boarding, as
Bolitho had waved his arm to signal the Spanish master to strike and
avoid bloodshed, Tilby had died.

Not in the heat and terror of close action or under an enemy
broadside, but quietly and without fuss while he had stood at the foot of
the foremast, his favourite place where he usually kept an eye on the
workings of his ship. Dalkeith had examined him and reported that the
boatswain's heart had given out, like a clock which had run its course
and could take no more.

His death made a deep impression on everyone who had known him.
To die in such a way was unthinkable. Tilby, who had survived battles
at sea and countless drunken brawls in taverns the world over, had gone
without a man seeing his passing.

When Tyrrell had collected his possessions Bolitho had been
dismayed to see that there was hardly anything to barter amongst the
company and thereby raise money for dependants he might have in
England. Two small wood carvings of ships he had once served, and one
of them was broken, a collection of foreign coins, and his silver call
which had been presented to him by no less a person than Captain
Oliver of the *Menelaus* where he had served as a boatswain's mate.
Poor Tilby, he had not even learned to write his own name, and his
language was limited to the profane for much of the time. But he knew
ships, and he knew *Sparrow* like his own body.

Harry Glass, the senior boatswain's mate, had been promoted in his
place, but like most of the others seemed unable to accept that he was

now independent of Tilby's booming voice and ever-vigilant eye.

As he watched the cutter rising from its chocks on the gundeck Bolitho wondered if indeed Tilby had anyone ashore to grieve for him. He touched the sun-heated taffrail and shuddered. He was captain now, the realization of a dream which had been with him since he could remember. If the war suddenly ended, or other circumstances forced him to leave the Navy, he would drop from his present foothold like a falling stone. Not being confirmed to post-rank, he would end up as a mere lieutenant on half-pay, and all this would just be a mocking memory. But how much worse for those like Tilby. He ran his eyes quickly across the men nearest to him as they worked at the braces to set *Sparrow* before the wind again. They had nothing. A little prize money if they were fortunate, some bounty maybe from a charitable captain, otherwise they would be thrown on the beach less able to face the demands of the outside world than when they had volunteered or been pressed into service. It was unjust. Worse, it was dishonourable to treat men so shabbily, when without their sacrifice and courage their country would have fallen to an enemy years ago.

He began to pace the deck, his chin sunk on his chest. Perhaps one day they could change it. Make the Navy a Service where men from all walks of life would be as glad as he was to serve in reasonable security.

'Deck thar! Breakers on the larboard bow!'

He came out of his thoughts and said, 'Bring her round two points, Mr Buckle. We will give those reefs a wide berth until we are clear.'

'Aye, sir.'

He turned his attention to the other sloop, noting that Maulby had managed to repaint his hull in spite of the heat. *Fawn* was exactly the same colour as *Sparrow,* and to any uncertain eye would appear a twin. It was another part of Bolitho's hard-won experience. When sailing separately, the fact they looked so similar helped to keep the enemy or his spies guessing. Like the flag locker, which he had stocked with almost every foreign flag in the book. Deception and surprise had been the enemy's game. Bolitho was reaping the benefit of their past success and turning the tables against them.

'West nor'-west, sir! Steady as she goes!'

'Very well.' He glanced at the compass and at the set of the main topsails. 'Not much of a wind, Mr Buckle, but it suffices for the present.'

All afternoon and into early evening the two sloops continued on the same tack, with the wind showing no sign of changing in strength or bearing.

The first dog watch was just drawing to a close and Bolitho was making another attempt to complete his letter when a sail was reported to the south-west. Signalling *Fawn* to remain in company, Bolitho altered course to investigate, but as the newcomer showed no sign of running he guessed it was a friendly ship. The masthead soon confirmed that she was in fact the flotilla's little schooner *Lucifer*, a vessel kept as busy if not busier than any of them, carrying despatches and poking into coves and bays where even sloops found little room to move in safety.

In the dull bronze sunlight she made a pretty sight, with her big fore-and-aft sails spread like wings across her narrow hull as she tacked towards the sloops, her signal flags soaring aloft to break in brightly coloured squares.

Bethune called, '*Have despatches on board*, sir!'

Bolitho looked at Tyrrell. 'Heave to, if you please.' To Bethune he added, 'Make to *Fawn*, *Remain in close company*.' He crossed to the rail as Tyrrell lowered his speaking trumpet. 'You can never be sure. She might have good news for us.'

Tyrrell gripped the rail, grimacing with pain as, with sails slapping fussily, *Sparrow* came up into the wind.

'Damn this leg!' In a calmer tone he said, 'Good or bad it's grand to see a friend. I was beginning to think we had th' bloody sea to ourselves.'

A jolly-boat was already on its way, and Bolitho saw that Lieutenant Odell, the schooner's captain, was coming in person, and felt a sudden twinge of hopeful excitement.

Odell clambered up the side and doffed his hat to the quarterdeck. He was a quick, darting young man, and was said to be slightly mad. But he seemed calm enough, and when he reached the cabin handed Bolitho his bulky envelope before saying, 'I have just come from Captain Colquhoun.' He took a glass of wine from Fitch and stared at it. 'He is much excited.'

Bolitho slit open the envelope and ran his eyes quickly over the scrawling hand of Colquhoun's personal clerk.

Tyrrell stood just inside the door, and Bolitho was well aware of Buckle's shadow across the skylight above the table. Not actually eavesdropping, but if he happened to hear anything, well . . .

He looked up and said, 'Captain Colquhoun took a fishing boat and questioned the crew.' He flattened the damp paper on the table. 'That was a week ago.'

Odell held the empty glass in front of him and waited until Fitch had refilled it before saying dryly, 'Actually, I caught the boat, sir,' he shrugged disdainfully, 'but the good Captain Colquhoun seemed to take over, as it were.'

Bolitho eyed him gravely. 'It also states here that the crew provided valuable information about the Frenchman.' He beckoned to Tyrrell and pushed the unfinished letter from his chart. 'The *flute* was sighted here, close inshore,' his finger rested on the western end of Grand

Bahama Island, 'right amongst the islets. She was carrying out repairs, according to the fishermen.'

Tyrrell nodded slowly. 'It sounds likely. If th' Frenchman knew a hunt was mounted, he would take th' most hazardous passage amongst th' islands to throw us off. It don't signify he's still there of course.'

Bolitho nodded. 'A week back. Allow another few days before that for the fishing boat to reach the place where *Lucifer* sighted her.' He snatched up his dividers and bent over the chart. 'Thirty leagues from our present position. We could be off the island by noon tomorrow if the wind holds.'

Odell said wearily, 'But I understand that Captain Colquhoun wishes you to flush her out and nothing more, sir?' He smiled. 'Or did I not comprehend the good captain's desires?'

Bolitho sat down and opened the despatches again. '*Bacchante* is to approach by the North West Providence Channel, while we remain to north'rd and harry the Frenchman if he tries to run for it.'

Odell nodded, satisfied. '*Bacchante* can be barely twenty miles from her attacking position by now, sir. I am to find her again and report that I have met you and that you *understand* the instructions.'

Bolitho glanced at him quickly. 'Thank you. I do understand.'

The lieutenant stood up and reached for his hat. 'Then I will return to my ship. I have no wish to be caught in these waters after dark.'

Together they watched the lieutenant being rowed back to his schooner.

Then Tyrrell said heavily, 'Seems clear enough to me. Cap'n Colquhoun is set on taking th' Frog as a prize, all to himself, while we just act as beaters.'

'There is something which bothers me far more.' Bolitho rubbed his chin. 'The fishing boat was a small one, according to the despatches. Too frail to be out in deep water where she might *expect* to find *Bacchante* or some other frigate. It was a mere fluke that she met with *Lucifer*, for as we know, Jethro, schooners in the King's service are rare out here.'

Tyrrell's eyes glistened in the dying sunlight. 'You mean that th' fishermen were looking for *another* ship?'

Bolitho met his gaze. 'Aye.'

'But there's only us an' the *Fawn* between here an' th' inshore squadron, an' their nearest patrol must be four hundred miles away.'

'Exactly.' Bolitho stared astern at the other sloop, her topsails already painted in deepening shadows. 'And who would know that better than some island fisherman, eh?'

Tyrrell breathed out slowly. 'Hell, you're saying *we* was meant to get the information, but once Colquhoun got his hands on 'em they acted for their own safety.'

'I don't know.' Bolitho walked to the nettings and back to the compass, seeing neither. 'But *Fawn*'s captain said something to me a while ago. That our exploits were getting well known, which is another way of saying they have been hurting the enemy.'

Tyrrell nodded. 'A trap. Is it likely?' He waved one hand towards the sea. 'Surely we're not that important!'

'It depends what the enemy intends.'

Bolitho turned away, feeling a chill on his spine. It was a new sensation, uncanny. To think that someone might be discussing him, planning and scheming like runners after a wanted criminal.

But it was certainly how it appeared, how he must anticipate it if he was to prepare himself. Fleets and valuable convoys stayed to the east or west of the Bahama Islands, so it was much more likely that the enemy was out after one particular prize.

He said, 'We will show a stern lantern for *Fawn*'s benefit tonight. At dawn I will tell Commander Maulby what I think.' He grinned, suddenly amused by his unusual caution. 'Or maybe by that time I will have driven my ghosts away.'

Tyrrell watched him doubtfully. 'To our enemy, th' Frogs in particular, you're like a thorn.' He frowned. 'There's only one way to deal with thorns, you tear 'em out and stamp on 'em!'

Bolitho nodded. 'I agree. We will continue with our new course, but be prepared to treat every event as a trick and a ruse until proved otherwise.'

He looked abeam for the *Lucifer*, but she was little more than a blur in the damp evening haze. He cursed Colquhoun for not supplying more information about the fishing boat, where it came from, or the reliability of its crew. Yet he could almost feel sorry for him. He was obviously beset with anxiety about his own future, and now there was the chance of catching a rich prize, and probably military information as well, he could think of little else.

He went below to his cabin and stared at the chart beneath a gently spiralling lantern. Between his hands the islands, the countless tentacles of reefs and shallows were like the neck of some gigantic bag, around which Colquhoun's flotilla, accidentally or otherwise, were converging to close with the finality of a noose.

Bolitho sighed and turned to lean from one of the windows. In the shaded stern lantern's beam the small frothing wake glowed like blue wool, and beyond it the horizon had faded to mingle with the first pale stars.

Then he touched the scar beneath the lock of hair, noting that it was hurting, throbbing in time with his heart. He knew he was uneasy, more so because he could not find a proper reason for it.

Overhead he heard Graves murmuring as he took over the watch, and

Tyrrell's limping step as he walked towards the companion ladder. Normal, regular sounds which usually gave him a sense of pleasure. Now, perhaps because they represented people he had come to know, and not merely extensions of the ship's efficiency, he was suddenly afraid. Not of an enemy or the ever-present shadow of death, but of his responsibility which their trust had given him.

11

Strategy and Spite

Bolitho was hastily tying his neckcloth when Tyrrell thrust his head through the cabin skylight and called, '*Bacchante*'s just signalled, sir! *Capn's to repair aboard!*'

'I will come up directly.'

He threw on his coat and took a quick glance round the cabin. He did not see Colquhoun very often, but he had learned it was best to forget nothing.

On deck he found the gig being swayed over the gangway, and when he glanced abeam he saw *Fawn*'s boat already in the water and Maulby hurrying down into it with his usual agility.

It was early afternoon and the deck burning hot through his shoes. All night, with *Fawn* keeping as close as safety allowed, they had driven south, with the sprawling barrier of sandbars and shallows some ten miles off the larboard beam. But it had taken longer than he had hoped to find Colquhoun's *Bacchante*, and almost as soon as the masthead had sighted her topsails the wind had fallen away to a mere breath, allowing the sun to tighten its grip over them like a furnace.

As he waited for the gig's crew to man their boat he turned to stare across the opposite beam, towards the distorted hump of blue and purple which he knew to be the western tip of Grand Bahama. Colquhoun was taking no chances. He was standing well clear of the land, either to give himself sea-room, or to prevent the enemy from seeing his intentions.

'Ready, sir.'

He ran down to the entry port and said to Tyrrell, 'Keep a sharp lookout for inquisitive craft of any kind. Send a cutter after 'em if they draw near. Don't wait for my orders.'

Then he was in the gig and settling himself on a hot thwart as Stockdale swung the tiller and sent the boat dipping and swaying towards the frigate. *Bacchante* was hove-to, her sails flapping loosely, showing her copper as she rolled unsteadily in the swell. She was a fine ship, he thought. Clean-cut and designed by a craftsman. Thirty-six guns and the ability to live off her own resources for many months, she was, or should be, every young captain's ambition. It did not seem to fit Colquhoun at all.

Stockdale was muttering under his breath, and Bolitho knew he was cursing his opposite number in *Fawn*, who always seemed to manage to get his boat anywhere just that bit faster. The gig turned swiftly, oars backing in close unison, the bowman hooking on to the frigate's main chains as *Bacchante*'s shadow gave them brief respite from the glare.

Bolitho clambered up the side, doffing his hat and regaining his composure while the calls shrilled in salute and a squad of red-coated marines slapped their muskets to the present.

The first lieutenant, a gaunt, harassed-looking man, bobbed his head in welcome.

'The captain is aft, sir. He is preparing his strategy, otherwise . . .'

Maulby stepped from the shade of the gangway and took his arm. '*Otherwise*, my friend, he would have had the good grace to meet us at the entry port, eh?' He laughed at the lieutenant's embarrassment. 'You, sir, deserve rich recognition for your penance aboard this ship.'

Together they strode beneath the poop, automatically ducking their heads despite the ample room above.

A marine stamped his boots together and threw open the cabin door, his eyes never blinking or shifting until both officers had stepped over the coaming.

Colquhoun was standing by the stern windows, studying his watch with obvious impatience.

'So you have arrived, gentlemen.' He sat down at his table. 'Eventually.'

Bolitho relaxed slightly. So it was to be this way.

He replied, 'We had adverse winds overnight, sir.'

Maulby added calmly, 'And I thought you might be closer inshore, sir. We seem to be somewhat, er, out of touch with affairs at present.' He glanced towards his own ship as she rolled uneasily about a cable from *Bacchante*'s quarter. 'But I expect you have a reason for that, sir.'

Colquhoun stared at him fixedly, as if to seek out the truth of his words. Fortunately he seemed quite oblivious to Maulby's sarcasm.

He snapped, 'Look at my chart.' They gathered round and he tapped it with some brass dividers. 'The Frenchman is here. I sent a cutter under sail before dawn to investigate.' He looked up, his eyes triumphant. 'So there's an end to speculation.'

Bolitho leaned closer. What a formidable place. From the western tip of the main island the main chain of reefs and bars ran northward for about forty miles to link with the notorious Matanilla Shoal. The latter then turned eastward, enclosing the great span of open water known as the Little Bahama Bank like one monstrous snare. In places the water was only feet deep, and the fathoms were few and far between.

According to Colquhoun's marks on the chart, the French ship had passed through or around one of the cays to rest up on the other side of the island. It was perfect for anyone trying to avoid a skirmish. For on this side and elsewhere in the channel the sea bottom was over two hundred fathoms, and any hope of a close attack was foiled by the steepness of the island's face. Whereas on the other side, within the Little Bahama Bank, the water was very shallow and sandy, ideal for a master who wished to careen his ship and carry out temporary repairs.

'Was your cutter seen, sir?' Maulby did not look up.

'Of course not!' Colquhoun seemed angry even at the simple suggestion. 'My first lieutenant was in charge. He knows what would happen to him if he allowed such carelessness.' He calmed himself with an effort. 'He saw many lights on the water. The cutter pulled through the surf and between two sandbars and watched the enemy at work. She's big, probably a forty-gun frigate with some armament removed. Must have touched bottom and sustained damage sometime after entering the islands.'

Bolitho glanced at his profile. Colquhoun was very excited, there was no doubt about it, despite his efforts to conceal his true emotions. There was a strong smell of brandy, and he guessed he had been celebrating privately the victory already in his pocket.

He asked quietly, 'What do you intend, sir?'

Colquhoun looked at him searchingly. 'I am working on the assumption that the enemy is near finished repairs. Now, he will either continue on passage, or make Martinique again if he is badly holed and needing greater help. Either way, we must act at once and avoid another chase.'

'I would suggest a boat action, sir. We could cross the bar from two directions and cut her out before they know what is happening. With men and boats from all three ships we can swamp her defences with darkness on our side.'

Colquhoun said mildly, 'With *you* in overall command of the boats, no doubt?'

Bolitho flushed angrily. 'Your frigate is too large by half to be of use in those confined waters, sir! If the Frenchman makes a run for it, or decides to show fight, you will be needed to present your ship to him and without delay.'

'Easy, Bolitho.' Colquhoun was smiling gently. 'You rise quickly to my words. Such haste to speak tends to show guilt more than conviction.'

He turned swiftly before Bolitho could reply. 'You, Maulby, will take *Fawn* across the bar tonight, under sweeps if required, but I want you in position *at dawn tomorrow*.' He leaned over the chart again. 'If the enemy is repaired enough to make sail he will no doubt hope for one of three possible channels. To the north his passage could be adversely affected by wind and tide. South is more likely, in which case *Bacchante* will be well placed to take him as he tacks around the point. But if he is still laid up or careened, you will be able to rake him there and then. He will see no use in firing back at you. Just a few more holes will be sufficient to render him immovable, or long enough for us to present more drastic measures.' He wagged one finger. 'But I know those Frogs. They'll not fight if the odds are so well laid.'

Across his bowed shoulders Maulby looked at Bolitho and shrugged.

Bolitho said nothing, knowing Colquhoun was waiting for him to protest. *Sparrow* was better suited to the task as defined by Colquhoun. Her armament was heavier, and her thirty-two pounders were far more accurate and deadly than *Fawn*'s lesser battery of nine-pounders. He knew that any such suggestion, however, would only bear out Colquhoun's earlier hint that he was greedy for more success and fame, or that he was a better man than Maulby for the mission.

Maulby asked slowly, 'Will you send men overland, sir?'

Colquhoun still did not look at them. 'God in heaven! Where is all this stuff of combat I have been reading in the *Gazette*? I am beginning to wonder at its substance!'

Bolitho said, 'It is a sensible suggestion, sir. I would prefer a boat action by night, but in daylight a force of men, including your marines, would be able to . . .' He got no further.

Colquhoun straightened like a steel spring. 'Enough of this! My plan leaves no room for nervous fumbling about the rocks like a lot of damn lizards! That Frenchman is as good as taken, and I intend to sail her into port intact and with her cargo or whatever ready for closer inspection!'

He walked from the table and stared at a half-filled decanter on his desk. As he reached out for it Bolitho saw his hand was shaking with anger or agitation. His voice was equally unsteady as he continued, 'And *you*, Bolitho, will close from the north. Stay out of sight until the time of attack and then make contact with me for further orders.' His fingers closed around the decanter like claws. 'That is all. My clerk will give you written details of attack as you leave.'

They left the cabin and walked in silence to the quarterdeck.

Maulby spoke first. 'It should be *your* doing, Dick. I agree with you about trying to cut the enemy out, but either way, it is your right to lead if Colquhoun intends to stand offshore.'

Bolitho touched his shoulder. 'I wish you all success, but you know that. You are more than due for promotion, and I hope this will bring it for you.'

Maulby grimaced. 'I'll not deny that I'd relish the chance. But I would wish it done with less bitterness.' He glanced aft. 'That man will be the death of me with his bloody moods.'

Bolitho bit his lip, trying to find the right words.

'Look, John, take good care. I know Colquhoun is desperate for his victory, but I do not share his scorn for Frenchmen. They fight well, they fight with courage. They are not given to empty gestures, even in the cannon's mouth.'

Maulby nodded, his eyes grave. 'Have no fear. If that Frenchman decides to match gun for gun with me I will haul off and await support.'

Bolitho forced a smile. Maulby was lying to ease his troubled mind. Lying as he would probably do under similar conditions. Before and after a fight at sea there was always room for recriminations and counter-proposals, but once joined in battle there was usually one thought. To fight, to keep on firing until the enemy broke or the tide turned against you.

'Boats alongside!' The first lieutenant greeted them with a tired smile. 'Is it done, sir?'

Maulby held up his written orders. 'Aye. Done.'

The lieutenant sighed. 'I have made a small sketch which may be of some help for you, sir. The tide-race is bad there, and the surf no better. But if the French could enter, then you should have less hardship.'

The two gigs were hooked on to the chains, and Bolitho said with sudden urgency, 'I will be making sail directly if I am to take station by dawn.' He held out his hand. 'I wish I was comng with you.'

Maulby returned the clasp. 'I, too.' He grinned. 'But at least you will be spared the sight of *Fawn* as she makes Colquhoun both rich and famous in one blow.'

Stockdale stood up in the gig as Bolitho descended the frigate's side, his eyes puzzled.

As the boat shoved off and the oars picked up the stroke, he hissed, 'Then we're not fightin', sir?'

Bolitho sighed. Secret orders, plans of battle, meant nothing to the lower deck. Stockdale had not left the gig, but he and probably every Jack in the flotilla knew what was happening.

'Not this time, Stockdale!'

He had already forgotten Colquhoun's snub, the calculated attempt to drive a rift between him and Maulby. He was thinking of *Fawn*'s task, the chances of success without prolonging the attack so that Colquhoun could blame Maulby for the delay.

'It ain't right, sir.' Stockdale was muttering from the tiller.

Bolitho glared at him. 'Just attend to your work! I have had a bellyful of strategy for one day!'

Stockdale studied the captain's squared shoulders, the way he was gripping his hanger so that the fingers showed white through his tan. *It ain't no use you blowin' off at me, my lad, it still ain't right, an' wot's more, you knows it!*

With his secret rebuff held firmly in his mind Stockdale eased the tiller bar and headed straight for the *Sparrow*.

As the bowman hooked on to the chains Bolitho turned abruptly and said, 'But thank you for your concern.'

Stockdale stood and removed his hat while Bolitho reached for the sloop's side.

He grinned broadly at his back. 'Thankee, sir!'

Tyrrell was no less ready to speak out. 'But that's a strange choice! Commander Maulby's a fine officer, but . . .'

Bolitho swung round. 'Prepare to get the ship under way. Rig the royal yards as soon as we are under command, for I want to make all speed with what wind there is!' He relented again. 'Just do as I *ask*, Mr Tyrrell, and let us have no more of it.'

Buckle ambled across the deck as Bolitho hurried below to rid himself of his heavy dress coat.

'What d'you make of it, Mr Tyrrell?'

Tyrrell frowned. 'That damn Colquhoun! I never took to th' man. Like bloody Ransome, his eyes are slits for the Devil to peer through!'

Buckle shook his head. 'Cap'n's worried, there's no doubt on that.'

'Not for himself.' Tyrrell watched the men hauling at the boat tackles as the gig bobbed above the gangway. 'That is equally certain.'

Bolitho's voice rose sharply through the skylight. 'When you have *finished*, gentlemen, I would be obliged if you would attend to my orders!'

Buckle looked at Tyrrell and grinned sheepishly.

'That's more like it! Our Dick's not the one to brood too long!'

Within the hour *Sparrow* was ghosting slowly to the north-west, her yards alive with canvas, as with all sail set she left her consorts further and still further astern.

The wind rose very slightly, and by the time the first stars appeared above the raked masts they had logged nearly fifty miles. Back along the same course they had used to join Colquhoun with such haste the previous night.

But there was nothing anyone could do about it, and there were some who were inwardly pleased to be spared *Fawn*'s uncomfortable passage through the shoals.

On the quarterdeck Lieutenant Graves leaned against the rail, half watching the loosely flapping sails, partly listening to the creak of the wheel, an occasional voice from his seamen on watch. He was thinking about his home in Chatham and the news he had received in a rare letter from England. His was not a seafaring family, and his father had owned a small but flourishing grocer's shop where Graves and his sister had been born and had grown up together. His mother, a sickly woman, died a year before *Sparrow* had sailed from the Thames, and in the past

years his father had apparently taken to drink. The business had fallen
into debt, and his sister, probably out of desperation, had married an
impoverished lieutenant in the army garrison.

She had written asking for money, for herself and to try to keep their
father from a debtors' prison. Graves had sent all he had, which had
been little enough. His share of *Sparrow*'s prize money would help
considerably, but until he received more news from home he was
unwilling to sign it over when it had been so hard to come by. If only he
had been better moulded to dealing with the ways of the Navy. Like the
captain, whose seafaring background and famous ancestors put him
apart from men like himself. Or even Tyrrell, who seemed indifferent to
all authority, although God knew he could ill afford to be so. He
remembered exactly when Tyrrell's sister had come aboard. They had
been in Kingston, Jamaica, where she had been living with friends,
waiting until the *troubles*, as she called them, in America were over. A
vivacious, lively girl, with none of Tyrrell's casual attitudes. To Graves
she had appeared like some sort of angel, an answer to everything he
had ever dreamed. She came from a settled, prosperous family, and as a
wife would have given him the chance to better himself, find his rightful
place in the world instead of remaining unsure and cautious. Tyrrell had
seen his intentions clearly enough, but had neither encouraged nor
come out directly against him. Then, the fool had had an argument with
Captain Ransome over a man being punished. Graves could no longer
remember if the punishment was just or not, nor did he care. All that
remained clear was that Ransome had acted swiftly and had used all his
charm, which was considerable, and his obvious skill on the girl's
defences to break his own chances as well as alienating her brother
completely. But Graves still blamed Tyrrell, hated him whenever he
thought of her and the way she had looked when Ransome had finally
put her ashore in Antigua.

He gripped the rail until the pain steadied him. Where was she now?
Someone said she had sailed for America again, others mentioned a
passing Indiaman which had gone south to Trinidad. Would she ever
think of him? He turned away, angry with himself for daring to hope
after so long. Why could he never be confident when it was most
needed? Perhaps he had been too long in that damned grocer's shop,
hearing his father grovelling to the *quality*, bowing and scraping to
customers who ran up bills far greater than his own debts.

The worry about his sister, the uncertainty about himself, had taken
their toll in other ways, too. He had sensed it after the fight with the
Bonaventure, even though he had been aboard *Sparrow* with the
rescued passengers. Suppose the captain had failed to grapple her long
enough to carry out his wild plan? Would he have had the strength to
turn *Sparrow* against orders and attempt to rescue Bolitho and his men?

But for Buckle and some of the others he doubted if he would have done so even when both grappled ships had burst into flames. They had seen the great pall of smoke from the horizon itself.

And later, when they had closed with the other prizes and had exchanged shots with privateers, he had felt the fear spreading inside him like some loathsome disease. Nobody had noticed. Yet. He shook himself and crossed to the weather side, trying to clear his mind in the cool breeze.

The two midshipmen were standing by the lee nettings, and Bethune said quietly, 'Mr Graves seems worried.'

The new midshipman, Fowler, ignored the comment. 'Now look here.' He had a lisp, which became more evident whenever he was trying to appear innocent before his superiors. Now it was barely noticeable. 'I have to supervise swabbing the cable tier tomorrow.'

Bethune was watching the lieutenant. 'I know. It's your turn.'

Fowler showed his small teeth. 'You do it for me. When we rejoin the fleet I will speak with the admiral.'

Bethune gaped at him. 'For *me*?'

'Perhaps.'

Bethune's gratitude was pathetic. 'Oh, if only . . .' He nodded firmly. 'Yes. I will take charge of the cable party. Anything else I can do . . .'

The youth regarded him coolly. 'I will let you know.'

Throughout the ship the company lived out their hopes and dreams in their own way.

In his tiny cabin Tyrrell was sitting on his sea-chest massaging his wounded thigh, while on the other side of the bulkhead Bolitho finished his letter to his father.

In the dimly lit wardroom Dalkeith was drowsing over a glass of rum, hearing Buckle re-telling a yarn about some woman or other in Bristol, while young Heyward listened to him with his eyes closed.

Right forward above the plunging beakhead, his hair blown by wind and drifting spray, Yule, the gunner, squatted with his back against a stanchion, a bottle between his knees, his blurred mind thinking of Tilby, the good times they had shared together.

Deep in the hold, a lantern above his narrow head, Lock, the purser, inspected a cask of lemons, examining each one like some robber with his booty, while he made notes in a ledger.

And below her pale canvas *Sparrow* held them all. Oblivious to their various troubles and pleasures, indifferent even to the sea. For she needed none of them, and seemed content.

As soon as Bolitho reached the quarterdeck, he knew the wind was changing against them, and rapidly. He had been in a deep sleep when a master's mate had groped into the cabin to tell him that Lieutenant Heyward was requesting advice.

It was only halfway through the middle watch, and the stars still very bright above the mastheads, but as he hurried across the deck, his bare feet soundless on the damp planking, he heard the topsails shaking violently, the responding chorus from stays and shrouds.

Buckle was beside the wheel, and like himself was wearing only his breeches, evidence, if it was still needed, of Heyward's unwillingness to call for help until it was almost too late.

'Well?' He peered at the slanting compass bowl, seeing the helmsmen's eyes glowing faintly in the binnacle light. 'I'm waiting, Mr Heyward.'

He did not wish to fluster the young lieutenant, and at another time could appreciate his wishing to control his own watch without showing uncertainty. But this was not the time, and in such dangerous waters they would have to act fast.

Heyward explained, 'The wind backed a point or so, and I had my watch trim the yards.' He gestured vaguely above his head. 'But now it has backed at a faster rate, I fear maybe from the north-east.'

Buckle muttered, 'We'll never be able to change tack in time to reach the head o' the shoals, sir.' He glared at the compass. '*Never!*'

Bolitho rubbed his chin, feeling the wind playing across his bare shoulders. Heyward had been foolish to let *Sparrow* have her head like this. Maybe he expected the wind to veer again, as it often did hereabouts, but whatever he thought or hoped, the ship's bow was now pointing almost north-west by north, and she was not holding that course very well either. Every minute was taking them further from the chain of shoals, and it would waste hours of wearing and tacking to fight round again towards their station as Colquhoun had directed.

Heyward said miserably, 'I'm sorry about this, sir. I—I thought I could hold her.'

Bolitho was thinking busily. 'You cannot help the wind. But in future you must learn to call me the moment you are unsure of anything. I'll not think worse of you.' He looked at Buckle. 'What is your opinion? We have four hours before dawn.'

Buckle was adamant. 'Impossible.' He sighed. 'I'm afraid we must remain close-hauled and try to wear ship in perhaps three hours or so.'

Bolitho pictured the chart in his mind, recalling vividly the nearest sandbars, the set of the tide.

'Call all hands, Mr Heyward. We will wear ship directly.'

'But, *sir!*' Buckle sounded anxious. 'We'll never be able to take up our proper course! With the wind staying steady from the nor-'east it's not possible.'

Bolitho heard the shrill of calls below decks, the sudden stampede of feet on gangways and ladders. 'I agree. Mr Buckle.' He paused as Tyrrell came out of the gloom, dragging his leg badly as he tried to buckle his belt. 'I intend to pass *through* the bars.' He looked at Tyrrell. 'If we stay as we are we will be unable to offer assistance if it is needed when daylight comes. Once inside the bank we will at least be able to use the wind if an opportunity presents itself.'

Graves ran to the quarterdeck, his feet very loud above the hushed voices. He had evidently found time to put on his shoes.

Bolitho said, 'Very well. Leadsmen in the chains, and then get the royals and t'gallants off her.' He was speaking fast in time with his thoughts. 'Tell the bosun to unleash the sweeps in case the wind drops altogether.'

Tyrrell nodded. 'Aye, aye, sir. I reckon we stand a fair chance of getting through. Th' set of th' tide is in our favour.' He hesitated. 'When it drops a piece we may find it bothersome.'

Bolitho smiled in spite of his thoughts. 'Well spoken!'

Shouts came along the gundeck where petty officers completed their count of topmen and hands for the braces. So well did most of them know the ship that darkness made little or no difference to them.

Bolitho nodded. 'Shorten sail, Mr Tyrrell.' He lowered his voice. 'Quick as you can.'

Within minutes all canvas had vanished from the upper yards, and with her topsails and courses thrusting noisily to the wind *Sparrow* lifted and staggered in an uncomfortable swell.

Bolitho gripped the weather nettings, watching the thin slivers of spray darting across the gangway, the extreme angle of the yards as with sail and helm Buckle tried to hold her as close to the wind as he dared.

And all the while he was thinking rapidly. Once the ship had gone about the nearest strip of sandbar and shoal would lie some ten miles across the bows. A false estimate of speed and distance, a wrong or careless description on the chart, and he might drive her hard aground. But in his heart he knew the risk was worthwhile. No one could blame him for keeping to his original orders and thereby allow the wind to carry him away from the area. Colquhoun would probably be pleased to have him as far off as possible if only to deny *Sparrow* even the role of spectator for the final act. By ignoring the rigid span of his orders he might lay himself open to reprimand, but with luck he would be better placed to give *Fawn* assistance if the Frenchman decided to fight. With the wind backed to the north-east, Colquhoun would be hard put to remain in his own sector when the time came, and that in itself would offer some excuse for Bolitho's action.

'Ready, sir!'

He tightened his jaw. 'Put the helm down!'

He tensed, feeling the sea dragging against the weeded keel in a strong undertow.

'Helm's a'lee, sir!'

Through the darkness he saw the headsails shaking wildly, heard the tramp of feet as the men hauled steadily at the braces to get the yards round.

'Off tacks and sheets!' Graves's voice was hoarse above the din of canvas and blocks.

'Mainsail haul!'

A man fell in the darkness and a voice yelled harshly to restore calm on the gundeck.

Bolitho gripped the nettings, his body tilting with the hull as *Sparrow* lifted her jib-boom, hesitated and then sliced heavily across the wind.

'Braces there!' Tyrrell was leaning over the rail as if to seek out individual seamen in the gloom. 'Heave, lads! *Harder!*'

Sparrow resisted awhile longer, then with sails filling and booming again she heeled over on the opposite tack, the spray sluicing up over the gangways and drenching the men beneath.

Bolitho had to shout to make himself heard above the noise. 'Close as you can, Mr Buckle!'

'Aye, sir.' He sounded breathless. 'Full an' bye!'

More uncomfortable minutes while men scampered above and along the gangways. A pull here and belay. Men hauling busily at halliards, while in the bows the selected hands took their leads and lines to the forechains in readiness to begin sounding.

Eventually even Buckle seemed satisfied. 'Sou' by east, sir!'

'Very good.'

Bolitho peered up at the hard-braced yards. Not even a frigate could sail this close to the wind. Nothing could.

Tyrrell staggered towards him, his shirt plastered to his body. 'You wanted this, didn't you, sir?' He was shouting, but his voice was matched by the surge of water alongside. 'You were worried about *Fawn*?' He cursed as his foot slipped and then clapped his hands to his thigh.

Bolitho supported him and waited for the hull to sway upright again. 'Easy, Jethro! Is it painful?'

Tyrrell showed his teeth. 'Dalkeith said there might be some small splinters left in th' bone. Them pistol balls can split open when they cut into a man.' He stood up gingerly and grimaced. 'Not too bad.'

Bolitho watched the topmen slithering down stays and shrouds and then said, 'Yes. I suppose I did want it. I cannot explain my fears.' He shrugged and added, 'So I will not try.'

He pushed his uncertainties away. 'Now, Jethro, I want our people to have breakfast and a tot of blackstrap. No sense in waiting for daylight, and I imagine they are too well drenched to sleep just now.' He ticked off the points on his fingers. 'Then have the fires doused, and muster the hands at quarters. We will not clear for action, but I intend that every available man is on deck when we cross the bar.'

Tyrrell was watching him intently. 'What about Heyward? Are you going to log him?'

Bolitho shook his head. 'He's learned his lesson, so there's no harm done. When I was a junior lieutenant I once fell alsleep on watch.' His teeth showed white in the darkness. 'I'm not proud of the fact, but by God I never did it again!'

He moved to the hatch cover and paused. 'I will go below and get into some clothes. It'll never do for our people to see their captain like this in daylight.' He laughed, the sound carrying up to a solitary man working on the mainyard. 'I may live like a savage, but I see no cause to look like one!'

Tyrrell turned back to the rail, easing his leg as the pain lanced through it. He had just seen yet another Bolitho. Naked to the waist, his black hair plastered over his forehead, he had looked as young, if not younger than Heyward. In such a moment Tyrrell had been touched by his concern for the hands as he had been impressed by his cheerful recklessness over the approaching sandbars.

Heyward came from the gundeck and waited to resume his duty.

Tyrrell said, 'Dismiss th' watch below. Then have th' petty officers lay aft for instructions.'

Heyward asked glumly, 'Will this go badly for me?'

Tyrrell clapped him on the arm. 'God, boy, *no!*' He laughed at his astonishment. 'You did th' cap'n a favour! If you *had* called him earlier he'd have been forced to change tack. Your *mistake* allowed him to take another course of action.' He strolled away whistling to himself, his bare feet slapping on the spray-drenched planking.

Heyward walked up the tilting deck and joined Buckle by the wheel. 'I don't think I understand.'

Buckle studied him dubiously. 'Well, don't you try, that's my advice.' He shuffled towards the hatch and added, 'An' next time you feels like playing God with my ship, I'd be obliged if you'd pass the word *first.*'

Heyward glanced at the compass and crossed to the weather side. There was more to being lieutenant of the watch than holding a commission, he decided wearily. He looked at the taut mainsail and grimaced. It had been a near thing, and at one time he had felt stricken by the swift change of events, so that he had imagined the ship was running wild, carrying him and all aboard like some uncontrollable juggernaut. Now, in these last moments, he had learned something. If it all happened again he would know what to do. Of that he was quite certain.

Stockdale was waiting in the cabin with Bolitho's shirt, and after handing him a towel asked, 'Did you *really* fall asleep on watch, sir?'

Bolitho rubbed his chest and arms, feeling the salt drying on his lips like another skin.

'Almost.' Was nothing secret from Stockdale? 'But we have to embroider things a little sometimes.'

He stepped out of his sodden breeches and threw them across the cabin. As he continued to towel his naked body he listened to Heyward's measured tread across the deck above.

Then he added quietly, 'I once knew of a lieutenant who beat a man for giving a false report from the masthead. After that the seaman was too frightened to say anything, and when there *was* danger he held his tongue for fear he would get another beating. As a result, the ship was driven ashore and the lieutenant drowned.'

Stockdale watched him warily. 'Serve 'im right.'

Bolitho sighed. Moralizing was wasted on Stockdale.

The big coxswain shook out a clean pair of breeches and handed them across. For another minute or so he did not speak, but his forehead was wrinkled in thought.

Then he asked, 'An' wot 'appened to the seaman, sir?'

Bolitho stared at him. 'I am afraid he was flogged for neglect of duty.'

Stockdale's battered face lit up in a broad grin.

'Proves me point then, don't it, sir? There ain't no justice in th' world for any of us!'

Bolitho sat down, one leg still tangled in the breeches. As was often the case, Stockdale had had the last word.

12

A Twist of Fate

Lieutenant Tyrrell gripped the quarterdeck rail and peered fixedly along the starboard gangway.

'God damn this mist!' He leaned across the rail, straining his eyes forward in an effort to see beyond the forecastle. 'And God damn our luck!'

Bolitho said nothing but moved to the opposite side of the deck. Since before dawn, when with leads going and every ear and eye pitched to the shouted depths, the sounds of distant surf and the occasional feather of warning spray in the darkness, he had been aware of the thickening sea mist. It was not unusual in these waters at the time of year, but he had expected it to pass quickly, to clear with the first hint of morning sunlight.

Now, as he stared abeam, he knew it was thicker than ever. Moving steadily with the wind, it wreathed between the shrouds and seemed to cling to the rigging like pale weed. Above the topsail yards he could see nothing, and apart from a clear patch of water below the quarterdeck, the sea was equally hidden. Keeping pace with the ship's cautious progress, the mist cut away all impression of movement, so that it felt as if *Sparrow* was suspended in cloud like some phantom vessel.

A voice below the quarterdeck called, 'By th' mark five!'

The seaman's call was hushed as the sounding was passed from mouth to mouth from the leadsmen in the forechains. Once over the bar, Bolitho had ordered the ship to be cleared for action, and with the enfolding mist shutting out both sight and sound, it was necessary to take every precaution.

He glanced at the maintopsail again. It was drawing quite well, taking the sloop steadily across the shallows, the flapping canvas shining with moisture in the grey light to show that somewhere above the mist there was a sun and maybe a sight of land, too.

'Deep four!'

Bolitho walked aft to the wheel where Buckle stood with his men, the mist moving through his splayed legs and making him appear like a spectre.

He stiffened as Bolitho approached and reported, 'She's holding well, sir. Sou' by east as afore.'

From the gundeck came a scrape of wood, and when he turned Bolitho saw one of the long sweeps swaying above the water before coming into line with the rest. He had ordered the sweeps to be run out an hour earlier, for if the wind dropped or they came upon some unexpected shoal, they would be the only means of working clear.

'Deck there!' The masthead's voice seemed to come from the mist itself. 'Ship on th' starboard quarter!'

Bolitho stared upwards, aware for the first time that the mist was tinged yellow like North Sea fog. Sunlight at last. Far above the deck, isolated by a layer of mist, the lookout had sighted another vessel.

He saw Tyrrell and the others watching him, caught in their various attitudes by the lookout's sharp call.

Bolitho said, 'I shall go aloft, Mr Tyrrell.' He unbuckled his sword and handed it to Stockdale. 'Keep good watch and ensure that the anchor can be dropped instantly if need be.'

He hurried to the gangway, his mind torn between the unexpected sighting of a strange ship and his rising nausea at the prospect of a climb to the lookout.

Then he swung himself out on to the main shrouds and gripped the gently quivering ratlines with as much force as if the ship had been in a full gale. Through the ratlines he saw Graves below on the gun deck, shoulders hunched, his eyes looking neither right nor left.

Bethune was close by him, one hand resting on a twelve-pounder, the other shading his eyes as he peered up at the mist. All along the ship men stood like crude statuary, bare backs shining with moisture which dripped ceaselessly from the sails and rigging, so that they appeared to be sweating, as if they had just been in battle.

Here and there a checked shirt, or the darker blue and white of a gunner's mate, stood out from the rest, as if the artist had found more time to complete their postures before passing on to some other part of the picture.

'By th' mark five.' The chant came aft from the forecastle like a dirge.

In his mind Bolitho pictured the chart. The tide was on the turn now. Soon even the so-called safe channels between the shoals and the sandbars would be drawn closer together, like great jaws closing around a capture.

He gritted his teeth and started to climb. When he paused to draw breath the ship had lost her outline in the mist. Only the guns and oblong hatchways stood out with any clarity, and aft by the taffrail Buckle and the others seemed to be cut in halves by the following tendrils of haze.

Up and up. At the maintop he swarmed quickly through the lubber's hole rather than tackle the additional agony of hanging by fingers and toes from the futtock shrouds. A seaman gaped at him as he passed and was still staring as Bolitho increased his rate of climb until he, too, was lost from view.

A few moments later Bolitho stared up at the main topgallant yard with something like awe. For there, above it, clean and empty of cloud, the sky was bright blue, and as he started up the last ratlines he saw the taut stays and shrouds shining like copper in the early sunlight.

The lookout, legs swinging carelessly from the crosstrees, moved over to allow the captain to climb up beside him.

Bolitho gripped a stay with one hand and tried to control his rapid breathing.

'Ah, Taylor, you have a good perch up here.'

The maintopman gave a slow grin. 'Aye, sir.' He had a soft North Country burr, and his homely voice did more than he would have dreamed possible to steady Bolitho's sickness.

He raised a bronzed arm. 'There she be, sir!'

Bolitho twisted round, trying not to look at the vibrating mast as it vanished below into the mist. For a moment longer he could see nothing. Then, as the sluggish wind stirred the mist into movement he saw the raked topmasts and flapping pendant of a frigate some three miles away on the starboard quarter.

He forgot his precarious position, the nausea of the dizzy climb, everything in fact but the other ship.

The lookout said, 'There be breakers yonder, too, sir. I reckon that frigate's on t'other side o' the bar.'

Bolitho looked at him gravely. 'You know her, don't you?'

The man nodded. 'Aye, sir. She's *Bacchante*, Cap'n Colquhoun's command flag is at the fore.' He watched Bolitho's impassive face. 'Anyway, I was in 'er once, two years back.'

Bolitho nodded. He had known it was *Bacchante*, too. Perhaps he had been hoping he was mistaken, that the mist and light were playing tricks.

But there was no doubting Taylor's conviction. It was typical of such seamen as he. Once they had served with or aboard a ship they seemed to know her under any condition. Taylor had only seen the frigate's upper yards, but he had recognized her instantly.

Bolitho touched his arm. 'Keep a good watch on her, Taylor.' He slung his leg over the edge. 'You've done well.'

Then he was climbing and slipping downwards, his mind grappling with the new encounter. Once, when he peered over his shoulder he thought he saw hazed sunlight on the water, further away from the hull. So the mist was thinning after all. But it was too late now, if things went wrong.

Tyrrell was waiting for him by the quarterdeck rail, his eyes anxious as Bolitho jumped down from the shrouds and hurried towards him.

'It's *Bacchante!*'

Bolitho stared past him at the upturned faces on the gundeck, the faint leap of spray as the leadsman made yet another cast.

'Quarter less five!'

He turned to Tyrrell. 'Colquhoun must have stood well clear of land during the night. When the wind backed it caught him out, as it did us. He must have been driven miles along the Channel.' He turned away, his voice suddenly bitter. 'The damn fool should have stayed closer inshore! Now he's useless out there beyond the shoals! It'd take him near half a day to beat back into an attacking position!'

Tyrrell's hand rasped over his chin. 'What'll we do? With the tide on th' turn we'll have to look sharp if we're to close with th' Frogs.' He glanced at Buckle. 'My guess is we should stand away and try again later.'

Buckle nodded slowly. 'Mine, too. If Cap'n Colquhoun's plan has gone off at half-cock then we can't be expected to do better.'

Bolitho ignored him. 'Pass the word, Mr Tyrrell. Withdraw sweeps and have the guns loaded and run out. Gun by gun, if you please, with as little noise as possible.' He studied Buckle's dubious expression and added quietly, 'I *know* the risk. So brail up the courses and have the bosun prepare a stream anchor in case we have to take the way off her directly.' He thrust his hands behind his back. 'You can think me mad, Mr Buckle.' He heard the sweeps thumping inboard on to their racks and the slow rumble of trucks as the first cannon were hauled towards the open ports. 'And maybe I am. But somewhere out there is a British sloop like ourselves. Thanks to others she is quite alone now, and God knows, if I am *not* mad then *Fawn* is going to need every bit of help she can get!'

The big main course rose billowing and protesting to its yard as men worked busily to bring it under control and lay bare the decks from bow to quarterdeck.

A gunner's mate called huskily, 'Loaded an' run out, sir!'

Tyrrell strode aft, his speaking trumpet jammed beneath his arm.

Bolitho met his gaze and smiled briefly. 'You were faster this time.'

Then together, with their backs to the helmsmen and an apprehensive Buckle, they leaned on the rail and stared directly ahead. The mist was still all around them, but thinner, and as he watched Bolitho knew it was at last outpacing the ship, moving stealthily through the shrouds and away across the lee bow. There was sunlight, too. Not much, but he saw it reflecting faintly from the ship's bell and playing on a black twelve-pounder ball which one gun captain had removed from a shot garland and was changing from hand to hand, testing its perfection or otherwise.

Bolitho asked softly, 'How far now, in your opinion?'

Tyrrell raised his injured leg and winced. 'Th' wind stays regular from th' nor'-east. Our course is sou' by east.' He was thinking aloud. 'Th' soundings have found no lie in th' chart.' He made up his mind. 'I reckon we're about six mile from th' place where *Fawn* crossed through th' shoals.' He turned and added firmly, 'You'll have to put about soon, sir. You'll be hard aground if you keep on this tack much longer.'

The chant seemed to float aft to mock him. 'By th' mark three!'

Lieutenant Heyward, who was standing very still by the quarterdeck ladder, murmured, 'Holy God!'

Bolitho said, 'If the Frenchman is still there, then there must be ample room for him to work clear.'

Tyrrell eyed him sadly. 'Aye. But by th' time we reach that far we'll be in no position to go about. Th' Frog can thumb his nose at us.'

Bolitho pictured the disembodied masts and yards of Colquhoun's frigate and gripped his hands together to steady his nerves and restrain his rising anger. That fool Colquhoun. So eager to keep the spoils to himself he had failed to anticipate a change of wind. So keen to keep *Sparrow* out of the victory that he had now left the gate open for the enemy to run free if he so desired. *Fawn* could not bring her to battle even if she could catch her.

'An' a quarter less three!'

He grasped the nettings and tried not to imagine the sea's bottom rising slowly and steadily towards the keel.

It was no use. He swung away from the nettings, his sudden movement making Midshipman Fowler start back in alarm. He was risking the ship and the life of everyone aboard. *Fawn* was probably anchored, or had already found the enemy gone. His apprehensions, his personal doubts would cut little cloth with the relatives of those drowned by his risking *Sparrow* for a whim.

He said harshly, 'We will wear ship. I intend to cross the bar and rejoin *Bacchante* as soon as the mist clears.' He saw Buckle nod with relief and Tyrrell watching him with grave understanding. 'Convey my compliments to Mr Graves and have the guns . . .' He swung round as several voices shouted at once.

Tyrrell said tersely, 'Gunfire, by God!'

Bolitho froze, listening intently to the intermittent cracks and the heavier crash of larger weapons.

'Belay that last order, Mr Tyrrell!' He watched as a shaft of sunlight ran down the trunk of the mainmast like molten gold. 'We will not be blind for long!'

More minutes dragged by, with every man aboard listening to the distant gunfire.

Bolitho found that he could see beyond the tapering jib-boom, and

when he glanced abeam he saw a writhing necklace of surf to mark the
nearest prongs of reef. Perhaps it was the mist, or back echoes from the
hidden land, but the gunfire did not sound right. He could pick out the
sharper bark of *Fawn*'s nine-pounders from the enemy's heavier
artillery, but there were other explosions from varying bearings which
seemed totally at odds with the circumstances.

Sunlight swept down across the damp planking and raised more haze
from the dripping shrouds and hammock nettings, and then, like some
fantastic curtain, the mist was drawn aside, laying bare the drama with
each detail sharp in the morning light.

There was the tip of the island, hard blue against an empty sky, and
the intermingled patterns of surf and swirling currents to show the
nearness of the bar. And dead ahead of *Sparrow*'s slow approach, her
hull seemingly pinioned on the jib-boom, was Maulby's *Fawn*.

Further away, with masts and furled sails still shrouded in departing
mist, lay the Frenchman, half hidden in shadow, the outline blurred into
the landmass beyond. She was firing rapidly, her battery flashing long
orange tongues, her flag clearly visible above the gunsmoke.

It was only then Bolitho realized that *Fawn* was still anchored.
Sickened, he watched the sharp waterspouts bursting all around her, the
occasional fountain of spray as a ball smashed hard alongside.

Buckle called hoarsely, 'He's cut his cable, sir!'

Maulby's men were already running out the long sweeps to try to
work clear of the murderous barrage, while from her own deck the guns
maintained a brisk fire towards the enemy.

Bolitho gripped the rail as *Fawn*'s foretopmast staggered and then
reeled down in a great welter of spray and smoke. He heard Tyrrell's
voice as if in a dream, saw him pointing wildly, as more flashes sparkled,
not from the Frenchman but from the headland and low down as well,
probably on some small beach.

What a perfect trap. Maulby must have been caught by the mist, and
after making sure the enemy was still apparently moored close inshore,
had anchored to await Colquhoun's support. No wonder *Bacchante*'s
first lieutenant had reported so much activity. The French captain had
taken time to land artillery so that any attacker would be caught in
one devastating arc of fire from which there was small chance of escape.

The sweeps were out now, rising and falling like wings, bringing the
little sloop round until she was pointing away from the enemy and
towards the bar and the open sea.

A chorus of cries and groans came from the gundeck as the larboard
bank of sweeps flew in wild confusion, the splintered blades whirling
high into the air before splashing around the ship in fragments.

Bolitho raised a telescope and held it trained on *Fawn*'s quarterdeck.
He saw running figures, faces magnified in the lens and made more

terrible by distance and silence. Open mouths, gesturing arms as men ran to hack away the wreckage and keep at least some of the guns firing. A spar fell across his small encircled world, so that he flinched as if expecting to feel the shock of its impact on the deck. A seaman was running and stumbling along one gangway, his face apparently shot away, his terror agonizing to watch as he fell and was mercifully lost alongside.

Someone had kept his head, and high above the deck Bolitho saw the maintopsail billowing free to the wind, the sudden response beneath *Fawn*'s gilded figurehead as she began to gather way.

He felt Buckle shaking his arm and turned as he shouted desperately, 'We *must* go about, sir!' He pointed frantically towards the glittering water and at a mass of brown weed which glided so close to its surface. 'We'll be ashore this instant!'

Bolitho looked past him. 'Prepare to anchor, Mr Tyrrell!' He did not recognize his voice. If was like steel against steel. 'Have the cutters swayed out and prepare to lay a kedge anchor directly.' He waited until Tyrrell had run to the rail and the first dazed men had swarmed out along the yards. 'We will remain *here*.'

Moving more slowly, *Sparrow* edged into the shallows, and when she passed above one sandbar it was possible to see her own shadow before the water deepened once more.

Bolitho continued to pass his orders, making each one separate and detached from the next while he forced himself to concentrate, to shut his ears to the gunfire, to shield his eyes from *Fawn*'s slow and methodical destruction.

The cutters were lowered, and as ordered, Glass, the boatswain, took one of them to lay out a small kedge. With sails brailed up, and loosely anchored from bow and stern, *Sparrow* finally came to rest.

Then and only then did Bolitho raise his glass again and turn it on the *Fawn*. Listing badly, and all but her mizzen shot away, she was still trying to work clear of the bombardment. It was hopeless, for although her rudder seemed intact, and the spanker and crossjack were giving her some sort of steerage way, she was badly hampered by a mass of dragging spars and canvas, and appeared to have few men left who were able to cut it adrift. She was hit again and again, the splintered sections of timber and planking plummeting in the shallows, floating with and astern of her like blood from a wounded beast.

She gave a violent lurch, and as her mizzen came down to join the rest of her spars, Bolitho knew she had driven aground. She was broaching to, her deck tilting towards him as the first savage spines ground into her bilges and keel. It was finished.

He closed the glass and handed it to someone nearby. He saw no individual faces, heard no voices he could recognize. His own was as strange and unnatural as before.

'The Frenchman lies on our larboard bow.' How quiet it was now. The enemy had ceased fire, for as *Fawn* lay gripped on a shoal she was at last out of reach from those guns. Smoke drifted above the headland, and Bolitho pictured the French artillerymen sponging out the muzzles, watching perhaps the unexpected arrival of another sloop. One more victim. 'The range is less than a mile. He is well moored to present a perfect deception.' He knew Tyrrell and the rest were watching him. Transfixed. 'Equally, he cannot hurt us. We on the other hand . . .' He turned despite his guard to see *Fawn*'s beakhead and bowsprit tear away and drop into the swirling current beneath her stem. He continued tonelessly. 'We can hit him, and *hard*!'

Graves was on the ladder, his face pale from shock or at seeing the other ship destroyed so cruelly.

Bolitho looked at him. 'Get the larboard bow-chaser to work. You will open fire when ready. Pass your requirements to the bosun. By using the anchor cables you will be able to traverse at will.' He turned to Tyrrell. 'Have the capstan manned at once.'

Graves was halfway along the deck when Bolitho's voice brought him stockstill in his tracks.

'Fetch Mr Yule! Tell him I want him to build a small furnace where he can heat shot for your gun. Take good care that it is done right and well.' He shifted his eyes to the enemy ship. 'We have time now. Plenty of it.'

Then he walked to the netting and waited for Tyrrell to come aft again.

Tyrrell said quietly, 'You were right after all, sir. It was *us* they were after. Good God Almighty, it was *us* we just watched being destroyed!'

Bolitho studied him gravely. 'Aye, Jethro.' He recalled with stark clarity Maulby's words to him at their last meeting. Of Colquhoun. *That man will be the death of me* . . .

He swung round, his voice harsh again. 'What the hell is the delay?'

He was answered by a loud bang from forward, and was in time to see the fall of shot some half a cable from the enemy.

An order was passed down the deck and the men at the capstan bars took the strain, tautening the cable very slightly so that *Sparrow*'s bows edged round to give Graves's crew a better traverse.

Bang! The ball shrieked away, this time slapping down in line with the enemy's poop.

Bolitho had to grip his hands to steady himself. The next ball would strike. He knew it would. From then on . . . He beckoned to Stockdale.

'Away gig. Pipe for the second cutter to head for *Fawn*. We may yet pick up some of her people.'

He saw Dalkeith below the ladder, already dressed in his long, stained apron.

Another bang came from the bow-chaser, and he saw the brown smoke billowing through the beakhead, hiding the actual fall of shot. But a voice yelled, 'Got 'er! Fine on th' quarter!'

He said, half to himself, 'Not pop-guns this time, Mr Frenchman! *Not this time!*'

'Gig's ready, sir!' Even Stockdale sounded shocked.

'Take charge until I return, Mr Tyrrell.' He waited for him to drag his leg down to the entry port. 'We will work out of here on the next tide.'

He heard dull hammering as Yule and his mates constructed a crude furnace. It was dangerous, even foolhardy under normal circumstances to consider heating shot aboard ship. A tinder-dry hull, cordage and canvas, tar and gunpowder. But this was not normal. *Sparrow* was anchored in sheltered waters. A floating gun-platform. It was merely a matter of accuracy and patience.

Tyrrell asked awkwardly, 'How long do we keep fighting, sir?'

Bolitho swung himself out above the gentle slapping cat's-paws and green reflections.

'Until the enemy is destroyed.' He looked away. '*Completely.*'

'Aye, sir.'

Tyrrell watched Bolitho climb into the gig, the quick flurry of oars as Stockdale guided it towards the hulk which had once been *Fawn*.

Then he walked slowly to the quarterdeck rail and shaded his eyes to watch the enemy ship. There was little sign of damage, but the balls were hitting her regularly now. Shortly, the heated shot would be cradled from Yule's furnace, and then . . . he shivered despite the growing sunlight. Like most sailors he feared fire more than anything.

Heyward joined him and asked quietly, 'Did he mean it?'

Tyrrell thought of Bolitho's eyes, the despair and hurt when *Fawn* had been taken by the trap. 'Aye, he did.'

He flinched as a gun fired from the Frenchman's deck, and saw the ball throw up a thin column almost a cable short. Seamen not employed on the capstan or boats were watching from the gangways and shrouds, some even made wagers as to the next shot. As each French ball fell short they cheered or jeered, spectators only, and as yet unaware that but for a twist of fate they and not *Fawn*'s people would have died under those cannon.

Tyrrell continued, 'Colquhoun brought us to this. If our cap'n had been given his rightful position to attack we'd have got clear.' He banged his palms together. 'Arrogant bastard! An' he just sits out there like some sort of god while we finish his mess for him!'

Another bang echoed across the water and he saw a spar fall from the enemy's mainmast. Very slowly, or so it appeared, like a leaf from a tree in autumn.

Midshipman Fowler called, 'Our boats are standing off the wreck, sir!'

He was pale, but as he raised his telescope his hand was as steady as a gun.

Tyrrell looked at him coldly. *And there's another one. Like Ransome, like Colquhoun. Without humanity or feelings.*

Wreck was how he had described *Fawn*. *Yet moments ago she had been a living, vital creature. A way of life for her people and those who would have come after.*

Savagely he said, 'Get aloft, Mr Fowler, and take your glass with you! Keep an eye open for *Bacchante* beyond th' reef and watch for her signals.'

If any.

Then as the gun banged out again he made himself walk to the opposite side leaving Heyward to his thoughts.

Bolitho heard the gun's regular bombardment even as the gig hooked on to *Fawn*'s listing side, and with some of its men he climbed aboard.

'The cutter first!' He gestured to Bethune who was staring at the bloody shambles like a man in a trance. 'Full load, and then the gig.'

Stockdale followed him up the slanting deck, over smashed boats and tangled rigging. Once as they passed a hatchway Bolitho saw a green glow, and when he peered below he saw the sea surging jubilantly through a great gash in the hull, the reflected sunlight playing on two bobbing corpses. Huge patches of blood, upended guns around which the dazed survivors staggered down towards the waiting boats. There seemed very few of them.

Bolitho wiped his face with his shirt-sleeve. *Us*, Tyrrell had said. It was not difficult to understand.

He paused on the quarterdeck ladder and looked down at Maulby. He had been crushed by a fallen spar, his features frozen in the agony of the moment. There was a small smudge of blood on his cheek, and there were flies crawling on his face.

He said hoarsely, 'Take him, Stockdale.'

Stockdale bent down and then muttered, 'Can't be done, sir. 'E's 'eld fast.'

Bolitho knelt over the spar and covered his face with a scrap of canvas. *Rest easy, old friend. Stay with your ship. You are in the best of company today.*

The deck gave a quick shiver. She was beginning to break up. The sea, the tide and the unlashed guns would soon finish what the enemy had begun.

Bethune's voice came up from alongside where the cutter rose and plunged in a dangerous swell. 'All off, sir!'

'Thank you.'

Bolitho heard the sea crashing through the deck below, swamping the wardroom and on into the stern cabin. One like his own. There was no time to retrieve anything now. He bent down and unclipped Maulby's sword.

He handed it to Stockdale. 'Someone in England might like it.'

He made himself take one long glance around him. Remembering every detail. Holding it.

Then he followed Stockdale into the gig. He did not look back, nor did he hear the sounds of *Fawn*'s final misery. He was thinking of Maulby. His drawling voice. Feeling his last handshake.

Tyrrell met him and then said, 'Mr Yule has th' furnace ready, sir.'

Bolitho looked at him emptily. 'Douse it, if you please.'

'Sir?'

'I'll not burn men for doing their duty. The Frenchman is too badly holed now to get away. We will send a boat across under a flag of truce. I don't think he'll wish to prolong senseless killing.'

Tyrrell breathed out slowly. 'Aye, sir. I'll attend to it.'

When he turned back from passing the order to cease fire he found that Bolitho had left the deck.

He saw Stockdale carrying the sword and wiping it with a scrap of waste, his battered face totally engrossed in the task. He thought of Tilby's two model ships. Like Maulby's sword. Was that all that was left of a man?

He was still pondering about it when *Bacchante*'s topmasts hove in sight and she hoisted her first signal.

It was evening before *Sparrow* was able to close with the frigate. For almost as soon as she had worked clear of the bar the wind veered and gained considerably in strength, so that it was necessary to use every effort to beat clear of those treacherous breakers. In open waters again, with the darkening slab of Grand Bahama some five miles abeam, *Sparrow* reduced sail and hove-to within a cable of Colquhoun's ship.

As he sat in the crazily tossing gig Bolitho watched the frigate and the last signal for him to repair on board being hauled down to the deck. It had been hoisted for some time, but like Colquhoun's previous ones, he had ignored it. Had not even made an acknowledgement.

Spray lanced back from the oars and dashed across his face. It helped to calm him, if only slightly. His sorrow was matched by anger, his self-control by an eagerness to confront Colquhoun.

The gig turned and rose dizzily on a steep swell, the bowman almost pitching overboard as he hooked on to the chains and made fast.

Bolitho clambered up the frigate's tumblehome, for once ignoring the sea which swirled along the hull as if to pluck him away.

Colquhoun was not at the entry port, and the first lieutenant said quickly, 'By God, sir, I am sorry for what happened.'

Bolitho eyed him gravely. 'Thank you. The fault was not of your making.'

Then without another word or a glance at the swaying side party he strode aft to the cabin.

Colquhoun was standing by the windows, as if he had not moved since their last encounter. In the lanterns' yellow glare his face looked stiff and unsmiling, and when he spoke his tone was like that of a much older man.

'It took you long enough! How dare you ignore my signals!'

Bolitho faced him coldly. The anger in Colquhoun's voice was as false as his composure, and he saw one hand twitching badly against his white breeches.

'Your earlier signals were made to *Fawn*, sir.' He saw him start and continued slowly, 'But she was already in pieces and her people mostly killed in battle or drowned when she struck.'

Colquhoun nodded jerkily, his brows tightening as if he was trying to keep a grip on his emotions.

'That is beside the point. You disobeyed my orders. You crossed the bar without permission. You . . .'

Bolitho said, 'I did what I considered to be my duty.' It was no use. He could feel his control slipping away like an icy yard beneath a topman. 'But for your lust after glory we would have taken the Frenchman together, without loss. We had all the advantage, for the enemy knew nothing of your full strength. She was after one prize only. *Sparrow*.' He turned away, trying to hide his grief. 'Because of you, Maulby and his men were killed, his ship lost. Because of your senseless rigidity, your failure to see beyond prize money, you could not help when the time came.' He swung round again, his voice harsh. 'Well, the Frenchman is taken! What d'you want now, a bloody knighthood?'

Surprisingly, Colquhoun's voice was very low, and as he spoke he kept his eyes on some point away from Bolitho.

'I will ignore your outburst.' He paused. 'Ah, I remember now, you have young Fowler aboard. It would have done no good to lose him in battle.' He was speaking more quickly, the disjointed sentences falling from his lips in time with his thoughts. 'The admiral will expect a full report. I shall . . .'

Bolitho watched him, sickened. 'I have the written orders you originally gave me. The ones which were to send me as far from the point of attack as you could invent.' Despite Colquhoun's pathetic explanations and excuses he forced himself to go on. 'If I had obeyed them, or the wind had remained constant, *Fawn* would still have perished. What would you have done then? Sent the little *Lucifer* maybe?'

Colquhoun walked to his desk and pulled a decanter from its rack. Some of the brandy slopped over his hand but he did not seem to notice it.

'I received orders some while back. When we had run the French *flute* to ground, or given up the search, we are ordered to proceed to New York. The flotilla is to be reduced.' He swallowed half a glass of brandy and had to fight to regain his breath. '*Bacchante* will be returned to fleet duties.'

Bolitho stared at him. Any compassion or pity he might have harboured behind his anger was gone with that admission.

In a low tone he asked, 'All this while, and you *knew* we were to go to New York?' He listened to his own voice, wondering how he could sound so calm. 'You thought it was a last chance to prove yourself. A great show of victory, with you entering port, a fine fat prize under your colours! Yet because of your greed you could not see the real danger, and *Fawn* has paid dearly for your ignorance!'

Colquhoun lifted his eyes and watched him desperately.

'In New York things might seem different. Remember, I was the one who helped you . . .' He broke off and swallowed another drink. 'I needed that prize! I've *earned* it!'

Bolitho moved towards the door, keeping his eyes on Colquhoun's quivering shoulders.

He said, 'I sent *Fawn*'s remaining lieutenant to take charge of the *flute*. Surrender was arranged by Lieutenant Heyward.' He made himself keep to the details, if only to stop Colquhoun from pleading. 'The French ship'll not be much use again. I suggest you send your marines to take charge and await the military, who'll wish to escort the prisoners elsewhere.'

Colquhoun leaned against the stern windows, his voice muffled by sounds of sea and rudder.

'It will mean a court martial.' His shoulders stiffened. 'You will be ordered to attend.'

Bolitho nodded. 'It would seem so.'

Colquhoun waved one hand towards the cabin without turning.

'All this gone. In just a moment of bad circumstances. Fate.'

'Maulby probably thought that, too.' Bolitho rested his fingers on the door.

Colquhoun pushed himself from the windows and lurched across the cabin.

'So you've won in the end, eh?' His voice cracked. 'You and your *bloody* Sparrow!'

Bolitho saw the man's anguish and answered, 'Three years ago when I was given *Sparrow* I thought command was everything, all a man could desire. Then maybe I would have agreed with your decisions, no matter what they entailed. Now I know better, perhaps after all, thanks to you. Command is one thing. But responsibility, the duty to those who depend on you, is the greater burden. We must share the guilt for Maulby's death.' He saw Colquhoun staring at him incredulously but continued, 'Your folly blinded you to everything but future advancement. My crime was pride. A pride which goaded the enemy into laying a snare for me, and one which cost *Fawn*'s people dearly.' He opened the door. 'I hope I never forget it. Nor you.'

He walked quickly to the quarterdeck and heard the door slam behind him, the slap of a musket as the sentry returned to a more relaxed stance.

By the gangway he found the first lieutenant waiting for him. Across the heaving water, its crests and troughs already painted with shadows, he saw *Sparrow* swaying unsteadily against the first pale stars. A lantern gleamed from her taffrail, and he thought he saw the splash of oars to mark where Stockdale held the gig in readiness. He could have waited in vain. Colquhoun might have made one last gesture by throwing him under arrest for his outburst. That he had not was proof enough of his true guilt. More, that Colquhoun was well aware of what he had done.

He said, 'We are to rejoin the Flag at New York.'

The lieutenant watched the gig bobbing towards the side and replied sadly, 'I'll not be sorry to quit this place.'

Bolitho sighed. 'Aye. A defeat is a bad business. But a victory can often bring the greater pain.'

The lieutenant watched him climb into the gig and pull clear.

So young, yet with so much responsibility. Not for me. Even as the thought crossed his mind he knew it was a lie, and upon looking round the darkening deck he wondered if Colquhoun's error had brought him any nearer to his own promotion.

13

No Better Epitaph

Almost immediately after dropping anchor at Sandy Hook, *Sparrow* and her company were thrown into the urgent work of a short but well-deserved overhaul. Under the wintry eye of a senior dockyard officer the ship was careened and the thick growth of weed cut and cleaned from her hull. Bolitho was able to send Lock ashore, and with more careful bribes obtained fresh provisions as well as replacements for some of the fouler casks of beef and pork.

In the midst of all this activity, which continued from dawn to dusk, he was occasionally visited by a scholarly lieutenant of the Commander-in-Chief's staff. He took statements from Bolitho and Tyrrell and compared them with notations in the log at the time of *Fawn*'s destruction, as well as those leading up to the actual attack. Buckle was required to display and explain each section of the charts used, and was instantly reduced to mumbling confusion under the lieutenant's skilful examination. But as the day followed the next, and *Sparrow* regained her original trim appearance, the bitter memories of *Fawn*'s loss, even the display of hot anger in Colquhoun's cabin, became blurred, if not erased from Bolitho's mind.

He had been kept continuously busy with the affairs of his ship, never knowing for sure when his next orders would arrive, and had spent any spare moments studying the wider aspects of the war on land. When the summons to appear at a court martial was delivered to him, it came as something like a shock.

Three weeks had gone by since he had confronted Colquhoun in *Bacchante*'s cabin and almost every day had been occupied with incident and activity.

Only certain details stood out with stark clarity in his mind. The picture of slaughter and desolation on *Fawn*'s shattered deck. Maulby's face, the flies crawling over his contorted features. Young Heyward's obvious pride at being given the task of receiving the Frenchman's surrender, and the *Fawn*'s one surviving officer who had gone to take charge of the enemy until the marines arrived. Maulby'd lieutenant had been like a man coming out of the shadow of death itself. His movements disjointed, his face stricken from the sights and sounds he had endured.

On the morning of the court martial Bolitho stood on *Sparrow*'s quarterdeck with Tyrrell and Buckle, aware of the many watching eyes, of his men, and those on nearby ships at anchor.

Tyrrell shifted his leg and muttered, 'I may be called as witness, but by God I feel like a guilty man!'

Bolitho watched the gig moving towards the entry port, and noticed that Stockdale and the oarsmen were dressed in their best clothes. Conscious, too, of this moment perhaps.

As well they might, he thought grimly. It was Colquhoun's day, but it was not unknown for a drowning man to drag others down with him.

He shifted his gaze to the old seventy-four which lay some three cables distant. The *Parthian*, where he had been given his instructions for rescuing the soldiers and General Blundell's bullion from the Delaware. How long ago it seemed now. An eternity.

The gig made fast and Tyrrell said abruptly, 'That bastard deserves to hang!'

Bolitho followed the others to the entry port, trying once again to find his true feelings. It was difficult to go on hating Colquhoun. His weakness had perhaps been too human, which made it harder to condemn after the first anger had passed.

As eight o'clock came and the bells chimed from each anchored ship-of-war, a solitary gun crashed out from the *Parthian*'s side, and the court martial Jack broke simultaneously from her gaff. It was time.

Graves stood with the rigid side party, his face expressionless as they climbed into the gig. He was not implicated, and Bolitho wondered if he saw his chances of promotion reflected in the court martial flag.

Once through *Parthian*'s gilded entry port and past the marine guard and assembled band, Bolitho felt a rising sense of disgust. The two-decker's quarterdeck was thronged with visitors. Senior officers, some of them military, several prosperous-looking civilians and a solitary artist gave the impression of a carefree outing rather than a trial. The artist, a bearded, intent little man, busied himself from every angle, making quick sketches, dotting in detail of uniform or title, hardly pausing between each capture.

He saw Bolitho and hurried between the chattering throng, his pad already poised in readiness.

'Ah, good sir! Captain Bolitho?' The pencil hovered and then darted down. 'I am so glad to see you at last. I have heard much of your exploits.' He paused and smiled shyly. 'I wish I could have been aboard your ship to take sketches. The people at home need to be told . . .'

Tyrrell murmured, 'For Christ's sake!'

A master-at-arms opened a door and the visitors began to filter aft towards the great cabin. Left isolated and ill at ease in their best uniforms, the witnesses remained on the quarterdeck.

Bolitho said quietly, 'At some other time maybe.'

He turned his head to watch a marine captain with drawn sword marching aft to the cabin. Just the sight of it made him feel sick. The grim array. Like the crowds at Tyburn, or the jeering fools who stood for hours to watch some wretch choking out his life on a village gibbet.

The artist's smile faded. 'I understand. I thought . . .'

Bolitho replied, 'I know what you thought. That I'd be pleased to see a man fall from office!' He did not hide his contempt.

'That, too.' The artist's eyes flickered in the sunlight as he made a quick alteration to his sketch. 'I also imagined you might see your future made stronger by this man's disgrace.' He shrugged as Bolitho turned on him angrily. 'That I am wrong on both counts makes me a fool, and you an even better man than they say you are.'

Bolitho looked at him sadly. 'What *they* say will count for little today.'

A lieutenant called, 'This way, gentlemen.'

They followed him in order of seniority and filed into the ship's wardroom.

The artist passed quickly and vanished towards the great cabin as Tyrrell growled. 'God, what is happening to us? Will they make pictures of th' Day of Judgement, too?'

All morning the wearing business went on. Witnesses were called and evidence mounted. Factual and hearsay, technical or just plain imagination, it seemed to take an eternity to get it down in writing. There were occasional pauses for refreshment and to allow the visitors to stretch their legs on the quarterdeck.

Throughout the whole morning Bolitho hardly spoke. Around him, their faces displaying either confidence or uncertainty, the rest of the witnesses waited their turn. Odell off the schooner *Lucifer*, his quick, agitated movements only adding to the tension. *Bacchante*'s first lieutenant and sailing master. *Fawn*'s surviving lieutenant and a blinded seaman who had stood beside Maulby when he had been struck down.

In seniority, or as their value directed, the witnesses dwindled until only Bolitho and Tyrrell remained. Through the open ports Bolitho saw boats plying between the ships and the shore, the haze of smoke from a nearby spit of sand where a man was burning driftwood.

It was stiflingly hot. The first day of May. He pictured what it would be like at home. In Falmouth. Sometimes he thought he would never see it again. Tiny pale dots of sheep on the hills and headland. Noisy cows in the lane below the house, always inquisitive as they passed the gates, as if they had never seen them before. And in the town square, where the coaches loaded up for Plymouth or the horses were changed for another route to the west, there would be plenty of laughter and good cheer. For if the war was a threat, so, too, was winter, and that was well behind them until the next time. Now, the fishermen could put to sea in safety, and the fields and markets would show the evidence of their labours and rewards.

'Mr Tyrrell.' The lieutenant held the door open. 'This way.'

Tyrrell picked up his hat and looked at him. 'Soon now, sir.' Then Bolitho was alone.

It did not take very long. Tyrrell's evidence was purely factual and concerned the times of crossing the bar and commencing the attack. In all events, he was obeying orders. He was safe.

When his call came Bolitho followed the lieutenant into the cabin without remembering hearing his name announced.

It was packed with seated figures, and right aft, behind a table which reached almost from side to side, he saw the officers of the court. In the centre, as President, was Sir Evelyn Christie, flanked by ten captains of varying status and seniority, none of whom was known to Bolitho.

Rear-Admiral Christie eyed him bleakly. 'Your sworn statement has been read and submitted in evidence.'

He sounded clipped and formal, so that Bolitho was suddenly reminded of their last meeting. The difference almost amounted to hostility.

'We have heard of the plan to take the *flute,* of the events leading to her discovery, including evidence given by *Lucifer*'s captain and that of your own officers.' He paused and ruffled through some papers. 'In your statement you said that you had advised your senior officer against a cutting-out expedition of the kind which was eventually employed?'

Bolitho cleared his throat. 'I thought that under the circumstances . . .'

The nearest captain snapped, 'Yes or no!'

'Yes.' Bolitho kept his eyes on the admiral. 'I gave my opinion.'

The admiral leaned back slowly. 'The accused has already stated that is *not* the case. He gave you your orders only after you had insisted that your ship would be better placed to the north of the Bank.'

In the sudden silence Bolitho could feel his heart pounding like a hammer. He wanted to turn his head and look at Colquhoun, but knew that any such attempt would be immediately seen as guilt.

The senior captain at the table said abruptly, 'Were there any witnesses as to what occurred when these decisions were reached?'

Bolitho faced him. 'Only Commander Maulby, sir.'

'I see.'

Bolitho felt the cabin closing in around him, saw the nearest faces watching him like a row of greedy birds.

The admiral sighed. 'I will continue. After leaving the other vessels you proceeded towards your allotted station.'

'Yes, sir.'

The admiral looked up with a jerk. 'Then why did you cross the bar?' He slapped one hand on the papers, bringing a mingled gasp from the spectators. '*Was it guilt*? Did you at last realize that Captain Colquhoun was right and that he needed your support in the south?'

'No, sir.' He could feel his hands shaking, the sweat like ice-rime between his shoulders. 'I have stated my reasons. We lost the wind, I had no option but to tack when I did.' Pictures flashed through his mind like parts of a nightmare. Heyward, ashamed at losing control of the ship. Buckle, doubtful and anxious for her safety as he had told him his intentions. He heard himself add quietly, 'Commander Maulby was my friend.'

The senior member of the court regarded him flatly. 'Really?'

Bolitho turned his head and saw Colquhoun for the first time. He was shocked to see the change in him. He was very pale, and in the reflected light his skin was the texture of wax. He was standing with his arms limp at his sides, his body moving only slightly to the gentle tilt of the deck. But his eyes were the worst part. They were fixed on Bolitho's face, on his mouth when he spoke, and shone with such incredible hatred that Bolitho exclaimed, 'Tell them the truth!'

Colquhoun made as if to step forward, but his escort, the marine captain, touched his arm and he relaxed again.

The admiral snapped, 'That will do, Captain Bolitho! I'll have no exchanges in this court!'

The senior captain coughed discreetly and continued, 'The rest we know. The French deception, and your destruction of their *flute*. all of which is above criticism. Despite obvious dangers you managed to rescue some of *Fawn*'s company, and several of her wounded are now alive and recovering, thanks to your efforts.'

Bolitho watched him emptily. He had done his duty, but the lies already told by Colquhoun about his character, and his statement which only Maulby could confirm, made a mockery of it. He looked down at Colquhoun's sword on the table. His own might lie there soon. He found he cared little about that, but the slur on his name he could not bear.

The admiral looked around the crowded cabin. 'I think we have heard enough before we withdraw, gentlemen?'

Bolitho swayed. A long lunch. More delays. It was torture.

Like most of those present he jerked round as a chair at the rear of the court went over with a loud clatter.

A husky voice shouted, 'No, dammee, I won't keep still! In God's name, I've given me eyes for the King! Ain't I allowed to speak the truth?'

The admiral rasped, 'Keep silent there! Or I will call the officer of the guard!'

But it was no use. Most of the visitors were on their feet, all talking and shouting at once. Bolitho saw that some had even climbed on to their chairs to see what was happening behind them.

The admiral sat speechless, while the rest of the court waited for him to carry out his threat.

The voices died away, and the crowded figures parted to allow the small artist to come aft to the table. He was leading the seaman who had been blinded aboard *Fawn* and who had already stated briefly what he knew of the preparations to cut the cable and escape the French artillery.

Now, in his ragged trousers and borrowed blue coat, with his head tilted as if to sniff out those nearest him, he approached the table.

The admiral said gravely, 'Very well, Richards.' He waited for the people to sit down again. 'What is this you wish to say?'

The seaman reached out and gripped the edge of the table, his bandaged eyes trained above the admiral's head.

'I were *there*, sir. Right there on th' quarterdeck with Cap'n Maulby!'

Nobody moved or spoke except the blind seaman named Richards.

Bolitho watched his hand as it moved vaguely in the air, saw his chest heaving as he relived those last terrible moments.

He said huskily, 'The Frogs had our measure, sir. We was all but dismasted an' with more'n half our brave lads cut down.'

The senior captain made as if to interrupt but the admiral's gold-laced cuff froze him to stillness.

'Th' sweeps was shot away, but all th' time Cap'n Maulby was shoutin' and cussin' in his same old style.' Beneath the stiff bandage the man's mouth twisted in a smile. 'An' he could cuss when given the occasion, sir.' The smile faded. 'I were quartermaster an' alone at th' wheel. The master was down an' so was my mate, both killed. The first lieutenant were below havin' his arm off, an' it was then that th' cap'n turns to me an' cries, '*God damn that Colquhoun, Richards! He's done for us this day!*' His head drooped and his fingers slipped from the table as he repeated brokenly, 'That's what he said. *He's done for us this day.*'

The admiral asked quietly, 'And then what happened?'

Richards waited for a few moments to compose himself. Still nobody moved or even whispered. Beyond the stern windows the wheeling gulls seemed too loud to be real.

Then he said, 'Mr Fox, th' second lieutenant, had just gone forrard, I think to seek some men for th' pumps. Several balls from th' Frog guns ashore came inboard an' killed Mr Midshipman Vasey. He were only fourteen but a good lad when he put his mind to it. When he fell, th' cap'n shouts to me. "*If Richard Bolitho was with us today as he wanted to be, then by God we'd show 'em, artillery or no*"!'

The admiral snapped. 'Are you absolutely certain? He said those very words?'

Richards nodded his head. 'Aye, sir. I'm not likely to forget 'em. For it was then that we was hit again and th' cro'jack yard came down to th' deck. It took Cap'n Maulby with it. He never cried out.' He nodded again, very slowly. 'He were a good cap'n, even if he did cuss more'n most.'

'I see.' The admiral glanced at his senior captain. Then he asked, 'Do you recall anything more?'

'We struck th' reef, sir. Th' mizzen come down an' a bloody swivel, beggin' your pardon, sir, exploded on th' rail and took away me sight. I don't remember much else till I come-to aboard th' *Sparrow*'.

'Thank you.' The admiral gestured to a marine orderly. 'I will see that you are taken care of.'

Richards groped up to knuckle his forehead and then said, 'Thankee, sir. I hopes you'll forgive me, but I had to speak me piece.'

He was guided between the watching faces, and as the cabin door closed a slow murmur began to grow like combined anger.

The admiral snapped, 'I will not order you to be silent again!'

'Surely you're not going to believe that lying hound?' Colquhoun's voice was shrill. 'That . . . that . . . *half-wit*!'

The marine captain stepped forward to restrain him but faltered as the admiral said calmly, 'Pray continue, Captain Colquhoun.'

'Oh, I knew about Bolitho and Maulby all right! As thick as thieves!' Colquhoun had turned slightly, his arms outstretched as if to embrace the court. 'And I was well aware that Bolitho wanted all the glory for himself. That was why I sent him to the north and gave Maulby the chance to prove himself.' He was speaking very rapidly, and his face was shining with sweat. 'I saw through Bolitho's little game from the start, which was why he tried to condemn me. I knew he wanted to take the Frenchman for himself without giving me time to take up my proper attacking station. An attack overland and with boats indeed!' He stopped, his jaw hanging open with astonishment.

The admiral said coldly, 'So he did *not* agree with your plan of attack, Captain Colquhoun? Your testimony was a lie?'

Colquhoun turned and stared at him, his mouth still open, as if he had been struck by a pistol ball and was beginning to feel its first searing agony.

'I–I . . .' He reeled away from the table. 'I only wanted . . .' he could not go on.

'March the accused out, Captain Reece!'

Bolitho watched Colquhoun as he lurched past the assembled officers, his gait less steady than the blind seaman's had been. It was incredible. Yet despite what had happened he could sense neither release nor satisfaction. Shame, pity, he did not know what he really felt.

'You may stand down, Captain Bolitho.' The admiral eyed him calmly. 'It will be placed on record that you and your people acted and behaved in the best traditions of the Service.' He turned to the cabin at large. 'Court will reassemble in two hours. That is all.'

Outside the stuffy cabin it felt like a different world. Faces swam around him, hands gripped him, and many voices called greetings and congratulations.

Tyrrell and Odell, with Buckle bringing up the rear, managed to guide him to a quieter part of the upper deck to await their respective boats. Bolitho saw the small artist and strode across to him.

'Thank you for what you did.' He held out his hand. 'I was hard on you earlier.' He looked around. 'Where is that man Richards? I would like to thank him, too. It took true courage to act as he did.'

'He's already gone across to a transport, Captain. I asked him to wait, but . . .' he shrugged sadly.

Bolitho nodded. 'I understand. Here we all are, congratulating ourselves, while he has nothing to look forward to and no eyes to see what awaits him either.'

The little man smiled, his gaze on Bolitho's face, as if seeking to discover something.

'My name is Majendie. I would like to speak with you again.'

Bolitho clapped him on the shoulder, forcing a smile.

'Then join me in my ship. If we must wait two hours, then I'd rather do it where I have a sense of freedom.'

The court assembled at the exact moment prescribed, and Bolitho found he was barely able to take his eyes from Colquhoun's sword. It was pointed towards him, the hilt on the opposite side of the table.

The senior captain's voice was lost, too, in his confused thoughts and memories. He heard fragments like 'hazarding the lives of men under your command, the ships used at your direction'. And later: '. . . did lay false evidence to smear the name of a King's officer and thereby bring discredit on this court'. There was a lot more, but Bolitho heard other voices intermingled with the cold summing-up. Maulby, Tyrrell, even Bethune, they were all in it. And above all, the blind seaman, Richards. *He were a good cap'n.* Surely there was no better epitaph for any man?

He jerked from his thoughts as the admiral said, 'The sentence is that you be dismissed your ship and be confined under close arrest until such time you may be transported to England.'

Colquhoun stared at the grave-faced officers and then at his sword.

Dismissed his ship. Bolitho looked away. They should have hanged him. It would have been kinder.

A voice broke the silence, 'Prisoner and escort, quick *march*!'

It was over.

As the orderlies ushered the chattering spectators towards the quarterdeck, Rear-Admiral Christie came round the table and held out his hand.

'Well *done,* Bolitho.' He shook Bolitho's hand warmly. 'I have great hopes for young officers of your cut.' He saw Bolitho's uncertainty and smiled. 'It grieved me to treat you as I did. But I had to have your name cleared of that slur. Right or wrong, it would have marked you for the rest of your service.' He sighed wearily. 'Only Colquhoun could do it, and it took poor Richards to spark the flint.'

'Yes, sir. I see that now.'

The admiral picked up his hat and studied it.

'Come ashore with me tonight. The Governor is holding a reception. A ghastly business, but it does no harm to see 'em enjoying themselves.' He seemed to sense Bolitho's mood. 'Take it as an order!'

'Thank you, Sir Evelyn.'

Bolitho watched him as he walked to his adjoining cabin. An invitation ashore. The admiral could just as easily have sentenced him to ignominy, if fate had not stepped in to aid him.

He let out a long breath. When did you ever cease to learn about such complex matters?

Then he strode out to look for his gig amongst the many boats alongside.

The reception that evening proved to be more breathtaking and unnerving than Bolitho had imagined it could be. As he handed his hat to a bewigged Negro footman and waited for Rear-Admiral Christie to exchange a few words with another flag officer, he stared up and around the great pillared hall, at the teeming throng of colourful figures who seemed to fill every inch of floor space and a handsome balcony as well. The scarlet coats of the military were very much in the majority, interspersed with velvets and brocades of their ladies, the familiar blue of sea-officers, although Bolitho noted with some alarm that most of the latter appeared to be admirals of one sort or another. Marine officers, too, their white facings and silver buttons distinguishing them from the soldiers, and so many civilians it was a wonder that New York had not come to a standstill. Along one side there were alcoves where Negro footmen and servants were kept busy at long tables, the contents of which were enough to make Bolitho think he was dreaming. The nation was at war, yet those tables were groaning under the weight of food and delicacies of every kind. Meats and huge portions of pie, tempting fruits and a glittering array of silver punch-bowls which were being refilled even as he watched.

Christie rejoined him and murmured, 'Take a good look at 'em,

Bolitho. A man needs to know whom he is serving as well as his cause!'

A footman in green livery met them at the top of the marble stairs, and after a cursory glance addressed the assembled guests in a voice which would have fitted a foretopman in a gale. 'Sir Evelyn Christie, Knight of the Bath, Rear-Admiral of the Red.' He did not bother to announce Bolitho, probably taking him as a mere side aide, or some dependent relative.

Not that it mattered. There was no break in the tide of laughter and conversation, and hardly anybody turned to examine the newcomers.

Christie moved nimbly through the fringe of the crowd, nodding to a face here, pausing to pat a sleeve or bow to a lady there. It was hard to see him in his role that morning. President of the court. Answerable to nobody when he passed his sentence.

Bolitho followed the admiral's slight figure until they reached a table at the far end of the hall. Beyond it and the perspiring footmen a doorway opened on to a great lawn, where he could see a fountain shining in the reflected glow of lanterns.

'Well?' Christie waited until each had a heavy goblet in his hand. 'What do you make of 'em?'

Bolitho turned to study the press of figures by the alcove, hearing the strings of some invisible orchestra as they joined in a lively quadrille. How anyone could find room to dance he could not imagine.

'It's like a fairyland, sir.'

Christie regarded him with amusement. 'Fools' paradise is a better description!'

Bolitho tasted the wine. Like the goblet, it was perfect. He relaxed slightly. The question had put him on guard, but the admiral's comment had shown that he had no intention of testing him.

Christie added, 'A town under siege, and we must accept that is the true position here, is always unreal. It is crammed with refugees and tricksters, merchants out for quick profit who care little for which side they trade with. And as always in a campaign of any size, there are two armies.'

Bolitho watched him, momentarily forgetting the noise and bustle around him, the despair and anxiety of the morning. As he had believed from the first, Christie's austere appearance hid a rapier-sharp mind. A brain which could sift and examine each challenge and problem, discarding everything that was superfluous.

'*Two* armies, sir?'

The admiral signalled for fresh goblets. 'Drink your fill. You'll not find wine like this elsewhere. Yes, we have the military who daily face the enemy, search out his weakness or try to contain his attacks. Soldiers who live on their feet. Know nothing of clean beds or good food.' He smiled sadly. 'Like those you saved in Delaware Bay. *Real* soldiers.'

'And the others?'

Christie grimaced. 'Behind every great army there is the *organization*.' He gestured towards the crowd. 'The military government, the secretariat, and the traders who live off the fighting like leeches.'

Bolitho eyed the swaying figures outside the alcove with growing uncertainty. He had always mistrusted people of the sort described, but it seemed impossible that it was all so blatant, so dishonest as the admiral had said. And yet . . . he thought of the cheerful, chattering visitors at the court martial. Spectators to a man's disgrace, but seeing it only as something to break the boredom of their own world.

Christie watched him thoughtfully. 'God alone knows how this war will end. We are fighting too many enemies, over too vast a span of the world to hope for some spectacular victory. But you, and those like you, must be warned if we are to have any chance of honour, let alone mastery over our adversaries.'

The wine was very strong, and the heat of the hall helped to break Bolitho's caution.

'But, Sir Evelyn, surely here in New York, after all that has happened since the rebellion, they must be aware of the true facts?'

He shrugged, a weary gesture. 'The general staff is too busy with its own affairs to retain much concern for what is happening here. And the Governor, if we may call him so, spends so much time in chasing giddy young girls and enjoying his mounting riches, that he has no wish to alter matters. He was once an army quartermaster, therefore an accomplished thief, and is ably supported by a Lieutenant Governor who was originally a customs officer in a city which was renowned only for its smuggling!' He chuckled. 'So between them they have tied this place into a bag for their own booty. No merchant or shipmaster can enter or leave without permits, from which our *leaders* reap a rich profit. New York is crammed with refugees, and the Governor decided that city, church and college moneys should be gathered into a fund for their relief.'

Bolitho frowned. 'Surely *that* was in good faith?'

'Maybe. But most of it has been squandered away. Balls and dances, receptions such as this, misses and whores, hanger-on and favourites. It all takes a great deal of money and support.'

'I see.'

In fact he did not. When he thought of his ship, the daily risk of injury and death with little comfort or relief, the manner in which every fighting man was facing a determined enemy, he was appalled.

Christie said, 'To me duty stands before all else. I would hang anyone who acted otherwise. But these . . .' he did not hide his contempt, 'these maggots deserve no loyalty. If we must fight a war, we should also ensure they have no gain from our sacrifice!'

Then he smiled, the sudden relaxing of the lines around his eyes and mouth altering him yet again.

'There, Bolitho, you have learned the next lesson, eh? First you command respect, then a ship. Next you achieve control of more and larger vessels. This is the way of ambition, without which no officer is worth a wet fuse to me.'

He yawned. 'Now I must be off.' He held up one hand. 'But you remain and continue your education.'

'Will you not stay to meet the Governor, sir?'

Something like panic at the thought of being left abandoned made him show his inner feelings.

Christie smiled cheerfully. 'Nobody will meet him tonight. He merely holds these affairs to pay off old debts and to keep his pot a'boiling.' He beckoned to a footman. 'So enjoy yourself. You have earned it, although I daresay you'd wish rather for London, eh?'

Bolitho grinned. 'Not London, sir.'

'Ah, of course.' The admiral watched the footman approaching with his hat and boatcloak. 'A son of the soil. I forgot.' Then with a nod he moved through the door to merge quickly with the deep shadows of the lawn.

Bolitho found an empty corner at the end of the table and tried to decide what he should eat. He had to have something, for the wine was doing its work well. He felt unusually light-headed, although he knew that drink was not entirely to blame. By leaving him to fend for himself the admiral had momentarily cut the strings of control. He had given him his head to act and think as he wanted. He could not recall it ever happening like this before.

A thickset post-captain, his face blotchy with heat and good wine, thrust past him and carved a huge piece of pie, adding several other sorts of cold meat to his plate before any footman could assist him. Bolitho thought of Bethune. The plate would have satisfied even his appetite for several days.

The senior captain turned and focused his eyes on him.

'Ah. What ship?'

'*Sparrow*, sir.' Bolitho watched him squinting as if to clear his vision.

'Never heard of her.' He frowned. 'What's yer name, eh?'

'Richard Bolitho, sir.'

The captain shook his head. 'Never heard of *you* either.' He ambled back into the crowd, brushing some of the meat against a pillar without even pausing.

Bolitho smiled. In these surroundings you soon found a proper awareness of your status.

'Why, *Captain*!' The voice made him swing round. 'It is! I just *knew* it was you!'

Bolitho stared at the girl for several seconds without recognition. She was dressed in a beautiful, low-cut gown, the colour of tawny port wine, and her hair, which hung in ringlets across her bare shoulders, shone beneath the chandeliers like silk.

He exclaimed, 'Miss Hardwicke! I did not know you were here, in America.'

He felt as foolish as he sounded, but her sudden appearance had caught him entirely aback. She was lovely, more so than he remembered since that far-off day. When she had defied her uncle, General Blundell, had shouted and kicked as his seamen had carried her bodily from the Indiaman before his fight with the *Bonaventure*.

And yet she was exactly the same. The smile, half amused, partly mocking. The violet eyes which seemed to strip away his defences and leave him like some inarticulate ploughman.

She turned to the tall officer at her side, wearing a frogged jacket of the dragoons, and said, 'He was so young, so *serious*, I think all the ladies on board fell in love with the poor man.'

The dragoon eyed Bolitho coldly. 'I think we must hurry, Susannah. I would wish you to meet the general.'

She reached out and laid a white-gloved hand on Bolitho's sleeve.

'It is good to see you again! I have often thought about you and your little ship.' Her smile faded and she became suddenly serious. 'You look well, Captain. Very well. A little older perhaps. A little less . . .' the smile crept back again, 'of the boy dressed as a man?'

He flushed, but was conscious of pleasure to match his confusion.

'Well, I suppose . . .'

But she was already turning away as two more escorts pushed from the jostling crowd to join her.

Then she seemed to make up her mind.

'Will you dine with me, Captain?' She studied him thoughtfully. 'I will send a servant with the invitation.'

'Yes.' The words came out in a rush. 'I would like that very much. Thank you.'

She gave a mock curtsy, bringing back the memory of their first meeting like a stab in the heart.

'Then it is settled.'

The crowd eddied and swayed and seemed to swallow her up completely.

Bolitho took another goblet and walked unsteadily towards the lawn. Susannah, the dragoon had called her. It was perfect for her.

He stopped beside the tinkling fountain and stared at it for several minutes. The reception had turned out to be a success after all, and made the morning seem just a blurred memory.

14

Join the Ladies

Three days after the Governor's reception the *Sparrow* was to all intents ready for sea again. Bolitho had carried out a careful inspection, and under Lock's anxious scrutiny had signed the final manifest for stores and supplies. The last days had been uneventful, almost lazy, and Bolitho found it easier to understand, if not share, New York's apparent lethargy. It was an unreal existence, with the war seen only at the end of a marching column of soldiers, or in some colourful account of the news-sheets.

The flotilla's other surviving sloop, *Heron*, had recently dropped anchor at Sandy Hook, and was now waiting hopefully for a similar overhaul.

On this particular forenoon Bolitho sat in his cabin enjoying a glass of good claret with *Heron*'s commander, Thomas Farr. The latter had been a lieutenant at their last meeting, but Maulby's death had given him a well-deserved promotion. He was elderly for his rank, probably ten years or so older than himself, Bolitho decided. A big, broad-shouldered man, uncouth, and with a ripe turn of phrase which reminded him vaguely of Tilby. He had come to his present appointment by a roundabout route. Sent to sea as a boy of eight years old, he had been in merchant service for most of his life. Coasters and mail-packets, Indiamen and humbler craft, he had eventually risen to command a collier brig out of Cardiff. With England embroiled in war he had offered his services to the Navy and been gratefully accepted. For if his manners and background marked him apart from many of his brother officers, his experience and skill in sail put him well ahead of them. Paradoxically, *Heron* was smaller than *Sparrow*, and like her commander had begun life as a merchantman. Consequently, her armament of fourteen guns was of lesser size. She had already gathered several good prizes, nonetheless.

Farr sprawled untidily on the stern bench and raised his glass to the sunlight.

'Bloody fine stuff! Though give me a tankard of English ale an' you can spit this against the wall!' He laughed and allowed Bolitho to pour another glass.

Bolitho smiled. How things had changed for all of them. Looking back to that moment at Antigua when he had gone to meet Colquhoun it was hard to recall just how the years and weeks had affected them as individuals. Then, as he had looked from Colquhoun's window in the headquarters building, he had seen the flotilla as a whole, had wondered what his command would be like. So many other doubts and fears had plagued him on that morning.

Now, *Fawn* was gone, and *Bacchante* had sailed only the previous day to rejoin the fleet under Rodney. Her captain had been appointed from the flagship, and Bolitho wondered if Colquhoun had been able to watch her clear the anchorage from wherever he was being held in custody.

Only *Sparrow* and *Heron* remained now. Apart from the little schooner *Lucifer* of course, and she was almost a rule unto herself. She would stay on her stop-and-search patrols of small coasting craft, or continue probing into coves and creeks in search for enemy blockade-runners.

Farr watched him comfortably and remarked, 'Well, you are doing famously, I hear. Reception with the mighty, wine with the admiral! By the living Jesus, there'll be no saying where you'll end up. Probably on some ambassador's staff, with a dozen little girls to dance to your tune, eh?' He laughed loudly.

Bolitho shrugged. 'Not for me, I have seen enough.'

He thought quickly of the girl. She had not written to him. Nor had he seen her, although he had made it his business to pass by way of her residence when he had been ashore on ship's affairs.

It was a fine house, not much smaller than where he had attended the reception. There had been soldiers at the gates, and he guessed that its owner held some sort of government appointment. He had tried to tell himself not to be foolish, so naive as to expect someone of her background to remember him beyond a momentary meeting. In Falmouth the Bolitho family was much respected, its land and property giving work and substance to many. Bolitho's own recent gains in prize money had made him feel independent for the first time in his life, so that he had lost sight of reality when it came to people like Susannah Hardwicke. Her family probably spent more in a week than he had earned since taking command of *Sparrow*. She was accustomed to travel, even when others were held still by war or lack of means. She would know the best people, and her name would be accepted in any of the great houses from London to Scotland. He sighed. He could not see her as the lady of the house in Falmouth. Entertaining ruddy-faced farmers and their wives, attending local fairs and the rough and tumble of a community which lived so close to nature.

Farr seemed to sense his mood and asked, 'What about the war, Bolitho? Where is it getting us?' He waved his glass. 'Sometimes I get to thinking we will go on patrolling an' running after bloody smugglers till we die of old age.'

Bolitho stood up and moved restlessly to the windows. There was plenty of evidence of power nearby. Ships-of-the-line, frigates and all the rest. And yet they gave an appearance of waiting. But for what?

He said, 'Cornwallis seems intent on retaking Virginia. His soldiers are doing well, I hear.'

'You don't sound too damn confident!'

Bolitho looked at him. 'The army is pinched back to its lines. They can no longer rely on supplies or support by land. Everything must move by sea. It is no way for an army to fight.'

Farr grunted. 'Not our concern. You worry too much. Anyway, I think we should leave 'em all to their own games. We should go home an' smash hell out of the Frogs. The bloody Dons would soon call for peace, an' the Dutch have no liking for their so-called allies anyway. *Then* we can come back to America an' have another go at 'em.'

Bolitho smiled. 'I fear we *would* die of old age if we followed that course.'

He heard a shouted challenge, the scrape of a boat alongside. He realized that his mind had recorded it, but that he felt at ease, even remote. When he had first come aboard there had been neither sound nor event which had not caught his immediate attention. Perhaps at last he was accepting his true role.

Graves appeared in the cabin door with a familiar sealed envelope.

'Guardboat, sir.' He darted a glance at *Heron*'s commander. 'Sailing orders, I expect.'

Bolitho nodded. 'Carry on, Mr Graves. I will inform you directly.'

The lieutenant hesitated. 'This letter was delivered also, sir.'

It was small, and the handwriting was almost hidden by a seal. *Office of the Military Government*.

As the door closed Farr asked thickly, '*Graves?* No bloody relative of our admiral, I trust!'

Bolitho grinned. With Rodney in the West Indies, and further restricted by bad health, the command of American waters came under the flag of Rear-Admiral Thomas Graves. Lacking the wisdom of Rodney, the hard-won respect of Hood, he was looked upon by most of the fleet's officers as a fair but cautious commander. He believed utterly in the rigid rules of fighting, and had never been known to change one jot of their interpretation. Several senior captains had put down suggestions for improving the system of signalling between ships engaged in close action. Graves had said icily, according to the many stories circulating amongst the fleet, 'My captains know their function. That should be enough for any man.'

Bolitho replied, 'No. Perhaps it would be better if he were. We might know more of what is happening.'

Farr stood up and belched. 'Good wine. Better company. I'll leave you to yer sealed orders. If all the written despatches from all the admirals in the world was laced together we'd have enough to cover the

Equator, an' that's a fact! God's teeth, I sometimes think we choke on paper!'

He shambled out of the cabin, refusing Bolitho's offer to see him over the side by saying, 'If I can't manage on me own by now, then it's time I was weighted with a pair of round-shot and dropped overboard!'

Bolitho settled down at the table and slit open the canvas envelope, although his eyes rested mainly on the smaller one.

The orders were briefer than usual. Being in all respects ready for sea, His Britannic Majesty's Sloop-of-War *Sparrow* would weigh and proceed at the earliest convenience the following day. She would carry out an independent patrol, eastward to Montauk Point at the top of Long Island and thence via Block Island to the approaches of Newport itself.

He contained his rising excitement with some difficulty and made himself concentrate on the sparse requirements of the patrol. He was not to become involved with enemy forces other than at his own discretion. His eye rested on the last words. How they reminded him of Colquhoun. So brief, yet concealing the very precariousness of his own position should he act wrongly.

But here at last was something direct to carry out. Not merely harrying blockade-runners or seeking some sly privateer. This was French territory. The fringe of the second greatest sea-power on earth. Beneath the flag captain's scrawling signature he saw that Rear-Admiral Christie had added his own. How typical of the man. A sign of his trust, and the extent of his arm.

He stood up and rapped on the skylight.

'Midshipman of the watch!'

He saw Bethune's face above him and called, 'My compliments to the first lieutenant. I would like to see him at once.' He paused. 'I thought you were on watch earlier?'

Bethune dropped his eyes. 'Aye, sir. That is true. But . . .'

Bolitho said quietly, 'In future you will take your watches as laid down. I suppose Mr Fowler should have been on duty?'

'I promised him, sir.' Bethune looked uneasy. 'I owed him a relief.'

'Very well. But remember my orders. I'll have no *retired* officers in this ship!'

He sat down again. He should have noticed what was happening. Poor Bethune was no match for the Fowlers of this world. He smiled in spite of his concern. He was a fine one to talk.

He slit open the second envelope and came up with a jerk against the table.

My dear Captain. I would be so pleased if you could dine with us this evening. I feel wretched at this inexcusable delay and hope for instant forgiveness. As you read this letter I am watching your ship through my uncle's telescope. So that I shall not be held in suspense, please show yourself.

It was signed, *Susannah Hardwicke.*

Bolitho stood up and winced as his skull collided with a deck beam. Pausing only to lock his orders in the cabin strongbox, he hurried out of the door and up the companion ladder. Her uncle's telescope. So General Blundell was here, too. It would explain the sentries at the gates.

But even this fact did not depress him. He almost collided with Tyrrell as he came limping aft, his arms spattered with grease.

'Sorry I was adrift when you called for me, sir. I was in th' cable tier.'

Bolitho smiled. 'Taking the opportunity of an empty tier to look for rot, eh?'

Tyrrell rubbed his thigh. 'Aye. But she's fine. Sound as a bell.'

Bolitho walked to the nettings and shaded his eyes against the fierce glare. The distant houses were almost lost in haze, their outlines quivering and intermingling as if they were melting in the heat.

Tyrrell watched him questioningly. 'Something wrong, sir?'

Bolitho beckoned to Bethune and took his telescope. It was no better. The one trained upon *Sparrow* was probably a huge affair. Very slowly he raised his arm and waved it from side to side.

Behind him Tyrrell and Bethune stood stockstill, each as puzzled as the other by the captain's strange behaviour.

Bolitho turned and saw Tyrrell's face. 'Er, I was just waving to someone.'

Tyrrell looked past him at the anchored ships and busy harbour craft. 'I see, sir.'

'No you don't, Jethro, but no matter.' He clapped his shoulder. 'Come below and I will tell you what we are about. You will be in charge of the ship this evening, for I am dining ashore.'

A slow grin spread across the lieutenant's face. 'Oh, I *see*, sir!'

They were examining a chart and discussing the sailing orders when they heard Bethune yell, 'Avast there! Stand still, that man!' Then there was a splash and more shouts along the gundeck.

Bolitho and Tyrrell hurried to the quarterdeck again to find Bethune and most of the unemployed hands lining the larboard gangway or clinging to the shrouds.

A man was in the water, arms striking out strongly, his dark hair glossy in the spray and sunlight.

Bethune panted, 'It was Lockhart, sir! He dived overboard before I could stop him!'

Tyrrell murmured, 'A good seaman. Never any trouble. I know him well.'

Bolitho kept his eyes on the swimmer. 'A colonist?'

'Aye. Came from Newhaven some years back. He's done it now, poor devil.' There was no anger in Tyrrell's voice. If anything it was pity.

Bolitho heard the men near him exchanging guesses at the swimmer's success of getting ashore. It was a long way to go.

He had known many deserters during his life at sea. Often he had found room for sympathy, although he had thought their actions to be wrong. Few men would volunteer for the harsh demands of service in a King's ship, especially as nobody ever knew for sure if he would regain his home in safety. Seaports were full of those who had returned. Cripples and men made old before their time in many cases. But as yet, no one had found a better way of crewing the fleet. Once pressed, most men accepted it, could even be relied upon to take others by similar methods. The sailor's old rule, 'If I'm here, why not him?' carried a lot of weight in ships-of-war.

But this was different. The seaman, Lockhart, had seemed nothing out of the ordinary. A good worker and rarely adrift for his watch or station. Yet all the while he must have been brooding over his proper homeland, and the stay in New York had done the rest. Even now, as he thrashed steadily past an anchored two-decker, he was no doubt thinking only of his goal. Some vague mental picture of house and family, or parents who had almost forgotten what he looked like.

A faint crack came from the two-decker's beakhead, and Bolitho saw a red-coated marine already ramming another ball into his musket for a further shot at the lone swimmer.

A growl of anger came from *Sparrow*'s seamen. Whatever they thought of the man's desertion, or of the man himself, had nothing to do with their reaction. He was one of their own, and the marine sentry was momentarily an enemy.

Yule, the gunner, muttered, 'That damn bullock should be shot down hisself, the bloody bastard!'

The marine did not fire again, but sauntered to the end of his little platform to watch the swimmer, like a wildfowler who has given his quarry best for the time being. Or so it appeared. Then as a guardboat swept round the stern of another two-decker, Bolitho knew why he had not bothered to shoot.

The longboat was moving swiftly, the oars sending it through the glittering water like a blue fish. In the sternsheets he saw several marines, a midshipman with a raised telescope trained on the seaman.

Yule observed dourly, ' 'E'll not escape now.'

Tyrrell said, 'It's out of our hands.'

'Aye.'

Bolitho felt suddenly heavy, the pleasure of the letter spoiled by this man's despair. Nobody who had *run* from a King's ship could expect mercy. It was to be hoped he was hanged rather than face the horror of flogging round the fleet. He chilled. If he was to be hanged . . . He stared up at *Sparrow*'s mainyard, his eyes desperate. There was no doubt where the execution would be carried out. Even Christie would make sure of that. An example. A warning clear to all aboard and throughout the nearby ships. He tried not to watch the guardboat as it swept down on the tiny, bobbing head.

His own friends, *Sparrow*'s loyal seamen, would be forced to witness the halter being set around his neck before they, and they alone, were ordered to run him up to the yard. After all they had endured together, this sickening act might drive a wedge between officers and men and destroy what they had achieved.

Tyrrell gasped, 'Look, sir!'

Bolitho snatched a glass and trained it beyond the guardboat. He was just in time to see the man, Lockhart, treading water, turning to stare either at the boat or perhaps at *Sparrow* herself. Then, even as the boat's oars backed water and a marine groped over the stemhead for the man's hair, he threw up his hands and disappeared beneath the surface.

Nobody spoke, and Bolitho found himself holding his breath, perhaps like the man who had vanished so suddenly. Sailors were usually poor swimmers. Perhaps he had got cramp. In a moment he would break surface nearby and the guardboat would haul him on board. Seconds, minutes passed, and then at a shouted command the guardboat resumed its leisurely patrol between the anchored ships.

Bolitho said quietly, 'I thank God for that. If he had to suffer, I am glad it was gently done.'

Tyrrell watched him dully. 'That's true.' He turned with sudden anger on the gunner. 'Mr Yule! Clear these idlers off th' gangway or I'll find 'em some harder work for their wits to dwell on!'

He was unusually disturbed, and Bolitho wondered if he was comparing his own fate with that of the drowned seaman.

He said, 'Make an entry in the log, Mr Tyrrell.'

'Sir?' Tyrrell faced him grimly. 'As a deserter?'

Bolitho looked past him at the seamen as they wandered towards the gun deck again.

'We do not *know* for certain he was deserting. Mark him as *Discharged–Dead*.' He walked to the hatch. 'His relatives will have enough to bear without the weight of shame also.'

Tyrrell watched him go, his breathing returning slowly to normal. It would not help Lockhart. He was beyond reach. But Bolitho's order would ensure that his name carried no stigma, and his loss would be recorded with those who had fallen in battle, in fights which he had also suffered without complaint. It was a small distinction. But even so, he knew that only Bolitho would have thought of it.

When Bolitho climbed from his gig he was astonished to find a smartly painted carriage waiting for him on the jetty. A liveried Negro doffed his tricorn hat and beamed hugely.

'Good evenin', Sah.' He opened the carriage door with a flourish while Stockdale and the gig's crew watched in silent admiration.

Bolitho paused. 'Er, do not wait, Stockdale. I will return to the ship in a local boat.'

He was strangely elated, and conscious of watching townsfolk on the road above the jetty, an envious glance from a passing marine major.

Stockdale touched his hat. 'If you says so, sir. I *could* come along with you . . .'

'No. I'll have full need of you tomorrow.' He felt suddenly reckless and pulled a coin from his pocket. 'Here, buy some grog for the gig's crew. But not too much for safety's sake, eh?'

He climbed into the coach and sank back against the blue cushions as with a jerk the horses took the first strain at their harness.

With his hat on his knees he watched the passing houses and people, Stockdale, even the ship, temporarily forgotten. Once, when the coach reined to a halt to allow a heavy wagon to cross ahead of it, he heard a faraway murmur of cannon fire. It was a fine evening, and the steady westerly wind was dry and warm. Sounds carried easily in such conditions. Even so, it was hard to connect the distant gunfire with the brightly lit houses, the occasional snatches of music and song from taverns along the road. Some army battery testing its guns perhaps. But more likely a nervous duel between opposing pickets where the two armies lay in watchful readiness.

It did not take long to reach the house, and as he stepped down from the coach he realized there were other guests arriving, too. Again he called himself a fool for imagining he alone would be entertained this evening.

Servants glided from the shadows, and like magic his hat and boatcloak were spirited away.

A footman opened some doors and announced, 'Captain Richard Bolitho of His Britannic Majesty's Ship *Sparrow*.'

How different from the reception, he thought. As he walked into a fine, high-ceilinged room he was conscious of comfort and luxury mixed with an air of intimacy which had been lacking before.

At the end of the room General Sir James Blundell watched his approach in silence, and then called gruffly, 'You are an unexpected guest, Bolitho.' His heavy features yielded slightly. 'My niece told me of your arrival.' He thrust out his hand. 'You are welcome here.'

The general had changed very little. Heavier perhaps, but otherwise the same man. In one hand he was holding a brandy glass, and Bolitho was reminded of his stay aboard *Sparrow*, of his obvious contempt for the men who had carried him to safety.

Something of their first meeting must have circulated amongst his friends, for upon Blundell's show of greeting the room came alive again with laughter and noisy conversation. It was as if they had all been waiting to see how Blundell would react. Bolitho's own feelings were of course unimportant. He could always be told to leave.

Bolitho felt the girl's hand on his arm and turned to find her smiling up at him. With a nod to her uncle she steered him towards the other side of the room, the guests moving aside for her as if she were royalty.

She said, 'I saw you today. Thank you for coming.' She patted his cuff. 'I thought you were splendid just now. Uncle can be rather troublesome.'

Bolitho returned her smile. 'I think I can appreciate that. After all, he lost a great deal of bullion because of me.'

She wrinkled her nose. 'I have no doubt he will have recovered it by insurance elsewhere.' She gestured to a servant. 'Some wine before dinner.'

'Thank you.'

He saw several officers, mostly military, watching him intently. Envy, resentment, curiosity, it was all there.

She said, 'Sir James is Adjutant General now. I came out here with him after our return to England.' She watched his face as he sipped the wine. 'I am glad I came. England is full of woe because of the war.'

Bolitho tore his mind from what she had just said of her uncle. Christie had already spoken scathingly about the Governor and his assistant. With Blundell involved in controlling the city, there seemed little hope of improvement.

As the girl turned to curtsy to a white-haired man and his lady he let his eyes devour her as if seeing her for the last time. The curve of her neck as she bowed to her guests, the way her hair seemed to float across her bare shoulders. It was beautiful hair. Golden brown, like the wing of a young thrush.

He smiled awkwardly as she looked up at him.

'*Really*, Captain! You make a girl feel indecent the way you stare so!' She laughed. 'I suppose you sailors are so long away from civilization you cannot control your ways!' She clutched his arm, her mouth quivering with amusement. 'Do not fret! There is no need to be so serious about it. I really must teach you to accept what is there, to enjoy what is yours by right.'

'I am sorry. You are most likely right about me.' He looked at the marble floor and grinned. 'At sea I can stand upright. Here, I feel as if the deck is moving!'

She stepped back and regarded him searchingly. 'Well, I shall have to see what can be done about that.' She tapped her lips with a slim fan. 'Everyone is talking about you, what you have done, how you faced that awful court martial and made fools of them.'

'It was not exactly like that . . .'

She ignored him. 'Of course *they* will not mention any of this. Some are probably afraid you will turn into a wild, bloodthirsty sea-dog!' She laughed gaily. 'Others see in your success something of their own failure.'

A footman was whispering to the general and she added quickly, 'I will have to leave you to your own devices for dinner. I am hostess tonight.'

He said, 'Oh, I thought . . .' To cover his confusion he asked, 'Is Lady Blundell not here, too?'

'She stays in England. My uncle's habits are those of a soldier. I think she is content to keep them well away from her.' She held his arm again. 'But do not look so sad. I will see you later. We must talk of your future. I know people who can help you. Put you where you deserve, instead of . . .' She did not finish.

A gong boomed and the footman intoned, 'My lords, ladies and gentlemen. Dinner is now served.'

They followed the general and his niece into an even greater room, and Bolitho found himself paired off with a dark-haired little woman who was apparently the wife of a staff officer. He was not present, and with something like gloom Bolitho thought he would be saddled with her for the rest of the evening.

The dinner matched the room. Every course larger, more extravagantly prepared than the one before. His stomach had long become used to the sparse fare aboard ship and the varying efforts of many seacooks. No one else seemed to find difficulty, however, and he could only marvel at the way the plates emptied without any apparent break in conversation.

There were many toasts, with the wines as varied as their reasons for drinking them.

After the loyal toast to King George there were all the usual ones. *Death to the French. Confusion to our enemies. A curse on Washington.* As the wine flowed they became as meaningless as they were incoherent.

The lady at Bolitho's side dropped her fan, but as he bent to collect it she reached below the tablecloth and seized his wrist, holding it against her thigh for several seconds. It seemed like an hour, and he thought every eye at the table must be on him. But she was the only one, and her face was filled with such desire that he could almost feel her control slipping away.

He returned the fan and said, 'Easy, ma'am, there are quite a few courses yet.'

She stared at him, open-mouthed, and then gave a secret smile.

'God what it is to find a real man!'

Bolitho forced himself to take another portion of chicken, if only to regain his wits. He could feel her knee pressing into his leg, and was very aware that whenever she required something from the table she seemed to need it from across his arm. Each time she lingered over the motion, letting her shoulder or breast touch for just a few moments more every time.

He glanced desperately along the table and saw the girl watching him. It was hard to understand her expression when she was so far away. Part amused, part watchful.

His companion was saying casually, 'My husband is much older than I. He cares more for his damned office than for me.'

She reached for some butter, allowing her breast to touch his sleeve while she kept her eyes on his.

'I expect you have been to many places, Captain. How I *wish* I could take a ship somewhere. Away from this place. And *him*.'

At last the meal was over, and with a scraping of chairs the men rose to allow their ladies to withdraw. Even at the last moment Bolitho's companion persisted with her campaign, like a frigate cutting out a ship which was totally outmatched from the start.

She whispered, 'I have a room here. I will send a servant to guide you.'

As she moved from the table he saw her stagger but recover instantly. It would take more than wine to break her, he thought anxiously.

The doors closed again and the men moved their seats closer to the head of the table.

More brandy, and some black cheroots which Blundell said had come from *some damned rascal who tried to avoid his dues*.

'I hear you are now on our local patrols, Bolitho.' Blundell's harsh voice reduced the other guests to attentive silence.

'Yes, Sir James.'

Bolitho eyed him evenly. Blundell was well informed, considering he had only received his orders that afternoon.

'Good. We need a few captains with the will to guard our lifelines, what!' Blundell's features were crimson from the extent of the dinner. 'These damn Yankees have had too much their own way, I say!'

There was a growl of approval, and someone called tipsily, 'Thash th' bloody truth, shir!' He shrank under Blundell's withering gaze.

Bolitho asked quickly, 'Colonel Foley, sir. Is he still in America?'

'He has a battalion under Cornwallis.' Blundell seemed disinterested. 'Best bloody place for him, too.'

Bolitho allowed the conversation to flow around him like a protective cloak. He heard little about the war. Horse breeding, and the cost of keeping house in New York. The affair of some unfortunate artillery captain who had been found in bed with a dragoon's wife. The growing difficulty of obtaining good brandy, even at smugglers' prices.

Bolitho thought of Christie's summing up. *Two armies*, he had said. How true it now seemed. Colonel Foley, whether he was a likeable man or not, was one of those fighting for his country's cause, and his life. Around this table sat a goodly proportion of the other sort. Spoiled, cosseted and completely selfish, he wished he could be rid of them.

Blundell heaved himself upright. 'We will join the ladies, God help us!'

When Bolitho glanced at the ornate French clock he saw it was almost midnight. It seemed incredible that time could pass so swiftly. But despite the hour there was no lessening in the pace. A small string orchestra struck up a lively dance, and laughing noisily the guests pushed and jostled towards the sound of music.

Bolitho walked slowly through the connecting rooms, watching for Susannah Hardwicke and keeping a wary eye open for his earlier companion.

As he passed a book-lined study he saw Blundell speaking with a group of men, most of whom were prosperous-looking civilians. One, very tall and broad-shouldered, stood partly in shadow, but the side of his face which was visible in the candlelight made Bolitho start with shock then pity. It had been scoured away, the skin burned almost to the bone from hairline to chin, so that it had the appearance of some grotesque mask. He seemed to feel Bolitho's eyes on him, and after a quick glance turned his back, hiding himself in shadow.

No wonder he had not joined the others at dinner. It was easy to imagine the agony of that disfigurement, the torment which had left him so scarred.

'Ah, there you are!' She came out of another room and rested her hand on his arm. 'Take me into the garden.'

They walked in silence, and he felt her dress swishing against his legs, the warmth of her body.

'You were absolutely splendid, Captain.' She paused and looked at him, her eyes bright. 'That poor woman. I thought for an instant you would fall to her.'

'Oh, you saw.' Bolitho felt uneasy. 'She has gone, it seems.'

'Yes.' She led him into the garden. 'I sent her off.' She laughed, the sound carrying through the shrubs like an echo. 'I cannot have her interfering with *my* captain, now can I?'

'I hope you were easy with her?'

'Actually, she burst into tears. It was all rather pathetic.'

She turned inside his arm, her full dress spreading out behind her like pale gold.

'I must leave you now, Captain.'

'But . . . but I thought we were going to talk?'

'Later.' She studied him gravely. 'I have plans for your future, as I told you earlier, did I not?'

'I weigh anchor tomorrow.' He felt wretched. Helpless.

'I *know* that, silly!' She reached up and touched his lips. 'Do not frown. I cannot allow it. When you come back I will introduce you to some friends of mine. You will not regret it.' Her gloved fingers moved gently to his cheek. 'And neither, I trust, shall I.'

A servant appeared through the gloom. 'Carriage ready, Missy.'

She nodded. To Bolitho she said, 'After you have left I will try and clear these dreary people from the house.' She tilted her head and faced him calmly. 'You may kiss my shoulder, if you wish.'

Her skin was surprisingly cool, and as soft as a peach.

She twisted away from him and called, 'Be good, Captain, and take care of yourself. When you return I will be here.' Then she laughed and ran lightly up the terrace into the house.

The coach was waiting for him as he walked dazedly through the shadowed garden and on to the carriageway. His hat and cloak were on the seat, and strapped to the boot was a large wooden box.

The footman's teeth shone in a white crescent. 'Missy Susannah had the kitchen pack some food for you, Sah.' He chuckled. 'Nothin' but the best, she said.'

Bolitho climbed into the coach and sank against the cushions. He could still feel her skin against his mouth, smell the perfume from her hair. A girl who could drive a man mad, even if he was not halfway there already.

At the end of the jetty he found a waterman nodding over his oars, and had to call several times to attract his attention.

'Wot ship, sir?'

'*Sparrow*.'

Just saying the name helped to steady his racing thoughts. Before he stepped down into the dory he turned to look at the coach, but it had already disappeared. Like one more part of the dream.

The waterman was grumbling to himself as he hauled the heavy box down the steps. Not enough to offend a ship's captain, but enough to add slightly to his fare.

Bolitho wrapped his cloak around him and felt the sea-breeze cold against his face. Still westerly. It would be good to get away again. If only to find time to collect himself and examine his hopes for the future.

15

A Good Likeness

Sparrow's new mission to investigate the strength of French shipping at Newport proved to be more difficult than Bolitho had expected. The passage from Sandy Hook to the eastern extremes of Long Island showed nothing but promise for a quick completion and an equally swift return. But the weather decided otherwise, and in a savage westerly gale the little sloop was driven and battered continuously, so that Bolitho had to run with it rather than risk damage to spars and canvas.

Even when the wind moderated it took many more days to beat back again, and hardly an hour passed without the need to shorten sail or lay the ship on a tack which would take her away rather than toward her goal.

New York's entertainment seemed a long way behind, and Bolitho found the reality of driving his ship against wind and tide more than enough to occupy his energy. Even so, he found plenty of time to think about Susannah Hardwicke. Pacing the deck, hair whipping in the wind, his shirt often drenched with spray, he remembered their parting, the hint of an embrace which he could recall as clearly as if it had just occurred.

He suspected that his officers knew or guessed what had happened in New York, if only because of their careful silence.

The drudgery of fighting against the wind, the constant demands on every man aboard, were eased in part by the presence of their passenger. Rupert Majendie, true to his word, had arrived within minutes of weighing, complete with sketching and painting materials, and a repertoire of stories which did more than pay for his keep on board. When the sea and wind calmed he would be seen with his pad, sketching seamen at their daily tasks or catching them at their relaxation off watch, dancing or making small models and scrimshaw work. If the weather was less friendly he would disappear below to find fresh scope for his busy hands with only a swinging lantern to guide his pencil or brush. He and Dalkeith had become firm friends, which was hardly surprising. Each came from another sphere of culture and high intellect, with far more to discuss than the average sailor.

At the end of three long weeks, and with each day adding to his frustration, Bolitho decided to wait no more. He called Tyrrell to the cabin and unrolled his chart.

'We will close with the shore at daylight tomorrow, Jethro. The wind is still strong, but I see no other choice.'

Tyrrell let his eyes move across the chart. The approaches to Rhode Island were always a problem with a prevailing westerly wind. To be caught in a full gale might mean being driven eastwards again, and once within the jaws of the mainland and Newport itself there would be little room for manoeuvre. Under normal conditions it required patience and understanding. But with the French in control of the area it was something else entirely.

As if reading his thoughts, Bolitho said quietly, 'I'd not wish to be caught on a lee shore. But if we stay out here in open water, we might as well admit failure.'

'Aye.' Tyrrell straightened his back. 'I doubt th' Frogs'll have much in th' way of ships anyway. They depend on their batteries to defend themselves.'

Bolitho smiled, some of the strain slipping from his face. 'Good. Pass the word. I'll want the very best eyes at the mastheads tomorrow.'

But true to Buckle's gloomy prediction, the next morning was something of a disappointment. The sky was clouded over and the wind, which made the topsails bluster and crack despite their trim, told there was rain nearby. And yet the air felt sultry and oppressive, affecting the hands as they went to their stations for changing tack. The welcome stay in harbour, followed by the nervous uncertainty of thrashing this way and that at the wind's discretion, had taken their toll. There were plenty of curses and not a few blows from boatswain's mates before *Sparrow* laid herself over on the larboard tack, her plunging beakhead pointing towards the shore once again.

A grey day. Bolitho gripped the weather nettings and mopped his forehead with his shirt-sleeve. His skin and clothing were wringing wet, as much from sweat as from flying spray.

Only Majendie seemed content to remain on deck willingly, his pencil busy, his thin body and jutting beard dripping with moisture.

'Land ho! Fine on the weather bow!'

Bolitho tried not to show his satisfaction and relief. With the dull visibility and blustery wind you could not be too secure with mere calculations. He looked up at the masthead pendant. The wind had backed slightly. He stared at the pendant until his eyes watered. There was no doubt about it. Good for a steady approach. Not so comforting if they had to turn and run. 'Bring her up a point, Mr Buckle.'

'Aye, aye, sir.'

Buckle dabbed his face with a handkerchief before passing his orders. He would be well aware of the difficulties, Bolitho thought. There was no sanity in worrying him further.

To Majendie he said, 'I hope you are getting it all down. You will make your fortune when you return to England.'

Buckle yelled, 'Nor' nor'-east, sir! Full an' bye!'

'Very good. Hold her so.'

Bolitho walked a couple of paces and thought of the girl in New York. What would she think of him now? Crumpled and soaked to the skin, his shirt more patches than original cloth. He smiled to himself, not seeing Majendie's pencil as it recorded his mood.

Tyrrell limped up the deck and joined him by the nettings.

'I reckon that Newport is 'bout five miles off th' starboard bow, sir.' He looked up with surprise as a shaft of watery sunlight played across the bulking hull like a lantern beam. 'Hell, you can never tell in these waters.'

'Deck thar! Ships at anchor to nor'-east!'

Tyrrell rubbed his hands. 'Frogs may be assembling a convoy. Our inshore squadron'll catch 'em if we carry th' word fast enough.'

The lookout yelled again. 'Six, no *eight* sail-o'-the-line, sir!'

Graves staggered from the rail as *Sparrow* lurched sickeningly into a deep trough.

'The man's mad!' He spluttered as spray burst above the nettings and cascaded over him like hail. 'A couple of frigates at most, if you ask me!'

Bolitho tried to ignore the buzz of speculation and doubt around him. De Grasse had a powerful fleet in the West Indies, that was well known. His subordinate, de Barras, who commanded at Newport, had no such strength. His usefulness was placed in frigates and smaller craft and in quick forays against British coastal trade. De Barras had made one attempt to challenge the New York forces off Cape Henry earlier in the year, but the action had been desultory and ineffective. He had retired to his defences and had remained there.

He said, 'Aloft with you, Mr Graves. Tell me what you see.'

Graves hurried to the shrouds muttering, 'That fool. Can't be ships-of-the-line. Can't be.'

Bolitho stared after him. Graves was acting very strangely. It was as if he dreaded what he might discover. Afraid? No. That seemed unlikely. He had been aboard long enough to know the risks and rewards of the game.

'Deck there!' It was another seaman clinging high above the mizzen yard. 'Sail on the larboard quarter!'

'Damn!' Tyrrell snatched a telescope and hurried with it to the taffrail.

Mist and spray, the distance made worse by *Sparrow*'s drunken motion, it took time to find the newcomer.

Tyrrell snapped, 'Frigate. No doubt, sir.'

Bolitho nodded. The other ship was clawing close inshore, coming around the jutting headland with every available sail set to the wind.

Buckle cupped his hands. 'Stand by to come about!'

'*Belay that!*' Bolitho's voice held the master motionless. 'We have got this far. Let us see what there is to see and *then* run.'

Graves came lurching from the gangway, his shirt torn from his rapid descent.

He gasped, 'He was right, sir. Eight of the line. Maybe two frigates, and a whole clutter of supply ships anchored closer in.'

Bolitho thought of his talk with Farr at Sandy Hook, his own reaction at seeing the British two-deckers nearby. Waiting, he had thought, but what for? And were these Frenchmen doing likewise?

Tyrrell said, 'Can't be none of de Grasse's ships, sir. Our patrols, even blind ones, would've seen 'em!'

Bolitho met his stare. 'I agree. It's a gathering for something. We must inform the admiral directly.'

Buckle shouted, 'Frigate closing fast, sir. Less than three miles, by my reckoning.'

Bolitho nodded. 'Very well, run up French colours, and prepare to come about.'

The flag rose swiftly to the gaff, to be greeted by an immediate blast of cannon from the frigate's forecastle.

Bolitho smiled grimly. 'He's not deceived. So hoist our own, if you please.'

Buckle crossed to Bolitho's side, his features screwed tight with worry.

'I think maybe we should wear ship, sir. That Frenchman'll be up to us afore we knows it otherwise.'

Bolitho shook his head. 'We would lose too much time. The frigate might chase us all the way to Nantucket or run us aground.' He swung on Graves. 'Clear away the bow-chasers. Load but do not run out.' He clapped him on the forearm, seeing him start with alarm. 'Lively, man! Or Mr Frenchman'll be aboard for grog!'

Men scampered wildly to their stations, some pausing only to peer over the hammock nettings at the other ship which was driving purposefully towards the larboard quarter. She was much nearer, but in the bursting spray her hull was almost lost to view. Only her bulging courses and topsails displayed her captain's eagerness to do battle.

'Ready about!' Bolitho had his hands on his hips as he peered aloft at the slashing pendant. 'Stand by on the quarterdeck!'

'Put the helm down!' He felt the deck stagger, and wondered how *Sparrow* would appear to the enemy. Running? Preparing to fight?

He almost fell as the ship heeled and tilted still further to the thrust of sail and rudder.

'Helm a'lee, sir!' Buckle added his own weight to the wheel.

Headsails flailing about like mad things, yards bending to the contest between braces and booming canvas, it was a picture of confusion as

Sparrow heeled sickeningly round into the wind. The sea surged up and over the beakhead, and men fell cursing and sprawling, some being washed into the gundeck scuppers like corpses.

Majendie clung to the nettings, his pad already sodden with spray as he stared transfixed at the sloop's wild turn across the wind.

Tyrrell's voice rose above the pandemonium like a trumpet. 'Braces there! Heave, my lads! Bosun, drive 'em hard today!'

Bolitho tried not to watch his ship's torment, but concentrated instead on the frigate. As *Sparrow* swung and plunged round on to her new tack, the wet sails thrusting her over until the lee gangway was awash, he saw the enemy's topmasts appear suddenly above the starboard bow. Barely a mile between them, but the violent turn had had the desired effect. Instead of closing comfortably on *Sparrow*'s larboard quarter, she now lay across the opposite bow and on a dangerously converging tack.

'Starboard chaser!' Bolitho had to repeat the order before young Fowler heard him and scurried forward to find Graves.

He yelled at Tyrrell, 'He must be made to think we are going to fight!'

Faintly from forward he heard the squeal of chocks as the gun crew hauled the thirty-two-pounder to its port. It would not be easy for them. With the ship lying hard over it would be like dragging it uphill.

'Fire!'

The smoke whipped inboard above the forecastle as the bow-chaser roared its challenge at the enemy.

Nobody reported a fall of shot, and at such an angle it was likely the ball had passed clean above the other ship.

Bolitho felt his jaw tighten into a grin. The enemy's forecourse was being brailed up, her topgallants disappearing as if by remote hand as they shortened sail to fight the impudent *Sparrow*.

'Fire!'

Again the gun hurled its heavy ball into the murky confusion of sea and drifting spume.

Bolitho looked at Buckle. 'Stand by!' He strode to the rail and touched Tyrrell's arm. 'Get the forecourse on her! Hands aloft and loose t'gallants! 'Tis time for a little prudence!'

As the great foresail billowed and then hardened to the wind Bolitho felt the hull steady and hold firm to its thrust. Right above the deck the topmen were busy releasing the topgallant sails, so that as he peered aloft the mainmast seemed to be bending forward like a tree in a storm.

When he turned towards the French frigate again he saw that his plan had worked well. She was trying to reset her foresail, but the momentary pause to present her broadside had cost her dearly. She was plunging past the *Sparrow*'s quarter a full three cables clear.

By the time she had regained her control of wind and tack she would be well astern. Also, *Sparrow*'s sudden manoeuvre had now given her the wind-gage.

A ripple of flashes spouted from the frigate's side. Balls plunged into the sea nearby, although with so many white-horses on each beam it was hard to tell shot from spray.

Overhead a ball whined between the masts, and a seaman fell from the mainyard, hitting the sea alongside without surfacing until he was far astern.

Majendie said hoarsely, 'The poor fellow! God rest his soul!'

Bolitho nodded. 'Aye. That was bad luck.'

He stared along the gundeck where his men worked like demons to retrim the yards and secure halliards which were swollen with damp. Hardly one of them had looked up as the man had fallen. Later perhaps they would mourn. But maybe, like himself, they were thanking God that *Sparrow* had answered their call, and had not scorned their efforts to drag her into the wind and risk demasting or crippling her to lie an easy prize under the enemy's guns.

'Steer due south, Mr Buckle. We will gain some room before we attempt to wear.'

Buckle gazed astern. The frigate was going about, the heart gone from her original challenge.

'There he goes, God rot him!' Buckle grinned at his helmsmen. 'Thought we were going to surrender without a fight, did he?'

Majendie watched Bolitho's strained face. 'Many would have done, Captain. Even I, a landsman, know you were badly matched.'

Bolitho forced a smile. 'But we did *not* fight, my friend.' He glanced briefly astern. 'Not *this* time.'

He shut the picture of the falling topman from his mind. It was to be hoped he died instantly. To see his ship sailing on without him would make his last moments on earth worse than death itself.

'Now, fetch Mr Graves and the lookouts. We will put all our information together.' He caught Majendie's arm as a deep plunge all but threw him down the quarterdeck ladder. 'Steady there! I may want you to make some sketches for the admiral. It seems the fashionable thing to do these days.'

When at last he was satisfied with *Sparrow*'s course and trim he walked aft and looked for the land. But it was lost from view, and he guessed that rain covered the headland and the frigate which had so nearly caught them in a trap.

He stripped off his shirt and mopped his neck and chest with it. Majendie watched him and then peered glumly at his sodden pad. That, he decided would have been the best sketch of all.

Bolitho read carefully through his prepared report and then thrust it into an envelope. Stockdale stood beside the table, a candle and wax ready to seal it, now that it seemed there was nothing more to add.

Bolitho leaned back and stretched his arms. For two whole days they had fought their way south-west, losing sight of land and intent only on gaining advantage over the wind. Tacking back and forth for hours at a time to record but a few miles in actual progress. It had been hard work for everyone, but now that the wind had decided to back still further *Sparrow* had at last been able to turn towards the mainland. With luck they would anchor at Sandy Hook tomorrow. He glanced at the open log book and smiled. It was sobering to realize that in the time it had taken to reach Newport, fight the adverse weather and return to Sandy Hook by this frustrating and delaying method, he could have sailed his ship clear across the Atlantic to Falmouth with days to spare.

'Will I seal it now, sir?' Stockdale watched him patiently.

'I think so.'

He closed his eyes, memorizing the statements he had obtained from Graves and the lookouts. They differed in small details, but one thing was clear. It seemed more than likely to expect a combined Franco/American attack on New York, and soon. He found some satisfaction in the fact that if the weather had delayed his swift return, then it would equally hamper the enemy.

'Deck there! Sail on th' weather bow!'

Bolitho pushed Stockdale's candle aside. 'Later.' Then he hurried from the cabin.

Because of the *Sparrow*'s need to gain advantage from the wind they had driven far to the south-west. Now, having at last found the wind's favour, the compass pointed north-west by north, with Sandy Hook some ninety miles ahead. The afternoon was hot but clear, and even from the deck it was possible to see the small pyramid of canvas to show that the other vessel was standing on a converging tack.

'Bring her up a point. Steer nor'-west.'

He took a glass from Bethune and steadied it above the nettings.

The masthead called, 'Brigantine, sir!'

He looked at Tyrrell. 'Ours probably.'

It was the only sail they had sighted since narrowly avoiding action with the French frigate. It was always good to meet a friendly ship, and he would pass some of his news across to her, in case she was making for the north and might pass too close to the enemy's squadron at Newport.

With the wind blowing keenly it did not take long for both ships to draw near one another.

'He intends to pass to lee'rd.' Bolitho raised the glass again.

Brigantines were untidy-looking ships. Square-rigged on the foremast, and with a schooner's fore-and-aft sail on the main, they appeared ill-designed, but were known capable of outdistancing even a frigate under good conditions.

Bolitho said, 'Signal her to heave to. I will speak with her master.'

Tyrrell said, 'Anyway, she's English. No doubt about that.'

Flags soared up the newcomer's yards and broke to the wind.

Bethune shouted, 'She's the *Five Sisters*, sir!' He fumbled with his book while Fowler stood a little apart, his mouth set in an expression of disdain. 'Shown here as under warrant to the Governor at New York.'

'Thought as much.' Tyrrell frowned. 'Law unto themselves, and crewed by some real rascals, I can tell you.' He sighed. 'Still, a warrant keeps 'em safe from th' press and risking their precious necks.'

The brigantine had crossed *Sparrow*'s bows and was moving steadily on the starboard tack. Bolitho could see the red and gold flag at her fore, the trim semblance of order usually found in a government-sponsored vessel. She was drawing closer, and would eventually pass less than half a cable clear.

Bolitho saw Majendie and Dalkeith by the nettings. The former scribbling frantically, the surgeon peering over his shoulder with obvious interest.

'She's heaving to, sir.'

The brigantine was coming up into the wind, her canvas aback and the big mainsail diminishing steadily as the seamen took charge of it.

Bolitho nodded approvingly. It had been well executed.

'Luff, Mr Tyrrell. I will hail her while she rides under our lee.'

The crash and boom of flapping canvas made any sort of conversation difficult, for as *Sparrow* turned closer into the wind and her way was reduced to a crawl, every sail and shroud seemed intent on drowning Bolitho's voice.

He held the speaking trumpet in both hands and shouted, '*Where are you bound?*'

Across the short wave-crests he heard the reply.

'Montego Bay! Jamaica!'

Tyrrell remarked, 'Bit off course, I'd say.'

The voice came again. 'We were chased by a Spanish frigate yesterday. Gave him the slip during the night, but you might report him for me.'

The brigantine was falling downwind and her yards were moving restlessly to show her master was eager to be on his way.

Bolitho lowered the trumpet. There was no point in detaining her longer. And he would get precious little thanks for so doing by the New York authorities. It was odd to realize that she probably came under the control of men like Blundell, who knew nothing and cared less for the sea.

He heard Dalkeith murmur, 'By God, that captain's face! I've never seen such cruel burns and know a man to live!'

Bolitho snapped, 'Give me that glass!' He snatched it from the astonished surgeon and levelled it on the other ship's poop.

Through the black rigging and loosely flapping sails he saw him. His coat collar was turned up to his ears despite the heat, and his hat was drawn firmly almost to eye-level. Bolitho realized that the brigatine's captain had not only lost half his face, but an eye as well, and he was holding his head at a stiff, unnatural angle as he trained the remaining one on the sloop.

So the brigantine had something to do with Blundell. He could picture them murmuring together in the study, the scarred face half hidden in shadow.

Buckle called worriedly, 'Permission to get the ship under way, sir? We're riding a bit close.'

'Very well.'

Bolitho waved to the men on the brigantine's deck and turned to watch Majendie again. He was hanging on the netting, scribbling and shading, smoothing out and adding detail even as the *Five Sisters* reset her foresail and began to gather way downwind.

Dalkeith grinned. 'Not bad, Rupert! I daresay some of our naval companions will assist you with detail of rigging, eh?'

Tyrrell limped over to him and peered across his narrow shoulder. He seized the pad and exclaimed, 'Holy God! If I didn't know for sure . . .'

Bolitho strode to his side. The picture was of the brigantine's poop, with officers and seamen caught in realistic attitudes, even if, as Dalkeith had hinted, the details of rigging were imperfect.

He felt himself go cold as he saw Majendie's drawing of the ship's captain. Distance and scale had wiped away the terrible scars, so that he stood out like a figure from the past. He looked at Tyrrell, who was still watching his face.

Tyrrell said quietly, 'You remember, sir? You were too busy fighting and guarding me from attack.' He turned to stare at the other ship. 'But after I took that ball in my thigh I had plenty of time to watch *that* bugger.'

Bolitho tried to clear the dryness from his throat. With stark clarity he saw the fury and hatred of battle as if it had been yesterday. The *Sparrow*'s seamen being cut down and driven from *Bonaventure*'s decks. And the privateer's captain, standing like some detached onlooker, calling on him to strike and surrender.

He snapped, 'Put the ship about! Hands aloft and set t'gallants!'

To Majendie he added softly, 'Thanks to you, I think we may solve a mystery today.'

The instant *Sparrow* showed her intentions, and even as the fore topgallant sail bellied from its yard, the brigantine also increased her canvas and headed away.

'Clear for action, sir?'

'No.'

He watched the jib-boom edging round until it fastened on the brigantine's starboard quarter like a bridge. In fact she was two cables clear and showed no sign of losing her lead.

'It must be quickly done. We will go alongside and grapple. Tell Mr Graves to loose off a ball from the larboard bow-chaser. Lively now!'

Buckle said grimly, 'We're overhauling him, sir.'

Bolitho nodded. Tyrrell understood what was happening, but so far nobody else had even hinted surprise at his actions. To all intents he was chasing a government vessel with which, minutes earlier, he had been exchanging pleasantries.

Bang. The bow-chaser's black muzzle lurched inboard on its tackles, and Bolitho saw the waterspout shoot upwards within a boat's length of the brigantine's side.

'She's shortening sail now!' Buckle sounded satisfied.

'Pass the word for Mr Graves to muster a boarding party!' Bolitho watched narrowly as the other ship began to yaw heavily in a procession of troughs. 'Mr Heyward, take charge of the gun deck! Mr Bethune, accompany the second lieutenant!'

Men scampered to the larboard gangway, cutlasses bared, and some carrying muskets above their heads to avoid misfiring into their companions.

'Steady, Mr Buckle!' Bolitho held out his hand and looked up at the yards. Sails were vanishing briskly, and as the forecourse rose booming and writhing to its yard he saw the brigantine slipping under the larboard bow, as if both ships were being drawn together by hawsers. '*Steady!*'

Along the gangway picked seamen swung their grapnels, while others scurried forward to fend off the first contact.

Across the shortening range Bolitho heard, 'Stand away there! I command you to keep clear! I will have the law on your head!'

Bolitho felt his tension easing. If he had harboured doubts they were gone now. There was no mistaking that voice. Too many of *Sparrow*'s seamen had died that day aboard *Bonaventure* for him ever to forget.

He raised the trumpet. 'Take in your sails and bring to *instantly*!'

He heard the grumble of chocks and guessed the brigantine's crew were well able to see the big thirty-two-pounder as it was run out again.

Warily, and with great skill, both vessels slowly edged round, their progress through the choppy water falling almost to nothing, their seamen taking in canvas and trimming yards in harmony with the change of rudder. It was perfectly done, and with little more than a shudder *Sparrow* nudged against the brigantine's hull and ground forward before coming to rest with her bowsprit level with the other's foremast. Grapnels flew from the gangway, and Bolitho saw Graves waving his men forward, and Bethune swinging out on the fore shrouds, his dirk seeming too small for so heavy a midshipman.

Tyrrell rested his hands on the rail and said, 'She carries a deck cargo as well.' He pointed to a large canvas hump below the forecastle. 'Booty for th' master, no doubt!'

Even as he finished speaking, and as the first seaman jumped out and down on to the brigantine's bulwark, the deck cargo revealed itself. Hands tore the canvas away to uncover a sturdy twelve-pounder which was rigged in the centre of the deck, its bulk controlled by tackles and ring-bolts.

The crash of its explosion was matched only by the shriek of grape-shot as it burst with terrifying impact along *Sparrow*'s gangway. Men and pieces of flesh flew in bloody profusion, and through the rolling bank of brown smoke Bolitho saw some of them smashed to the opposite side of the deck.

Then came the shouting, and from the brigantine's poop and main hatch he saw some fifty men charging to the attack.

He groped for his hangar, but realized he had forgotten to bring it from the cabin. Everywhere men were shouting and screaming and above it all came an increasing rasp of steel, the bang and whine of musket fire.

A seaman fell bodily from the netting and knocked Tyrrell against the rail. His leg doubled under him and his face contorted with pain.

Bolitho yelled, 'Take charge, Mr Buckle!'

He snatched a cutlass from the dead seaman's belt and ran to the gangway. His eyes smarted in smoke, and he felt several balls fan past him, one severing a netting like an invisible knife.

The brigantine stood no chance against *Sparrow*'s cannon. But, grappled together like this, the fight could easily turn against them. He had done this very thing himself and knew the odds.

He vaulted wildly on to the main shrouds and then saw with astonishment that Graves was still below him on the gundeck. He was yelling at his men, but seemed unable to follow them. Of Bethune there was no sign, and he realized that Heyward had gone forward to meet a rush of boarders who were trying to climb across the beakhead.

He slipped and almost dropped between the hulls, and then with a gasp he was on the brigantine's deck. A pistol exploded beside his face, nearly blinding him, but he slashed out with the heavy cutlass, felt a brief impact and heard someone scream.

'The poop!' He thrust his way between some of his men and saw Bethune using a musket like a club, his hair blowing wildly as he tried to rally what remained of his boarding party. 'Take the poop, lads!'

Somebody raised a cracked cheer, and with fresh heart the seamen lunged aft. Feet and legs kicked and swayed above groaning wounded and corpses alike. There was no time to reload muskets, and it was blade to blade at close quarters.

Through the struggling, interlocked figures Bolitho saw the ship's wheel, a master's mate standing alone beside it, while others lay in various attitudes of death around him to show that aboard *Sparrow* someone had mustered a few sharp-shooters in the maintop.

Then all at once, they were face to face. Bolitho, with his shirt torn almost to his waist, his hair plastered across his forehead and the cutlass outstretched towards his enemy.

The other captain stood quite motionless, his sword held easily and angled across his front. Close to, his face was even more terrible, but there was no doubting his agility as he suddenly darted forward.

The blades came together with a sharp clang. Sparks flew as they ground inwards until both hilts locked and each man tested the weight of his adversary's arm.

Bolitho looked into the unwinking eye, felt the heat of his breath, the quivering tension in his shoulder as with a curse he thrust Bolitho back against the wheel, withdrawing his sword and striking forward in two swift movements. Again and again, strike, parry, guard. The cutlass felt like a lead weight, and each movement became an agony. Bolitho saw the other man's mouth set in a grim smile. He knew he was winning.

Beyond the rail the fighting continued as before, but above it he heard Tyrrell yell from the quarterdeck, 'Help th' cap'n! For Christ's sake, *help him*!'

As they circled each other like jungle cats, Bolitho saw Stockdale slashing and hacking to try to reach him. But he was fighting at least three men, and his bellows were those of an anguished bull.

Bolitho lifted the cutlass and levelled it at the other man's waist. He could raise it no further. His muscles seemed to be cracking. If only he could change hands. But he would die if he attempted it.

The sword flicked out, its point cutting through his sleeve and touching his skin like a white-hot iron. He could feel blood running down his arm, saw the man's single eye gleaming through a mist of pain like some glowing stone.

The brigantine's captain shouted, 'Now, Cap'n! This is the moment! For *you*!'

He moved so quickly that Bolitho hardly saw the blade coming. It caught the cutlass within inches of the hilt, turned it from his fingers like something plucked from a child, and sent it flying over the rail.

There was a loud crack, and Bolitho felt the ball pass his shoulder, the heat so fierce it must have missed him by an inch. It struck the other man in the throat, hurling him aside even as the sword made its final lunge. For a moment longer he kicked and convulsed in his blood and then lay still.

Bolitho saw Dalkeith throw one leg over the bulwark and climb up beside him, a pistol smoking in his hand.

Throughout the two ships there was stricken silence, and the brigantine's crew stood or lay to await quarter from their attackers.

Bolitho said, 'Thank you. That was close.'

Dalkeith did not seem to hear him. He said brokenly, 'They killed Majendie. Shot him down like a dog as he tried to save a wounded man.'

Bolitho felt the surgeon's fingers on his arm as he ripped his shirt into a deft bandage.

Majendie gone, and so many others, too. He looked down at the dead man by the bulwark. If he had kept his head he might have got away with the deception. But for Majendie he certainly would have done. Perhaps, like himself, he had never forgotten that day aboard the privateer, and once more fate had decided to end the memory in its own way.

He turned to survey the two vessels. There was much to be done, a lot to be discovered before they reached Sandy Hook.

Some of his men gave a hoarse cheer as he walked to the bulwark, but most were too spent even to move.

Anger, disgust, as well as a sense of loss, flooded through him as he walked amongst his gasping seamen. To think men had died because of treachery and to gain riches for others who remained aloof from blame.

'But not *this* time!' He spoke aloud without realizing it. 'Somebody will pay dearly for today's grief!'

Then he thought of the girl in New York and wondered how he could protect her when the truth became known.

16

One Man's Loss . . .

Rear-Admiral Sir Evelyn Christie rose from behind a table crammed with documents and leaned forward to offer his hand.

'Welcome.' He gestured to a chair. 'Good to meet you again.'

Bolitho sat down and watched the admiral as he moved towards the stern gallery. It was stiflingly hot, and even though there was a regular breeze across Sandy Hook, the air in the flagship's great cabin was lifeless.

Christie added abruptly, 'I am sorry to have kept you so long. But the politics of high command are no area for a young captain.' He smiled. 'Your courage is beyond doubt, but here in New York they would eat you alive.'

Bolitho tried to relax. For three days after dropping anchor he had been to all intents confined to his ship. Once his report had been spirited to the flagship and his wounded landed for care ashore, he had been left in little doubt as to his own position. No actual command had been issued, but the Officer-of-the-Guard had told him that his presence aboard would be in everyone's best interests until word from the admiral.

He began, 'If I have done wrong, sir, then . . .'

Christie looked at him sternly. '*Wrong*? Quite the reverse. But you have certainly set a fox amongst the geese this time.' He shrugged. 'But you did not come aboard to hear what you already know. Your action in capturing the brigantine *Five Sisters*, the seizure of certain documents before her master could dispose of them, far outweigh individual discomfort elsewhere.'

'Thank you, sir.' He was still uncertain where Christie's comments were leading.

'It now seems evident that the brigantine's master, one Matthew Crozier, intended to pass information either to an enemy vessel or to some spy along the coast. That would explain his being so far off course, his excuse of avoiding a Spanish frigate. But there can be no doubt as to his main mission. Whilst on passage for Jamaica he was to deliver a message for the Comte de Grasse at Martinique. My people have examined the despatch most thoroughly.' He eyed Bolitho steadily. 'In it they found full details of our defences and all available ships-of-war. Deployments, both sea and military, even to the extent of our strength under Cornwallis.' He picked up a document and studied it for several seconds. 'One way or t'other, this will be a year to remember.'

Bolitho shifted in his chair. 'How could a privateersman like Crozier obtain a warrant to work for the British?'

Christie smiled wryly. 'He owned the brigantine. It was no doubt purchased by his own side. The crew were hand-picked. The sweepings of a dozen ports and almost as many countries. With small vessels in such demand his deception was not so very difficult. Even on his official voyages he was apparently smuggling.' He turned away, his shoulders suddenly rigid. 'Mostly for those in power in New York!'

'May I ask if they are to be punished?'

Christie turned and shrugged. 'If you mean General Blundell, then you may be assured he will be leaving America very soon. After that I am equally certain he will be saved by influence and powerful friends at home. Distance and time are great healers where the guilty are concerned. But others will certainly go to the wall, and I have been told that the Military Command intends to use your discovery to rid itself, in part at least, of the parasites who have lived too long off its back.'

He smiled at Bolitho's grave features. 'Pour some madeira. It will do us both good.' He continued in the same unruffled tone. 'Admiral Graves is well pleased with you. He has sent the schooner *Lucifer* to Antigua to inform Admiral Rodney of the situation here. Patrols have been ordered to Newport to watch de Barras's squadron, although, as you well know, it is hard to see what is happening there. In fact, everything is being done with the forces available to watch over local waters to see which way the tiger will pounce.'

He took a glass from Bolitho's hand and asked, '*Sparrow*, is she in good repair?'

Bolitho nodded. It was still difficult to keep pace with the small admiral. 'My carpenter has almost completed repairs to the gangway and . . .'

Christie nodded briskly. 'In any case, *that* can be finished at sea. I want you to take on full supplies, for three months at least. My flag captain has it in hand. He might even find you some seamen to replace those lost in battle. I have sent *Heron* to the south'rd again, but my other inshore patrols are too well spread for comfort. I need every available ship, especially yours.' He smiled. 'And you.'

'Thank you, sir.' He put down the glass. 'Newport again?'

The admiral shook his head. 'You will join Farr and his *Heron*.'

Bolitho stared at him. 'But, sir, I thought you needed ships to watch de Barras?'

Christie picked up the decanter and examined it thoughtfully. 'I may do so later. But for the present I want you out of Sandy Hook. Away from those who will try to bring you down. You have made enemies by your actions. As I said just now, you are no match for the devious ways of politics.'

'I am prepared to take that risk, sir.'

'*I am not!*' Christie's voice was hard. Like it had been at the court martial in this very cabin. 'To you, your ship and her affairs are paramount. But I must think on a wider scope, and my superiors wider still. If it is thought best for you to lead my whole squadron against de Barras, then that is how it will be. And if your ship must be sacrificed like a tethered animal in a snare, then that, too, will be ordered!' He relented. 'Forgive me. That was unpardonable.' He waved one hand above his charts. 'The enemy is powerful, but not so that he can attack everywhere at once. He can strike against New York, for deprived of it we have no pretence at government in America. Or he can turn his iron on General Cornwallis's army in the field, for without that we are just as pointless. Either way there will be a battle, and I believe that a sea fight will decide our course and that of history for years to come.'

Feet pounded overhead and Bolitho heard the bark of commands, the scrape of tackles and blocks. Even the old *Parthian* was preparing to sail, to show her readiness for whatever the enemy intended.

Bolitho stood up. 'When can I expect my orders, sir?'

'Before sunset. I would advise you to contain your, er, other interests, until some later date.' He proffered his hand. 'The heart is a fine thing, but I would prefer you to rest your judgements on the brain.'

Bolitho walked out to the sunlight, his mind buzzing with all Christie had said and the greater part which he had left unspoken. It was all so unfair. A sailor stood to his gun in battle until told otherwise. Or he struggled aloft in a shrieking gale, frozen with icy spray, and scared half to death. But he obeyed. It was the way of things, or had been in Bolitho's experience. Until now.

Yet Blundell's kind ignored such distinctions, could and did use their personal authority for gain, even when the country was fighting for its life. No wonder those like Crozier could prosper and achieve more results than an army of paid spies. Crozier had been doing his duty in the only way he knew. By ignoring the dangers, Blundell had committed little better than treason.

He stopped by the entry port and stared at the waiting gig with sudden anxiety. So why had he not told Christie of Crozier's presence in Blundell's house? There would have been no hiding from conspiracy had that piece of news been released. He swore under his breath and signalled to Stockdale.

Fool, fool! Perhaps he should have told her first. To allow her time to disassociate herself from her uncle's affairs.

The flag captain joined him by the port. 'I have had the water hoys sent over to *Sparrow*. Another lighter will be alongside within the hour. If your people turn with a will, you should have all the stores aboard before dusk.'

Bolitho eyed him curiously. Such calm assurance, yet this captain had not only his own ship and the whims of an admiral to consider, he must concern himself with the needs of every officer and man in the squadron. He was jolted by his discovery. It was like seeing Christie's charts on the cabin table. To all but himself, *Sparrow* and her company were just a tiny part of the whole.

He doffed his hat to the shrill calls and shining bayonets and clambered down to the gig. He said nothing as the boat pulled lustily across the anchorage, and Stockdale for once seemed content to leave him in peace.

He was in his cabin with Lock studying the latest return of ship's stores when Graves entered to announce the arrival of another hoy carrying fresh water.

As the purser scuttled away to watch over the casks before they were lowered into the hold, Bolitho said, 'I was meaning to have a word with you, Mr Graves.' He saw the lieutenant stiffen, the way his fingers locked into his coat. Poor Graves. He looked like an old man, and even his tan could not hide the shadows under his eyes, the pinched lines at each side of his mouth. How did you begin to ask an officer if he was a coward? He added, 'Are you troubled about something?'

Graves swallowed hard. 'My father is dead, sir. Some weeks back. I just received a letter.'

'I am sorry to hear that, Mr Graves.' Bolitho watched his face with sudden compassion. 'It is harder to bear when you are out of reach, as we are.'

'Yes.' Graves did not even blink. 'He had been, er, ill for some while.'

The door swung open and Tyrrell limped noisily into the cabin. He did not appear to see Graves as he exclaimed, 'By God, Cap'n! I've had news!' He leaned on the table, all his excitement and pleasure welling out of him in an uncontrollable flood. 'My sister. She's safe an' well! I met a man who was a trapper in th' country. He said she's living with our uncle. That's about twenty mile to th' north of our old farmstead.' He grinned widely. 'Safe! I still can't believe I'm awake.' He turned and saw Graves for the first time. 'Oh hell! I'm sorry. I forgot myself with th' fair excitement of it all.'

Graves was staring at him glassily, and his fingers had screwed his coat into two tight balls.

Tyrrell asked, 'What's wrong? You sick or something?'

Graves muttered, 'I must go. If you'll excuse me, sir.' He almost ran from the cabin.

Bolitho stood up. 'It *was* good news, Jethro.' He looked at the open door. 'I am afraid Graves just brought some of a sadder note. His father.'

Tyrrell sighed. 'I'm sorry. I thought maybe it was something I said . . .'

'In what way?'

Tyrrell shrugged. 'No matter. He was once in hopes of courting my sister.' He smiled at some secret memory. 'It all seems a long way back now.'

Bolitho tried not to think about Graves's stunned expression.

'One day you'll be able to join your sister again. I am very glad for you.'

Tyrrell nodded, his eyes dreamy. 'Aye. One day.' He nodded more firmly. 'I don't feel quite so lost any more.'

Midshipman Fowler stepped neatly over the coaming and removed his hat. 'The lighterman brought you a letter, sir.' His lisp was very pronounced. 'He insisted I give it to you myself.'

'Thank you.'

Bolitho held it in his fingers. Like the other one which he had locked in his strong-box. Her own hand.

He opened it quickly and then said, 'I'll be ashore for an hour. Maybe longer. Call away my gig.'

Fowler ran from the cabin, his sharp voice calling for the boat's crew.

Tyrrell asked quietly, 'Is it wise, sir?'

'What the hell do you mean by that?' Bolitho swung towards him, caught off guard by his question.

Tyrrell frowned. 'I met several people when I was ordering some new cordage, sir. It's well known all over New York what you've done. Most are laughing fit to burst that your action has unmasked these bloody scabs and traitors. But some think you'll be in real danger while you're here. There'll be plenty more quaking in their beds. Wondering what you discovered, an' when th' soldiers are going to bang on *their* door.'

Bolitho dropped his eyes. 'I'm sorry about my anger. But have no fear. I've no intention of parading my back for the benefit of that sort.'

Tyrrell watched him as he snatched up his hat and fretted impatiently for Fitch to adjust his swordbelt.

Then he said, 'I'll rest easier when we're at sea again.'

Bolitho hurried past him. 'And that will be tonight, my cautious friend. So stir yourself and watch over the provisions!' He smiled at Tyrrell's concern. 'But beware. There may be an assassin hiding in the salf beef!'

Tyrrell saw him over the side but remained by the rail for a long while, despite the sun and the pain in his thigh.

There was a small carriage waiting for Bolitho at the end of the jetty. It was a shabby affair and not in the least like the one which had carried him to the general's residence. But the driver was the same Negro, and as soon as Bolitho was inside he cracked the whip and urged the horses into a brisk trot.

They rattled through several narrow streets and then out into a quiet road which was lined by sturdy houses, most of which seemed to be occupied by some of the city's refugees. The buildings had lost their façade of well-being, and where there had been gardens there were piles of discarded boxes and sorry-looking vehicles. At many of the windows he saw women and children staring out at the road below. They had the lost look of uprooted people with little to do but wait and hope.

The coach wheeled through a pair of sagging gates and towards another such house. Except that this one was empty, its windows bare in the sunlight like blind eyes.

For an instant he recalled Tyrrell's warning, but as the coach slid to a halt he saw the girl beside the house, her gown reflected in a partly overgrown pond.

He hurried towards her, his heart pounding in time with his shoes.

'I came as fast as I could!' He took her hands in his and studied her warmly. 'But why must we meet here?'

She tossed her head, throwing the hair from her shoulder in the way he had remembered in the weeks he had been away.

'It is better so. I cannot bear the watching eyes. The sneers behind my back.' There was little emotion in her voice. 'But we will go inside now. I must speak with you.'

Their shoes rang hollowly on the bare boards. It had been a fine house, but now the plaster was flaking and the walls were heavy with cobwebs.

She walked to a window and said, 'My uncle is in serious trouble, but I expect you know. He was perhaps foolish but no more than many here.'

Bolitho slipped his hand beneath her arm. 'I do not want you to be involved, Susannah.'

His insistence, or the use of her name, made her turn and face him.

'But I *am* involved, as you put it.'

'No. The smuggling and other offences could have had nothing to do with you. Nobody would ever believe it.'

She stared at him calmly. 'Nor does it matter. But one hint of treason would ruin my uncle and all connected with him.' She gripped his arm. 'That man, Crozier, have you spoken of his presence at our house? Please, I must know. For if you remain silent, all may yet be well.'

Bolitho turned away. 'Believe me, I can save you from that. Your uncle will be sent to England. There is no reason why you cannot remain here.'

'*Here?*' She stood back from him. 'What use is that?'

'I—I thought, given time you might see your way to becoming my wife.' In the empty room his words seemed to come back to mock him.

'Marry you?' She brushed her hair from her forehead. 'Is that what you thought?'

'Yes. I had cause to hope.' He watched her despairingly. 'You hinted that. . .'

She replied sharply, 'I hinted no such proposal, Captain! If things had gone as I had planned, well then maybe . . .'

He tried again. 'But nothing *need* change for us.'

She continued as if he had not spoken. 'I did think that with some help from my friends you might one day amount to something. A position in London, perhaps even a seat in Parliament. All is possible if the will is there.' She lifted her eyes to his face again. 'Did you really expect me to marry a sea-officer? Live from day to day waiting for one ship after the other to drop anchor? There are other lives beyond your miserable Service, *Captain*!'

'It is my life.' He felt the walls closing in on him. The air forced from his lungs as if he was drowning.

'The path of duty.' She walked to the window and looked down at the carriage. 'You were a fool to think of my sharing such an existence. An even bigger one if you continue to do so!' She turned easily, her eyes flashing. 'There's more to living than catching some poor smuggler in the King's name!'

Bolitho said, 'I did not tell of Crozier being with your uncle. But it is certain to come out when the authorities have finished their inquiries.' He added bitterly, 'Rats always turn on one another when the pickings are few.'

She breathed out slowly, one hand resting lightly below her heart. 'Stay a few minutes while I go to my carriage. I have no wish to be seen here.'

Bolitho reached out his arms and then let them drop to his sides. He was defeated. Had been so for longer than he had understood.

Yet in the dusty sunlight, as she stood watching him, her violet eyes holding him at a distance, he knew that if there was anything he could do or say to keep her he would use it.

She moved to the door. 'You are a strange man. But I can see no future for you.' Then she was gone, her shoes fading on the staircase until he was quite alone.

He did not remember how long he stood in that empty room. Minutes? An hour? When at last he walked down the stairs and into the overgrown garden he realized that even the shabby carriage had gone. He crossed to the pond and stared at his own reflection.

If she had been angry, or frightened, anything he could have recognized, he might still have known what to do. There had not even been contempt. She had dismissed him with no more thought than if she had been rejecting a useless servant.

A foot scraped on stone and he swung round, seeing in those seconds four dark figures lined against the ragged bushes.

'*Easy*, Cap'n!' One of them had a drawn sword, and he saw the others were also well armed. 'There's no sense in strugglin'!'

Bolitho backed up to the pond, his fingers on his hanger.

Another of the men chuckled. 'Aye, that's right, Cap'n. Somewhere for us'n to hide yer corpse when we've done with you. Most considerate, eh, lads?'

Bolitho remained quite still. He knew it was useless to bargain with any of them. They had the looks of professional criminals, men who worked for a fee, no matter what the final cost might be to them. He was suddenly very calm, as if their arrival had driven away his other despair like a cold wind.

'Then I'll take a couple with me!'

He snatched out his hanger and waited for them to attack. Two carried pistols, but there were probably military patrols nearby and a shot might bring them running.

Steel clashed with steel, and he saw the leader's grin fade to an intent frown as they locked blades together. He ducked as one man struck at his neck, twisted his hanger and slashed him across the face, hearing him scream as he tumbled back into the bushes.

'Damn you, you bloody bastard!' Another dived forward, his sword sweeping under Bolitho's guard. But it glanced from his belt buckle and he was able to thrust him aside with the hilt, catching him on the jaw with such force it almost tore the hanger from his grip.

The garden swam in a mist of pain as something struck him savagely on the forehead, and he realized that one of them had hurled a stone. He hit out with the hanger but felt it pass through air. Someone laughed, and another called hoarsely, '*Now*, 'Arry! In the guts!'

Feet pounded through the shrubs, and Bolitho was pushed aside by someone in a blue coat who shouted, 'At 'em, lads! Cut 'em down!'

Swords grated and sparked, and a body rolled thrashing into the pond, the blood staining the surface like red weed.

Bolitho lurched to his feet, realizing that Heyward and Tyrrell were driving the two attackers against the house, while Dalkeith stood watchfully nearby, his beautiful pistols shining in the sunlight.

Heyward brought his man to his knees and jumped back to let him roll silently on to his face and stay there.

The sole survivor threw down his heavy sword and yelled, 'Quarter! Quarter!'

Tyrrell swayed awkwardly on his crippled leg and said harshly, 'Quarter be damned!'

The sword took him in the chest, holding him to the wall for an endless moment before allowing him to slide beside his companion.

Tyrrell sheathed his blade and limped to Bolitho's side.

'All well, Cap'n?' He reached out to steady him. 'Just in time, it seems.'

Heyward stepped over one of the corpses. 'Someone wanted you dead, sir.'

Bolitho looked from one to the next, the emotion rising to mingle with his understanding.

Tyrrell grinned. 'You see, I was right.'

Bolitho nodded heavily. *Someone wanted you dead.* But the worst part was knowing that she had realized his peril and had done nothing. He glanced at the corpse sprawled in the pond.

'What can I say? How can I find words?'

Dalkeith murmured, 'Let's say it was for Rupert Majendie, too.'

Tyrrell slipped his arm over Heyward's slim shoulder for support.

'Aye, that'll do.' He glanced at Bolitho and held his gaze. 'You've done plenty for us. An' in *Sparrow* we look after our own!'

Then together they walked out to the road and towards the sea.

17

Mistaken Identity

Bolitho leaned back in his chair and stared wearily at the open log. He was stripped to the waist, but could feel no benefit in the overheated cabin. He touched his mouth with the pen, wondering what he should write, when there was nothing to report. Around and above him the ship swayed and dipped in a gentle south-easterly breeze, and he pitied the watch on deck, sweating out another day of relentless glare and fierce sunlight. Even the *Sparrow* seemed to be voicing her protest. The timbers groaned and trembled to the motion, dried out by salt and heat, and through the open windows he saw the carved scrollwork by the sill splitting open, the paint flaking away to reveal bare wood.

Once on station north of the Little Bahama Bank he had anticipated being recalled to more active duty within a matter of weeks. But like most of his men, he had long since given up hope. Week followed week, with *Sparrow* and her attendant sloop, *Heron*, dragging their wearying patrol through July, each dawn bringing an empty horizon, and every hour tightening its grip on their small, isolated existence.

And now it was August. Perhaps Christie had insisted on three months' supplies because he had had no intention of recalling *Sparrow* until the end of that time. Maybe they had all been forgotten, or the war was over. It was as if the whole patrol area had been drained of movement. Unlike their last visit to the Bahama Banks, when they had taken prizes or had gossiped with lawful merchantmen, they had seen nothing. Their routine varied little. Usually they kept *Heron*'s topsails just within sight below the horizon, and on a parallel tack swept back and forth well clear of reefs and shoals. With the masthead lookouts of both sloops able to see one another, it was possible to sweep an area some sixty miles wide, unless the weather changed against them. Even a real storm would be welcome. But the agonizing discomfort was getting everyone down, not least himself.

There was a tap at the door and Dalkeith entered, his round face shining with sweat. The forenoon watch had half run its course, and Bolitho had found it necessary to meet the surgeon at this time every day when he had completed his inspection of the sick.

He gestured to a chair. 'Well?'

Dalkeith groaned and shifted his bulk carefully to avoid the glare from the open skylight.

'Two more down today, sir. I've got them below. A few days' rest might revive 'em for a while.'

Bolitho nodded. It was getting serious. Too much heat and not enough fresh food or fruit. Lock had already opened the last barrel of lemons. After that . . .

Dalkeith had been carrying a glass of water which he now stood on the table. It was the colour of tobacco juice. Without comment he took a flat bottle from his pocket and looked at Bolitho for permission to pour himself a stiff glass of rum.

Again, it was one of their little routines. Although how the plump surgeon could stomach rum in this heat was beyond Bolitho.

Dalkeith smacked his lips. 'Better'n this water.' He frowned. 'If we can't get a fresh supply of drinking water I'll not answer for the consequences, sir.'

'I'll do what I can. Maybe we can close with some small island and find a stream. But I am not too hopeful hereabouts. Was that all?'

Dalkeith hesitated. 'I'm supposed to hold my peace, but friendship and duty rarely go hand in hand. It's the first lieutenant.'

'Mr Tyrrell?' Bolitho tensed. 'What about him?'

'His leg. He tries to pretend it's all right, but I'm not happy about it.' He dropped his eyes. 'Worse, I'm getting anxious.'

'I see.' He had noticed Tyrrell's limp getting more pronounced, but whenever he had mentioned it he had replied, 'It'll pass. Nothin' to bite on!'

'What d'you advise?'

Dalkeith sighed. 'I can probe for more splinters. But if that fails . . .' He took another swallow of neat rum. 'I might have to cut it off.'

'Oh God.'

Bolitho walked to the windows and leaned out over the transom. Below, the sea looked very clear, and he could see small darting fish in the rudder's frothing wake.

Behind him he heard Dalkeith add firmly, 'I could do it, of course. But it would have to be while he is still strong. Before the pain and this damn heat gets him down like some of the others.'

Bolitho turned, feeling the sun across his bared back.

'I was not doubting your ability. You've proved that more than enough.'

Dalkeith said grimly, 'I was at a fine hospital in London before I left England.' He grimaced. 'We practised on the poor and worked for the wealthy. It was a hard training ground, but very useful.'

'Will you return when the war is over?' He tried not to think of Tyrrell being held on a table, the saw poised above his leg.

Dalkeith shook his head. 'No. I'll settle out here somewhere. Maybe in America, who can tell?' He gave a wry smile. 'I am afraid that I had to leave England in somewhat of a hurry. A matter of honour over a lady.'

'I have wondered these three years where you found your skill with pistols.'

Dalkeith nodded. 'Unfortunately, I shot the wrong man. His death was considered a greater loss than mine, so I caught the packet from Dover, and eventually, two years later, I arrived in the Indies.'

'Thank you for telling me.' Bolitho massaged his stomach with the palm of one hand. 'I will see what I can do to obtain a berth in another ship, if and when we are ordered home.'

The surgeon lurched to his feet. 'I would appreciate that.' He watched Bolitho doubtfully. 'And Tyrrell?'

'I'll speak with him.' He turned away. 'In God's name, what do I say? How would I feel if it were me?'

Dalkeith rested his hand on the bulkhead until *Sparrow* had completed a slow uproll.

'I can't answer. I'm just a surgeon.'

'Aye.' Bolitho looked at him gravely. 'And I'm just a captain.'

Midshipman Bethune clattered through the wardroom and paused outside the cabin.

'Mr Graves's respects, sir. *Heron* has signalled she has sighted an unknown sail to the east'rd.'

'Very well. I'll come up.'

Dalkeith waited for Bethune to go. 'Recall to New York, sir? If so, I could take Tyrrell to a hospital. They have facilities, proper care.'

Bolitho shook his head. 'I fear not. That sail will be from the south'rd to be on such a bearing. Friend or foe, we have yet to see.'

He heard Dalkeith sigh as he left him and hurried up the ladder to the quarterdeck.

He glanced quickly at the helmsman who called hoarsely, 'Nor' nor'-west, sir!' His lips were cracked in the heat.

Graves reported, 'Our masthead has not sighted her yet, sir.' His mouth jerked at one corner and he added quickly, 'Could be anything.'

It was an empty moment, but Bolitho knew it was merely to cover his embarrassment. He had seen the growing strain on Graves perhaps worst of all. Now the twitch in his jaw laid bare his inner torment like the mark of some disease.

'Very well. Call the hands and prepare to run down on *Heron*. Get the t'gallants on her and lay her on the starboard tack.' He saw Buckle climbing wearily through the hatchway and called, 'A sail, Mr Buckle! Maybe it'll bring us luck today!'

The master pouted. ''Bout time, sir.'

Bolitho heard the familiar limping step and turned to see Tyrrell walking from the larboard gangway.

Tyrrell grinned. 'A sail, did I hear, sir?' He shaded his eyes as he watched the men mustering at their stations. 'Now there's a thing indeed!'

Bolitho bit his lip. It made it more painful to see Tyrrell's new contentment. To know what must be done. That was if Dalkeith knew his trade. And he did.

On the horizon he could see *Heron*'s sails glinting brightly, and knew Farr would wait for him to join him. To break the monotony if nothing else.

Within the hour the stranger had identified herself. It was the *Lucifer*, her great schooner sails spread like wings as she ran before the wind, the spray bursting above her jib-boom in a lively silver pattern.

Fowler was in the lee shrouds with a telescope, his small, piggy face glowing with heat.

'From *Lucifer. Have despatches on board.*' He looked down at the quarterdeck as if proud of his revelation.

'Heave to, Mr Tyrrell.'

Bolitho watched the mad dash aboard *Lucifer* to shorten sail and put her about before running down beneath *Sparrow*'s lee. A fine little vessel. Had she been his instead of *Sparrow* he wondered if his life would have been changed to the same extent.

He saw the haste with which the schooner's boat was being hoisted out above the water. Something acted like a small warning in his mind, and he said, 'Signal *Heron*. Captain repair on board.'

'Aye, aye, sir!' Fowler snapped his fingers and continued to do so until the flags had broken from *Sparrow*'s yard.

Farr's gig hooked on the chains within minutes of *Lucifer*'s jolly-boat.

Odell had come aboard in person, and as he removed his hat to the quarterdeck and darted a sharp glance at Bolitho's bare torso, Farr climbed up beside him and said cheerfully, 'By God, what brings you here, man? Were you pining for us in Antigua?'

Odell walked a few paces clear and then faced them.

'The French are out, sir.'

For a moment nobody spoke. Bolitho held the words in his mind, yet was also aware of those about him. Stockdale by the hatchway, slightly stooped as if to hear better. Buckle and Tyrrell, their faces showing astonishment and more. Relief perhaps that the guessing was over.

'Come below.'

Bolitho led them to his cabin, the heat and the drudgery of patrol forgotten.

Odell sat on the edge of a chair, his features giving little hint of strain at driving his command all those miles from Antigua.

Bolitho said quietly, 'Now, tell us.'

'I carried the despatches to the fleet as ordered.'

Odell had a quick, erratic manner of speaking, nodding his head in time with his words. It was not hard to see how he got his reputation for being slightly mad. A man on a knife-edge, Bolitho suspected. But there was no doubting the accuracy of his report.

'Admiral Rodney despatched a fleet of fourteen ships-of-the-line to assist our forces at New York.'

Farr muttered, 'By God, that's more like it. I've no stomach for our Admiral Graves.'

Odell's eyes flashed dangerously at the interruption.

He snapped, 'Rodney has sailed for England. He is a sick man. Hood commands the reinforcements.'

Farr was unabashed. 'Ah well, even better. I've served Admiral Hood and respect him.'

Bolitho said, 'Let us hear all of it. I suspect there is more.'

Odell nodded. 'The Comte de Grasse set sail with some twenty sail-of-the-line. The patrols reported that he was escorting the season's convoy clear of the islands.'

Bolitho said, 'That is quite usual, I believe.'

'Yes. But de Grasse has not been seen since.' The words fell into the cabin like round-shot.

Farr exclaimed, 'A whole fleet! Disappeared? It's bloody impossible!'

'But fact.' Odell glared at him. 'Admiral Hood's ships must have passed this area well to the east'rd. And there are several frigates searching elsewhere.' He spread his hands. 'But of de Grasse there is no sign.'

'God!' Farr looked at Bolitho. 'What d'you make of that?'

Odell said testily, 'I could relish a glass, sir. I am as dry as a pauper's loaf.'

Bolitho opened his cupboard and handed him a decanter.

He said, 'Hood will join with Graves at Sandy Hook. They will still be outnumbered, but can give good account if de Grasse chooses to head their way.'

Farr said less firmly, 'And Hood will show the damn Frogs, eh?'

Bolitho replied, 'His fleet is larger than Admiral Graves's. But Graves is senior now that Rodney has gone home.' He looked at Farr's anxious face. 'I am afraid Graves will lead our forces if and when the time comes.'

He turned to Odell, who was drinking his second glass of wine.

'Do you know anything else?'

He shrugged. 'I understood that Admiral Hood will examine Chesapeake Bay while on passage to New York. Some believe the French may strike at Cornwallis's army from the sea. If not, then New York is to be the melting pot.'

Bolitho made himself sit down. It was strange to be so moved by Odell's information. For months, even years, they had expected some great confrontation at sea. There had been skirmishes and bitter ship-to-ship actions in plenty. But this was what they had all known would happen sooner or later. Who commanded the waters around

America controlled the destiny of those who fought within its boundaries.

He said, 'One thing is certain, we are doing no good here.'

Farr asked, 'Are you saying *we* should join the fleet?'

'Something like that.'

He tried to clear his mind, put Odell's brief facts into perspective. De Grasse could be anywhere, but it was ridiculous to imagine he had sailed back to France, his mission left incomplete. Without his presence in the Indies, the British would be able to throw every ship and man into the fight for America, and de Grasse was astute enough to know his own value.

He moved to the table and pulled a chart from its rack. It was close on seven hundred miles to Cape Henry at the mouth of Chesapeake Bay. With the wind remaining friendly they could make landfall in five days. If Admiral Hood's ships were lying there he could request further orders. Sloops would be more than useful for searching close inshore or relaying signals in a fleet action.

Bolitho said slowly, 'I intend to head north. To the Chesapeake.'

Farr stood up and exclaimed, 'Good! I'm with you.'

Odell asked, 'Are you taking full responsibility, sir?' His eyes were opaque.

'Yes. I would wish you to remain here in case any ships come this way. If they do, you can come after us with all haste.'

'Very well, sir.' Odell added calmly, 'I would like it in writing.'

'Damn your eyes, you impudent puppy!' Farr thumped the table with his fist. 'Where's your bloody trust?'

Odell shrugged. 'I trust Captain Bolitho, have no doubts, *sir*.' He gave a quick smile. 'But if he and you are both killed, who is to say I only obeyed orders?'

Bolitho nodded. 'That is fair. I will do it directly.' He saw the two men watching each other with open hostility. 'Easy now. Right or wrong, it will be good to move again. So let's not start with disharmony, eh?'

Odell showed his teeth. 'I meant no offence, sir.'

Farr swallowed hard. 'In that case, I suppose . . .' He grinned broadly. 'But by God, Odell, you push me to the limit!'

'A glass together.'

Bolitho wanted to go on deck, to share his views with Tyrrell and the others. But he knew this moment was equally vital. Just a few seconds, which each would remember when the other ships were mere silhouettes.

He raised his glass. 'What shall it be, my friends?'

Farr met his eye and smiled. He at least understood. 'To *us*, Dick. That will do fine for me.'

Bolitho placed his empty glass on the table. A simple toast. But, King,

Cause, even Country were too remote, the future too uncertain. They had only each other and their three little ships to sustain them.

With legs braced against *Sparrow*'s uncomfortable, corkscrewing motion, Bolitho levelled a telescope across the nettings and waited for the shoreline to settle in the lens. It was close on sunset, and as the dull orange glow withdrew beyond the nearest shoulder of land he forced himself to concentrate on what he saw, rather than what he had anticipated from his charts. Around him other glasses were also trained, and he heard Tyrrell's heavy breathing at his side, the squeak of a pencil on Buckle's slate by the wheel.

Within a few miles of Cape Henry, the southernmost cape at the entrance of Chesapeake Bay, the wind had backed sharply, and backed again. A full day had been added to their previously fast passage, and as they had clawed desperately from a lee shore, had fought to obtain sea room, Bolitho had watched the bay fading across the quarter with something like anger. And now, after their long beat back towards the entrance, he was faced by a new decision. To lie offshore until dawn, or take his chance and thrust between Cape Henry and the northern headland in what would certainly be total darkness.

Tyrrell lowered his glass. 'I know this entrance well. There's a great middle-ground which reaches into th' bay. With care you can pass either side, but with th' wind under our coat-tails I'd suggest trying th' southern channel. If you stay to lee'rd of th' middle-ground you can hold mebbe three miles clear of Cape Henry.' He rubbed his chin. 'If you misjudge and tack too far to south'rd, you'll have to move lively. There are shoals off th' cape, an' bad ones at that.'

Bolitho shifted the telescope to watch some dancing red flashes far inland.

Tyrrell remarked, 'Cannon. Good way off.'

Bolitho nodded. If Tyrrell was feeling the strain of drawing so near to his home territory he did not show it.

Tyrrell continued, 'Up beyond York River, I reckon. Heavy artillery, by th' looks of it.'

Heyward, who was standing nearby, said, 'No sign of any ships, sir.'

'There wouldn't be.' Tyrrell was watching Bolitho. 'Just around Cape Henry lies Lynnhaven Bay. Good shelter where big ships anchor sometimes when there's foul weather around. No, you'd not even see a fleet from out here.' He paused. 'You'd have to go inside th' old Chesapeake.'

Bolitho handed the glass to Fowler. 'I agree. If we wait longer the wind might veer. We'd be on a lee shore again and lose more time fighting clear from it.'

He turned to look for *Heron*. Her reefed topsails were still holding the fast fading sunlight, but beyond her the sea was in deep shadow.

'Show the signal lantern to *Heron*. Captain Farr knows what to do.'

He turned to Tyrrell. 'The place is badly charted.'

Tyrrell grinned, his eyes glowing in the dull light. 'Unless things have changed, I reckon I can take us through.'

Fowler called, 'Signal passed, sir!'

Bolitho made up his mind. 'Alter course two points to starboard.' To Tyrrell he added slowly, 'I hate entering any bay like this one. I feel more secure in open sea.'

The lieutenant sighed. 'Aye. Th' Chesapeake is a brute in many ways. North to south it measures close on a hundred an' forty miles. You can sail a fair-sized craft right up to Baltimore without too much hardship. But it measures less'n thirty across, an' that's only where the Patow-mack flows into it.'

Buckle called, 'Course sou'-west, sir.'

'Very well.'

Bolitho watched the nearest headland of Cape Charles losing its bronze crest as the sun finally dipped behind a line of hills.

'You may clear for action, Mr Tyrrell. Better safe than sorry.'

He wondered briefly what Farr was thinking as he tacked to follow *Sparrow*'s shadow towards the dark mass of land. Doubt, regret, even mistrust. You could hardly blame him. It was like groping for coal in a shuttered cellar.

Under his shoes he felt the planks quiver to the hurrying seamen, the thud of screens being torn down and mess tables dragged clear of tackles and guns. That was another difference he had found in *Sparrow*. Even clearing for action had a sort of intimacy which was lacking in a ship-of-the-line. In *Trojan* the hands had scurried to quarters, urged on by the drums' staccato beat and the blare of a marine's bugle. Sometimes you never knew men who did not serve in your own watch or division. But here it was entirely different. Men nodded to each other as they dashed to their stations, a grin here, a brief touch of hands there. In many ways it made death harder to accept, a man's cries too personal to ignore.

'Cleared for action, sir.'

'Good.' Bolitho gripped the nettings and watched the tiny feathers of surf far abeam. 'Alter course another point.'

'Aye, sir.' Buckle was muttering to his helmsmen. Then, 'Sou'-west by south, sir.'

'Hold her steady.'

He moved restlessly below the great spanker, seeing a faint glow on the boom from the compass bowl.

There were already plenty of stars in the velvet sky, and there would be a moon on the water in a few hours. But by then he must be inside the bay.

Tyrrell joined him by the wheel. 'It's a strange feeling. My sister'll be no more than fifty miles from where I'm standing. I can still remember it clearly. Th' York River, th' place in th' woods where we used to get together as kids . . .' He turned and said sharply, 'Let her fall off a point, Mr Buckle! Mr Bethune, take some men forrard and trim the foreyard again!' He waited until he was satisfied with the ship's head and the bearing of the nearest cape and continued, 'It's a funny business all round.'

Bolitho agreed. After the first few weeks he had not thought much about Susannah Hardwicke. Now, as he pictured an unknown girl out there in the darkness beyond the occasional flash of gunfire, he realized how their lives had become merged. Tyrrell's sister, and Graves's secret longing for her. Dalkeith's affair of honour which had cost him his career and almost his life. And himself? He was surprised he could still not examine her memory without regret and a sense of loss.

When he looked again he realized that Cape Charles had merged with the shadows. A quick glance at Tyrrell reassured him. He seemed relaxed, even cheerful, as he stood where he could watch the compass and the set of the spanker overhead. But for the treacherous span of middle-ground, they could have sailed boldly between the capes with a comfortable four miles or more on either beam.

Tyrrell said, 'We will alter course again, with your permission, sir.'

'She's in your hands.'

Tyrrell grinned. 'Aye, aye, sir.' To Buckle he called, 'Steer west by north, full an' bye!'

Then he cupped his hands and yelled, 'Pipe th' hands to th' braces!'

With the helm down and the seamen hauling at the braces, *Sparrow* turned her bows towards the land. Voices called in the gloom, and above the decks the paler shapes of arms and legs moved busily about the yards.

'West by north, sir!' Buckle peered at the flapping sails as the ship heeled still further, close-hauled on the starboard tack.

Tyrrell limped from side to side, his arm darting out to catch a man's attention, or his voice sending another to pass his orders right forward where Graves was equally busy.

'Right, lads! Belay there!' He cocked his head as if to listen to the chorus of shrouds and vibrating halliards. 'She's loving it!'

Bolitho walked up to the weather side and felt the cold spray across his face. Tyrrell had come and gone through these capes many times in his father's schooner. Perhaps that memory, and the realization that his sister was now safe and close at hand, made him forget the purpose of their mission, the chance of danger with each passing minute.

'Breakers on the weather bow!' The lookout sounded nervous.

But Tyrrell called, 'Breakers be damned! That'll be th' middle-

ground.' His teeth gleamed in the darkness. 'True as a bloody arrow, if I
do say so myself!'

Bolitho smiled at his excitement. *Breakers be damned!* He had used
much the same phrase and tone when he had driven his sword through
the man who had almost killed him beside the pond.

The massive, looming shoulder of Cape Henry hardened from the
darkness on the larboard beam, and for a brief instant Bolitho imagined
they were too close, that the wind had thrust them further downwind
than Tyrrell had allowed.

He dragged his eyes to the opposite side, and through the spray and
across the deep inshore swell he saw a revolving patch of white. The
middle-ground was clearly marked by the swirl of broken water, but if
Tyrrell had misjudged his approach it would have been too late to avoid it.

Tyrrell shouted, 'Once saw a damn fine Dutchman aground there!
She broke her back!'

Buckle muttered, 'That's bloody encouraging!'

Bolitho peered astern. 'I hope *Heron*'s seen our entrance.'

'She'll be fine.' Tyrrell hurried to the side and studied the darker
wedge of land. 'She draws less and is better to handle close-hauled.' He
patted the rail. 'But *Sparrow*'ll do for me!'

'Take in the forecourse, if you please.' Bolitho pitched his ear to the
sea's changing sounds. The hollow boom of surf against rocks, the
deeper note of water exploring a cave or some narrow gully below the
headland. 'Then the spanker.'

Under topsails and jib *Sparrow* crept deeper into the bay, her stem
rising and plunging across tiderace and swell alike, her helmsmen
tensed at the wheel, fingers sensing her will almost as soon as she did.

Minutes dragged by, then an half-hour. With eyes straining into the
darkness, and other men poised at gun-port tackles and braces, the
sloop tacked delicately below the cape.

Then Tyrrell said, 'No ships here, sir. Lynnhaven lies abeam now.
Any squadron at anchor, ours or th' Frogs, would be showing some sort
of light. To deter an enemy, if for no other reason.'

'That makes good sense.'

Bolitho walked away to hide his disappointment. Odell had been
right to ask for written orders, for if Bolitho had misjudged Hood's
whereabouts this badly he could be equally at fault for quitting his
proper station in the south.

A series of dull explosions echoed across the water, and one bright
stab of flame, as if some powder had been accidentally fired.

He ran his fingers through his hair, wondering what he should do
next. Sail on for New York? It seemed the only solution.

Tyrrell said quietly, 'If we are to beat clear of th' cape, then I suggest
we wear ship now.' He paused. 'Or anchor.'

Bolitho joined him by the compass. 'Then we anchor. We must make contact with the army. They at least should know what is happening.'

Tyrrell sighed. 'It's hard to think that there's a damn great army out there across our bows. Poor bastards. If they are in Yorktown as Odell was led to believe, then they are well placed. But it'll be no comfort if they come under siege.'

'Let's waste no more time.' Bolitho beckoned to Fowler. 'Show the lantern again. Captain Farr will anchor when he sees the signal.'

The topsails stirred noisily as *Sparrow* turned obediently into the wind, her anchor throwing up a sheet of spray like some disturbed water-spirit.

Buckle called, 'Easy with that light, Mr Fowler! Enough is enough!'

Tyrrell dropped his voice. 'No matter. We'll have been sighted from th' moment we weathered th' cape.'

Bolitho looked at him. It was not difficult to picture some scurrying messenger or a mounted man riding through the darkness to warn of their arrival. He felt much as he had done in Delaware Bay. Cut off and restricted, with only the vaguest idea of what was happening.

Tyrrell said, 'I can take a boat, sir. If th' army is encamped in th' town, then they'll be well shielded around th' next spit of land along York River.' He sounded suddenly on edge. 'God, this quiet disturbs me more'n gunfire! My grandfather was a soldier. Used to make my flesh creep with his yarns of night fighting.'

Bolitho watched the topmen sliding down to the deck, seemingly indifferent to the closeness of land or a possible enemy.

'Rig boarding nets and have half the twelve-pounders loaded with grape.'

Tyrrell nodded. 'Aye. An' I'll put some good hands on th' swivels, too. No sense in being rushed by some crazy boat attack.' He waited and then asked, 'Shall I go?'

'Very well. Take both cutters. Mr Graves can command the second one. Mr Fowler will go with you in case we need any signals made.'

A voice called, '*Heron*'s anchored, sir!'

But when Bolitho looked across the nettings he could see nothing. The lookout must have caught a brief glimpse of her reefed topsails as she edged around the cape, or the splash of her anchor when she let go.

Tackles creaked and jerked as both cutters were swayed over the gangways before the decks were sealed off in a web of nets. That could be left safely to the boatswain. Not too taut to afford a grip to some daring boarder, just slack enough to confuse him, to allow a pike or bayonet to catch him before he could slip free.

Men shuffled across the deck, and he heard an occasional clink of steel, the thud of oars being released from their lashings.

Graves came aft, his breeches white in the darkness.

'You know what to do?' Bolitho looked at each in turn. 'Mr Tyrrell
will lead. Muffle your oars, and watch out for enemy pickets.'

Graves sounded breathless. 'How will we recognize our own
soldiers?'

Bolitho could imagine his mouth jerking uncontrollably and was
tempted to keep him on board. But Tyrrell was all important. He knew
the lay of the land like his own cabin. It needed an experienced officer to
back him if things went wrong.

He heard Tyrrell reply calmly, 'Easy. Th' Frogs speak French!'

Graves swung round and then controlled himself with an effort.

'I–I didn't ask for your sarcasm! It's all right for you. This is your
country.'

'That will do!' Bolitho stepped closer. 'Remember, our people are
depending on you. So let's have none of this bickering.'

Tyrrell eased his sword in its sheath. 'I'm sorry, sir. It was my fault.'
He rested his hand on Graves's shoulder. 'Forget I spoke, eh?'

Fowler's voice came up from the boats. 'All ready, sir!'

Bolitho walked to the gangway. 'Be back by dawn.' He touched
Tyrrell's arm. 'How is the pain now?'

'Hardly feel a thing, sir.' Tyrrell stood back to allow his men to
clamber into the cutters. 'A bit of exercise will do me good.'

The boats shoved off and pulled steadily into the darkness. Within
minutes they had vanished, and a watchful silence settled over those
who stood at the loaded guns on either beam.

Bolitho sought out Stockdale and said, 'Have the gig lowered. I may
want word carried to *Heron*.' He saw Bethune's plump outline by the
rail and added, 'You take the gig and pull round the ship. I will signal if I
need a message passed.'

Bethune hesitated. 'I would have willingly gone with the first
lieutenant, sir.'

'I know that.' It was hard to believe that in the midst of all this
confusion Bethune had managed to see his choice of Fowler as a
personal slur. 'He is very young. I need all the *men* I can get to manage
the ship.' It was a lame explanation, but it seemed to suffice.

It was cool under the stars, and after the heat of the day, a gentle
relief. Bolitho kept the seamen in short watches, so that those not on
lookout or standing at the guns might snatch a few moments' rest.

Likewise the officers stood watch and watch, and when he was
relieved by Heyward, Bolitho squatted against the mainmast trunk and
rested his head in his hands.

He felt someone gripping his wrist and knew he must have fallen
asleep.

Heyward was crouching beside him, his voice a fierce whisper. 'Boat
approaching, sir, maybe two.'

Bolitho scrambled to his feet, his mind grappling with Heyward's words. Surely they were not returning already. They could not even have reached the first part of their destination.

Heyward said, 'It's not the gig. She's away on the starboard quarter.'

Bolitho cupped his hands around his ears. Above the slap of water alongside he heard oars and the squeak of a tiller.

A boatswain's mate asked, 'Shall I call a challenge, sir?'

'No.' Why had he said that? 'Not yet.'

He strained his eyes and tried to pick out the splash of oars amidst the lapping cat's-paws of the bay. It had to be Tyrrell returning for he was coming straight for the ship without caution or hesitation.

A thin shaft of moonlight had made a small rippling pattern across the water, and as he watched a longboat glided into it, the oars moving unhurriedly.

Before it slid once more into shadows Bolitho saw the gleam of crossbelts, some soldiers wearing shakos crowded in the sternsheets.

Heyward gasped hoarsely, 'Holy God, they're French!'

The boatswain's mate whispered, 'There's another one astern of 'er!'

Thoughts and wild ideas flooded through Bolitho's mind as he watched the boats' slow approach. Tyrrell and his men captured and being returned for parley. The French coming to announce that Yorktown was theirs and to demand *Sparrow*'s surrender.

He moved quickly to the gangway and cupped his hands. '*Ohé! Du canot! Qui va la?*'

There was a babble of voices from the boat and he heard someone laughing.

To Heyward he snapped, 'Quick, recall the gig! We'll catch these beauties with any luck!'

The first boat was already grinding alongside, and Bolitho held his breath, half expecting one of his own men to fire.

From a corner of his eye he saw a cream of spray, and thanked God that the gig's crew had kept their wits. It was sweeping around the stern, and he could imagine Stockdale willing his men to pull with all their strength.

Heyward came back, the signal lantern still in his hand.

Bolitho shouted, '*Now!*'

Even as the first men appeared on the chains and clung uncertainly to the nets, a line of armed seamen leapt on to the gangway with levelled muskets, while Glass, the boatswain, swung a swivel gun and trained it threateningly.

There was a chorus of shouts and a musket stabbed fire though the night. The ball slammed into the rail and brought a savage fusilade of shots from Heyward's marksmen.

Glass depressed the swivel and jerked the lanyard, changing the crowded boat into a screaming, bloody shambles.

It was more than enough for the second boat. The crash of musket fire, the devastating hail of canister from Glass's swivel were sufficient to render the oars motionless. Hardly a man moved as the gig tore alongside and made fast, and across the choppy water Stockdale bawled, 'Got 'er, sir!' A pause and he called again, 'There's a dozen English prisoners in this 'un!'

Bolitho turned away, feeling sick. He saw Dalkeith and his mates climbing down to the boat alongside and pictured the whimpering carnage he would find there. It could just as easily have been the second boat, and the canister would have carved its bloody path amongst their own people.

He said harshly, 'Get those men aboard, Mr Heyward. Then send the gig to *Heron*. Farr will be wondering what the hell we are about.'

He waited beside the entry port, as with boarding nets lifted the first dazed men were pushed or hauled aboard. The second boatload, French and English alike, came with obvious relief. The French glad to have been spared their companions' slaughter. The English redcoats had different reasons, but their stunned disbelief was pitiful to watch.

Bedraggled and filthy, they were more like scarecrows than trained soldiers.

Bolitho said, 'Take the prisoners below, Mr Glass.' To the redcoats he added, 'Have no fear. This is a King's ship.'

One, a young ensign, stepped forward and exclaimed, 'I thank you, Captain. We all do.'

Bolitho gripped his hand. 'You will get all the rest and help I can offer. But first I must know what's happening here.'

The officer rubbed his eyes with his knuckles. 'We were taken several days back. It was a skirmish with one of their patrols. Most of my men were killed.' He rocked on his feet. 'I still cannot believe we are saved . . .'

Bolitho persisted, 'Is General Cornwallis holding Yorktown?'

'Yes. But as I expect you know, sir, Washington and the French general, Rochambeau, crossed the Hudson some weeks back to the head of Chesapeake Bay. They have a great army massed around Yorktown. A musket behind every tree. But when we heard that an English squadron had looked into the bay we thought we were relieved. I understand a little French and heard the guards speaking of their arrival.'

Heyward said, 'Hood's ships.'

Bolitho nodded. 'When was this?'

The ensign shrugged. 'Three days back. I have lost count of time.'

Bolitho tried to shut out the pitiful cries alongside. He knew little French. Little more than he had used to deceive the boat, but sufficient to recognize pleading. A man being held while Dalkeith got busy with his knife.

Three days back. That fitted what Odell had reported. Hood must have taken a quick look into the bay, and finding no sign of de Grasse had pushed on for New York.

The ensign added weakly, 'The French are expecting their own fleet. That was why, when someone hailed them in their own language, they . . .'

'*What?*' Bolitho seized his arm, his voice harsh despite the man's condition. 'Expecting their own fleet?'

The ensign stared at him. 'But I thought . . . I imagined our ships had gone to fight them off, sir!'

'No.' He released his arm. 'I fear that when they reach New York and discover their mistake it will be too late.'

'Then the army is done for, sir.' The ensign walked unsteadily to the rail. 'All this.' He shouted across the dark water. 'All for *bloody nothing!*'

Dalkeith appeared on deck and with a brief nod took the officer's arm.

Bolitho said, 'Take care of them for me.'

He turned away. They would be prisoners again very soon unless he could decide what to do.

Buckle was watching him anxiously. 'What about Mr Tyrrell, sir?'

'D'you imagine I've not thought about him?' He saw Buckle recoil. 'We will pass the word to *Heron* immediately. If she can work clear tonight Farr must carry the news to Admiral Graves. There might still be time.' He saw the purser hovering by the hatch. 'Fetch some paper and I will write a note for Farr.'

To Buckle he added, 'I'm sorry I abused you. It was a fair question.'

He looked towards the land. 'We will weigh at first light and move closer inshore. Have the sweeps ready in case the wind loses us. I'll not throw Tyrrell and his men away without a fight.' He remembered the lieutenant's words in that far-off garden. *In* Sparrow *we look after our own.* He added quietly, 'We've all come too far together for that.'

Dalkeith crossed the deck as Bolitho walked to the taffrail. To Buckle he whispered, 'What's the captain going to do?'

Buckle shrugged. 'Something crazy, I expect.'

The surgeon wiped his hands on a piece of waste. 'But you approve, nonetheless?'

Buckle grinned. 'Don't make much difference what I think, does it? But I s'pect he'll think of something.' He added vehemently, 'I bloody well hope so, for all our sakes!'

18

Only the Brave

Stockdale padded across the quarterdeck and held out a pewter mug.

' 'Ere, sir. Some coffee.'

Bolitho took it and held it to his lips. It was barely hot, but cleared the dryness from his throat.

Stockdale added thickly, 'The galley fire was doused, so I 'ad to warm it on a lantern in the shot locker.'

Bolitho looked at him. Was it imagination, or were Stockdale's features growing more distinct in the gloom? He shivered. More likely he had been too long on deck, waiting and wondering. Yet he could do no good by pacing the deck and going over his ideas again and again.

'It was a kind thought.' He handed him the mug. 'I feel awake now.'

He peered up at the rigging and furled sails. The stars were still there, but paler. That was no illusion.

'Where is the wind?'

Stockdale considered the question. 'As afore, sir. Nor' nor'-east, if I'm not mistook.'

Bolitho bit his lip. He had already decided it was so. Stockdale was usually right, but his confirmation did little to help.

He said, 'Rouse the master. He is by the hatchway.'

Buckle sprang to his feet, wide awake at Stockdale's first touch.

'What is it? An attack?'

'Easy, Mr Buckle.' Bolitho beckoned him to the rail. 'The wind has dropped, but still too far north'rd to help us.'

The master said nothing and waited to see what the captain had in mind.

'If we are to be of any use, we must drive higher into the bay. It would take hours of tacking back and forth, with little to show for our pains. But if we stay here at anchor we can help neither the first lieutenant nor ourselves if an enemy arrives.'

Buckle yawned. 'That's true enough.'

'So call all hands and run out the sweeps. We will get under way and not wait for the dawn.'

Buckle pulled out his watch and held it against the compass light.

'Hmm. It'll be a hard pull, sir. But the current will not be too much against us.'

He walked to the nettings and kicked a shadowy figure who was sleeping soundly on the bare planks.

'Up, boy! Tell Mr Glass to call the hands. Jump to it!'

Bolitho went quickly to his cabin and concentrated for several minutes on his chart. Recalling what Tyrrell had told him, and adding the information to what he knew already, he settled on his plan of action. Beyond the cabin he could hear the tramp of feet at the capstan, the regular clink of a pawl as the cable came inboard.

He put on his coat and adjusted his swordbelt. How strange the cabin looked in the solitary lantern's light. Cleared for action like the rest of his ship, the guns creaking gently behind their sealed ports, powder and shot, rammers and sponges, all within easy reach. But no one stood near them, for like the remainder of the gundeck, every hand would be needed to raise anchor and man the long sweeps. The latter had got them out of trouble before. This time they might do the same for Tyrrell and his men.

He left the cabin and ran swiftly up the ladder.

It was lighter. There could be no doubt about it. A sort of greyness above Cape Henry, and he could see the swirl of currents well clear of the hull.

He saw the long sweeps swaying above the water on either beam, the men hunched around them, chattering quietly while they awaited an order from aft.

Heyward touched his hat. 'Anchor's hove short, sir.' He sounded tense and very alert.

Bolitho strode from side to side, watching the ship's swing towards the shore, the ripple of water below the gangways.

'How does it feel? From midshipman to first lieutenant with barely a pause?'

He did not hear Heyward's reply, and knew he had only asked the question to cover his own anxiety. If the men lost control of the sweeps he would have to anchor immediately. Even then he might be driven too close inshore for comfort.

From forward he heard Bethune's cry, 'Anchor's aweigh, sir!' The patter of feet as men ran from the capstan bars to add their weight on the sweeps.

Then Glass's voice, 'Steady! *Stand by!*'

Bolitho gripped his hands together until the fingers almost cracked. Why the hell was he leaving it so late? In a moment the ship would be aground.

'Give way all!'

The sweeps swayed forward, dipped and then came steadily aft.

Behind him Bolitho heard the wheel easing gently, and Buckle's quiet cursing as he endured the tension in his own style. He tried to relax his muscles. Glass had been right to make sure of that first stroke. But it was one thing to know it, another to remain aloof in the face of danger to his ship.

Up and down, forward to aft, the sweeps creaked busily but without undue haste, until Buckle called, 'Steerage way, sir!'

'Good. Hold her due north, if you please.'

Heyward removed his coat. 'I'll go and lend a hand, sir.'

'Yes. Make sure we have every available man working. Those redcoats as well, if they have the strength.' He checked him as he ran for the ladder. 'There is no need to tell the soldiers we are heading *towards* the enemy, Mr Heyward!' He saw him grin. 'They'll find out soon enough.'

Buckle and a solitary seaman stood at the wheel, and Bolitho walked right aft to the taffrail without speaking. He saw the nearest cape more clearly now, the pattern of white-caps at its base to mark some small cove. An empty place. When daylight came, and *Heron* was seen to be gone, his men might question his action, and rightly. But if their presence was to be of any use to the admiral, then they must learn everything possible. The released soldiers had told them much. But a lot could have changed since they had been taken. He smiled grimly. He was deluding himself. But for Tyrrell and the others, would he really have remained here in the bay?

He heard shouts on deck and someone speaking in French. Heyward was more than a good companion, he was proving to be an excellent officer. Without further consultation, and at the risk of his captain's displeasure, he had released the French prisoners and put them to work. All strong, beefy soldiers who had led a fairly comfortable life guarding prisoners, they would make a small but significant difference to the heavy sweeps.

Some gulls rose screaming angrily from the water where they had been sleeping as the *Sparrow* moved amongst them at a slow but steady crawl. Time dragged by, and Bolitho saw that the soldiers' coats were red again instead of black as they had appeared in the darkness. Faces regained personality, and he was able to see those who were standing the strain and others who were being relieved at more frequent intervals to regain their breath.

A blacker shadow loomed and held firm across the starboard bow. That must be the inner side of Cape Charles, he decided, with Tyrrell's middle-ground some distance below it.

'Bring her up a point, Mr Buckle.' He heard the helm squeak. 'We must pass the cape with the mainland to larboard. There'll not be too much water in the channel, so hold her steady.'

'Aye, sir. Nor' by east it is!'

The ship was heading almost directly into the wind, and he could feel it on his face, smell the land and its freshness in the dawn air. But it was more sheltered, and he was relieved to see the sweeps were still moving in unison, although the actual progress was probably less than a knot.

He sought out the young ensign and called him aft. He arrived panting on the quarterdeck, and Bolitho said, 'Look abeam. How near are your outposts?'

The soldier peered across the larboard nettings and raised one arm.

'That bit of land, sir. That'll be the turning point. A lot of sand there. We lost some barges a few weeks back when they ran ashore. A mile or so further and you'll be able to see the mouth of York River just beyond a pair of small islands.'

Bolitho smiled. 'I expect you're surprised we're heading this way.'

The ensign shrugged. 'I am past surprise, sir.' He stiffened. 'I heard a bugle. That'll be our lads.' He tapped the rail with his fingers, his face engrossed. Then there was a long-drawn-out trumpet call, which sent a cloud of gulls flapping and squeaking from the land. He said, 'The Frogs. Always a minute behind our reveille.'

Bolitho tried to break him from his mood. 'What of the Americans?'

The ensign sighed. 'They have artillery over the river. They'll start firing at first light. More effective than any damn bugle!'

Bolitho turned towards Buckle. 'We will keep on this course as long as our people have strength for it. The wind will favour us when we finally go about, but I want to get as far above York River as I can.'

He looked aloft and saw the masthead pendant for the first time. It was flapping gently astern, but showed no warning of a strengthening wind. If it got up now, his men would be unable to hold the stroke. Even with Tyrrell's boat crews it would have been hard. Without them, impossible.

When he glanced abeam he saw the overhanging spur of Cape Charles, and far beyond it, like a thin gold thread, the horizon. Showing its face to the sun which was easing into view, parting sea from sky, night from day.

There was a muffled bang, and seconds later he saw the telltale white fin of spray to mark where a ball had ploughed into the bay.

The ensign remarked indifferently, 'They'll never reach you at this range. You've a good half a mile to play with.'

'Where is the battery?'

The soldier studied him curiously. 'Everywhere, sir. There are guns right round this sector. Yorktown and its approaches are hemmed in a ring of iron. Our army has the sea at its back.' He suddenly looked very young and vulnerable. 'Only the fleet can bring relief.'

Bolitho pictured Farr's *Heron* making all haste towards New York. Even there he might find Hood gone, perhaps further still to Newport to contain de Barras.

He thought too, of Odell's solitary vigil in his *Lucifer*. If the French did come by way of the little used Bahama Channel, he would need no encouragement to make sail and run.

He blinked as a shaft of sunlight played across the distant cape and coloured the yards and stays like honey. He pulled out his watch. Tyrrell should have made his contact with Cornwallis's pickets and be on his way back to Lynnhaven by now. By weighing and putting the men to the sweeps, their meeting should have been brought forward by an hour at least.

Glass ran up the ladder, his chest heaving from exertion.

'Can't hold 'em much longer, sir!' He peered down at the sweeps, at their sluggish rise and fall. 'Shall I put the rope's end to 'em, sir?'

'You will not.' Bolitho looked away. There was no malice in Glass, nor was he prone to unnecessary force. It was just that he did not know what else to do. 'Tell them. Another half hour. Then we make sail, or anchor.'

Glass shifted awkwardly. 'It'd be better from you, sir.'

Bolitho walked to the rail and called, 'One more turn of the glass, lads!' He heard groans, the mingled curses and gasps from those still hidden in shadow. 'It's that or leave our people out there to fend for themselves! Remember, it might have been you!'

He turned away, not knowing if his words had achieved anything but resentment.

Glass watched critically and then spat on his hands. 'That done it, sir! Better already!'

Bolitho sighed. The stroke looked as weary as before, but if the boatswain was satisfied then . . .

He swung round as a voice called, 'Boat, sir! Fine on the larboard bow!'

Bolitho gripped the rail. 'Just the one?'

'Aye, sir.'

'Bring her round two points to larboard.'

Bolitho tried not to think about the missing boat. He felt the hull yaw, the stroke failing as the helm went over.

The soldier said quietly, 'No closer, I pray you. You'll be in cannon-shot before long.'

Bolitho ignored him, '*Pull*, lads! Come on, do your damndest!'

One man fell exhausted from a loom and was dragged away by Dalkeith.

The lookout yelled, 'It's the second cutter, sir! Mr Graves!'

Dalkeith heaved himself up the ladder and stood at the rail.

'I *know* what you're thinking, sir.' He did not flinch under Bolitho's cold stare. 'He'd not leave you. Not for anything.'

Bolitho looked past his shoulder at a patch of land. In the strengthening light he saw tall trees and a round hill beyond. They were motionless. The sweeps were only keeping *Sparrow* steady against wind and current. In a minute she would start to pay-off and drift inshore. They had done their best. It was not enough.

He snapped, 'Damn your eyes, Mr Dalkeith! I'll not be lectured by you!'

He leaned over the rail. 'Mr Heyward! Stand by to let go the anchor!'

Bolitho waited while men ran to the call and Glass sent others to bear down on the flagging sweeps where exhausted sailors had fallen to the deck. He heard a bang and saw a ball ricochet across the water to throw up a plume of spray very close to the approaching cutter. The boat was moving rapidly towards him, and he could see Graves by the tiller, his hat awry as he beat out the time to his oarsmen.

'Ready, sir!'

He chopped with his arm. 'Let go!'

Even as the anchor took grip and the hull swung carelessly to the cable, he yelled, 'Withdraw sweeps! Mr Glass, *get those men on their feet!*'

Dalkeith stood his ground. 'You can't blame yourself, sir.' He met Bolitho's gaze stubbornly. 'Curse me if you will, but I'll not stand by and see you torment yourself.'

The cutter was hooking on to the main chains, and he heard Graves shouting at the men on deck to make fast his lines.

He said quietly, 'Thank you for your concern. But there is no one else *to* blame.'

He made himself wait by the rail until Graves had scrabbled aboard, and then called sharply, 'Lay aft, if you please! The boatswain can deal with the cutter.'

Graves hurried towards him, his face twitching violently.

Bolitho asked, 'Where are the others?' He kept his voice very calm, but was conscious of his whole being screaming at Graves's stricken face.

'We grounded in some shallows, sir. Both boats separated. It was the first lieutenant's idea. A patrol of soldiers had signalled where we should secure the boats, but there was some shooting. Enemy marksmen, I believe.'

'And then?' He could feel others standing nearby, see Heyward's frozen expression as he listened to Graves's quick erratic account.

'In the darkness we were all trying to take cover. I lost a man, and Tyrrell sent word for us to stay hidden in the creek.' He shook his head vaguely. 'The balls were flying everywhere. Tyrrell was going to meet one of the officers. They knew we were coming, apparently. Their scouts had seen us.' His mouth jerked uncontrollably. 'We stayed there waiting, and then there was more firing, and I heard men charging through the brush, there must have been a platoon or more!'

'Did you not think of going to assist Mr Tyrrell?'

Graves stared at him, his eyes blank. 'We were in mortal danger! I sent Fowler to find the others, but . . .'

'You did *what?*' Bolitho reached out and gripped his coat. 'You sent that boy on his own?'

'He – he volunteered, sir.' Graves looked down at Bolitho's hand on his coat. 'When he failed to return I decided to' – he raised his eyes, suddenly composed – 'to obey your orders and withdraw to the ship.'

Bolitho released his hold and turned away. He felt sick and appalled with what Graves had done. The lieutenant's pathetic defiance made it worse, if that were possible. He had obeyed orders. So his crime was acceptable.

A puff of smoke rose above the nearest spit of land, and he saw the ball drop within half a cable of the ship. Even now, some officer might be ordering up a heavier gun. One which would make short work of so promising a target.

He heard himself say, 'Tell Mr Yule to run out the larboard bow-chaser and lay it on that gunsmoke. He will fire with grape until I order otherwise. It might cool their eagerness.'

He walked past Graves without a glance.

'Have the cutter manned at once.' He looked down at the silent seamen on the gundeck. 'I want volunteers for . . .' He swallowed as the assembled men moved towards the side as if drawn by wires. 'Thank you. But just a boat's crew. Mr Glass, see to it at once!'

To Heyward he added, 'You will remain here.' He did not look at Graves. 'If I fall *you* will assist the master in getting the ship under way, understood?'

Heyward nodded, his eyes filling his face.

Dalkeith touched his arm. '*Look*, sir!'

It was the other cutter, or what was left of it. Even in the poor light it was possible to see the splintered gunwale, the few remaining oars which moved it so slowly on the uneasy water.

There was a bang and another waterspout shot skyward just beyond it. The hidden gun had shifted to a smaller but closer target.

Bolitho flinched as Yule's crew fired their first shot from forward, saw the trees quiver as if in a freak gust as the packed grape scythed towards the drifting smoke.

'A glass!'

He hardly dared to raise it to his eye. Then he saw the cutter, the scars in its side left by musket balls, the lolling corpses still propped between the remaining oarsmen. Then he saw Tyrrell. He was sitting on the gunwale right aft, someone draped across his knees as he steered the boat past the white patch left by the enemy's ball.

He said quietly, 'Thank God.'

The bow-chaser hurled itself inboard again, dragging him from his thoughts, his overwhelming relief.

He shouted, 'Mr Bethune, take the cutter and assist Mr Tyrrell!' He looked for Buckle. 'Get the hands aloft and prepare to loose tops'ls!'

All exhaustion and dread at Graves's report seemed to be fading as men tore to their stations. The cutter was pulling from the side, Bethune standing upright as he urged his crew to greater efforts.

Dalkeith said, 'Well, sir . . .' He got no further.

One of the topmen who had reached the uppermost yard before his companions yelled, 'Deck there! Sail comin around th' 'eadland!'

Bolitho snatched a glass and trained it above the nettings. She was standing well out from the bay, but was already tacking frantically towards Cape Henry. It was the *Lucifer*.

Odell would be shocked to find no fleet, nor even *Heron* at anchor. He tensed. There was damage to the schooner's mizzen, and she was handling sluggishly as she tried to beat closer to the entrance. She must have been caught unprepared by another ship, perhaps under cover of darkness. There was no mistaking the flapping rents in her great foresail, the uneven spread of rigging.

He saw flags breaking to the wind, and held the glass motionless while his lips spelled out the brief signal.

He turned to Buckle. '*Enemy in sight.*'

'God A'mighty.'

'Mr Heyward!' He saw him swing round from the capstan.

'Stand by to cut the cable! We will not recover the boats, but make sail as soon as our people are aboard!'

He heard a chorus of shouts, and when he turned aft he saw *Lucifer* folding her great sails like the wings of a dying bird. She must have risked everything to reach him with her news, even to make that one vital signal. She had driven too close and had struck the shoals which Tyrrell had described so vividly.

He made himself walk to the rail and look for the boats. Tyrrell's cutter was almost awash, but Bethune was there, and he saw the wounded being hauled across, a patch of scarlet to mark at least one soldier in the party.

Several more guns were firing now, and balls threw up tall splashes in the pale sunlight like a line of leaping dolphins.

Some of the topmen gave a ragged cheer as Bethune cast the waterlogged cutter adrift and headed back towards *Sparrow*.

Bolitho turned towards Graves who was standing much as before. 'Take charge of your guns.' He kept his voice formal without understanding why or how. He could picture *Lucifer*'s frail hull breaking up on the rocks and Tyrrell's shattered boat trying to reach *Sparrow*. He could even see young Fowler, a mere child, running through some unknown woods while shots shrieked all about him. 'Do your duty. That is all I ask of you.' He looked away. 'All I will ever ask of you again.'

He heard the boat grind alongside and saw Tyrrell and the others being dragged through the entry port, being clapped on the shoulders and bombarded with questions and cheers.

Bolitho strode towards him and saw with sudden despair that Tyrrell was carrying Midshipman Fowler. It must have been his body across his legs in the boat.

Tyrrell looked at him steadily and gave a tired grin. 'He's all right, sir. He was crying fit to break his heart, an' then fell asleep in th' boat.' He handed the midshipman to some seamen. 'Worn out, poor little bugger.' He saw Graves and added flatly, 'But he's got guts. Plenty of 'em.' Then he strode forward and gripped Bolitho's hands. 'He's not th' only one, it seems.'

A new voice drawled, 'Pon my *word*, I knew we'd meet again!'

It was Colonel Foley. A bandage round his throat, his uniform in tatters, but somehow remaining as impeccable as Bolitho remembered him.

Bolitho said, 'I, too.' He looked at Tyrrell. 'We are in for some warm work today, I fear. *Lucifer*'s done for, and we must leave quickly if we are to avoid her fate.'

'Aye.' Tyrrell limped towards the wheel. 'I'd guess as much.'

A cry from aloft brought every eye towards the headland. Very slowly, their yards braced round in the sunlight, a frigate and a deep-hulled transport were passing level with the wrecked schooner.

Bolitho said simply, 'Sooner than I thought.' He looked at Heyward. 'We will cut the cable.' To Tyrrell he added, 'Then you may pass the word to load and run out.'

The cutter and its dead oarsmen drifted away from the side, a discarded reminder of their sacrifice.

Bethune hurried aft, his face glowing with excitement.

Bolitho said, 'Well done. I'll see you a lieutenant yet, despite what *you* do to the contrary.'

He felt suddenly composed, even relaxed. 'Run up the colours! We'll show the army we're not leaving them to no purpose!'

The cable cut, and with her topsails bellying to the wind, *Sparrow* tilted round in a tight arc, the thunder of her canvas drowning the gunfire from the trees, her seamen too busy even to think beyond their work and the need to reach the open sea.

By the time *Sparrow* had gone about and settled on her course towards the capes, there could be no doubt in anyone's mind as to the enemy's intentions. Even as Tyrrell reported all guns loaded and run out, Bolitho raised his glass to examine yet another ship as she rounded the southern headland. One more heavy transport, and beyond her he could see the billowing topsails of a protective frigate.

Tyrrell said, 'God's teeth, a fleet and nothing less!'

Buckle called, 'Steady as she goes, sir! Sou' by west!'

The first transport had already dropped anchor, and through his glass Bolitho saw her boats being lowered with swift precision, the glint of sunlight on weapons and uniforms as soldiers clambered down ladders and nets in a manner which spoke of much practice. He shifted his glass to the second large vessel. She, too, was crammed with soldiers, and there were limbers on her upper deck, and her yards were festooned with heavy tackles, the kind used for lowering horses into boats or lighters.

Colonel Foley drawled, 'We heard Rochambeau was expecting reinforcements. It would appear they have arrived.'

Bolitho glanced at him. 'What is your mission now?'

'If you can get me to New York I have despatches for General Clinton. They may not help Cornwallis, but he will be glad to know what is happening here.' He gave a brief smile. 'I heard that you dealt severely with our old friend Blundell? Not before time.' He raised one eyebrow. 'You met his niece again, I understand?'

Bolitho watched the jib-boom swing very slightly and settle on the outthrust wedge of headland. How could they speak so calmly and detachedly when death lay so close at hand?

He replied, 'Yes. She will be in England now.'

Foley gave a sigh. 'I am relieved. I recognize all the signs, Captain. She wanted you to quit the Service and join her train of admirers, eh?' He held up one hand. 'Do not bother to reply! It is plain on your face, as it must have been on mine.'

Bolitho smiled gravely. 'Something of the sort.'

'When she tired of me I was sent to serve under Cornwallis. A favour as it turned out. And you?'

Tyrrell stepped back from the rail. 'She almost had him killed!'

Foley shook his head. 'A formidable woman indeed.'

'Deck there! Ship-o'-the-line roundin' the cape!'

Bolitho felt a chill on his spine as he thought of Odell's dash from the south. Day by day and at each dawn he would look astern at the pursuing ships. It must have been a nightmare for every man aboard.

The boats from the two transports were pulling towards the land now, and he could see the hulls deep in the water as testimony of the numbers they carried.

'Set the t'gallants, Mr Tyrrell. We will need all our wind today.'

Foley drew his sabre and turned it over in his hands. 'You are not merely running away, I take it?'

Bolitho shook his head. 'Those two frigates are shortening sail, Colonel. They intend to rake us when we attempt to clear the middleground.' He pointed towards the anchored transports. 'There is our course. Close inshore, where we'll be least expected.'

Foley grimaced. 'Or welcome, I suspect.'

Bolitho looked at Buckle. 'When we go about you must lay her as close as you can to Cape Henry.'

'Aye, sir.' Buckle was peering through shrouds and stays, his eyes fixed on the ships.

Bolitho raised his glass again. The two frigates were under minimum canvas standing before the wind with some difficulty as they waited for the small sloop to dash past them. Less than a mile now. He watched them narrowly, noting their drift, the sun gleaming on their broadsides and on the raised telescopes of their officers.

He snapped, 'How many boats in the water?'

Bethune called, 'At least thirty!'

'Good.'

Bolitho imagined the packed soldiers who would be watching *Sparrow*'s apparent dash for safety. A spectacle to drive away their own doubts and fears of what lay ahead on the American mainland.

Bolitho drew his hanger and held it above his head. Along the gun-deck he saw the crews crouching at the tackles, each captain peering aft, a slow-match held ready. In the maintop two swivels were training this way and that, a seaman squatting on the barricade with fresh canister cradled to his chest. Curiously, as he ran his eyes quickly over his command, he was reminded of Colquhoun's words so long ago. *When all others are looking aft at you.*

He heard a sharp bang, and seconds later the high-pitched whine of a ball whipping overhead. One of the frigates had fired a ranging shot. But he kept his eyes on the nearest transport as she swung to her cable, her high poop towards the beach. Aboard the frigates the gun crews would be betting with each other. How many balls would they get off before the *Sparrow* was overwhelmed by their cross-fire or she struck her colours?

He brought down his hanger with a flourish. '*Now!*'

The wheel creaked noisily, and as men hauled at the braces to retrim the yards, *Sparrow*'s stem began to turn. Bolitho held his breath, watching the frigates slipping further and further down the larboard bow, while the nearest transport and then the great spread of oared boats swam across the jib-boom, and beyond them the land opened up as if to receive their onrushing charge.

'Hold her!'

Bolitho ran to the nettings, his mind hanging on to Tyrrell's words of Lynnhaven Bay, the depths and currents, the dangers and margin of survival.

Buckle's helmsmen cursed and spun the wheel against the opposite thrust of wind and sea, and as spray leapt above the beakhead Bolitho saw the nearest boats careering off course, the realization and horror of his intentions at last only too clear.

Gunfire thudded across the bay, and balls whimpered and splashed very near to the hull. But the two frigates had been taken by surprise, and as *Sparrow* lunged towards the shore, Bolitho knew that within minutes she would be screened from their fire by the first transport.

He could feel the madness surging through him like fever, and as he yelled down at the gundeck he knew it was infectious, saw the men poised at their open ports like half-naked demons.

'*Stand by!*' The hanger was above his head again. 'Full depression!'

He saw the nearest muzzles dipping towards the creaming water, the gun captains dancing from side to side while their men stood ready with charges and fresh shot for the next barrage, and the one after that.

'As you bear!' The hanger hovered, holding the fresh sunlight like gold. '*Fire!*'

The air was blasted apart by the ragged broadsides from either beam. As the dense smoke swirled inboard, and the gun crews yelled and cheered above the squeak of trucks, the clatter of handspikes and rammers, Bolitho saw the next spitting tongues from forward, the double-shotted charges smashing into boats and soldiers, the whirl of splinters and spray. Above the decks the braced topsails quivered to each explosion, the smoke fanning out on either side in a choking fog while the guns roared out again and again.

Sharper cracks from muskets, the metallic bangs of swivels, made words impossible. It was a nightmare, a world in torment. Boats lurched into the hull and Bolitho felt the deck shake as *Sparrow*'s stem smashed into a launch, breaking it in two and spilling out the overloaded soldiers in a kicking, screaming profusion.

A transport was firing now, her upper tier cutting over the scattered boats and slapping through *Sparrow*'s canvas like great fists.

A ball burst through the nettings, and Bolitho heard shrill screams as two seamen were pulped against the opposite side. He saw Fowler walking dazedly past the dismembered corpses, his face set as if in deep thought. He noticed that he was snapping his fingers.

The hull gave another great lurch, and below his feet he felt the enemy's iron smashing through the gundeck, the attendant rumble of a twelve-pounder being overturned.

Another longboat lurched down the starboard side, some men firing with their muskets, others scrambling over the frantic sailors at the oars. Balls thudded into the rail and bulwark, and a seaman fell choking on blood as one took him in the throat.

Bolitho ran to the side and wiped his streaming eyes to peer astern. The surface was littered with smashed boats and drifting woodwork. Men, too, some swimming, others fading beneath the water under their weight of weapons and equipment.

Foley was reloading a musket and shouting, 'A few less for our boys to fight!' He leaned over the nettings and shot down a soldier even as he stood to fire at the sloop.

Bolitho strained his eyes towards the shore. It was near enough. Almost too close.

'Bring her about!' He had to repeat the order before Buckle understood.

With blocks screaming and her yards braced round once more, *Sparrow* heeled dangerously on the larboard tack, her bows seemingly pointed straight at the land.

And there was the second transport, swinging drunkenly across the bow, her gun-ports already flashing and tearing the air apart with shot.

A ball ripped through the quarterdeck rail, splitting it apart like matchwood, and cutting down a master's mate who was yelling to the hands at the mizzen braces. Blood splashed across Bolitho's breeches, and he saw other men falling on the gundeck, the protective nets above it jerking with fallen cordage and torn canvas.

A quick glance aloft told him the masthead pendant was streaming almost abeam. They were as close to the wind as they could be. Enough or too little made no difference now. There was no room to go about, nor time to change tack.

Tyrrell yelled, 'Rake that bastard's poop!' He gestured to the nearest gun captains. 'Grape! Bring them down!'

He stared at Bolitho, his eyes glazed with fatigue, the fury of battle.

'She's coming round!' He caught a seaman as he dropped from the nettings, his face a mask of blood. 'Another for th' surgeon!' He turned to Bolitho again and then gave a short cry, his hands to his thigh as he fell.

Bolitho knelt beside him, holding his shoulders as more balls blasted splinters from the deck. Tyrrell stared up at him, his eyes dark with pain.

'S'all right.' He gritted his teeth. 'It's th' same bloody leg!'

Bolitho saw Dalkeith stooping and running across the deck, some of his men at his back.

Tyrrell added weakly, 'I knew it had to come off. Now there's no excuse, eh?' Then he fainted.

From the littered gundeck Graves watched him fall, although his mind was cringing to the noise and the stench of death.

He screamed, 'Run out!' He thrust at a wild-eyed seaman. 'Point! *Ready!*' He stared fixedly at the towering sails of the transport as it rose ponderously abeam. '*Fire!*

The deck lurched beneath his feet, and he saw two men blasted into crimson fragments, their screams cut short before they reached the stained planking. But somewhere in his reeling mind he was thinking of Tyrrell. He must be dead, *God rot him.* His sister would be all alone now. One day, maybe sooner than the others realized, he would find her. *Take her for himself.*

A gunner's mate gaped up at him, his mouth like a black hole as he bellowed, 'Look out, sir! For Christ's sake . . .' His words were lost in the grating crash of timber as the main topgallant yard plunged through the nets like a great tree. It gouged into the planking and further still to the deck below. As its trailing rigging and severed halliards thundered between the blazing guns Graves died, his body impaled under the broken spar.

At the quarterdeck rail Bolitho saw him die, and knew that the months of patrol duty, the storms and the fights, had at last broken the yard which they had once fished so carefully after another battle, a thousand years ago.

But Heyward was there, his voice rallying the gun crews as the anchored transport faded into the smoke, her hull pitted with holes from the bow-chaser's merciless bombardment.

The wind fanned the smoke inside, and with something like disbelief he saw the sheer of Cape Henry pulling back like a huge door, the horizon glittering beyond it in welcome.

Fowler slipped and fell on some blood and sobbed, 'It's no use! I can't . . .'

Bethune strode towards him. 'You can and you damn well will!'

The young midshipman turned and blinked at him. '*What?*'

Bethune grinned, his face black with powder smoke. 'You heard me! So jump to it, *boy!*'

'Mr Buckle!' Bolitho winced as some stray shots shrieked through the shrouds and brought down more lengths of cordage. 'I want you to . . .'

But the master took no notice. He was sitting with his back to the hatchway, hands to his chest as if in prayer. His eyes were open, but the spreading pattern of blood around him told its own story.

Glass and a solitary seaman stood at the unprotected wheel, their eyes wild, their legs straddled amidst dead and dying.

Bolitho snapped, 'As close as you can. *Lucifer*'s remains will guide you clear of the shoal.'

As sunlight enveloped the sloop from stem to stern and her yards swung yet again to take her out of the bay, Bolitho saw the great array of ships coming down from the southern horizon and filling the sea. It was a fantastic spectacle. Squadron by squadron, the ships-of-the-line appearing to overlap as they headed purposefully towards the Chesapeake.

Foley murmured, 'De Grasse. I have never seen such a fleet.'

Bolitho tore his eyes away and hurried to the taffrail. There was no sign of pursuit from the bay, nor had he expected one. The two frigates would be guarding their new anchorage and trying to rescue some of the soldiers who had escaped *Sparrow*'s fury. He turned towards the wheel where Heyward and Bethune stood watching him.

'We will wear ship directly.' He saw Dalkeith and called, 'Tell me!'

Dalkeith eyed him sadly. 'It's done. He's sleeping now. But I am confident.'

Bolitho wiped his face and felt Stockdale steady his arm as the ship pitched heavily to the freshening wind.

So much still to do. Repairs to be carried out even as they avoided the oncoming might of France. To find Admiral Graves and tell him of the enemy's arrival. To bury their dead. His mind felt numb.

Yule, the gunner, clattered up a sagging ladder and barked, 'Any spare hands, sir! I need 'em for the pumps!'

Bolitho faced him. 'Get them elsewhere.'

He looked around at the sprawled bodies caught in their various attitudes of death.

'Only the brave lie here.'

He looked up, startled, as from high above the deck he heard someone singing. Beyond the pitted canvas and dangling rigging, to where the topgallant yard had splintered apart before falling to kill Graves, he saw a solitary seaman working in the sunlight, his marlin-spike glinting as he spliced a broken stay. The sounds of sea and booming sails were too loud for him to hear the words, but the tune seemed familiar and strangely sad.

Foley joined him and said quietly, 'If they can sing like that, after what they've done.' He turned away, unable to watch Bolitho's face. 'Then, by God, I *envy* you!'

Epilogue

Two days after fighting out of the bay, *Sparrow*'s lookouts sighted the van of Admiral Graves's fleet bearing down the coast of Maryland. The occasion was both exciting and bitter, for with many of her company wounded or killed it was hard not to feel emotion. Well ahead of the fleet, her signal flags rippling in the sunlight, *Heron* stood before the wind, a small symbol of what they had endured and achieved together.

Bolitho could remember the moment exactly, as with his men he had waited on the splintered quarterdeck while his signals were passed to *Heron* and repeated to the flagship.

When the reply had been received, Bethune had turned, his face suddenly matured.

'*Flag* to *Sparrow,* sir. *You will lead. Yours is the honour.*'

For an admiral who disliked superfluous signalling, Admiral Graves had done them proudly.

Once again, *Sparrow* had gone about, her torn sails and battered hull acting like a pointer to the great ships-of-the-line which followed obediently in her wake.

Once in sight of the bay, and with the knowledge that the French were still there, *Sparrow*'s role had become that of a mere spectator to a battle which was to leave its mark on all who took part. A warning to young officers like Bolitho, a grim lesson to the hidebound who had for so long fought by the book, a book which had become outdated by hard experience.

Perhaps Admiral Graves had expected, even hoped, up to the last moment that the French had quit the Chesapeake or at worst de Barras's smaller squadron would be there, having slipped past his patrols and escaped from Newport some days earlier. *Sparrow*'s signal had put paid to any such belief, and the sight of such a grand array must have filled him with misgivings. But if his fleet was inferior to de Grasse's in both ships and guns, he had much in his favour. The wind gave him the advantage, and as Tyrrell had so often predicted, the treacherous middle-ground between the Chesapeake's capes was soon to show its impartiality to those who braved it.

With the British bearing down on the bay, and de Barras's reinforcements not yet in close company, de Grasse decided to weigh and meet them in open water. An adverse wind and tide, the dangerous spit of middle-ground, soon told him he was unable to leave his protective anchorage as a complete fleet. Squadron by squadron, his ships fought their way around Cape Henry, with *Lucifer*'s skeleton close by as a warning to the foolhardy or the careless.

This should have been Graves's great opportunity. To signal *General Chase* and allow his captains to fall on the enemy before he could reassemble and proclaim his superiority. Had there been a Hawke or a Keppel in command there was little doubt in anyone's mind that the effect would have been devastating.

But once again Graves faltered, his mind grasping the written word of the 'Fighting Instructions' and seeing no other alternative.

His flagship hoisted the rigid signal to form line of battle, and it remained flying throughout the action. The delay allowed de Grasse to assemble his fleet and when the two adversaries finally drove together it was impossible for the rearmost British ships even to engage. By evening, failing light forced the fleets to disengage, and driven by a strong north-easterly both soon lost contact.

When at last Graves was able to re-form his squadrons, the French had beaten back into the Chesapeake. They did not leave it again, and after further hesitation Graves ordered his frustrated captains to sail for New York.

Helpless and beyond reach of the action itself, Bolitho had watched much of the tactics and guessed far more of what was happening. He left the deck at regular intervals to speak with Tyrrell in the sick-bay, holding his hand as he tried to describe the sequence of events.

He could recall each visit exactly. Tyrrell's face very pale in the lanternlight, his mouth clenched against the agony. And around him, groaning or sobbing quietly, the others who had suffered, and some who were beyond pain.

Tyrrell had said hoarsely, 'That's th' army finished.' He had gripped Bolitho's hand with some of his old vigour. 'But *we* did what we could!'

Later at Sandy Hook, as *Sparrow* had carried out repairs and Bolitho had received orders to sail for England with the admiral's despatches and news of the battle, the blow had fallen.

Cut off from the sea, his ammunition and supplies exhausted, Cornwallis and his whole army capitulated.

True to his reputation, General Washington had allowed the British to surrender with both honour and dignity, but it was a crushing defeat, nevertheless.

Couriers who had brought the news of the surrender told of the British military band which led their soldiers into Washington's camp. They had been playing 'The World Turned Upside Down', which gave some hint of what they thought about their situation if nothing else.

Under low cloud and a steady drizzle *Sparrow* weighed and turned her stern to Sandy Hook for the last time. Her company reacted to their sailing orders with mixed feelings. Some mourned old friends whom they had buried at sea or left crippled to await more comfortable transport. Others were almost afraid of what they might find in England after so long. And there were plenty who turned their backs on America and dreamed only of that moment when they would step ashore in their own country, thankful at being spared the pain and despair, grateful even to see the leaden sky above the mastheads.

When not required on deck Bolitho spent much of the voyage alone in his cabin. It made contact less painful, the losses of familiar faces easier to bear.

He could remember his last handshake with Tyrrell as he had said his farewells at a New York hospital. Dalkeith had been there, too, and it had been a sad parting. It was still hard to think of Tyrrell with one leg, nor did he want to. One thing seemed certain, Tyrrell was without despair.

'After this, I'm going home.' He had said it several times. 'I don't know how or when, but by th' Lord I'll get there!'

Dalkeith had been appointed to an accommodation ship off Sandy Hook, and had added quietly, 'Reckon they'll need a good doctor, too, eh, Jethro?' He had given his deep chuckle. 'So here's me hand on it!'

Bolitho shivered and pulled his coat more closely across his body. It was cold and very damp, and the bulkhead was dripping with condensation. He glanced at the open log book. It was the first day of January 1782, another year for all of them. He stood up and walked slowly from the cabin, his legs taking the pitch and plunge without conscious thought or effort. Over three and a half years since he had stepped into this ship which had become so much a part of him.

He climbed the ladder and saw Heyward at the weather nettings. It would be worse for him. He had been aboard since he had commissioned five years back. He walked across to him, seeing the grey mist swirling through the dripping shrouds, the spray bursting high above the gangway.

'Well, Mr Heyward, the English Channel. Yonder, with any sort of luck, lies the Isle of Wight. We will anchor at Spithead before dark.'

Heyward looked at him steadily. 'It's a strange feeling, sir.' He shrugged. 'I'm not sure if I want to leave the ship now.'

Bolitho nodded. 'It is often the case. *Sparrow* is no different from the rest of us. She needs proper overhaul in the yard, and she is to be fitted with these new carronades we keep hearing about. She'll not be the same after this.' He saw Bethune climbing from the gun deck, his jaw working on a stale biscuit. 'I doubt if any of us will.'

'Land ho! Fine on th' starboard bow!'

Bolitho took a glass. 'Wight. You'd better let her fall off a point.' He watched Heyward hurry to the rail with his speaking trumpet. It could have been Tyrrell.

Then he looked around the rain-soaked deck at the seamen by the mizzen braces, their faces and arms even darker in the hostile grey light.

A tan-sailed yawl bobbed past, a bearded man waving from the tiller. On the other beam he saw a smudge of land through the drizzle and mist. England. He gripped the rail hard. After so long and so much.

'Steady as she goes, sir!' Heyward joined him again.

Bethune stood on his opposite side and murmured, 'I feel as if I've grown up in *Sparrow*.'

Bolitho thrust his arms around their shoulders.

'We *all* did.'

Then he turned away and said formally, 'Muster your anchor party and tell the gunner to prepare a salute.'

He began to pace slowly up and down the weather side, seeing the busy seamen around him, and many more. Buckle and Tilby, Graves and the artist Majendie.

He paused and touched the rail, the scars where balls had cut down so many of his men.

A frigate loomed through the mist on an opposite tack, her flags very bright against the murky backcloth.

Fowler called, '*What ship?* sir.'

Bolitho nodded. 'Hoist our number.'

Sparrow, sloop-of-war, had come home.